Patrick Francis Moran

Memoir of the Ven. Oliver Plunket

Archbishop of Armagh and primate of all Ireland. Second Edition

Patrick Francis Moran

Memoir of the Ven. Oliver Plunket
Archbishop of Armagh and primate of all Ireland. Second Edition

ISBN/EAN: 9783337092627

Printed in Europe, USA, Canada, Australia, Japan

Cover: Foto ©Raphael Reischuk / pixelio.de

More available books at **www.hansebooks.com**

MEMOIR

OF THE

VEN. OLIVER PLUNKET

Archbishop of Armagh and Primate of All Ireland

WHO SUFFERED DEATH FOR THE CATHOLIC FAITH IN THE
YEAR 1681

BY

CARDINAL MORAN

Archbishop of Sydney

SECOND EDITION

BROWNE & NOLAN, Ltd.
NASSAU-STREET, DUBLIN
Printers and Publishers
1895

Printed by Browne & Nolan, Ltd., *Dublin.*

CONTENTS

CHAPTER I.

CHAPTER II.

CHAPTER III.

CHAPTER IV.

CHAPTER V.

CHAPTER VI.

CHAPTER VII.

CHAPTER VIII.

CHAPTER IX.

CHAPTER X.

CHAPTER XI.

CHAPTER XII.

CHAPTER XIII.

CHAPTER XIV.

CHAPTER XV.

CHAPTER XVI.

CHAPTER XVII.

CHAPTER XVIII.

CHAPTER XIX.

CHAPTER XX.

CHAPTER XXI.

CHAPTER XXII.

CHAPTER XXIII.

CHAPTER XXIV.

CHAPTER XXV. PAGE

CHAPTER XXVI.

CHAPTER XXVII.

CHAPTER XXVIII.

CHAPTER XXIX.

CHAPTER XXX.

ADDITIONAL NOTE.

MEMOIR

OF THE

VEN. OLIVER PLUNKET,

Archbishop of Armagh and Primate of all Ireland.

CHAPTER I.

EARLY LIFE OF DR. PLUNKET.

OLIVER PLUNKET, the subject of these memoirs, was born at Loughcrew, in the county of Meath, in the year 1629. He was by birth connected with many of the most illustrious families of Ireland, and was a near relative of Dr. Patrick Plunket, who successively ruled the dioceses of Ardagh and Meath; as also of Dr. Peter Talbot, Archbishop of Dublin, who, in a letter addressed to him before his appointment to the see of Armagh, styles himself *his cousin.* The Bishop of Ardagh, just mentioned, in a letter of the 19th of October, 1668, thus writes to Dr. Oliver Plunket himself, then Agent of the Irish Clergy in Rome :—

" As regards your relatives, the Earls of Fingall and Roscommon have re-acquired their lands and property, which were in the hands of Cromwell's officers, and to the great delight of all friends, the castle of Killiney (Killeen), six (?) miles from Dublin, has been restored to Lord Fingall. The Baron of Dunsany not having recovered any of his estates, is reduced to great poverty : but the Baron of Louth has obtained a partial restitution of what he lost.*

* This agrees with the statement of De Burgo : " Tres fuere simul suntque gentis Plunketanæ proceres, comes nimirum Fingallus, atque Barones Dunsanius et Louthanus. Cæterum antistes Oliverius prodiit e domo Plunketorum de Loughcrew in Midensi agro Lageniæ, teste Lodgeo. vol. i., p. 156,"—*Hibernia Dominic.*, p. 130, n. (t).

B

Mr. Nicholas Plunket, of Dunsaile,* has got back all his former possessions. The other Plunkets of Tatrath, Balrath, and Preston have not as yet got back their castles, which are all still in the hands of the Cromwellians and Londoners, having been purchased by them from the Parliament in the time of the Rebellion."

Oliver, at an early age, displayed a desire to devote himself to the sacred ministry, and his education, until his sixteenth year, was confided to his own relative, Dr. Patrick Plunket, then titular Abbot of St. Mary's, Dublin. This we learn from a letter of the illustrious teacher himself, who, when the buds had put forth their flowers, and the little plant had become a full-grown tree, recalled to mind with delight the labour of former years, and the anxious care with which he had scattered in his tender mind the fruitful seeds of virtue and learning. This letter is addressed to the Secretary of the Sacred Congregation of Propaganda :—

"During twenty-two years I ruled the diocese of Ardagh, nor did I abandon the Church entrusted to me until the persecution of Cromwell, when I suffered exile for seven years. As soon as the king, having obtained possession of his hereditary dominions, restored to my dear brother and nephews their castles and possessions confiscated by Cromwell, I obtained permission to return to my native country, in which I was the only bishop to perform the pontifical functions. Promptly and faithfully I carried into effect in the very city of Dublin(though not without imminent danger) the Decrees of the Sacred Congregation against the false and schismatical brethren, and on every occasion will I intrepidly continue to execute them, even though now in my old age all my blood should be shed; nay, it would be a glorious thing for me to exchange for martyrdom, through reverence for the Apostolic See, the few years of life which yet remain. Rome, as a watchful and holy mother, was not unmindful of my labours; and you, a true lover of Ireland, being the proposer and promoter of my cause, the Holy See and the Sacred Congregation transferred me from the lowly diocese of Ardagh to that of Meath, the most flourishing in the whole kingdom, where, dwelling in my own home, I may superintend my whole flock. For this favour, and for having increased the number of our bishops, I render to you, and ever shall render, all the thanks in my power; *as also for the affection displayed by you towards Dr. Oliver, who is closely united to me by birth. Having educated him from his infancy till his sixteenth year, I sent him to Rome to pursue his studies at the fountain-head of truth, and I now take pride in his having*

* Dunsoghly.

merited your patronage: neither do I believe that my judgment is led astray by flesh and blood, when I assert that he burns with ardent zeal for the Apostolic See, and for the spiritual progress of our country. I earnestly commend him to your protection.

"So much regarding private matters ; let us now pass to public affairs.

" In these kingdoms three Parliaments will soon be summoned, whose principal object will be to repress the fanatics, the Independents, and the Presbyterians. The number of these Dissenters has increased, whilst the Protestants have dwindled away almost to nothing. Thanks be to God, the number of the Catholics is daily increasing, to whom, if I mistake not, the king will now be favorable, for it is his interest to conciliate them, that aided by them and the Protestants he may have a strong party to oppose to the fanatics and Presbyterians, who are the enemies of all monarchy.

" The Bishop of Kilmore, being continually infirm in body, and sometimes too in mind, is not able to repress the dissensions which have arisen in his diocese, the only remedy would be to give him a coadjutor. I propose to you a person renowned for his learning and piety, who during the persecution of Cromwell never abandoned the sheep entrusted to his charge. For six years he dwelt by day in the caverns and rocks, and by night offered the holy sacrifice and refreshed the scattered flock. His name is Robert Plunket, Pastor of Kilbride, and son of the Baron of Locriff, not far from the Diocese of Kilmore. If in your charity you seek to remedy the aforesaid evils, you will be good enough to nominate him or some other coadjutor.

" In this my Diocese of Meath, than which no other is more extensive in the whole kingdom, there are about eighty secular priests, learned and exemplary men ; there are also many belonging to the Regular clergy, Dominicans, Augustinians, Franciscans, and some Fathers of the Society, who with great applause attend to the education of youth, so that the heretics themselves send their children to their schools.

" I have placed so clearly before our Catholics the iniquities of Walsh* and Taafe, that these two unhappy men have been obliged to quit the kingdom. They now live privately in London, seeking the patronage of the Court, in order to assail us. Against them and their followers I will be ever ready to carry out your Decrees

" I remain, Your Excellency's most obliged and devoted servant,

" PATRICK, of Meath.

" Killiney in Meath, 22nd June, 1669."

* A brief account of Father Peter Walsh is given in Brennan's *Eccles. History of Ireland*, t. ii., p 203. Father Taafe was brother of Lord Carlingford. Walsh was the great promoter of a profession of pretended Catholic principles called the *Remonstrance* (compiled in 1661), which contained many things derogatory from the dignity of the Holy See. He was also an intimate friend of Lord Ormond, a perfidious enemy of Ireland and its religion, who availed himself of the agency of Walsh to excite dissensions in the Catholic body.

In 1643, Father Peter Francis Scarampo was sent by the Holy See on a special mission to Ireland. He was a man filled with the spirit of God, and during his stay among the Irish Confederates, heaven seemed to smile on their cause and to crown their efforts with success. In 1645, the Supreme Council petitioned the Holy Father to have a Nuncio to represent him in Ireland, after the manner of great Catholic kingdoms, and at the same time solicited him to confer this dignity on Father Scarampo ; but the humble disciple of St. Philip* offered a most decided opposition to this project, in so much so, that Innocent X., when permitting him by a Brief of the 5th of May, 1645, to return to Rome, expressed regret that through the holy man's humility the Church in Ireland, and with it in a manner the universal Church, should be deprived of his eminent services.

A few months later .Father Scarampo, accompanied by five youths,† was seen hastening towards the Irish coast. A frigate was there awaiting him to bear him and his companions to Flanders. The people flocked around him in thousands to receive for the last time the blessing of one whom they loved, and to pray in return that God would shower down His benedictions on the good Oratorian, and on the youthful Levites whom he was leading with him to the sanctuaries of Rome, there to drink in at the very source

* The following extract from a Vallicellian MS Life of Father Scarampo will be interesting to many of our readers. The writer says :—" I remember that meeting one day with Cardinal Panzirolo, then Secretary of State of Pope Innocent X., he said to me : ' Your Father Scarampo through humility has not accepted the title of Nuncio, but he has fulfilled all the duties of an excellent Nuncio.' And again, Father Wadding, a religious of that exemplary life and learning which the whole world knows said to me frequently : ' I will not call your Father Scarampo by any other name than that of Apostle of Ireland for he truly deserves this title.' "

† From the Archives of Vallicelli, Barberini, Colleg Hib. de Urbe.— The departure of Father Scarampo for Rome is erroneously referred by some writers to 1647 ; not only do the various authorities above referred to, mention it as having occurred in 1645, but Dr. Plunket in many of his letters states that he lived in Rome *for twenty-five years*, which necessarily requires his arrival in that city before the close of 1645.

the pure streams of truth with which one day they might refresh their native land.

One of these youths was the future martyr-Archbishop of Armagh, then in his sixteenth year. The holy Oratorian seems to have even then cherished a special affection for *Don Oliverio*, as he loved to style him—an affection increased with each succeeding year, which was faithfully responded to by Dr. Plunket.

A journey from Ireland to Flanders was not without its dangers at this period. The narrow seas were covered with cruisers of the rival states, and pirates also continually infested the British Channel. The Nuncio Rinuccini,* in the month of October of this very year (1645), when sailing from France to Ireland, had more than once with difficulty escaped from the pursuit of the Parliamentary squadron ; and Father Scarampo, with his young companions, now incurred like dangers when sailing from the Irish shores. Pursued for twenty-four hours, says his biographer,† by two large vessels, they were more than once in imminent danger of falling into the hands of the enemy. On arriving in Flanders new perils awaited them. When travelling through the country they were seized by bandits, and it was only by the payment of a large sum of money that they obtained their liberation. But Providence having safely conducted them through these and many other trials, at length, before the close of the year 1645, they arrived in the Eternal City, and knelt together around the tombs of the Apostles.

Here we must depart awhile from chronological order, that we may be the better enabled to appreciate the warmth of affection with which, in later years, Dr. Plunket repaid

---

* See the *History of The Confederation of Kilkenny*, by the learned Rev. C. P. Meehan, page 106, *seq*. See also Castlehaven's *Memoirs*, and *Nunziatura in Irlanda di Mgr. Rinuccini*, Firenze, 1844, page 67. The fullest details of this journey of Rinuccini are preserved in a MS. letter, written from Limerick on 10th November, 1645, by a companion of the Nuncio, which is preserved in Archiv. Irish College, Rome.

† Arrighi, MS. Life of Vallicelli, and Barberini libraries; also, letter of Scarampo, which we shall afterwards give in full.

the paternal kindness of the good Oratorian. In 1656, the
city of Rome was ravaged by the plague. A central hospital for those stricken by the frightful malady was established
in the island of St. Bartholomew. All who, impelled by
charity, entered within its walls to minister to the wants of
its inmates were deemed devoted to certain death. Nevertheless, many were the zealous priests who sought this
martyrdom of charity; and to judge from the records of the
time, none displayed in a higher degree that heroism of
divine love than Father Peter Francis Scarampo. Scarce,
however, had he entered upon his arduous mission in
the pestilential wards of the hospital, than the members
of his order, and his other many friends in Rome,
wrote letters urging him to abandon the theatre of such
imminent danger, and to reserve for other labours his
precious life.

The only letter of this apostolic man, which is now
preserved in the Vallicellian archives, was written in reply
to one of these friendly remonstrances, and, in the style of
those times, bears the address, "To my Very Reverend
Master, Mr. Oliver Plunket, at St. Girolamo della Carità
(Rome)." This letter is truly valuable, not only as disclosing
to us the noble sentiments of charity and faith which
animated the zealous Father of the Oratory, and his ardent
affection for Dr. Plunket; but as also recording those facts of
their journey to Rome, which, otherwise, perhaps, should
have remained wholly unknown to us. I translate it entire
from the original letter, in the handwriting of Father
Scarampo :—*

" Why do you fear, O you of little faith? Should we desist from
a work which is truly ours, which God wishes us to perform, which
is pleasing to Him ? I have almost completed my sixtieth year, and
never before did such an occasion present itself of satisfying for my

---

* This letter is incomplete, not only in the MS. Lives, but also in that
published by Arringhi. The authors of these lives are also inaccurate in
copying some of the sentences.

sins, and perhaps should I live as many more, such another would not be granted to me: shall I therefore be idle and allow it to be lost? But. you say, you shall die? What matter; even at the Chiesa Nuova and everywhere else we must die. Relatives, friends, masters, acquaintances, dependants, subjects, penitents will grieve ; but all these, if they do not die themselves before me will have, at some other time, to weep my death. Would it then be proper for me not to face death, in order to pass perhaps eight, ten, fifteen years more in a painful old age, even should death not prematurely assail me? and yet it will be vain for it to assail me, should not the Lord of death so will it. The same God who snatched both me and you from that death with which the piratical ships threatened us in the English Channel—who freed me from snares in my long and continual journeys—who, in Flanders, by ransom, liberated us from robbers, and who in His power guided us through many other more imminent and certain dangers, which you have never known or heard of—He too is present in the hospital, should I be seized with the pestilence in St. Bartholomew's. In Him do I confide. How. therefore, do you say to my soul, change your quarters and return? He who sees all things, will He be unwatchful of me?

" So much about myself. As to you, place your trust in God, and He will do everything. If I have shown you any love or kindness—for I conferred no benefit—to whom are you indebted? to Him who is the bestower of all gifts, the Father of charity and of kindness ; what He performed through me—I repeat it—if it was any good, He can perform the same still better through another. Be of good courage! rest not for your support on reeds, of which I am one of the most fragile. I will do what you desire: I will commend you to my Fathers, Virgil and Marianus : nor need you ever entertain any doubt of their charity. When I have leisure I shall give the testimonial letters. I shall speak about you to Cardinal Barberini, or perhaps I may write to him. Would that I could in like manner assist Mr Baron.* Father Virgil will not speak to his Holiness in his favour, unless he be solicited to do so. Let him continue his petitions to Monsignor Ferrini, the Pope's Almoner ; let him also send a petition to Monsignor Piccolomini, which if he himself is not in favour. Dr. Creagh† will not, I think, refuse to take charge of. I wish I were able, and I would do it. Kiss his hand for me.

* From the form of salutation subsequently added it is clear that this was an Irish priest. Probably he was Father Wilfred Baron, nephew of the celebrated Father Wadding, and author of many justly celebrated works. He was a Franciscan, for many years resident in Rome.

† This was Dr. John Creagh, Domestic Prelate to Alexander VII. He was brother of the celebrated mayor of that name, so distinguished during the siege of Limerick, and uncle of Dr. Creagh, subsequently Archbishop of Dublin.

Salute also Father Luke * and his charge, Father Young † and his, not forgetting Dr. Creagh, and all the other Irish. Thank them for their prayers ; and as these are most necessary for me, have them frequently offered up for me ; and I embrace you from my heart.

" From the island of St. Bartholomew, the Feast of St. Francis (4th Oct.).

" Your most faithful and devoted servant,

" PET. FR. SCARAMPO.

" P.S.—Having applied both mind and hand to the drawing up of the desired testimonials, I am in doubt as to what is to be written ; for you have most unexceptional vouchers as to your birth, journey, life in the city, and in the college, and in the house of St. Girolamo. However, if there is anything special that you desire, send me a copy which I may sign, or which I may re-write with my own hand."

This letter clearly evinces the lively interest with which Father Scarampo sought to provide for his young friend. Indeed, so great was the solicitude which he continually displayed in his regard, that Father Scarampo's brother, on one occasion, said to Dr. Plunket‡ :—" Father Peter Francis does for you what he would never consent to do for me ; for he readily goes on every occasion to speak to the cardinals in your favour ; and this he never once did for me, though I frequently solicited him to do so, even on some matters of great importance."

A few days passed on from the date of the above letter, and the fears of the friends of Father Scarampo were too sadly realized. Struck down by the pestilence, contracted in attending the sick, he breathed his last on the 14th of October, 1656, offering up his life as a holocaust of charity. He was interred in the church of St. Nereus and Achilles,

---

* Father Luke Wadding, the renowned author of the *Annals of the Franciscan Order*. In the letters of the time he never receives from his friends any other name than *Padre Luca*.

† He was a Jesuit, at this time Rector of the Irish College, Rome.

‡ See MS. Lives, Barberini, Vallicelli, and Arringhi. " Sappiate che il Padre Pier Francesco mio fratello fa per voi quel tanto che non ha giammai voluto far per me ; mentre si prontamente va in vostro servizio all' occorrenza a parlare ai Cardinali. Cosa di che quantunque esso da me nei miei interessi pregato non volle giammai fare."

and the following simple inscription was placed upon his tomb :--

" To Peter Francis Scarampo,
Superior of the Roman Congregation of the Oratory,
Who, inflamed with the ardour of charity,
And ministering to those infected by pestilence,
Being seized with the same contagion,
Received as his reward a wished-for death.
The day before the Ides of October, 1656.
Of his age the 60th."*

Amongst the MSS. of the Vallicellian, there is, on a flying-sheet, another beautiful inscription, composed by some of Father Scarampo's admiring friends, and not improbably by our own Dr. Plunket. It is as follows:—

" Peter Francis Mary Scarampo, from Saone,
Superior of the Congregation of the Orat. of S. Philip Neri in Rome.
From nature he received nobility ;
This he increased by his life
By his death he rendered it undying.
During the contagion
He embraced the heroism of charity,
And losing life he attained it,
In the year of salvation 1656, of his age the 60th,
The day before the Ides of October." †

In the letter cited above, Father Scarampo had commended Dr. Plunket to the care of Father Virgilius Spada. This

---

* D. O. M.
Petro Francisco Scarampo,
Romæ Congnis Oratorii Præposito
Qui dum fervore charitatis accensus
Pestilentia laborantibus u'tro ministrat
Eodem morbo correptus
Optatam mortem pro mercede recepit.
Prid. Id. Oct. MDCLVI.
Ætat. Suæ LX

† Franciscus Maria Scarampus Saonensis.
Congñis Oratorii S. Philippi Nerii Romæ Præpositus.
Nobilitatem naturâ meruit
Vitâ auxit
Morte reddidit Immortalem:
Grassante lue
Majorem charitatem amplexus
Vitam dum perdidit invenit.
Anno Salutis MDCLVI. Æt. suæ LX.
Pridie Idus Octobris

priest was a member of the Oratory, and had been for some
time Superior-General of the Order. During the pestilence he
had entered the hospital with Father Scarampo, and had ever
been his constant companion in his labours of love. To him
Dr. Plunket, whilst weeping for his departed friend and
benefactor, now turned for consolation; and the fragment
of the letter which still remains, addressed by him to Father
Spada, will better express than any words of ours the
bereavement and sorrow which overwhelmed him. It is
preserved in the Vallicellian and Barberini manuscript life
of Father Scarampo :—

" Ireland has lost its untiring protector and efficacious benefactor
in the death of Fr. Peter Francis Scarampo ; and I, in particular,
have lost a father more dear to me than my earthly father, for he
conducted me from Ireland, encountering in so long a journey many
dangers from pirates and bandits, and bringing me to Rome at his
own expense, and also maintaining me for three years in the city and
in our college ; * and even when I had completed my studies, his
assistance, whether temporal or spiritual, was never wanting to me.
God alone knows how afflicting his death is to me, especially at the
present time, when all Ireland is overrun and laid waste by heresy.
Of my relatives, some are dead, others have been sent into exile, and
all Ireland is reduced to extreme misery : this overwhelms me with
an inexpressible sadness, for I am now deprived of father and of
friends, and I should die through grief were I not consoled by the
consideration that I have not altogether lost Father Scarampo: for
I may say that he in part remains, our good God having retained
your reverence in life, who, as it is known to all, were united with
him in friendship, and in charity, and in disposition, so as even to
desire to be his companion in death, from which, though God
preserved you, yet he did not deprive you of its merit."

But it is time to resume our narrative, and pursue the
career of Dr. Plunket as student, and subsequently as
professor, in Rome.

* There being but a limited number of burses in the college, his
expenses were defrayed for a time by Father Scarampo until a burse
would become vacant.

CHAPTER II.

THE Irish College for the secular clergy in Rome, like most of the other Irish Continental institutions, dates its origin from the times of persecution. Gregory XIII. (1572-85) had more than once contemplated the establishment of such an asylum for our nation, but the demands for arms and supplies made on him by the Irish princes then combating for their lives and religion, consumed the various sums set aside by him for this purpose. The bishops of Ireland, however, persevered in their petition, and in a *Relatio status* of the Irish Church presented to Rome in 1625,* the foundation of an Irish college is insisted on as a necessary means for supplying our suffering island with virtuous and learned pastors, and maintaining its connection with the centre of Catholic unity.

Among other papers bearing on this subject, one preserved in the Barberini archives gives the following *resumé* of the motives then urged to attain this end :—

1. "Lest such faithful and loyal children of the Holy Roman Church, more so even than all other Christians, should seem not children, but orphans.

2. "That at home they may be the more confirmed in their usual constancy in suffering persecution, seeing that they are dear to the chief Pastor of Christendom.

3. "That the modesty and piety of the Irish may be made known in Rome, where hitherto, since the time of the persecution, some rude stragglers had excited prejudices against the whole nation by their sad ambition and ignorance.

4. "That through this foundation of a seminary, the same fruits, and perhaps in still greater abundance, may be gathered, which were sought for in the establishment of the seminaries of other nations.

5. "Because, without such a seminary the restoration of discipline among us would be impossible, as Ireland would remain in

* *Archiv. de Prop. Fid.*

ignorance of the discipline of the Roman Church, by which the Christian faith must be propagated and sustained.

6. "Because, by the same institution, the adjoining islands, and the greater part of Scotland will be succoured, in which scarcely a vestige of religion n w remains, and in which the Irish language alone is used."

Notwithstanding the repeated solicitations of the Irish bishops, it was only in the year 1627 that the college was at length established, through the munificence of Cardinal Ludovisi, nephew of Gregory XV., and through the untiring exertions of the illustrious ornament of the Franciscan Order i i the seventeenth century, Father Luke Wadding. This wonderful man, having already founded the Convent of St. Isidore for the members of his own order, earnestly laboured to have a similar institution opened for the secular clergy. An occasion soon presented itself, and, indeed, a truly propitious one. Urban VIII. had, on his accession to the Papal throne, nominated Cardinal Ludovisi Protector of Ireland This cardinal was distinguished even in Rome by his liberality and munificence One monument alone—the Church of St. Ignatius—which is due to his piety, should suffice to immortalize his fame. It was his desire, in which he was confirmed by his most intimate friend, Luke Wadding, to render to the Irish Church some important service calculated to perpetuate the memory of his protectorate "It was not a difficult matter," says the simple narrative from which we learn these particulars, "to convince his Eminence that no other work was more worthy of his munificence, or could render more lasting service to the Irish Church, than the foundation of a missionary college for the youth of that nation." * Without delay this idea was carried into effect; and we learn, from many sources, that it was the intention of his Eminence, not merely t) found the college, but to endow it with sufficient funds for

* MS. History of the College, written in 1678 : " P. Lucas Waddingus, O.S.F., Cardinali apprime charus proposuit rem quam adductis rationibus, facile ostendit esse munificentiâ Principis dignissimam, Hiberniae prae caeteris proficuam et mole sua amplam ac perennem, erectionem videlicet seminarii ad educandam in Urbe juventutem ad usum missionum."

the maintenance of a large number of students. Death, however, cut short his beneficent designs, and the sum which he was able to bequeath for its endowment being comparatively small, during the one hundred and seventy years which the college lasted, till its suppression by the French usurpers of Rome, in 1798, it was scarcely ever able to receive more than eight students within its walls.

At the period of which we now treat it was under the direction of the Jesuit Fathers, and it sent forth so many learned and distinguished missionaries, who shed lustre on the Irish hierarchy, to which many of them were raised, that it won for itself in Rome the title of nursery of bishops, " seminarium episcoporum." Indeed, the seventeenth century may be justly considered a glorious era in the history of the Irish College.*

Of the five students conducted to Rome by Father Scarampo, three were placed in the Irish College, two of whom, Drs. Plunket and Brennan, were destined, as Archbishops of Armagh and Cashel, to become pillars of the Irish Church in the days of her severest trials ; whilst he third, Father Walsh,† having completed his course of studies, entered the congregation of the oratory, and made, first, Perugia, and then Rome, the theatre of his missionary labours.

On arriving at Rome, Dr. Plunket devoted himself, for some time, to the study of rhetoric, under Professor Dandoni.

---

* For instance, the following prelates, contemporary with Dr. Plunket, and whose names will more than once recur in the following pages, were educated in the Ludovisian Irish College :—Dr. Brennan, Bishop of Waterford and Lismore, and thence transferred to the Archdiocese of Cashel ; Luke Plunket, Vicar-Apostolic of Raphoe, afterwards of Derry ; Ronan Maginn. Vicar-Apostolic of Dromore ; Dr. Cusack, Bishop of Meath ; Dr. Peter Creagh, Bishop of Cork and Cloyne, afterwards Archbishop of Dublin, &c.

† From the Vallicellian MS. Life of Father Scarampo we learn that in 1669 it was the intention of the Sacred Congregation to confer on Father Walsh the Archbishopric of Cashel, his native diocese ; he being prevented by sickness from accepting that dignity, Dr. William Burgatt was appointed to that see.

In the following year, 1646, he was admitted a student of the Irish College. There he applied himself with great diligence for eight years to the study of mathematics, philosophy, and theology ; * subsequently he attended the lectures on Canon Law of the celebrated Jurisconsult, Mariscotti,† in the halls of the Roman University called the Sapienza.

With what ardour and proficiency he applied to these studies, we learn from a paper presented to the Sacred Congregation of Propaganda, in 1669, by the then Rector of the Irish College, Father Edward Locke :—

"I, the undersigned, certify that the very Reverend Dr. Oliver Plunket, of the Diocese of Meath, in the Province of Armagh, in Ireland, is of Catholic parentage, descended from an illustrious family ; on the father's side from the most illustrious Earls of Fingall, and on the mother's side from the most illustrious Earls of Roscommon, being also connected by birth with the most illustrious Oliver Plunket, Baron of Louth, first Nobleman of the Diocese of Armagh : and in this our Irish College he devoted himself with such ardour to philosophy, theology, and mathematics, that in the Roman College of the Society of Jesus he was justly ranked amongst the foremost in talent, diligence, and progress in his studies ; these speculative studies being completed, he pursued with abundant fruit the course of Civil and Canon Law, under Mark Anthony de Mariscotti, Professor in the Roman Sapienza, and everywhere and at all times he was a model of gentleness, integrity, and piety.

" EDWARD LOCKE,
" *Rector of the Irish College de Urbe.*
" Rome, 8th June, 1669."

It was the rule of the Irish College that the students after their ordination should return to Ireland ; and they were obliged solemnly to avow their intention of discharging this duty, should they not be exempted from it by their superiors. Such was the state of Ireland in 1654, the date of the ordination of Dr. Plunket, that there were great

---

* Amongst those who at this period attracted by their learning foreign students to the halls of the Roman College, we may mention Father Pallavicino, afterwards cardinal of Holy Church.

† Mark Anthony de Marascotti was one of the most learned Jurisconsults of the seventeenth century.

obstacles to preventing him from entering immediately on his sacred mission. Indeed, nothing can be more sad than the spectacle then presented by our Church. The ruthless invasion of Cromwell had rendered like unto a desert the fairest plains of Ireland: her cities were desolate, and the country deluged with the blood of the inhabitants; many of the survivors of the dreadful massacres had been sent to undergo a lengthened martyrdom in the Barbadoes, or the swamps of Savannah : all colleges and seminaries had been suppressed, religious houses dissolved, the clergy proscribed, the Bishops put to death or driven into exile, the churches all ruined : in a word, the long meditated purpose of the enemies of Ireland, and of Ireland's creed, seemed to have been realized. But still the spark of faith was not extinguished, and faithful pastors, concealed in the recesses of the forests and the fastnesses of the mountains, gathered together the remnants of their scattered flocks, and broke to them the bread of eternal life.

Fearing to enter on this arduous mission without further preparation, Dr. Plunket, on the 14th June, 1654, thus addressed the General of the Jesuits.

"I, Oliver Plunket, your most humble petitioner, student of the Irish College, having completed my philosophical and theological studies, considering the impossibility of now returning to Ireland (as your paternity well knows), in accordance with the rules of this College, and with the oath which I have taken, humbly request of you Most Rev. Father, that I may be allowed to continue in Rome, and dwell with the fathers of St. Girolamo della Carità. I promise, however, and declare that I will be ever ready to return to Ireland whensoever you, Rev. Father, or my superiors shall so command.

"Rome, 14th June, 1654."

The permission sought for was readily accorded, and for three years Dr. Plunket devoted himself to study and the unostentatious exercise of the sacred ministry in the silent retreat of St. Girolamo. In 1657, however, his fame for theological learning being wide-spread in Rome,* he was appointed

* "Essendo nota la sua grave dottrina nella Sacra Teologia fu eletto l'anno 1657, per lettore di questa sacra facoltà nel Collegio de Prop. Fide."—Marangoni, page 117.

professor in the College of Propaganda, where for twelve years he continued to lecture on Speculative, Controversial, and Moral Theology. He was at the same time Consultor of the Sacred Congregation of the Index, and of other Congregations. In a letter of the 15th September, 1674, Dr. Plunket thus alludes to his labours in promoting study in these schools :—

" I spent in Rome twenty-five years (1645-1669), and for twelve of these I served the Sacred Congregation in the chairs of Theology and Controversy. I also served the Sacred Congregation of the Index, as you are aware. The state in which I found the course of studies in Propaganda, and the progress which they had made before I left Rome, may be learned from the Very Rev. Fathers Libelli, Laurea, Spinola, Sommaschio, and the Rector Bonvicini, who were the Prefects of Studies during my time, and are acquainted with the matters to which I refer."

Dr. Plunket, whilst prosecuting his studies at the Roman College, became acquainted with the celebrated Father Pallavicino, then filling one of the chairs of the Roman College, which had been illustrated by the learning of Suarez, De Lugo, and Toledo. When the literary and theological labours of the great historian of the Council of Trent were rewarded by his promotion to the Roman purple, Dr. Plunket continued to enjoy his friendship, and to live with him on terms of the most cordial intimacy. In a letter addressed to Cardinal Casanatti, 15th August, 1676, the Archbishop of Armagh thus writes :—

" Whilst your Eminence was Secretary of Propaganda I had the honour of enjoying your erudite and learned conversation, in company with His Eminence Pallavicino, of happy memory; and I must in sincerity declare that from such conversation I derived great instruction. Of this and many other favours received from your Eminence, I, although in these remote parts of the world, retain a lively recollection, and I never forget you in the Holy Sacrifice of the Mass, praying the divine Majesty to grant to you long life and every prosperity for the good of all, and especially of this afflicted country."

Of those whose society he thus enjoyed, many afterwards attained the highest dignities in the Church ; and among others, Monsignor Odescalchi, who in 1676 was raised to the Chair of Peter, assuming the name of Innocent XI. The letter written by Dr. Plunket, then Archbishop of Armagh, on the occasion of this elevation, and addressed to the Cardinal Prefect of Propaganda, exhibits many features of· the life of Dr. Plunket in Rome at this period. It bears the date 11th August, 1677 :—

" MAY IT PLEASE YOUR EMINENCE,—It would be difficult to express with what spiritual consolation and joy the Catholics of this kingdom, lay and ecclesiastic, have received the announcement of the merited exaltation of our Holy Father to the Chair of St. Peter, as I have already declared to Monsignor Tanari, the Internuncio, a prelate, indeed, of great prudence, and of extraordinary zeal for the affairs of the Church in this nation, who, on the first news of the election, communicated to us the intelligence. The heretics themselves, who surely are no lovers of the faith of St. Peter, entertain, nevertheless, a special veneration for his present successor ; and the English and Scotch, who during the past years visited Rome for sight-seeing, returned greatly edified, and reduced to silence their own preachers and ministers, who from the pulpit proclaimed all sorts of fables and falsehoods about Rome. The courtesy and kindness shown to the Protestants who visit Rome are of great advantage to the poor Catholics of this country. Whilst professing Theology and Contro- versy in the College of Propaganda for many years, I had experience of the sanctity of our Holy Father, and of the great esteem in which he was held by all for wisdom, prudence, and holiness. I was par- ticularly intimate with D. Marcantonio Odescalchi. I often assisted him when he served the poor and ragged and needy, many of whom were covered with vermin. He gathered them into an asylum, and clothed them at his expense ; with his own hands he cleansed them, fed them, &c. I am morally certain that God granted to his Church so holy a head through the merit, in great part, of the saintly D. Marcantonio. This being the case, your Eminence will easily imagine with what joy I received the intelligence of the exaltation of our Holy Father ; hence I feel compelled to announce to the people what I saw and what I experienced, that thus they too may raise their hands in thanksgiving to the Divine Majesty, and supplicate for the long life of his Holiness. The Irish are especially bound to do this in consequence of the great tenderness and compassion ever dis- played towards them by the Holy See. During the persecutions which they sustained these hundred years past, and which we still have to sustain, rather than abandon the ancient faith, they suffer with joy the plunder of all their goods, and the privation of all offices and dignities ; and I am sure the Holy Father will ever with spiritual care promote and preserve the holy faith in this kingdom, and remove all obstacles which might impede its progress.

" I pray your Eminence to inform his Holiness, that there has been lately published here, in English, in a new form, the pestiferous

C

history of *Soave*,* which is a continual tirade against the Popes, and against the Council of Trent, with the life of that impostor, as though he were a hero. As the poison has been thus spread, an antidote indeed is necessary : such would be the history of the same Council, by Cardinal Pallavicino, if translated into English ; should the duty of translating it be imposed on Dr. Leyburne, Auditor of his Eminence Cardinal Howard, he being a learned man, and versed in the English, Latin, and Italian languages, would perform the task most successfully. You cannot imagine what injury has been done by that pest of a writer, Soave : all the nobility, gentry, merchants, &c., read his history, and it is the more detrimental as it pretends to be written by a religious of our communion. I request you once more to propose this matter to the Holy Father, that without delay the necessary remedy may be provided, which indeed would be the above-mentioned translation ; and offering you my homage, I shall ever be,

" Your Eminence's most devoted and obliged servant,

✠ " OLIVER OF ARMAGH.

" Dublin, 11th August, 1677.

" To his Eminence Cardinal Cybo, &c., &c.'

Dr. Plunket enjoyed, moreover, a close intimacy with the Cerri family, and especially with Monsignor Cerri, with whom, as Secretary of the Sacred Congregation de Prop Fide, he maintained in after life an uninterrupted correspondence and constant friendship. On being made acquainted with the appointment of his old friend and fellow-student to the high office of Secretary of Propaganda, Dr. Plunket thus wrote to him, recounting the first occasion of his intimacy with that family :—

" MOST REVEREND LORD,—A letter from any member of the house of Cerri would be at any time most gratifying to me ; but the letter of your Excellency, of the 11th of June last, was especially so, not only for its own merits, but on account of the many obligations which I owe to the revered memory of your father, who was my master and benefactor. My intimacy with him commenced in this way :—Father Peter Francis Scarampo was confessor of the pious and devout lady, your mother; she gave frequent accounts to D. Francesco (your father) of the great prudence and virtue of this F. Scarampo, priest of the Chiesa Nuova; and D. Francesco being intimately acquainted with, and esteemed by

---

* The assumed name of Father Paul Sarpi, a Venetian apostate friar, of the Order of the Servites, author of a history of the Council of Trent, famous for distorting facts, and misrepresenting doctrines.

Cardinal Barberini, excited in his Eminence a great affection for Father Scarampo, who, after discharging the mission of papal minister in Ireland, conducted me thence to Rome. When the pestilence broke out in that city, Father Scarampo, by a pious stratagem, obtained permission to assist those who were infected in the island of St. Bartholomew, and there he afterwards got sick, and died in the odour of sanctity. A little while before his death he wrote a letter to D. Francesco, recommending me to his protection, which was of great advantage to me, as through his intercession I soon afterwards obtained the chair of Theology, and subsequently of Controversy, in the College de Propaganda Fide, where I continued to teach till I was appointed to the Primatial See of this kingdom, about nine years ago ; so that your excellency, *haereditario jure*, as if by inheritance, is my master and protector ; and I in these remote quarters of the Christian world make continual remembrance of D. Francesco in the most holy sacrifice of the Mass, and I pray for the prosperity of the whole house of Cerri, and I induce other priests to do the same. I am, moreover, obliged to your Excellency for the favour conferred on Dr. James Cusack,* who is a learned and prudent man, and has laboured here with great zeal for the last sixteen years. The venerable Bishop of Meath was well deserving of this favour, having served the Sacred Congregation, as bishop, for nearly thirty years, during all the fury of the persecution.

"OLIVER OF ARMAGH.

"Dublin, 30th August, 1678."

In little more than twelve months from the date of this letter, Monsignor Cerri was hurried to a premature grave ; and Dr. Plunket, writing on the 30th November of the following year, thus expresses his sorrow at that event :—

"I am exceedingly grieved at the death of Monsignor Cerri. He was my fellow-student in the city of Rome, and his father, M. Francis Cerri, was my most dear friend. I shall have the holy sacrifice and prayers offered up for the repose of his soul by the clergy of the province of Armagh, for they are indeed under an obligation of doing so on account of the fatigues which he sustained for them when Secretary of the Sacred Congregation."

We have already remarked that Dr. Plunket, in 1654, entered the house of the Oratory at St. Girolamo della Carità. The justly-renowned Rubricist, Catalani, in his commentary on the Roman Pontifical,† affirms that he became a member of the Oratory ; but from the petition

* He had been lately appointed Coadjutor Bishop of Meath.
† Vol. iii., page 313 (ed. Paris, 1852).

presented by him to the General of the Jesuits, in June, 1654, it is manifest that he intended merely to reside there; and in the sketch of his life by Marangoni, to which Catalani refers as his authority, it is only said that:—

"Having completed his studies about the year 1654, he procured a place among the fathers of the house of St. Girolamo della Carità, where he was admitted, and he obtained permission to reside there till such time as his superiors would judge it opportune to send him to Ireland." *

Even to the present day the house of St. Girolamo continues to be a place of peaceful retreat, where many members of the secular clergy take up their abode, devoting themselves at the same time to the pursuits of study, and to the exercise of the ecclesiastical ministry.

Marangoni was a learned oratorian, whose writings have acquired for him a universal fame. In the appendix to his work, *Life of the Servant of God, Father Buonsignore Cacciaguerra*, page 116, he gives a chapter entitled "Life of Father Oliver Plunket, afterwards Archbishop of Armagh, and Primate of Ireland." This life extends from the 116th to the 124th page, and contains little more than the translation of Dr. Plunket's discourse at Tyburn. Nevertheless, the few additional sentences that are added are of inestimable value, as illustrating this period of Dr. Plunket's life, and supplying some facts which we would seek for in vain from other sources. He commences his narrative by declaring that Dr. Plunket "should be ranked amongst the most illustrious personages whose virtuous lives adorned the Oratory of St. Girolamo della Carità."† This house had been founded by St. Philip; many of his early disciples had lived there, and it had ever been the abode of virtue and learning, and hence these words of the learned oratorian

---

* "Terminati gli studj circa l'ano 1654 (it was, as we have seen, precisely June, 1654), procurò di avere luogo tra i Padri di questa Casa di S. Girolamo della Carità ove fu ammesso ed impetrò la facoltà di potervisi trattener quanto fosse piaciuto a chi spettava di rimandarlo con opportunità propria in Ibernia."

† "Uno de' piu celebri soggetti che hanno illustrato questa Casa di S. Girolamo della Carità."—Page 116.

show how eminent was the fame of sanctity to which
Dr. Plunket had attained, and how distinguished were his
missionary labours in Rome.

Marangoni then describes the occupations of Dr. Plunket
whilst living at St. Girolamo :—

" Here it is incredible with what zeal he burned for the salvation
of souls. In the house itself, and in the city, he wholly devoted
himself to devout exercises ; frequently did he visit the sanctuaries
steeped with the blood of so many martyrs, and he ardently sighed
for the opportunity of sacrificing himself for the salvation of his
countrymen. He, moreover, frequented the hospital of Santo Spirito,
and employed himself even in the most abject ministrations, serving
the poor infirm to the edification and wonder of the very officials
and assistants of that place." *

Rome is truly rich in sacred monuments. Its very soil,
so often bedewed with martyrs' blood, shed for the Catholic
faith ; the treasures of the relics of countless saints which it
conceals ; its sanctuaries and shrines—present resistless
attractions to the fervent soul. The great founder of the
Oratory, St. Philip, never allowed a day to pass without
rekindling, at these shrines, the flames of divine love.
Dr. Plunket seems to have taken him for his model, and to
have daily visited these holy places with special ardour of
devotion. As we have seen, Father Scarampo presented in
his life a true model of Christian solicitude for the poor
and the infirm : and the devotedness which Dr. Plunket
displayed in the public hospitals in assisting them and
in ministering to their wants, sufficiently attests what
progress he had made in this sacred school of virtue.
Marangoni speaks only of the hospital of Santo Spirito ;
but from the incidental reference made by Dr. Plunket
himself in his letter to the Prefect of Propaganda, when

* " Qui è incredibile il zelo grande per la salute dei prossimi di cui
avvampava il suo cuore ; si applicò tutto agli esercizi divoti e dentro e
fuori di casa; frequentava la visita dei santuarii bagnati col sangue di
tanti Martiri venerati sospirava ardentemente l'opportunità di sacrificare
se stesso per la salute dei suoi. · Visitava frequentemente l'ospedale di
S. Spirito ove si esercitava ne' ministerj anco piu abietti in servizio dei
poveri infermi, con edificazione ed ammirazione dé medici uffiziali e
servienti di quel luogo."—Page 116.

speaking of D. Marcontonio Odescalchi, we learn that he visited other hospitals with like charity and zeal.

It was when visiting Santo Spirito, that a holy priest announced to him his future martyrdom, which gave occasion to the humble prelate to betray the ardent desire with which he burned in his inmost soul to attain that glorious crown. We shall allow the learned Marangoni to narrate this fact in his own words :—

"I cannot here omit to relate a fact [he says] which is attested by Father James Mochi, a priest yet living, and Dean of the Fathers of this house of St. Girolamo, who at that time was engaged in attending the hospital of Santo Spirito, so frequented by Father Oliver, who also was well known to him : he therefore attests that Dr. Oliver Plunket, having gone in his episcopal dress to visit that hospital, before his departure from Rome, when standing at the door which looks towards the castle of St. Angelo, and bidding farewell to the then prior, D. Jerome Mieskow, a Polish priest of extraordinary sanctity of life; the latter, embracing him, and, as if prophesying, said to him : 'My Lord, you are now going to shed your blood for the Catholic faith.' And he being wholly inflamed with the desire of thus shedding his blood for Christ, replied with humilty : 'I am unworthy of such a favour; nevertheless, aid me with your prayers, that this my desire may be fulfilled.' " *

* " Non tralascierò qui di notare ciò cheattesta il P. Giacomo Mochi sacerdote ancora vivente e Decano de' Padri di questa casa, che allora si ritrovava all' assistenza del sudetto Archispedale di S. Spirito tanto frequentato dal P. Oliverio da lui molto ben conosciuto : riferisce che portatosi in abito Prelatizio, a visitare quel luogo, nell' atto del licenziarsi che fece sulla porta del medesimo luogo, che guarda il castello col Priore che era allora il Sig. D. Girolamo Mieskovio Polaceo Sacerdote di gran bontà di vita, abbraciandolo questi quasi profetando nell' abbracciarlo, gli disse : Monsignore voi ora andate a spargere il sangue per la fede Cattolica : ed egli che n' era tutto acceso di desiderio gli rispose con umiltà : 'Non ne sono degno, ma pure aiutatemi colle vostre orazioni acciò questa brama si adempisca.' "

CHAPTER III

DR. PLUNKET AS AGENT OF THE IRISH CLERGY AT ROME.

At the close of the year 1668 there were only two Catholic
bishops living in Ireland, Dr. Patrick Plunket, Bishop of
Ardagh, and Dr. Owen M'Sweeney, Bishop of Kilmore.* On
the Continent three other members of our hierarchy, the
Bishop of Kilfenora, the Bishop of Ferns, and the Archbishop
of Armagh,† lived in exile. No wonder, then, that the
widowed churches of Ireland should have hailed with joy
the 21st January, 1669, the day on which the Sacred
Congregation of Propaganda nominated four new bishops to
vacant sees; i.e., Dr. Peter Talbot to the Archiepiscopal See
of Dublin, Dr. William Burgatt to Cashel, Dr. James Lynch
to Tuam, and Dr. Phelan to Ossory.

The Irish ecclesiastics scattered throughout the Continent
shared in the common jubilee; and amongst other letters
written on this occasion I find one addressed to the Secretary
of Propaganda, by Rev. Dr. Fallon,‡ Professor of Theology in
the University of Bologna, who thus writes to thank the
Sacred Congregation for the favour conferred on the Church
of Ireland :—

" Most Reverend Monsignor,—I lately received letters from
Dr. Plunket, by which I was able sufficiently to understand the great
solicitude and benevolence of your excellency in succouring our
country, which is so poor, and menaced by so many dangers : wherefore, may God grant to you His blessing, and may you during your
whole lifetime enjoy the good things of Jerusalem. I certainly am
of opinion that your selection could not fall on persons better suited.

---

* Dr. French, writing on the Continent in 1667, speaks of Dr. M'Sweeny
as then dead. This is an error; for the letters of the Archbishop of
Armagh, and the other prelates, in 1668 and 1669, more than once speak
of him as yet living, although retired in the most remote part of the
country, and subject to continual infirmities both in body and mind.

† Dr. Edmund O'Reilly died in Paris, in March, 1669.

‡ Dr. Fallon was for twenty-five years Professor of Theology in the
University of Bologna.

and more prudent than those you have selected for the spiritual government of our falling kingdom of Ireland. I myself know almost all of them to be of a most virtuous and exemplary life; and, I doubt not, that they are full of zeal for the Catholic faith : wherefore I return thanks, not indeed proportionate, but as far as is in my power, to the bestower of so great a gift, devoting myself perpetually to your service; praying that you may enjoy a long and happy life, for the propagation of the faith, and the direction of the Church of Ireland.

"GREGORY FALLON.

"Bologna, 20th July, 1669.
"To the Secretary of the Cong. de Prop. Fid."

During this period of persecution our Irish hierarchy was more than once on the verge of destruction; and if our Church at the present day does not present the sad desolation of England and Scotland, we are indebted under heaven to those indefatigable men who laboured in season and out of season to preserve unbroken, despite the efforts of the enemies of our holy faith, the succession of our chief pastors.

No one laboured more strenuously than Dr. Plunket in attaining this happy result. He had already been for some time agent in the Roman Court for his relative the Bishop of Ardagh; but no sooner were the new bishops nominated by the Holy See than he was chosen by them their common representative in Rome. The letter addressed to him by Peter Talbot, the justly celebrated Archbishop of Dublin, is exceedingly interesting under many respects. He thus writes :—

"The Bishop of Ferns has requested me to unite with him in constituting you our agent in the Roman Court, for the Province of Dublin, to which request I have most readily assented, well knowing your zeal for the faith, and the affection you bear your friends; and that you will correspond to the confidence placed in you, and give full satisfaction to all.

"I was consecrated in Antwerp, on Sunday last * (the 8th of May), and I now return in haste to London to meet Peter Walsh, and oppose his infamous efforts against God, the king, and his country;

---

* There is here a marginal note, "16th May, 1669;" but this cannot be correct. Comp. letter of Dr. Talbot, written on the 15th May, 1669 (styl. vet.), which was Sunday. He says he was consecrated on the preceding Sunday, that is, the 8th of May (styl. vet.).

and, although he pretends nothing but allegiance to the king, I know that this is only a mantle with which such plotters ever seek to mask their evil designs.

"Until such time as you shall be able to procure the pallium for me, I have obtained a Brief, authorizing me to exercise its prerogatives and privileges. Nevertheless, I beseech you to ask for it in the same manner as it was granted to my predecessors, and that as soon as possible.

"Neither I nor my province shall present any petition in the Roman Court without giving intelligence to you and Rev. Dr. Brennan, and we hope that no attention will be paid to anyone else. I say this, because I have heard that a memorial was presented to the Sacred Congregation, or to the Holy Father, soliciting the power to absolve those who incurred the censures of Rinuccini; this would occasion great disorder, as there is a rigorous edict of the king against all who would ask for such an absolution; and I believe it is not the desire of the Sacred Congregation that any noise should be made in this matter: it is well that we should have the power of absolving *in coro conscientiœ* all such as have any scruples on this head, but it would be unwise to send any public document to that effect.

"In the Province of Armagh there is such confusion that I suppose an Archbishop will soon be appointed. I have proposed three: Patrick Everard, a learned man, of noble and ancient lineage; he studied in Seville, in Spain, and is a good theologian and preacher; Thomas Fitzsymons, and a certain Dr. Nugent. Everard is the best suited.

"Your most affectionate Cousin,

"PETER OF DUBLIN." *

Before Dr. Plunket could represent to the Sacred Congregation the views of the Archbishop of Dublin regarding the censures of Rinuccini, the power of absolving from them had already been despatched from Rome. The Internuncio writes on the 18th of April, acknowledging the receipt of these faculties for the Irish bishops; and we find Dr. Talbot, in the postscript to his letter of the 15th May, thus referring to the letter he had just received, conveying the power of absolving from these censures :—

"I have received the letters of your Eminence, dated 27th April, by which faculty is granted to absolve all who solicit absolution from

* This letter is without date, being only a copy of the original letter. There is the following note in the handwriting of Dr. Plunket :—

"*Dr Talbot started from Brussels on the 28th May, for London, as I have been informed by Bartholomew Plunket, President of the Irish Seminary in Brussels.*"

the censures fulminated by Rinuccini. I embrace with due obedience
and humility the paternal goodness of His Holiness ; but it seems to
me that the publication of such a faculty would be attended with
great danger ; as it was enacted by a law of the King and Parliament
of Ireland, that anyone asking to be absolved from the censures of
Rinuccini should be incapable of acquiring property or receiving any
inheritance, and by far the greater number of Catholics applaud this
law ; nor do I remember anyone having had recourse for absolution
from these censures to those who formerly received a like faculty ;
for all, with one accord, attribute the ruin of our country to the
divisions occasioned by these censures. Nor are they the ignorant
alone who say this, but even the greater part of the clergy, secular
and regular, warmly contend that the censures were invalid. Wherefore it surprises me how a petition to absolve from them could be
presented to His Holiness in the name of the Catholic bishops of
Ireland. I indeed deem it very proper that we should have power to
absolve in the tribunal of penance all such as recur to us ; but should
this become known, the whole hierarchy of Ireland would be exposed
to great risk, and the Irish laity would be compelled to declare by
public document that they never gave any commission to have such
a request forwarded to His Holiness. Wherefore I think it expedient,
and I stated so to his Excellency the Internuncio, that this faculty
should be given by word of mouth to the Archbishops, but that the
letters of your Eminence should in nowise be transmitted to Ireland,
till such time as an answer may be received to this difficulty, which
with due submission I propose.

" PETER OF DUBLIN.

" Brussels, 15th May, 1669."

The result was that this faculty of absolving from the
censures of Rinuccini was not published ;* and we find some
years later the same subject engaging the attention of the
Sacred Congregation and of our Irish bishops.

The predecessors of Dr. Plunket, as representatives of the

---

* Nothing can be more groundless than the assertions of Charles
O'Conor, in his *Historical Address*, as to the refusal of the Holy See to
grant absolution from the censures of Rinuccini. Before the Nuncio
took his departure from Ireland he gave faculty to the Archbishop of
Armagh to absolve from these censures, and to sub-delegate such faculty
to any others he might deem fit. On his death, Alexander VII. by
special Brief, gave a like faculty to the Bishops of Raphoe, Cork,
Leighlin, and Clonfert (1655); on the death of the Bishop of Raphoe,
the newly appointed Archbishop of Armagh was, a few years later,
nominated in his place: and in 1665, another Brief seems to have been
addressed to all the surviving bishops, empowering them in like manner
to absolve from these censures. On another occasion we may, perhaps,
discuss more fully the merits of some of Dr. O'Conor's statements in his
Historical Addresses, &c.

Irish bishops in Rome, had filled that office with prudence, and conciliated for themselves and for the Irish Church the esteem of the authorities in that city. Dr. Burgatt, who, as we have seen, was at this time appointed Archbishop of Cashel, had held that office for many years; and Dr. O'Dwyer, whose name is so justly illustrious as connected with the national Confederation, and subsequently as Bishop of Limerick, was in the early half of this century deputed, on more than one occasion, to act as the agent of the Irish bishops at the Papal court. Those who, during the latter years of the seventeenth century, were appointed to the same office were not unworthy of their predecessors ; and the names of Dr. Brennan, Dr. Creagh, Dr. Sleyn, and Dr. Michael Plunket sufficiently attest the solicitude of the Irish prelates in sending worthy representatives to the central see of the Catholic world.

The principal efforts of Dr. Plunket were directed against the machinations of Taafe and Peter Walsh, who left no stone unturned to find patrons and abettors for their well-known "Remonstrance." Indeed, through the zeal and labours of Dr. Talbot, both before and after his appointment to the episcopate, this remonstrance was soon wholly discredited in Ireland ; and Dr. Plunket laboured with equal ardour in Rome to second his efforts, and make known to the authorities there the iniquitous designs of the Remonstrants. The Archbishop of Dublin, on the 4th of July, 1669, thus wrote to Dr. Plunket, congratulating him on his labours in the cause of the Irish Church, and supplying at the same time much interesting information regarding Peter Walsh :—

" DEAREST COUSIN,—I have received your four letters, all treating of the same matter, and I am much obliged for your efforts to promote the public welfare of our country, and I hope that in its own good time you shall receive the fruit of your labours. We know by experience the benevolence and favour of Monsignor Baldeschi : our prayers and hearts are his. When the occasion presents itself, thank the Cardinal Barberini, and tell him how I esteem his counsel not to enter into disputes with Walsh ; I discredit him, however, in the esteem of those who are in authority and of men of learning. Here he is so concealed and unknown that no one can tell where he lives

He has made many offers, and shown more than once a desire to submit to Holy Church ; but when it comes to the point, he wishes to maintain his opinions and to justify himself. Through others I hold out to him hopes of clemency and pardon, should he return to the truth, and retire to some Catholic country to one of his convents or monasteries. In my opinion, it would be time that his Superiors should oblige him, under penalty of incurring censure, to retire to Flanders, which precept or command should be sent to him without delay, for it is his boast that he has never disobeyed them.

" Yours, &c.,

" PETER OF DUBLIN.

" London, 4th July, 1669."

A paper regarding Walsh and his associates, presented by Dr. Plunket to Propaganda in May, 1669, contains many further particulars on this subject, which he states were gleaned from letters of Dr. French, and Bartholomew Plunket, President of the Irish College in Brussels, written on the 13th of April, 1669 :—

" Walsh has sent an agent to London to seek a continuation of the protection of the Queen, but her Majesty has withdrawn her protection from him. This agent also sought to procure for Walsh the favour of the new Viceroy; but he received for answer that if the new Viceroy found Walsh in Ireland on his arrival, he would send him to the scaffold.

" F. Taafe is gone to London, and is waiting to receive money and a safe conduct from Monsignor, the Internuncio, to pass into Flanders.

" Ormond, now that he has lost all power, puts himself forward, and pretends to be a well-wisher of his country. The King makes a display of affection towards him, but his intimacy with the Duke of York gives displeasure, and it is thought that for this reason he was deprived of his office.

" The Catholic gentry of Ireland lately sent Sir Nicholas Plunket as their agent to London, to obtain from the King a restoration of their property on the occasion of the change of government ; but it is feared that nothing will be gained, as many in the Court are interested in the plunder, the Duke of York receiving annually two hundred thousand scudi * (£50,000), and Ormond a like sum." †

The Taafe to whom reference is made in this letter is

---

* According to the relative exchange of that time, four scudi were deemed equivalent to £1.

† Plowden, *Hist. Review of State of Ireland*, t. i., p. 175, gives the testimony of a writer, who states that "the gifts and grants to Ormond amount to £630,000 ;" all which gifts were continued by Parliament.

almost unknown in the published histories of this period, and yet few events attracted more attention for many years, or threatened our Irish Church with such imminent danger, as the imposture which he devised, and which can scarcely find a parallel in the ecclesiastical annals of any country. To support the ruinous fabric of the Remonstrance, this companion of Peter Walsh forged a Bull from the Holy See, empowering him, though a simple friar, to act as Vicar-Apostolic of all Ireland, and depose, as he should think fit, the local vicars and bishops, and make many other arbitrary arrangements for the due reformation of the Irish Church, all his plans, however, having for their chief object to discredit and depose whosoever had been opposed to the Remonstrance, and to place the ecclesiastical authority of the country in the hands of its favourers and abettors. So artful was the forgery, and so ingenious its author, that he procured the recognition and authentication of his Bull, not only from Ormond and the English Government, but even from Dr. Darcy, Bishop of Dromore, and Dr. Patrick Plunket, Bishop of Ardagh. The particulars of the confusion which ensued in many dioceses, and of the sums which were levied on various ecclesiastics, in virtue of this pretended authority, belong to the life of Dr. Edmund O'Reilly, to whom we are chiefly indebted for having unmasked this iniquitous imposture. A letter addressed to Dr. Oliver Plunket by the Bishop of Ardagh, in 1668, evinces the zeal with which that good prelate sought to amend his error, committed in recognising Taafe ; whilst at the same time it affords much additional information regarding our Irish Church at this period :—

"Dublin, 19th Oct. (styl. vet.), 1668.

"I have received your letter, which was most gratifying to me and to all your friends, as well for the news concerning your health as for the information regarding the pretended Commission of Taafe, authenticated, as he pretended, by Card. Roberti and by a public notary. Few or none dared to oppose his Commission in the commencement, through reverence for the Apostolic See, and F. Taafe made various copies, and sent Visitators with them throughout the whole kingdom, who for the most part were those who had signed the rash and scandalous formula of Peter Walsh. When I saw the Commissioners whom he employed, I commenced to doubt of the validity of the Commission, and I rejected it, as the whole kingdom knows, even before the letters came from Rome, and I made this known by a public deed ; for when one of the Visitators of Taafe had excommunicated the Vicar-General of our Primate, the Archbishop of Armagh, I declared the excommunication null. This exceedingly annoyed Taafe, and in all his subsequent letters he declared me his enemy, which, indeed, affected me very little. When, thanks to divine Providence, the letters and orders of the Sacred Congregation, written in the name of the Holy Father, came to me, I, laying aside all human respect for family or parentage, rigorously executed them, and, presenting myself to Taafe in this city, exhorted him most pressingly to be obedient to the Holy See, it being a human fault to err, but a truly diabolical one to persevere in error. He, in the beginning, despised my exhortation, and with a fierce oath exclaimed that the Queen Mother, who had obtained for him this Commission from two Sovereign Pontiffs, would maintain him in spite of all his opponents; and he boasted that he would send me and all the clergy of Ireland into exile. I answered, that we were all ready to suffer in so just a cause, but that with God's aid he would not be able to prevail in any way against us. Taafe afterwards, reflecting on matters, thought better to write to me, declaring that he would submit to the commands of the Holy See and of the Sacred Congregation, as I announce to his Eminence Cardinal Barberini in the enclosed letter, which you will hand to him without delay.

" For the rest, it would be tedious to describe all the particulars of the manner of proceeding of this friar : *ex ungue leonem.* He has commanded all his Visitators to exact twenty scudi from each Vicar-General, and four scudi from each Parish Priest ; and he commanded that in case of poverty, and of their not being able to pay this sum, they should on three successive Sundays, *intra Missarum Solemnia,* ask it as alms from the people. His manner of life gives occasion to great scandal. May God grant him repentance, and give him grace to change his life."

Taafe went through all this farce more as the dupe of Peter Walsh than through any malice of his own. After repeated summonses he at length repaired to the Eternal City, and for many years he led a retired life in the Convent of St. Isidore.

On the same day on which the bishops were nominated to the vacant sees, Dr. Patrick Plunket was transferred from Ardagh to Meath. Dr. Oliver Plunket, when petitioning for this translation, assigned as its motive the sad condition to which the diocese of Ardagh had been reduced since the devastation of Cromwell. " No two Catholics," he says, " have been left in possession of their hereditary estates, and the whole country is parcelled out between the soldiers of Cromwell and the merchants of London, who purchased it from that tyrant or from Parliament."*

In the month of April following Dr. Plunket obtained for the same prelate the faculty of conferring Holy Orders "*extra tempora et non servatis interstitiis ;*" as also " of consecrating the holy oils in the presence of at least five priests ; but not on any other day except Holy Thursday, unless necessity should require the contrary." † The most important petition, however, presented by him to the Secretary of the Sacred Congregation was addressed in the name of all the bishops, and was as follows :—

" To establish peace and order in the thirty-six dioceses, which are in the four provinces of the kingdom of Ireland, whose secular clergy amounts to the number of a thousand, the regulars, moreover, being six hundred, and the Catholic population two millions, we supplicate your Excellency, through the great zeal and affection you bear our kingdom, to consider the following points :—

" 1. That until such time as the sees of Ireland be provided with Bishops and Vicars Apostolic, the Bishops already appointed may nominate Vicars-General to the dioceses which are vacant, or may become vacant, that thus all occasion of schism may be removed.

" 2. That the Vicars Apostolic, should they be constituted, may be made dependent on the resident Bishop of the Province.

" 3. That on any day of Lent the Bishops may consecrate the Holy Oils.

" 4. That the Bishops may have the faculty of blessing a Crucifix, which being kissed by the dying, may communicate to them the indulgence *in articulo mortis*, and that he may bless one such Crucifix for each Parish Priest.

" 5. That the Bishops may be enabled to communicate their faculties to such Irish Priests, as moved by the Spirit of God, may feel a vocation to undertake the arduous mission of the American islands to succour the many thousands of Irish Catholics sent thither into exile by the tyrant Cromwell, and who, through the want of Priests, run great risk of their eternal salvation.

* " Non vi sono due Signori Cattolici in possesso dei loro Castelli o possessioni essendo quasi tutta (la diocesi) distribuita tra i soldati di Cromwello tiranno e tra i Mercanti di Londra, i quali l'hanno comprato dal Parlamento o dal detto Cromwello."

† " Consecrandi olea cum quinque saltem Sacerdotibus, non extra diem Coenae Dni. nisi necessitas aliud urgeat."

" 6. That by one Order or one Brief, an indulgence may be granted to all the Cathedrals, Churches and Parishes of Ireland on their titular feast, their dedication, the festivals of our Lord, of the Blessed Virgin, and the holy Apostles. I said in virtue of one Brief or Order ; for to multiply Briefs for every Church would be too tedious and dangerous in a country ruled by heretics, where there are rigorous penal laws against any such communication with Rome ; and that this indulgence may be gained wherever the Parish Priest says Mass, for we have no fixed Churches or Oratories, but celebrate the Holy Sacrifice often in the fields, now at one place, now at another, and often too in the castles of the nobility and gentry." . . .

These faculties seem to have been accorded by the Holy Father ; but when, a little later, Dr. Plunket, as Archbishop of Armagh, represented the imminent danger of being detected by the Government spies, and the difficulty of assembling so many priests, and hence further solicited the faculty of consecrating the oils with the assistance of only *two priests,* he received for answer from the Secretary of the Holy Office that this case had been already provided for (*jam provisum est*) in the faculties communicated to bishops in heretical countries (*in locis infidelium*).

Whilst Dr. Plunket thus laboured in the Eternal City to promote the interests of the Irish Church, he displayed an equal solicitude in providing for the wants of his suffering countrymen who perchance had taken refuge in that common asylum of all the faithful. I find one instance especially recorded in a MS. account of some of the early students of the Irish College.* In the month of April, 1666, Dr. Edmund O'Reilly, Archbishop of Armagh, took his departure from Rome. A few days before his leaving an ecclesiastic arrived from Ireland, and solicited admission to the Irish College. No burse, however, was vacant in the College, and as the young traveller's funds were exhausted, a sad alternative presented itself to his mind. No sooner was this case of distress made known to Dr. Plunket, than he set to work to satisfy the pious desires of the young man, and obtaining a contribution of 30 scudi from the Primate, from

* Archiv. Colleg. Hib. de Urbe.

various other individuals an additional sum of 50 scudi, and supplying 20 scudi, the sum which was yet wanting, from his own scanty funds, he succeeded in placing him within the College walls, and maintaining him there till such time as he was able to enjoy a burse of that institution.

It was perhaps at this period that Dr. Plunket composed the Irish poem to which O'Reilly, in his *Irish Writers*, refers as commencing with the words, " Oh Tara of the Kings!" During his infancy he had often roamed about the royal hill, and it cannot surprise us that in after-life his soul should dwell with rapture on the ancient glories of his country clustered around its summit.   Such reminiscences especially could not fail to recur to his mind when standing amidst the ruined trophies of the persecutors of the Christian name, he contemplated from afar the struggles of his countrymen, and the persecutions which they endured, not so much in the cause of nationality as for the faith of their fathers.   One quatrain of this poem is preserved in the Egerton manuscript (British Museum, No. 146), with the heading " The saying of Primate Plunket, who was put to death in London," and has been thus translated :—

" Tara of Kings ! bright was thy fame in days of yore,
When Cormac, son of Conn, the royal sceptre bore ;
Now the rude Sass'nach reaps corn on the sacred soil,
Where Brehons, and brave chiefs gave laws to Erin's Isle."

CHAPTER IV.

DR. PLUNKET NOMINATED ARCHBISHOP OF ARMAGH.

ON the 9th of July, 1669, Dr. Oliver Plunket was nominated by the Sacred Congregation Archbishop of Armagh.   His illustrious predecessor had been compelled, by the storm of persecution which laid waste our island, to seek an asylum on the Continent, and some months had now elapsed since death closed his eventful career.   Having been almost wholly deprived for many years of the presence of its chief spiritual

D

pastor, the Church of Armagh was torn by dissensions, and the germs of many scandals had appeared in some of the districts subject to the primatial see. Hence, urgent were the solicitations of the Irish prelates to have a successor appointed without delay, who might heal these wounds, and restore peace and tranquillity to the desolate flocks. None more forcibly represented to the Holy See the necessity of appointing at once a distinguished prelate to the vacant church, than the Most Rev. Peter Talbot, the lately consecrated Archbishop of Dublin. On the 15th of May, 1669, he thus writes to the Cardinal Prefect of Propaganda:—

"With due reverence I have received here in Brussels, the Apostolic letters and the faculties, together with a letter of your Eminence, addressed to me, and another addressed to the clergy of Dublin; and on last Sunday I was consecrated in Antwerp. I confess that the burden imposed on me by His Holiness far exceeds my strength, which I know to be slight indeed. But I hope that the spirit which rules the whole Church, and distributes its graces and gifts according to the exigency of the office which each one discharges, will also grant to me such aid as may enable me to guard from the wolves the flock committed to my charge, and to repel the last efforts of Peter Walsh; who, not content with his past persecution, now again leaves no stone unturned to obtain a confirmation in his infamous office of government satellite and spy, that thus he may continue in his schism. To attain this dignity, he is preparing for a journey to England, strengthened by the solicitations of some heretics, and the commendatory letters of the pseudo-Primate of Armagh. But these arms will but little aid the cause of the discredited and foolish man, who received a fatal blow in the fall of the Duke of Ormond, or at least in his removal from the government of Ireland. As for me, both by my own desire, and by the counsel of my friends, I hasten to London in order to oppose Walsh, and confirm the royal ministers in their sentiments and hatred of his iniquities. Thence I shall proceed direct to Dublin, and soon acquaint your Eminence with the present state of matters, and my future hopes.

"But as no part of Ireland stands so much in need of a proper Pastor and Primate as the province of Armagh, in which the clergy is split into factions, giving occasion of great scandal not only to the Irish Catholics, but also to the English and Scotch Protestants, who are very numerous in Ulster, I cannot delay to acquaint your Eminence with the necessity of promptly nominating an Archbishop for Armagh. For though it is not expedient for the present to create many bishops, lest Ormond should say that the Papal authority had received a sudden and dangerous increase in Ireland since his withdrawal ; nevertheless, the Bishop of Armagh added to the other three Archbishops can give no occasion of evil report or envy, especially should he be a person not displeasing to the Court. Three have been proposed to me by those best acquainted with matters and persons. *D. Patrick Everard*, a learned theologian, exceedingly pious and prudent. He suffered much for the Catholic faith during the thirty-six years which he strenuously and untiringly laboured in cultivating the vineyard of the Lord, and in rooting out vices in the province of Armagh, of which he is a native, and he is descended from a noble and ancient family. His prudence appears even from the fact that in all the dissensions of the clergy of his province, he was never known to be the author or promoter of factions ; and whilst there was no more determined enemy of the Remonstrants, no one, at the same time, was less obnoxious to the Government. He opposed and condemned the Dublin approval of the Sorbonic propositions; he is well skilled in the Irish language, preaches also in English, and is dear to both nations; nor will his appointment be displeasing to the king. The second proposed to me for the Primacy is *D. Thomas Fitzsymons*, or *M ic Symons*, to whom nothing is objected excepting his having signed the Dublin formula. The third is *Dr. Nugent*, who lives in Spain, and I believe taught there ; but I do not deem him so well suited as Dr. Everard.

" Moreover, as the province of Armagh is so vast, that at least two suffragans may be required, and as the Bishop of Kilmore is either delirious or deficient in many things, I would recommend *D. Oliver Dease*, Vicar-General of Meath, as worthy of the see of Ardagh, or of Clogher, especially as the only objection made to him is that of age ; whilst, nevertheless, he is of a robust constitution. Surely the number of years during which he has fought the battles of God, should favour, rather than impede, the promotion of one who is thus at the same time full of merits and of years.

" No public danger can now be feared from Father James Taafe, for he is so deficient as well in cash as in prudence. that he can be of harm only to himself : he is deemed a solemn impostor by all He daily promises to start for Belgium, and, I am sure, he will be faithful to his promise, for without money it will be difficult for him to remain any length of time in England. . . .

" PETER OF DUBLIN.

" Brussels, 15th May, 1669. (styl. vet.)"

Besides those here proposed by Dr. Talbot, many others were recommended to the Sacred Congregation as worthy to succeed to the Primatial See. Some difficulty, however, was met with in regard to each of them. Dr. Everard, for instance, a member of the Society of Jesus, was Rector of the Irish College of Antwerp, and the only pillar of its support ; and his removal from it threatened to deprive the

nation of that ecclesiastical resource. Dr. Nugent was
advanced in years, and the merits of Dr. Fitzsimons had not
as yet been sufficiently attested to justify his nomination to
that important see. "But why delay," said the Holy Father,
"in discussing the dubious merits of others, whilst we have
here in Rome, a native of that island, whose merits are
known to us all, and whose labours in this city have
already added so many wreaths to the peerless glory of
the 'Island of Saints.' Let D. Oliver Plunket be Archbishop
of Armagh."*

This appointment, whilst it filled with terror and dismay
the sowers of dissension and the enemies of our holy faith,
called forth the applause of the true lovers of Ireland, and of
the watchful guardians of that chosen portion of the Church
of God. The illustrious Bishop of Ferns thus writes from
his place of exile to the Archbishop of Cesarea, then Secretary
of the Sacred Congregation of Propaganda :—

"Most Illustrious and Rev. Lord,—Applauding and rejoicing,
I have hastened hither from Gand to the most Reverend and
Illustrious Internuncio of Belgium, to return all possible thanks to
our Holy Father, in the name of my countrymen, for having crowned
with the mitre of Armagh the noble and distinguished Oliver Plunket,
Doctor of Theology. . . To your influence we owe it, that such a
prelate, of noble birth, and adorned with exalted talents, benevolence,
and virtue (and yet of no proud conceit) should be raised to the
government of the Primatial Church, the Spirit of God leading the
minds of their Eminences to this conclusion. It came from on high
(such is my opinion), that whilst your Excellency wisely laid open
this matter to the Holy Father, he should place this excellent man
on the mountain of the Church, in which office he will be a light to
all who hope in the Lord.

"The Holy Father acted holily and justly, in promoting a devoted

---

* His contemporary, Arsdekin, thus writes: "Præbuit div. Providentia
occasionem, per quam acquisitum tot annis solidæ sapientiæ thesaurum in
patria insuam latius erogaret. Postulabatur a Sum. Pont. Clemente IX.
præsul idoneus qui Ecclesiam Armacanam cum suprema Primatis potestate
in Hibernia administraret . . . Demum sua Sanctitas omnibus pro rei
gravitate expensis in hanc sententiam conclusit: Non est cur diutius
consultemus de incertis, quando rem certam ante oculos habemus. En
virum probatæ virtutis, consummatæ doctrinæ, diuturnæ experientiæ in
ipsa urbis Romæ luce omnibus dotibus conspicuum Oliverium Plunketum:
hunc ego Archepiscopum. Armacanum, hunc ego Hiberniæ Primatem
Apostolica auctoritate constituo."—(*Theol. Trip.*, tom. iii., p. 227.)

child of the Roman See, rather than one who, having favoured Walsh the Philistine, when combating against the Ark of God, nowise deserved to be honoured by the Church. . . Do you, in the meantime, most illustrious Lord, pursue your course; for by your counsel, affection, and efforts, the falling hierarchy of the Irish Church has commenced to exalt itself above heresy and error; according to your piety, promote the members of both Clergy, but only such as are faithful servants of God, soldiers of Christ, champions of the Cross devoted to the Holy See, and holily fulfilling their vows to God. I lovingly kiss your consecrated hands.

"In all things your most obedient servant,

"NICHOLAS, Bishop of Ferns.

"Brussels, 30th August, 1669."

Dr. James Dowley, lately appointed Vicar Apostolic of Limerick, writes in like manner, congratulating the Holy See on the happy appointment made to Armagh :—

"MOST ILLUSTRIOUS AND REV. LORD,—I return exceeding thanks to your Excellency for my election in the last Congregation (through your solicitude and care) as Vicar Apostolic of Limerick, whilst I also find that it is your intention to exalt me, though unworthy, to a still higher dignity.*

"Most pleasing to all was the appointment of Dr. Plunket, and I doubt not but it will be agreeable to the Government, to the secular clergy, and to the nobility; and all this we owe to your Excellency. We shall soon return to our country, when I shall give you an account of the flock committed to my charge.

"JAMES DOWLEY.

"Paris, 23rd August, 1669.

"To the Archbishop of Cæsarea, &c."

The ornament of the College of St. Sulpice, in Paris, was at this time Dr. John O'Molony, who a few years later was appointed bishop of the ancient see of Killaloe. He too thus returned thanks to the Sacred Congregation for the favour now conferred on the Irish Church :—†

"New favours require the expression of new gratitude, and the renewal of benefits can only be requited by the renewal of thanks· giving. Not long ago, though unknown to your Excellency, yet, laying aside all fear of temerity, I addressed to you letters expressive

---

* Some years later he was appointed *Bishop* of that see.
† Dr. Malony, in 1671, was appointed Bishop of Killaloe. During the exile of the royal family on the Continent he was attached to the Court; subsequently he was Dean of Cashel, Canon of Rouen, in France, &c.

of my sincere gratitude for the great watchfulness and solicitude which you displayed for the welfare of our Church, as though it alone occupied your attention, though on you rests the burden of so large a portion of the whole Catholic world. You had already laid the foundations of our edifice, erected the pillars, and given shepherds to feed the sheep and the lambs : but now, that the work should not remain imperfect, you have crowned the edifice, and provided a Pastor for the Pastors themselves, appointing the Archbishop of Armagh. For it is not of the Diocese of Armagh alone that he has the administration, to whom the primacy and guardianship of all Ireland is entrusted. One therefore in a thousand had to be chosen, suited to bear so great a burden. That one you have found: one than whom none other better or more pleasing could be found; with whom (that your wise solicitude for our distracted and afflicted country should be wanting in nothing) you have been pleased to associate his Suffragan of Ardagh, a most worthy and grave man.* With what thanksgiving, then, or praises I should extol you, I know not, for your benefits exceed all thanks and all praise: I therefore supplicate you to return yourself due thanks, that thus those whom you have eternally bound to you by your benefits may be still more closely bound by your becoming minister of their thanksgiving : whilst I, the last of your disciples, who am not worthy to be called your disciple, shall never be unmindful of your benefits, but will ever be, your Excellency's

"Most obliged servant,

"J. O'MOLONY.

"Paris, 16th August, 1669."

More interesting still is the letter addressed to the Secretary of Propaganda, Monsignor Baldeschi, by the illustrious Archbishop of Dublin, who rejoices in like manner in the happy choice of the Holy Father, and assigns, as his motive for not having already proposed Dr. Plunket in the first place for the see of Armagh, the request of that prelate, who had expressed a desire to prolong yet awhile his stay in the Eternal City :—

"MOST ILLUSTRIOUS AND REV. LORD,—Most agreeable to me were the Roman letters by which I learned the promotion of the most Illustrious and Reverend Oliver Plunket to the see of Armagh ; nor less pleasing to all good men was the announcement of what had been done against the Remonstrants as well in Spain as in Ireland, although as yet we are ignorant of the particulars, for which I anxiously look forward ; and all this must be attributed to the piety

* Gerard Farrell, O.S.D., who for a short time had acted in the Roman Curia as agent of Dr. Edmund O'Reilly, was on the same day appointed Vicar Apostolic of Ardagh.

and zeal of your Excellency. Certainly no one could be appointed better suited than Dr. Oliver Plunket, whom I myself would have proposed in the first place, were it not that he had written to me, stating his desire not to enter for some years on the Irish mission, until he should have completed some works which he was preparing for the press.

"Peter Walsh talks of signing a submission to the Holy See; whether, however, with sincerity or not we shall learn very soon; for he knows that I leave London within a few days, and he promises to do more within that time than I can easily give him credit for. However, he can do but little harm, as he dares not return to Ireland; and his capital enemy, the Earl of Orrery, remains here in England, caressed by the King and Buckingham. Perhaps this may induce Walsh, though late, to think seriously of conversion to the Catholic faith and religious discipline.

"In the month of October the Parliament will assemble, and we are in dread of persecution if liberty of conscience be not granted. The King, however, has little to fear, for he has won over some of the heads of the different factions. I have hurriedly written those few lines, as the bearer is taking his departure; but I shall write at greater length from Dublin. In the meantime, &c., &c.,

"PETER OF DUBLIN,
"Primate of Ireland.

"London, 11th August (styl. vet.), 1669."

The Bulls appointing Dr. Plunket Archbishop of Armagh were despatched to the Internuncio in Brussels, and the decree of the Sacred Congregation was conveyed to him, destining Belgium as the place of consecration. This had already been deemed the more prudent course in the case of the bishops appointed in the preceding January; and in the life of Dr. Brennan and other prelates, we see the same course pursued in their regard; for it was supposed that by being consecrated in Rome the prejudices of the Government would be more awakened, and the bishops rendered more obnoxious in their future labours. But Dr. Plunket was too attached to Rome not to ardently desire to receive the sacred consecration within its hallowed walls, amidst its sanctuaries and shrines. He wished to go forth from Rome fully armed for the spiritual fight, as so many apostles and martyrs had hitherto gone forth, to scatter the heavenly seed, to reap the good harvest; and perhaps, too, consummating his course like them, to receive the martyr's crown. Hence he addressed an energetic petition to the Sacred

Congregation, to have its order reversed, and sacred consecration imparted to him in the Eternal City. " No one," he
thus concludes, " was ever known to be obliged to leave
Rome and seek elsewhere the holy gift of consecration,
save, perhaps, Dr. Burgatt ; and, as if by fate, his Brief
strayed from place to place, and only after great delay, and
beset by many dangers, could that prelate receive consecration ; let, then, this crowning favour be added to the many
others I have received, and I shall ever more and more be
bound in union with the Holy See and the Sacred Congregation." There are many passages of this letter which disclose
further particulars connected with the subjects of these
memoirs, and some facts relating to the history of the
Irish Church, which are otherwise unrecorded :—

" The whole Irish nation [he says] and especially the poor house
of Plunket, have received so many favours and benefits from your
Excellency, that neither heart, nor tongue, nor deeds, can ever
render due thanks to so pious and beneficent a protector.

" Monsignor Plunket obtained the episcopate of Meath, which is
the most fruitful and largest in the whole kingdom, and where his
nephews have the greatest part of their lands. Dr. James Phelan,
actual chaplain of the Lady Mary Plunket, niece of Monsignor
Plunket, has been promoted to Ossory ; and lately we have had the
appointment, as Vicar Apostolic of Ardagh, of D. Gerard Farrell,
who was for many years chaplain to the sister of Monsignor Plunket,
and in Rome to Sir Nicholas Plunket, ambassador of the Irish
Catholics to that city, who received knighthood from Innocent X.

" The Primate, who died in France within the month of March
last, belonged to the province of Dublin ; his predecessor was Hugh
O'Reilly, of the Diocese of Kilmore; his predecessor again was
Peter Lombard, of Waterford, in the province of Cashel, who was
highly esteemed by Clement VIII., and Paul V. ; the predecessor of
Lombard was Richard Creagh ; his predecessor was of the house of
Netterville, in the diocese of Meath, and the predecessor of Netterville was of the Dowdall family, also of the diocese of Meath : and
if I mistake not, a certain Octavianus Palladius, a Florentine, was
Archbishop of Armagh, and transferred the residence of the Primates
from Armagh to Drogheda, which is the second city of the kingdom,
half of which is in the diocese of Armagh, and the other half in
Meath, being divided by the river Boyne. . . . I have seen myself
(for he died within my own time) Malachy O'Queely, of the province
of Cashel, Archbishop of Tuam ; and at present, Dr. Lynch is Bishop
of Kilfenora, although a native of the diocese of Tuam.

" The nephew of Monsignor Plunket, that is, Lord Fingall, whilst
commanding the infantry in the Royal army, was made prisoner by

the Cromwellians not far from Dublin, and put to death in the tower of Dublin. Monsignor Plunket then, with Sir Nicholas, his brother, and Lord Fingall, his grand-nephew, lived in exile in France and Flanders during the whole time of the Cromwellians. The king being restored, Dr. Plunket returned without delay, and being the only Bishop capable of performing the Pontifical functions, he ordained in the very capital during many years, *two hundred and fifty priests*, from all parts of the kingdom, administered the sacrament of Confirmation to a large number, and faithfully carried out the commands of the Sacred Congregation. . . .

" It is, indeed, true, that it is not a matter of prudence to promote those who took a prominent part in the various factions during the late war, and are held in positive abhorrence by the king; but I believe that it is not desirable to advance those who seek for promotion through the English Court, for such persons always adopt the doctrines of the Sorbonne, and should any question arise, they will adhere to the king, and not to the Apostolic See; and, ordinarily speaking, they are restless, ambitious, and flatterers; seeking evil report, and listening not to truth; and pursuing their own interests, not those of Jesus Christ. . . And, were the Holy Father to appoint persons truly great and affectionate towards the Holy See, such as the late Primate and the Bishop of Ferns, and two other bishops put to death in Ireland, even though they should find little favour at court, I am sure that their death or exile would be of great glory and honour to the Apostolic Church, which 'sanguine et persecutione martyrum et confessorum crevit, crescit, et crescet (by the blood and sufferings of her confessors and martyrs ever increased, increases, and will yet increase). Thrasamund, Arian King of the Vandals, in Africa, in order to root out the Catholics, published a decree, that no more Catholic bishops should be consecrated. What then did the Catholic bishops do? They consecrated in one day, seventy-two bishops; wherefore, the infuriated Thrasamund sent them and many others into exile, into Sardinia. And yet, Symmachus, writing to St. Fulgentius, and to the other exiled bishops, deemed the Church of Christ triumphant in these her glorious champions."

Dr. Plunket adds, that, "on one occasion Innocent appointed twelve bishops for Ireland," and concludes as we have cited above.

The Primate-Elect, however, appealed in vain: the decision had been made, and the Sacred Congregation was inexorable. Thus frustrated in his holy design, he wished, at least, to be the bearer to his afflicted Church of a sacred treasure, of which, through the violence of the persecution, it had been long deprived. Its history is as follows:—

In 1648, the Most Rev. John Bapt. Scanarola, a noble

citizen of Modena, and Bishop of Sidonia, admiring the generous spirit of self-sacrifice and religious zeal which the Irish nation then displayed, whilst combating around the altar and the throne, presented to the primatial see of Armagh a cross of massive gold, containing relics of the holy wood of the Cross, of the Blessed Virgin, St. Joseph, and other saints, and entrusted it to the care of the illustrious Bishop of Ferns, Dr. French, who was then in Rome on an embassy from the confederate Council to the Holy Father. It was a condition, however, of this gift that it should be ever preserved in the Cathedral Church, and with due solemnity exposed to the veneration of the faithful. But Dr. French knew too well the sad condition of the Church of Armagh, at that period, to guarantee these conditions. He had seen the fury of the storm which had lately swept unchecked over the northern province; and hence he recommended a delay of a little while till order should be again restored, and religious liberty be achieved by the arms of the Confederates. In 1654, Monsignor Scanarola formally renewed his donation to the Cathedral of Armagh, and, by act of public notary, declared Father Luke Wadding and other members of the Franciscan convent of St. Isidore, the depositaries and guardians of his gift, until the conditions referred to above could safely be carried out.

Dr. Plunket deemed that such a time had now arrived, and anxious to be himself the bearer of this precious relic to his afflicted flock, addressed the following petition to the Holy Father :—

"In the tenth year of Innocent X., of happy memory, when Cromwell drove the clergy of Ireland into exile, and destroyed our church, Monsignor Scanarola presented a cross of gold, with a relic of the most holy Cross, to the Church of Armagh, with the annexed condition, that it should be publicly exposed for veneration. Now that, through the mercy of God, the persecution of Cromwell has passed, and as, through the clemency of his present Majesty, we enjoy such liberty that the Catholics have public oratories. and even the Regular Clergy have opened their novitiates, your petitioner most humbly supplicates your Holiness to command the Friars of the Reformed Order at St. Isidore's, who hold that cross in their custody, to consign it to me for the consolation and devotion of the Catholics in the province of Armagh, who will ever pray for the welfare of your Holiness."

As in his subsequent letters, Dr. Plunket never renews his solicitations for this holy relic, it seems probable that his petition had a favourable result ; but I have been unable to find any certain record of its success.

Before we come to the consecration of this successor of Ireland's glorious apostle, one other fact remains to be recorded. Dr. Plunket had acquired, during his residence in Rome, a small vineyard on the declivity of the hill whose summit is crowned by castle Gandolfo, and adjoining the farm then belonging to the Irish College, but known in after years as the *villeggiatura* of the novitiate of the Jesuits of St. Andrew on the Quirinal. Before taking his departure from the Eternal City, Dr. Plunket presented this vineyard to the Irish College, anxious to testify his affection for the nursery of his youth, in which he had been trained to the sacred ministry, and whose brightest glory he himself was soon to become by his apostolic labours and heroic martyrdom. It seems that he left several of his books to the same college, many of which were lost when its library was scattered during the French invasion of Rome. Some, however, still remain, and one in particular is carefully treasured in its archives, having the simple record written with his own hand :—" Oliver Plunkette, Collegio Hibern. dedit." We will hereafter see that in his last letter addressed to his relative Michael Plunket, then student of the college, the only dying memorial which he bequeathes, is one to the same loved abode of his early years. " The pictures which are there I leave to the place where you are, and where I got my first education ; would there were *cornici* (frames) to them." How dear these paintings would now be to every Irish Catholic, and how sad that they, as most of the other memorials of the old Irish College, should have been plundered at the period of the invasion of Rome by the French republicans towards the close of the last century !

CHAPTER V.

CONSECRATION OF DR. PLUNKET.

From a commendatory letter addressed by the General Superior of the Dominicans, Father Peter Mary Passerino, to the Provincial of the Order in Ireland, we learn that Dr. Plunket took his departure from the Eternal City towards the close of August, 1669. Father Passerino, in this letter, extols the virtues of the Archbishop-Elect, and speaks of his merits as known to the whole city :—

" The bearer of this letter, the Most Rev. and Illustrious Archbishop of Armagh, and Primate of the kingdom of Ireland, departs from Rome ; and as we wish him a happy journey to his destination, so we desire that he may be greeted on his arrival with your reverential homage, and that of your subjects. In this matter to remind you of the obligation by which all are bound, it would suffice to recall to mind the exalted dignity of so great a Primate and Archbishop ; but even this dignity is equalled by the many and great merits of the same most worthy prelate, which are known to the whole city of Rome, so that on this account our devoted homage must be in every respect redoubled. Let, therefore, your paternity be attentive, that on all occasions our Order may display peculiar devotion and reverence towards so excellent a prelate, and that the most benign affection which he openly professes for the Dominican family may never be defrauded of the due return of gratitude and recognition. Thus may you prosper with those subject to your care, and be often mindful of us and our companions in your Holy Mass and prayers.

" Rome, 24th August, 1669.

" Fr. Peter Mary Passerino."

The incidents of Dr. Plunket's journey from Rome to Brussels are unknown to us. It was not an age of railways and steamboats, when that road may be run over in little more than two days. Two months at least were then required for that journey, and it was only in the beginning of November, 1669, that the Archbishop-Elect entered the city of Brussels. A few months earlier in the same year Dr. Burgatt, the Archbishop-Elect of Cashel, pursued the same homeward course ; and from a letter of his, written at Milan, we may

learn the difficulties which beset travellers in those days, from
the want of conveyances, the broken roads, and the continual
overflowing of the rivers:—

"It was not without difficulty that we arrived here on yesterday,
the little mountain streams being swollen into torrents by the heavy
rains, and consequently impeding our progress. We remained at
Bologna eight days (all the vehicles being engaged by the local
nobility—I know not for what feast or amusement) ; the overflowing
of the Po detained us two days in Padua: yesterday our boat sailed
for five entire miles over trees, and corn-fields, and vineyards, the
whole country being inundated by the river. Neither is it possible
for us to get away from this city, the same cause preventing us. I
hope in the divine mercy that all these obstacles will prepare, at
least, a peaceful port for us at the close of our journey. We have
learned nothing from Ireland or other parts worth communicating.
We shall leave as soon as possible. In the meantime your Excellency
will be pleased to expedite everything connected with the progress
and peace of our Church, which also Dr. Plunket will take care to
suggest. . . .
Milan, 5th May, 1669."

It was in the beginning of November that the Internunzio
in Brussels welcomed our Archbishop-Elect to his hospitality,* and this worthy representative of the Holy See soon
discovered that his guest was truly what his Roman friends
had already proclaimed him to be, full of zeal for the propagation of the faith, and one who by his merits and wisdom
would render still more illustrious the exalted dignity to
which he had been destined.

"I was in Liège [he thus writes to the Sacred Congregation]
when Monsignor Plunket arrived here. On my return to Brussels
I welcomed him to my house, where he still remains. I have written
to the Bishop of Ghent to arrange for his consecration, as from that
city he can without delay continue his journey to Ireland. I am still
awaiting his answer. I have found in Monsignor Plunket most
excellent qualities, and his zeal to labour for the glory of God gives
grounds for the greatest hopes. I am consoled and rejoiced that the
favours of our Holy Father are so well conferred."

The Bishop of Ghent was invited to consecrate the Elect
of Armagh, and an illustrious member of the Irish hierarchy,

* Dr. Plunket, writing on the 22nd September (styl. vet.), 1672 (that
is, 2nd October), says: "Three years all to one month have now elapsed
since I had the honour of being caressed by your Excellency in your
Palace at Brussels."

Dr. French, Bishop of Ferns, then living in exile in that city
was to be one of the assistants. This glorious Confessor
hastened to Brussels to welcome the Prelate whom he had
long admired, and who was now about to become the
pillar of our ancient Church. On Saturday, the 22nd of
November, he once more hastened from Brussels towards
Ghent, accompanied by Dr. Plunket, and the following day
was destined for the consecration. But a slight illness of the
consecrating Prelate supervened, and it was only on the
30th of November, 1669,* in the private chapel of the
Episcopal Palace, that Dr. Plunket at length received from
the Bishop of Ghent, the solemn imposition of hands, and
was consecrated Archbishop of Armagh. But the Bishop
of Ferns claims it as his special right to announce the
consecration of his illustrious friend, and we must now allow
him to speak for himself:—

"I present a concise narrative of the consecration of the most
illustrious Archbishop of Armagh. His Excellency the Internunzio
wrote most kind letters to the Bishop of this diocese, requesting him
to perform it, and he most readily acquiesced. But I, on receiving
this news, set out at once for Brussels to conduct hither his Grace of
Armagh, bound by gratitude to render him this homage. A slight
fever seized our excellent Bishop on the Saturday before the 24th
Sunday after Pentecost, which had been fixed for Dr. Plunket's consecration ; wherefore that ceremony was deferred till the first Sunday
in Advent, on which day it was devoutly and happily performed in
the Capella of the Palace, without noise, and with closed doors ; for
such was the desire of the Archbishop of Armagh. Remaining here
for eight days after his consecration, he passed his time in dispatching
letters and examining my writings. These are two small works,
viz., *A Refutation of the wicked Remonstrance, or the Protestation of
Walsh;* and *A Bulwark for the House of God*, that is, a just defence
of the religious congregations profanely lacerated with the
greatest impiety, fury, and madness by those who envied the
innocence, probity, and efforts of the clergy of Ireland, who
strenuously laboured to sustain the kingdom of Christ, and earnestly
asserted the honour, and dignity, and power of the Holy See. In the
foremost rank of these persecutors Peter Walsh led the way, not

* Airoldi writes on the 23rd November, 1669 :—"Partì ieri mattina
verso Gante per ricevere ivi consacrazione Monsig. Plunket." He again
writes on the 30th :—"Doveva Domenica passata seguire in Gante la
consacrazione di Monsignor Plunket, ma certa indisposizione di quel
Monsignor Vescovo ha fatto differir la consacrazione sino al giorno d'
oggi."

only amongst the orthodox, but also amongst the Protestants. His Grace of Armagh left with me in writing his testimony as to the irreproachable integrity of the aforesaid works in point of morality and faith.

"These things I deemed proper to state to you regarding the consecration, delay, and occupation in this city of his Grace of Armagh, to whom I pray all things most prosperous, as also to your Excellency, who by your influence caused him to be placed as a pillar in the Church of God. I most reverently kiss your sacred hands.

"NICHOLAS OF FERNS.

"Ghent, 19th December, 1669."

During the age of persecution the Bishops of Belgium displayed for the persecuted members of our Irish Church true Christian sympathy and charity; and we learn from some letters of those times, that they not only admitted to their hospitality the Irish prelates who sought consecration at their hands, but, moreover, on the day of consecration, presented to them rich gifts, generally a precious ring, and other ornaments for the sacred functions of their ministry. Dr. Plunket continued in Ghent for eight days after his consecration, and thence setting out for England, arrived in London about the middle of December, 1669. Even during his short stay in Belgium, his attention was wholly engaged in the promotion of the interests of our holy faith. Through his solicitations, the learned Jesuit, Arsdekin, a native of Kilkenny, and at this time lecturing on divinity in the University of Louvain,* composed his learned work, entitled *Theologia Universa Tripartita*, which acquired for the author a universal fame, in a few years passing through more than ten editions on the Continent. From the letter of Dr. French, we also see with what an interest he encouraged that exiled prelate in his invaluable writings, which are all so replete with the love of our country and of our holy faith.

* "Pergit igitur Apostolica auctoritate ac monitis instructus iter in Hiberniam per Belgium instituere, ubi cum et ego tunc Lovanii illius alloquis fruitus essem, inter primos auctor fuit ut hoc opus in Missionariorum Apostolicorum subsidium elaborarem, quo etiam titulo singulari, illum sibi inter primos Patronos vindicare debet."—(*Th. Tripart.*, pag. 227, tom. iii.)

Before hastening to the scene of his future labours, Dr. Plunket delayed some time in London, and it was only about the month of March, 1670, that he arrived in Ireland. He had many relatives and acquaintances at Court, and as the opening of Parliament was fixed for the beginning of February, he awaited there, anxious to use his influence in seeking to mitigate the rigour of those measures which many members had already vauntingly prepared for his suffering country. His letter, addressed from London, to the Cardinal Protector of Ireland, Cardinal Barberini, presents a most interesting narrative, being a detailed record of his stay in that city :—

" I presented the letters of your Eminence to the Queen, who gave me a most gratifying audience, and passed a high eulogium on your Eminence for the affection which you have ever displayed towards her, as also towards the King, and the entire nation ; and she added that persons sent by your Eminence had always been excellent and well disposed towards his Majesty, and that she had like hopes for me. I spoke with some who are familiar with the King, and they told me that he often refers to your Eminence with affection and regard. I also consigned your Eminence's letter to the Rev. Father Howard, Grand Almoner, a truly worthy man. He secretly lodged me for ten days in his own apartments in the Royal Palace ; with great kindness he often, too, conducted me in his carriage to see the principal curiosities of the city ; he is truly hospitable and munificent, and the refuge of all foreign Catholics; and he enjoys great favour with the King and Queen, and is loved by all, even by the Protestants, for his great gentleness and courtesy. I request your Eminence to thank him in your next letters for the kindness which he showed me, through esteem for your Eminence. Father Fernandez also, in consequence of your Eminence's letters, made many professions of readiness to serve me, and showed great courtesy. In my opinion, he is not very influential, and has but little weight with the Queen : est bonus vir, he is a good simple man.

" Walsh is here, hated by all; everyone holds him to have been excommunicated by the Commissary-General of Flanders. He received a command to withdraw to that country, under pain of excommunication, but he appealed to the General, and should the General send him such an order, he will appeal to the Pope, and from the Pope he will appeal to a Council, and from the Council to the tribunal of God. He is a lost man. Father Taafe will do well not to return any more to this quarter of the world, his very name is so abhorred by all. The Parliament will reassemble on the 14th of February, which was the day fixed in the prorogation ; when the Parliament is prorogued, the preceding sessions are of little avail,

The King asked for eight millions of scudi,* in order to pay his debts : but the Parliament declared they would only grant one million of scudi, and two hundred thousand more should France declare war against the Dutch. As the Government has no money we shall continue neutral. The Parliament often engages the King in foreign wars, and then refuses to grant supplies, in order that in his need he may be dependent on them ; and King James (the First) in order that he should not be thus dependent on the Parliament, never consented to embark in war, though he was instigated to it by the Parliament, in favour of the heretics of France and Germany. General Monk died this morning, lamented by all ; he was a man of moderation and courage. It is thought that Prince Rupert, or the Duke of Monmouth (natural son of the King) will be the future General. Here the cold is so intense that the wine of Spain was frozen in my chalice; for many years they have not experienced so rigid a season. A heavy fall of snow succeeded the ice, so that it is morally impossible to travel till this cold shall have passed. I have no desire, however, to remain in London, knowing the intention of the Court. The adherents of Walsh, or rather Walsh himself, sends to some of the Ministers of Court anonymous letters, full of falsehoods about my presence here ; but their malignity is known and they themselves are despised. A letter was written to the King, stating that Father Howard concealed three hundred priests in the Royal Palace, who made their rounds every night seeking to make proselytes for the Pope. These fabulous stories do this much good, that no credence is given to the writers even when they tell a little truth. The Duke of Ormond will do his utmost to excite some storm against the clergy, in order to molest Monsignor Talbot, Archbishop of Dublin, for whom he entertains a mortal hatred. Not to tire you further, I make a profound reverence.

"Your most devoted and obliged servant,

"OLIVER, Archbishop of Armagh,

"And Primate of Ireland.

"London, 30th December, 1669."

On the 18th of June, in the following year, Dr. Plunket again writes to the same Cardinal, and though his letter anticipates the matter of some of the subsequent chapters, yet it is all so interesting, that the reader will be glad to peruse it in full :—

"The continual favours which I received from your Eminence in Rome encourage me to lay before you a brief narrative of what has occurred since my departure from that city. Having arrived in London (as I already notified to your Eminence), I received that

* Two millions of pounds sterling.

E

courtesy from the Queen which she professes to be her desire to show
to all who come under the protection of your Eminence. I found
that the gentlemen of this Court, who have been in Rome, proclaim
to every one the great kindness and generosity of your Eminence,
and profess their obligations for the attention they received in that
city, on account of which the Catholics in England receive many
favours from them.

" I afterwards arrived in Ireland, in the month of March, and
hastened immediately to my residence : and I held two Synods, and
two Ordinations, and in a month and a-half I administered Confirmation to more than ten thousand persons, though throughout my
province I think there yet remain more than fifty thousand persons
to be confirmed. I remarked throughout the country, wherever I
went, that for every heretic there are twenty Catholics. The new
Viceroy is a man of great moderation ;. he willingly receives the
Catholics, and he treats privately with the ecclesiastics, and promises
them protection whilst they attend to their own functions, without
intriguing in the political affairs of Government. I found that four
of the principal persons in Court were secretly Catholics, and these
maintain the Viceroy in his favourable sentiments and esteem for the
Catholics ; so much so, that not long since he wrote a long letter to
the King in favour of the Irish clergy, declaring that they were good
subjects, and worthy of the favours of his Majesty. This is all that
now occurs to me, in order not to fatigue your Eminence, to whom
I pray every happiness, and make a profound reverence.

> " OLIVER OF ARMAGH,
> " Primate of Ireland.

" Dublin, 18th June, 1670."

Despite the intense cold which then prevailed, Dr. Plunket
resolved to delay no longer in the English capital, anxious
to avail himself of the approaching Lent to visit and console
his flock, and administer to them the consolations of religion.
At Holyhead he was detained for twelve days by contrary
winds; but at length, on Monday, about the middle of March,
1670, he was welcomed by his many friends who awaited
his arrival on the Irish shores. Before the close of the week
he thus announced to Monsignor Baldeschi the various
incidents of his journey from London to the Irish capital:—

" I at length arrived in this city on Monday last, and I may say
that I suffered more from London to Holyhead (where I went on
board of a vessel) than during the remainder of the journey from
Rome to London—excessive cold, stormy winds, and a heavy fall of
snow · and then when a thaw set in, the rivers became so swollen

that three times I was up to my knees in water in the carriage: I was detained twelve days at Holyhead in consequence of contrary winds; and then, after a rail of ten hours, I arrived in this port, where the many welcomes and caresses of my friends mitigated the sorrow with which I was oppressed on account of my departure from Rome.

" Sir Nicholas Plunket at once invited me to his house, and gave me his carriage : the Earl of Fingall, who is my cousin, invited me to his country seat. The Baron of Louth will give me board and lodging in my own diocese as long as I please, and I am resolved to accept the invitation of this gentleman, as he lives in the very centre of my mission : there are also three other knights who are married to three of my cousins, and who vie with each other in seeing which of them shall receive me into his house.

" I was also consoled to find the Bishop of Meath, though sixty-eight years old, yet so robust and so fresh, that he seemed to be no more than fifty: he has scarcely a grey hair in his head, and he sends his sincere respects to your Excellency. I write about these matters to your Excellency, knowing that you will be pleased to learn the happy success of one who reveres and loves you.

" I set out upon my journey despite the severity of the weather, that during the Lent I might be able to discharge part of my duty in my province; but I shall find it difficult to assemble five priests when consecrating the Holy Oils, especially during Holy Week, when all are occupied in hearing confessions : so I pray your Excellency to obtain for me the privilege of consecrating the Holy Oils with the assistance of only two priests."

Unfortunately this letter is without date; it seems to have been delayed for some time on the road, and it was only on the 7th of July that it was laid before the Sacred Congregation in Rome.

CHAPTER VI.

POLICY OF THE GOVERNMENT IN IRELAND AT THE BEGINNING
OF DR. PLUNKET'S EPISCOPACY.

AT this period the storm of persecution, which, from the first landing of Cromwell on the Irish shore, had desolated the island, commenced to subside. The Puritanical fanaticism of the Protestant faction required indeed the enactment from year to year of new penal and oppressive laws; but the administration of the Government being entrusted to wiser and less bigoted men, and better lovers of Ireland, these strokes fell more lightly upon the people, and at intervals Catholics were enabled to practise in peace the holy exercises of their religion. The Duke of Ormond, indeed, to the last, proved himself an insidious enemy of the Irish Catholics, and, ever intent on his own personal aggrandisement, had unceasingly laboured to root out Catholicity and lay desolate the sanctuary; and it was only when he saw the reins of power about to fall from his grasp, and rival statesmen gaining the favour of the King, that he began to deem it necessary to conciliate the Catholics, and hold out to them some hopes of a liberal administration.

We have seen in the third chapter how, on the dawn of peace upon the horizon, it was the first care of the Holy See—ever watchful of the interests of our afflicted Church—to appoint pastors to the widowed sees of Ireland. Its hierarchy, indeed, had remained unbroken despite the efforts of persecution; and when, on the 21st of January, 1669, the Archbishops of Dublin, Cashel, Tuam, and the Bishop of Ossory, were appointed by Rome, there were yet five bishops who had survived the scenes of suffering and trial, and now handed down to new champions that precious inheritance of unsullied faith which they themselves had received from their fathers. It was the same temporary calm that enabled the Sacred Congregation of Cardinals, on the demise of Dr. O'Reilly, to deliberate without delay on the appointment of his successor in the person of Dr. Plunket to the primatial see of Armagh.

On the 14th of February, 1669, Ormond was deprived of the Lord Lieutenancy, and this disgrace of their insidious enemy inspired with new hopes the great body of the Catholics. The appointment of John, Lord Roberts, of Truro, was hailed as the dawn of a more impartial administration: he is described by his biographers as a staunch Presbyterian, obstinate, jealous, and proud, but at the same time just in his government. Some acts, however, of his viceroyalty—if they may not be attributed to the fanaticism of individuals rather than to the Government— would not be out of place in the bitterest days of persecution. One instance connected with the subject of these memoirs will suffice.

Amongst the Rawdon papers we find a letter from Lord Conway to his brother-in-law, Sir George Rawdon, then residing near Lisburn, County Antrim, which discloses to us the benign designs of the Government officials in regard to the newly-appointed primate : —

LETTER CVI.

> " From the Lord Conway to his brother-in-law, Sir George
> Rawdon."

" DEAR BROTHER,—I have been all this day with my Lord Lieutenant, or employed about his commands, and I am but newly come home from him. Though it be very late, yet I am to give you notice, by his command, that the King hath privately informed him of two persons sent from Rome, that lie lurking in this country to do mischief. One is Signore Agnetti, an Italian employed by the College de Propaganda Fide, the other is Plunket, a member of the same college, and designed titular Archbishop of Armagh. If you can dexterously find them out, and apprehend them, 'twill be an acceptable service. But I told him I did not think they kept their residence in our parts (about Lisburn); however, he thinks it is his duty to search everywhere.

" CONWAY.

" Dublin, 20th Nov., 1669."

Such were the sentiments even of those who were esteemed the most just and impartial of our rulers ! The person who, in the above document, is indicated by the name *Agnetti*, is the canon *Claudius Agretti*, who for many years was first secretary of the Papal Internunzio in Brussels, and for some time, too, discharged the office of pro-Internunzio. At the period of which we speak he had been sent on a mission to Ireland with instructions from the Holy See connected with the forgeries of Taafe and the Remonstrance of Peter Walsh. He was probably as yet in Ireland at the date of Lord Conway's letter, though on the eve of his departure from it; as we find that on the 14th of December following he writes to Rome announcing his return to Brussels, and transmitting a paper, which he styles "a narrative of his pilgrimage to Ireland." The Government, however, were misinformed as to the presence of Dr. Plunket in the country, and though they had received intelligence of his appointment to the Primatial See, yet they were wholly astray as to his movements; and at the date of Lord Conway's despatch he was living with the Internunzio in Brussels, awaiting in peace the day appointed for his consecration. Aware of the feelings that existed, Dr. Plunket, on his arrival in Ireland, some months later, considered it prudent to avoid appearing in public as long as this administration lasted, and only performed his sacred functions and visited his flock by night or in disguise.

The Government of Lord Roberts was of short duration, and on the 21st of May, 1670, Lord Berkeley, of Stratton, was sworn in as Viceroy of Ireland. The private instructions which he then received inculcated the necessity of showing special favour to those who had signed the Remonstrance of Peter Walsh, and of shielding them from their more orthodox opponents. The twentieth article of these instructions was as follows:—

" Several popish clergy, since the return of the Duke of Ormond hither, have exercised their jurisdiction, to the great grief of the Remonstrants. If so, execute the laws against the titular archbishops, bishops, and vicars general that have threatened or excommunicated the Remonstrants; and see that you protect such Remonstrants as have not withdrawn their subscriptions."

The other articles recommend energy and zeal in the propagation of the Protestant religion; thus, in the fourteenth article, we read: "Endeavour to bring all to a conformity in the religion by law established, and acquaint us with what difficulties you meet with therein." And in the very beginning of the Instructions: "Forasmuch as all good success doth rest upon the service of God above all things, you are to settle good orders in the Church, that

God may be better served in the true established religion, and the people by that means be reduced from their errors in religion, wherein they have been too long most unhappily and perniciously seduced; and never more than since the late fatal rebellion, which hath produced too plentiful a seed-time of atheism, superstition, and schism."*

A special subject of these Instructions is *the building and repairing of Protestant churches.* The wars of Cromwell not only laid in ruins the few places of Catholic worship which, despite the preceding persecutions, had remained in the hands of the Catholics, but involved in the same destruction those venerable structures, which though raised by our Catholic forefathers, had, nevertheless, been appropriated to Protestant worship. Dean Swift, in a sermon on the martyrdom of King Charles I., whilst he delineates the evils of Puritanical zeal, presents a vivid description of the utter demolition of the Irish churches :—

"Another consequence [he says] of this horrid rebellion and murder was the destroying or defacing of such vast numbers of God's houses. If a stranger should now travel in England, and observe the churches in his way, he could not otherwise conclude, than that some vast army of Turks or heathens had been sent on purpose to ruin and blot out all marks of Christianity. They spared neither the statues of saints, nor ancient prelates, nor kings, nor benefactors : broke down the tombs and monuments of men famous in their generations ; seized the vessels of silver set apart for the holiest use ; tore down the most innocent ornaments both within and without ; made the houses of prayer dens of thieves or stables for cattle. These were the mildest effects of Puritan zeal and devotion for Christ; and this was what themselves affected to call a thorough reformation. In this kingdom (Ireland), those ravages were not so easily seen ; for, the people here being too poor to raise such noble temples, *the mean ones we had were not defaced, but totally destroyed.*"

The spiritual decay of the Protestant Church at the time of which we speak, was not less apparent than the ruin of its material edifices ; and the Instructions given to Lord Berkeley justly speak of *the atheism, superstition, and schism* which had desolated their establishment since the era of the

* Cox, *Charles II*, page 9.

Revolution.   Dr. Williams, Protestant Bishop of Ossory, who
died in 1672, has left us a tract in which he details the sad
condition both of the Protestant clergy and people in his
diocese, and he adds that it was *not much better in all Ireland.*
We shall give a few extracts which may serve to confirm the
foregoing statement of Dean Swift, at the same time that
they disclose to us the prevaling destitution.

"If you walk through Ireland, as I rode, from Carlingford to
Dublin, and from Dublin to Kilkenny, and in my visitation thrice
over the diocese of Ossory, I believe that throughout all your travel
you shall find it as I found it in all ways that I went, scarce one
church standing and sufficiently repaired, for seven (I speak within
compass) that are ruined and have only walls without ornaments, and
most of them without roofs, without doors, without windows, but the
holes to receive the winds, to entertain the congregation. . .
I do believe that out of about a hundred churches that our ((Catholic)
forefathers built and sufficiently endowed in the diocese of Ossory,
there are not twenty standing, nor ten well repaired at this day. . . .
As God is without churches for His people to meet in—to serve Him,
so He is without servants enabled to do Him service, to praise His
name, and to teach His people. But why have we not such churchmen
as are able to instruct God's people?" &c. (pages 2-6)

The conclusion to which this learned bishop arrives is
identical with what is oftentimes proclaimed in Protestant
meetings in our times, namely, that "Popery can never be
suppressed, and the true Protestant religion planted," without an augmentation of the means and livings of the Protestant clergy, and without many new grants to the Protestant
establishment.   Even the most thoroughly Protestant districts
were no better circumstanced, and the Protestant Bishop of
Derry, in a statement made to the King in council, on the
13th of May, 1670, gives a forcible description of the sad
spiritual condition even of the city and county of Londonderry.*

The documents, indeed, to which we have just referred
seem to limit this spiritual decay in the Protestant Church
of Ireland to the period of Cromwell's invasion, and ascribe
it to the persecution of the Puritans, and to the want of

---

* See Mant's *History of the Church of Ireland,* vol. i.

means in the Protestant clergy. But impartial history testifies far otherwise. Thus in the diocese of Meath, in 1622, according to Usher's own report, though there were 243 livings, there were only half-a-dozen churches in good repair, ninety churches being in ruins, and sixty others in a ruinous condition ; we learn also from Leland, that long before the rebellion of 1640, "ignorance, negligence, and corruption of manners prevailed among the Established clergy ; * and Stuart, in his *Historical Memoirs of Armagh*, is not less explicit. " The parishes," he says, " were either filled with careless and immoral pastors, or sequestered by avaricious bishops in *commendam*. Divine service was not performed except in great towns and cities." Even the Lord Deputy Wentworth styles "the clergy unlearned," and " the people untaught ; " and assigns as its cause " the non-residence of the Protestant clergy, occasioned by unlimited, shameful numbers of spiritual promotions, with care of souls, which they hold by *commendams ;* the rites and ceremonies of the Church run over, without decency of habit, order, or gravity, in the course of their service; the (Protestant) bishops alienating their very houses and demesnes to their children, and farming out their jurisdiction to mean and unworthy persons." † As to the number of those who had embraced the Protestant doctrines, they must have been but few indeed. Stuart, in the work already referred to (page 266), informs us that forty years after the commencement of the Reformation an inquiry was made into the religious state of the country, from which it resulted " *that the people had not adopted the Protestant religion.*" Dr. Kelly, the late lamented Professor of Ecclesiastical History in the College of Maynooth, calculated the relative proportion of Catholics to Protestants, in 1630, to have been eleven to two.‡ Dr. Plunket, however, more than once states that, with the exception of Dublin, the Catholics in his time, as compared to Protestants,

* *History of Ireland*, vol. iii.
† See *State Letters*, vol. i., page 187.
‡ O'Sullivan's *Hist. Cath.*, page 343, in not. (Dublin, 1850).

were as twenty to one.* Such, then, were the fruits of Protestantism in Ireland, after a struggle of more than one hundred years, though it was ever supported by all the wealth and power which earth could command.† And what were the effects of the boasted Reformation? The temples of the living God were destroyed ; divine service was interrupted ; ignorance and immorality had spread through the land, and the endowments of the Catholic Church, destined for the support of religion and the poor, were handed over to foreign Protestant Bishops and ministers, whose only object it was to aggrandize themselves, and to transmit to their children large properties, accumulated from the spoils of the Catholic Church·

Without attaching much importance to the instructions which he had received, Lord Berkeley seems to have devoted all his energies to the unbiassed administration of justice and the consolidation of public order in the kingdom. Dr. Plunket often speaks of him as a man nowise hostile to the Catholics, but, on the contrary, anxious to show them favour and protection. Thus, in his letter of the 18th of June, 1670, addressed to the Cardinal Protector of Ireland, he states :—

" The Viceroy of this kingdom shows himself favourable to the Catholics, not only in consequence of his natural mildness of disposition, but still more on account of his being acquainted with the benign intentions of his Majesty in reference to his Catholic subjects, so that ecclesiastics may freely appear in public without suffering any annoyance, even when they are recognised as such. The Viceroy himself privately treats some members of the clergy with great courtesy, exhorting them to live peaceably, without tumult, and without meddling in State matters, attending solely to their ecclesiastical functions, on which condition he promises them every protection ; and, indeed, it seems that this protection will be afforded should that condition be fulfilled. I perceive that some of his court are secretly Catholics, as are also some of the principal members of the Government, who suggest to him kind measures for the Catholics. May God grant us a long enjoyment of this calm, and bestow many years on your Eminence for the public good of the Christian Church."

* See letters, 18th June, 1670, and 20th June, 1670.
† See further illustration of this matter in Chapter VII.

In another letter of the same date, addressed to Cardinal Barberini, which we have given in full in the last chapter (page 49), he repeats the sentiment, and adds :—

" I found that four of the principal persons of Court were secretly Catholics, and these maintain the Viceroy in his favourable sentiments and esteem for the Catholics ; so much so, that not long since he wrote a long letter to the King in favour of the Irish clergy, declaring them good subjects, and worthy of the favour of his Majesty."

In another letter, dated from Dublin two days later (20th June, 1670), and addressed to the newly-appointed Pontiff, Clement X., congratulating him on his accession to the chair of St. Peter, he thus writes :—

" We experience in this kingdom, Holy Father, the benign influence of the King of England in favour of the Catholics, so that all enjoy great liberty and ease. Ecclesiastics may be publicly known, and are permitted to exercise their functions without any impediment. Our Viceroy is a man of great moderation and equity ; he looks on the Catholics with benevolence, and treats privately with some of the clergy, exhorting them to act with discretion ; and for this purpose he secretly called me to his presence on many occasions, and promised me his assistance in correcting any members of the clergy of scandalous life. I discover in him some spark of religion, and I find that many even of the leading members of his Court are secretly Catholics. The nobles who are natives of this country are all Catholics, with the exception of three or four ; and comparing the Catholics with the heretics throughout the kingdom, we find that there are twenty Catholics for one Protestant, if we except Dublin, which is the metropolis, and in which the Viceroy resides, where the heretics have a majority."

Writing on the 16th of April, 1671, he styles Lord Berkeley *a moderate and prudent man*, and adds : " Should our Viceroy be changed, God knows what will come to pass." At this time the leaders of the bigoted faction left no stone unturned to achieve the ruin of the Viceroy, and to substitute in his stead his avowed enemy—who was at the same time the mortal enemy of the Catholics—the Earl of Orrery. In a postscript to his letter of 27th September, 1671, Dr. Plunket states the following fact regarding Orrery :—" As I have already made known to you, the Earl of Orrery, a few days since, expelled from Limerick by a public edict all the Catholics. A nice gain we would have made had this man been appointed our Viceroy, as some persons most anxiously desired. '

This fact of the edict published against the Catholics by Lord Orrery is further explained by Dr. Plunket in a letter written on the following day, the 28th September, 1671 : —

" I sent another parcel to Dr. Dowley, Bishop of Limerick. This poor man is yet in trouble, the Earl of Orrery having published a few days ago an edict commanding all Catholic ecclesiastics or laymen to depart from, and live no longer in, that city. Some desired that he, instead of Berkeley, should be our Viceroy : a good bargain we would have made. I do not know how our Viceroy Berkeley, who is now returned to the helm, will take these proceedings of Orrery. Orrery is no friend of the Viceroy, and some are of opinion that these edicts are published by Orrery on purpose. He is a cunning politician ; should the Viceroy recall these decrees, then Orrery may assail him as being a patron of the Catholics, and already in various meetings he has styled Lord Berkeley *a Catholic*, that thus he might excite against him the enmity of the heretics, who hate the Catholics."

At length, by misrepresentation and calumny, the enemies of Lord Berkeley succeeded in obtaining an order for his removal, and though he did not actually abandon the reins of government till August, 1672, his removal was determined on, and notified to him as early as the preceding May, as we learn from Dr. Plunket, who thus writes to the Internunzio on the 14th May, 1672 :—

" *Tandem aliquando* (at length) we have a certainty of the removal of our good Viceroy, as he himself has communicated the intelligence to me on yesterday morning, when I was with him for two hours. His departure is a great loss to us ; he would have promoted our interests, and carried out punctually in the cities the last proclamation of the King in our favour, for in some cities it meets with opposition, which, however, I hope will be overcome. His successor, the Earl of Essex, is represented to us by Father Howard and Father Patrick * as a moderate and prudent man ; e *fructibus ejus cognoscemus eum* (by his fruits we shall know him). The Lord Chancellor, who is also the Protestant Archbishop of Dublin, had

---

* Father Howard was afterwards known as Cardinal Norfolk ; Father Patrick was brother of Dr. Magin, Vicar-Apostolic of Dromore, and was at this time Chaplain at the Spanish Embassy, London.

great differences with the present Viceroy about the government of this city, which matter did but little service to the good Viceroy, and at length they have come to an open rupture. The other Viceroy will arrive about the middle of June. We shall never have one like to the present."

The character of Lord Berkeley is admirably drawn by Mr. O'Conor in his *History of the Irish Catholics* (page 104) :—

"Lord Berkeley was a man of probity and moderate principles who substituted a mild and merciful administration for the unrelenting tyranny of oppressors; the penal statutes of Elizabeth were relaxed, the public exercise of the Catholic religion allowed, its professors were admitted to all situations of trust and emolument, civil and military, to all franchises and corporations, to the rights and privileges of subjects, protected in their persons and properties, invested with political power, with shrievalties and magistracies, to secure them against oppression and injustice. Under this system Ireland began to flourish and prosper, to recover from the miseries of the late war, and the desolation of Cromwell; arts and manufactures revived."

We cannot be surprised that such a Viceroy should secretly encourage Dr. Plunket, not only in the correction of public abuses, but also in the establishment of schools, for which purpose he even seems to have placed various sums of money at the disposal of the Primate.*

Arthur, Earl of Essex, assumed the Lord Lieutenancy, on the 5th of August, 1672. Howsoever desirous he may have been to pursue the conciliatory course of his predecessor, he was soon compelled by the jealous bigotry of the Protestant faction, and the Puritanical fanaticism of the English Parliament, to lay aside all semblance of toleration and seek by stringent measures to compel the bishops to fly for safety to the Continent, and abandon the flocks entrusted to their care. Dr. Plunkett exhorted his fellow-pastors to remain in the country, and conceal themselves till the storm would have passed, or, if necessity should be, to imitate the example of the bishops of the first centuries, and fearlessly

* Dr. Plunket occasionally speaks of this as a pension from the bounty of the King.

lay down their lives for their flocks.*   In company with
Rev. Dr. Brennan, his former companion in the Irish
College in Rome, now Bishop of Waterford and Lismore
he chose a place of retreat in his own diocese; the only
provision which he had made, was one *of books and candles*,
as he states in one of his letters ; and often did he and his
companion run the risk of death from the cold and fatigue,
and the want of the necessary means of subsistence.   This
storm, too, subsided, and the latter days of Essex's administration were comparatively mild, or at least not marked
by any special deeds of hostility towards the Catholics.
This Viceroy seems to have entertained a high personal
esteem for the Primate, and when MacMoyer and his
fellow-apostates had, by their perjured testimony, procured
sentence of death against Dr. Plunket, Essex joined with
Lord Berkeley in soliciting his pardon, and, as Echard
informs us, "told his Majesty that the witnesses must
needs be perjured, for those things sworn against him could
not possibly be true."

Even the Duke of Ormond when resuming the viceroyalty,
in August, 1677, was compelled for a while to hold out the
hand of friendship to the Catholics, and to assume the mask
of moderation and impartial justice.   Dr. Plunket often
speaks of his government as being at this period peaceful
and mild ; but when, in the following year, circumstances
began to change, and the court party in England proclaimed
their hostility to the Catholic faith, this old betrayer of
Ireland hesitated not to sacrifice his convictions to interest,
and to inaugurate and promote that persecution whose
crowning deed was the glorious martyrdom of the Archbishop
of Armagh.

---

* See letter 12th November, 1673·

CHAPTER VII.

WE have seen, towards the close of the fifth chapter, how the newly consecrated primate, as soon as circumstances permitted, abandoned the British capital and hastened to his diocese, anxious to enter, without delay, on the field of his spiritual labours, and break to the flock intrusted to him the bread of eternal life. The first fruits of his pastoral zeal are thus briefly enumerated in the letter already cited of the 18th June, 1670 (p. 49) :—" I held two Synods and two Ordinations, and in a month and a-half I administered Confirmation to more than ten thousand persons, though throughout my province I think there yet remain more than fifty thousand persons to be confirmed." Nor was this the fervour of a momentary impulse : it was the fruit of the ardent zeal and humble spirit of self-sacrifice which he had so long cherished at the tombs of the Apostles. His subsequent career reveals to us at every step manifest traces of the same Apostolic spirit, and it seems difficult to conceive how one man could, in so short a career, effect so much good, overcome so many difficulties, and undergo so many trials.* " How great his industry," cries out his learned contemporary and friend, Father Arsdekin, " in appointing fit pastors to guard the fold : how wondrous his labours throughout the vast districts of Ulster to strengthen the faith of its people, ever devoted children of the . Roman Church ; and what was still more arduous, how untiring his vigilance to preserve from the teeth of the

---

* About the year 1740 a charge having been made in Rome regarding the administration of the Ludovisian College against the Jesuit Fathers, the then Rector drew up a statement in reply. Referring to some distinguished students of the College, he thus concisely describes the merits of Dr. Plunket : "*fu martire glorioso per la santa fede e meriterebbe un libro intero di glorioso elogio.*"

wolves and from the errors of heresy the fold entrusted to his care."*

In like manner the Oratorian Father, to whose sketch of Dr. Plunket's life we have already referred, exclaims: "Who can worthily relate with what solicitude he laboured to restore piety and raise up religion, and with what care he sought to appoint worthy pastors to his flock, and to confirm in the faith the Catholics scattered through the vast province of Ulster!"

Indeed the labours of Dr. Plunket, even in the first months of his episcopate, would have sufficed to render his name illustrious in the Irish Church, and entitle him to the veneration of posterity. Before three months had passed from his arrival on our shores—that is, before the close of June, 1670—he had already solemnized two Synods of his clergy, and, moreover, convened and presided at a General Synod of the Irish bishops which was held in Dublin; and before the month of September in the same year we find him summoning a Provincial Council of Ulster, and enacting many salutary decrees for the correction of abuses and the advancement of ecclesiastical discipline in that province. This Synod, justly celebrated in the ecclesiastical annals of our country,* was held at Clones; and the representatives of the respective dioceses soon after re-assembled privately in Armagh, and thence addressed a letter of thanksgiving to the authorities in Rome for having destined as their primate a prelate of such ability and piety. No words can better describe the untiring labours of Dr. Plunket, and the fruitful efforts of his zeal during the first months of his episcopate, than this letter of the assembled clergy of the province of Armagh; it is dated the 8th of October, 1670, and is as follows:—

"MOST ILLUSTRIOUS AND REVEREND LORD,—When we send letters to your Excellency we consider ourselves addressing the Apostolic See. We have not written sooner to your Excellency regarding our most illustrious Primate, for we waited till his merits should be

* Theo. Tripart., tom. iii., page 227.

known to us by experience. And now that we have had this experience, we render exceeding thanks to the Apostolic See for having placed over us such a pastor and teacher. Since his arrival in the province of Armagh, he is unceasing in his labours; to the great utility of the province he convoked Diocesan Synods, and instructed the clergy by word and by example, and in the ordinations which he held he promoted none but such as were worthy, and only after they had passed a rigorous examination. He celebrated a Provincial Council in the town of Clones, in which many salutary decrees were made; and, to the great joy of the whole clergy, and of all the Catholics, the jurisdiction of Terence O'Kelly, Vicar of Derry, was suspended, what many hitherto had sought to accomplish, but always without success. He introduced the Fathers of the Society of Jesus into the diocese of Armagh to educate the youth and instruct the younger clergy, and built for them a house and schools at his own expense. In the dioceses of Armagh, Kilmore, Clogher, Derry, Down, Connor, and Dromore, although far separated from each other, he administered Confirmation to thousands in the woods and mountains, heedless of winds and rain. Lately, too, he achieved a work from which great advantage will be derived by the Catholic body, for there were many of the more noble families who had lost their properties, and, being proclaimed outlaws in public edicts, were subsequently guilty of many outrages; these, by his admonitions, he brought back to a better course; he, moreover, obtained pardon for their crimes, and not only procured this pardon for themselves, but also for all their receivers; and thus, hundreds and hundreds of Catholic families have been freed from imminent danger to their body and soul, and properties. Truly, he is so assiduous in good works, his life and conduct are so exemplary, that he has won for himself and clergy the love and reverence even of the enemies of our faith: and since his arrival amongst us the clergy have not been subjected to persecution.

"We, therefore, return repeated thanks to the Apostolic See for having promoted him to this dignity, and we shall ever pray for the repose of the soul of that holy Pontiff who sent such a man amongst us, as likewise for all who concurred in his promotion, amongst whom we do not hesitate to reckon your Excellency, whose most obedient servants we shall ever remain.

> " PATRICK DALY, Vic.-Gen. of Armagh.
> " PATRICK O'MULDERG, Vic.-Gen. Down and Connor.
> " RONAN MAGIN, Dean and Vic.-Gen. Dromore.
> " EUGENE CONNALL, Vic.-Gen. Derry and Raphoe.
> " THOMAS FITZSYMONS, Archdeac. and Vic.-Gen. Kilmore.
> " PATRICK COLLYN, Vic.-Gen. Clogher.

" To the Most Illustrious Monsig. Baldeschi, &c., &c., &c

" Armagh, 8th Oct., 1670."

One of the crowning deeds of Dr. Plunket's episcopate was another Provincial Synod, which, despite the fury of the persecution then let loose against the Catholics, was convened in Ardpatrick, in August, 1668. Once more the assembled prelates and clergy resolved to testify their affection for this worthy successor of St. Patrick, and their admiration of his untiring zeal. Their letter is addressed to the cardinals of the Sacred Congregation of Propaganda, and is dated 27th August, 1678 :—

" We, the undersigned, have assembled in Provincial Council, being convoked by the Most Illustrious and Rev. Oliver Plunket, Archbishop of Armagh, Primate of all Ireland, and our Metropolitan, for the purpose of correcting many and grave abuses.

" How great was the necessity for this Council, is proved by the Decrees which we have enacted, and which our Metropolitan will transmit to your Eminences to be examined, and should you so judge, approved, as calculated to remedy the abuses, and suited to the circumstances of the times.

"Moreover, to silence those who speak evil things, we have deemed it our duty to make known to your Eminences the manner of government of the same Most Illustrious and Rev. Metropolitan, who was sent amongst us about nine years since by his Holiness and your Eminences.

" We, therefore, declare that the aforesaid Most Illustrious Metropolitan has laboured much, exercising his sacred functions, not only in his own, but also in other dioceses. During the late persecution he abandoned not the flock entrusted to him, though he was exposed to extreme danger of losing his life; he erected schools and provided masters and teachers, that the clergy and youth might be instructed in literature, piety, cases of conscience, and other matters relating to their office : he held two Provincial Councils, in which salutary decrees were enacted for the reformation of morals : he, moreover, rewarded the good and punished the bad, as far as circumstances and the laws of this kingdom allowed : he laboured much, and not without praise, in preaching the word of God : he instructed the people by word and example : he also exercised hospitality, so as to excite the admiration of all, although he scarcely received annually 200 crowns from his diocese : and he performed all other things which became an Archbishop and Metropolitan, as far as they could be done in this kingdom : in fine. to our great service and consolation he renewed, or rather established anew, at great expense, correspondence with the Holy See, which for many years before his arrival had been interrupted, or rather become extinct. For all which things we gratefully acknowledge ourselves indebted to his Holiness and to your Eminences, who, by your solicitude. provided for us so learned and vigilant a Metropolitan : and we shall ever pray the Divine Majesty to preserve his Holiness and your Eminences.

" From the Provincial Council, held in Ardpatrick, the 27th day of August, 1678, we, your most humble and obsequious children and servants,

" PATRICK, Bishop of Meath.
" FR. PATRICK, Bishop of Clogher, and Administrator of Kilmore.
" PATRICK O'MULDERG, Vicar-General of Connor.
" LUKE PLUNKET, Vicar-General of Derry, and Procurator of the Diocese of Raphoe.
" JAMES CUSACK, Procurator of the Vicar Apostolic of Ardagh.
" PATRICK O'BRUIN, Vicar-General of Down, and Procurator of Rev. Henry Mackey, Vicar-General of Dromore.
" CHRISTOPHER PLUNKET, Archdeacon of Meath.
" HENRY HUGO, Procurator of Chapter of Armagh.
" PATRICK PLUNKET, Vicar-General of County Louth.
" BERNARD MAGORKE, Dean of Armagh, and Consultor in the Council.
" ARNOLD MATTHEWS, Archdeacon of Clogher."

The date of this letter brings us within a few months of the imprisonment of Dr. Plunket, and during this interval he was engaged, as we learn from his subsequent correspondence, in a laborious visitation of the suffragan dioceses of Armagh, as had been determined on by the assembled prelates at the Council to which we have just referred.*

* We have already referred to the testimony of his contemporary, Arsdekin, as to his indefatigable zeal and labours: page 227 (*Thoel. Trip.*, tom. iii.),he thus writes :—" In Hiberniam ubi pervenit ibi demum campum animo suo et Apostolicis laboribus parem invenit. Quis valeat dicendo complecti quantum illi insudandum fuit ut plurima in rebus ac moribus iniquitate temporum collapsa restauraret, ut pluribus locis idoneos animarum curatores præficeret, ut per latissima Ultoniæ plagas populum illum Ro.nanæ fidei semper tenacissimum opportunis ubique documentis confirmaret. Sed quod omnium maxime arduum, quanta illi vigilantia tot annis incumbendum fuit ut gregem suum uli.que lup's admixtum ab eorum dentibus et erroribus illæsum conservaret. Cum alia non suppeterent accusationis capita, adornantur criminationes occultæ quibus hic tam validus Ecclesiæ Romanæ propugnator, vel opprimi possit vel extingui." The renowned oratorian Catalani writes still more forcibly. After adducing the example of St. Malachy, Archbishop of Armagh, to illustrate the proper manner of performing the Episcopal visitation, he adds : " Certe S. Malachiam Archiepum Armacanum, imitatus est Oliverius Plunket, ejusdem Ecclesiæ Armacanæ antistes atque totius Hiberniæ Primas a Clemente IX. Pont. Max. ob eximiis

In the letter addressed from the Synod of Clones, mention
Is made of the blessing he conferred on many Catholic
families, by obtaining their pardon from the Government
They were the descendants of those whose lands and properties had been seized on in the Confiscation of Ulster.
Vowing revenge on their oppressors, they had formed themselves into predatory bands, and sought subsistence by
making incessant inroads on, and plundering the holders of
their former possessions. They were known as *Tories*, and
were proclaimed outlaws by the Government, whilst all who
harboured them were subjected to fines and imprisonment,
and sometimes even to death. Whosoever was guilty of any
crime, and fled from justice—all who could escape from
prison, or might prefer to peaceful labour a bandit career,
were received with welcome by the Tories. Degenerating,
too, from their original purpose, they often levied taxes on
whole districts, and, plundering whithersoever they went,
involved innocent and guilty in one common ruin. Those
who escaped from the *Tories* were sure to feel the hand
of the military sent in pursuit of them, and the guilt of
being favourers or harbourers of bandits was often deemed

ejus animi dotes constitutus anno 1670 (?) ætatis suæ 41. Quamquam
enim missus osset ad lupos, stetit in medio luporum Pastor intrepidus,
totamque Provinciam circumiens, perquirebat anhelus, quem Christo
acquireret; paratus et animam suam dare pro ovibus partes boni Pastoris
explevit; quamobrem licet sub alio prætextu violatarum scilicet Regis
Angliæ legum, in odium Catholicæ Religionis crudelissimam mortem
oppetiit die 1 Julii, 1681. Vitæ illius compendium Italico idiomate
scripsit noster Joannes Marangonus una cum aliis vitis servorum Dei qui
nostræ Congni. Oratorii S. Hieronymi charitatis nomen dederunt. Unus
enim ex iis fuit Oliverius, inter nostros adscitus anno 1654, extatque hodie
ejus effigies inter alias illustrium Patrum in aula domus cum hac
inscriptione: P. Oliverius e Comitibus Plunket, Hybern. in Coll. de Prop.
Fid. S. Theol. et Controver. lector, Archiep. Armacanus ac tot. Hibernicæ
Primas ob. Kal. Jul. 1681." There is still in the house of St. Giralmo an
ancient portrait of Dr. Plunket. The inscription which it presents is
somewhat different from that given by Catalani; it is as follows:—
" P. Oliverius Plunket, hujus Oratorii Sac. a Clemente IX. Ardmacan.
Archiep. et Hibern. Primas renunciatus ob Ecclesiasticam Disciplinam
propugnandam apud Regem a fidei desertoribus calumniatus Londini
gladio aliisque cruciatibus transfossus hanc domum S. Hieronymi de
caritate glorioso fine condecoravit. 1 Julii, 1681."

sufficiently proved by the fact of being spared in their devastations. Thus, many districts, especially of Armagh, were kept in continual terror, and none could devise means for establishing tranquillity and peace. Dr. Plunket, immediately after his arrival in his diocese, went in person to seek out these bands of Tories in their hiding-places : having found them, he made known to them the wickedness of their career, and exhorted them to desist from their guilty course. They listened to the voice of their pastor, and promised obedience. He then hastened to the Viceroy and did not cease his solicitations till he was himself the bearer of a Proclamation announcing pardon to all who should submit. Those who were most guilty, and were looked up to as the leaders of the bands, he himself conducted to Dublin, and placed on board of vessels bound for France : the names of many of these outlaws soon became illustrious in the military services of France and Spain.

This was not the only occasion in which Dr. Plunket procured the peace of the northern districts. In the Province of Ulster there was a numerous family which for years had received the opprobrious name of *Magouna*. They were descended from the ancient sept of the O'Reillys, and had received that surname on account of some members of the family who apostatized from the faith of their fathers in the time of Elizabeth. In vain did the descendants of these families, when they returned to the bosom of the Catholic Church, seek to resume their ancient name. The O'Reillys refused to acknowledge them as members of their illustrious sept, and continued to address them as a dishonoured branch by the epithet *Magouna*. Many quarrels and continual disputes and recriminations hence arose, and the whole Catholic body seemed split into two irreconcilable factions, some defending the apostate family, others continuing its reproach. The Primate long sought to reconcile the conflicting parties, and terminate this quarrel. At length, in 1672, he published a decree, which he caused to be privately printed in Dublin, and afterwards communicated to all the contentious leaders, by which he prohibited, under pain of censure, the future application of the opprobrious epithet to the converted family, commanding that their original name of O'Reilly should be restored to them. All parties respected this solemn decision of the Primate, and thus this controversy disappears from our history. There were some indeed who deemed this decree imprudent, and even made it a subject of accusation against Dr. Plunket, as if he had usurped the King's prerogative, to whom was reserved by law the privilege of changing family names : but the decree of the Primate was dictated by zeal for the welfare of the flock intrusted to him; and whilst he thus healed their dissensions, and re-established charity and peace, he merely restored to prodigal but repentant children the inheritance of their true family name, which, *in the eyes of the law*, they had never lost.*

Another occasion presented itself, about the same period, for displaying his pastoral love for his suffering people. We shall present it in the words of the Primate, from his letter of the 14th of May, 1672:—

"In part of my diocese, and in all the diocese of Clogher, the Chancellor of the Protestant bishop frequently molested, and still molests, in a most tyrannical manner, the poor Catholic farmers, as also some of the priests of that diocese. It is the custom here that for the baptism of Catholic children two giulj† should be paid to the priest, and four giulj to the Protestant minister. This latter payment is commanded by law, and although a great grievance, yet it has been tolerated and paid. But, in addition to this, the said Chancellor, whose name is John Linsy, cited to the tribunals and prosecuted the poor Catholics for bringing their children to the priests to be baptized, and thus procured the ruin of many poor Catholic families in the diocese referred to. I yesterday drew up a memorial to the Viceroy and Supreme Council against this extortion, and I showed it to the Protestant Primate and to the Protestant Bishop of Clogher. Both besought me not to present the memorial to the Viceroy, and promised that within fifteen days the Chancellor would be compelled to desist from this tyrannical manner of proceeding, by which he impoverished more than three hundred Catholic families."

---

* Ex archiv. de Propag. Fid. in not. MS,

† A giulio was at this time equal to 6d. ; a scudo to 5s. ; four scudi to £1.

Surely no people ever suffered more for their religion, and with more Christian patience, than the Irish. What was originally presented by Catholic parents, as a free and religious offering for the support of their devoted clergy, was now insisted on as a legal right by the ministers of the Protestant Establishment, and an action at law was granted to them for the recovery of such fees even from the Catholics. Curry in his *Review of the Civil Wars in Ireland*, states, in the words of Sir Edward Walker, that in the reign of Charles I. the Catholics of Ireland prayed " to be relieved from those exorbitant sums which they were obliged to pay for their christenings and marriages to the Protestant Clergy, and particularly to have the extravagant surplice fees, and the extraordinary warrants for levying them, abolished." The Irish Commons, too, in a Remonstrance, in 1640, distinctly charge the Ecclesiastical Courts of that period as guilty of " *barbarous and unjust exactions ;*" and give the following particulars of the extortions which were practised by the Protestant clergy :—

" In Connaught and elsewhere, sixpence per annum of every couple is paid for holy-water clerk : of every man that dies, a *multure*, by the name of *anointing money* : from a poor man that has but one cow they take that cow for *mortuary* : from one that is better able, his best garment for *mortuary*. If a woman, her best garment for *mortuary* ; and a gallon of drink for every brewing by the name of *Mary-gallons ;* for every beef that is killed for the funeral of any man, the hide and tallow, and they challenge a quarter besides ; fourpence or sixpence per annum from every parishioner for soul-money ; a ridge of winter corn, and a ridge of oats, for every plough, by the name of *St. Patrick's ridges:* for *portion-canons* the tenth part of the goods, after debts paid, &c."

Thus, whilst the Protestant clergy stigmatized the Catholic doctrines and practices as superstitious and idolatrous, they nevertheless insisted on receiving tenfold the offerings which in Catholic times were wont to accompany Catholic devotions.* The Chancellor, Linsy, however,

* From the character of the Protestant clergy given in the preceding chapter, these exactions cannot surprise us. In this same Remonstrance of the House of Commons (Comm'ns' *Journal*, vol. i., pp. 259-261) it is added that " *the exorbitant and barbarous exactions* of the Protestant

was not content with these exactions; he wished that, besides paying the parson, Catholics should become Protestants into the bargain; and because they resolved to listen to God rather than man, this so-called minister of the Gospel of charity, till checked in his ruthless career by the true pastoral zeal of the Primate, succeeded in reducing to abject misery and ruin more than three hundred poor families.

Dr. Plunket, writing to Rome on the 18th June, 1670, estimates the number of those to whom he had already administered the Sacrament of Confirmation at about ten thousand; and adds that no fewer than fifty thousand persons yet remained to receive it. By frequent visitations he sought to place within the reach of all the consolations of that holy sacrament; and so untiring were his labours, that on the 15th of December, 1673, he announced to the Secretary of Propaganda:—"*During the past four years I confirmed forty-eight thousand six hundred and fifty-five.*" And what renders this more surprising is, the many toils he had to undergo in order to administer this sacrament to them; for often having no other food than a little oaten bread, he had to seek out their abodes in the mountains and in the woods,* and often, too, was this sacrament administered under the broad canopy of heaven, both flock and pastor being alike exposed to the winds and rain.

The Synodical letter which we have cited refers also to the zealous solicitude of the Primate in instructing the

clergy were levied *especially on the poorer sort.*" Indeed, the Protestant mission was carried on as a mere money-making speculation. Burnet tells us that "the Chancellor bought his place, and hence thought he had a right to all the profits he could make out of it;" and this writer adds that "in the bishop's court bribes went about almost barefaced" (*Life of Bedel.* See also Mason's *Life of Bedel.*) The statement of Usher confirms Burnet's testimony; for, writing to Archbishop Laud, he says that, "such is the venality of all things sacred here (in Ireland), that I fear to mention anything about them."

* See letter of the Vicar-General of Raphoe, giving an account of the administration of Confirmation by Dr. Plunket in his diocese, 1st November, 1671; and also the letter of the assembled prelates, 8th October, 1670.

faithful, and announcing to them the saving doctrines of eternal life.* He allowed no motive to excuse him from this pastoral duty, and even when suffering from bodily sickness he continued to pursue the same career of love. Writing on the 2nd of August, 1678, under the assumed name of Thomas Cox, he thus makes known to the Sacred Congregation his labours during the preceding months :—

" The past two months were spent in a fatiguing and most laborious visitation of my diocese, of which I shall shortly give a full account to your Excellency . . . The distillation from my eyes, which was greatly increased by the laborious visitation in the mountains of the northern districts, scarcely allows me to write or read letters even as large as a snuff-box; but still it did not impede my tongue from preaching in both the English and Irish languages."

We shall afterwards have occasion to commemorate his sacrifices in order to maintain the schools which he opened for the education of the youthful portion of his flock, and which he entrusted to the Jesuit Fathers. It will suffice at present to quote a few words from his letter of the 22nd September, 1672, in which, speaking of these schools, he says :—

" Oh! what labours, what expenses, did I sustain in order to support them ; how many memorials were presented against me, and against the Viceroy, even to the Supreme Council . . . I solemnly avow, Monsignore, that I expended for them, during the past two years and two months, more than 400 scudi; and, moreover, they and I are in debt 200 scudi. I dressed in cloth of two shillings a yard. I had but one servant, and a boy to look after the horses, and I kept a most sparing table, in order to aid them."

Elsewhere Dr. Plunket (see letter of 7th of June, 1671) details the vast labour and expense which he incurred in corresponding with the Holy See ; whilst he also declares that in the commissions which he received from Rome it was his firm resolution to face all dangers, and to submit to calumny and persecution, rather than betray the cause of

* The Internunzio Airoldi, on the 19th September, 1671, acknowledges the receipt of a brief from the Holy See, through the Sacred Congregation, congratulating Dr. Plunket on his zeal and labours.

justice which was entrusted to him. His letter is as
follows :—

"I have received your most welcome letter, and I can avow to
your Excellency that I toil night and day in the affairs of my
mission, and that *non dedi requiem temporibus meis aut palpebris meis
dormitationem* (I give no rest to my brains or repose to my eyes),
and let all be for the greater glory of God and the service of the
Apostolic See—that is, the propagation and preservation of the
faith. For the future, however, I shall not have to labour so much,
as I now live with the fathers of the Society in the house which I
built near Dundalk. They assist me in resolving difficult cases,
and in writing letters to different parts of the kingdom when necessary. Hitherto, whilst living in the house of a friend, I was without
any assistance. The schools, too, succeed so well that even Protestant
gentlemen send their children to them, and defend them when some
ministers seek to molest us.

"I shall decide throughout my whole province regarding the
dispute between the Franciscans and Dominicans, according to the
commands of your Excellency, and I shall rest rather on your
authority than on my own. I must candidly declare that the
decision is arduous and full of difficulties : and after all my toils
I shall gather no other fruit than the thorns of calumnies and lies.
I shall summon only one procurator at a time from each of the
three controverted convents, and having taken their depositions and
proofs, I shall afterwards decide according to their testimonies and
proofs : *pereat mundus et fiat justitia. Si fractus illabatur orbis
impavidum ferient ruinæ.*

"I already wrote beseeching you to procure from the Sacred
Congregation some provision or missionary stipend for three fathers
of the Society who instruct the clergy and youth in this province :
otherwise I cannot support them. I wrote also for some assistance
for myself to enable me to visit the Scottish islands or the Hebrides,
otherwise I can do nothing. It will be necessary to bring a priest
and a servant with me, and to dress after the manner of these
people, which is very different from that of every other part of the
world. I moreover wrote to have some arrangement made for the
expenses of the letters, otherwise it will be impossible to correspond
for the future as I have hitherto done. I expended more than
100 scudi for letters this year. Generally the letters of the other
bishops and archbishops come inclosed in mine, and I pay out the
money without ever receiving anything in return. I shall spare no
labour in corresponding, but it is too much to bear the whole
burden. There is no one but myself that keeps up a regular and
continual correspondence with London, Antwerp, Brussels, and
Dublin.—And I shall ever be, your most affectionate and obliged
servant,

"OLIVER OF ARMAGH.

"7th June, 1671."

The spirit of religion—the desire to promote God's glory and propagate the blessings of our holy faith—which was the moving spring of all Dr. Plunket's labours, is here transparent in every line. In another letter addressed to the Internunzio, on the 28th September, 1671, he again avows these holy desires, and presents in detail the motives which spurred him on to toil incessantly in guarding the flock intrusted to him :—

" The despatches which I received [he says] were accompanied by a most kind letter from your Excellency, dated the 12th of August, and full of such courteous expressions, as would suffice to move the very travertine to activity and action. I will not fail to work with the pen, with the tongue, with all my slender energies, and this for three motives—1st, to serve the Divine Majesty; 2nd, through gratitude and the reverence which I owe to the Apostolic See for the education and honours which it conferred on me ; 3rd, because God commands me to obey and serve the Holy See, and its service is inseparable from that of Christ."

During the years of persecution which preceded the arrival of Dr. Plunket in Ireland, the priesthood had been so thinned by exile and the sword, that many districts were left wholly destitute of pastors. Dr. Patrick Plunket, Bishop of Meath, was, for a time, the only bishop in the country able to confer ordination, and during his episcopate of Ardagh alone, no fewer than 250 priests received at his hands the sacrament of Holy Orders. In the list of Irish priests registered in the year 1704, and published by the Government,* there were yet living more than ninety who represented themselves as ordained by this prelate. It is certain, however, that some of these must be referred to the Primate, as the date of ordination is more than once subsequent to the demise of the Bishop of Meath ; and about 120 others of the registered clergy refer their ordination to Dr. Plunket, Archbishop of Armagh. From the letters of the Primate, which we have already quoted, it is certain that, immediately on his arrival in Ireland in 1670, he held two ordinations ; and from the synodical

* See reprint in Battersby's *Directory* for 1838.

letters of Clones and Ardpatrick, it is sufficiently clear that he continued without intermission, during the subsequent years of his episcopate, to promote worthy ministers to the holy order of priesthood.

In his letter of 25th September, 1671, addressed to the Internunzio in Brussels, Dr. Plunket gives the following estimate of the number of the regular clergy, not only in his own diocese, but also throughout the whole province of Ulster : —

"The regular clergy of the province of Armagh form a large body : in it they have many convents, and a yet greater number of friars. They are principally Dominicans and Franciscans, and the latter are more numerous than the former. I confess, however, that the Dominicans have the more able preachers. I have visited all the convents of the province excepting those of Ardagh, and shall now give some account of them.

" In the diocese of Armagh there are two convents of Dominicans: one in Drogheda, consisting of three friars, of whom F. Bathews is grave, prudent, and learned ; the other convent is in Carlingford, consisting of five friars ; its prior, Eugene Cogly, is one of the best preachers of the kingdom. There are three convents of Franciscans in this diocese : one in Drogheda, of six friars, amongst whom there is a man of great prudence and modesty, and very learned, by name John Brady: he is definitor. The second convent is in Dundalk, consisting of four friars, two of whom preach pretty well; their names are Patrick Cassidy and Anthony Gearnon : the latter was a follower of Walsh, and I fear that he is yet inwardly such, though he professes the contrary. The third convent is in Armagh, of fourteen friars, amongst whom there is only one worth mentioning, named Bonaventure O'Quin, a learned and prudent man, though not expert in preaching.

" In my diocese there is a residence of discalced Carmelites, and there is one father who preaches very well, called F. Levin. There is also in Drogheda a residence of Capuchins, in which there are four friars; all four are men of merit, and two of them are good preachers, F. Dowdall and F. Verdon. There is, moreover, in the same city, a convent of Augustinians, composed of three friars: they are pretty good.

" In the united dioceses of Down and Connor there are two convents of Franciscans, one in Down of eight friars, two of whom are good preachers, F. Paul O'Neil and F. Paul O'Bryn; they have a novitiate there, as also in Carrickfergus, where they have a convent of six friars. Near Down, at ' Villa Nova,' the Dominicans have a convent of five friars, and the prior, F. Clement Byrne, is a learned preacher.

' In the diocese of Derry the Dominicans have two convents, one in the city of Lerry, of six friars; the prior, *F. Patrick O'Dyry*, is an exceedingly good man, and a great preacher. The other convent is in Culrahan, and consists of ten friars, the prior, *F. Dominic Loreman*, is famous for preaching. The Franciscans have in this diocese a residence of four friars. In the two convents of the Dominicans there are novitiates.

"In the diocese of Raphoe there are, in the convent of Donegal, eighteen friars, two of them distinguished, *F. Stephen Congall* and *F. Anthony Dogherty*, who had been provincial. Here also they have a novitiate.

"In the diocese of Clogher the Dominicans have a convent of eight friars, two of whom are good preachers, *F. Thomas MacMahon* and *F. Charles MacManus*. Here again they have a novitiate. There are two convents of Franciscans, one in Lisgaole, of six friars, two of whom are sufficiently good preachers, *F. Terenan* and *F. Macmalachin*. The other convent is in Monaghan, composed of seven friars, and one of them is a good preacher and learned man; his name is *F. Francis Maguire*.

"In the diocese of Meath the Dominicans have a convent at Trim, of five friars; they have also a novitiate there; amongst the friars there is one named *F. John Byrne*, a great and learned preacher, but quarrelsome. In this diocese there are two convents of Franciscans; there is one likewise at Trim of six friars; all were Valesians, but now pretend the contrary; the two most distinguished in this convent are of the *Tuite* family. The other convent is in Multifarnham, composed of ten friars; *F.* Geanor resides there. It has also a novitiate.

"In the diocese of Kilmore there is only one convent of Franciscans."

Some of the dioceses are here passed over in silence, but we have sufficient data to supply them from a *Relatio* or Report on the Province of Ulster, presented by Dr. Plunket in 1675, to the Sacred Congregation. From it we learn that in the diocese of Dromore there were no regular clergy. In the diocese of Clonmacnoise there was one convent of Franciscans, and in the diocese of Ardagh there were two convents of Franciscans, and one of Dominicans.

The same *Report* gives us the number of the secular clergy; there were forty secular priests in the diocese of Armagh, and about two hundred and fifty others divided between the ten remaining dioceses of the province.*

* As we have already seen, in Chapter III., Dr. Plunket, when agent for the Irish bishops in Rome, represented the total number of the secular clergy as 1,000, and the regulars 600. This account differs but little from that of Peter Walsh, in his *History of the Remonstrance*, who

The Holy Sacrifice seems to have been at this period for the most part celebrated in private houses, and such was the fury of the persecutors, that it was deemed a criminal offence in Catholics to seek to erect a public edifice for the service of God. Hence but few chapels were to be met with through the country, excepting those which, with the connivance of Ormond, had been erected by the Valesians. He wished by this privilege to win for Walsh and his fellow-Remonstrants special favour amongst the Catholics; but the people of Ireland were too devoted to the See of St. Peter to offer insult to his successor, no matter what might be the bribe held out to them. The Remonstrants soon ceased to hold any position among the Catholics, and the churches they erected passed into the hands of their orthodox opponents. We shall allow the Archbishop to describe the happy result as to his diocese in the following extract from his letter to the Internunzio, dated Dublin, 26th September, 1671:—

"To say the truth, our just and good God *qui mala permittit quia de malis novit benefacere* has drawn good from the evil deeds of Walsh. This man, about eight years ago, anxious to make a display of zeal, and thus more easily gain followers and attract the people, obtained from Ormond a toleration for chapels and convents in Dublin, and many other cities, but he wished that all the convents, and even all the provinces should be governed by his own adherents. Ormond being removed from the Viceroyalty, through the mercy of God, no other Viceroy molested or molests either the chapels or the convents. In the most wealthy and noble city of my diocese and of the whole province, there are three chapels, very beautiful and ornamented: the first belongs to the Capuchins, the second to the Reformed Franciscans, the third to the Jesuits. There is also one of the Augustinians, but it is rather poor. So that we may all repeat what is said of the sin of Adam—*O felix culpa* (oh happy fault); or again, *necessarium Adæ peccatum*. The above-mentioned city is called Drogheda, at five hours distance from Dublin; it is, next to Dublin, the best city in Ireland."

Before the close of 1673 the storm of persecution was once more let loose upon our country. The bishops and regular clergy were those against whom its fury was chiefly

reckons the number of Secular Priests as more than 1,000, and the Regulars as about 800, being divided as follows:—Franciscans, 400; Dominicans, 200; Augustinians, 100; and nearly 100 religious of the other various orders.

levelled.　Incredible were the privations and sufferings which Dr. Plunket was compelled to endure; but what most afflicted the tender heart of the good shepherd was to see his fold laid waste by the devouring wolves, and all the institutions, the fruits of years of unceasing toil, reduced to ruin.　He seems, indeed, in the zealous labours of his early episcopate to have foreseen the coming persecution, and in his letter of 29th September, 1671, he thus expresses himself :—

" I pray your Excellency to expedite the matters which I wrote to you about.　This is the time for doing good whilst the present Viceroy is with us.　We must act as the mariners at sea, who, when the wind is favourable, unfurl all their sail, and *inflatis velis* sweep the ocean with great velocity, but when the wind becomes contrary, they lower the sails, and seek some little port for refuge.　Whilst we have the present Viceroy, *we may sail*, and I will do all in my power to advance our spiritual interests, instruct the clergy, and educate them in science and theology."

His anticipations were too soon to be realised ; and, writing on the 15th of December, 1673, he draws a vivid picture of the sufferings he had then to undergo, and the poverty to which he was reduced :—

" Matters here have been very severe, the more so as the meeting of Parliament is at hand on the 7th of January next, so that I am in concealment, and Dr. Brennan is with me.　The lay Catholics are so much afraid of losing their property, that no one with anything to lose will give refuge to either ordinary or regulars, and although the regular clergy have some connivance to remain, yet the Catholics dread almost to admit them to say Mass in their houses.　The priests give nothing to the bishops or ordinary ; I sometimes find it difficult to procure even oaten bread, and the house where I and Dr. Brennan are is of straw, and covered or thatched in such a manner that from our bed we may see the stars, and at the head of our bed every slightest shower *refreshes* us ; but we are resolved rather to die from hunger and cold than to abandon our flocks.　It would be a shame for spiritual soldiers, educated in Rome, to become mercenaries.　We shall take no step without the order of your Eminences.

" There is nothing that occasions me more inward grief than to see the schools which were instituted by me, now destroyed after so many toils.　Oh! what will the Catholic youth do, which is both numerous and full of talent?　The schools continued till the close of November last, and commenced about the beginning of July, 1670, so that they lasted three years and five months, and indeed the fathers of the Society behaved well, and toiled exceedingly in them, and they generally had about 150 Catholic boys : I procured also a Master to instruct the young priests of the province of Armagh in cases of conscience and in the manner of teaching the catechism, &c. The Sacred Congregation assigned 150 scudi per annum to the fathers. I received this sum for two years, but I have already given 500 scudi to the fathers, for which I have the receipt of their Superior, Father Rice, a copy of which I sent to the Internunzio and Dr. Creagh : the allowance for 1673 has not been paid, so that I am now creditor for the allowance of one year and five months. I expended more than 200 scudi in various journeys, and in arranging the differences of the Dominicans and Franciscans in their different dioceses, by order of the Internunzio, Airoldi, and as Delegate of the Apostolic See : and I expended about 200 scudi in bringing Fathers Harold and Coppinger to submission to your Eminences, as I wrote in former letters : I expended 400 scudi in letters, whilst I only received 100 from your Eminences ; for I am obliged to keep up a correspondence with all parts of the kingdom, and also in London, in order to be able to give accurate information to your Eminences. Modesty prevents me from speaking, but, nevertheless, as it is the truth, I will say it : I gave more "Reports" to your Eminences, and corresponded better, than all the prelates of Ireland for the past 30 years, and Monsignors Baldeschi, Airoldi, and Falconieri can testify to the truth of this : I gave no rest *temporibus, calamo nut etiam equis* (to my brains and pen, or even to my horses) during the past four years, in a vast province of eleven dioceses, in all of which, besides myself, there was only one bishop, and he old and half decrepit, Dr. Plunket, Bishop of Meath, until the arrival, a short time ago, of the Bishop of Clogher, and of the Bishop of Down, a little before him : and although the Bishop of Down has been a year in the country, how many letters has he written to your Eminences ? I confirmed during the past four years forty-eight thousand six hundred and fifty-five, of whom I have kept the list, and there are some dioceses here that have not seen a bishop for forty years, though the Catholics are numerous in them. Now you see from all this, that the Sacred Congregation owes me 300 scudi for letters, and 150 for the schools for one year, and about 60 for five months; which make in all 410* scudi; and God knows I stand in need of it; for, since the dread of the Parliament commenced in the month of February last, I did not receive 10 scudi from my diocese, and at present, since the publication of the edict, not a coin is to be seen : with difficulty can a piece of oaten-bread be found, or a hut even of straw. May the Lord God be ever praised, and the most holy Mary. —I am, &c.

"OLIVER OF ARMAGH.

" 15th December, 1673.
" To Monsignor Cerri, Secretary of Propaganda."

* This should have been 510 : but Dr. Plunket was only desirous to have some assistance given him in his present distress, and does not seem to have been very solicitous about the precise sum.

Dr. Plunket, in many of his letters, had already announced this coming storm, and he received in return a consolatory letter from the Sacred Congregation exhorting him to courage and fortitude of soul.* The letter of Dr. Plunket, to which this consolatory brief was more immediately sent as a reply, is as follows:—

"I have received your letter of the 3rd inst., and I am rejoiced that your Excellency was pleased with the 'Report' which I sent regarding the state of Catholic affairs in this Kingdom; but I am sorry that this is far worse now than heretofore. The bishops are all now proscribed, as also the Vicars-General, and all the heads: the clergy are thus *achephali*,† and are like to *scopæ dissolutæ*.‡ No Catholics can keep or carry fire-arms; and they would not have been allowed even to retain their swords, were it not that the Viceroy was resolute, and at the same time inclined to clemency. It is now expected that no Catholic will be allowed to live in the cities. You must have heard from London with what audacity the Parliament sought to prevent the marriage of the Duke of York with a Catholic, although the marriage contract had been made with the consent of the King. The House of Commons also wished that no Catholic lord—that is, no marquis, earl, or baron—should have a vote in Parliament; and, moreover, it refused supplies for carrying on the war against the Dutch. It also desired that no Catholic should reside within five miles of London, and that all Catholics should have some distinctive mark, as the Jews in Rome. Similar were the beginnings of the Parliament in 1640 and 1641, which, with unheard-of tyranny, beheaded the father of the present King, who is a wise and clement sovereign. These unreasonable demands obliged the King to prorogue the Parliament till the 7th of January, and he would have dissolved it altogether were it not for two counsellors who dissuaded him. The Government here dare not moderate in any way our sentence of banishment, or give us a longer respite than the 1st of December, through dread of Parliament, which is so severe against the Catholics. I exhort my brethren to constancy, and not to abandon their flocks, but, imitating the pastors of the three first centuries, to retire to some corner of their districts till the storm shall have passed. I shall retire to some little hut in the woods or mountains of my diocese with a supply of candles and books. Nevertheless, you can continue to send your letters as usual, and I will try occasionally to send some account to you. You will be good enough not to send envelopes, as they cost as much as the

* So we find recorded amongst the diaries of the Congregation, held 26th February, 1674.
† Without a head.
‡ Untied brooms.

G

letters themselves: every letter with a cover, costs 46 *bajocchi;* *
without the cover it would only cost 23 bajocchi. Since May, I
only received 80 scudi from my diocese; and were it not for
Sir Nicholas Plunket, who gave me lodging and support, I would be
rather a pilgrim than a Prelate. The poverty of the Catholics,
occasioned by the many taxes, and by the last war with the Dutch, is
inconceivable and indescribable ; and hence the priests are poor, having
nothing but the offerings of the faithful to support them : the
poverty of the priests occasions the poverty of the bishops, for they
have nothing but their proxies—that is, four or five scudi from each
priest—but since the edict was published, the bishops cannot make
any visitations, or receive any proxies, and hence they are in a
most miserable condition; and as I spent all that I had in the
service of their Eminences, I hope they will compensate my expenses,
and labours, and faithfulness in serving them. I hope they will not
reply, *Cum hæc omnia feceritis dicite quia servi inutiles sumus.* The
Viceroy is very friendly towards me, as are also all the counsellors
of State, because I never take any part in political or civil affairs.
The schools which I erected gave them some annoyance; but I
satisfied the more moderate amongst them by explaining that they
were erected for no other purpose than to instruct the youth in the
Christian doctrine, and in literature, that thus they might be useful
for the State, and for the service of the King, and that otherwise they
would become vagrants, and rogues, and highway robbers, and
disturbers of the peace and of social order.

  " I already wrote to you on the 5th of this month that all the
convents were destroyed, and all the novices scattered about in the
houses of the laity.   This edict was far more efficacious than any
letter of the Father-General. During the past three years I wrote
without ceasing against the excessive number of novitiates, and against
the soliciting of alms at the parochial altars ; I also wrote a letter to
the Provincial Chapter of the Franciscans, of which I sent a copy to
your Excellency, though I cannot say whether it reached you or not;
but they deemed me their adversary, because I proposed these wise
counsels to them—*exitus acta probat.* The sheet comes to a close,†
but I shall never cease to be the most affectionate and devoted servant
of your Excellency. I pray you to send this letter to Monsig. Cerri,
whom I also pray to give a copy of all my letters to Dr. Creagh,
that he may expedite my affairs.

  " 12th November, 1673.

                                " OLIVER OF ARMAGH.

  " P.S.—The Bishop of Waterford will come to my district to
conceal himself, as his own city is full of fanatics and furious

---

  * The *bajocchi* was a little more than our halfpenny, being one-tenth of
sixpence.
  † In the original letter these words terminate the last page ; what
follows is written wherever a vacant space presented itself throughout
the letter.

Presbyterians. The Bishop of Meath is old and attacked with gout, and unable to move about. I think the Viceroy will have compassion on him, on account of the esteem he has for Sir Nicholas, brother of the Bishop."

The alarm consequent on the renewal of the persecution lasted till the close of the following year. During this time Dr. Plunket, with the Bishop of Waterford, lay concealed in the woods and mountainous districts. He found opportunity, however, in the beginning of 1674, to undertake a journey to the province of Tuam, having been commissioned by the Holy See to confer the Pallium on Dr. Lynch, the Archbishop of that province: in this excursion he penetrated as far as Galway, and in his letter to the S. Congregation he extols the devotion and hospitality of that good people.

Calumny seems to have been added to the sufferings of our Irish Bishops, and some individuals represented to the Holy See that the Pastors of the Irish Church were abandoning their flocks, and that no fewer than 14 Bishops had left that island on their way to Rome.* Nothing could be more false than this calumnious assertion. Dr. Plunket expresses his surprise how such a tale could be invented; and writing on the 15th September, 1674, whilst he repeats his solicitations for assistance, and details the sufferings to which he and Dr. Brennan were exposed, he declares, at the same time, their firm resolve to run all risks, and to endure imprisonment and torture sooner than abandon the flocks entrusted to their charge. The following is his letter in full: it is directed to the Internunzio in Brussels:—

" During the past month 1 received two of your letters, but the judges of assizes being on circuit in my district I retired to my usual place of concealment in the most remote parts of the province, and hence I was not able to correspond according as I desired, nor can I even at present do so, for during the past two months and a-half I ceased to correspond with my friends in Dublin and London, as also with those in the provinces of Cashel and Tuam ; so that I can give no ' Reports ' except in regard of my own diocese, and the cause of all this is the lightness of my purse. I declare to your Excellency

* Ex notis Archiv. S. Cong.

Coram Deo et non mentior, as the Apostle said, that all I have in this world does not exceed 80 scudi, and the usual charities of the faithful have ceased since the edicts; nor is there any chance, as far as I see, that the sums which I expended in serving their Eminences will be repaid to me, so that I find myself in a deplorable condition; but let all be for the glory of God and the salvation of my soul. Had I served the Duke of Mirandola, in correspondence and otherwise, as I served the Sacred Congregation these five years past, the baker's account would have been long since settled; had I the means I would spare no labour or industry in serving their Eminences, being obliged to it by every law of justice and gratitude; but what is out of my power I cannot do. There is no single letter which I send to your Excellency that does not cost me one giulio (6*d.*): for each letter that I receive from you I have to pay two giuli and a-half (15*l.*); there is no letter that I receive from Cashel or Tuam but costs me a carlino (4*d.*) in Dublin, and then 2½ bajocchi (1½*d.*) from Dublin to my residence. Then, too, I have to give some recompense to my agents in Dublin and London, who have the trouble of going to the post to receive the letters and transmit them to me; and in paying them for the post I was not very stinted; they would not have served me and wasted their time, and shoes, and paper and ink, were I not liberal with them. I may say the same of my correspondents in Tuam and Cashel, and, indeed, *digni erant mercedibus suis.* I doubt not but the purse of your Excellency must feel and experience the expense of letters: indeed, there has been no year that it did not cost me more than one hundred scudi (£25); and since the period of your coming to the Nunciature in Flanders it has cost me more than a hundred scudi: for, during the whole time of the persecution, which has now lasted a year all to one month, though I was concealed in the mountains, as was also the Bishop of Waterford, with the exception of the two past months, I always found some means, though not without difficulty, to procure letters from these quarters, but I may say (as experience sufficiently convinces me) that which our Saviour tells us—*cum hæc omnia feceritis dicite quia servi inutile sumus.*

I expended during the five years which are now passed all to one month, about 500 scudi (£125). I expended 200 scudi when commissioned as Delegate of the Apostolic See, in arranging the differences of the Dominicans and Franciscans, of Mr. Farrell and Gafney, and in reducing Coppinger and Harold to obedience to the Holy See, and I received only 100 scudi, which Monsig. Airoldi, predecessor of your Excellency, procured for me. God knows that I gave no rest to my brains, to my pen, or to my horses, in serving their Eminences, and I should ever continue to do so with alacrity and joy were it possible for me; but, as I have no means, how can you expect that I should do so, *ad impossibile nemo tenetur.* I was in Rome for twenty-five years, and for twelve of these I served the Sacred Congregation in the Chairs of Theology and Conferences; I also served the Sacred Congregation of the Index, as you are aware and in what a state I found the studies at Propaganda, and in what perfection I left them, the very Reverend Fathers Libelli, Laurea, Spinola, Sommaschi, and Bonvicini, the Rector will state; these Fathers were Prefects of Studies, and know it well. Then their Eminences destined me to the principal church in this kingdom, and God knows in what manner I laboured, and with what toils I promoted and preserved the cause of the Church. Modesty prevents me from speaking, but as it is the truth I may boldly declare it; I corresponded better and more frequently with their Eminences than all the prelates of the kingdom. Let the archives of Propaganda be looked to and explored, and you will touch with your hands the truth of what I say. I moreover wrote to some of their Eminences, as to Cardinals Barberini, Azzolini, and others, concerning the persecution and the misery of this country, which was so great, that in my diocese more than 500 Catholics died from starvation,* and the Bishop of Waterford and I were glad to get a morsel of oaten bread. But enough of these matters.

"As to the subject of your letters, I sent a copy of the last edict through two different channels; that is, by the post, and by a friend who was going to London. As to the story you heard of our prelates being on their way to Rome to take up their residence there, I cannot understand it; there is no bishop here who knows the language of Rome or has friends there, excepting the Bishop of Waterford and myself, and we will not abandon our flocks till we are compelled to do so ; we will first suffer imprisonment and other torments ; we have already suffered so much on the mountains, in huts and caverns, and we have acquired such a habit of it, that, for the future, suffering will be less severe and less troublesome. As to my diocese, all is peaceful, excepting two priests who are refractory. The Provincial of the Franciscans published a very imprudent order for all his friars to go to their residences, and live and seek alms as usual ; it is feared that this will cause new rigour of persecution, the more so, as the Parliament will meet on the 11th of November. Father Saul, the apostate, makes a great noise with his writings against our faith. I pray you to send this letter to Monsignor Ravizza, and I shall ever be your Excellency's most affectionate and obliged servant,

"THOMAS COX

"15th September, 1674.   "(Oliver of Armagh).
"To the Internunzio."

From the facts incidentally mentioned in this letter, we may form some idea of the misery to which our country was now reduced by continued oppression and the renewal of the persecution. In one diocese alone more than five hundred persons fell victims to famine, choosing rather to suffer death

---

* The Internunzio, writing in August, 1674, announces that a dreadful famine had set in in Ireland, and laid the whole country desolate.

itself than to barter for the mess of potage which was held out to them the precious inheritance of their faith. Amidst all their sufferings, however, the good shepherd clung to his sheep, their sorrows were his sorrows, their trials were his trials.

In the following years, though the Catholics at intervals enjoyed a partial calm, yet their sad condition and misery continued unabated. A little while before his arrest, in 1679, Dr. Plunket wrote to the Secretary of Propaganda that all he possessed in this world did not exceed 50 scudi ; and in another letter, written at the same time, he attests the desolation of his flock, occasioned by famine and the sword, and declares his resolution to sell even the sacred vessels themselves in order to relieve their misery. The continuance of persecution produced no change in his holy resolve to cling inseparably to his flock, and on the 15th of May, 1679, in his letter to the Internunzio, he calmly announces to him, " so many are the spies in search of me, that I am morally certain I shall be apprehended; but, nevertheless, I will remain with my own, nor will I abandon them till I be dragged to the sea-shore."

Many were the calumnies which, from time to time, were published against our primate. However, they only caused his true merit to shine forth with renewed brilliancy and lustre. We shall more than once have occasion to refer to these accusations hereafter ; for the present we shall merely cite a few testimonies of those best acquainted with our Irish Church as to his zeal and untiring labours. Thus the Internunzio, Falconieri, writes to the Sacred Congregation on 9th November, 1673 :—" *I cannot here omit to represent to the Sacred Congregation the zeal with which the Archbishop of Armagh labours for the propagation of the Catholic religion in his diocese, of which I have received most indubious proofs from various quarters;* "* and again, on 24th February, 1674,

---

* Non devo lasciare di rappresentarle il zelo col quale l'arcivescovo di Armagh procura la propagazione della Religione Cattolica nella sua diocesi avendo io ottimi riscontri da diverse parti. Archiv S.C.

transmitting to Rome a letter of the Primate, he adds; "Chiefly by his zeal are the affairs of the Catholic religion maintained in the kingdom of Ireland."* Peter Creagh who was so distinguished towards the close of the 17th century, as Archbishop of Dublin, also expresses himself in the same strain in his letter of 24th January, 1671, to Dr. Brennan, the agent of the Irish clergy in Rome:—

" I was in Dublin [he writes] during the Assembly of our bishops, and though there was some difference between the Archbishops of Armagh and Dublin as to the order of signature to the decrees, nevertheless this controversy was carried on so peaceably that its echo was scarcely heard beyond the precincts of the place of assembly. We experience great benefit from the formula of allegiance which the prelates presented to the Viceroy, and we are allowed to enjoy great liberty.

" All that has been written against the Archbishop of Armagh is mere calumny, proceeding from envy. He administers his province with great zeal and devotedness: he has put an end to many quarrels and scandals, and he has reduced to submission certain bands of outlaws who were a perpetual annoyance to the Catholics of the province. Now, thanks to God, there is nothing to disturb our tranquillity and peace."

The Archbishop of Cashel, too, in his letter of 6th April, 1677, after rejecting several calumnies with which Dr. Plunket was assailed, thus briefly adds his own invaluable testimony as to the zealous labours of the primate:—

" In my opinion, the present Archbishop of Armagh has attended more to the spiritual administration of that province than any of his predecessors for many years ; and I say this without wishing to lower in any way the merit of the preceding primates."

And again, after the glorious martyrdom of Dr. Plunket, the same Archbishop, when transmitting to Rome a narrative of his imprisonment and execution, writes :—

" In truth, his holy life merited for him this glorious death ; for during the twelve years of his residence here, he showed himself vigilant, zealous, and indefatigable above his predecessors, nor do we find within the memory of any of the present century that any primate or metropolitan visited his diocese and province with such

* Al di lui zelo s'appoggiano principalmente gli affari della Religione Cattolica in quel Regno.

solicitude and pastoral zeal as he did, reforming depraved morals amongst the people, and the scandalous lives of some of the clergy, chastising the guilty, rewarding the meritorious, consoling all, and benefiting, as far as was in his power, and succouring the needy: wherefore he was applauded and honoured by the clergy and people, with the exception of some wicked enemies of virtue and religious observance."

CHAPTER VIII.

DR. PLUNKET'S ZEAL IN CORRECTING ABUSES.

FROM the zeal displayed by Dr. Plunket in advancing the cause of God, and promoting the spiritual welfare of his flock, we may easily conclude with what ardour he would seek to root out any prevailing abuses, and bring back to the right path the straying sheep of his fold. Considering the circumstances of the times, these abuses were indeed but few; many of the Irish people in the fulness of their faith, and the simplicity of their hearts, receiving with submission the teaching of their pastors, realized in their lives, amidst the afflictions of this world, and the trials of persecution, all the sublime perfection of the Gospel. Nevertheless, there were those who neglected the practises of faith—prodigal children in the spiritual household, and these became the special objects of the good prelate's care. Several instances of this kind have already presented themselves; and when attempts were made to sow dissensions amongst the faithful, we have seen with what zealous ardour he laboured to reconcile his children and to preserve the blessings of peace.

In some districts of his province, Dr. Plunket found that drunkenness had cast deep root, and immediately all the energies of his soul were directed to eradicate it, and introduce holy temperance in its place. The better to effect that object, he resolved to propose in his own life a model of abstemiousness, which all might imitate; and not only did he avoid all excess, but, moreover, even at his meals he abstained altogether from the use of every exciting drink. All excesses in the clergy were, in like manner, most strictly prohibited, and he interdicted, under the severest censures, their frequenting drinking-houses ; his exhortations, confirmed by his own example, and by that of his clergy, were happily successful in converting many of the people from their evil ways, and in winning them back to the observance of the precepts of the Gospel. No words can better attest his zeal in correcting this abuse than his own letter to the Sacred Congregation—from which, too, we learn how successfully he strove to present in his own life, and that of his clergy, a model of temperance to the faithful :—

" Whilst visiting six dioceses of this province [he writes], I applied myself especially to root out the cursed vice of drunkenness, which is the parent and the nurse of all scandals and contentions. I commanded also, under penalty of privation of benefice, that no priest should frequent public houses, or drink whiskey, &c., &c. Indeed I have derived great fruit from this order ; and, as it is of little use to teach without practising, I myself never drink at meals. Give me an Irish priest without this vice, and he is assuredly a saint."

More than all, however, Dr. Plunket, was untiring in introducing regularity and discipline into some houses of the religious orders, where inobservance had crept in during the years of persecution. No spiritual labourers had culti-vated with greater zeal this portion of the vineyard of the Lord than the children of St. Francis. Not only had many illustrious members of the Irish hierarchy come forth from their ranks, but in the days of Ireland's peril, when the sword was unsheathed to smite the shepherds of the fold, the convents of St. Francis, scattered through the Continent, sent to our own shores, band after band of devoted cham-pions of the cross, who kept alive the flame of faith, and often, too, sealing their testimony with their blood, led on their faithful flocks to martyrdom. The glory of these heroic soldiers of Christ, is nowise obscured by the corrupt lives of some few who sought to make their holy habit a mask for their ambition, and a means of gratifying the vilest passions. At the time of which we speak, it cannot at all surprise us that the seed sown by Peter Walsh and Taafe

should bear its evil fruits; and that, whilst the learning
of Wadding, in Rome, and the evangelical labours of
Dr. Tyrrell, in Ireland, added new glories to the pages of
the Franciscan annals, some unworthy brethren bringing
contumely upon that name, and, violating their most sacred
vows, should, Judas-like, consummate their wickedness by
renouncing their saving faith, and even hesitate not to
persecute the most zealous of their fellow-labourers in the
ministry, and bring their saintly chief-pastor to the scaffold.

In many of the letters of Dr. Plunket, we may remark
how particularly he dwells on the irregularities and abuses
which had crept in amongst some houses of this order, and
how he refers to such abuses as the main source of any
scandals that then existed in the Irish Church. The
superiors of the Franciscan order were, indeed, no less
desirous than the Archbishop that these disorders should
be checked; and when, in 1669, the first measures were
taken by the Holy See to re-establish the purity of religious
discipline in Ireland, we find that the then Guardian of the
Fraciscans in Louvain addressed a letter, in the name of
his fellow-religious, to the Secretary of the Sacred Congregation, thanking him for his solicitude and watchfulness in
promoting that holy work :—

" When the Irish Franciscan province [he says], weakened by so
many assaults, tossed about by so many contrary winds, lacerated by
the dissensions of the wicked, disturbed by the ambition of some, was
hastening to its ruin, and seemed even on the brink of destruction, our
good God, who rejects not, nor despises those who hope in Him, but
from on high looks on them with an eye of mercy, and protects and
defends them with His omnipotence, at length was pleased to
stretch forth to us His assisting hand ; and you were the chief
instrument He made use of, by whose energy and prudence the waves
were calmed, the clouds scattered, and peace restored, our province
was re-established, religion promoted, the lovers of observance comforted, the contumacious repressed and humbled. Wherefore, in
most humble sentiments, prostrate before your Excellency, mindful
of so great a blessing, whose remembrance shall be undying amongst
us, we render to you all the thanks that are in our power ; and we
offer up our prayers to God that He, who is omnipotent, may deign
to long preserve your Excellency for the propagation of His holy
Church and the preserving of our province."

This letter is signed by Father Francis Fegan, Guardian of the College of St. Anthony (of Padua) in Louvain.

In the Barberini Archives there is another letter from the Franciscans in Ireland, in which they lament, in like manner, the ruin which some disorderly members had well-nigh brought upon that province, and return thanks to the Holy See for its watchful solicitude in checking their disorderly career.

In the Synod of Prelates convened by Dr. Plunket in Dublin, in June, 1670, more than one decree was enacted, ordering various reforms, especially in regard of some of the Novitiates of the Franciscans. As we shall see when speaking of that Synod, the religious being exempt from episcopal jurisdiction, such decrees, when subjected to the decision of Rome, were declared null and void; but the Secretary of Propaganda, when replying to the letter of the Archbishop conveying these decrees, deemed it necessary to assure him that the Sacred Congregation wholly approved of their substance, and moreover authorised him in the name of the Holy Father, to re-enact the same decrees, should the bishops deem it proper and expedient.

In his letter of the 25th September, 1671, Dr. Plunket goes to the very root of these evils, and exhorts the Holy See to strike a decisive blow which would at once remove such scandals from the Church :—

" Your Excellency [he says] sees how many novitiates there are ; they receive novices promiscuously and without choice, nor are they educated in a proper manner ; they neither attend to choir, nor observe the discipline of the order ; they treat with seculars of every description, and, the novitiate being ended, they are sent to quest in the cities and towns, whence it arises that many of them become unworthy members. It would be necessary to prohibit the reception of novices in this kingdom, where they cannot be trained in a proper manner ; let those who have a vocation be sent to Louvain, to Prague, to Rome, or to Capranica, to make their novitiate. But they will say they are poor and have not sufficient means for this journey. I reply that, nevertheless, they have means to send them to those convents or colleges to pursue their studies ; let them apply these funds to send them to the same convents to make their novitiate ; and it would be well that one of the four convents or colleges which I mentioned should be destined for a novitiate, where their vocations might be examined, for here *introducunt cœcos at claudos eosque cogunt ac compellunt intrare*, and while thus gourds are sown, it cannot be expected that melons should be gathered. Neither the Capuchins, nor the Jesuits, nor the Carmelites, have a novitiate here, being aware that they could not give novices a proper training in this kingdom. There is also another great disorder; the guardians, for instance, of Louvain and Prague, when they find a disorderly friar, to free themselves from his annoyance, procure an order for him to go to Ireland; the remedy for this might be that the Nuncios should examine such as are to be sent to us. At present they keep the good men, and send them to teach in the convents of Germany and Flanders, and France, and Italy, &c., whence they never come to the mission, but grow old and die on the Continent. It would be necessary to send without delay to Ireland, all the (Irish) friars that are not actually in the convents which I mentioned of Prague, Louvain, &c.; and, moreover, all those friars, who live unoccupied in these convents, that is not engaged in teaching, or as vicars, &c.

"I pray you to procure a remedy for these disorders, and I remain,

"Your most obedient and devoted servant,

"OLIVER PLUNKET.

"Dublin, 25th Sept., 1671."

"P.S.—The Earl of Orrery published a proclamation against all Catholics, ecclesiastics, or laymen in Limerick; he wishes that all should depart from the city; he is president of Munster, and but little friendly to the Viceroy who will assist us."

In the following year a Chapter of the Franciscan fathers was convened at Elphin, and in a letter* whose every sentence breathes the pastoral solicitude of the writer and

---

* We insert, in the original text, the letter referred to; our readers will admire its classical simplicity, and at the same time the lessons of wisdom which it dictates:—

"REVERENDI PATRES,—Appulsus in Hiberniam tanquam immeritus D. Patritii successor nihil habui antiquius, quam in cleri totius reformationem in Armac provincia ita incumbere ut idem qua doctrina, qua ecclica, disciplina apprime imbueretur. Et quamvis non pauca in clero religioso animadverterim, quæ mihi videbantur non usq. adeo eorum instituto consona, quæq. idem institutum etiam hoc in Regno minus deceant, illa tamen divulganda non censui, donec opportunitatem nanciscerer eadem superioribus alicubi congregatis indicandi. Cum igitur non ita pridem acceperim Superiores, et præcipuos Ordinis vestri Patres coetum Elphinæ celebraturos, mearum esse partium duxi nonnulla pro meo in Ordinem vestrum amore, et in provinciam meam zelo eid. cætui proponere, quibus mature perpensis meo, et plurium aliorum judicio, remedia quantocujus

his affectionate regard for the great order of St. Francis,
Dr. Plunket lays open to them the abuses which prevailed,
and suggest the means by which they might be remedied.
These exhortations of Dr. Plunket were not fruitless, but
the zealous Primate deemed all partial remedies insufficient
unless the occasion and very root of every abuse were
removed. Hence, in 1673, he renewed his solicitations to
the Internuncio, to have the various Novitiates suppressed,
writing as follows:—

" I have received your letter of the eighth of this month with the
enclosure for the Father General of the Franciscans, and I shall have
it safely delivered to him ; but, in my opinion, the multiplicity of
novitiates can never be remedied until the Holy See will take the
matter into its own hands, absolutely prohibiting the receiving of
novices in this kingdom, or at least prescribing that, as there is only

adhibenda sunt ; quibus fiet ut religiosi vestri optimo incolis exemplo, et
summo toti provinciæ splendori, ac commodo, sint deiuceps futuri.
" Inprimis igitur quot in Armacana provincia conventus, totidem isthic
propei modum tyrocinia reperire est ; a meo in Hiberniam adventu tyrones
admissi fuere Pontani, Dundalkiæ, Armachæ, Duni, Petrafargusiæ,
Dunegalliæ, Cavanachiæ, Athloniæ, et alibi. In hisce et tot aliis conventibus apud tyrones nec chori sunt, nec regularis observantia viget ;
inter servos, ancillas, advenas, aliosq. promiscue versantur. Iidem mensis
inservientes, quibus sæculares tam viri quam fœminæ accumbunt, mun
danis et futilibus intersunt colloquiis, quorum assuetudine fervor omnis, si
quem hauserint, religiosæ observantiæ et pietatis, nullo pæne negotio
evanescit   Insuper difficillime in his conventibus reperiri poterunt
novitiorum magistri, muneris tam eximii capaces, qui tyrones juxta
Instituti, et vocationis suæ normam, quo par est, honore, et fructu
instruant. Peracto tyrocinio hus illuc ruri vagantur, et conventuum
negotiis occupantur. Meo quidem quantulocumq. judicio, satius foret
unicum in provincia Armac* conventum assignare, in quo omnes istius
provinciæ novitii tyrocinium ponerent sumptibus eorum conventuum, a
quibus eo destinantur, ut procul a vulgi strepitu, et omnium illecebrarum
immunes soli Deo vacent, et solidarum fundamenta virtutum jaciant ;
vel certe (quod optabilius) in ultramarinas partes mittantur, puta Lovanium,
Romam, Pragam, vel Capranicam tyrocinii peragendi ergo ; quemadmodum enim anno tyrocinii expleto ad prædictas urbes studiorum, quidni
etiam tyrocinii causa proficiscantur ?   Hinc duplex (ut alia taceam
plurima) commodum in ssmum ordinem, quia in novitios, redundabit.
Inprimis aliorum ead. in domo commorantium fervor, et in virtutibus
progressus tyronibus stimulo erit, ne sacri Instituti spiritum divinitus
inditum remittant ; deinde tyrones in transmarinis partibus aberunt ab
omni periculo scandali, quo hic nonnulli patrum vestrorum tam eos, quam
sæculares, quos in novitiorum professione adhibent convivas, non possunt
non offendere, dum liberius vino adusto (vulgo aquavitæ) indulgent. Deo
certe gratissimum foret, si Patres omnes hoc genere potus omnino

one province, so also there shall be but one novitiate, or at most two.
It is certain that in my province there are twelve or thirteen novitiates.   There are also novitiates in the provinces of Cashel, Tuam,
and Dublin ; in all about thirty; they gather a crowd, and make
bundles of every sort of herbs ; they sow gourds, and how can they
gather melons?   Unless the Holy See will apply some remedy
to these novitiates, as was done by Innocent X. in my time in
Italy, the matter cannot be remedied.   A brief to the effect, either
that only one novitiate should be kept in this kingdom, or that the
novices should be sent beyond the seas, as is done by the Jesuits and
Capuchins, would be of the greatest use to this kingdom.—(18th
August, 1673)."

Another cause of annoyance to the Primate was found in
the divisions and dissensions of some unworthy and ambitious
members of this order.   We have seen how the Guardian of

abstinerent, a quo ipsi etiam sacerdotes sæculares, quia ego illis severe
interdixi, modo sibi temperant.

    "Alterum est, quod vobis proponendum habui æquum esse, ut cum
ssma. D. Francisci regula et Ordinis constitutiones mandent pedibus iter
conficiendum, id omnes exequantur, quod non difficilius hoc in Regno,
quam in Germania, Belgio, et alibi potest observari, quibus, in Regnis
religiosi viri incommoda anni tempestate pedibus. et quidem nudis iter
conficiunt, et pleriq. vestrum alias iisdem in locis fecerunt. Contra vero
in variis hic conventibus vix reperitur ullus sacerdos, qui non equo ipse,
et famulo equite. dum aliquo est proficiscendum, utatur: quæ famulorum
et equorum multiplicitas non potest non magno conventibus oneri esse,
quodq. sacellis aut eorum altaribus exornandis, ac libris emendis seponi
posset, inutili equorum famulorumq. gregi alendo impenditur ; multos
videre est nobiles, qui pedites incedunt, quidni id faciant ii, qui eo vi
Regulæ adstringuntur, quod catholicis æque ac heteredoxis esset ædifica-
tioni, et nullo incommodo hoc in Regno fieri potest.

    "Tertium hoc deniq. vos monitos velim, plerosq. seniorum put et
juniorum Patrum multos pretiosiorem pannum, pileos gallicos, et collaria
(vulgo cravatts) limbis dentatim textis ornata, et id genus alia sumptibus
non exiguis sibi comparare; quibus emendis abstinendum, potjus, et pecunia
in meliorem usum convertenda, tyronibus alendis, sacræ supellectili, libris
ac hujusmodi rebus emendis ordini vestro (quem multi vrum. dicunt gravi
rerum fere omnium penuria laborare) proficuis, vel deniq. tyronibus in
ultramarinas partes transvehendis.   Quam plurimi nobiles toto anno
Levidensa, seu nostrate panno vestiuntur.   Sed, inquies, hoc in Regno
inter heterodoxos versamur ; esto sane, ipsi tamen minime advertent, an
tu eques vel pedes incedas, an panno et pileo gallico, vel hibernico utaris,
an tyrocinium unum vel plura instituas.   Hæc in ordinis vestri et pro-
vincie meæ commodum insinuanda duxi, et responsum vestrum propediem
prestolabor.

    "Dublini, 30 Oct. 1672.
        "Vestrarum Paternitatum.   " Addictissimus,
                                            " OLIVERIUS ARMACH.

    · Patribus Ord. S. Franc. Congregatis Elphinæ."

Louvain referred to this same source of scandal, and, indeed, it was a natural consequence of those abuses which Dr. Plunket so laboured to check. A division of Ireland into two Franciscan provinces had long been contemplated by the superiors of that order, and urged by the Primate ; but those who fomented disorder, seeking to gratify their self-ambition, opposed this plan with all their might. On the 22nd of September, 1672, Dr. Plunket thus writes on this subject, referring to some of those unworthy members :—

" It is ambition that prevents their consenting to a division of the province, although they are sure, as many of them declared to myself, that it would be a source of perpetual peace to themselves and to others. The constant dissensions of the Franciscans have for many years disturbed the spiritual tranquillity of this kingdom, and they still disturb it, and occasion great scandal to our flock, and to our adversaries. They sometimes even bring their trials before the secular tribunals. They make such a medley of novices, without education or virtue, and without any selection, that it is no wonder that scandals arise. They should send their novices to be trained at Louvain, or Prague, or Rome. They have here about seventy convents, which, in a kingdom with only one provincial, cannot easily be governed. The Commissaries, Father James Darcy, and Father John Brady, get up factions here lest any division may be made. They have now the rod of government in their hands, and they hope to always have a finger in the management of matters, and they would sooner have it extend to the whole kingdom than to half. In three years it will fall to Armagh to have the Provincial, and this Brady is morally certain that he shall be elected ; and hence, he now does all in his power to prevent a division, for he wishes to govern all and not a part. It was once commanded in their Provincial Chapter that the province should be divided, but the war and other events prevented the decree from being carried into effect. Monsignore, I pray you not to attend to the complaints or threats of difficulties which some will propose against this division. Let a brief be published ordering the division to be made, so that Ulster and Connaught form one province, and Leinster and Munster another, and all difficulties will at once disappear."

The persecution which soon burst upon the country blasted at once all the hopes of the re-establishment of discipline, and in a postscript to his letter of the 15th December, 1673, Dr. Plunket briefly remarks :—

" All the convents and novitiates are destroyed, and the novices are scattered throughout the country; the last decree has also

terminated the disputes of the Dominicans and Franciscans, both
as to questing and as to the convents. Dr. Plunket, Bishop of
Meath, on account of his old age and the gout, has, though with
difficulty, received permission to remain."

With the return of a momentary calm, returned also some
of those disorders of which the Primate complained, and his
zealous desire that his ecclesiastical province should be a
model of discipline and perfection to the Catholic world, was
rekindled anew. Availing himself of the opportunity presented by his secretary and cousin, Michael Plunket, who
was about to start for Rome to enter upon a course of studies
at the Irish College in that City, the Archbishop wrote three
letters, all dated 15th August, 1676, addressed to the chief
authorities in Rome, recapitulating in them the various
abuses then prevailing, and the remedies by which they
might be removed. One of these letters is addressed to the
Cardinal Protector of Ireland, and is as follows:—

" I deem myself in conscience obliged to represent and lay before
your Eminence, with due submission, the measures which may conduce to the good of religion in this kingdom, and to point out the
abuses which now retard its propagation and maintenance. And in
the first place the novitiates of the Regulars do us much harm. They
receive a number of novices, and cannot give them proper instruction : they have no real convents, but live in a sort of huts, without
choir and without due education   In the province of Armagh alone,
the Franciscans had thirteen novitiates.

" 2ndly. Various Colleges were instituted in Rome, Salamanca, St.
Jago, Lisbon, &c., by some pious founders, to educate Secular Priests,
who, on finishing their studies. might return to labour in this vineyard : nevertheless the best students become Religious, and never
return to this country, and thus the intention of the founders is
frustrated, and the parishes here are left abandoned : a decree for
the various Irish Colleges, similar to that made in regard of the
Pontifical colleges, would remedy all this disorder.

" 3rdly. You will be pleased to intimate to the Superiors of the
Religious in Rome, that no Religious be sent hither with the title of
Missionary Apostolic without having first received faculty from the
Sacred Congregation, *et ab eadem mittatur*, which faculty they will be
obliged to present to the Ordinary in whose diocese they live. These
points being arranged and decreed, great harmony and peace will be
promoted here in ecclesiastical affairs. The bearer, Mr. Michael
Plunket, my cousin, who was also my Secretary for three years, will
give you a more minute detail of our affairs here, and of all we have
to suffer. He will act as our Agent until the arrival in Rome of

Dr. James Cusack,* who was educated in Rome, and was afterwards a great preacher in English and Irish, a good theologian and canonist, but who cannot commence his journey before next spring. In the meantime, I pray you to protect the bearer; and, making you a profound reverence, and wishing you every felicity, and a long life, I shall ever remain

"Your Eminence's

"Most humble and obliged, devoted servant,

"OLIVER OF ARMAGH.

"Dublin, 15th August, 1676."

In one of his last letters, transmitted together with the decrees of the Synod of Ardpatrick, and dated 10th of September, 1678, Dr. Plunket, writing under his usual assumed name, *Thomas Cox*, renews his solicitations to have the number of Novitiates lessened, and recommends the appointment of Dr. Tyrrell, Bishop of Clogher, who was an illustrious ornament of the Franciscan Order, as Apostolic Visitator of the Irish Province:—

"I have spoken [he says] with some of the superiors of the Franciscans, who have four convents in my district: in one there are only two friars, in another four, in the others seven or five; and I besought them to put them all the members in one or two convents, but they do not like to do it. Nothing stands in such need of reformation. I tire your Excellency and their Eminences with so many letters, but '*the zeal of the house of God hath eaten me up,*' and I would wish that my province, both as to the secular and the regular clergy, should be holy and good and observant. Monsignor Tyrrell was Secretary-General of the Order of St. Francis for twelve years; he was also Definitor General, Commissary, Visitator, &c., and no one knows their Rules better, and were he appointed by Brief Apostolic Visitator of the Franciscans in Ireland, I cannot say what good he would effect. Dear Monsignor, procure this favour from their Eminences, and you will render a great advantage to religion: and I conclude with a profound reverence."

* He had· at this time the charge of the parish of Duleek, diocese of Meath, and had been lately appointed Agent of the Irish bishops in Rome. In a letter of the same date as that given above, but addressed to Monsig. Cerri, Secretary of Propaganda, and in which the same grievances are reported without important variation, the Primate adds concerning Dr. Cusack:—"He studied in Rome, and laboured here for thirteen years with great success: he is a gentleman by birth, and more so by his deportment, and you will find him nowise inferior to the Agents his predecessors: he is a great preacher in English and Irish, and besides the speculative sciences is well versed in Canon Law, and I think will fully satisfy their Eminences. But he cannot be ready or begin his journey till spring."

We have seen how Dr. Plunket, in his letter of the 15th of August, 1676, referred to the small number of students that returned from the colleges in Rome and other parts of the Continent; in a preceding letter he had already indicated the same abuse, and together with it, a custom which was introduced by some of the Catholic gentry, and at this time had grown beyond all due bounds: he thus writes on the 18th of August, 1673:—

" The secular clergy is too numerous : every gentleman desires a chaplain, and is anxious to hear Mass in his room, under pretence of fear of the Government. They force the bishops to ordain priests, and afterwards they move the whole world in order to procure a parish for this priest, their dependent: the remedy for this would be to withdraw from me, and from all the archbishops and bishops of this kingdom, the faculty of ordaining *extra tempora*, and I beseech you to deprive us of this faculty. The Irish College in Rome only maintains seven, or at most eight students ; that is, two for each province: and of these some die in Rome, and some become religious, so that few remain for the secular clergy ; and so also it happens with two or three colleges in Spain. As to those of Flanders, if you except Louvain, which also maintains but few, the others are only for belles lettres. In a word, in the province of Armagh there are only three that were educated in Rome; that is, Dr. James Cusack, a man distinguished for his learning and prudence; Dr. Ronan Magin, also sufficiently learned, and now Vicar Apostolic of Dromore ; and a certain Eugene Colgan, Archdeacon of Derry, a very learned man, and of exemplary life. These are the fruits of the Irish College as regards my province. There are three dioceses of my province, that is to say, Raphoe, Derry, and Clogher, full of Protestants, Presbyterians, Anabaptists, Quakers, &c.: if you could obtain two places for each of these three dioceses, it would be of great advantage for the maintenance and propagation of the faith in this province and in these dioceses.

"Armagh, 18th August, 1673.

"OLIVER OF ARMAGH.

"To the Internuntio in Brussels."

Whilst the good Archbishop thus zealously laboured to effect these reforms, the enemies of our Church deemed it a fit opportunity to bring reproach upon the Irish Catholics, and heap calumny upon the Primate himself; and thus whilst, on the one hand, the evils were exaggerated, on the other, the manner of acting of the Archbishop was represented as most arbitrary and oppressive. To one of the accusations made against him Dr. Plunket thus alludes in his letter to Dr. Creagh, of 15th September, 1674:—

"I received your two letters, one of the 1st of May, and the other of the 21st of July, to which I replied more diffusely through a friend who was going to London. I now say, as to the principal points, that I never preached or spoke either before or after Mass against friars or regulars *in genere*, *specie aut in individuo*: so that all this is a mere calumny and falsehood."

To another somewhat similar accusation he refers in his letter of 30th August, 1678:—

"They published against me [he says] as I learned from his Eminence Cardinal Howard, that I made a decree in a Congregation or Synod of Armagh, to the effect that *the clerics with the four minor orders should take precedence of all the Regulars* of this kingdom. This information is manifestly false; and surely these insidious informers and forgers should be punished according to the ecclesiastical law and the canons."

In a letter of Dr. Brennan, under date 14th November, 1672, reference is made to these misrepresentations circulated by some discontented persons:—

"They consider the Archbishop of Armagh their adversary; they say that they have learned by letters from Rome, that he sent a report to the Sacred Congregation, full of lies and calumnies against them; forsooth, that they were of no use; that they became heretics; that they annoyed the bishops and priests. They even sent round a circular to be signed by the bishops in contradiction of the pretended accusations; this circular was sent to me for signature by the Father Commissary; I replied that I would attest the good affected by the order; that they do not become heretics, that they even convert many heretics; but that I would not attest that they maintain amicable relations with the bishops and priests, or that many of them do not exercise parochial functions *contradicente episcopo*, because I was aware of the contrary; in these terms I gave my attestations, and not otherwise."

Another important letter on this subject was addressed by Dr. Plunket to the Internuncio on the 26th of September, 1673, in which whilst he repudiates the calumnious accusations made against the Irish Church in Rome, he at the same time plainly states the true evils that required the solicitude of the Holy See:—

"Your letter of the 8th inst. wisely admonishes me to avoid all occasions which might give pretext to the threatened persecution. I

will be sure to carry it out to the letter, and indeed during the whole
past year, I took care that no synods or provincial councils or assemblies of the clergy should be held by the bishops, which indeed
proved of great advantage to those who conformed to my council.
The Archbishop of Dublin, however, held three or four assemblies in
Dublin itself, and provoked the rage of the whole Government, and
gave great umbrage to the Earl of Essex, our Viceroy, a wise and
prudent man, who does not willingly give annoyance to those who
live in peace. The same Archbishop, during the past four years,
waged an open war against the Duke of Ormond, who is the most
powerful subject of his Majesty in this kingdom, and you know that
it is not safe to assail the powerful, *nemo potentes aggredi tutus potest*.

"As to what you command, that I should write to Monsignor
Secretary, I shall obey; it will be necessary, however, for Monsignor
Secretary to give a copy of my letters to Dr. Creagh. that thus he
may refresh the memory of his Excellency, and expedite the transaction of our affairs; for Monsignor Secretary is often overwhelmed
with business touching the affairs of so many kingdoms and missions,
and I well know from my experience in Rome, that such an agent
is necessary to call his attention to our business. I believe that
Monsignor Ravizza is now returned from Portugal; if I write a
separate letter to Dr. Creagh, the expense will be increased; and hence
I pray you to write to the Monsignor, requesting him to show my
letter to Dr. Creagh.

"As to the dissensions of the Catholics, of which you speak, I
see here, on the contrary, great concord; nor do I see any divisions
whatsoever amongst ecclesiastics, and did such exist I should know
it, as I receive letters every week from all the archbishops and
bishops, and when any discord arises, they write to me at once; and
you may rest assured that, of all that happens, you shall have a
sincere and perfect account, without any partiality or passion.

"I wrote to you on former occasions that it is necessary to take
away from the bishops the faculty of ordaining *extra tempora*, and to
send a brief that no more novices be received amongst us. Such a
brief would affect great good, or rather an exceeding great good in
this kingdom. The Franciscans alone have twelve or thirteen
novitiates in the one province of Armagh; imagine, then, how many
there are in the other provinces. The Dominicans are more moderate
and circumspect; they have only five novitiates in my province; but
as there is only one provincial for each order, so also there should be
only one novitiate, or at most two; however, it will be better that
they should have none for a few years. I write continually on this
matter, because I see the great necessity there is for it, and I fear
that a great tempest will one day arise, unless a remedy be soon
applied to this root of many future disorders."

The zeal of Dr. Plunket was tempered by prudence and
charity, and even those who were most irregular and disorderly in their conduct were, on their conversion, treated

by him with special kindness and regard. We have an illustrious example of this in his receiving back to the bosom of
the Church a wretched apostate named Martin French.
This man had been a member of the Augustinian order, but
setting aside all laws, ecclesiastical and divine, had refused
to listen to the voice of his legitimate superiors, and even
summoned the Archbishop of Tuam before the secular courts,
accusing him, under the statute of *praemunire*—that is, of
exercising foreign jurisdiction in the British dominions. In
consequence of these accusations the Archbishop was detained
for many months in prison, and even for some time was in
great danger of being led to the scaffold. Dr Plunket, on the
24th of April, 1671, thus refers to the sufferings of this
Archbishop :—

"The good Archbishop of Tuam was imprisoned anew during
the past Lent, on the accusations of Martin French, and was found
guilty of *praemunire*—that is, of exercising foreign jurisdiction, but
now, having given security, he is allowed to be at liberty till the
next sessions of August ; but Nicholas Plunket, who is the best
lawyer in the kingdom, and the only defender that the poor
ecclesiastics have in such circumstances, writes that he should appeal
from the courts of Galway to the supreme jurisdiction of Dublin, in
which there is greater equity."

On the trial being sent to Dublin, French did not appear
to prosecute, and soon afterwards, touched by repentance,
he petitioned the Primate to pardon him his guilt and
readmit him to the bosom of the Holy Church. The good
prelate, moved by his prayers, and still more by the tears
which testified his horror for the course of crime he had
pursued, absolved him, in the name of the Holy See, from
the censures he had incurred, and wrote most pressing
letters to the Archbishop of Tuam, praying him to receive
back the prodigal child, and reinstate him in the household
of God. It was thus Dr. Lynch himself wrote, on the 17th
of September, 1671, to the Internunzio in Brussels. After
stating that French had repented of his crimes, he adds :—

"He had recourse to the most illustrious Lord Primate, who
freed him from censures, and more than once notified the same to us
by letters, praying also and beseeching us that we would admit to our

communion this man, no longer subject to censures or irregularities, and that we would cast every fault, if there were any, upon his own shoulders ; and to this testimony we have given every credence."

Dr. Plunket received instructions from Rome, in 1671, to remove from the Irish province, two religious who had been connected with the proceedings of Peter Walsh, by name Coppinger and Harold, and to place them in some convent of the Franciscan order on the Continent. In reply he writes, concerning Coppinger, that he will use all possible diligence, and that he has no doubt there would be no difficulty in inducing him to depart, especially as he had heard that " with the exception of these dissensions he was an excellent man."—(22nd Sept., 1672.)

In another letter Dr. Plunket gives further details regarding his success in executing this commission of the Holy See .—" As I wrote on a former occasion I intimated to Coppinger to meet me in the vicinity of Dublin. He obeyed, and undertook a long and toilsome journey. Many objections were made, but at length he submitted. If I am not deceived Father Coppinger is an exceedingly good man, and, moreover, a good religious ; and were it not that he was led astray in these late disturbances, he would deserve every favour : even his adversaries never had anything to reproach him with as to his conduct and morals. I pray you to send this letter to Rome. May the Almighty be ever praised : I have undertaken nothing since my arrival in this kingdom that has not been prospered by God."—3rd November, 1672.

Three days later he wrote again to the Internunzio confirming the same intelligence, and stating, moreover, that "he had exhorted Coppinger to present himself to the Archbishop of Dublin, and place his retractation in his hands." A letter of the same father was transmitted to Rome, written immediately after his first conference with the Primate, and in it, whilst he declares his submission to the superiors of his order, and to the Sacred Congregation, he adds : " The most illustrious Primate of this kingdom, some

weeks ago, wrote to me to meet him at Dublin.   I travelled
one hundred Irish miles, and suffered a great deal in this
inclement season, to meet his wishes : he proposed many
motives and strong reasons why I should obey the Very Rev.
Father Geanor, and other superiors of my order in this
kingdom."

As to Harold, Dr. Plunket was equally successful.   His
letter of the 20th of January, 1672, breathes his characteristic spirit of benevolence, and in it he particularly dwells
on the good qualities of this religious, and on the happy
fruits that might be expected from his zeal, should he obey
the commands of the Sacred Congregation :—

"To my great grief, the rumour prevails here and in London,
that the Viceroy will have to change his quarters and return to his
own country, and that the new Viceroy will be the Earl of Essex, a
man, they say, prudent and wise ; but we do not know what his
sentiments are towards the Catholics ; however, we must only sail
according to the winds. I received the amout of 60 scudi from
Monsignor Sarsefield, and Father Harold has been here for the last
four weeks at his own expense. I have not given him anything as
yet, and no ship can be found for those parts. I also have been here
(Dublin) for eighteen days, at great expense, with four horses and
three servants, for no other purpose than to see him embarked, and
to give him a part of the money here ; he shall receive the remainder
on his arrival at his destination *in termino ad quem*. I have at length
come to the resolution to allow him to pass through England, for I
do not see what injury can be done by it, especially as he himself is
indifferent as to what journey he should make. Moreover, at this
season of the year, it is somewhat dangerous to undertake a
long sea voyage—and, as I said, I do not know what injury can come
from his journey to England ; had he been desirous to go thither
to make any arrangement with Peter Walsh, he might have gone
there long since of his own accord, for he did not acknowledge the
authority of Father Geanor, but only of Coppinger. Moreover, he
promises to bring Walsh to a better sense of his duty, and to make
known his sentiments to your Excellency, and to do all in his power
to convince him of his folly. I shall give a third part of the
money here, and send the remainder to Father Howard, who can give
him the balance when embarking in London for Ostend or Dunkirk.
I deem Father Harold a man of honour, and, with the exception of
this late dissension, in which he sets himself to sustain the part of
Coppinger, a good man and an exemplary religious, well versed in
theology, and should he obey (and I think he will submit to all
the commands of your Excellency), he will be a very useful subject,
being also a good preacher in the Irish language. Monsignor,

this commission to bring him to submission has already cost me more than 40 scudi; but for the service of God and of the Holy See I would sell even the pectoral and the mitre."—(20th January, 1672.)

One of those lovers of inobservance who had occasioned most annoyance to the Primate was a Franciscan father named Felix O Neill. Amongst other things, in his over-zeal for the privileges of his order, he had broached many propositions which occasioned scandal to the laity and the clergy ; even after his being reconciled to the Primate, he seems to have retained a secret enmity against him, and many, too, imputed to him a share in that sacrilegious plot which a few years later led the holy Archbishop to Tyburn. But far, far, were all such sentiments of secret rancour from the bosom of Dr. Plunket. The following is the letter addressed to the Internuncio on receipt of the retractation of O'Neill, in which we may easily recognise the sentiments of the good pastor on finding the strayed one of his fold :—

" Father Felix O'Neill explains the propositions that he made use of ; that, forsooth, the flock is not bound to support the parish-priest, and that his Holiness could not suppress the Order of St. Francis. He explains them, as you will see, from the annexed letter, which he sent to the guardian of Dublin, and he is ready to submit himself to Holy Church, and to the Holy See. He also came to me, and he promises submission for the future; and he will do the same with the Bishop of Clogher; and I am greatly rejoiced at it, because this reconciliation will give great peace to my districts ; and as hitherto I deemed this Father Felix deserving of reprehension on account of his manner of teaching and acting, so now is he worthy of praise for having overcome himself by performing these generous acts of peace and reconciliation for the common good. And as he is of noble family, both by the father's and the mother's side, he can do great good in the whole province, in which he is closely related to the highest nobility. I am desirous to animate him and console him, that he may be reconciled with the Bishop of Clogher and with me, in order to propagate and preserve our holy faith in this kingdom; and I beseech you to write a courteous and loving letter to the same father, praising him and consoling him, as also to send this letter to Monsignor Cerri (Secretary of Propaganda), and I pray him to make this known to their Eminences, and to write likewise to the same father ; for this will be of great advantage to the spiritual interests and tranquillity of my districts, &c.

"THOMAS COX.
(Oliver of Armagh.)

" Dublin, 27th Sept., 1678."

Thus the interests of religion and the glory of God were the sole springs of every action of the Primate, and a paternal affection was sure to greet the sinner on his repentance. This truly divine, not human, zeal, implied another feature, which is not less clearly recognised in the actions of Dr. Plunket, namely, that when he discovered himself in error he did not hesitate to avow it, and retract the injury which, perchance, he might have done. A noble instance of this is presented in his letter of 21st September, 1678 :—

" Some time since you asked me for an account of Dr. Cornelius Daly, but as he was then in Paris, I besought you to write to that city, and soon after I received information that he was a Jansenist, factious, &c. I now find that the information thus conveyed to me was false, for as he at present is here in Ireland, I conversed with him ; and I find him wholly opposed to the Jansenists, and he subscribed in my presence the formula condemnatory of Jansenism ; and I find him well versed in theology, and in the canons, and in cases of conscience ; and he is, in my opinion, a modest, exact, and exemplary ecclesiastic, of grave and good deportment, being about forty years of age ; and, to say the truth, I saw but few returning from Paris with better ecclesiastical qualities ; and, in my humble opinion, he is deserving of any dignity that he may be promoted to. I pray your Excellency to write to Monsignor Cerri in his favour, that he may be appointed Vicar-Apostolic of Ardfert and Aghadoe, which two small dioceses have been united for forty years, as also to send this letter to Monsignor Cerri. Dr. Daly can affect great good in these dioceses ; he is a good preacher, and can labour well in propagating and preserving the faith ; and I remain with profound veneration,

" THOMAS COX.
(Oliver of Armagh.)

" 21st Sept., 1678.
" To M. Pruisson, Brussels."

Though the zeal of Dr. Plunket was more than ever exercised in correcting the abuses and disorders of some houses, or some members of the Franciscan institute, yet, far was the good prelate from seeking to reflect discredit on

that holy order, or from being animated with any sentiments
in its regard save those of esteem and love. We have
already seen how he extolled the zeal and learning of many
of its members, and how well he was aware of the glory
which was shed upon religion in Flanders, Germany, Italy,
and Spain, by the Irish children of St. Francis. But it was
his desire, as he himself avowed, that his province, "*both as
to the secular and the regular clergy should be holy, good, and
observant*" (10th Sept., 1678); and hence he laboured
incessantly that every disorder should be rooted out, and
every occasion of irregularity be removed; and even in his
dying words upon the scaffold he declared:—

" By preaching, and teaching, and statutes, have I endeavoured to
bring the clergy of which I had the care, to a due comportment,
according to their calling: and though thereby I did but my duty,
yet some who would not amend, had a prejudice for me; and
especially my accusers. to whom I did endeavour to do good. . .
But you see how I am requited; and how, by false oaths, they
brought me to this untimely death : which wicked act being a defect
of persons, ought not to reflect upon the order of St. Francis, or
upon the Roman Catholic clergy : it being well known that there
was a Judas among the twelve apostles, and a wicked man called
Nicholas among the seven deacons; and even, as one of the said
deacons, to wit, holy Stephen, did pray for those who stoned him to
death, so do I for those who, with perjuries spill my innocent
blood, saying, as St. Stephen did, 'O Lord, lay not this sin to
them.' "

There were some, however, who passing over the true
bounds of Christian charity, and imputing to the whole body
the irregularities and disorders of a few individual members,
heaped calumnies upon the Order of St. Francis, and soon
after the death of Dr. Plunket petitioned the Holy See, that
it might be wholly suppressed in Ireland. or, at least, that
those Colleges which the order possessed upon the Continent,
should be withdrawn from its guardianship. These
calumnies gave occasion to many of the Irish Bishops to
re-echo the sentiments of Dr. Plunket, and whilst they
condemned the scandalous life of some individuals of that
order, to extol the zeal and fruitful labours of the others.

We shall here present the letter written on this occasion, by the bosom friend of the deceased Primate, the Archbishop of Cashel, who, as he shared in the privations and perse-cutions of Dr. Plunket, so, too, we may rest assured, shared with him the noble sentiments which he now uttered in regard to the calumniated Order of St. Francis. This letter is dated 20th September, 1684, and is as follows :—

"The Franciscan fathers of this Kingdom, finding themselves accused before their Eminences (as they assert), for the many and frequent disorders committed by certain individuals of that order, and fearing that some stigma or chastisement might be inflicted to the detriment of the entire province, regarding the government of those colleges which they possess in Catholic countries : lately summoned here a provincial Chapter, and wrote various letters to persons of authority in Rome, excusing themselves, and praying that the disorders of individuals should not prejudice the common good of the province, and of the nation ; on this occasion they pressed me to concur in their petition, and add my supplication in their favour. I confess there are some amongst them of scandalous life, but these are very few, compared with the great number of fathers who are here of exemplary life, and of great zeal and learning, who labour incessantly, and with abundant fruit for the glory of God, and the salvation of souls. I may even add confidentially that the Franciscan fathers of strict observance in this kingdom do more good than any other religious order. I pray, therefore, your Excellency to grant your protection and favour to these fathers, procuring that they may continue in the government of their colleges, and that their agent may also exercise his office in the Roman Court as heretofore. I have no doubt that great advantage will accrue from this determination to our holy faith in these countries, and hence it is deserving of the benign protection of your zeal. May God grant to your Excellency many and happy years, for the benefit of Holy Church, and I remain, with sincere reverence, &c.

                    "JOHN, ARCHBISHOP OF CASHEL.

"20th September, 1684."

CHAPTER IX.

IN the preceding pages we were more than once obliged to refer incidentally to the schools erected by Dr. Plunket; but he refers so frequently in his letters to education, and supplies such abundant information regarding the Collegiate Institutions on the Continent for the instruction of the Irish Catholic youth, that we have deemed it expedient to devote a special chapter to the subject.

The thirst for knowledge ever displayed by the people of Ireland, from the first era of their enlightenment by Catholic faith, is proverbial. During her ages of peace and prosperity, seminaries and other institutions of learning were everywhere scattered throughout the land. Science, exiled from the Continent, found a secure asylum on the Irish shores; and from the monasteries and schools of Ireland went forth an innumerable host of holy and learned men to rekindle in the kingdoms of Europe the lamp of knowledge, and to confer on them the blessings of civilization and religion. St. Bernard writes that "from Ireland as from an overflowing stream, crowds of holy men descended on foreign nations; and a Saxon writer, Aldhelm,* describes Ireland as "rich in the wealth of science," and as thickly set with learned men as the poles are with stars." The German historian, Görres, contemplating the Irish Church at that period, cries out—"While the flames of war were blazing around her, the green Isle enjoyed the sweets of repose. When we look into the ecclesiastical life of this people, we are almost tempted to believe that some potent spirits transported over the sea the cells of the valley of the Nile, with all their hermits—its monasteries, with all their inmates, and had settled down in the Western Isle!—an Isle which in the lapse of three centuries gave eight hundred and fifty saints to

* See letter preserved in Usher's *Sylloge,*

the Church—won over to Christianity the north of Britain, and soon after a large portion of the yet pagan Germany ; and while it devoted the utmost attention to the sciences, cultivated with special care mystical contemplation in her religious communities as well as in the saints whom they produced." Eric of Auxerre, and other writers, speak with rapture of the learned men who, in the reign of Charlemagne hastened "in swarms" to the shores of France ; and even as late as the eleventh century we find that Sulgenus, the holy Bishop of St. David's, in Wales, went to Ireland to cultivate the pursuits of literature ; " since that country," adds his contemporary biographer, " is renowned for its wondrous wisdom."

" *Ivit ad Hibernos sophia mirabili claros.*" *

Six centuries of devastation, of plunder, and of ruin ensued ; religious persecution was added to national strife. and soon the garden became as a wilderness, and learning seemed exiled from the land. In the year 1581 it was enacted by Parliament that—

" Any person keeping a school-master who shall not repair to the Established Church shall forfeit £10 per month.

Other acts of Parliament followed in quick succession. We shall give but a brief epitome of them :—

" If a Catholic kept a school, or taught any person—Protestant or Catholic—any species of literature or science, such teacher was, for the crime of teaching, punishable by law by banishment ; and if he returned from banishment, he was subject to be hanged as a felon."

" If any Catholic, whether a child or adult, attended, in Ireland, a school kept by a Catholic, or was privately instructed by a Catholic, such Catholic, although a child in its early infancy, incurred a forfeiture of all its property, present or future "

" If a Catholic child, however young, was sent to any foreign country for education, such infant child incurred a similar penalty—that is, a forfeiture of all right to property, present or prospective."

" If any person in Ireland made any remittance in money or goods for the maintenance of any Irish child educated in a foreign country, such person incurred a similar forfeiture." †

* See Montalembert, *Les Moines d'Occident*, vol. ii., book 7th, where he treats of St. Columbanus and other Irish saints. See also *Ozanam Etudes Germaniques*, t. ii., p. 99.

† *Memoirs of Ireland*, &c., by D. O'Connell.

All this, however, did not suffice; and British legislation was said to have attained its perfection, and *pacified Ireland*, only when all our Catholic inhabitants were pent up in the narrow precincts of Connaught :—when emigration from the immediate district assigned to them was made punishable with death, without trial or form of law ;—when it was commanded that all priests should be hanged without mercy ;—that all the inhabitants should take the oath of abjuration, if presented to them, under penalty of forfeiting two-thirds of their goods and chattels ; and when, in fine, its legislature enacted regarding education—" that all Catholic children attaining the age of twelve years were to be taken from their parents and educated in England in the principles of the Protestant religion." * Thus nothing remained for our forefathers but to renounce the pursuit of learning, or to drink in, at poisoned sources, the waters of knowledge. The eager desire of some to penetrate the secrets of science induced them to frequent Protestant schools, and imperil the precious treasure of their faith. Often, however, even during this period of persecution, did the pastors raise their warning voices to make known to their flocks the snare which was laid for them ; and often did they lament the dread evils which threatened the nation, and which it seemed beyond their power to avert. Thus the bosom friend of our Primate, Dr. Brennan, then Bishop of Waterford, giving a " Report" of his Diocese to the Sacred Congregation, on the 20th September, 1675, writes :—

"A good education and instruction is much wanting for the Catholic youth of this country, for, in consequence of the penal laws, no Catholic is allowed to act as schoolmaster; so that our youth are obliged to seek instruction from Protestant teachers --a sad misfortune indeed, which will one day produce great evils." †

* See O'Conor's *History of the Irish Catholics.* The last ordinance of Parliament referred to was sanctioned in 1657. A very ancient MS. copy of this Act of Parliament is preserved in the Barberini Library.

† " Alla gioventu Cattolica di questo paese manca di molto la buona crudizione ed ammaestramento, mentre in vigore delle leggi penali non è lecito a niun Cattolico di fare il maestro di scuola, talche i nostri giovani sono necessitati d'imparare da maestri Protestanti ; cosa dolorosa che sarà di pregiudizio in tempo avvenire." (*Archiv. de Propag. Scritt. Rif. Irl.*, vol. iii.)

When he was transferred to Cashel his sentiments remained unchanged, and in another "Report" to the Holy See, dated from Kilcash, 9th November, 1687, he thus writes :—

"By the penal laws Catholics are prohibited to keep schools, in order that our students may be compelled to frequent the schools of Lutheran masters, to be there imbued with Protestant doctrine and morality. To repel this danger, some Catholic masters kept private schools to instruct the Catholic children in letters and in the principles of faith—not without their own great risk; and many of them, on this account, have suffered imprisonment and pecuniary fines."*

Dr. Plunket lamented no less than the Archbishop of Cashel the dangers arising from irreligious instruction. In one of his letters he writes that " *Irish talent is excellent and acute, especially that of Ulster;* " and adds, " but what does this avail when it cannot be cultivated ; the richest land without the plough-share or the spade can yield but little fruit ; and here, in consequence of the penal laws, we can have no fixed Catholic schools ;" and again, writing to the Internunzio on the 22nd September, 1672, he states that before the opening of his schools the Catholics were obliged " *to send their children to Protestant masters, and thus incur great danger as to their faith ; for you can well understand how easily young shoots receive a wrong bent, unless they be properly trained from the commencement.*" In a preceding letter, too (26th April, 1671), when praying for some assistance to support Catholic teachers, he adds : " *Let us aid the poor children, many of whom have been perverted by going to Protestant schools.*"

At every interval of peace and toleration, it was the first thought of the Catholic prelates to establish colleges and schools. Thus, in 1641, before the threats of extermination

* " Per le leggi sudette (penali) vien anche inibito ai Cattolici di tener scuole acciò li nostri studenti si necessitassero di frequentare le scuole di maestri Luterani per ivi imbeverlsi della dottrina e costumi Protestanti. Per oviare a questo pericolo, parecchi maestri Cattolici tenevano scuole private per instruir la gioventù Cattolica nelle lettere e nei principii della fede ; non senza pericolo di tali maestri, molti dei quali hanno patito le carceri e multe pecuniarie per tal esercizio." (*Archiv. Propagand.*)

compelled the Irish to rise in arms, and plunged once more the nation into all the horrors of invasion and civil strife, the Jesuit fathers had opened schools, *to the great joy* * of all the Catholics in Dublin, Drogheda, Kilkenny, Ross, Wexford, Clonmel, Waterford, Cashel, Cork, Limerick, and Galway. From a paper written not long after by Father William Salinger S.J., and entitled, "An Answer to some Calumnies against the Jesuit Order," we learn that Dr. Hugh O'Reilly, Archbishop of Armagh, had resolved on the establishment of two colleges, one of which should be placed at Armagh. Dr. Thomas Walsh, Archbishop of Cashel, founded one college, and collected a large sum of money for the establishment of another, but the sums collected by him were appropriated to other objects in consequence of the war. Dr. John De Burgo was engaged preparing for a like foundation; the Bishop of Meath had already opened one such institution and contemplated the establishment of another. Dr. Francis Kirwan, Bishop of Killala, had promoted the foundation of another seminary.

A like spirit seems to have animated the lay leaders of the Catholic party, and the renowned General of Ulster, Owen Roe O'Neil, who for his martial spirit and continual life in the camp, and struggles in the field of battle, we should suppose would have little leisure for reflecting on the necessity of Catholic instruction, had resolved on the establishment in Ulster of four colleges, " that from them, as he alleged, might proceed the reformation of morals, and the due and sufficient Christian education of the youth and people." He even had marked out the place and site for these colleges, and often publicly spoke of them.†

We learn moreover, from the "annual letters" of the Society of Jesus, that even when the country was laid

---

* Summo cum fructu et satisfactione.—MS. mox. citand.

† Sallinger, ut supra: Illmus Ultoniae Generalis Eugenius O'Nellus statuit ac promisit. ut in Ultonia, fundarentur collegia quatuor, unde dicebat ille, juventutis ac populi Christiana proba et urbana educatio et morum procederet reformatio; collegiis illis apta loca et commoda designavit ac publice saepius nominavit.

waste by the Cromwellians, and the clergy were everywhere forced to seek refuge in the woods and mountains; they endeavoured to keep alive the spark of learning as well as of religion, and in particular this is recorded of Father James Ford, who, in the middle of a vast bog, choosing out a spot of more than ordinary consistency, built a little house on it, whither a large number of youths soon flocked, who erected little huts all around, and then the good father instructed them, at the same time, in science and in virtue (*litterarum studiis et virtutum*); and the writer adds, that " the disciples vied with their master in enduring, not only with fortitude, but even with joy, all the inconveniences to which they were there exposed." (Status Soc. J. an. 1654.)

It cannot, then, surprise us that one of the first thoughts of Dr. Plunket on his arrival in Ireland should be to procure such Catholic schools ; and to realise, at least in part, the project of the great Ulster leader of the Catholic interests. Before the month of July, 1670, he had completed a college for three Jesuit fathers, and it soon numbered no fewer than 150 pupils within its walls.   To maintain this college, the good prelate, as we have seen in the last chapter, often deprived himself even of the necessaries of life, and clothed himself in the plainest raiment.   The Sacred Congregation of Propaganda soon came to his aid ; and till the time when a new outburst of persecution scattered to the winds this noble work of the Primate, 150 scudi were allowed each year for the maintenance of his teachers.   The Lord Lieutenant gave a tacit consent to the erection of this college, and many of the Protestant gentry, on witnessing its fruits, became its warm advocates, and even sought for their children the benefits of its instruction.   But the happy results and success of these schools will be best learned from the letters of the Archbishop himself.

One of the most interesting of these letters * is addressed

---

* I owe this letter to the kindness of my esteemed friend, Rev. C. P. Meehan, to whom all lovers of Ireland are so much indebted for his untiring zeal in promoting our national literature.

to Father Oliva, General of the Society of Jesus, and in it he acquaints him with the establishment of the college, and the happy fruits which were there produced by the zealous members of his order. It is a curious incident that the original of this letter is now preserved in the library of Trinity College ; it seems to have never reached its destination, having been, probably, intercepted by the government. It is as follows :—

"VERY REVEREND FATHER,—Dr. Creagh, the agent of the prelates of this kingdom in the Roman court, has written to me declaring his many obligations to your paternity for your affability, kindness, and patronage in his regard, which is of great assistance to him. Every one knows, and by long experience in Rome, I have learned how great a benefactor you are, and your kindness has been experienced in like manner by all my fellow-countrymen in Rome ; each and every one of whom attest your anxiety in their regard ; and as they cannot otherwise correspond to this kindness and prove their gratitude, than by loving and doing good to the members of your Order in this kingdom, I can assure you that in this they are not cold or negligent ; and the fathers, on the other hand, by the great good which they do, merit to be thus loved, praised, and caressed. I have three fathers in the diocese of Armagh, who by their virtue, learning, and labours, would suffice to enrich a kingdom.

"The founder of the Armagh Residence is Father Stephen Rice, a learned man, successful in preaching, prudent in his labours, and of profound religious virtue ; nor is he ever weary of teaching, instructing, and attending to the pupils and to the young priests, of whom he is the examiner and director. Oh! how much he had to suffer during the past two years and four months, in founding that residence *sudavit et alsit ;* and he is so modest, so reserved, that he seems as though he had come on yesterday from the novitiate of St. Andrew's. He was educated in Flanders, where, indeed, he was imbued with the true spirit of the society ; he retains that spirit, and is a son worthy of such a father as St. Ignatius ; in a word, Father Rice is another Father Young.*

"The second is Father Ignatius Browne, a celebrated preacher in the English language, a learned man, and of exemplary life. He was educated in Spain, and he preaches on every festival with great applause in the principal chapel.

"The third is Father Murphy, a good theologian, and good religious : he also preaches well in Irish, and is a young man of great talent.

"There is a lay-brother named Nicholas, who is like a real brother of Brother George of holy memory.

---

* A distinguished Irish Jesuit.

"In the schools there are 150 boys; they are for the greater part children of the Catholic nobility and gentry, and there are also about 40 children of the Protestant gentry. You may imagine what envy it excites in the Protestant masters and ministers to see the Protestant children coming to the schools of the society.

"In the city of my diocese, where their residence is, there are also houses of the Dominicans, Franciscans, Augustinians, and Capuchins; the city is called Drogheda, or *Dreat* in our English and Irish languages, and *Pontana* in Latin; it is distant from Dublin as far as Tivoli from Rome; it is a maritime port, situated on the noble river Boyne, or *Boina*, and from its bridge (*pons*) it derives its Latin name Pontana. It is well supplied with corn, with flesh of every description, and with fish. The country around is for the most part inhabited by orthodox noblemen and gentlemen, and in the city there are rich merchants and respectable artisans.

"When I introduced the fathers to my diocese, and the schools commenced to flourish, Dr. Talbot reprehended the undertaking as rash, imprudent, precipitous, and vain, and said that it would be short-lived, especially in such a busy city. But he was only half acquainted with the matter. The Viceroy, my Lord Berkeley, was most friendly to me, and esteemed me much more than I deserved— *et in verbo ipsius laxavi rete*—and I founded the residence; and the present Viceroy, the Earl of Essex, a wise, prudent, and moderate man, is nowise inferior to his predecessor in his kindness towards me, as also to the schools. As they have lasted these *two* years and four months, so we may hope that God, through the intercession of St. Ignatius, will grant them a longer duration. But be this as it may, whilst the wind is favourable, we must unfurl the sails and pursue our course, and when it becomes contrary or tempestuous, we shall lower them and seek shelter in some small port beneath a mountain or rock,

"Very reverend and dearest Father, paper fails me, but I shall never fail to be

"Your most affectionate and obliged servant,

"OLIVER OF ARMAGH,
"Primate of Ireland.

"Dublin, 22nd November, 1672."

At the date of this letter the schools had lasted two years and four months, and the fifth month was hastening to its close; for another year they continued to flourish and diffuse through the diocese of Armagh the blessings of Catholic education. But on the renewal of the persecution, towards the close of November, 1673, this work, the fruit of so much toil, was levelled to the ground, and the good Primate was forced to cry out in anguish of soul, " What shall the Catholic youth now do entrusted to my care?"* So well had these schools succeeded, that even Protestant gentlemen sent their children to them, and defended them when they were assailed by the ministers of the Established Church. (Letter of 7th June, 1671.) In his letter of the 12th November, 1673, as we have seen, Dr. Plunket mentions that when at first the Viceroy and those of the court took umbrage at the establishment of the schools, the more moderate amongst them were satisfied on his making known to them that the only object he had in view in instituting these schools "was to imbue the youth with a knowledge of the Christian doctrine, and to communicate instruction to them; and thus render them useful for the State and the service of the King, whilst otherwise they would become noxious members, rogues, highway robbers, and disturbers of the peace and social order."

A promise of an annual sum of 800 scudi had been held out to Dr. Plunket by the Court, probably as a sort of bait to win his favour for the doings of the Government; but finding that all the efforts of the Primate's zeal were directed to promote the glory of God and the interests of the Church, and that he was resolved to fearlessly denounce all obstacles to these holy ends, no matter whence they might proceed, this sum soon ceased to be paid to him. He had mainly relied on this Government aid for the maintenance of his schools; but when this resource failed, incredible were the privations that he endured and the efforts which he made to carry them on, till at length the Sacred Congregation of Propaganda granted to the Jesuit fathers connected with the schools the annual sum of 150 scudi, to be dated from the first establishment in his diocese.

When soliciting this aid from the Sacred Congregation, by letter of 26th April, 1671, Dr. Plunket gives many interesting details as to the manner in which the schools were carried on:

"The nobility and gentry of the whole province of Ulster, excepting three, are deprived of their lauds, and from being proprietors

* See letter of 15th December, 1673.

have become tenants: they have how no means to educate their children. The young priests who were ordained during the past seven years, in order to fill the places of those who were deceased, are very backward in learning, as they had no proper master to instruct them; in fact, Catholic teachers were not at all tolerated.

"I undertook an arduous' work : I invited the Jesuit fathers to my diocese; I built from the foundation a commodious house for them, as also two schools, where about 150 boys are educated and 25 ecclesiastics; and during the past nine months I supported two very learned and laborious Jesuits, with one lay-brother and one servant. One of the fathers instructs, for an hour in the morning and another hour in the afternoon, the ecclesiastics in cases of morality, as also in the manner of preaching and catechising; the same father teaches the rhetoricians for two hours in the morning and two hours in the evening : on the feast days and vacations he teaches the ceremonies and the manner of administering the sacraments, &c. The other Jesuit is occupied in teaching syntax and grammar, &c. Both, moreover, are engaged in preaching. For nine months I have supported them, and I had to purchase even the smallest articles of furniture for them."

He then states that for the future it would be necessary for him to have three Jesuits, who would be thus occupied:—

"The first will attend solely to the ecclesiastics; the second to the rhetoricians; the third will teach syntax and grammar to the younger boys. Your Excellency has conferred great benefits on this poor country, but I assure you it will not be the least to procure a missionary stipend for these three fathers. Let us aid the poor children, many of whom have been perverted by going to Protestant schools."

On this long-wished, for aid being granted, Dr. Plunket thus commences his letter of thanksgiving, addressed to the Internunzio, on 22nd September, 1672 :—

"I have received your most welcome letter of the 2nd September, and this whole kingdom is indebted to you for the stipend procured for the Jesuits They do a great deal of good: they have in Drogheda, in my diocese, 160 students. Oh! what toils had I to undergo, what efforts had I to make, to sustain them ! how many memorials were forwarded to the Viceroy and Supreme Council against me and against them ; and they give the more annoyance to our adversaries because they are in Drogheda (*i.e.*, *Pontana*), only four hours' journey from Dublin, where no Catholic school is allowed. And then to have there the Jesuits, whom they hate above all others, was the greatest eye-sore possible ; but now the very adversaries caress both me and them, in order to have permission for their children to come to them ; and, in reality, many Protestant boys come to them belonging to the principal families, who afterwards assist us in defending them. Monsignore, I solemnly assure you that I expended on them during the past two years and two months more than 400 scudi, and that already both they and I are in debt for 200 scudi. I dressed in cloth of one-half scudo a yard, I kept only one servant, and a boy to look after my horses, and my table was most sparing, in order to assist the Jesuits. The Viceroy gave me half a promise that he would not disturb them ; but as the money promised by the King was not granted, I confess that I found myself in difficulty to carry them on, and I was overwhelmed with melancholy ; but now your letter imparts great consolation.

"I thank you also for the aid in regard of the letters. It is now three years all to a month since I was welcomed to the palace of your Excellency in Brussels. Since then I wrote more letters than all the bishops of this kingdom : I gave no rest *temporibus aut calamo*, and I will glory in my infirmities, as St. Paul says : I laboured more than all the others : but the withdrawal of the pension gave me a check. Now, however, my courage has returned, and I hope the Jesuits will do more good for this kingdom than has been done within our memory. The Catholic gentry lost their possessions and estates in this kingdom, and for the most part have become tenants : it would be impossible for them to send their children to the Catholic kingdoms. Hence it is a great relief to them to have Catholic masters here. Before my arrival they were obliged to send their children to Protestant teachers, exposing their faith to great risk : for, as you will well understand, young plants easily receive a bad direction unless they be attended to from the beginning . . . The money can be sent to Mr. Daniel Arthur, an Irish Catholic merchant in London, and it may be consigned to Father Perez in Brussels, or to the Provincial of the English Jesuits, to be sent to Mr. Daniel Arthur, and thus I shall receive it here with some advantage, to compensate the difference of exchange between Brussels and London."

Sometimes the aid promised by Propaganda was, for a little while, delayed ; and hence, on more than one occasion, Dr. Plunket pours out his soul in pitiful laments, lest his poverty, and the absolute want of the necessary means, should compel him to close these schools.

On one occasion, too, the Superior of his schools seems to to have fallen into error when writing to some members of his order in Rome, as to the sum which he had hitherto received from the Archbishop. This gave occasion to complaints, and it was even asserted by some enemies of the Primate in Rome, that he had applied to other uses the sums granted to him for these schools. The Agent of the Irish

Church in Rome, Dr. Creagh, made known this matter to the Primate, and received in reply the following letter, which shows the accuracy with which he attended even to affairs of minor concern, and at the same time discloses to us his desire, if his means allowed it, to extend still more the benefit of these schools :—

"DEAR MR. CREAGH,—About the 15th of the past month I wrote you a long letter: but now, in consequence of yours of the 27th of June, which was handed to me by Father Rice, I find it necessary to write to you again on the same subject ; and when I read your letter for Father Rice, *erubuit* (he blushed): it must be that his memory failed him. I have his own receipt for every sum of money consigned to him – at one time £10, then £5 or £6, then £37 ; and I have also the bills in six different papers, each account being separate, of how the money was spent in butter, bread, coffee, repairs, &c., &c. ; and all this in his own handwriting. I have also two copies, written by his own hand, of the entire sum, in accordance with the letter sent to you last year, in which he thus writes :—' *Illmus. Dnus. Primas sumptibus nusquam in nostris alendis pepercit, ideoque liquido, mihi constat tam in varias ædes et supellectilem quam in nostrorum sustentationem impensas fuisse primo b'enario libras Anglicanas minimum centum viginti quinque ;*' that is, 500 scudi. Now, how can he say that he only received 150 scudi ? Is it not ridiculous to write things so contradictory ? But I attribute all to a defect of memory. I confess, indeed, that if I had received the sums spent in correspondence and otherwise in serving their Eminences, I would have given the whole of it to the fathers ; and if I received the 800 which were promised to me, I would have given 150 scudi of my own per annum, in addition to the sum granted by the Sacred Congregation. But neither have I received the former sums, nor the pension, nor have I received 20 scudi from my diocese during all this year. I leave it to yourself to think how I could be liberal, or look after the affairs of the Society, either in France or here. *I tell you**most solemnly, that I have in this world no more than £20, that is, 80 scudi ; so that I find myself in a most deplorable state after spending all I had in correspondence within the kingdom and abroad, and in the schools erected in my diocese ; and hence, as I wrote to Monsignor Ravizza and Monsignor Falconieri, I can no longer give him the reports on ecclesiastical matters in this kingdom, having no more to spend in letters, unless the Sacred Congregation give me some assistance. Things being so, send 100 scudi of this money to Monsig. Falconieri to my account, and keep 50 for expediting letters, and other matters, and give 12 scudi to Mr. Fitzsimons, and leave the burden on me of rendering an account to their Eminences of the sums received in support of the schools. I

* These words are in English in the original letter.

expended 500 scudi, and as yet I have only received 450, so that I am yet creditor for 50 scudi, and I have all the different sums and items in the handwriting of Father Rice. I cannot understand how you can have anything to do in this matter, having received the money as my agent, and by an order in my name ; leave the settling of the accounts to me ; put that part of the burden on me, but do you dispose of the money according to my directions.

" I never write to any Secretary or Minister of the King, nor did it ever come into my head that the Franciscans had acquired so much property and money ; for I know it to be all false : nor did I ever speak against the Franciscans or other Regulars, either before or after Mass, so that all this is a calumny : *ego autem cum nil contumelia dignum agam, mendacia sperno*, nor do they affect me in the least, *contumeliae, si irascare, agnitae videntur ; spretae obsolescunt*. And this will suffice in reply to yours of the 1st of September ; and I remain

" Your most affectionate servant,

" OLIVER OF ARMAGH, &c.

" Armagh, 1st October, 1674.

" P.S.—The Parliament is prorogued for eight months. I am of opinion that all that has been written against the Archbishops of Cashel and Tuam, and the Bishop of Killaloe, is false."

This confusion seems to have arisen from an unintentional mistake in the account sent by Father Rice to Rome which was at once remedied by that good father, and in the subsequent correspondence no further reference whatsoever is made to this matter. Soon after the intelligence had been conveyed to the Primate that Propaganda would aid him in the maintenance of these schools, he thus wrote to the Internunzio (31st January, 1672):—"I thank your Excellency for the stipend granted to the three Jesuit teachers in my diocese. Oh! what expense, what annoyance did these schools cost me; yet the great advantage which redounded to fifty young priests, gave me more spiritual consolation than I could have received temporal comfort from a treasury well filled with gold."

We shall add one other extract regarding these schools, from Dr. Plunket's letter of 26th September, 1673, to the Internunzio, in which he thus writes :—

" I am very glad that you received the letter of Father Rice, Superior of the Society in this kingdom, and that you sent it to Dr. Creagh, that thus he may be able to pay me the sums expended in the maintenance of the fathers who teach in my diocese. The schools were commenced in the beginning of July, 1670, and they have continued to the present; there are as many as forty children of the Protestant gentry in them, and even the Protestants are attentive that no annoyance should be given them. I already gave to the schools £125 sterling, and every pound is equal to four Italian scudi. I have received only 300 scudi from the Sacred Congregation, so that 200 scudi yet remain, 150 scudi are due for this year, 1673, and there can be no doubt as to the payment of these. I wrote to Monsignor Airoldi to procure for me my expenses in various matters which were executed by his orders. Then as to the expense of the letters, I declare to you, that I expended 400 scudi during the past four years, and yet the Sacred Congregation gave me only 100. In order to correspond well, I must have letters from all parts of the kingdom, and foreign letters from London and elsewhere, every week, and to this end I have a special correspondent in London. Had I served in correspondence, either the king of France or Spain. as I served their Eminences these four years past, my baker's account would be long since settled. I beseech you to excuse the prolixity of this letter, for I had no time to make it shorter, and I remain your most affectionate and obliged servant,

" OLIVER PLUNKET.

" 26 Sept., 1673.

" P.S.—I pray you to send this letter to the Monsignor Secretary."

It was not the local schools alone that engaged the attention of the zealous Primate. When visiting his own diocese, and the other dioceses of his province, he found many of the clergy lamentably deficient in those higher studies which should render them fitted to discharge the office of chief pastors, and rule with wisdom the church of God. It was, indeed, impossible that a country, so continually disturbed by wars and persecutions, could supply these studies; and, hence, Dr. Plunket turned his eyes to the Continent, and especially to Rome, earnestly soliciting the Sacred Congregation to have students sent to him from its colleges; and praying, at the same time, that the number of students and the efficiency of the national college in that city might be increased. This esteem for education in Rome was not a mere abstract sentiment in our Primate; we have seen that he was imbued with the conviction that his being educated at the fountain-head of Catholic truth, was a special blessing which he had received from God, and which imposed many special obligations on him ; and, hence, when overwhelmed by afflictions and persecutions, he was accustomed to re-awaken his courage by the reflection : "*it would be a shame for spiritual soldiers, educated in Rome, ever to become mercenaries.*" (Letter 15th December, 1673.)

Writing on the 27th of September, 1671, Dr. Plunket thus declares to the Sacred Congregation the wants of his province and diocese, and his anxious desire to receive some priests from Rome :—

"I am now in this kingdom for one year and seven months, and I think I presented so many relations of the spiritual affairs of my province that their Eminences may almost touch with their hands, and see with their eyes the condition in which it is, and the state of matters here : it is in many parts infirm, and there is danger that the malady will go on spreading and increasing, if their Eminences, the chief physicians, do not give some healing and preservative remedies. The ignorance, in general, is great, although the Irish talent is excellent and acute ; but what does this avail when it cannot be cultivated : the best soil without the spade or plough can produce but little fruit, and in consequence of the penal laws we cannot have fixed schools, and are in continual alarm ; and although I undertook what others would not attempt, to maintain schools during all this year, and support the Jesuits in my province at my own expense, building houses and schools for them, that they might instruct the priests in cases of conscience, and the youth in grammar and rhetoric, yet we were not able to have classes in philosophy, or theology, or controversy, and from this it must result that our priests will be *infra mediocritatem*, and we shall have none able to administer dioceses or answer and dispute with Protestants.

"Before the war, the Catholic gentry of Ulster held their properties and estates, but now only a few of them retain anything, such as the Marquis of Antrim, whose property extends for about thirty miles, and embraces vast estates and many castles, such as the Orsini and Savelli in Latium ; but even as these, so is he also up to his eyes in debt : Sir Henry O'Neile re-acquired about 4,000 scudi per annum, and a certain Maginis about 2,000 scudi : these are the only three Irish Catholic gentlemen who re-acquired their property ; all the others must seek as a favour to be allowed to hold by lease a small portion of their former estates, and it is deemed a great favour when this is granted to them. The people, that is, those who cultivate the land, are well off, and it is from these that the priests and friars receive their maintenance, and the same persons give some relief to those upon whom they were once dependent : but as to the nobility and gentry, they are wholly ruined, so that they can no longer maintain the children in Catholic Universities ; and, what is still more deplorable, they cannot give them even the necessary means to go to the

Continental Colleges without great difficulty, and hence their condition, merits compassion and assistance, for they lost all in order not to lose their faith in God, or their reverence in spiritual things for the Apostolic See.

"In my humble opinion it would be a great charity to aid the children, and grant them an education in Catholic countries, and especially in Rome. Those who are educated there are less suspected by government, Rome being a neutral country, neither attached to Spain nor to France; and, moreover, they are more faithful to the spiritual interests of the Holy See. It is seen by experience that no priest or friar educated in Rome ever became an adherent of Walsh or any other schismatic, but only such as received their education in France, Spain, or Louvain. Moreover, those educated in Rome are better acquainted with the desires of the Apostolic See, they know its principles, and are better able to correspond with it. The 'Piazza di Spagna,' the Propaganda, and, in a word, all Rome is a great book: how many nations with their various customs are seen there. Poles, Germans, Spaniards, French, Indians, Turks, Ethiopians, Africans, Americans, are met with, and one learns in what manner and with what judgment the varying opinions and conflicting interests of so many contrary nations are harmonized. A great deal, too, is learned in the changes of government: thus one day it is seen with what modesty and wisdom and moderation those deport themselves who, the day before or under another Pontiff, ruled everything, and were honoured by everyone: *æquam sciunt servare fidem rebus in arduis, in prosperis et adversis.* I especially remarked the prelates, Cajetan, Massimi, and another from Modena who was governor of Rome in the time of Alexander the 7th, of happy memory, and many others in the time of Innocent and Urban. One treats with cardinals and prelates of great wisdom and prudence, well versed and experienced in spiritual matters, and in the temporal affairs of so many monarchs and princes; and it is impossible that a person of moderate talent would not derive great profit, as well in science as in experience. And, indeed, to educate a missionary priest, there is no college in the world better suited than the Propaganda, where they are instructed for two hours every morning in theology, and after dinner for one hour in controversy, and afterwards, for half an hour or an hour, in cases of conscience. They learn to preach, and become masters of the Hebrew and Greek; they officiate in the Church, and are also exercised in Gregorian Chant: they receive, in a word, an education better suited for missionaries than that of any other college. And hence I anxiously supplicate that I may be allowed to send *a half dozen of the most talented young priests that I can find to be educated in that college,* that thus my miserable province of Ulster may have persons able to govern its churches, for if it pleased God to remove from us three who are in Ulster, Thomas Fitzsymons, Dr. Conwell, and Dr. Ronan Magin, there would be no others who, either by their learning or experience, would be adapted for, or capable of governing these churches. The other vicars-general, *non sunt mediocritatem prætergressi.* If you do not grant me this favour, we shall be without leaders, without pastors, and the wolves will devour our flocks. The Roman—that is, one educated in Rome—is he that is able and knows how to govern ; and hence well did the prince of poets sing—

> ' Tu regere imperio populos, Romane, memento . .
> Hæ tibi erunt artes,' &c.

I beseech you in the bowels of Christ, and by the affection which you bear to this impoverished province, to procure this favour, and I shall ever be your Excellency's

> " Most affectionate and obliged servant,
>
> " OLIVER PLUNKET.

"Dublin, 27th Sept., 1671."

In a letter written in the preceding May (13th May, 1671), Dr. Plunket had passed a like eulogy on the students from Rome :—

"It is worthy of remark [he says] that no priest educated in Rome adhered to Peter Walsh or the Remonstrance, but only those from France and Belgium : and hence out of the 150 boys I have here at school, I would wish to select half-a-dozen of the best, and send them to Rome—*ut remaneat semen in Israel.* Here I am able to instruct them pretty well in literature and morality, but not in dogmatic theology or controversies ; and thus we cannot prepare persons who will be fitted to be bishops or vicars general unless by sending them to the Continent—*oportet ut aliqui sint doctores qui possint reddere rationem eorum quæ credunt.* By degrees we shall be wholly destitute of such persons, unless we attend to their education : and, as I said, the education of Rome is the best."

Not long after the Primate addressed another letter to the Internunzio, in which we find detailed many particulars connected with the various national colleges scattered through the Continent :—

"In your last letter you commanded me to give you some account of the Irish colleges in the kingdoms governed by the orthodox princes, and I now obey in the best manner I can ; but I must imitate the painters of scenery, who present some objects most vividly and clearly, and others only in outline and obscurely ; or the historians, such as Guicciardino and others, who described matters, and especially the wars in Tuscany, and, indeed, of all Italy, in a most vivid manner but not in so prominent a manner, the victories of Spain and France. Had I now the notes which I left at home, I would be able to give a more precise narrative, but I believe I shall err in very few points of any importance.

"And to begin with the Irish College in Rome, it was founded by

Cardinal Ludovisi, nephew of Gregory the Fifteenth; he bequeathed to it a thousand scudi a-year, besides a good house and a good vineyard in Castle Gandalfo.and it maintains about seven or eight students, three Jesuits, and two servants.   But in a separate letter, 1 shall write more particularly about the college.   Its revenue is capable of supporting twelve students, who would be better prepared for this mission than they now are.   In Spain there are four colleges, all directed by the Fathers of the Society; one of them is in St. Jago, which supports at one time six, at another seven students; another in Salamanca, of the same kind, and another in Lisbon, which maintains eight or ten students.   These three colleges were founded by Philip the Second, and in doing so he proved himself a zealous Catholic and a good politician; by this means he won the affection of the Irish, and when the students returned to Ireland, they won for the Spaniards the hearts and the esteem of all their friends; in a word, they could speak of nothing but Spain, *totam spirabant Hispaniam ;* whence it happens that the Irish go more freely to serve the King of Spain than any other Prince.

"In France there is a college at Bourdeaux which maintains twenty-four students, as 1 have heard, founded by the archbishops of Bordeaux and others; but, contrary to the institution and intention of the founders, this college does not admit any excepting from Cashel and Munster; and the colleges of Spain do not willingly receive students from Ulster, which is a serious injury and a manifest injustice.   It truly moves one to compassion to see high families of the house of O'Neil, O'Donnel, Maguire, MacMahon, Maginnis, O'Cahan, O'Kelly, O'Ferrall, who were great princes till the time of Elizabeth and King James, in the memory of my father and of many who are yet living ; it moves one to compassion, I say, to see their children without property and without maintenance, and without means of education ; and yet for the faith they suffered joyfully the loss of property, *cum gaudio susceperunt direptionem bonorum ;* but it is intolerable that they should be excluded from college education, for the colleges were not founded for this or that province, but for the whole Kingdom.   As to the college in Rome, I can propose a plan according to which it may be able to support sixteen students, and with more profit to religion, than it now supports six ; but this must be kept as a secret much like that of the holy office till it be carried into execution.   At present, as I said, it maintains eight students, and three Jesuits, and two servants, in all thirteen ; it has a thousand scudi per annum, and a house and vineyard.   Let the house be sold, which is worth 6,000 scudi, as also the vineyard, which, with the house that is in it, is worth 2,000 more ; let these 8,000 scudi be put in the 'Montes Pietatis,' and they will give 240 scudi per annum, which, with the 1,000 scudi above, will make in all 1,240 scudi per annum ; and let the whole sum be given to the College of Propaganda *ut erigatur alumnatus Hibernicus,* which may also be called *alumnatus Hibernicus Ludovisianus,* for it was Cardinal Ludovisi that left the money, and instead of Jesuits and servants, it will maintain so many students. Of what use is it to keep a little college with so few students, whilst for the same funds a larger number can be maintained for the service of the Missions? But two difficulties have to be solved; the first is, how can the Testament of Cardinal Ludovisi be interfered with? I answer, that the Holy Father, by a brief, can arrange this, for it is nowise injurious to that Cardinal, or to his intentions: *supponetur enim interpretative Cardinalis quamvis defuncti consensus, ac fore ut idem Cardinalis consentiret si modo rixisset;* it being the intention of the Cardinal to propagate the faith, which is better realized by placing the students in Propaganda, where a larger number may be educated. It is certain that the Cardinal had the intention of erecting a larger and more numerous College, but *morte præventus,* he could not carry his noble ideas into execution. The second difficulty is, that the Jesuits will oppose the project. But this is of little matter, when we are acting for the greater glory of God. The money was left to maintain Priests for the missions and not Jesuits; and indeed, many of the students become Jesuits, and never return to their country, which is contrary to the intention of the Cardinal. But some one will say that the Ludovisi family will give opposition; to this I reply that the greater glory of God is to be preferred to such opposition; for there is no reasonable ground of complaint, and it is a greater glory for the Ludovisi family to have an *alumnatus* in so renowned a College, which is frequented by so many cardinals, than to have so small a college, which serves rather for the Jesuits than for carrying out the intention of the founder. But then, everyone knows how the Ludovisi family now stands, and that it will make little opposition when it is well informed about the matter: all that is wanted is determination and secrecy; and whilst our Holy Father is solicitous for the propagation of the faith, there will be but little difficulty in it.

"There is a college at Seville, which maintains sixteen students, and is supported by alms.

"The Bishop of Ferns can give better information about the colleges in Spain, and perhaps, also, about that in France. The Canon Joyce can give it concerning those in Flanders. There is a college, as I hear, in Toulouse; but I do not know in what state it is: I believe it is of little importance.

"OLIVER PLUNKET.

"30th September, 1671."

In another letter, written on the same day, he adds a postscript, in which he says:—

"I forgot a college founded in Alcala, by George de Passe Silviéra, a Portuguese; he left 5,000 scudi a-year, but a great deal has been expended in building. The Bishop of Ferns can give you an account of it."

It was about this period that another college first sprung into existence, which was destined in after times to hold an important position in the Irish Church. I refer to the national College in Paris. Ireland mainly owes the foundation of this college to the Right Rev. John O'Molony, Bishop of Killaloe. Before his appointment to that see in May, 1671, he had been for many years a distinguished student and professor in the seminary of St. Sulpice. The schools of that seminary were frequented by many youths from Ireland, anxious to prepare themselves for the ministry of the altar ; and Dr. O'Molony had frequent occasion to lament the many distractions and dangers to which they were exposed, living scattered through that gay and populous city, which, too, at this period, numbered amongst its clergy many warm advocates of the condemned doctrines of Jansenius. After his consecration, he continued for many months to reside in Paris, anxious to organize a special college in that city, into which his countrymen might be received. The Sacred Congregation of Propaganda, however, repeatedly urged him to hasten to his flock, and share with them the threatened dangers of persecution, and dispense to them the bread of life. Positive orders to that effect were sent to him on the 2nd of August, 1672 ; and in reply, the good prelate expressed his readiness to obey, but petitioned at the same time to be allowed to remain some time longer, as his labours were all directed to obtain this college for the Irish Church. This petition was seconded by letters of Dr. Plunket of Armagh, and Dr. Brennan of Waterford, as we find commemorated in a minute of Propaganda. Nevertheless, the Sacred Congregation remained inexorable, and we find Dr. O'Molony before the close of this year zealously labouring in many parts of Ireland. The Irish bishops, however, had warmly entered into his views regarding the establishment of a National College in Paris ; and early in the following year they deputed Dr. O'Molony to return as their deputy to that city, to urge the authorities there to patronize the institution of such a college.

No one was more zealous than Dr. Plunket in promoting this great work, and though the college was not opened till after his glorious martyrdom, yet the Irish Church owes in great part to his active co-operation and untiring zeal, that the chief obstacles were overcome, and that those difficulties were removed, which at first seemed to destroy all hopes of its future realization. His letter of the 14th of March, 1673, sufficiently evinces the interest which he took in the institution of this college, and how earnestly he co-operated with Dr. O'Molony in seeking to effect its establishment ; he thus writes :—

"All the prelates of this kingdom have subscribed an authorization for the Bishop of Killaloe to proceed to Paris, and procure for us a college ; and it is certain, that no one could be selected better suited to treat this matter, for he is a great friend of the Archbishop of Paris, and of the Ambassador of the King of France in London, and there are strong reasons and just grounds for hoping that the college will be founded. If so, it will be a great seminary for the missions of this kingdom, being in a city so rich, so desirous of procuring the propagation and maintenance of the faith, as their charity sufficiently proved during the last persecution of Cromwell, when the Parisians supported hundreds and hundreds of the ecclesiastics and students exiled during that tempest. It is certain that the Bishop of Killaloe will do more good by procuring for us that college, than he would did he remain in his diocese during his whole life-time ; and hence I pray your Excellency to treat this matter with the Holy Father and the Sacred Congregation in such a manner that they may not be displeased with the Bishop of Killaloe for this journey to Paris, since he travels at his own cost, and with the desire of procuring so great an advantage for us. He is a great friend of Colbert, the first Minister of State, and of the Archbishop of Paris, who will be the more favourable to him should he be allowed to exercise his functions (for the Archbishop will surely request him to do so on various occasions) ; and hence I pray you to procure from His Holiness and the Sacred Congregation permission for Dr. O'Molony, during his stay in Paris, on account of our ecclesiastical matters, to exercise the episcopal functions as often as he may be requested to do so by the Archbishop of that see. Monsignor, your Excellency has always favoured, in every emergency, this poor and afflicted Church, and we hope that there is no means conducive to the attainment of this great blessing, or tending to facilitate it, which you will not favour ; and therefore I beseech you with the most urgent entreaties to lay this affair before the Sacred Congregation in such a manner, that it may allow the Bishop of Killaloe to remain in Paris whilst this matter is pending, and to exercise his episcopal functions when requested by the Archbishop ; for it is on the aid of the Archbishop, and the communications which he presents, that the success of this undertaking must in a great measure depend. In conclusion, I remain, with a profound reverence.

"OLIVER OF ARMAGH.

"Dublin, 14th March, 1672 (styl. vet.)"

Early in Dr. Plunket's episcopate many complaints were presented to Rome, especially by the prelates of Ulster and Connaught, regarding the system of selecting students for the continental colleges. From a report of the Secretary of the Sacred Congregation on the 30th May, 1672, we learn that the chief colleges * for Irish students on the Continent were :—In Flanders : Louvain, Antwerp, Tournay, and Lisle. In Spain : Madrid, Seville, Salamanca, and Compostella (both founded by Philip the Second), Alcalà, and Valence. In Portugal, that of Lisbon, founded by Philip the Second. In Italy, the College of Rome, founded by Cardinal Ludovisi.

From other documents we learn that there were similar colleges in Bordeaux and Toulouse ; and it was principally in regard of these seminaries that complaints were presented to Rome. Writing on the 13th of May, 1671, Dr. Plunket laments that in many of the continental colleges, and in particular *in Bordeaux and Toulouse,* no students were admitted excepting from Munster or Cashel; and, he continues :—

"Were we to consider the extent of the provinces, and their relative necessities, students should, above all, be received from Armagh ; for in extent it is larger than Tuam and Dublin united together : and as to its necessities, God knows that they are great. I say it with tears in my eyes, that in all Ulster there are scarcely three gentlemen who re-acquired their lands seized by Cromwell, and thus the Catholics are unable to defray the expenses of the education of their children."

In the month of August of the same year he wrote again praying the Sacred Congregation to apply some remedy to this evil :—

"I already wrote to your Excellency [he says] to procure a brief enacting that students should be received alike from all the provinces, into the colleges of Spain, France, and other places. But as I have been informed that such a brief would be of no avail in France or

* In the Acts of the Congregation, held 31st of August, 1671, the Irish colleges are thus mentioned : "In Hispania : Salmaticense, Compostellanum, Hispalense, Complutense, Valentianum, Madritense. In Lusitania, Ulissiponense. In Gallia : Parisiense, Atrebatense, Burdigalense, Tolosanum, Agénse. In Belgio : Lovaniense, Antwerpiense, Tornacense, Insulense. In Italia : Ludovisianum Romae."

K

Spain, as the colleges of these countries were not founded by the Holy See, it might be better for the Sacred Congregation to address letters on the subject to the nuncios in these countries, and to the bishops in whose dioceses the colleges are situated. As to Spain, since its colleges are in the hands of the Jesuits, it would suffice to intimate to the General of the order, in the name of the Sacred Congregation, that an equal number of students should be admitted from each province. according to the institution of the colleges themselves. Great injury has been done to my province in this matter during the past twenty years. It is the superior of the Jesuits in this country that sends the students to these colleges; hence, the Father General could intimate to this superior to send none excepting *juxta æqualitatem Provinciarum et æqualiter ex Provinciis.*" These colleges were founded for the spiritual assistance of all Ireland, that secular priests might be educated there in virtue and learning, who afterwards might administer the parishes, &c. Now I pray your Excellency to consider that the nomination being thus in the hands of religious, he will surely be anxious to send such only as he sees disposed to become religious; and, hence, I would judge it better that the presentation or nomination of these students should be placed in the hands of the archbishops. The German College, Rome, is under the care of the Jesuits; nevertheless, the students are selected for it by the prelates of Germany, and not by the principals of the order. By this, however, I do not intend to prejudice that order; for the Jesuits are my friends, and do a great deal of good in my province."

The wished-for letter was addressed by the Sacred Congregation to the General of the Jesuit order, and in reply Father Oliva, a bright name in the roll of the most distinguished superiors of that illustrious society, not only promised to comply with this just desire of the Irish bishops, "who are so zealous, and have deserved so well of the Catholic faith;" but, moreover, assigns the true cause of some disorders which had sprung up in these colleges, and especially in the Irish college of Rome; that, namely, some of the students were not selected at all in Ireland, but though wholly unfit for sacred studies, were forced upon the superiors of these colleges by the influence and solicitations of some high relatives on the Continent.

CHAPTER X.

On the 21st of May, 1670, Lord Berkely, of Stratton, was sworn in as Viceroy of Ireland. This appointment filled the Irish Catholics with joy, and all were animated with the hope of a peaceful administration. One of its first fruits was the convocation of a General Synod of the Irish bishops, to be held in Dublin on the 17th of June, 1670. This Synod was convened by Dr. Plunket for a twofold purpose : first, to correct some abuses which had crept in during the preceding persecutions ; and, secondly, to draw up an amended formula or address of allegiance to the King. At this period the Irish Church numbered but six bishops in its hierarchy, and all hastened to take part in the deliberations of the Synod. The six bishops then in Ireland were Dr. Plunket, Archbishop of Armagh ; Dr. Peter Talbot, Archbishop of Dublin ; Dr. Burgatt, Archbishop of Cashel ; Dr. James Lynch, Archbishop of Tuam ; Dr. Patrick Plunket, Bishop of Meath ; and Dr. Phelan, Bishop of Ossory. The Vicars-General of the other sees were also present, and since the days of Rinuccini, this was the first assembly of clergy that merited the name of a national council.

On the 17th of June, 1670, these prelates assembled in Dublin, under the presidency of Dr. Oliver Plunket. Their deliberations were protracted for three days ; and a note of the Archives of Propaganda describes the Synod as having been held " in Bridge-street, in the house of Mr. Reynolds, at the foot of the bridge." We shall see in the next chapter how the decrees of this council were adopted in the provincial Synod of Clones, and republished amongst its statutes ; but we may now present a translation of them, together with a transcript from the original document transmitted to the Holy See.

TRANSLATION.

Some Statutes, decreed in Dublin on the 17th, 18th, and 20th of June, 1670, by the Archbishops and Bishops of Ireland, together assembled.*

1. "As we have been informed that the bodies of some deceased laymen, in various parts of this kingdom, have been laid out in public, on a bier, clothed in religious habits, we decree, and command, that for the future no corpse shall be thus laid out.

2. "Since it is the interest if all the clergy of Ireland that an agent and procurator be in Rome, to carry on and expedite their business, we decree that £50 sterling, of English money, be annually given to our agent in Rome, which sum shall be equally divided by the Metropolitans between the provinces; and, as the Rev. Dr. John Brennan, during the past year, has acted as our agent in that city, we decree that the said sum be paid to him.

3. "No public rites or unusual questing shall hereafter be introduced without having first consulted the ordinary of the diocese and obtained his permission.

4. "We command abstinence from flesh-meat on the feast of St. Mark (as also on the three days preceding the Ascension), except when it falls on Sunday, or in Easter week.

5. "We command all the Parish Priests to use every endeavour

---

* The following is the original text of the decrees :—

Statuta quædam acta Dublini, diebus 17. 18, et 20 Junii, 1670, ab Archiepis et Epis. Hiberniæ simul congregatis.

1. Cum nobis relatum sit nonnulla laicorum defunctorum corpora in diversis regni partibus in habitu Regularium palam et supra mensam exponi. statuimus et ordinamus ut nullum corpus in posterum taliter exponatur.

2. Cum toti Clero Hiberniæ necessarium sit ut agentem et procuratorem in urbe habeant ad sua negotia sollicitanda et expedienda, decernimus ut agenti nostro pro tempore existenti 50 libræ Anglicanæ annuatim solvantur, æqualiter, dividendæ per quatuor provincias per metropolitanos. Cum autem nostra negotia nunc agat R. D. Joan. Brennan ab uno jam anno, dictam summam ei solvendam decernimus.

3 Nulli ritus publici aut quæstus inusitati in posterum inducantur inconsultis locorum ordinariis ac sine ipsorum licentia.

4. Præcipimus abstinentiam a carnibus in die S. Marci (sicut in triduo ante Ascensionem). nisi venerit in Dominica aut hebdomada Paschæ.

5. Decernimus ut omnes Parochi toto conatu procurent ut clamores, et vociferationes fœminarum comitantium corpora defunctorum impediantur.

6. Statuimus ut nullus ordo Regularium occupet aut detineat conventus aut monasteria aliorum ordinum Regularium vel Clericalium absque authentica auctoritate aplica, et ordinariorum consensu.

7. Statuimus nullos Regulares in posterum publice ad altere mendicare

to prevent the clamour and vociferations of the women who accompany the funerals of the deceased.

6. " We decree that no religious order shall occupy or retain any convents or monasteries of other religious or clerical orders without an authentic authorization of the Holy See and the consent of the ordinary.

7. " We decree that no religious shall hereafter ask alms at the altar unless they belong to a community in which there are four religious, of whom two, at least, are priests; and, in general, no religious is to be allowed to quest publicly unless he be a priest, who may offer the Holy Sacrifice for the people, and thus relieve and assist the Parish Priest.

8. " We command, that should any member of the Franciscan order, within thirty days, refuse to acknowlege as his superior the Rev. Father Peter Geanor, whom we certify to be the ligitimate Franciscan Provincial, no Catholic, after the said thirty days, shall confess to him or assist at his Mass, or give him alms when publicly questing for the said order.

9. " We, moreover, decree that all the ordinaries shall command, in their respective dioceses, the Parish Priest and preachers to admonish and warn, under threat of divine vengeance, the people subject to their charge, to give no favour, aid, or assistance to robbers,

nisi sint ex conventu in quo quatuor sunt, ex quibus duo ad minus sint Sacerdotes, et facile non admittatur Regularis ad quæstus publice faciendos nisi fuerit Sacerdos ad celebrandum populo propter levamen et solamen parochorum.

8. Statuimus ut nulli fratrum Franciscanorum qui non obedierit intra 30 dies a die horum actuum suo superiori, scilicet Rev. P. Pet o Geanor quem nobis constat esse legitimum Franciscanorum Provincialem, ullus Catholicus confiteatur vel ejus sacrum audiat aut eleemosynas ei publice petenti elargiatur post illos 30 dies.

9. Decernimus insuper ut ordinarii omnes in suis respective diœcesibus imjungant Parochis ac prædicatoribus serio ac sub interminatione divinæ vindictæ monere populos sibi subditos nullum favorem, operam aut auxilium præbere latronibus aut viarum grassatoribus aliisque publicæ quietis perturbatoribus (vulgo I ories dictis.)

10. Quoniam Apus, præcipit ut fiant obsecrationes et orationes pro omnibus hominibus, pro Regibus et omnibus qui in sublimitate constituti sunt, parochi atque etiam regulares in suis conventibus diebus Dominicis moneant populu n ut singuli Deum or nt pro Serenissimis Carlo IIo et Catharina, Rege et Regina nostris, ut Deus eis omnem felicitatem et insuper prolem elargiri dignetur; item pro Exemo D. Pro-Rege Hiberniæ; necnon pro felici Angliæ, Hiberniæ et Scotiæ regimine, et eadem intentione dicantur iisdem diebus Litaniæ B.V.M. ante vel post Missam.

11. Denique decernimus et volumus ut nullum ex ordine subscribendi hisce actibus aliisque Scripturis, et Instrumentis hujus Congnis, præjudicium juri cujuspiam fiat.

Die, 20 Junii, 1670.

highwaymen, and other disturbers of the public peace, who are known as *Tories*.

10. "Since the Apostle commands supplications and prayers to be offered up for all men, for kings, and for all who are placed in authority, let the parish clergy, and also the regulars in their convents, admonish the people on Sundays, that all are to pray to God for the most serene Charles the Second and Catherine, our king and queen, that God may deign to grant to them prosperity and offspring, as also for our most excellent lord, the Viceroy of Ireland; and moreover, for the good government of England, Ireland, and Scotland, and with the same intention let the litanies of the Blessed Virgin be recited on the said days either before or after Mass.

11. "In fine we decree and intend that the rights of no one shall be prejudiced by the order of subscribing to these acts, and to the other documents and instruments of this Synod."

Another matter which engaged the attention of the bishops in the Synod, was the drawing up of an address to be presented to the Viceroy. Precisely four years had now elapsed since the Irish prelates, convened in Dublin, at the desire of Ormond, had presented to the Crown a declaration of loyalty and allegiance. On that occasion they rejected, it is true, the Valesian Remonstrance, but, then, they appended to their address three propositions,* which one would suppose any Government hostile to the Holy See would be glad to find presented to them. Yet that address was rejected with disdain, and the Viceroy ordered, without delay, the imprisonment of the assembled bishops; and renewed hostility against the Catholic priesthood seemed to be the only result of their well-intentioned deliberations. But what could not be obtained by petition, was won by the unflinching spirit of the Irish hierarchy, which, encouraged by the Holy See, refused to sacrifice to court-favour one jot of Catholic principle; and though the Primate died in exile, and the other prelates were compelled to endure sufferings and persecutions, yet the cause for which they combatted was sure to triumph, and the English ministers were glad in 1670, to receive from the Irish bishops that very address, which, even with its un-Irish appendix, they had disdainfully

* We may here remark that it was only by a deceptive explanation of these propositions that the Primate, Dr. Edmund O'Reilly, and the other members of the Synod, were induced to subscribe to them.

rejected four years before. We shall here present to the reader in parallel columns the Address of the bishops in June, 1670, and that rejected by the Government in June, 1666 :—

Address presented by the Bishops of Ireland to the Lord Viceroy of the Kingdom.

" To our most gracious King, Charles II., Monarch of Great Britain, France, and Ireland.

" We, your Majesty's subjects, the Clergy of the Roman Catholic Church, do hereby declare and solemnly protest before God and His angels, that we own and acknowledge your Majesty to be our lawful King, and the undoubted Monarch, as well of this your realm of Ireland, as of all other your Majesty's dominions ; and consequently, we confess ourselves bound in conscience to be obedient to your Majesty in all civil and temporal affairs as far as any other subjects can or ought to be to their princes, as the laws of God and nature require from us ; and therefore we promise that we, during life, will inviolably bear true allegiance to your Majesty, your lawful heirs and successors, and that no power on earth shall be able to withdraw us from our duty herein : and that we will, even to the loss of life and property, if occasion requires, assert and defend your Majesty's rights against any that shall invade the same, or attempt to deprive your Majesty, your lawful heirs and successors, of any part thereof. And, in order that this our sincere protestation may more clearly appear, we further declare the doctrine to be false and intolerable which teaches that any

Address presented in 1666. The Catholic Clergy's Remonstrance of Loyalty.

" We, your Majesty's subjects, the Roman Catholic clergy of the Kingdom of Ireland, together assembled, do hereby declare and solemnly protest before God and His holy angels, that we own and acknowledge your Majesty to be our true and lawful King, supreme lord, and undoubted sovereign, as well of this realm of Ireland, as of all other your Majesty's dominions ; consequently, we confess ourselves bound in conscience to be obedient to your Majesty in all civil and temporal affairs, as any subject ought to be to his prince, and as the laws of God and nature require at our hands. Therefore, we promise that we will inviolable bear true allegiance to your Majesty, your lawful heirs, and successors, and that no power on earth shall be able to withdraw us from our duty herein; and that we will, even to the loss of our blood, if occasion requires, assert your Majesty's rights against any that shall invade the same, or attempt to deprive yourself or your lawful heirs and successors of any part thereof. And to the end, this our sincere protestation may more clearly appear, we further declare that it is not our doctrine that subjects may be discharged, absolved, or freed from the. obligation of performing their duty of true obedience and allegiance to their prince ; much

private subject may lawfully kill his prince, the anointed of God. Wherefore, deeply persuaded of the abominable and sad consequences which ensue from its practice, we oblige ourselves to discover unto your Majesty or some of your ministers any attempts of that kind or rebellions against your Majesty's person, crown, or royal authority, which may come to our knowledge, that thus such horrid evils may be prevented.

" In fine, as we hold the afore-aforesaid things to be just and agreeable to good consciences, so we will preach them, and seek to inculcate them on our respective flocks, ready to confirm them with our oaths.

"In witness whereof we do hereunto subscribe the 18th day of June. 1670."

less may we allow of or pass as tolerable any doctrine that perniciously, and against the word of God, maintains that any private subject may lawfully kill or murder the anointed of God, his prince; wherefore, pursuant to the deep apprehension we have of the abomination and sad consequences of its practice, we do engage ourselves to discover to your Majesty, or some of your ministers, any attempt of that kind, rebellion or conspiracy against your Majesty's person, crown, or royal authority, that comes to our knowledge, whereby such horrid evils may be prevented. Finally, as we hold the premises to be agreeable to good conscience, so we religiously swear the due observance thereof to our utmost, and we will preach and teach the same to our respective flocks.

" In witness whereof, we do hereunto subscribe, the 15th day of June, 1666."—(See O'Conor's History, &c., App. xvi.)

Thus, the address of 1670 was identical, if not in every word, at least in substance, with that rejected in 1666, and still more, it was free from the three propositions adopted and subscribed to by the former assembly—propositions borrowed from the declarations of the Parisian clergy, which, howsoever they were explained to the Irish prelates, had originally been drawn up in a spirit of hostility and insult to Rome.*

* These propositions were as follows:—
" 1st. We do hereby declare that it is not our doctrine that the Pope hath any authority in temporal affairs over our sovereign lord King Charles the Second : yea, we promise that we will oppose them that will ·assert any power direct or indirect over him in civil and temporal affairs.
" 2. That it is our doctrine that our gracious King Charles the Second is so absolute and independent, that he acknowledgeth not, nor hath

Some writers, confiding too much on the authority of historians who were alike the enemies of Ireland and of our Catholic faith, have broached assertions regarding this Synod which are wholly repugnant to truth, and are alike discreditable to the Archbishop of Dublin and to the subject of these memoirs. Thus, it is gravely asserted that Dr. Talbot, on arriving in Ireland, found the prelates assembled in Dublin and this, too, in 1669)—that he at once introduced himself amongst them, announcing that the King had appointed him to oversee them all: that Dr. Plunket, "considering this an unwarranted assumption, desired to see the authority on which it was advanced, alleging that if there was in fact such an authority, he would submit to it. The other answered that he had not it under the great seal. To which Dr. Plunket replied, that the little seal would serve his turn, but until one or other was produced, he would take care to oversee Talbot, and expected to be obeyed.*

All these assertions are most unfounded, and are as little consonant to truth as is the date 1669, which some of these writers assign to the National Synod. It was Dr. Plunket, indeed, that convoked this Synod; but Dr. Talbot, who was long in Ireland before the Synod, was the chief bishop with whom he made arrangements for its convocation. The question of the primacy being as yet undecided, and the presidency of the Synod depending on who was to be considered the primate, Dr. Plunket proposed that the decision of the question should be left to the assembled prelates; but Dr. Talbot chose rather to refer it to the decision of the Holy See; to which the Archbishop of Armagh readily assented; and in the meantime, with the protest which is usually made in such cases, that the rights of the respective parties should

in civil and temporal affairs, any power above him under God; and that to be our constant doctrine, from which we shall never decline.

" 3rd. That it is our doctrine that we subjects owe such natural and just obedience unto our King, that no power, under any pretext soever, can either dispense with us or free us thereof."—(See Butler's *Memoirs, &c.*, vol. iii., p. 434.)

* These assertions have been repeated, almost in the very words of the text, by most of the modern writers on our Irish history.

receive no prejudice from the order of subscribing to the
the decress, &c. (as may be seen in the eleventh canon), the
presidency was ceded without any opposition to Dr. Plunket;
and the bishops proceeded with their deliberations in a most
perfect spirit of unity and peace.*   It was at the close of the
proceedings that a dispute arose, which, though of no importance in itself, yet gave some colouring to the fabrication of
the above monstrous tale.   In the letters of Dr. Plunket no
reference is made to this dispute, but in a note of Propaganda it is recorded that on the Synod being convened by
Dr. Plunket, principally for the purpose of drawing up a
declaration of allegiance to his Majesty, and when all the
assembled prelates had signed the proposed declaration, a
question arose as to who should present it to his Majesty.
Some proposed Sir Nicholas Plunket, who had been long
distinguished for his services in the Catholic cause, and, as
well in the deliberations of the Confederation of Kilkenny,
as in various embassies of which he formed a part, had given
clear proofs of his ability and prudence.   He was a near
relative of the Primate, and brother of the Bishop of Meath :
and in attestation of his services he had received the order
of knighthood from Pope Innocent the Tenth.   Dr. Talbot,
however, opposed his appointment to present their address,
alleging that he himself had long been intimate with the
Court and the Royal family, and that he had received an
authorization from the King to superintend the clergy in
civil matters of this kind.   Dr. Plunket demanded that this
commission from the King should be presented in writing
and under the King's seal; adding that then, without hesitation, all would leave in his hands the presentation of the
address.   Indeed, there can be but little doubt as to
Dr. Talbot's having received such a commission from the
court, especially as we find a letter addressed to him from
London, in September, 1672, by Dr. Patrick Magin, brother
of the Vicar-General of Dromore, conveying to him a similar

* See letter of Dr. Crengh, at page 76, where he states that the affairs
of this Synod were conducted with the greatest harmony.

commission, requesting him, in the name of Lord Arlington, to superintend the manner of acting of the Irish clergy, and to check the violence of some of the prelates. But on the present occasion either Dr. Talbot had not received this commission in writing or was unwilling to present it to the Synod; and hence the assembled bishops deputed Sir Nicholas to be the bearer of their declaration to the King.

On the second day of the Synod, a petition * was drawn up and despatched to the Holy See, soliciting the appointment of some new bishops to the vacant dioceses, and presenting at the same time the names of the clergymen whom they deemed most deserving of the episcopal dignity. Favours and dispensations are also solicited from the Holy

* We insert the original petition, which is as follows :—

" Illme. ac Rme. Dne.

" Cum Clemens Papa VIII. fel. Rec. die 13 Martii anno 1598, indultum quod incipit, Venerabiles fratres, concesserit Epis, per Hiberniam constitutis, commutandi abstinentiam a carnibus feria 4ᵃ et ab ovis feria 6ᵃ in Hibernia consuetam in alia pia opera. quod indultum aliqui Episcopi acceptarunt, alii non, quibus non obstantibus progressu temporis ubique observata fuit donec nonnulli in externis regnis (ubi consuetudo non abstinendi illis diebus viget) educati non absque scandalo et multorum dissensione, aliis applaudentibus, aliis contradicentibus, morem antiquum abstinendi transgrediuntur, quod sane multis est peccandi occasio. Quapropter nos infrascripti ut hujusmodi scandalis et dissensionibus opportunum adhibeatur remedium enixe rogamus Illmam. Dom Vestram ut auctoritate Aplica, Indulto Clementis nobis uti liceat, atque ut prædicta abstinentia unius cujusque devotioni relinquatur, maneantque fideles liberi ab ipsius observatione, quod in magnum animarum solatium cessurum non dubitamus.

" Cum insuper nonnulli Regulares prætextu privilegiorum, in 2⁰ et 2⁰ consanguinitatis et affinitatis gradu necnon inter levantem et levatum dispensent, ac præterea in omni irregularitate etiam ex defectu vel delicto publico proveniente, rogamus Illmam. Dom. Vestram ut Sacra Congregatio hujusmodi privilegio vel nobis concedi procuret vel a Regularibus auferri. Non enim consentaneum videtur ut quilibet Regularis in nostris Diœcesibus ad Episcopalis dignitatis vilipendium majora quam nos ipsi privilegia exercere valeat.

" Cum rursus tempore longi belli et saevæ persecutionis Cromwellianæ capitula in diversis Diœcesibus fuerint destructa, dignitariis et canonicis vel mortuis vel peremptis ; ex quo magnæ dissensiones et defectus etiam legitimæ electionis Vicariorum Generalium exortæ sunt, ut in posterum in omni eventu hujusmodi incommodis obex ponatur, supplicamur, Illm. Dni. Væ. ut nobis a S. Sᵉ et a S. Congᵒ facultatem impetret instituendi

Father, regarding the practice of abstinence as it then prevailed in Ireland, and various questions affecting the interests of the Irish Church.

The discipline of the Church regarding matrimonial dispensations within the prohibited degrees was, at the time of which we speak, rigorously maintained by the Holy See; and hence, not only was the general faculty of dispensing in them denied to the bishops, but repeated letters were also addressed by the Sacred Congregation to the superiors of the religious orders, withdrawing their faculties, and insisting on their conforming themselves to the established disciplinary laws.

The dispensation as to the abstinence from meat on

dignitarios et formale capitulum in illis Ecclesiis Cathedralibus in quibus hactenus extiterunt.

" Cum denique pro majori animarum consolatione et spirituali lucro multum conducant indulgentiæ plenariæ in diebus patronorum Ecclesiarum Cathedralium et Parochialium, rogamus Illmam. Dom. Vestram ut uno indulto seu brevi generali hujusmodi indulgentias concedi procuret omnibus rite dispositis qui in dictis diebus a primis Vesperis usque ad 2ᵃˢ locum in quo talium patronorum solemnitas celebrabitur, visitaverint.

" Quandoquidem in Hibernia messis sit multa, operarii vero et pastores pauci, sunt etenim triginta quatuor Diœceses et sex tantum Epi, qui administrandis sacramentis et instruendis populis non sufficerent, etiamsi nihil aliud toto vitæ tempore agerent præterquam soli confirmationis sacramento attendere; quibus accedit magnam clero existimationem et venerationem etiam apud adversarios ex congruo Eporum. numero (sicut experti sumus) oriri, rogamus Illmam. Dom. Vestram ut in unaquaque Hibᵐ provincia nonnullos novis Epos instituendos S. Sanctitati et s. Congregationi proponat.

" Subjicimus autem hic nomina illorum Ecclorum. quos tantæ dignitati ac muneri aptos et idoneos in Dno. judicamus.

" PRO PROVINCIA ARDMACANA.

" R. D. Patricius Daly, I.U.D., qui a 30 annis Vic. Generalem agit in Diœcesi Ardmacana, vir magnæ charitatis et integerrimæ vitæ pro Diœcesi Clogherensi.

" R. D. Oliverus Dease, vir doctus et in rebus Ecclesiasticis bene versatus qui etiam a 30 annis Vic. fuit Gen. Midensis, pro Diœcesi Kilmorensi.

" R. D. Thomas Fitzsymons, Vic. Gen. Kilmorensis, S. T. Licentiatus pro Diœcesi Derrensi.

" PRO PROVINCIA DUBLINEN.

" R. D. Lucas Wadding, Vic. Gen. Fernensis, vir doctis et pius quem

Wednesdays, and from eggs on Fridays, which long usage had established in our Irish Church, was readily granted by the Sacred Congregation ; and on the 3rd of August, 1671, we find a brief addressed to the Irish bishops, granting dispensation to those who had violated the law for the past, and empowering the respective ordinaries, at any future time (perpetuis futuris temporibus), to dispense in regard to such abstinence.

The indulgence for the feasts of patron saints was also granted ; and, in compliance with the desire of the Council to have new members added to the Irish hierarchy, we find, in the following year, no fewer than six bishops

Epis Fernen. pro suo Coadjutore desiderat, cum ipse ob senectutem ac adversam valetudi nem alia que causas gregi adesse non possit.

"R. D. Gulielmus Phelan, S.T.D. et Cancellarius Ossorien, ac Prot. Aplicus. vir egregie doctus, pro Diœcesi Leghlinensi.

"R. Pater Nicholaus Netterville, Soc. Jesu, vir doctrina et verbi Dei prædicatione celebris pro Diœc. Kildarensi.

"PRO PROVINCIA CASSELLENSI.

"R. D. Joannes Brennan, S.T.D. et Professor. vir doctrina, prudentia, et vitæ integritate conspicuus, ut Væ Illmæ. Dni satis notum est, pro Diœcesibus Waterforden, et Lismoren, canonice unitis.

"R. D. Jacobus Dulæus. Vic. Aplicus. Limerican. cujus etiam doctrina et vitæ integritas Illmæ. Dni. Vræ. probe nota est, pro Diœcesi Limericen.

"R. D. Dermitius Hederman. S.T. Licentiatus, vir magnæ doctrinæ et pietatis pro Diœcesibus Ardfertensi et Aghadœnsi canonice unitis.

"R. D. Thadæus O'Brien, S.T.D., vel R. D. Joannes Swiny, S.T.D., vel R. D. Gulielmus Goold, S.T.D., pro Diœcesibus Corcagiensi et Cloynensi unitis.

"R. D. Joannes Molony, vir doctus et prudens S.T.D., vel R. D. Thomas Kennedy, vel R. D. Thomas Gripha, pro Diœcesi Laonensi.

"PRO PROV. TUAMENSI.

"R. D. Georgius Fallon, S.T.D. et Professor Bononiæ, vel R. Pater Patricius Kerovan, Augustinianus, vel R. D. Thomas Bourke, S.T.D., pro Diœcesi Elphinensi.

"R. Pater Thadæus Keogh, Dominicanus et S.T. Magister, vel R. D. Michael Linch. S.T.D., pro Diœcesi Clonfertensi.

"Quibus omnibus simul congregati subscribimus die 18 Junii, 1670, Dublini

"OLIVERUS ARDMACANUS, ETC.
"JACOBUS TUAMENSIS, ETC.
"JACOBUS OSSORIEN.

"GUIL. CASSELEN, ETC.
"PETRUS DUBLINENSIS, ETC.
"PATRITIUS MIDENSIS.

"Illmo. et Rmo. Duo Baldeschi, Sro Cnis de Prop. Fide, Secretario Romam."

and five vicars-apostolic appointed to the Irish sees, viz. :—

Dr. John Brennan, to the united dioceses of Waterford and Lismore.
Dr. John O'Molony, to Killaloe.
Dr. Patrick Duffy, to Clogher.
Dr. Thaddeus Keogh, to Clonfert.
Dr. Dominick de Burgo, to Elphin.
Dr. Daniel Mackey, to Down and Connor.
Ronan Magin, Vicar-Apostolic of Dromore.
Eugene Conwell, Vicar-Apostolic of Derry.
Patrick Dempsey, Vicar-Apostolic of Kildare.
John de Burgo, Vicar-Apostolic of Killala.
Michael Lynch, Vicar-Apostolic of Kilmacduagh.

CHAPTER XI.

PROVINCIAL SYNOD OF ARMAGH, HELD IN CLONES, 1670.

THE first provincial Synod of Armagh, in the seventeenth century, was held in the year 1614 ; and having been convened during the intolerant administration of Chichester, it sufficiently proves the anxious desire of the prelates of that province to maintain Catholic morality and discipline in their primitive purity and integrity. In that year some of the bishops were in exile, and several sees were vacant, and all the dioceses of the province of Armagh were administered by vicars-general ; and hence we find the name of no bishop appended to the synodical decrees then enacted. More than once these decrees received the sanction of succeeding synods ; but with the new era which seemed to open for the Irish Church during the peaceful administration of Berkeley, Dr. Plunket deemed it expedient to make further efforts to root out all abuses, and to reduce to perfect order the disciplinary regulations of the districts intrusted to his care.

For this purpose, immediately on landing in Ireland, he set about visiting the different dioceses of his provinces, convening their respective clergy, and deliberating on the reforms which it might be necessary to introduce; and afterwards, before the close of 1670, he summoned, in the town of Clones, of the diocese of Clogher, a general Synod of the whole province. Many of the vicars-general who assisted at this Synod assembled soon after in the town of Armagh, and testified by letter their gratitude to the Holy See for having appointed so indefatigable a prelate to the primatial see, and they briefly set forth the principal works which he had performed since his arrival in Ireland, especially referring to the suspension of Terence O'Kelly, Vicar of Derry.* The Terence O'Kelly to whom reference is here made (his name is erroneously printed Terence O'Reilly in some recent publications) had many years before been appointed Vicar Apostolic of Derry ; and when attempts were made to remove him for some public crimes of which he had rendered himself guilty, he more than once had had recourse to the civil authorities to maintain himself in his dignity. The Father Taafe already mentioned (p. 3), on coming to Ireland with a pretended authority to hold a visitation throughout the whole island, sought to give a colour to his mission by promulgating sentence of deposition against the Vicar of Derry. So just was this sentence, that many were induced to admit as genuine the authority from which it proceeded, and Ronan Magin, Vicar-General of Dromore, accepted a commission to carry it into execution. He accordingly set out, in company with some others, to be bearer to the guilty vicar of the decree of Taafe, suspending him from the exercise of all his spiritual functions. However the object of this journey became known to O'Kelly ; and Ronan Magin, on his arrival in Derry, found the military with a warrant for his arrest on a charge of *præmunire ;* that is, of exercising foreign jurisdiction in the British dominions. He was accordingly seized and brought to Dublin for trial ; and it was only by the intercession of many high members of the Court in London that he was soon after conducted to that city, and

* See chapter vi., page 64, where their letter is quoted.

having been subjected to a nominal trial, was restored to liberty.*

Dr. Plunket had better success with the unfortunate Vicar ; and having first received from him a promise that he would submit to the decision of the Provincial Council, invited him to be present at its deliberations. A decree of deposition was consequently enacted in the Synod ; and as we shall see in the twelfth chapter, the Archbishop himself carried it into effect, and appointed Eugene Conwell † his successor in the office of Vicar-General of the diocese of Derry.

The Synod of Clones was held on the 23rd of August, 1670 ; and, in addition to the Archbishop and Dr. Patrick Plunket, Bishop of Meath, there were present at it— Patrick Daly, Vicar-General of Armagh ; Oliver Dease, Vicar-General of Meath ; Terence O'Kelly, Vicar Apostolic of Derry ; Cornelius Gaffney, Vicar-General of Ardagh ; Patrick O'Mulderig, Vicar-General of Down and Connor ; Rouan Magin, Dean and Vicar-General of Dromore ; Thomas Fitzsimons, Archdeacon and Vicar-General of Kilmore ; Patrick Cullen, Vicar-General of Clogher ; Edmund Junge, Vicar-General of Clonmacnoise ; Eugene Conwell, Vicar-General of Raphoe ; and then elected Coadjutor Vicar of Derry. There were also present Father John Byrne, Superior of the Dominicans, and Father John Brady, Superior of the Franciscans.

Dr. Oliver Dease was appointed Procurator of the Synod, and Dr. Thomas Fitzsimons its Secretary ; and after the celebration of the Holy Sacrifice and the invocation of the Holy Ghost to guide them in their deliberations, the assembled prelates formally protested that their only object in this Council was to promote the glory of the Almighty, the interests of the Catholic Church, and the tranquillity and peace of the kingdom ; that thus, whilst they rendered to

---

* Letter of the Internuncio, June, 1669.

† The letter of Dr. Conwell, from which many of the preceding particulars have been taken, refers this appointment to the end of August, which well agrees with the date which the decrees of Clones present.

Cæsar the things which were Cæsar's, they might render to God the things which were of God.

The decrees which were enacted are twenty-eight in number, and are all directed to the removal of every scandal from the sanctuary, the sanctification of the faithful, and the celebration of the Holy Mysteries and Rites of the Church with due solemnity and decorum. The parish priests were commanded to have a fixed place of residence; the vicars-general were prohibited to be absent from their dioceses, without special leave from their Metropolitan, for more than two months; and to all the clergy, it was inter-dicted to frequent public taverns and market-places, and after the third admonition, such as refused to obey were to be deprived of all ecclesiastical benefices. Whatsoever ecclesiastic should have recourse to the lay tribunals, to obtain a benefice or sacred office, was, by the very fact, declared incapable of such benefice or office, and the laity who would take a part in such interference, were subjected to excommunication. It was further commanded, that in each diocese, there should be destined synodal examiners, and two masters of ceremonies, the approbation of one of whom, at least, would be required before any priest could be permitted to celebrate the Holy Sacrifice. No priest was allowed to celebrate twice on Sundays or holidays, excepting in case of necessity, without an express permis-sion from his Diocesan Superior. No questing of the religious should be allowed in the churches, without a written permission from the Ordinary; and the parish priest was permitted to make collections at the altar only four times each year. One *solidus*, or shilling, was fixed as the alms for the Holy Sacrifice; and two *solidi* were the annual stipend which each family should contribute to the support of the parish priest; and should any parish priest fix a smaller sum, he was to be fined by the Ordinary. For the support of the bishops, it was fixed that *five solidi* should be given once a-year by each of the parish priests. All drinking at wakes, and all night-wakes were prohibited.

L

The decrees of the Council of |Trent were declared to be received as they had been hitherto received in all the dioceses; and, in fine, the assembled prelates gave their sanction to the various statutes which had been enacted in the Episcopal Synod of Dublin, in the month of June of the same year, concerning which latter Synod we shall speak more at length in a subsequent chapter.*

CHAPTER XII.

PROVINCIAL SYNOD OF ARDPATRICK, NEAR LOUTH, IN 1678.

Succeeding years bring with them new exigencies regarding the disciplinary laws of the Church ; former decrees may be neglected, or perhaps have fallen into oblivion ; new social circumstances may have arisen to require new arrangements

---

* We insert here in full the decrees of the Synod of Clones, so justly celebrated in the modern jurisprudence of our Church.

"Acta, Statuta et Decreta facta et ordinata in Concilio Provinciali Ardmacano celebrato in oppido de Clunes, Diœcesis Clogherensis ejusdem Provinciæ die 23 Augusti, 1670, præsidente Illmo. ac Revmo. Domino D. Oliverio Archiepiscopo Ardmacano totius Hib. Primate et praesento Illmo. et Revmo. Do. D. Patritio Epo. Midensi cum suis respective Vicariis Generalibus, viz. :—Reverendis admodum DD. Patricio Daly et Oliverio Daise ; item Reverendis DD. Terentio O'Kelly, Vic. Apostolico Derriensi; Cornelio Gaffney, Vic. Gen. Ardaghaden ; Patricio O'Mulderig, Vic. Gen. Dunen. et Connoren. ; Ronano Magin, Vic. Gen. Dromoren; Thoma Fitzsimons, Vic. Gen. Kilmoren; Patricio Cullen, Vic. Gen. Clogheron; Oliverio Daise, Procuratore; adm. Rev. D. Edmundo Jauge, Vic Gen. Clonmacnoisensi ; Doctore Eugenio Conwell, Vic. Gen. Rapotensi, tum instituto Derriensi ; et Revv. PP. Joanne Byrne, Ord. Praed. et Joanne Brady, min obs. provincialibus, etc.

"Post Sacrum et invocato Spiritu Sancto, dicto hymno Veni Creator, etc., declarandum esse duximus et per presentes declaramus, protestamur, ac totum facimus, Nos nihil aliud in hac nostra conventione ac Synodo meditari velle aut intendere, praeter quam Dei gloriam omnipotentis, Religionis Catholicæ exaltationem, Regis ac Reginæ salutem et conservationem, et totius Regni tranquillitatem et pacem, reddentes Cæsari quæ sunt Cæsaris, et quæ Dei Deo : itaque sancimus et ordinamus ut sequitur.

1. " Statuimus et ordinamus ut in exequiis nullæ fiant compotationes nec vigiliæ nocturnæ ab occasu ad ortum solis, nec admittantur nisi consanguinei et proximi amici.

2. "Ut Sacerdotes et Clerici tabernas et nundinas non frequentent, quod si tertio admoniti non obediant, beneficiis priventur.

3. "Ut omnes Sacerdotes non admittant ancillas nisi bonæ famæ et de

in the outward discipline of the Church ; and perhaps, too, abuses may have crept in to call for the pruning hand of the pastor, or demand the enactment of canonical punishments to chastise, the guilty and check the vicious in their criminal career. Hence, wisely has the Church decreed that her provincial synods should be renewed at stated intervals, and that her pastors, assembled in the spirit of God, should deliberate together on the spiritual necessities of their flocks.

Though the year 1678 already presented forebodings of the approaching tempest which was soon to render desolate so many of the Irish sees, yet Dr. Plunket resolved not to defer any longer the celebration of his second provincial synod, and he accordingly convened it for the month of August, 1678. One bishop had been added to the province of Armagh since its pastors had last assembled in 1670, at

quibus nulla prorsus sit suspicio ;. admittantur cognatæ usque ad tertium vel quartum gradum ; et nullæ prorsus in cubiculo sacerdotis dormiant.

4. " Ut omnes Parochi domicilium fixum habeant sub pœna arbitraria.

5. " Ut nullus sacerdos seu clericus quamcumque fœminam equitando retro se gerat.

6. " Nullus Vicarius Generalis ultra duos menses a sua diœcesi, absque speciali licentia Metropolitani, absit.

7. " Ut clericus quicumque qui pro beneficio aut officio obtinendo, aut pro se vindicando de suo superiore aut competitore recurrerit ad brachium sæculare, præter infamiæ notam eo ipso incurrendæ, sit ipso facto inhabilis et incapax beneficii aut officii pro quo taliter recurrit et laicus se immiscens huic casui sit excommunicatus.

8. " Ut nullus sacerdos seu sæcularis seu regularis substituatur in parœciis sine approbatione ordinarii loci.

9. " Ut in qualibet diœcesi sint examinatores Synodales et duo magistri cæremoniarum, sine quorum aut saltem unius de ipsis approbatione nullus admittatur ad celebrandum.

10. " Ut nullus parochus quæstus ad sua altaria fieri permittat sine expressa ordinarii licentia in scriptis accepta.

11. " Ut nullius ordinis aut religionis fratres qui in diœcesi aliqua a memoria nostra aut parentum, conventus aut residentias non habuerint, ad inibi residendum de novo admittantur ; et parochi talibus religiosis mendicare aut praedicare ad altare non permittant sine licentia ordinarii in scriptis sub pœna excommunicationis.

12. " Statuimus et ordinamus ut quicumque defunctum, qui vivus specialem sibi non elegit sepulturam, extra parœciam propriam ad aliam sepeliendum transtulerint, a divinis arceantur donec eorum ordinario se sistant et pœna arbitraria mulctentur.

13. " Ut nulla sacerdos sive regularis sive sæcularis sub pœna

Clones, viz., Dr. Patrick Tyrrell, Bishop of Clogher and Administrator of Kilmore, a man renowned, even on the Continent, for his knowledge of ecclesiastical jurisprudence, and at the same time a zealous co-operator with the Primate in carrying into execution the disciplinary laws of the Church. Dr. Conwell had in the interval passed to a happy eternity, and his successor, Luke Plunket, bore in the present synod not only the title of Vicar-General of Derry, but also Procurator of the diocese of Raphoe. Dr. James Cusack, who took part in this synod as Procurator of the Vicar-Apostolic of Ardagh, had already been appointed Coadjutor of the Bishop of Meath, but was not as yet consecrated; and we find three others also present, Edward Dromgole, Henry Hugo, and Bernard Magork, whose names were afterwards transmitted to Rome as worthy to be successors of the martyred primate, and the first of whom

suspensionis ipso facto incurrendæ, diebus Dominicis vel festivis, bis celebret nisi gravi necessitate urgente et præsertim in eodem altari absque expressa ordinarii in scriptis licentia.

14. " Ut nullus Parochus quæstus pecuniarios exigat ad altare nisi quater in anno.

15. " Ut designetur locus aliquis conveniens Parocho et Parochianis in quo Missa habeatur sive sacerdos duo habeat altaria, sive unum tantum ; quod si parochiani dissenserint, electio et designatio loci sit penes sacerdotem ipsum; quod si parochus in hoc partialis fuerit sit penes Ordinarium.

16. " Parochus a conjugalibus æqualiter pro salarii annualis stipendio duos solidos Anglicanos exigat ; qui de hac summa aliorum Parochorum præjudicio aliquid remiserit ad decem solidos Anglicanos mulctetur.

17. " Taxa ordinaria pro celebrantis Missam labore, sit unus solidus, et qui plus vel minus exigat ab ordinario puniatur.

18. " Statuimus et ordinamus ut nullus audeat in impedimentis matrimonii dispensare virtute indulti alicujus aut privilegii nisi ejus auctoritas sit ab ordinario approbata et in hoc etiam actu includimus Regulares sub pœna suspensionis ad arbitrium ordinarii. Deinde præcipimus et stricte mandamus sub eadem pœna ut nullus parochus accipiat hujusmodi dispensationes, etiam a Regularibus Societatis Jesu, absque ordinariorum respective licentia.

19. " Statuimus et ordinamus ut nullus ordinarius pro dimissorialibus aliquid recipiat alioquin tamquam simoniacus a Metropolitano puniatur.

20. " Statuimus et ordinamus ut nullus ordinarius pecunias pro visitatione accipiat nisi actu visitet, quod si contrarium fecerit, puniatur, juxta arbitrium Metropolitani.

21. " Statuimus et ordinamus ut omnes sacerdotes juvenes qui a sexennio ordinati sunt, studia prosequi cogantur etiam privatione

governed the Church of Armagh for three years, having been constituted by the Holy Father Vicar Apostolic of that see.

This synod was opened with all solemnity; first, the Litanies of the Saints were chanted; then an exhortation was addressed to the assembled prelates, and with the hymn of the Holy Ghost, *Veni Creator Spiritus*, they invoked the Father of heavenly counsels to guide them in their deliberations. Afterwards was renewed the protest of the former council, that their only object in thus assembling was " to promote the glory of God, and procure the advancement of the Catholic faith, the salvation of souls, the tranquillity of the kingdom, rendering to Cæsar the things which are of Cæsar, and to God the things which are of God."

beneficiorum ; qui si Parochias habeant concedimus eis licentiam substituendi alios sacerdotes ab ordinario approbatos, et ad quinquennium emolumentum quod cum substituto paciscantur annue accipiendi ; qui nullas vero parochias habent ab aliis Parochis adjuventur.

22. " Recipimus et admittimus SS. Concilium Tridentinum im omnibus Diœcesibus sicut hactenus receptum est.

23. " Statuimus et ordinamus ut nullus fiat de novo sacerdos, nisi attestetur ordinarius se habere necessitatem claudi illi demissoriales et illum habere ad curam animarum sufficientem doctrinam.

24. " Ut quicumque sacerdos assistet matrimonio sine tribus præviis denuntiationibus suspendatur et mulctetur ad arbitrium ordinarii et ipse ordinarius dispensans sine causa mulctetur ad arbitrium Metropolitani.

25. " Statuimus et ordinamus ut quarta pars funeralium cedat ordinario sicuti in concilio Provinciali sub Illustrissimo Primate Edmundo O'Reilly numero 8 statutum est : quoad legata vero pia, cedant ei cui determinate legata sunt, salvo jure Parochorum et ordinarii quoad quartem partem parochialem et episcopalem juxta mentem concilii Tridentini sess. 25 de Reform cap. 13.

26. " Statuimus et ordinamus ut omnes Parochi ante finem duorum mensium habeant exemplar horum actuum et aliorum actuum conciliorum Provincialium, eosque quolibet mense legant et in synodis Diœcesanis publice perlegantur. ac insuper inter Missarum solemnia, statuta populum concernentia publicentur.

27. " Statuimus et ordinamus ut quilibet Parochus in quacunque diœcesi totius Provinciæ det Metropolitano pro una vice tantum quinque solidos monetæ Anglicanæ.

28. " Tandem accipimus omnia statuta acta Dublinii diebus 17, 18, et 20 Junii, 1670, ab Archiepiscopis et Episcopis Hiberniæ simul congregatis quorum primum est.

[Here follow the decrees of the Synod of Dublin, given above in Chap X. page 132.]

It was then decreed by the assembled prelates:—

1. That the clergy should warn the faithful against aiding or countenancing the bodies of lawless bandits, who were called *Tories*, and who, under the pretence of defending the national rights, then infested the country; and that they (the clergy), should likewise make known to their flocks what dishonour the deeds of these wicked men brought upon their religion and country.

2. That the doctrine which declared that the appointments of the Holy See to particular dioceses, required for their validity the acceptance of the clergy and laity of these dioceses, was erroneous, and that the oaths taken not to acknowledge any who would not be thus accepted were damnable and not binding before God.

3. That, whilst they lament the ignorance of some who would fain affirm that the *postulation* of the clergy or laity, or of both, or the *presentation* of the lay nobility, is binding on the Holy Father when appointing bishops to the vacant sees, they at the same time declare "such practice and doctrine to be schismatical and contrary to the canons," and decree that "such as, in consequence of similar presentations or postulations, impede the appointments made by the Holy See, are subjected to censures reserved to the Supreme Pontiff."

4. The fourth decree condemns "as perverse and erroneous, the ravings of those who affirm that it belongs to the people to choose their own pastors, and to fix for them, independently of the Ordinary, the stipend to be given to them.

5. That teaching is declared erroneous and contrary to the Scripture, which would affirm that no stipend is due by the faithful to their lawful pastors.

6. The doctrine is likewise condemned which declared it lawful to take the goods of Protestants, or of any others whosoever, the owners not being cognizant or willing; and, it is added, that such persons acting unlawfully are obliged to restitution.

7. The clergy are prohibited to admit those pupils who

are called *Dallas;* and the violators of this decree incurred the penalty of deprivation of benefice or office.

8. It was prohibited to priests to drink whiskey in any public house or public assembly, and any one guilty of this crime should be subjected to a fine of ten *solidi,** to be given to the Vicars-General and Vicars-Forane of the diocese.

9. No priest should frequent the public markets without the permission of the Ordinary, and the transgressors of this law were also subjected to a fine of ten *solidi.*

10. It was enacted that every month, with the exception of the three winter months, conferences should be held in each of the districts of the Vicars-Forane, and any priest who absented himself from these conferences incurred a penalty of five *solidi.*

11. That those who publicly defame their superiors should not be admitted to the sacraments, till they either establish their charges before the proper tribunals, or give satisfaction to the injured party.

12. None of the laity should receive the aspersory, but only be sprinkled with holy water, according to the rite of the Church.

13. Neither the Ordinary nor the Metropolitan has power to dispense in the irregularity arising from the public violation of censures, and any such dispensations hitherto accorded are declared to have been invalid.

14. Every priest who refuses due obedience to his ecclesiastical superior incurs suspension from his benefice or office for three months, and if after three months he should continue contumacious, he is declared *ipso facto* incapable of any ecclesiastical benefice in that province.

15. Penalties are then enacted against any of the clergy who should attempt to offer the Holy Sacrifice, without having observed strict fast from the preceding midnight.

16. Each parish priest was commanded to have within three years, at least, one silver chalice of the value of fifty

---

* The *solidus* was equal to one shilling.

solidi, with decent vestments, all which should be left to the parish on the demise or departure of the parish priest.

17. The seventeenth decree regards clergymen dying intestate, and each diocese is directed to adopt the regulation of the Metropolitan Church in regard of the disposal of their property.

18. It is decreed that the four *testilia*, which were due to the parochial clergy four times in the year, were part of the stipend due by the faithful to their pastors.

19. The rights and customs of the archdeacons when conferring benefices should remain unaltered.

20. It was declared that Dr. Patrick Tyrrell, Bishop of Clogher, having received a full and legitimate appointment to the administration of Kilmore, all Catholics, whether clergy or laity, were obliged to show every reverence and obedience to him, and all who should contumaciously persist in opposing him, were subjected to ecclesiastical censures reserved to his Holiness.

21. Those who should contract marriage within the prohibited degrees, without having received a dispensation, were to be excluded from the Holy Sacrifice and the sacrament of the altar.

22. When controversies arose between different dioceses, or between adjoining parishes of the same diocese, as to their respective limits, the *Ancient Register* should be followed.

23. The decree of the Council of Trent regarding clandestine marriages is enacted ; that is, all marriages are declared null when celebrated without the presence of the parish priest, and of at least two witnesses.

24. The most illustrious Primate was requested to form part of a commission, for which the Bishop of Clogher and the Rev. Bernard Magork, Dean and Vicar-General of Armagh, as well as Dr. Edward Dromgole, were especially deputed, and which should propose to the various religious orders some regulations to be observed. These regulations especially regarded the manner of questing for alms, and they, moreover, commanded that no religious should

celebrate the Holy Sacrifice, except once each day, or exercise parochial duties without a written approbation from the ordinary. No member, too, of a religious order should be permitted to seek for alms in any parish, unless some member of the same order administered spiritual assistance there by preaching and catechising the people, when requested to do so by the parish priest.

25. The Primate was requested to undertake a general visitation of the whole province.

26. In fine, it was decreed that all the clergy, whether present or absent, should unceasingly offer up their prayers to the Divine Majesty for the safety of the most serene King Charles II., of the Queen and Royal Family, and especially of the then Viceroy; for the tranquillity of the nation, and for peace amongst Christian princes, and that they should command their flocks to offer similar prayers; and all these decrees are declared to be directed to the greater glory of God, of the Blessed Virgin, and of St. Patrick (the patron of Ireland), and St. Augustine, on whose feast, and under whose invocation, this holy synod was concluded.*

* We add here in full the original decrees enacted in the Provincial Council of Ardpatrick, as sent by Dr. Plunket to the Internuncio in Brussels.

In Nomine Dni. Amen.

Acta, Statuta, et Decreta facta et ordinata in conc. provinciali in loco de Ardpatrickprope Louth in Diœc. Armachana die 28 mensis Augusti, 1678, præsidente Illmo. et Rmo. D.D., Oliverio Armachano Metropolitano ac totius Hiberniæ Primate, præsentibus Illmis et Revmis D.D., *Patritio Midensi,*et *Patritio Clogheren.* administratore Kilmoren. Rev. admodum, D.D. *Jacobo Cusaco,* S.T.D., procuratore Vic. Aplici Ardaghaden; *Patritio óMulderig.* Vic. Connoren; *Edwardo Drumgole,* S.T.D., procuratore Vic. Glis Clonmacnoisen; *Luca Plunket,* Abbate S. Thomæ Vic. Gn. Derren. et procuratore Rapoten; *Patritio Bruin,* Vic. Gn. Dunen. procre Vic. Glis. Dromoren; *Henrico Hugonio,* S.T.D., procre Capituli Armachani; *Christophoro Plunketo archidiac.* Clogheren.; *Bernardo Magork* Decano Armachano; *Patritio Plunketo, Vic. Louthen.* Post litanias omnium SS., concionem, ac invocationem Spiritus Scti., lecto hymno Veni Creator Spiritus, declarandum esse duximus, sicut per præsentes declaramus, nos in hacce nra. Cngne nihil meditari aut intendere, quam Dei omnipotentis groriam, Cath. Religionis exaltationem, reddentes ea, quæ sunt Cæsaris, Cæsari, et quæ sunt Dei, Deo.

1. Statuimus ergo et in ordinamus, ut omnes Parochi et curam

When transmitting the decrees of Ardpatrick to the
Internunzio in Brussels, Dr. Plunket requested him to forward them to Rome, promising an explanation of some of
them in a future letter. On the 10th of September he
consequently addressed a letter to the Internunzio, and the
explanations which he presents, though few in number,
serve, nevertheless, to illustrate many customs of the Irish
Church in the seventeenth century. In the first place, he

animarum habentes prædicent contra latrones, vulgo *Tories*, et contra
fautores eorum ac receptores, et exponant, in quanto periculo animarum
suarum, et corporum versantur, et quam nigram notam inurant et
Religioni, ac Nationi, ac quantum jacturam patriotis suis inferant
impediendo commercium, ac ipsos reddendo obnoxios multis aliis
gravaminibus.

2. Decernimus contra spargentes illam doctrinam, quod provisiones
Eccliarum factæ a summo Pontifice dependeant ab acceptatione cleri,
et populi, et juramentum præstitum ab Ecclesiasticis et laicis de non
acceptandis superioribus absq. mutuo consensu esse damnabilem, ac
perinde doctrinam illam damnamus velut erroneam, et declaramus
unumquemq. obligari ad revocationem talis juramenti, et ad illud non
servandum.

3. Cum proh dolor, tam crassa sit ignorantia aliquorum ut existiment
postulationem aut cleri aut populi, aut utriusq. aut præsentationem
nobilium sæcularium ligare manus summo Pontifici, declaramus
hujusmodi praxim et doctrinam esse schismaticam, et contra canones.
Declaramus insuper impedientes vi istarum postulationum, aut præsen-
tationum, executionem provisionum a summo Pontifice factarum, aut
fiendarum incurrere censuras ipsi summo Pontifici reservatas.

4. Damnamus tanquam doctrinam perversam ac erroneam quorumdam
deliria, qui dicunt penes populum esse, assumere sibi, quos volunt,
pastores, et taxare quantum stipendii sit ipsis debitum, invitis ordinariis.

5. Damnamus doctrinam illorum qui dicunt, aut prædicant non deberi
stipendium exercentibus curam animarum, tanquam erroneam et contra-
riam S. Scripturæ.

6. Damnamus doctrinam illorum qui tenent aut docent licere accipere
bona protestantium, aut aliorum quorumcunq. ipsis insciis et invitis, velut
erroneam, et nullatenus excusantem a restitutione.

7. Decernimus, ut nullus Sacerdos adoptet, aut acceptet alumnos,
vulgo *Dallas*, directe vel indirecte, per se vel per alium, et qui hoc
decretum transgressus fuerit, careat beneficio et officio ad arbitrium
ordinarii.

8. Decernimus et statuimus, ut nullus Sacerdos bibat aquam stillatam
in ulla popina, aut congressu publico sub pœna decem solidor. applican-
dorum Vic. generalibus et Foraneis.

9. Decernimus, ut nullus Sacerdos profiscatur ad nundinas, vel fora
absq. licentia ordinarii in scriptis, et qui hoc decretum violaverit, solvat
decem solidos Vic. suo Foraneo.

10. Decernimus et statuimus, ut quolibet mense exceptis tribus
mensibus hyemalibus, fiant conferentiæ casuum conscientiæ in districtibus

explains who were the *dallas* spoken of in the seventh
decree :—

"Some wicked priests [he says] becoming *nutritors* (fosterers)
took to their care the children of Protestants, that thus they themselves might be defended against their ecclesiastical superiors : these
children were called *dallas.*"

He then presents the true meaning of the 16th and 17th
decrees. These, at first sight, would seem to imply that

singulor. vicariorum Foraneor, et qui aberit, solvat quinque solidos
præsentibus.

11. Decernimus, et statuimus, ut qui suos superiores diffamant,
tamdiu arceantur ab administratione sacramentor., donec probaverint
crimen superiori imputatum coram Judice competente, aut satisfaciant
parti læsæ.

12. Decernimus, ac statuimus, ut nullus sacerdos sive sæcularis, sive
reglis. ulli sæculari porrigat aspersorium, sed aqua tantum aspergatur
juxta-ritum Ecclesiæ.

13. Declaramus nec metropolitanum, nec ordinarium dispensare posse
in irregularitate proveniente ex publica violatione censurarum, et
dispensationes hactenus super his concessas invalidas fuisse.

14. "Decernimus et statuimus, ut quicumq. Sacerdos, cujuscumq.
gradus aut auctoritatis, fuerit inobediens suo superiori, privetur per tres
menses officio et beneficio, et si post tres menses non resipuerit, sit ipso
facto incapax beneficii in illa provincia.

15. "Decernimus et statuimus, ut Sacerdotes compotantes a media
nocte, et postea mane celebrantes pro prima vice arceantur a celebratione
missæ, et ab administratione sacramentor. per mensem, pro secunda vice
per bimestre, si tertia vice per annum.

16. "Decernimus et statuimus, ut singuli parochi habeant intra
triennium calicem argenteum valoris 50 ad minus solidorum cum
paramentis decentibus, quæ teneantur relinquere parochiæ, quandocumq.
ex parochia discedant.

17. "Decernimus et statuimus quantum ad spolia Sacerdotum curam
animar. habentium, ut unaquæq. diœcesis observet consuetudinem eccliæ.
Metropolitanæ.

18. "Declaramus quatuor testilia, quæ debentur Sacerdotibus curatis
quater in anno esse partem stipendii pastoribus debiti.

19. "Decernimus ut illæsa permaneant jura et consuetudines
Archidiaconorum quoad possessues dandas illis, quibus conferuntur
beneficia.

20. "Cum nobis constat Illmum. ac Rmum. D. Patritium Clogheren,
plenum ac legitimum habere jus ad administrandam Diœcesin Kilmoren.
declaramus omnes Ecclicos. et sæculares Catholicus ipsi omnem
obedieutiam ac reverentiam præstare debere tanquam suo superiori, et
omnes ei contumaciter contradicentes incurrere censuras reservatas suæ
Sanctitati.

21. "Decernimus, ut qui nubunt in gradibus prohibitis sine dispensa-
tione arceantur a missa et sacris.

22. "Decernimus et statuimus, ut quando est controversia inter

the Irish churches were not at this time provided with proper vestments and sacred vessels. However, we learn from Dr. Plunket that such a conclusion would be wholly erroneous :—

" As to the 16th and 17th decrees : it is true that all the pastors, with few exceptions, have chalices of silver and decent vestments; but that the terms might be general, and that the few exceptional priests might repair their neglect, and that when the priest leave the parish or die, these things might not be lost, but left to the parishes in which they lived, the above decrees were made."

In the 18th the word *testile* is used to designate the coin, four of which were given four times each year to the

diversas diœceses de limitibus, et inter parochias intra eamd. diœcesin, procedatur secundum antiquum Registrum.

23. "Declaramus, quod nullum matrimonium in posterum contrahendum inter Ecclesiæ Romanæ Catholicos sit validum absque præsentia parochi, et duorum testium.

24. "Rogamus Illmum. et Rmum. Nostrum Metropolitanum, et deputamus Illmum. ac Rmum. Patricium Clogheren. ac Rdos. admodum Dnos. Bernardum Magork Decanum, ac Vic. Gen. Armachanum, Edvardum Drumgole, S.T.D., vel eorum tres aliquos, ut tractent cum superioribus Regularium in Provincia Armachana, ut faciant sequentia puncta obervari a suis, nisi vel leges, vel privilegia ostenderint in contrarium : quod si non ostenderint, statuimus, et ordinamus, ut singuli Ordinarii in suis respective diœcesibus illa faciant promulgari et observari tanquam statuta diœcesana.

I. "Ut non admittantur ac mendicandum Regulares Conventuum, in quibus non est competens numerus fratrum juxta ipsor. constitutiones ad observandam regularem disciplinam.

II. "Ut Regulares, per se et non per procuratores sæculares mendicent.

III. "Ut Regulares in villis privatis non erigant altari ad convocandum populum illius villæ ad mendicandum.

IV. "Cum varii Regulares diversis conventibus assignati a suis Superiorib. vivant toto fere anno domibus sæcularium, cogantur a suis Superioribus vivere convertibus sub regulari observantia.

V. "Ut non binent sacra sine licentia Ordinarii in scriptis.

VI. "Ut non prædicent, instruant, aut catechizent populum sine approbatione Ordinarii in scriptis.

VII. "Ut nullus Regularis admittatur ad mendicandum in parochia, nisi aliquis illius Ordinis prædicet aut catechizet in ead. parochia, si requiratur a parocho.

25. "Ob necessarios ac graves momenti rationes rogamus Illmum. ac Rmum. D. Nrum. Metropolitanum, ut visitet singulas diœceses totius provinciæ quamprimum ac convenienter fieri poterit.

26. "Demum statuimus, ut omnes tam hic præsentes, quam absentes Sacerdotes incessantib. precibus divinam majestatem orent pro incolumitate Serenissimi Regis. Nri. Caroli II., Reginæ nræ., ac Regiæ familiæ,

parochial clergy ; and Dr. Plunket explains this term as follows :—

"Each 'testile' is equal to about *four bajocchi,** 2½d.*, which each family gives four times in the year to the pastors ; and as some doubted whether this formed part of the parochial stipend, the decree declared that they were a part of the said stipend."

His next remark is of great importance as serving to place in its true light the history of the promulgation in Ireland of the Tridentine decree regarding clandestine marriages :—

"As to the 23rd decree [he writes], the Council of Trent was received here at the time of Rinuccini, and also in this Province at the time of Elizabeth, but whereas doubts were raised in some parts whether this promulgation regarded the decree on matrimony, and as, moreover, we do not here dare to speak openly of the Council of Trent, it being contrary to the laws, we enacted the decree in an equivalent manner; we do not here dare to excommunicate or announce censures in express and formal words, but in equivalent terms, for otherwise we should incur præmunire."

It may not be uninteresting to the reader if we here commemorate some facts connected with the promulgation of the Council of Trent in the Irish Church. Dr. Plunket refers its publication in the province of Armagh to the reign of Queen Elizabeth ; and we learn from the "Appendix Consultationis Provincialis" of Armagh (held in 1614), that some of the Irish bishops, that is,

ac præsentis Proregis, pro tranquillitate patriæ, ac pace inter Xnos principes, idque commendent orationibus suorum respective gregum ; atque hæc ad majorem Dei, Deiparæ, ac sanctorum Patritii nri. Patroni ac Augustini.

The following words are added in Italian : —
"Questi sono li atti del Conc. Provinle. ultimamente celebrato. Farà grazia di mandarli a Mr. Cerri e di tener una copia appresso di se. Con una altra lettera ne do più esatto ragguaglio.
"Di V. S. Illma.
"Dmo. Serv.
"Thomas Cox."
(Oliver Plunket.)
A Mr. Internunzio in Brussels.

* The *bajocco* is an Italian coin a little more than a *halfpenny*, ten of them, according to the exchange of those days, being equal to sixpence.

" Redmundus Derriensis, Donaldus Rapotensis, Cornelius
Dunen. et Conorensis, Edmundus Ardaghadensis, Ricardus
Kilmorensis,Cornelius Clogherensis,et Eugenius Aghadensis,"
assembled in the Diocese of Clogher, before the year 1589,*
and addressed an order to the clergy that the Council of
Trent should be received by all, and they especially insisted
on the reception in each parish of the decree *de reformatione matrimonii*. In many of the parishes, however, the
subsequent promulgation of the decree regarding matrimony
is extremely doubtful ; and it is certain that in some parishes
it never was promulgated. Even in many of the districts
in which it was received, the irruptions of the invaders, and
the frequent devastation of the country, and the influx of
foreign settlers, soon obliterated every vestige of its publication ; and hence we find, early in the seventeenth century,
some of the Irish clergy petitioning the Holy See to declare
to them what course they should pursue. We have not
been able to discover what answer was given by Rome ; †
but Dr. Plunket informs us, that, at the time of Rinuccini,
the solemn promulgation of the decrees of Trent was
proposed for the whole island. The manifold afflictions,
however, which desolated the Irish Church, and in particular the province of Ulster, during the devastations of
Cromwell, occasioned in some districts an inobservance,
especially of the decree regarding clandestine marriages,
which fully justified the Synod of Ardpatrick in enacting
its 23rd decree.

The concluding portion of Dr. Plunket's letter has already
been presented to the reader in the eighth chapter. He

* One of the above-mentioned bishops, Donald or Donagh M'Congal,
Bishop of Raphoe, died in 1589, as we learn from the Four Masters.
Another of the bishops, Cornelius O'Dubhana, of Down and Connor, was
not appointed bishop before 1532.

† A paper presented to Propaganda by Dr. Edmund Dwyer (as agent
of the Irish clergy), in 1636, in the name of the Archbishop of Armagh,
complains of some religious who presumed to exercise their faculties
without the permission of the ordinary, and adds : — " *Advertendum est
receptum et publicatum in Provincia Ardmachana, observarique ad unguem*
(decretum Trid.)."

dwells on the necessity of restricting the number of the religious houses, and declares that his dwelling so continually on this subject proceeded solely from his zeal to promote the glory of God, and his desire to see all the clergy of his province, whether regular or secular, holy, good, and perfect; in fine, he prays the Holy See to appoint Dr. Tyrrell (Bishop of Clogher) Apostolic Visitor of the Franciscan Order in Ireland, and declares that great good would redound from such a measure in the maintenance of the Catholic faith in its integrity and purity.

APPENDIX.

Letter of the Bishop of Ferns on the promulgation of the Council of Trent in Ireland.

As the following letter is connected with the matter treated of in the preceding chapter, we judge it opportune to present it to the reader in its original form. It was, however, written without preparation, as the illustrious Prelate himself informs us; and this sufficiently accounts for some historical inaccuracies which are to be met with in it :—

" ILLME. ET REVME. DNE.

" Binis gravibusque postulationibus Gratiac Vrae, an in Hybernia vigeat observantia Constitutionum S. Concilii Tridentini, et an Hyberni agnoscant easdem Constitutiones, tanquam obligatorias, apposite respondere, agnosco negotium esse supra vires ingenii mei; quod imperium vestrum ad me perlatum fuit tantum heri vesperi ad medium decimae. Nilominus ad ambas quaestiones sic repono cum humilitate; Constitutionum S. Tridentini Concilii ad fidem ac Religionem spectantium, quales esse censeo de peccato originali, justificatione, canone ac usu librorum divinorum, de institutione, excellentia, usu, effectu et essentialibus sacramentorum in genere, et de quovis in particulari, de Sacrificio Missae etc., viget observantia in Hybernia sicut in aliis provinciis Catholicis et constanter viguit. Hoc unum circa Sacramentum Matrimcnii advertendum quod etsi celebretur apud nos coram Parochó et testibus quemadmodum S. Concilium Tridentinum ordinavit; tamen etiam num validum est ac ratum Matrimonium clandestinum si non subsint impedimenta dirimentia ; puniuntur tamen sic Matrimonium contrahentes; etiam publicantur denunciationes ante Matrimonium ut in his regionibus, et Parochi eas omittentes severe plectuntur.

" Reformationibus interim S. Tridentini Concilii et Constitu-

tionibus circa mores ac disciplinam non idem habetur honor ut in
aliis Catholicis Regnis; earum non viget observantia in Hybernia;
loquor de decretis e.g. circa seminaria, hospitalia reparationem
Ecclesiarum, beneficiorum dispositionem, Clericorum tam saecula-
rium quam regularium correctionem, brachii saecularis invocationem
etc. Ex hoc responso ad quaestionem primam, sequitur secundum.

" Nimirum Hybernos non agnoscere tanquam obligatorias constitutiones morum et disciplinae passim in sessionibus de Reformatione
contentas; ratio est quia sunt observatu difficiles et moraliter
impossibiles; unde non possunt nos obligare: non dico hoc prove-
nire e defectu promulgationis; scimus enim legem Pontificiam in
curia Romana publicatam, obligandi vim habere in toto orbe
terrarum, quatenus est ex sua parte, sed nos non obligant quia non
erant ab Hybernis receptae et approbatae; nec vere poterant esse
loco et tempori et nationi convenientes, praedominante et atrociter
furente in regno illo haeresi, quae Angliam totam, et Hyberniam
pro magnâ parte inquinavit : gladium gessit, et etiamnunc gerit.
magistratus haereticus: ideo parum poterant ordinarii in materia
correctionis : non habuerunt Episcopi carceres, non poterant requi-
rere brachium saeculare, gladium magistratus haeretici qui spernit
anathemata et excommunicationes Ecclesiae Catholicae; et si forte
ordinarii attentaverint interdicere, suspendere a divinis, aut excom-
municare subditos suos, imminebat illis periculum carcerum atque
exilii ; aliquando capite plexi sunt propter exercitium jurisdictionis
Catholicae quam haeretici vocant potestatem foraneam seu papalem.
Ob hoc factum, ut nulla Congregatio Ecclesiastica Nationalis *in
quantum scire potui* in unum coetum coaluerit ad recipiendum S. Trid.
Concilium. Hoc enim erat capitale crimen et perduellio. Poterat
fateor tempore belli Catholici recipi S. Trid. Concilium sed hactenus
in nulla Ecclesiastica Congregatione, cui interfui, fuit propositum :
quidam dicunt a multis annis fuisse receptum in quodam Concilio
provinciali Provinciae Ardmachanae, quod non credo; super hoc
poterit Illmus. D. Armachanus Primas totius Hyberniae consuli et
interrogari. Malui quaestionibus propositis hoc responsum raptim
elaboratum praebere, quam mandato vestro non parere. Hac
occasione utor subscribendi me hoc 2° Junii, Gandavi, 1671.
" Illmae. D. Vrae addictmum. et humum. famulum,

" NICOLAUM FERNENSEM.

" Illmac. Dno. Internuntio Aplico." *

---

* Dr. French was mistaken in regard to the promulgation of the decree
of the Council of Trent on clandestine marriages in Armagh. It does
not, however, appear that this decree was published in Dublin until the
year 1827, when it was solemnly promulgated in all the parishes on the
the 2nd December. (See *Carrriere De Matr.*, vol. ii., page 406, on the
promulgation of the decree of the Council of Trent.)

CHAPTER XIII.

THE labours of Dr. Plunket were not confined to his own immediate diocese. According to the canonical legislation of those times, it was a privilege formerly attached to the dignity of archbishop and primate, that he who enjoyed it might perform a visitation in the dioceses subject to his primacy ; and Dr. Plunket, partly resting on this privilege, partly through a special commission received from the Holy See, and often, too, at the request of the local diocesan authorities, more than once undertook a visitation of the dioceses of the province of Ulster. Indeed, this seems to have been one of the earliest cares of our Primate ; and in his letter of the 16th of April, 1671, he speaks of the visitation which he had already made of six of his suffragan dioceses ; in which visitation, as he in the same place informs us, he had principally directed his efforts to the rooting out of the cursed vice of drunkenness. The items of his *Relatio*, or report, regarding the united dioceses of Down and Connor, are the only record of this visitation which we have been able to discover amongst the letters of Dr. Plunket. This Relation is dated the 1st November, 1670, and is directed to Monsignor Baldeschi, Secretary of the Sacred Congregation of Propaganda :—

" *Relation concerning the canonically united dioceses of Down and Connor.*

" These united dioceses are about 50 miles in length and 15 in breadth : they are rather mountainous than level, and abound in milk, oats, and barley. Great peace is enjoyed there.

" There are about two thousand five hundred Catholic families. The Marquis of Antrim, a good Catholic, is very powerful and very zealous ; there is no other Catholic that has property there. Thanks to God, the Catholics enjoy great toleration.

" There is no bishop, but a Vicar-General, by name Patrick O'Mulderig, an old man, 60 years of age, a good and practical priest.

M

though not distinguished for literature ; he lives with his brother in a private house, and has converted many to the faith.

"The cathedral churches of Down and Connor are now roofless, but [that of Down is very celebrated as being the burial-place of Saint Patrick, Columba, and Bridget, according to the old distich—

'*Ili tres in Duno, tumulo tumulantur in uno*
Brigida Patritius atque Columba pius.' *

In Down, also, was born the celebrated Doctor Scotus.

"In the diocese of Down there is a convent of Dominicans, but the friars live at lodgings. There are five Dominicans, but only one is of great fame. viz., Clement O'Byrne, who is a good preacher, and produces much fruit.

"There is also a convent of Franciscans, who are twelve in number, and amongst them Paul O'Bryn, Paul O'Neill, and James O'Iliny are [the most distinguished in point of preaching and producing fruit.

"In the convent of Carrickfergus, in the diocese of Connor, there are ten Franciscans, of whom only five are priests ; amongst these Hugh O'Dornan and Daniel O'Mellon are distinguished in preaching. There is also a certain Paul O'Haran, who is well versed in literature.

"The Dominicans have a convent in Culrahan, in which there are only four friars, and of these only two are priests, one of whom, James Crolly, is a good preacher.

"The parish priests are supported by a stipend which the Catholics give them—namely, every family, in addition to the uncertain sums, contributes *four Julii* (2s.) every year. At baptism *two Julii* (1s.) are given, at marriage *four*, and at extreme unction *two*, and also at every burial each family, according to its own pleasure, give some alms.

"There are many boys well suited for study, but there is a great want of Catholic schools, as the Protestants do not allow Catholic masters. There is, nevertheless, a certain William Flaherty, a priest, a good rhetorician, who keeps a school in Down.

"There are no nuns, excepting four of the Franciscan order.

"At the time of Cromwell there was a violent persecution, and whosoever brought in the head of a priest received 20 scudi (£5) ; but under the present king there is great toleration and sufficient connivance."

It seems to have been during this first visitation that the Primate appointed a Vicar-General to administer the diocese of Raphoe, and also delivered to Eugene Conwell a Brief from the Holy See, constituting him Vicar-Apostolic of

---

* In Down three saints are buried in one grave —Patrick, Bridget, and Columkill.

Derry. The latter wrote as follows to the Secretary of Propaganda on the 1st of November, 1671 :—

" A few years since, having completed my studies in Brabant, and read the course of philosophy and theology, his Eminence, Cardinal Rospigliosi, then Internunzio in Brussels, sent me to this kingdom, granting me the privilege of Missionery Apostolic ; and I, obeying his commands, laboured in this vineyard, instructing and preaching, not impelled indeed by any desire of promotion or impulse of ambition. Yet it pleased our most illustrious Primate to appoint me to the government of this diocese, about the end of August last year, after he had deprived of the use of all jurisdiction, Terence Kelly, the Vicar Apostolic, on account of his grievous crimes : the Provincal Council, assembled in Clones, sanctioned his deposition, and Terence Kelly himself previously consented to whatever judgment the Provincial Synod should decree : than which step, indeed nothing more useful ever happened to this province, as the deposition of this Terence struck terror into all those who imitated his depraved example. I confess that I laboured much in this diocese, with the sole hope of an eternal reward ; but see how, even in this world, the few labours which I sustained are rewarded beyond their merit by the Brief of the Holy Father. And not only the Brief, but also the letters of Cardinal Anthony (Barberini), signed also by your Excellency, were handed to me by our primate, who indeed undertook a long and difficult journey to this northern district of this country, to be himself the bearer of this Brief and Letters, and the whole Clergy of the diocese being assembled, he read the Apostolic Brief and Letters together. But the Archdeacon of Derry, with all his might, protested against this Brief, affirming that it was null on account of Terence Kelly being yet alive at the time of its being expedited, and, as he was Vicar-Apostolic, he could not be deposed either by Metropolitan or Synod. Then, too, as the formula *tametsi de Vicareo Generali seu Capitulari fuerit provisum* was inserted in the Brief, he argued that it was surreptitious, on account of the additional words *seu de Apostolico* not having been added. And, in fine, he contended that the Brief was given under a false impression, as I was not a native of that diocese, but a stranger, I could not govern it : for they thus style me a stranger, though I am an Irishman and a native of the adjoining diocese. But the most Illustrious Primate replied that every Vicar was movable at the will of him who appointed him : and and as Terence Kelly was Vicar-Apostolic according to the pleasure of the Holy See, so did his authority cease by the very fact of a new appointment being made. He then also clearly established that a Vicar-General should rather be a stranger than a native ; and all peaceably agreed to his decision. Before the promulgation of this Brief in Synod, the Primate performed a work most useful to this Diocese, suspending Patrick Colgan, who was guilty of much wickedness and crimes. He nowhere spares any priest who is habitually bad, and thus he has acquired great fame amongst both Catholics and heretics : nor can it be said or imagined how great a benefit this province has received from his continual labours—the erection of schools—the correction of the clergy, whom he instructs both by word and example—his many journeys—and the decision of so many controversies, so that all this province enjoys peace and tranquillity. May I also mention that he is so esteemed by the Protestants, that even the Protestant nobility vie with each other in receiving him as their guest, and enjoying his society; whence it happens that for his sake they do not molest our clergy. The Lord Primate had also a conference with the Protestant Bishop of Derry,* who is eminent amongst his own for learning : they discussed several points of controversy, and the Primate so solved his doubts, that this Protestant bishop afterwards declared that he had never received such satisfaction from any one; nor did he afterwards cease to extol him, and in my own hearing he declared that as *he was first in dignity, so too was he first in learning amongst the Papists.* I, as far as in my power, will work and labour to walk in his footsteps, and I will strive to fulfil the duty imposed upon me. In the meantime I return to your Eminence all the thanks in my power, for whose safety and welfare all Ireland is bound to pray to the Most High, and above all others.

" Your most humble and devoted servant,

" EUGENE CONWELL,

" Vic. Ap. of Derry.

" Derry, 1st November, 1671."

The letter of the Vicar-General of Raphoe, bearing the same date, is not less important, and sets forth in detail many interesting particulars regarding that ancient diocese :

" For nineteen years I cultivated in France and Italy the studies of speculative and moral divinity, as also those appertaining to ecclesiastical Jurisprudence ; and whilst I was in Rome, Alexander VII., of happy memory, granted to me, *in commendam*, the Abbey of St. Thomas, in Dublin. Six years since, I received the care of souls in the diocese of Meath, but I was not long allowed to remain in that diocese. For our most Illustrious Primate called me to his diocese, and conferred on me the Priory of Rath, which had annexed to it the care of souls. How I would have wished that the Primate had allowed me thus to live in private, and attached to the service of one particular church, and not place me on the eminence of an entire diocese. I was obliged to obey his Grace and accept the Vicar-Generalship of the diocese of Raphoe ; and in order that I might obtain peaceable possession, the Primate himself accompanied me through these rugged paths, truly like to those of the Alps or Apennines. Here the harvest is great, and these

---

* Dr. Roger Boyle who in the following year (1672) was transferred to Clogher.

districts, though otherwise abounding in sterile mountains, yet are ripe for the sickle, but the labourers are few, and even these are but little acquainted with the art of arts—that is, the guidance of souls. There are about fourteen priests, of whom one alone passed the boundaries of this country ; and he, though he completed his studies at Louvain, is not altogether of a sound mind. His·name is Lewis Gallagher. The others learned superficially grammar and poetry—and, after the manner of the country, some cases of conscience. The diocese itself is, for the most part, sterile, and produces only barley and oats, and its riches consist in oxen, horses, and swine. The whole diocese does not annually yield more than £15 of English money—that is, sixty scudi Italian. But the Primate promises me a better support, and has already given me in advance 20 scudi. Impelled solely by spiritual motives have I embraced this province in a region so sterile, rough, and rugged. I confess, too, that the exhortations of the most illustrious Primate, confirmed by his own example, moved me very much : for often has he confirmed the children in these mountains and woods, and often, too, has he had no other food than oaten bread, salt butter, and stirabout, and no drink but milk. We are all amazed how a man of such a delicate constitution, and so delicately (as I myself have known) reared in Rome, should be able to undergo so many labours, so many journeys, so many rugged and difficult things. Assuredly, unless he adopt another manner of living and acting, he will lose his health, and will become useless to himself and to others. Stimulated, therefore, by his example, I will reside on these mountains, that thus I may merit our Redeemer's grace, and the esteem of the Holy See and the Sacred Congregation. I will make your Excellency acquainted with whatever occurs. One thing I forgot to mention, that the Presbyterians possess the better and more fertile part of this diocese, whilst the poor Catholics hold the mountains and woods, and have no other possessions than their flocks. According to the civil nomenclature, this district is called Tyrconnell, and its chieftain was a famous prince, the Earl of Tyrconnell, of the illustrious family of O'Donnel, who, about the beginning of James the First's reign, after a long war, fled to Rome, where, if I mistake not, he died a youth of seventeen years of age. A scion of that so illustrious family yet remains, and is supported by his kinsmen and friends, all his possessions having been confiscated to the crown, and thus he is reduced to great straits. This being my first letter, I shall not any longer detain your Excellency, and I ask your blessing, &c.

On the 28th of September, 1671, Dr. Plunket despatched a long letter to the Internunzio, acknowledging the receipt of the nominations for Derry, Dromore, and Ardagh, and also of the order from the Holy See prohibiting the Irish bishops to exercise the episcopal functions in foreign kingdoms, even though they had the consent of the respective ordinaries. The most important portion of the letter is, however, that which regards the diocese of Meath and its venerable Bishop, Dr. Patrick Plunket. A complaint had been lodged against this Prelate, that he resided at a distance from his diocese, and neglected the spiritual wants of his children ; and as his actual residence in Dublin gave some colouring to this accusation, the Sacred Congregation had sent an order, to be communicated by the Primate, that he should choose some place of residence within the limits of his own diocese. The reply, however, of the Primate seems to have fully satisfied the authorities in Rome, and we find no further mention made of this matter in the subsequent letters. We give this important letter at full length :—

" The despatches consigned to Father Howard all reached me, and though they have been somewhat tossed and tattered, yet they can be read. I received the despatches for Eugene Conwell and Ronan Magin,* and their execution, I am morally certain, will have no difficulty. I have also received that for Gerald Ferrall,† but its execution will be difficult, for he is opposed by a man well versed in canon law, especially *quoad partem practitium*, who, though an old man, is lively and energetic, and having served his flock for thirty years, without ever abandoning it, even during the persecution of Cromwell, has with him the hearts of the clergy and laity ; and, to say the truth, without some risk it is difficult to compel him by censures to yield through dread of the statute *præmunire*, made in the 2nd year of Queen Elizabeth ; about which statute I shall send you a separate paper, for it is a curious thing to see how it began, and what has been its progress. The penalty of him who transgresses this statute, or recognises, *facto, verbo, vel opere*, a foreign jurisdiction, is imprisonment for one year, and the confiscation of all his movable property. Father Nugent, as I already wrote, is in prison in Wexford for violating this law, and as your Excellency well said, this fact will be of great prejudice to the Catholics : as by this example and precedent other evil-designing persons will take courage to accuse other ecclesiastics of *præmunire :* this word means *præmunire auctoritatem Regis adversus extrinsecam jurisdictionem quamcunque spiritualem aut temporalem ;* and this law was in force *in beneficialibus* even in the time of Edward the III., King of England, although he was a Catholic ; and in this they imitated the French, and in part, too, our Flemish friends. For the present I deem it

* Appointed Vicar-Apostolic of Dromore.
† Vicar Apostolic of Ardagh.

better to abstain from the execution of the brief of Ferrall, 'till I receive the decree of the Sacred Congregation, which, as your Excellency informed me in yours of the 11th of this month, will come in due time ; and when it arrives, I shall carry it out, though this should cost me my life, *doce quod jubes, et jube quod vis, faciam quod jubes.* I received also the printed order that the bishops of this kingdom should not exercise the *pontificalia* in foreign kingdoms, *etiam cum consensu ordinariorum*, and I intimated it to the Bishop of Meath : I also sent a parcel of them to the Archbishop of Dublin, and another parcel to the Archbishop of Cashel, and another to the Archbishop of Tuam, who, through the mercy of God, is now out of his trials, as Friar Martin (French) did not appear at the last sessions against him or the others, so that all are now liberated. There was a beautiful document prepared by Sir Nicholas Plunket, in favour of the Archbishop, expressing the illegality and errors of the process; and it was presented to the judges before their departure from Dublin to proceed to the sessions of Galway. I sent another parcel of them to Dr. Dowley of Limerick ; this poor man is yet in troubles, the Earl of Orrery having, a few days since, published an edict commanding all Catholics, both ecclesiastics and laity to depart from, and not live in, the said city. Some were desirous that this man, in preference to Berkeley, should be our Viceroy : a nice bargain we should have made. I do not know how our Viceroy Berkeley will take these proceedings of Orrery. Orrery is no friend of the Viceroy, and some suppose that he published these edicts on purpose; he is an astute politician ; should the Viceroy recall these edicts, then he will proclaim him a favourer of the Catholics, and indeed he already more than once announced at different meetings that Berkeley was a Catholic, that thus he might excite against him the hatred of the heretics, who are all filled with hatred against the Catholics.

" I do not deem it prudent to show the order that I received, or the letter of Cardinal Anthony to the Bishop of Meath ; he is in a tertian fever for the last twenty days, which is dangerous in an old man of seventy years of age, the more so as the information given to the Sacred Congregation is so false that nothing can be more so. There is no year that he does not consecrate the holy oils in his diocese and ordain ecclesiastics and priests, and visit his entire diocese; and there is no corner of his diocese in which he has not administered the sacrament of confirmation, so that I do not know what countenance those can have who write lies so manifest and so palpable ; and he being within a distance of five, or at most six, miles from his diocese, is in a convenient spot for hearing his subjects ; and it is certain that were there a bishopric at the ' Torre de Mezzavia,' near Frascati, or at the ' Torre Nuova,' of Princess Aldobrandini, no one would find fault with the bishop for residing, for the most part, in Rome. I saw many who wrote lies under some semblance of truth, but those who wrote such barefaced ones to so venerable a Congregation must assuredly be *perfrictæ frontis.* How many things, too, have they not written about me, which, nevertheless, were found to be false. There is one consolation, that lies are short-lived, and that their authors so lose esteem and confidence, that afterwards their testimony is not received even when they state the truth, as Aristotle well said:—*hoc unum mendaciis acquirit mendax ut veritatem dicenti fides non adhibeatur;* and, as St. Gregory writes, some deem it a great policy—*cor machinationibus tegere, mentem verbis velare, et quae vera falsa ostendere et quæ falsa sunt vera demonstrare;* and he adds : *hæc mentis duplicitas prudentia ac urbanitas appellatur;* but, nevertheless, they are deceived, and instead of being esteemed prudent, they lose the confidence of all, and are considered unworthy of enjoying human intercourse, of which lies are most destructive. I assure you there is not, in the whole kingdom of Ireland, and scarcely even on the Continent, a diocese better governed or administered than Meath. Nevertheless I shall carry out whatever you write to me, and give to the Bishop of Meath the letter to that effect, should you so command, and should the reasons which I have adduced seem insufficient; but I would not deem it advisable to communicate it to him in the present circumstances of his serious illness. I may also add, that he is old, and often subject to attacks of the gout and other infirmities, whilst, in the country parts, there are no physicians or apothecaries; and it is certain that he has lost his health and grown old in the service of the Sacred Congregation during the past twenty-four years, during seven of which he alone exercised the pontifical functions in the whole kingdom, all the other bishops having fled. Considering these things, I leave it to your Excellency to consider whether he should be obliged to a physical or mathematical residence, whilst he is morally present and resident in the diocese, and omitting no duty of a most vigilant prelate, as I can, in conscience, attest. Would to God, that those who physically reside in their dioceses would discharge their duty as the Bishop of Meath does, and has done for the past. But enough of this.

"I also received the decree against the Jesuit fathers on the point of matrimonial dispensations, and I shall intimate it to the three fathers who are in my diocese, but I must say that they behave with great prudence and submission, and never interfere in such matters.. I also received a decree of Cardinal Anthony, of happy memory, by which he approves of the deposition of Terence O'Kelly, Vicar-Apostolic of Derry. This miserable and unhappy man died during the summer. May God preserve us, *sicut vixit ita morixit,* as the people say. I received at the same time two letters from Monsignor Baldeschi, on the 27th of June, in which he replies to the six heads of my letter to his Excellency, of the 24th of April, and in it he speaks of Father Duffy; but this will require a special answer from me: the other also is dated the 27th, and in it he holds out hopes that the three Jesuit fathers who teach the young priests in my diocese shall receive the provision of missionary priests, which will enrich my province, both as to morality and learning, and God will remunerate his Excellency for this, and so many other benefits which he has conferred on this poor kingdom.

" In fine, I received a letter of his Eminence Cardinal Anthony, and I do not understand it. The Archbishop of Dublin and I read it over together; it is said in it, that the bishops who assembled in Dublin in June last year, made a decree good, indeed, and just, but as they had no jurisdiction over the exempt regulars, such a decree was informal and null. The decree, however, is not specified in the letter of his Eminence, and hence, we do not know what answer to make. I hope that in your next letter you will give us some information about that decree or statute, that we may be able to carry out the intentions of their Eminences.

" All these despatches and letters were accompanied by a most courteous one of your Excellency, of the 12th August, so full of kindness, and of such affectionate expressions, that they should excite the very travertine to activity and motion. I will not cease to work with the pen, with the tongue, and with all my slender faculties, and this for three motives :—1st. To serve the Divine Majesty. 2nd. Through gratitude, and the duty which I owe to the Apostolic See for the education and honours which I received from it. 3rd. Because God commands that I should obey and serve the Holy See, its service being inseparable from that of Christ. I cannot complain of slowness in the despatch of business in Rome, knowing, as I do, by certain and attested experience, that more resolutions have been made since Monsignor Baldeschi was appointed Secretary, and your Excellency Internuncio, than during the twelve preceding years, *quod scimus loquimur, et quod vidimus testamur.*

" If Father Duffy and Mr. Daniel Mackey have been made bishops, I will do all in my power to defend them against the attacks of their enemies, and to assist them when they come into the kingdom. Now that they are made, there is no remedy.* Aristotle expressed it well when praising the poet Agatho—*hoc unum diis negamus ut quod jactum est infectum fieri nequeat.* With great labour I examined in three dioceses, in the month of July last, the dispute between the Dominicans and Franciscans, and I ran great risk even of losing my health. Before delivering judgment, I took three consultors with me, *ut non inniterer prudentiæ meæ,* that is, the Bishop of Meath, Oliver Dease, a man of sound judgment and prudence, and Thomas Fitzsymons ; and I gave judgment in favour of the Dominicans, and I will send a copy of it to your Excellency. I left in my house near Dundalk the list or catalogue of the colleges, and of those who have charge of them, and in a few days I will send it to your Excellency, and I make you a profound reverence.

" Dublin, 28th September, 1671."

During the months of February and March of 1674, Dr. Plunket left his place of concealment in the remote parts of his diocese, and, despite the storm of persecution

* We shall see just now that Dr. Plunket wrote repeatedly against the appointment of any more bishops, for some time, in Ireland.

which then raged through the country, wished to be himself
the bearer of the *pallium* to the illustrious Archbishop of
Tuam.   During this visit the most distinguished ecclesiastics
of that province hastened to welcome him amongst them.
But he does not seem to have penetrated far into the country,
probably not beyond the city of Galway, the religion and
hospitality of whose inhabitants he especially extols.   On
the 10th of March, 1674, he sent the following narrative
of this visitation to Monsignor Baldeschi, Secretary of
Propaganda :—

" From the beginning of February to the 10th of March, I have
been travelling in the province of Tuam, to which I went in order
to give the pallium to the Archbishop of Tuam, who is a prelate
most prudent and ecclesiastical.   I spoke also with the Bishop of
Clonfert, who is a grave and prudent man, and beloved by all.   I
saw Dr. Michael Lynch, Vicar-Apostolic of Kilmacduagh, a learned
and grave man, and a famous preacher.   I had also in my company
for ten days, Maurice Durcan, the Vicar-General of Achonry, who is
a doctor in theology, and a grave man.   I enjoyed the society, too,
for fifteen days, of Dr. J. Dowley, who was Vicar-General of Tuam
for thirty-five years, during the whole time of the persecution, and
suffered very much, and as the Catholics of the diocese inform me,
sæviente persecutione he kept alive the spark of religion which
remained in the diocese, and in the whole province, and he is the
best casuist of the entire province, as I learned from the Archbishop.
The city of Galway, although small, is very beautiful, and two-thirds
of the inhabitants are Catholic ; but they are poor, having lost
all their properties.   Oh! what a devout and hospitable people.
They support no less than three communities, one of the Dominicans,
another of the Augustinians, and a third of the Franciscans.   The
Dominicans have the best and most ornamented church that is in the
entire kingdom.   All three communities live with the greatest regularity and decorum.   The city is exceedingly strong, and is a maritime
port.   It was the last place in the kingdom attacked by Cromwell,
and it resisted a long time.   The Superior, or, as they call him,
the Warden of the Secular Clergy in the city of Galway, and in nine
or ten adjoining parishes, pretends to exemption from the jurisdiction of the Archbishop, and on this head disorders frequently
arise ; but, as far as I could see, the Warden is in the wrong, and is
not exempt from the jurisdiction of the ordinary ; but regarding this
matter, I leave all to the Archbishop, as it is his business.
" The Parliament gave liberty of conscience to the Presbyterians,
Protestants, Anabaptists, &c., but would not grant it to the Catholics ;
nay more, it seeks to induce the King to retract the declaration made
in favour of the Catholics.   The King, however, is firm, and does not

wish to consent to the desires of Parliament on that head, and we hope that he may continue in this good resolution, although some are of opinion, that the want of money will oblige him to do what he would not otherwise consent to. I pray you to excuse this besmeared letter,* as the servant, when making my bed, upset the ink-bottle, and as the post leaves in two hours, and is at a distance from me, I have no time to re-write the letter. In the meantime I pray you, &c.

"10th March, 1673 (styl. vet).

"OLIVER OF ARMAGH."

The only other " Relatio " of the visitations performed by the Primate is dated 6th March, 1675. It regards the entire province of Armagh, and is as follows :—

" The first diocese is Armagh, 70 miles in length, and about 20 in width. In it there are about forty parish priests, three houses of Franciscans, and two of Dominicans, one Augustinian, and one Carmelite community, and a residence of the Capuchins. It is divided into three counties—Louth, Tyrone, and Armagh, and there are two Vicars-General, Patrick Plunket, and Phelim O'Connogan.

" 2. The diocese of Meath, which is the first suffragan diocese, is 60 miles in length, and 30 in width ; it has seventy parish priests ; two houses of Dominicans ; two of Franciscans ; one of Augustinians ; one of Discalced Carmelites ; and two residences of the Capuchins. The bishop is Dr. Patrick Plunket—an excellent ecclesiastical prelate. The Catholics possess more property in this diocese than in all the other dioceses of the province.

" 3. The diocese of Clogher is about 50 miles long, and 16 wide ; it has thirty-five parish priests ; two houses of Franciscans, and one of the Dominicans. The bishop is Dr Patrick Duffy, formerly a Franciscan friar. No Catholic has any property in the diocese, and all are tenants under Protestant or Presbyterian landlords.

" 4. The diocese of Derry is about 55 miles in length, and 20 in breadth ; it has thirty parish priests ; it has for Vicar-General, Luke Plunket, a man of learning, and who governs it admirably. There are two communities of Dominicans. All the Catholics in it are tenants.

" 5. The diocese of Kilmore is 50 miles in length, and 20 in breadth ; there are in it about twenty-six parish priests, and two houses of Franciscans. All the Catholics, with the exception of two, are only tenants. The Vicar-General is Thomas Symons, a very learned and eloquent man. He was professor of theology in Belgium.

" 6. The diocese of Raphoe is about 40 miles long, and 16 wide ;

---

* The latter sheet of the original letter is all besmeared with ink, hence the remark in the text. The ink seems to have been wiped off whilst it was yet fresh, and thus the text is perfectly legible.

it has eighteen parish priests, and there is in it one house of
Franciscans. The Vicar-General is Bernard Magorck, a learned and
exemplary man.

" 7. The diocese of Connor is about 30 miles long, and 15 wide ; it
has about twelve parish priests, and a community of Franciscans ; all
its Catholics, with the exception of three, are tenants. The Vicar-
General is Terence O'Mulderig, of fair learning, and of exemplary life.

" 8. The diocese of Dromore is 20 miles long, and 12 in breadth ;
there are sixteen parish priests, but no regulars. All the Catholics,
with the exception of one, are tenants. The Vicar-General, was
appointed by Apostolic Brief, and is sufficiently learned ; he studied
theology, and received the doctorate in Rome. His name is
Ronan Magin.

" The diocese of Down is about 30 miles long, and 14 wide ; it has
a house of Franciscans, and one of Dominicans. All the Catholics,
excepting one, are tenants; there are fourteen parish priests, and
on account of its great vicinity, and of its having no one sufficiently
qualified, it is administered by the aforesaid Ronan Magin.

" 10. The diocese of Ardagh is about 40 miles long, and 16 wide ;
there are twenty-four parish priests; two houses of Franciscans, and
one of the Dominicans. There are only four Catholic gentlemen of
property ; all the others are tenants. The Vicar is Gerard Ferrall,
who was appointed by Apostolic Brief.

" 11. The diocese of Clocmacnoise is about 20 miles in length,
and 16 in width ; it has seven parish priests, and one community of
Franciscans ; all the Catholics there are tenants, with the exception
of four. The Vicar-General is Dionysius Coffey, and although he does
not possess great learning, he is, nevertheless, a man of saintly life.

" The Protestant bishops and ministers possess all the churches
and ecclesiastical revenues : the Catholic priests and bishops
have only the alms and the offerings which are made by the poor
Catholics ; they are, indeed, like those of the early Church. All the
above-mentioned dioceses, with the exception of Meath and Clonmacnoise, are in the northern division of Ireland, called Ulster. There
are various sects in it, Protestants, Presbyterians (who reject
episcopal government), Anabaptists, and Quakers. The Presbyterians prevail both in numbers and influence over the other three ;
they do not frequent the Protestant churches; they have their
ministers chosen by the elders, or senior laymen of their sect, and
they do not admit ordination from bishops ; they hate the sign of
the cross—they do not allow any fixed prayer, but only that which
is dictated at the moment by the Holy Ghost—they do not even allow
the ' Our Father '—they have churches of their own, but use no bells."

Before the close of 1678 Dr. Plunket seems to have again
performed a visitation of his suffragan dioceses, and on this
occasion the establishment of peace in the dioceses of Clogher
and Kilmore principally engaged his attention.

On more than one occasion we have referred to the eulogies passed by Dr. Plunket on the zeal and merits of Dr. Patrick Tyrrell, the learned Bishop of Clogher. He was a member of the order of St. Francis, and had held some of the highest offices in various houses of that order on the Continent. On being destined by the Holy See to the government of the ancient diocese of Clogher, he zealously co-operated with the Primate in reforming abuses and building up the spiritual sanctuary laid waste for so many years. Such, however, was the extreme poverty of that see, that in 1677 he petitioned the Sacred Congregation to have annexed to it the administration of the neighbouring diocese of Kilmore. The Primate supported his petition, stating, that only by adding such administrations could the poverty of the Irish dioceses be provided for. On this petition being granted by the Holy See, the existing Vicar of Kilmore, whose learning had often been commended by the Primate, but whose pride seems to have been commensurate with his learning, refused to obey the authority of Dr. Tyrrell, and endeavoured to support this insubordination, not only by pretending some informalities in the Brief of the Holy See, but also by broaching principles which, at this period, had become fashionable in the French schools. Dr. Plunket in consequence set out in person in company with Dr. Tyrrell, and, visiting the disturbed parishes of this diocese, refuted the erroneous principles of Fitzsymons, or Symons, and brought its clergy to a sense of due sub-mission to their legitimate pastor.

The happy results of this visitation, especially as to the peace established in the diocese of Clogher, are thus described by Dr. Tyrrell in a letter to the Internunzio, dated the 19th of March, 1678 :—

"The Archbishop of Armagh communicated to me that portion of the most kind letter of your Excellency of the 4th inst. (directed to him), which regarded me, and from it I perceive how sincere, cordial, and efficacious, were the most benign representations of your Excellency to their Eminences in my favour in regard of the administration of Kilmore, and it cuts off all controversy about the deposition of Symons, at the same time that it succours my

necessities; and hence I thank your Excellency with the most
humble and warmest thanks which a truly grateful heart can express,
and I shall ever remain most obliged to your incomparable piety
and zeal, and excessive kindness.

"The letters which Father Felix O'Neil, at the instance of your
Excellency, wrote to the clergy of Clogher, exhorting them to due
obedience to me, their bishop, arrived two months after the said
clergy had asked pardon for their fault, ably and learnedly convinced
by the Archbishop of Armagh, and by myself, as far as my weak
ability could contribute to it; and hence, these letters not being
necessary for the desired effect, were not published by me, though
they were most gratifying to me, and most esteemed as a proof of
the great zeal of your Excellency, which caused them to be written."

He adds, however, a complaint, that, despite this apparent
submission of Father Felix, he had been secretly instigating
the clergy to persist in their disobedience, and in disturbing
"that peace which was so fully established by the writings
of the Primate and myself, which so clearly refuted the
erroneous principle which had led them astray, as to the
jus postulandi, that they had nothing to reply, except
peccavimus, injuste egimus, iniquitatem fecimus."

In his letter of 27th October, 1678, Dr. Plunket informs
us that, at the request of the assembled prelates of Ardpatrick, he had undertaken a visitation of his province;
that he commenced with the diocese of Meath; that thence
he proceeded to Clonmacnoise, and, whilst engaged in the
visitation of this diocese, the news first reached him of the
persecution having burst forth anew, and of the arrest of
the Archbishop of Dublin. The months of June and July
of the same year were spent in the visitation of his own
immediate diocese, though at this time the Archbishop was
suffering from a painful malady in the eyes. In his letter
to the Internunzio, announcing this visitation, he details
many further particulars regarding the dioceses of Ardagh,
Meath, Derry, Clogher, and Kilmore. It is dated the 2nd
of August, 1678, and is especially interesting, as disclosing
to us how little Dr. Plunket allowed himself to be biased by
family interests, when the cause of religion was at stake:—

"During the past two months I was engaged in a fatiguing and
most laborious visitation of my diocese, of which I shall soon send

a further narrative to your Excellency. After my return I received two letters of your Excellency of the 11th of June, and of the 16th of July, from which I learn that the Bishops of Meath and Kildare, and Dr. Cusack, have received your favours, and these favours have been conferred on truly worthy persons, and hence our whole nation is obliged for them to their Eminences in Rome and to your Excellency. To his Eminence Cardinal Altieri and to Monsignor Cerri I shall reply in a few days; but the inflammation of my eyes, which was much increased by the laborious visitation of the northern mountains, scarcely allows me to write, or to read even letters as large as a snuff-box. It did not, however, prevent my tongue from preaching, in both the English and Irish languages.

"Christopher Farrell, a Dominican,* is a relative of mine; but, nevertheless, *caro et sanguis nihil mihi revelabit,* contrary to the good of religion, and of the mission. He is not distinguished either by his learning or personal qualities. Moreover, the diocese of Ardagh has not a revenue of eighty scudi a year, and I think the resolution of their Eminences is wise, not to multiply our bishops without necessity. With every submission I state my humble opinion on this subject. The diocese of Ardagh is contiguous, and as if intermixed with the diocese of Meath, and has been for many years without a bishop, without confirmation, &c. Their Eminences might grant the administration of that diocese to Dr. Cusack, the coadjutor of the Bishop of Meath; thus the two difficulties prudently referred to by your Excellency would be removed, and that diocese would be provided with an active and learned superior. I do not think that any further bishops are required for the province of Armagh, excepting in the diocese of Derry, which is very far to the north, and has been without a bishop for eighty years. Luke Plunket, the Vicar of Derry, during the past spring, when coming to me for the consecration of the chalices and altars, during the difficult journey, fell from his horse and broke his right arm in four places; now, however, thanks be to God, he is better. He is renowned for his labours, and by his good administration in six years he brought that uncouth people to great discipline and order.

" Dr. Tyrrell, by his last visitation, restored the diocese of Clogher to such peace, concord, and ecclesiastical discipline, that he is deserving of every praise. He laboured very much, and also took possession of the diocese of Kilmore, and, after performing a visitation of it, he will give a relation to your Excellency. Thomas Fitzsymons fought against him, and said in my presence (Monsignor Tyrrell and Dr. Edward Dromgole, a learned and exemplary man, were present), that the Bulls of the Holy Father depend *ab acceptatione cleri et populi,* and he stated in writing that the Bishop of Clogher *non debet de jure admitti* as administrator of the diocese of Kilmore. Dr. Dromgole, however. refuted him; and in truth, it is a doctrine worthy only of a blacksmith."

* He had lately been petitioned for as Bishop by the Vicar-Apostolic and the clergy of Ardagh.

In many of his letters Dr. Plunket refers to the great poverty which prevailed in many of the dioceses of Ireland, and this was the chief motive which impelled him, at different intervals during his episcopate, to urge on the Holy See the necessity of not adding new members to the hierarchy. As early as the 16th of March, 1672, he addressed a letter to the Internunzio most earnestly commending this matter, and suggesting, at the same time, an easy remedy for the administration of the vacant churches :—

" I have heard from different quarters [he says] that bishops are to be appointed for this province. I deem myself obliged in conscience to express my sentiment on this matter. There are in this province about ten dioceses, and it is as large as the provinces of Tuam and Dublin together. This province can afford competent support to five bishops, if they be distributed in a proper manner, and agreeably to the wants of the province. The Bishop of Meath can easily govern his diocese, and hold, at the same time, the administration of Clonmacnoise : the Bishop of Kilmore can, in the same way, administer the diocese of Ardagh ; the Archbishop of Armagh that of Clogher ; the Bishop of Derry that of Raphoe ; and the Bishop of Down and Connor can administer Dromore ; and thus five bishops will suffice. The five bishoprics which are given in administration are small and poor, and have but few priests. Now, as to the subject, I think the most eligible are the following three :— Thomas Fitzsymons, a learned and exemplary man, a good theologian and canonist ; Oliver Dease is also a learned man, and of great experience, having been for thirty years Vicar-General of Meath ; Dr. James Cusack, who was educated in Rome, is also a learned and exemplary man. These three are the most distinguished subjects of the province, and are secular priests.

" OLIVER OF ARMAGH.

" Armagh, 16th March, 1672."

Succeeding years did not produce any change in this sentiment of Dr. Plunket. In his letter of the 15th of September, 1677, he not only insists with greater earnestness on this measure, but more fully also declares to us the poverty to which the bishops of Ireland were subject :—

" Neither in Munster nor in any other province is there a bishopric now vacant that has an annual revenue of one hundred scudi, with the exception of Derry. In Munster, that is in the province of Cashel, two bishoprics are vacant, namely, Ardfert and Emly. The riches of these does not annually yield eighty scudi ; now you yourself will judge, how could a bishop (why do I say a bishop, how could his servant) support and clothe himself with eighty scudi a year ? They are obliged to support themselves here with shame and ignominy to the mitre and pastoral. You will be good enough to pay particular attention to what I am now going to say. No bishop in Ireland has two servants, and it is one and the same that acts as his servant and stable-boy, and it is the stable-boy that serves the bishop's Mass. Moreover, none of them have their own house ; to procure food they go to-day to the house of one gentleman, and to-morrow to the house of another, not without their shame ; and indeed the gentry are now tired of these visits. Whether or not this be a humiliation of the pastoral authority, I will leave it to be decided by the prudence of your Excellency. From this it also arises that the poor prelates are the servants of the gentry, and if they do not give the parishes according to the wishes of the gentry to persons often undeserving, they will incur their displeasure ; *tandem est turpis egastas, ac homines ridiculos facit*, poverty compels the bishops to perform things unbecoming their dignity.

" These things being so, I beseech you, through the love of Christ, to represent to their Eminences what I write, with all reverence, as being well acquainted with all the different parts of this kingdom. I have three servants, but my friends support them, and give hay and oats to my horses. However, were it not for their charity, the stable-boy would also be the server of my Mass. I have never had 200 scudi of revenue, and the third part of that revenue (and even more) goes in the expense of correspondence within the kingdom and with foreign parts. Letters are sent to me from all parts, because they know that I alone keep a fixed and regular correspondence in Dublin, &c., and that my diocese is only half-a-day's journey from Dublin. I charge the Canon Jones with many letters to be sent to Rome, and I do not pay him anything in return ; I only apply all my Masses during the year for his intention. Were their Eminences thoroughly acquainted with the state of the kingdom, and the poverty of the Catholics, they would make no bishops here excepting such as are absolutely necessary. In the province of Cashel there are at present living, besides the Archbishop, four suffragan bishops; that is, in the sees of Killaloe, Kilfenora, Cork, and Limerick. They are sufficient, and more than sufficient.

" OLIVER OF ARMAGH.

" 15th September, 1677."

Even when detained in prison, and awaiting his trial on a charge of high treason, Dr. Plunket had his thoughts fixed on the churches entrusted to him ; and fearful lest new dangers might beset his spiritual charge, more than once addressed to the Sacred Congregation his ardent request that no new bishops should be created for some time. The following extracts from his letters of the 19th and 24th of

June, 1680, not only express this sentiment of the Primate, but, moreover, present some particulars connected with other prelates of Ireland and the most distinguished of the clergy of Ulster at this period :—

" I declare and solemnly consider that nothing more injurious to the spiritual interest of the kingdom could be done than to appoint new bishops in these disastrous times ; for this would provoke the Government to enact more rigorous decrees, and would give further pretext to a renewal of the persecution ; and all, as well the laity as the clergy, would exclaim that their Eminences were the cause of their tribulations ; and it would seem that it was done on purpose to defy and goad on the Protestants . . . Seek for further information on this subject from the Archbishop of Cashel and Dr. Forstall of Kildare, who are prelates remarkable for their learning, prudence, gravity, and sanctity of life, and who would be not only fit, but would even deserve to be appointed to the sees of Toledo or Paris ; and you will surely find that they share in my sentiments."

He next assigns the subjects whom he deems most worthy to be chosen, should the Sacred Congregation deem it expedient to make any appointment to the vacant sees :—

" We have here Dr. Edward Dromgole, a preacher and famous theologian and canonist ; Bernard Magork, Vicar of Armagh, a grave, learned, and exemplary man ; Dr. Henry Hugo, my Vicar-General, who taught philosophy here, and also was educated at Rome ; Luke Plunket, a renowned canonist and moral theologian, who suffered imprisonment and exile, and being full of zeal, returned to this country about six months since. All these *ferunt pondus diei et aestus ;* they defend the flock and feed it ; *patiuntur in exequtione ; laborant ac sudant in vinea Domini.*"

CHAPTER XIV.

VISITATION OF VARIOUS DIOCESES, CONTINUED.

WE have reserved for this chapter some particular information connected with a few of the suffragan and other sees, which we shall distribute under their respective heads.

§ 1.—DIOCESE OF CLOGHER.

On the 12th of May, 1671, Dr. Patrick Duffy was appointed by the Holy See Bishop of Clogher. Few of the newly-nominated prelates seem to have so incurred the hostility of the Government as this learned bishop.

"I sent to you [thus writes Dr. Plunket to the Internunzio on 29th September, 1671], through Mgr. Howard, a cipher, that thus I may be able to communicate more freely with their Eminences concerning the spiritual affairs of this nation. I sent also, through the same channel, the decision come to, after great fatigue and labour, in the matter of the Dominicans and Fransciscans. My decree is based on justice and *si fractus illabatur orbis, impavidum ferient ruinæ.*

" Some time since the Viceroy sent for me, and, after many compliments and affectionate expressions, began to speak of matters of which, he said, he had been informed in London. He said that about ten new bishops had been made; but I replied that he must be misinformed, as there were not so many. No matter, he added, I will not permit Father Duffy to stop in this kingdom. In reply, I besought him not to give credence to false reports; that Father Duffy was in high repute upon the Continent; and that these reports proceeded from enmity, or from envy of the abilities of Dr. Duffy. He replied, he must employ his talents in other parts, and he commanded me to write this to the Internunzio, to whom he gave great praise. The Viceroy added, that as regarded the other bishops, he would close his eyes; and he also said that he was nowise hostile to the Holy See or to its defenders, and that his consort shared his sentiments; so that he even sent his sons to school to the Jesuits in France."

A few days later Dr. Plunket was summoned to another audience with the Viceroy. Well might the Archbishop be surprised at the unusual honours thus lavished on him : " *Seu fortuna mea est,*" he writes, adopting the words of the Roman orator, " *seu sors, seu principis error, maximus exiguo tempore crevit honor.*" The subject of conversation in this interview was the late appointment to the see of Clogher :—

" He spoke to me at great length [writes Dr. Plunket, on 2nd October, 1671], about the new bishops, and against Dr. Duffy, saying that he had heard strange things, and received the worst accounts about him from one of the ministers of the English Government, who knew him well. I said that Dr. Duffy was calumniated by evil, designing persons. Oh, no, he replied, that minister was acquainted with him in Spain ten years ago. I added that I never heard it even whispered that Dr. Duffy had done anything prejudicial to the King, or to the interests of the country. The Viceroy then entered into a long discourse, to the effect that

Duffy and my predecessor sought to make the people of Ulster submit to Cromwell, and that he himself had heard many things about this matter in Flanders; that Colonel Philip O'Reilly had taken part in this matter, and suffered the due penalty in Flanders At length he concluded by saying: Write to Monsignori Airoldi and Baldeschi not to allow Duffy to come to this kingdom; but as to the other bishops he would close his eyes, as it was not the intention of the King that any should be molested who had not sided against him."

How it must have pained the noble-hearted Primate to hear from the lips of the minister these calumnies against his venerated predecessor, and against his friend of Clogher! The English spies on the Continent were ever busy inventing tales to gratify the anxious bigots at home, and these were treasured up till the occasion might present itself of making the pastors of the Church their victims, or at least of debarring them from the exercise of their sacred ministry. Despite these threats of the Viceroy, Dr. Duffy fearlessly hastened to his spiritual flock, and for four years, till his death, continued, in season and out of season, to break to them the bread of life.

His successor, Dr. Patrick Tyrrell, had no sooner arrived in his diocese, than he found a still worse storm excited against him. A few unworthy members of the clergy broached principles which were at this time widely circulated in the schools of France, and sought to maintain that the people and clergy enjoyed an inherent right to elect their own pastors. As Dr. Plunket shared with the former bishop the perils of persecution, so did he share with Dr. Tyrrell the labour of combatting these schismatical principles. We shall, however, allow Dr. Tyrrell to detail the history of this controversy.

Soon after his arrival in Ireland he thus writes, on 17th December, 1676, to the Internunzio in Brussels:—

" Being one of the four bishops lately consecrated for Ireland, I deem it my duty to acquaint your Excellency with my movements, as I should have done before this had an occasion presented itself.

" I arrived safely, thanks to God, in Limerick, a maritime city of this kingdom; and although, through the indiscretion of a certain priest, a severe perquisition was made to discover me, nevertheless

Providence, through the instrumentality of some good Catholics freed me from this danger. I was obliged, however, to conceal myself for awhile. This storm being over, I went to visit the Primate, my Metropolitan; and, having presented to him my briefs, he placed me in peaceful possession of my diocese of Clogher, *nemine prorsus reclamante*."

He then details the scandalous manner in which two of the priests went around exciting the others against him. To remedy the consequent disorders, Dr. Tyrrell convoked a synod of the clergy of the diocese :—

"From my discourse [he thus continues] a diversity of opinion arose amongst them, so that some returned to their due obedience, whilst others asked for the term of one month to deliberate. Although I replied that I could allow no such terms when treating of the submission due to the Holy Apostolic See and to their legitimate pastor, nevertheless, as it is dangerous here to unsheathe the sword of ecclesiastical censure, except as a last remedy, I deemed it better to avail myself of some excuse, and absent myself for some time, the more so as the Primate wished to employ me in confirming the faithful of some other dioceses (as I had already done in my own). The term which they asked for being expired, I again returned, and cited the refractory to appear. The Primate cited them also, yet they refused to obey; and hence we were obliged to proceed against them as contumacious, and to act as best we could in these parts, and as prudence dictated to us in the circumstances I suspended from their office, and from the administration of the sacraments, the two ring-leaders, hoping that their chastisement would suffice to strike terror into the rest.

"The others are all submissive, and I hope that in a short time all will return to obedience. The clergy are fifty in number, of whom forty-two have the care of souls. As yet I have not been able to make the visitation of my diocese, partly on account of these disorders, partly on account of the weather being so rigid in these parts; but as soon as possible I shall visit it, with God's aid, and shall then give more minute details.

"Should you wish to honour me with your esteemed commands, be pleased to direct them as follows : *for Mr. John Wariu, in Dublin.*

"Fr. PATRICK OF CLOGHER.

"Louth, 17th Dec., 1676."

In another letter of the 31st December, he again writes :—

"About thirteen days ago, I sent some account to your Excellency of the disturbances which a few priests of the diocese of Clogher excited against me, their lawful pastor . . I do nothing without consulting the Archbishop of Armagh, who has great experience,

courage, and zeal. I have no doubt but that in a little while everything will go right; however, I foresee that some annoyances await
me; if our blessed God wish so, His will be done. I do not shun
this labour now, since His Divine Majesty has imposed this burden
on my shoulders, although I foresaw, indeed, that it was too weighty
for me."

On the 14th of the following February (1677), he gives
some particulars of the first origin of the opposition thus
made to him :—

" The opposition [he says] is not a personal one, that is, directed
personally against me ; on the contrary, they had resolved not to
admit not only as Bishop, but even as Vicar-General, anyone unless
he were a native of the diocese of Clogher, even though he should
belong to the province of Armagh, as I do, being a native of the
first suffragan diocese ; that is to say, of Meath."

" Before the arrival of my predecessor all this was planned, and
was occasioned by the appointment of a Vicar-General, who, though
a native of the province, belonged to another diocese, and who was
nominated by our Metropolitan, at the request of the greater part of
the clergy, and resided at the distance of only two or three miles
from that diocese. This vicar* was a man of virtue, and learning,
and zeal, and being anxious to reform some abuses among the
clergy, provoked the displeasure of a few, who made an agreement
amongst themselves not to admit, for the future, any superior for
the diocese excepting one from the place itself, de gremio loci.

" Nothing was heard of this agreement during the lifetime of my
predecessor, Dr. Duffy, for it so happened that he was a native of
the diocese. But immediately on his death, the clergy renewed that
agreement. . . .

" In a few days, I start on the visitation of my diocese, that thus
I may be able to detail more minutely its present state. Up to the
present it was impossible to do so, partly on account of the
disorders, and partly because the winter was exceedingly severe
in these parts. I understand, however, that the diocese is very
extensive and very poor. I have not received, as yet, the value of
one pin from it; and though I should receive all that is usual
granted to a bishop, it would not suffice for the maintenance of one
priest, and much less for the support of a bishop who is obliged to

* The Vicar-General, thus nominated, was Dr. Edward Dromgole,
often extolled in the letters of the Primate, and who on the martyrdom
of Dr. Plunket, governed the diocese of Armagh, as Vicar-Apostolic.
As early as 22nd August, 1673, Dr. Plunket thus wrote concerning
him:—" Mr. Edward Dromgole is one of the best priests I have ; he is
well versed in speculative theology and in morality; he has great talent
for preaching, and is of an exemplary life; he was for a short time
Vicar-General of Clogher, and he governed that diocese well.

keep, at least, one servant and a chaplain, no matter how poor he may be. I hear all the prelates lamenting the misery that they endure; may God compensate it by the abundance of His heavenly graces.

"The Parliament of England keeps us in apprehension of new persecutions, but the mercy of God comforts us with the firm resolution to either suffer or die *aut pati aut mori* for our spiritual flocks.

"Fr. Patrick of Clogher.

"Clogher, 14th February, 1677."

Through the exertions of Dr. Tyrrell, seconded by the untiring labours of the Primate, peace was soon restored throughout his diocese ; and we find, during the subsequent years, that, in the rebuilding up of the Church of God, the restoring of discipline, the correcting of abuses, the celebration of synods, Dr. Plunket had no more devoted assistant, no more zealous co-operator, than the Bishop of Clogher.

See the chapter on *Jansenism in Ireland,* for some further particulars regarding the exertions of Dr. Plunket in this controversy.

§ 2.—Meath.

The name of Dr. Patrick Plunket, Bishop of Ardagh,* and afterwards of Meath, has more than once been introduced in these pages. He it was that trained the opening intellect of his relative, the subject of these memoirs; for many years he was almost the only bishop in Ireland exercising episcopal functions, and if, at the time of his consecration, sunshine seemed to smile upon the island, the close of his eventful episcopate was darkened by a gathering storm, which whilst he hastened to his eternal rest, held men's minds in suspense, and burst forth in all its fury. The primate thus communicates to the Holy See the intelligence of the demise of this holy prelate :—

"'To your most kind letter of the 10th of October, I did not send an answer, not having any news of importance to communicate. But now I must give you the sad intelligence of the death of Dr. Patrick Plunket, Bishop of Meath, a prelate distinguished by

* In the Life of the celebrated Abbot de Rancé, by Chateaubriand, it is stated that he received the abbatial consecration in the year 1664, at the hands " of the Irish Bishop of Ardagh."

his birth, sincerity, integrity of life, his skill and experience in ecclesiastical matters, and his great watchfulness over his pastoral charge during the long space of thirty-three years; and although he was son of one of the first nobility of the kingdom, yet he never pursued any of the vain pleasures of this world. He was at first abbot of St. Mary's, near Dublin. About thirty-three years ago Innocent X. honoured him with the mitre of Ardagh, and Clement X. transferred him to the diocese of Meath. For many years there was no other bishop in Ireland, all having fled in consequence of the fiery persecution of Cromwell. He continually enjoyed the protection, or, at least, the connivance, of the State on account of his birth and moderation; he was an enemy to all temporal and political intrigues, and his nephew being married to the niece of the Duke of Ormond, our Viceroy, and *vice versa*, one of his nieces having for husband the nephew of the Viceroy, he had a written protection during the two late persecutions. He died poor because he lived rich, and devoted to alms-deeds; his right hand knew not what his left hand performed; he never denied an alms to a poor man, and he gave many secret charities to the bashful poor, respectable men and widows, of whom we have now a large number since the massacre of Cromwell. He had no more than one thousand scudi when dying. All the ornaments of his chapel, and his books and pontificals, he bequeathed to me during my life, and on my death to the diocese of Meath. He died on the 18th of this month, the day dedicated to the consecration of the Basilicas of St. Peter and Paul (for whom he entertained a most ardent devotion), and in the seventy-sixth year of his age ; and I recommend the soul of this great prelate to your Excellency when offering the most Holy Sacrifice.

" The death of Monsignor Cerri afflicted me very much ; he was my fellow-student in Rome, and his father, M. Francis Cerri, was my most warm friend; I will get all the clergy of the province of Armagh to offer up the Holy Sacrifice and prayers for the repose of his soul; and they have an obligation to do so, on account of his labours for them whilst secretary to the Sacred Congregation.

"We are here like sick persons, who, when they commence to become convalescent, rise prematurely from bed, to fall with greater impetus, *quo lapsu graviore cadant.* As the persecution commences, or appears to commence to decline, the regulars begin to frequent the cities and their convents with too much publicity and impru-dence, which makes us fear another proclamation ; and although the prudent prelates, and Catholic nobility *arguant, obsecrent, increpent,* they obstinately refuse to listen. Would you believe that the Franciscans of my diocese opened a novitiate during the past summer. The Capuchins educate their novices in Charleville, and do not send them to this country till they have acquired virtue and experience. If the Dominicans and Franciscans would also prepare their novices in some Catholic country where they have convents, we should not have here so many refractory persons and apostates.

I, for my part, having so often admonished their eminences, have done all that I could do.

"Dr. Brennan of Cashel obtained the administration of the diocese of Waterford and Lismore, and everyone readily obeyed. To Monsignor Forstall the favour was also granted of the administration of Leighlin ; and the clergy did not say one word in opposition, though they only received authentic copies of the Brief, precisely such as those of Dr. Tyrrell for Kilmore."

He then condemns the obstinacy of some of the clergy in the last-named diocese, who still refused to acknowledge Dr. Tyrrell for their bishop, and adds :—

"It is said that the Parliament will be dissolved, and that the King, by his own authority, nominates and constitutes the Sheriffs, that is, his Lieutenants in the counties or provinces, which was hitherto the privilege of the Lord High Chancellor and of the Judges. The fanatics and sectarians of those kingdoms are but little pleased with the return of the Duke of York : *ut ut sit, non debemus desperare meliora lapsis* (no matter what he may have been, we can hope better things from him after his conversion). The Government here both was and is very moderate, considering the disastrous circumstances of the times. It is gradually becoming manifest that all this conspiracy, the cause of the shedding of so much Catholic blood, was got up by the Presbyterians, who are hostile both to the monarchy and to the hierarchy. By the next post I shall write to Monsignor Cybo. His uncle acquired great fame for skill and goodness, and integrity, which makes us hope that his nephew, in an office so important for the propagation of the faith, shall be imitator of the heroic virtues of his uncle.

"I heard by a letter from Paris, that a Nuncio had been appointed for that court ; you will be kind enough to honour me with a few lines, mentioning his name, surname, whence he comes, and what offices he has held ; in the meantime I deem it more expedient to await the arrival of that prelate in Paris, to put in order and harmony some matters connected with that city—a subaltern cannot arrange things so well. I will ever pray to God for the repose of Monsignor Dandoni, who was an intimate friend of mine. His brother was my professor of rhetoric.

"The exile knight who visited you, was here accused of high treason, *criminum læsæ majestatis;* that is, of procuring by foreign troops to destroy the present Government and the Protestant religion. But the villains who accused him gave conflicting evidence at the trial, so I think the prosecution will cease. I recommend my own pecuniary interests to you, as from the month of May to the present I have not received ten scudi from the diocese. You will be good enough to send this letter to Monsignor Cybo, and keep a minute of anything that you may deem necessary.

"I remain, &c.

"30th November, 1679."

For some years Dr. Patrick Plunket had been subject to grievous infirmities ; and hence, on the 9th of March, 1678, being in his seventy-fourth year, he petitioned the Holy See to grant him a Coadjutor in the person of Dr. James Cusack, who was at this time Vicar-General of Meath. On the following day the primate wrote to Rome soliciting the same favour, and the appointment of Dr. Cusack on 5th October, 1678, as bishop of Casensis and Coadjutor of Meath, was the result of these solicitations. The letter of the Primate, which details many interesting facts connected with the diocese, and which, as we have said, bears the date 10th of March, 1678, is as follows :—

" Dr. Patrick Plunket, Bishop of Meath, now in his 74th year and so reduced by the gout and other infirmities, that he cannot, without imminent danger, attend to his diocese, has petitioned the Sacred Congregation to have a Coadjutor appointed to him in the person of Dr. James Cusack, who studied philosophy and theology in Rome, and during the past sixteen years, laboured with great fruit on this mission, preaching, teaching, and administering the sacraments. He is also so skilled in canon law, that from all parts of the kingdom they recur to him for the decision of their legal disputes. During the past six years he discharged the office of Vicar-General of Meath to the satisfaction of all ; even the Protestant magistrates respect him for his many good qualities. The good old Bishop of Meath, who toiled here for fifty-three years, being part of the time missionary, and part of the time bishop, and yet never claimed any assistance from the Sacred Congregation, merits this favour and consolation. Dr. Cusack, too, after studying in Rome and completing his course with *eclât*, and labouring here so faithfully and untiringly for many years, will, I hope, be honoured by their Eminences, thus giving a stimulus to others to labour in like manner."

The merits of Dr. James Cusack had already been more than once appreciated in the Irish Church; and in 1676, the bishops destined him as their representative to the Holy See. Various occupations, however, delayed his departure from Ireland, and his preparations were not yet completed, when he received from Rome his appointment as Coadjutor Bishop of Meath. In many of his previous letters, Dr. Plunket had repeated the same eulogies which we have just seen in his letter of 10th March, 1678.

Thus, on the 15th August, 1676, he styles him a good canonist and theologian, and a distinguished preacher in both languages, *i.e.*, English and Irish. "He studied in Rome," he adds, "and laboured here for thirteen years with great fruit and zeal." In another letter of 18th August, 1673, he styles him a man renowned for his learning and prudence ; and as early as 1671 he earnestly recommended his appointment as Vicar-Apostolic of the then vacant see of Clogher.

Yet this affectionate esteem for Dr. Cusack could produce no bias in the mind of Dr. Plunket, when it was his duty to act as judge of controversies in which this distinguished ecclesiastic was a contending party.

In 1670 and 1671 the parish priests of the diocese of Meath entered into a resolution to tolerate no longer the system then pursued by the Irish members of the order of St. Francis of soliciting the alms of the faithful at the parochial Mass. Immemorial custom, however, had given its sanction to their thus soliciting alms, and the parish priests seemed to have overstepped their limits when they assumed to themselves the power of abrogating this usage. Dr. Cusack was chosen agent by the clergy to carry out their resolution, and when the Bishop of Meath decided in favour of the Franciscan order, he appealed first to the Archbishop of Armagh, and then to Rome, that the decree of his ordinary might be reversed.

Dr. Oliver Plunket appointed as his delegates to examine this cause Oliver Dease, Vicar-General of Meath ; Philip Draycott, Parish Priest of St. Peter's, Drogheda, and Vicar-General of Armagh ; and Patrick Everard, a distinguished theologian. These summoned a meeting of the contending parties, but three days before the appointed time some adherents of Peter Walsh, fearing the result of the conference, informed the Government, and, at their solicitation, an order was sent to the Primate prohibiting this assembly. Dr. Plunket, in consequence, published a temporary decrees by which he commanded the parish priests to allow *pendente*

lite the religious of the order of St. Francis to quest, as
heretofore, at the parochial Mass. It was in consequence
of this decree that Dr. Cusack, in the name of the parish
priests, appealed to the judgment of the Holy See ; though
he soon afterwards withdrew this appeal, and, in a letter to
the Sacred Congregation, declared the readiness of the
clergy to abide by the decision of the Archbishop of Armagh.
No one more than Dr. Plunket deprecated the abuses which
gave scandal to the faithful people of Meath and other
dioceses, but he was desirous that these abuses should be
checked by the legitimate authority, whilst the just rights
of the religious orders should be, at the same time, maintained. Thus, he more than once declared in his letters
to the Sacred Congregation that this custom ought to be
abrogated ; and that, if the Sacred Congregation would not
make a special decree on the subject, the bishops of his
province at the next provincial council were resolved to
submit to their Eminences some remedy for these abuses.
Till such time, however, as the proper remedy might be
thus applied by the legitimate authority, he decided in the
present controversy that the immemorial usage of the
Franciscan order should be confirmed, whilst, at the same
time, the members of that order were admonished to avoid
the abuses which had, heretofore, afforded such just grounds
of complaint. This decision of the primate was confirmed
by the Sacred Congregation on 11th January, 1672.*

* We shall add two letters of Dr. Cusack which throw considerable
light on the entire controversy.

"Duæ Epistolæ Jacobi Cusack ad Illmum. et Rmum. D. Archiepum.
Cæsareæ Romam.

"Illme. et Revme. Dne.

"Viget in hoc regno a multis annis consuetudo, seu, ut verius dicam,
corruptela admittendi regulares aliquos, Carmelitas scilicet, Augustini-
anos, Dominicanos, et Franciscanos diebus dnicis. et festis ad mendicandum
publice ante sacrum parochiale. Et quia solent quandoq. prædicti
regulares ante mendicationem conciorari, quo potius scandalizatur, quam
ædificatur populus, cui finis harum concionum videtur mendicatio, unde
emanavit proverbium illud *istas conciones habere caudas*, quia nimirum
post conciones aut oves aut agnos aut aliquid emendicant; statuerunt
regni Præsules, ne quo die concionaturus accederet regularis, permitte-
retur mendicare. Hac de causa repulsus quidam Pater Dominicanus a

§ 3.—The Diocese of Derry.

The letters of Dr. Conwell and of the Vicar-General of Raphoe, which were given in the chapter on the zeal and apostolic labours of Dr. Plunket, anticipate much of what should be said in the present article. It was not without great risk and toil that the Primate succeeded in deposing Terence Kelly, the Vicar-General of Derry, whom his predecessors had sought in vain to correct. Dr. Conwell, whom he substituted in the administration of the diocese, is spoken of in the contemporary records as a man of distinguished zeal and learning, and the Holy See soon sanctioned his appointment, constituting him Vicar-Apostolic of Derry:

parocho, quia nimirum contra statuta nostræ diœcesis post concionem vellet etiam invito pastore mendicare, adjunctis sibi Franciscanis aliquot, qui cum pastoribus aliquibus antea contendebant, accedit ad Illm. et R. Patritium Midensem, conqueriturq. se et Franciscanos a tribus parochis Midensis diœcesis impeditos, quominus eleemosynas suas secundum consuetudinem antiquam diœcesis corrogare possent. Fulminat Midensis, inaudita parte, suspensionem latæ sententiæ S. Pontifici reservatam in quemcunq. parochum suum, regulares secundum antiquam diœcesis consuetudinem emendicantes impedire tentantem. Exultanc et insultant parochis regulares, jactant nobis invitis consuetudinis suæ beneficio seso fruituros, minas et pericula obstrepentibus intendunt. Graviter commovet res hæc parochos et pungit, lædi hac suhjectione dignitatem suam agerrime ferunt, præcisamq. censura illa libertatem, qua regulares aut pro sua benevolentia admittebant, aut pro arbitrio rejiciebant, indignabantur. Quid multis? Primi parochi, quibus ostensa est censura, quosq. frustra territant regulares, nomine suo et totius cleri Midensis Ardmachanum appellant, apostolos a Midensi obtinent: Ardmachanus autem totam causam delegat admodum Rdis. DD. Oliverio Lease, Vico. Gli. Miden. Philippo Draycott nuper Vico. Gli. Ardmeno. et Pastori St. Petri Pontanæ, et Patritio Everardo Theologo emerito. Hi locum et diem citatis partibus constituunt; sed triduo ante præfixam diem interdicit Ardmacanus, ne conveniamus, significans, hoc pro-regis jussu factum, cui regulares aliqui delegati citationem eo consilio ostenderunt, ut conventio nra. ipsius auctoritate disturbaretur. Verum regulares nunc palam Ardmenum. incusant, et conventum nrum. ejus opera in gratiam Midensis interdictum ajunt. Quidquid sit, cum pro-rex vir alioquin humanissimus et cui nos omnes quamplurimum debemus, paulo ante synodum provincialem permiserit, et quotidie longe frequentiores conventus etiam in urbibus et oppidis permittat, certum videtur, quod nec nostrum, qui ruri habendus erat. et ad quem soli ordinum superiores quatuor, et ego cleri procurator citatus eram, interpellasset, nisi ut aliquibus nostris gratificaretur.

" Jam præcipit Ardmacanus appellantibus fratres ut antea ad mendicandum admitti pendente lite, quam data opportunitate decidendam spondet

his delicate constitution, however, did not long sustain the incessant labours of that vast and important diocese.

In the beginning of 1673 Dr. Plunket transferred the Vicar-General of Raphoe, Dr. Luke Plunket, to the diocese of Derry; and when, in 1677, a momentary calm seemed to smile upon the Irish Church, we find a petition presented by the Primate, that a bishop should be granted, and this vicar-general be consecrated for that ancient see.

A letter of the Nunzio, of 21st August, 1677, besides referring to this desire of the Archbishop of Armagh, presents many interesting particulars connected with this diocese :—

" The Vicar of Derry informs me, that, through the mercy of God, great peace is enjoyed in that diocese, and that order is maintained there, not only by his own exertions, but by the union of the clergy, who, moreover, are not called on to contribute much for his support as he possesses a sufficient private patrimony. For two years he

Sed mihi consultius visum est Ssum. in Christo Patrem, et D. N. Clementem X. P.O.M. appellare ; nec cui appellationem meam potius qum Illmæ. et Rmæ. Dni. Vræ. exhibendam transmitterem, attentius considerando inveni : qui oculus es S. Cngnis. de Propda Fide a longe prospiciens quæ in locis omnibus hæresi infectis geruntur. Nec aliud rogo, quam (cum non suppetat, unde personaliter causam prosequar) ut res delegatis ab Ardmacano iterum auctoritate Aplica. committatur, aut aliis quibusvis, et onerentur eorum conscientiæ, ut consideratis etiam circumstantiis loci et temporis, quod justum videbitur, exequantur, ut ad omnipotentis Dei honorem et populi ædificationem tam barbarus mendicandi modus ad altaria, cujus fusiorem descriptionem brevi transmittam, e medio tollatur. Quod si forte non convenit ab Illma. et Rma. Dne. Vra. hanc appellationem exhiberi, dignabitur saltem cleri nostri agentem instruere, quo pacto causam nram. administrare et curare debeat.

" Interim Dnem. V. I. et R. Omnipotens ad propagatnem suæ fidei diu sospitet, quod ex animo apprecatur,

" Dnis. Vræ, I. et R.
" Obsqmus.
" JACOBUS CUSACUS.

" Dublinii, 6 Febrii., 1671."

SECOND LETTER.

" Illme. et Revme. Dne.

" Postquam transmisi appellationem ad Illm. et R. Dnem. Vram. Ssmo. Patri Nro. exhibendam, rogarunt regulares quidam controversiam iterum committi cisdem delegatis decidendam. Arrisit mihi, quod optarunt, et utramq. manum dedi, ut liti finis hic imponeretur, renuntiavi appellationi factæ, et cum ex adversa valetudine abfuissent delegati duo,

exercised the function of Vicar-General of Raphoe, and is for five years in his present position; he was twice cast into prison by the Protestants, and accused of acting with authority delegated by the Holy See, yet he was each time set at liberty, and declared innocent through the want of evidence against him. He laments his being at the distance of one hundred miles from the residence of the nearest bishop, and this in a mountainous country, so that not being visited by other bishops, and Derry itself being without a bishop more than a hundred years, almost the whole mass of the people is without the Sacrament of Confirmation, and deprived of those advantages which the presence of a bishop would confer on it. He requested me to grant him the faculty of consecrating altars and chalices; but as I had no such power, I answered that I would petition your Excellency, as I now do, to obtain it for him.

"All the preceding statements are confirmed by the Archbishop of Armagh, who, moreover, writes that he administered confirmation in that diocese to old men sixty years of age; and after passing a high eulogy on the learning and merits of the Vicar-General, he declares that if the Sacred Congregation is desirous of appointing a bishop to the see of Derry, he would be the best qualified both in

acquievimus communi consensu judicio et sententiæ Illmi. et Rmi. Oliveri Ardmacni. et Rdi. admodum D. Dni. Oliveri Dease Vicarii Glis. Miden. eorumq. quos ipsis in consilium adhibere videorentur. Audierunt utriusq. partis rationes, et argumenta, sed cum mihi persuadeam Illmum. et Rmum. Ardmcnum. in causis gravioribus nihil agere inconsulta Illm. et R. Dne. Vra. in rebus gerendis experientissima, visum est meas rationes, et adversorum argumentorum solutionem eo transmittere, ut collatis eisd. cum argumentis regularium, qui ! in Dno. faciendum sit, ex consilio et sententia sua significet. Addidit mihi ad hoc animum, quod referat Ardmacnus Illm. et Rvm. D. Vram. strenue laborare, ne quid ullibi de hierarchiæ dignitate detrahatur, cujus veritatis evidentissimum habemus in hoc regno testimonium, ubi collapsam pene hierarchiam tot præsulum creatione in pristinum quasi statum vestra præcipue industria restituit, cum Neoterici nostri extremam pastoribus ipsis ruinam palam minabantur, quasi vero ipsi convenientiorem modum fidei propagandæ missionarios suos (qui a pinguioribus divelli sese non facile patiuntur) excogitare possent, quam Christus ipse Dnus omnipotens, omnibonus, omnisapiens per Epos. et parochos. Hi sunt qui per ostium intrarunt in ovile, et non ascenderunt aliunde: Christus ostium est juxta illud; ego sum ostium. His Christus committit ovile. De istis videtur prophetice dictum Hier. 22. Non mittebam prophetas, et ipsi currebant, non loquebar ad eos, et ipsi prophetabant. Et certe ausim dicere, si Ecclesiastica Hierarchia in Anglia et Scotia nondum concidisset, nunquam in eis sic fides defecisset. Sed hæc nunc missafacio Deus O. M. Illmam. et Rmam. Dncm. vram. ad decus et tutelam Ecclesiæ nræ. et ad majorem sui nominis gloriam ubique propagandam diu sospitet, idq. ex intimo corde apprecatur

"Dnis. Vræ. &c.,

"Obsqmus.
"JACOBUS CUSACK."

regard of his own talents, and on account of his having sufficient
private means ; he adds that he has very few equals in Ireland, and
that the only defect is his delicate constitution."

We have a letter of Dr. Plunket, written on 4th of
August, 1677, to the Secretary of the Sacred Congregation,
which dwells at length on the same subject :—

" It is my duty to represent to their Excellencies whatever may
tend to promote the propagation of the faith, and ecclesiastical
discipline in this kingdom, and especially in the province of Armagh.
Now it is certain that great advantages would accrue to our holy
religion by granting a bishop to the diocese of Derry. This diocese
is the most remote in this kingdom, and has about thirty parish
priests and about six thousand Catholic families. These are at a
distance of more than a hundred miles from me and from every other
bishop ; and hence, for the consecration of chalices and altar-stones,
as well as for the ordinations, they are obliged to make a long and
difficult journey ; and as there was no bishop there for more than a
hundred years, many persons are met with at a very advanced age
who never received the Sacrament of Confirmation. It was with
difficulty that I found a proper vicar who would undertake the
mission in these remote districts, till about five years ago God
moved Luke Plunket, a learned and exemplary man, to accept the
burden of the Government of that diocese ; he passed nineteen years
in Italy and France ; he is rich in earthly wealth, but still more so
in zeal for the glory of God : he suffered much in the exercise of his
ministry : he was imprisoned and prosecuted by the Protestants,
but his defence was so prudent that he was liberated. On one
occasion, though sick, he was dragged, at midnight, two miles away
to prison ; yet such was his zeal, that no persecution could force
him to abandon his flock. *Vere tulit pondus diei et œstus.* Your
Excellency will be good enough to propose the matter to their
Eminences, that thus Don Luca may be appointed to the see of
Derry : this will be a great favour to the Catholics of these districts :
if it be not granted, let an Apostolic Brief at least be sent, giving
him faculty to consecrate chalices and portable altars. As he has a
rich patrimony he could support his dignity with decorum, besides
the blessings that would accrue to the Catholics of that diocese.
                                        " OLIVER OF ARMAGH.
    " Dublin, 4th August, 1677."

A few days later in the same month, the Internunzio
transmitted from Brussels some information which had
been asked for by the Secretary of the Sacred Congregation
as to the means of support of the clergy of this diocese :—

" By the Archbishop of Armagh [he says] as well as by Dr. Luke
Plunket, I have been informed that there are no fixed boundaries

for the parishes, nor a fixed revenue for the parish priests in the diocese of Derry; it is customary to assign to the care of each priest a sufficient number of Catholic families, who by their offerings and alms contribute to his support."

The plan proposed to the Holy See by the Primate could not be realized, for scarce were these letters received in Rome when intelligence was brought that the long-threatening storm of persecution had burst, with all its fury, upon the afflicted island; and from subsequent records we learn that the Vicar of Derry was one of those who enjoyed the happy honour of sharing with the Primate the sufferings and chains of his imprisonment.

§ 4.—KILDARE.

In the letter of the Primate, 2nd August, 1678, mention is made of the requested favours having been granted, not only to the Bishop of Meath and Dr. Cusack, but also to the Bishop of Kildare. The favour solicited by Dr. Plunket for this prelate was the administration of the adjoining diocese of Leighlin. Dr. Forstall was a prelate of great virtue and learning, and before his appointment to the see of Kildare, he had held high ecclesiastical offices in Vienna, in which he won for himself even the esteem and favour of the Imperial Court. He was, however, a member of the Order of St. Augustine, all whose convents had been destroyed or impoverished throughout the kingdom; and, as the diocese of Kildare presented at this period no means of subsistence, yielding to the Bishop a revenue of only fifty-six scudi per annum, that is to say, little more than £1 per month, he was obliged to have recourse to Rome, *the common mother of all*, soliciting aid in his distress. Dr. Plunket was mainly instrumental in procuring for him the administration of the diocese of Leighlin; and in his letter of the 20th of August, 1677, whilst he suggests the means by which the worthy prelate (whom he elsewhere declares fit to govern the most important dioceses of the world) might be relieved, he especially commends

o

this provision for the diocese of Leighlin, as whilst i^t
succoured the indigence of the Bishop, it would, at the
same time, be a source of great spiritual blessings to
that venerable see. The following is the letter of the
Primate :—

" The great affection which your Eminence has ever displayed for
me and for this nation, is the cause of my so often inconveniencing
you both for myself and for my friends, amongst whom is
Dr. Forstall, a grave and learned prelate, and here esteemed by all ;
he is bishop of Kildare, which diocese is amongst the poorest of this
kingdom, having only fifteen priests, and yielding no more than £15,
that is, about fifty-six scudi of Roman money. It is certain that
many of the chaplains of the ' Madonna dei Monti '* receive a great
deal more, and this poverty of the bishops renders them the servants
of the laity, and makes them ridiculous and contemptible. The
manner of succouring this worthy prelate is either to destine an
annual sum for him from the Sacred Congregation, such as is
granted to the bishops of the East ; or, if not, to grant to him the
administration of the diocese of Leighlin, adjoining that of Kildare,
which, although it has not more than fifteen or sixteen priests, and
gives a revenue of only fifty or sixty scudi, nevertheless will be a
great relief to Dr. Forstall : this measure would be of great spiritual
advantage to the Leighlin diocese, since the said prelate could
administer there the Sacraments of Confirmation and Orders, and
consecrate chalices or altars, &c. ; and it is certain that it would be
a source of greater profit and spiritual consolation to this diocese to
be administered by a bishop (since it cannot support a bishop for
itself) than by a vicar-general who, *ut plurimum*, is not a person of
such learning, and does not enjoy so great authority.

" I, therefore, pray your Eminence to propose to his Holiness
and to the Sacred Congregation, either to assign an annual sum to
Dr. Forstall, or otherwise to grant him the administration of
Leighlin diocese, which is contiguous to and adjoining the diocese
of Kildare : this is a matter worthy of your charity and great zeal,
and I remain, &c.

" OLIVER OF ARMAGH.

" Dublin, 20th of August, 1667.

" To his Eminence the Cardinal
        Colonna, &c."

During the next month this same petition was renewed,
and the petition of the Primate was confirmed by the

* A church not far from the old Irish College in Rome; it is also at
present the parochial church of the national college in that city.

suffrage of Dr. Plunket, of Meath, and Dr. Tyrrell, of Clogher.*

As we have seen in the letter above referred to (30th November, 1679), this favour was accorded by the Holy See. The diocese of Leighlin, however, was not allowed to enjoy long this administration. Before the close of the year 1679 Dr. Forstall was cast into prison ; and even after his liberation the fury of persecution compelled him to seek for safety in the woods and mountains, till, in 1683, he closed his earthly career an exile in the diocese of Cashel.

§ 5 —Kilfenora.

On the 22nd of January, 1647, Dr. Andrew Lynch was elected by the Sacred Congregation Bishop of Kilfenora. His episcopate embraced one of the saddest epochs in the history of the Irish Church. During the persecution conse-quent on the invasion of Cromwell he fled to France, and acted for many years as suffragan or assistant-bishop to the Archbishop of Rouen.

In 1671 the Sacred Congregation deliberated on the propriety of transferring this prelate to the then vacant see of Cork, and of uniting his small diocese with the adjoining see of Killaloe. The opinion of Dr. Plunket was solicited

---

* The following is the joint memorial of these three bishops to the Sacred Congregation :—

" Nos infrascripti habentes optimam notitiam et informationem status Diœceseos Kildarensis, attestamur ejus districtum esse unum ex pau-perioribus totius Hiberniæ : in ea Epum. non habere domum, hortum, agrum aut paramenta ulla ecclesiastica nec moris esse ut laici aut seculares Catholici viritim contributionem ullam aut subsidium pendant Episcopo, et quod caput est fidem facimus in ea non esse nisi 15 Pastores aut Curatos quorum singuli singulas libras æris Anglicani annuatim Ep's opo solvunt; et consequenter proventus et emolumenta annua Episcopi se tantum extendere ad 15 libras Anglicanas, seu ad quinqua-ginta sex circiter scutata monetæ Romanæ : ac proinde affirmamus impossibile prorsus esse ut Epus. spectatis emolumentis e diœcesi pro-venientibus nisi aliunde ei succurratur, possit residere, se sustentare, aut eas functiones et fructus facere qui residentiam requirunt.

" Datum in diversis respective refugii nostri locis mense Septembri, 1677.

" Oliverius Armachanus, T.H.P.
" Patritius Midiæ Epus.
" Patritius Epus Clogheren."

through the Nunzio as to the propriety of this union ; and the following fragment of a letter, written by him in reply, was transmitted to the Sacred Congregation before the close of 1672 :—

"31st Jan , 1672.—As regards the union of the diocese of Kilfenora with Killaloe, I think it would be well ; for Kilfenora has no more than four or five priests."

In the preceding months the Internunzio had presented a similar recommendation to Rome. His letter of 17th October, 1671, is as follows :—

" The Bishop of Kilfenora, who is now in France, and though sixty-five years of age, is nevertheless robust and strong, was obliged to abandon his diocese on account of its being so reduced and impoverished, and to retire to France to acquire subsistance, acting as suffragan of the Archbishop of Rouen. Moreover, he had but little duty in his own diocese, as it is only ten Italian miles in extent, and even in the most flourishing times of the Church had only nine priests, that number being now reduced to four. It forms as if a corner of the diocese of Killaloe, and adjoins the diocese of Kilmacduagh, so that it would be well to have it incorporated with either of these dioceses, not to have a bishop confined to so small a district, which is wholly insufficient for his support ; for in Ireland the bishops subsist by the charitable offerings of the people and the voluntary contributions of the poor priests. Shou'd the Sacred Congregation adopt this plan, the present Bishop of Kilfenora might be transferred to the see of Cork, which is in the same province of Cashel, and is very extensive and rich, whilst it is, at the same time, very remote from the residence of the other bishops who are now in Ireland. This sentiment has been approved by Dr. O'Molony (Bishop of Killaloe), the Bishop of Ferns, and Dr. Dempsey, who also requested me to supplicate your Excellency for this favour, as the Bishop of Kilfenora is most anxious to return to labour in Ireland, whilst it would be impossible for him to return to his former residence. The account I have received of this bishop represents him as a man very learned and virtuous. The Archbishop of Armagh writes that the Bishop of Meath is seriously ill, and on account of his being so old there is great danger of his passing to a better world."

The good Bishop of Kilfenora, however, declined the proffered translation to the see of Cork ; and, continuing to reside in France, some few years later, in the diocese which had yielded him a refuge, found also a tomb.

CHAPTER XV.

For some years before the departure of Dr. Plunket from the Eternal City, the missions in the Hebrides and Highlands of Scotland had engaged the attention of the Sacred Congregation ; and he had not as yet reached Belgium, when, by order of the Holy Father, he was appointed, on the 17th of September, 1669, the superior of these missions, with an injunction to procure spiritual pastors for that desolate flock.*

At an early period of the persecution against the Catholics of Great Britain, all priests were compelled to fly from the Scottish islands, and as these were too poor to attract the attention of the reformed ministers, their inhabitants were left almost wholly immersed in the grossest ignorance. We find at intervals, however, some heroic priests, especially from the neighbouring shores of Ireland, fearlessly risking their lives in order to administer to these poor islanders the sacraments of the Church, and break to them the bread of life. The records of the Jesuit missions, as well as those of the Orders of St. Francis and St. Vincent,† present illustrious examples of such true Christian heroism. We shall take one from the Annual Letters of the Jesuit fathers. About the year 1650 Father David Galvins was

---

* Atti, &c., 17th Sept., 1669 : "Ssmus. mandavit deputari in superiorem illius missionis modernum Archiepum. Armacnum qui ad illas insulas operarios mittat."

† In the Life of St. Vincent, l. ii., c. 1, sect. xi., there is an account of the missionary labours of the Lazaristes in the Hebrides, and of the success which they obtained. St. Vincent, it is there stated, selected two Irish priests for the mission of the Hebrides, to whom a third was added, Scotch by birth. There is an interesting letter inserted in the same chapter, written by one of those missionaries, the Rev. Mr. Duignin, or Duggan, which gives an accurate account of his labours in the Western Islands,

renowned throughout the Irish province for his piety and
zeal; three times did he set out for the missions of Scotland.
On the first occasion he travelled as a merchant, yet could
convert none of the islanders to the profession of the Catholic
faith, such was their terror of the Duke of Argyle, a bitter
enemy of the Catholics, and lord of that territory. When
returning to Ireland, overwhelmed with sadness at the bad
success of his journey, the Scotch sailors, who, themselves,
were imbued with Calvinism, surprised that though he
styled himself a merchant, yet he had purchased no goods,
asked him for what object he had undertaken so long a
journey? The good father replied that he was, indeed, a
merchant, but of merchandise far more precious than all
earthly goods, and that he sought for souls redeemed by the
most precious blood of Jesus Christ. The sailors, reasoning
amongst themselves, declared with one accord that that
religion should be true which could inspire such a desire for
the salvation of souls ; and before the vessel reached the
Irish coast, he had the consolation of receiving these straying children into the fold of Christ. On his second and
third mission his labours were crowned with abundant
fruit: in some districts, whole towns, parents as well as
children, received the Sacrament of Baptism ; and on one
occasion, so incessant was his toil in instructing the poor
mountaineers, that for five months he never changed his
garments, though often compelled to rest at night exposed
to the rain and the inclemency of the weather. Such was
the hatred conceived against him by the heretics, that they
publicly sent round his likeness in order to secure his arrest;
but the good father safely passed through their hands,
though not without a manifest interposition of Providence ;
and sometimes, too, employing the artifice of declaring
himself a merchant, and bringing around some sacks of corn
as if they were samples, the better to disguise his true
mission.*

* See " Relatio rerum quarumdam mirabi ium quae contigerunt in
missione Hibernica Soc. Jesu ab anno 1641. usque ad an. 1650," compiled
from the " Litteræ annuæ Soc. Jes." in Archiv. Col. Hib. de Urbe,

In 1662 Alexander Winster was appointed prefect of all the Scottish missions, and in his "Report" to the Sacred Congregation he states that there were six thousand Catholics in Scotland, and that the Highlanders used the Irish language; the clergy consisted of eleven Jesuits, three Dominicans, two Franciscans, and six secular priests, all being maintained by the Sacred Congregation of Propaganda. These priests, however, were, for the most part, confined to the Lowlands, and but few could be found who would embrace the mission to the Scoto-Irish, as they called the inhabitants of the Hebrides and Highlands. We have seen in the Second Chapter how the Irish Bishops urged, as a motive for the establishment of the Irish College in Rome, that thus they might be the better able to supply missionaries for the Scotch districts. Dr. Burgatt, too, when agent of the Irish Clergy in Rome, petitioning the Holy Father, in 1668, that bishops might be destined to the vacant sees in Ireland, assigns this, amongst other reasons, that thus the Scottish Church might be succoured, for at this time it was almost wholly destitute of pastors. "The Scotch (he says) have but few ecclesiastics of their own nation; fruitful missions, however, were often given there from Ireland, for they freely receive instruction from the Irish priests on account of their having the same language as well as the same origin. In particular, the Scottish islanders so hate the English, that they even seem to shun those who speak the English language."*

As soon as Dr. Plunket had expedited matters more immediately connected with his own diocese, he resolved to visit and procure pastors for this scattered portion of Christ's fold :—

" The visitation of the Hebrides yet remains [he thus writes on the 23rd February, 1671] ; but if the Sacred Congregation does not

---

* " Scoti vix ullos habent suæ gentis ecclesiasticos : ex Hibernia illuc fieri solebunt fructuosæ missiones : Hibernos enim libentur audiunt propter communionem linguæ necnon et originis. Odio ita prosequuntur Anglos (præsertim, insulares Scoti) ut etiam ipsorum linguam loquentes vulgo aversari videantur." Relat. Ec. Hib. a Gul. Burgatt, &c.

write a letter to the Marquis of Antrim, we shall be able to effect nothing. This nobleman has great influence in these islands, but he is in every respect not unlike Mgr. Albrici, good and prudent, but slow and scrupulous in everything. I remember that Mgr. Albrici could not find in all Italy a servant to suit him : the Florentine was too talky ; the Milanese was giddy; the Romagnese was stupid ; the Neapolitan was quick with the fingers ; the Roman was too sad. And so it is very difficult to find people to suit the Marquis of Antrim. I proposed to him no fewer than twenty priests, but he had something to say against every one of them ; and in regard to Ronan Magin—a man truly suited for the task—he remarked that he seemed too hasty and presumptuous and proud. The chief cause of the delay, however, is the treaty of union between Scotland and England, as I mentioned in a former letter. The Marquis sent three priests to these islands to administer the Sacraments of Penance and the Eucharist during the Lent ; after Easter they returned, and they would not consent to remain in them for the whole year, as they have good parishes in the County Antrim. Moreover, they are very old, and but ill-suited for the labour of these islands. A courteous letter to this nobleman, commending his piety and his zeal for the spiritual profit of these souls, and commemorating also the piety of his ancestors, will be very efficacious in promoting this matter. I was with him for three days at his house at Dunluce ; it is a noble building ; the palace is perched on a high rock, which is lashed on every side by the sea : it is only twelve miles distant from the largest of the Hebrides. Mgr. this letter is necessary, as the Marquis is the only Catholic nobleman who can assist me in this mission, and without his aid I shall have to run many risks."

This letter of the Primate was read in the Congregation of 13th of July, 1671, and at the same time that the wished-for letter was directed to the Marquis of Antrim, a missionary stipend was decreed to three priests whom the Archbishop of Armagh should destine for these missions.

Whatever may have been the judgment of the Marquis of Antrim in regard of the subjects proposed by Dr. Plunket for the Scottish mission, it is manifest from the letters of the Primate, that he omitted no diligence in choosing missioners well suited for that holy work. Thus, he writes in 1670, immediately after his arrival in Ireland :—

" When I next assemble the vicars of the province, I shall send to your Excellency the names of the missionaries for the Scottish islands : three have already offered themselves for that mission, but before I accept them, I will examine them as to learning, and I will go to their own district, in order to see what is the tenor of their lives. You may rest assured that those that I will send shall be men of sufficient learning and of holy life. Their stipend might be the same as is given to the other missionaries of Scotland, especially as these islands are even poorer than Scotland itself. When I transmit to you their names and the attestation of their merits, I am sure that your Excellency, in the fulness of your zeal, will do all that is necessary for the advancement of this holy work. There is one missionary in this island named White, who is supported there by Daniel Arthur, an Irish merchant of London."

Before the above-mentioned decree was enacted by the Sacred Congregation, Dr. Plunket had addressed another letter repeating his former demands, and soliciting pecuniary aid to enable him to execute the commission entrusted to him by the Holy See.

"I need some assistance [he says, in his letter of 7th June, 1671] to enable me to visit the Scottish islands, that is, the Hebrides without your assistance I can do nothing, It will be necessary for me to bring a priest and a servant with me, and to dress after the manner of these people, which is very different from that of every other part of the globe."

In his subsequent letters, Dr. Plunket makes no further petition for any aid: hence, we may conclude that the wished-for favours were granted to the missionaries in those islands. He continued, however, to take a great interest in this mission; and writing to the Secretary of the Sacred Congregation on the 29th September, 1671, he thus earnestly recommends it to their care :—

"I recommend to] you the Scottish islands. The poor creatures are dying from spiritual hunger, having none to break to them the bread of Christ; ecce jam regiones albæ sunt ad messem; let us reap the harvest while it is ripe, and let us gather in the vintage before it is destroyed by the hail and the tempest."

I have met with only one formal "Relatio" on the Scottish Islands, presented by Dr. Plunket to the Sacred Congregation. It is dated the 2nd of September, 1671, and the Primate takes care to add that his information regarding this mission was received from Father Francis MacDonel, an excellent Franciscan missionary, who had laboured with great fruit for many years in those islands :—

"The first of these islands is called Buyth (Bute) in Irish, boad, and is nineteen miles in length, and five in width; its lord is one of the Stuart family. There is no Catholic on it, through the want of missionaries. The inhabitants, however, are all well disposed towards the faith, and they are reckoned at about twenty thousand.

"Another island, called, Arran, is twenty miles in length, and eight in breadth. All its inhabitants, who are reckoned at twelve thousand, would profess the Catholic faith had they anyone to preach it to them. At present they are, to all appearance, heretics, and are subject to several masters, among whom the property of the island is divided.

"The island of Isla is twenty-four miles long and ten broad: it has eight thousand souls, who change their religion at the will of their master; they were formerly Presbyterians, but they are at present Protestants. The proprietor of the island is a member of the Campbell family, who, in Irish, are called Maccalin.

"The island of Dura is twenty-six miles long, and six in width, and has only two thousand inhabitants. Its owner is the Marquis of Argyle, the head of the Campbell family. All are heretics. This marquis was in Rome, and was treated with great kindness by Father Dempster, the then Rector of the Scots' College, and when this father, some time afterwards, fell into the hands of the heretics in Scotland, the marquis had a great part in rescuing him from the rigour of the law, for he would not, on any account, give evidence against him. The marquis's grandfather was an excellent Catholic, but his father was a desperate heretic, the chief plotter of all the machinations against the late king, and for this reason he was executed in the present reign ; the son should also have forfeited his property, but through the clemency of the King, it was restored to him ; he is a man of great ability. Annexed to this are several other smaller islands, Lunghe, Sile, Colasa, Kersera, and Lismore. The largest of these is not more than six miles in length.

"The island of Mule is twenty miles long and twelve in width, and has six thousand souls, all heretics. The proprietor is MacLein, whom the Irish call Macalin.

"The island of Tyreyke is ten miles long and four broad, with two thousand souls. Its proprietor is the aforesaid MacLein, and the inhabitants are outwardly heretics.

"The island of Coll is twelve miles in length and three in width, and has scarcely one thousand souls. It is subject to the same owner as the preceding two.

"The island of Whist, thirty miles long and eight broad, has twelve thousand souls, and is subject to two owners. Lord Clanranel owns half of it, and all his tenants are Catholics. The other half belongs to Sir James MacDonel, and his tenants are part Catholics, part heretics. The only priest is the Franciscan Father Francis MacDonel. Belonging to the same Lord Clanranel are other islands called Claim, Roma, Egg, and Muc; they have about one thousand souls, all Catholics.

"The island of Barra is six miles long and three wide ; the owner is MacNeil; it has one thousand inhabitants (Catholic). The owner

MacNeil, is also Catholic. There is a Dominican missionary, Father George Fannin, who labours there successfully.

"The island of Lennse is thirty miles long and ten broad, and has four thousand souls, all heretics. The owner is the Earl of Siforth, of the family of Macchegni. This nobleman is very influential, and well disposed towards the Catholic faith. He persuaded the Royal Council of Edinburgh not to disturb the Irish priests among the Highlanders, assigning as his motive, that since those priests led the natives to observe the Catholic faith, there are fewer robberies and other crimes ; and, what was formerly a thing unheard of, restitution of stolen goods is now frequently made. For this reason, the Royal Council allowed Father Whyte to continue his mission among them. A priest named Monro has also lately gone to those parts, and he is on good terms with the same nobleman.

"The island of Skye is thirty miles long and twenty broad, and has six thousand souls. The owners of the island are Sir James MacDonel, who owns half of it; and MacLuid, who holds the remainder. There are some Catholics in the Island, but they suffer very much from the heretical ministers.

"In all the aforesaid islands, the working class speak no language but the Irish ; but the gentry, besides the Irish, speak a corrupt dialect of the English language.

"The proprietors of the islands hold vast territories, also on the mainland of Scotland, and the people speak only Irish, and are well disposed towards the Catholic faith. They retain many of its rites and traditions, and they despise the Protestant ministers, although the proprietors themselves, for political motives, profess Protestantism.

"In these islands, there is no wheat, but barley and oats and *spelta* are cultivated. Cows and oxen, horses, sheep and deer are in great abundance, as are also fish and birds of every description. Great quantities of fish are taken.

"There are no forests in these islands, and the fruit trees do not yield fruit, on account of the fierce sea-breeze, particularly from the north, which blights and withers everything.

"In the islands, there are several monuments of the early saints, and many ruins of the ancient churches destroyed by the heretics. So general was the ruin of the churches, that the ministers at present preach in private houses, and hold their services there. All these islands are subject to a pseudo-bishop, who is styled Bishop of the Isles, who, however, never resides there. He, for the most part, lives at the Court, and is quite content, and gives no trouble, that he regularly receives his revenues. To this is, in a great measure, due the toleration which the islanders enjoy in the matter of religion. The ministers, too, who live among them, are very moderate, and, if there were a sufficient number of missionaries, there is no doubt that many of those ministers would be themselves converted, as happened in the parish of Glenlivet on the mainland, which is, in consequence, to the present day, almost entirely Catholic.

"The ordinary beverage which is used is milk, in summer; and boiled water, mixed with flour, in winter; and seldom, even among the richest of the gentry, will you find cider or beer. Hence it is that the missionaries suffer a good deal until they get accustomed to the climate and the food of the country; the more so, as they have to travel about by night, in order to escape the violence of the persecution. The people give nothing, even as alms, to the missionaries, but they are compelled to support the Protestant parsons.

"The missionaries receive nothing on the occasion of marriages, funerals, or baptisms, and they depend entirely for their maintenance on the aid received from the Sacred Congregation. The missionaries on the mainland, for the most part, live in the houses of the Catholic gentry; and thus are amply provided for.

"The missionary, in the Hebrides Islands, has to keep a servant who carries the sacred vestments, and also brings, from place to place, a portable bed, which is used in the summer season. The missionary must also buy his own flour, for the inhabitants subsist on milk, butter, and cheese. From all this it is clear that the missionaries must be reduced to great straits, as they have to provide themselves with everything, whilst they receive only fifty scudi a year from the Sacred Congregation, and even that amount not complete, on account of the exchange which has to be paid on it

"In order to propagate and maintain the faith in these islands, the following things are absolutely necessary :—

"1st. To send thither missionaries who speak the Irish language and are men of virtue, inflamed with zeal for the salvation of souls.

"2nd. To select native youths, who may be supported and educated in the colleges of the Continent, for these, as missionaries, will be far more acceptable to the islanders than strangers. The safest means for sending letters to the islands, is to address them to Dublin, and to forward them from Dublin to Belcastel, to Mr. Daniel Magee, who is a Catholic. He will send them on to Mr. Daniel Groam MacDonel, who lives in Kentyre,'that is the head of the mainland.

"3rd. It would be of great advantage to the interests of religion, to make some provision, and to grant a salary to a Catholic schoolmaster, for the children are in extreme need of some instruction. About ten years ago, Eugene MacAlaster was appointed to teach school at Glengary, in the Highlands, and about two years ago, two others were selected, but there has been no tidings as to whether they undertook the task.

"4th. It would be most useful were the Sacred Congregation to write commendatory letters to Gillenan MacNeil, the lord of Barra Island, who is a Catholic, and to the above-mentioned Daniel MacDonel of Moidort, and to the Lord Clanranel, who though a heretic, is most favourable to the Catholics, and is married to a Catholic wife, who, together with about five hundred others, were converted to the faith by the aforesaid Father Francis MacDonel."

At the end of the " Relatio " is added :—

"Such is the report regarding the Hebrides Islands given to the Archbishop of Armagh, by Father Francis MacDonel, on the occasion of his coming to the said Archbishop to receive the holy oils. The Archbishop further states that he would have wished to proceed in person to those islands to see everything with his own eyes, but that *spiritus quidem promptus est, crumena autem infecta.* He gives great praise to Father Francis as an excellent missionary."

To illustrate this " Relatio " of Dr. Plunket, it will not be out of place to present some extracts from two other narratives of these missions, forwarded to the Sacred Congregation in the year 1669. One of these was written by Dr. Winster, who, as we have seen was for many years prefect of the mission in the Scottish Islands. He states that :—

" The mountainous districts are barren and during five or six months of the year, scarcely yield to the inhabitants sufficient oaten or barley-bread; towards the sea there is an abundance of fish, and everywhere there are large flocks of sheep and cattle ; the people live on cheese, milk, and butter ; the lower classes, however, are often without bread.

" The Highlands have no commerce with foreign nations, but sell their cattle to the inhabitants of the Lowlands, and are thus enabled to purchase flour ; this is the reason why the missionaries who visit these districts are obliged not only to bring with them bread and wine for the Holy Sacrifice, but also food and every other necessary, not without very great inconvenience.

" There are no post-offices, and no means of sending letters unless a person sends them by hand to the chief city of the kingdom.

" The language of the inhabitants is the Irish, wherefore only natives of Ireland are suited for these missions, till such times as priests from the districts themselves be educated in the col'eges on the Continent.

" The Catholics live in peace in the district of Glengarry, under Earl MacDonnell ; also in those mountain districts which belong to the Marquis of Huntley, and in the islands of Uist, Barra, and Morar, which are the most remote from the Government residences.

" Such is the severity of the laws, that the practice of the Catholic religion is not allowed ; in the Highlands, however, and remote islands, these laws are not carried into execution.

" The present missionaries are two Franciscan friars, viz., Father Mark and Father Francis MacDonnell, sent thither by the Sacred Congregation ; there is also one secular priest (a missionary of the

Sacred Congregation), whose name is Francis White,* and a schoolmaster in the Glengarry district named Eugene MacAlaster. The
Father White, whom I have mentioned, often visits the islands and
the lands of Glengarry, and all the mountain districts, as far as he is
able, and in doing so he endures great fatigue and suffering; willingly, however, on account of his great zeal for the salvation of
souls; hence all this country is greatly indebted to him, and he is a
native of Ireland.

" The schoolmaster is scarcely tolerated in Glengarry, despite the
protection of the lord of that territory; and there is but little hope
of another master being found to succeed the present one in that
toilsome position.

" There was also another Irish missionary in the Highlands,
named Duigen; he, however, has left that mission, and now Father
White alone remains.

" The few missionaries who are in the mountainous districts are
wholly insufficient for the wants of the Catholics, especially in
winter, when the roads are almost wholly impracticable; wherefore
we pray that other Irish priests may be sent thither, and Father
White undertakes to find such priests through his brother,† who is
vicar in the diocese of Limerick in Ireland; this is the more necessary,
as the Franciscans, on account of their bad health, cannot long
continue on that mission."

The second report was made by a Scotch priest after
visiting all the districts of this mission. He writes:—

" The Highland families are, for the most part, Catholic, or
prepared to be so, if they had priests to instruct them; those, however, of the Lowlands are most fierce heretics, and hate the
Highlanders on account of their religion.

" The Highlanders are of an excellent disposition, quick of intellect,
and taking a special delight in the pursuit of knowledge; they are
desirous of novelties, and have an unbounded passion for ingenious
inventions, so that no greater favour can be conferred on them than
to educate their children, and render them suited to become priests
or ecclesiastics.

" Their untiring constancy in all matters is truly surprising, and
is admitted and extolled even by their enemies, particularly in regard
of religion, which they continue to profess. as much as the severity
of the persecution, and the total want of priests permit.

" Their arms are, two-edged swords, large shields, bows and

---

* In a letter written 25th September, 1679, Dr. Winster announces the
death of this missionary, and adds, that " he might justly be styled the
Apostle of the Hebrides and neighbouring districts," *a gran ragione si
può chiamare Apostolo degli Ebridi e paesi vicini.*

† This was Dr. Gaspar White, Vicar Capit. of Limerick, till the
appointment of Dr. Dowley as Vicar-Apostolic in 1669.

arrows, which they still continue to use, adding to them, however, firearms, which they manage with admirable dexterity.

" They still retain the language and costume of their earliest forefathers, so that their dress is not very dissimilar from that of the ancient statues in Rome, loosely covered from the waist to the knee, and a *bonnet* on the head.

" Almost all the families are Catholic, or disposed to receive the Catholic faith, if, for no other reason, at least to imitate their ancestors, who were so zealous in the cause of religion. Nay more, many of these families have suffered, and actually suffer, for this sole reason, not only in Parliament, where the nobility of the Lowlands have a large majority, but also in the courts of justice, where they are oppressed by the greater number and authority of their enemies; and the heretic judges give sentence against them, even though their cause be most just, deeming them rebels for not conforming to the Established Religion.

" The remaining Scoto-Irish are heretics, more through ignorance than malice; they cease not, however, to cherish a great esteem for the Catholics, as appears in many things.

" If a priest visit them they show him more respect, and honour him more than their own ministers.* In fact, the heretics amongst the Highlanders surpass in reverence for our priests the very Catholics of the Lowlands.

" They, moreover, retain many Catholic usages, such as making the Sign of the Cross, the Invocation of Saints, and sprinkling themselves with holy water, which they anxiously ask from their Catholic neighbours.

" In sickness they make pilgrimages to the ruins of the old churches and chapels which yet remain, as of the most noble monastery of Iona, where St. Columba was abbot, also of the chapels of Ghierlock, and Appercrosse, and Glengarry, which were once dedicated to the saints. They also visit the holy wells, which yet retain the names of the saints to whom they were dedicated; and it has often pleased the Most High to restore to their health those who visited these ruins or drank at these wells, invoking the aid of the saints.

" The enmity of the Lowlanders has been a source of great injury to the Scoto-Irish, especially since heresy began to domineer in Scotland; for the inhabitants of the Lowlands being most furious heretics (with the exception of some few whom the Catholic missionaries restored to the bosom of the Church), and seeing the Highlanders most constant in the faith, and that there is no hope of alienating them from the Catholic Church, seek, by all possible means, to excite odium against them, designating them barbarians,

---

* In an addition to this "Report," made, I presume, by the agent of the Scottish Church in Rome, it is said, "The priest is styled by the islanders, and known by the name, *coronatus;* they venerate and caress him much more than their own preachers."

impious, enemies of the reformed creed, &c. ; and they hesitate not
to affirm of them everything that can be suggested by detraction
and their own excessive hatred ; and they even deem it a glorious
deed to show contempt for, or cast ridicule on, a Highlander." *

CHAPTER XVI.

THE REVENUE OF THE IRISH SEES.

ONE of the first acts of the *reformed* Church in Ireland was
to appropriate to itself everything that the piety of our forefathers had offered to God for the support of the ministers
of the altar. Nor did this suffice ; taxes were levied, new
appropriations made, new government grants sanctioned, in
order to advance the interests of the Protestant Church.
However, all was fruitless. The ministers of that Church
could never say *enough*. When they were upbraided with
the failure of their mission and preaching, they always
imputed it to the want of sufficient means ; but despite
every additional increase, the curse of barrenness ever
weighed upon their ministry.

As early as 1576, Sir Henry Sydney, who had six times
been at the head of the Irish Government, in a report to
the Queen, declares, "Your Majesty may believe it, that,
upon the face of the earth where Christ is professed, there
is not a church in so miserable a case, the misery of which
consisteth in these three particulars—the ruin of the very
temples themselves, the want of good ministers to serve in
them, competent living for the ministers." Thirty years
later we find another *Report* from Sir John Davies to
Robert, Earl of Salisbury. Speaking of the dioceses of
Kilmore and Ardagh, he says: "The vicarages are so
poorly endowed, that ten of them, being united, will
scarce suffice to maintain an honest minister . . . But the

---

* Lord Macaulay has manifested the same spirit in our own times,
never omitting any opportunity to blacken the character and religion
of the Scoto-Irish.

incumbents, both parsons and vicars, did appear to be such poor, ragged, ignorant creatures, as we could not esteem any of them worthy of the meanest of these livings." Nevertheless, in the same page, he informs us that "the bishop, Robert Draper, is a man of this country birth, worth well-nigh £400 a-year. He doth live now in these parts, where he hath two bishoprics ; but there is no divine service or sermon to be heard within either of his dioceses." *

Again, when Bishop Bedell complained to the Lord Deputy that "in this kingdom of his Majesty, the Pope hath another kingdom far greater in number ;"† in other words, that Protestantism had been as yet unable to make any progress in Ireland, the Parliament, without delay, "passed several Acts for improving the temporal estates of the Church ;"‡ so much so, that the prelates and clergy assembled at Dublin presented an address to the King (Charles I.), in which, after commemorating how they had lately been "dejected and depressed to the lowest degree of misery § and contempt by the wars and confusion of former times, having their churches ruined, their habitations left desolate, their possessions alienated, their persons scorned, their very lives hourly subject to the bloody attempts of rebellious traitors," they declare, "that the bounty and piety of his sacred Majesty, and of his blessed father, had not only made restitution of that which the iniquity of former ages had robbed them of, but also enriched them with new and princely endowments, which favours did become more sweet whilst entertained by them as pledges of his future unexhausted goodness." The benevolence of the Crown did not even stop here ; and a little before Dr. Plunket's appointment to the see of Armagh, we find a

---

* Davies, *Tracts*, page 266.
† Strafford, *Letters*, i. 147.
‡ See Mant, i. 482.
§ Thomas Moygne, Protestant Bishop of Kilmore and Ardagh, in 1625, when giving a general prospect of the Irish Establishment, declares that "in consequence of the poverty of the clergy, "the Church will soon be brought to decay."—(See Parr's *Collection*, page 322.)

large portion of the forfeited property of those who had
lost their lives in defence of the royal cause, and who
nevertheless were designated, with an unheard-of ingrati-
tude, *Irish Papists, rebels, and enemies*, allotted to increase
the revenues of the ministers of the Protestant Church.
(14 & 15 Charles II., chap. 2.)

In one of his letters, Dr. Plunket values the revenues of
the Protestant Archbishop of Armagh at 20,000 scudi, or
£5,000. In 1539 the valuation of the see amounted to
only £183 17s. 5½d.; in 1618 it had increased to £400; in
1635, as we learn from Sir James Ware, the rents amounted
to £735 4s. 4d. per annum ; and thus they gradually swelled,
until, at the present day, we find the gross amount of the
yearly revenues of the see, as stated in the Report of the
Ecclesiastical Commissioners, to be £17,669 16s. 7d.

Whilst, despite all human efforts, and this ever-increasing
revenue, the Protestant Church in Ireland, was seen subject
to a gradual decay, we are supplied by Dr. Plunket with
accurate intelligence as to the earthly means with which the
Catholic priests and bishops were supported whilst they
cheerfully led on their flocks to martyrdom, and overcame,
in an unceasing victory, all the powers of this world leagued
against them. In many of his letters the Primate will be
found to dwell upon this subject; but we shall select two
as sufficient for our present purpose. In one of these,
whilst he petitions the Holy See to succour the Bishop of
Kildare, he draws a general picture of the poverty of the
Irish Church : and in the other he presents in detail the
individual revenues of the various sees.

The first letter is dated from Dublin, the 13th of August,
1677 :—

" Since the beginning of the heresy and schism in this kingdom,
no parish priest or prelate of the orthodox creed had any possessions, lands, or fixed revenue, the churches, with all their emoluments
being seized on by the Protestant ministers, who continue to enjoy
them to the present day ; so that our ecclesiastics are obliged to
depend for their support on the oblations of the poor Catholic
families who, according to their means, make certain offerings to
their parish priests ; that is, about two shillings in the year; and,

generally speaking, the bishops have no other revenue than the offering of £1, which is annually made by each of the parish priests; so that the greater the number of the parish priests, the larger will be the revenue of the bishops. Some dioceses have sixty priests; others forty; others thirty; others fifteen; others only seven, as Clonmacnoise, Kilfenora, &c. Hence it arises that in some dioceses it is impossible for a bishop to have sufficient revenue to support a clerk of S. Girolamo della Carità.* It is certain that Dr. Forstall, of Kildare, whose little diocese is only five or six miles from Dublin, and, having only fifteen priests, yields him no more than £15 per annum, has not sufficient revenue to maintain a servant, even of a low grade. I don't know how poor religious can subsist when they are appointed bishops, for such revenue cannot suffice to support a bishop's servant : and this extreme poverty renders their dignity despicable with Catholics, as well as Protestants. The Viceroy on one occasion said to me that he was not, and never would be, a persecutor of ecclesiastics ; but that he was surprised how bishops were sent to this kingdom without their having sufficient means for their support. I told his Excellency, in reply, that our prelates imitated those of the primitive Church. Yes, he said, but they are far different from those of France and Spain. But, I replied, the bishops of France and Spain, when it may be necessary, are ready to act in the same manner. I must say, however, that at the present day it does not suit the episcopal dignity to be held by mendicants ; and the poverty of the bishops prevents their conversing with the Protestants, from which great good might be derived. Now, few of the bishops have a better opportunity of communicating with the Protestants than the Bishop of Kildare, who is a learned, prudent, and grave prelate, and esteemed by all who know him. As his church does not yield him more than £15 per annum, he might receive the administration of the adjoining diocese of Leighlin, which has likewise about fifteen or sixteen priests, and thus he might be able to live *juxta miserias patriae.* The diocese of Leighlin, of itself, would not be able to maintain a bishop ; and it would be better that it should be held in administration by a learned bishop than be governed by a vicar-capitular. A bishop could administer confirmation there, consecrate chalices and altars ; and he would also be a greater consolation to the Catholics than a vicar-general. I beseech you, therefore, to see that this worthy prelate, Dr. Forstall, may, in addition to his own diocese, receive the administration of Leighlin, which measure will redound to the greater glory of God and the consolation of the Leighlin Catholics, and is deserving of the charity and zeal of your Excellency."

Besides this general picture of the extreme poverty of the Irish sees, we have another letter of Dr. Plunket, in which

---

* The church to which Dr. Plunket was attached whilst in Rome.

he presents in detail the precise revenues of nearly all the
various dioceses. It was written about the close of the
year 1673, and is as follows :—

"On the Vigil of Christmas, Mgr. Daniel Makcy, Bishop of
Down and Connor, most perfectly obeyed the last edict, and
departed not only from Ireland, but also from the world, to enjoy
now, as we hope, a country and a kingdom where he will be free from
the Parliament of England and its edicts. He was a good theologian, educated in Spain, and chaplain for many years of D. Pedro of
Aragon. At his death he had no more than thirty-five bajocchi
(eighteen pence), so that to have even a private funeral it was
necessary to sell a part of his goods.

"I take the present opportunity of sending to the Sacred
Congregation an account of a matter of some importance ; and the
effect of this report will be, I hope, to prevent, for some time, the
appointment of any more bishops for this kingdom; and my
opinion is based on the poverty of the various dioceses, which is
indeed, astounding. The following is the annual revenue of all my'
suffragan sees :—

			£	s.
"The primatial see of Armagh ...		...	62	0
„ diocese of Meath	...	...	70	0
„ „ Clogher	...	...	45	0
„ „ Derry...	...	...	40	0
„ united dioceses of Down and Connor			25	0
„ diocese of Raphoe	...	...	20	0
„ „ Kilmore	...	...	35	0
„ „ Ardagh	...	...	30	0
„ „ Dromore	...	...	17	10
„ „ Clonmacnoise ...		...	7	10

These are all the sees, with their revenues, in the province of
Armagh. You may hence reflect and ponder how little it becomes
the dignity of the episcopal character to be bishops in dioceses which
cannot yield a sufficient support.

"Moreover, I know for certain, that the metropolitan sees of
Dublin, and Cashel, and Tuam do not yield £40 each per annum.
It is true that the diocese of Elphin, which is a suffragan see of the
Archbishop of Tuam, yields about £50, and the diocese of Killaloe,
in the province of Cashel, yields about £55; but of the other
dioceses not one exceeds £25.

"The churches of Ireland, however, as they are in the hands of
the Protestants, are very rich ; for instance, the Protestant Primate
derives from the lands and possessions of the church of Armagh
£5,000 per annum, and the Protestant Archbishop of Dublin has
about £3,000. But the Catholic Primate and Archbishop have only
the revenues which I mentioned above ; whence you may conclude

how inexpedient it is to appoint any more bishops in this kingdom ; and should any such be appointed, it will be necessary for the Sacred Congregation to supply them with revenues, as it does for the bishops in the Indies, and *ad orientales infidelibum plagas.* I have two suffragans, Dr. Plunket, Bishop of Meath, brother of the Earl of Fingall, who, for the past twenty-six years has served the Sacred Congregation with the greatest integrity, even at a time when there was no other bishop to act in Ireland. The other is Dr. Patrick Duffy, Bishop of Clogher, who even ventured to take possession of his see at the moment when the persecution was about to burst forth.

" The Archbishop of Tuam has two suffragans, that is, the Bishops of Clonfert and Elphin.

" The Archbishop of Cashel has two also in his province, the Bishops of Waterford and Killaloe : there is also a third, but he lives in France, viz., the Bishop of Kilfenora.

" The Archbishop of Dublin has one suffragan, the Bishop of Ossory, who is in Ireland; and another, the Bishop of Ferns, a worthy prelate, but who, for many years past, has fixed his domicile in France. In my humble judgment the Metropolitan, with one suffragan bishop, would be quite sufficient in each province.

" From this report a question of curiosity will, perhaps, suggest itself to your Excellency—how, forsooth, I and the other prelates succeed in making out these few shillings ? Each parish priest gives us per annum for *proxy* one pound sterling, which is equal to twenty shillings, or four scudi. But you will ask how is the parish priest maintained ? I answer, that each family or each head of a family gives four juli, that is, two shillings per annum to the parish priest; then for his trouble in baptism he receives one shilling ; for every matrimony, 1s. 6d., or three juli. From which it follows, that where there are most Catholic families, there the parish priest is richest ; I should rather say, less poor and miserable. In the diocese of Down and Connor, as also in many other dioceses, there is a large number of Presbyterians (who are especially numerous in Ulster), of Anabaptists, and Quakers, and hence these dioceses are exceedingly poor. And it must here be remarked, that the Presbyterians, who are an offshoot of Protestantism, are more numerous than Catholics and Protestants together.

" You thus see the state of the ecclesiastical riches of the Catholic bishops of this kingdom, and I assure you that during the past four years I would have been reduced to beggary, were it not for a few pence that I had set aside, but which are now wholly exhausted.

" I pray you to send this letter to Mgr. Ravizza, who is the present Secretary of Propaganda, as I have been informed. I already requested you to direct your letters to me thus—*For Mr. Thomas Cox, Dublin,* and they will surely reach me without being intercepted. I now make my reverence to you from my hiding-place, on the Feast of the Holy Innocents, 1673. 1 wish you a most happy new year, replete with every felicity."

The revenue of £62 for the diocese of Armagh was the normal sum which the Archbishop should receive, considering the number of clergy in the diocese; but when the persecution was let loose with redoubled fury against the Irish Church, many of the priests were scattered, and all were reduced to such poverty that few could contribute anything to the support of their chief pastor; and hence we more than once find Dr. Plunket, in his subsequent letters, declaring that at intervals he did not receive twenty scudi, that is, £5 per annum from his diocese, and, whilst a small thatched hut was his only residence, oaten bread with a little milk was often his only sustenance.

CHAPTER XVII.

SOME SPECIAL EVENTS OF DR. PLUNKET'S EPISCOPATE.

1670.

THE accusations which, from time to time, were made against the Primate by those whose enmity he had awakened by his spirit of religion, and his zeal in the correction of abuses, gave him more than once occasion to refer in his correspondence with the Holy See to some facts of the early years of his episcopate, which, perhaps, would otherwise have remained wholly unknown to us.   Thus, in 1672, he was accused of having deported himself during his episcopate in a manner unbecoming his sacred character.   In reply Dr. Plunket thus writes on the 2nd April, 1672 :—

" Monsignor, I predicted some time ago that should I publish the decree in favour of the Dominicans, endless calumnies would be circulated against me.   I assure your Excellency, that since the present Viceroy came to this kingdom (that is to say, during the past two years), there is no living being that can accuse me of having performed an action unbecoming of my sacred character.   I pray you to mark well this assertion.   Yes; *distingue tempora et conciliabis Scripturas.*   During the time of Roberts, the preceding Viceroy, who was my enemy and persecuted me, I was obliged, in order to conceal

myself, to go under the name of *Captain Bruno* (Brown), with my
sword, and a wig, and pistols, &c.; this lasted for two or three
months."

Thus we learn that during the first months of his episcopate, whilst the Primate was visiting his diocese, and
administering Confirmation and convening diocesan synods,
the sword of persecution was all the while suspended over
his head, and that he was obliged to disguise himself under
the dress and manner of a layman.

A little later, in consequence of some representations
made in Rome, unfavourable to the Primate, the Secretary of
the Sacred Congregation deemed it his duty to convey to him
a strong, yet friendly admonition. This elicited the beautiful
answer of Dr. Plunket, dated 23rd February, 1671:—

" I received your most welcome letter of the 20th December, and
I assure you that though it was conceived in strong terms, yet when
I reflected on all the circumstances, it afforded me much more
comfort than affliction; for I knew that the correction was truly
fraternal, given by one who loved me with sincere affection, and I
am sure that that *amor erat mutuus*, for I ever loved and revered your
Excellency as my benefactor, and as the promoter of the spiritual
good of my country. as is well known to all in this northern world.
Moreover, I was well aware that all that was said against me was
false, and that it proceeded merely from envy; everything that I
undertook as to the removal of abuses and the promotion of the
spiritual good of my country being blessed with success by God;
and this, although many of the things that I undertook were arduous,
such as the opening of public schools, the holding of a Provincial
Synod in the celebrated town of Clones, and especially the obtaining
pardon for a large number of outlawed gentlemen, and for hundreds
of Catholic families who were prosecuted by Government for having
intercourse with them. The most difficult task, however, was the
removal of Terence Kelly, Vicar of Derry. He had such influence
with the Protestants that he made my two immediate predecessors
tremble, and procured the imprisonment of more than one visitator.
I went in person to the diocese of Derry; convoked the clergy,
suspended his jurisdiction, and appointed in his stead Dr. Conwell,
a learned and holy man. I was accused before the lay tribunal, but
the unfortunate man found that he was anticipated even in the
court of the Viceroy, and in that of the Governor of Ulster, the
Earl of Charlemont; and then he cried out in a loud voice, ' *The
Italian Primate, the Roman Primate has unhorsed me.*' The Earl of
Charlemont has not molested even one ecclesiastic since my arrival
here; he is also so friendly with me, that on one occasion, seeing me

somewhat afraid, he said to me, ' Have no fear, no one shall dare touch you ; and when you want to administer confirmation, don't go any more to the mountains, but come to the court-yard of my palace.' He made me a present during my life of a garden and excellent orchard, with two fields, and a fine house. It is in an excellent position. As to the Viceroy, it is notorious that he has such an esteem for me, as even to conciliate in my behalf the favour of the King. Dr. Brennan, who has my cipher, will tell more to your Excellency. Suffice it to say that he granted me the lives of three Catholics who had been prosecuted and condemned in the City of Enniskillen. The Earl of Drogheda allows me to have a public church, with bells, &c., in my diocese, within his district, which are exempt from the royal jurisdiction. No fewer than nine times have I been accused before the Viceroy, on account of the schools, and for exercising foreign jurisdiction. This nobleman, however, always brought the charges to his own court, and thus they were quashed. " In the province of Munster the Earl of Orrery has prohibited assemblages for Mass : the Earl of Kingstown, too, has expelled the clergy from the city of Galway, the capital of the province of Tuam : and the accusations of Martin French against the Archbishop of Tuam have been admitted. In Dublin, the schools which were commenced at Saggart have been upset, and the Remonstrants give annoyance to the Archbishop and others, summoning them before the Court of the Viceroy. Yet in my province I have had no annoyance, nor has any accusation been admitted either against me or against any of my clergy, although I drove away all the Remonstrants, so that not one of them remains."

Another letter of Dr. Plunket, written on the 30th December, 1670, and addressed to Dr. Brennan, then agent for the Irish clergy in the Eternal City, gives many particulars as to the events of this year :—

" It was most consoling to me to receive intelligence that Mgr. Baldeschi was pleased with the course that I have pursued in my province, and you may assure him that the best relations exist between me and Dr. Talbot, and that on various occasions I most earnestly exerted myself with the Viceroy in his behalf, and that were it not for my interference he would have been expelled long since from the kingdom.

" The agent of the Duke of Ormond is a certain Mr. Matthews, with whom I never spoke one syllable. Mr. John Patrick is as much an agent of Ormond as you are : on the other hand, he is a good Catholic, and of great influence with the Viceroy, and he is a mortal enemy of Walsh, and on these accounts I have held communication with h'm. There is, however, a coolness between him and Dr. Talbot, on account of some family matters.

" The Bishop of Meath visited his diocese twice this year, and this is as certain as that you made the visitation of the Seven Churches.

"I more than once wrote to you, that the Viceroy is nowise a friend of Ormond, and much less of Peter Walsh, whom he regards as a great schemer : the Viceroy, however, does not always make known his mind on this matter. John Everard, a Franciscan, agent of Walsh in this kingdom, presented a memorial to the Council of State in Dublin against those Franciscan friars who went from this province to the General Chapter held last year, saying that they went thither to procure the condemnation of Walsh ; I hope, however, it will be unsuccessful, on account of the aversion of the Viceroy for Walsh.

"The Earl of Orrery, President of the province of Cashel, published a proclamation against the assembling together of Catholics for Mass; he afterwards started for England ; he is a mortal enemy of the Viceroy. The President of Tuam has also begun to give annoyance to the Catholics in the city of Galway.

"In the province of Armagh the clergy and Catholics enjoy a perfect peace. The Earl of Charlemont, being friendly with me, defends me in every emergency. Being once in the town of Dungannon to administer Confirmation, and the Governor of the place having prevented me from doing so, the Earl not only severely reproved the Governor, but told me to go to his own palace, when I pleased, to give Confirmation, or to say Mass there if I wished.

"The magistrate of the city of Armagh having made an order to the effect that all the Catholics should accompany him to the heretical service every Sunday, under penalty of a half-crown per head, for each time they would absent themselves, I appealed to the President of the province against this decree, and he cancelled it, and commanded that neither clergy nor Catholic laity should be molested.

"Dr. James Cusack has been put in nomination for the Vicariate Apostolic of Clogher in this province. I can attest that he is a man of great merit for his learning, and prudence and earnestness in opposing Walsh.

"Mr. Thomas Fitzsymons deports himself so well in this province, that I know no one more deserving than he is. There is another named Patrick Mulderig, Vicar-General of Down, who labours with great fruit and zeal. Both one and the other deserve the patronage of Mgr. Baldeschi, should it be intended to nominate pastors for the vacant dioceses of this province."

On the 10th of the same month (10th December, 1670) Dr. Plunket pointed out some disorders which he had met with in his visitations, and which may serve to convey a more complete idea of the state of the province of Armagh at this period :—

"Having journeyed a good deal during the past summer, and made the visitation of six dioceses, it becomes my duty to mention some abuses that I remarked, that thus the Sacred Congregation may apply due remedies. The first is, a warm dispute between the Dominicans and Franciscans, especially in the County Fermanagh, where they dispute not only about the limits of their questing, but also about the convent itself. A remedy would have been applied to this in our Council of Clones, were it not that their Procurators said that they would arrange the matter amongst themselves, and prevent all scandals for the future. In the month of October I wished again to terminate the matter, but they again told me that their Procurators in Rome had brought the matter before the Sacred Congregation; the question being thus before a higher tribunal I did not think it proper to put my hands in it.

" Another dispute exists between the secular and regular clergy about questing at the Altar during the Parochial Mass.

" But there is another still greater disorder, viz., that in not one of the ten dioceses of this province is there a canonical and legitimate Chapter, nor are there any Canons or Dignitaries legitimately appointed. The Priests and Vicars *auctoritate propria* nominate the Archdeacons, Deacons, Treasurers, Canons, &c. In all the dioceses that I visited, I declared the Chapters null, as the forming of Chapters and the nomination of Dignitaries belonged to the Holy See, and not to the clergy of the diocese. I, consequently, have written requesting authority from the Holy See to institute Chapters in these dioceses, that thus the election of the Vicars Capitular may be valid; or should it be more pleasing, the names of five or six subjects of each diocese can be transmitted to Rome, and thus the Bulls of nomination may be expedited in form. I will be happy to do whatever the Sacred Congregation may command to reform these abuses."

In the month of July of this year Dr. Brennan, agent of the Irish Bishops, presented to the Sacred Congregation a petition in the names of " Oliver Plunket, Archbishop of Armagh and Primate of Ireland, Peter Talbot, Archbishop of Dublin, William Burgatt, Archbishop of Cashel, and James Lynch, Archbishop of Tuam," that the Archiepiscopal Pallium might be granted to them. Before the close of the year two Palliums were transmitted to Dr. Plunket for himself and the Archbishop of Dublin. It was only at a later period that the same sacred badge of union with the Apostolic See was granted to the other Archbishops.

1671.

On the 26th September, 1671, the Internunzio in Brussels thus writes to the Secretary of the Sacred Congregation :—

"Father Howard * has written, informing me that the Viceroy, Berkeley, has left London for Ireland, and that he had held many pleasing conversations with him about the affairs of that kingdom. He adds, that the King, at his solicitation and that of Berkeley, had granted to the Archbishop of Armagh an annual sum of £200, and that the Viceroy took on himself the charge of having that sum paid from the Irish revenue of the King.

" Howard also mentions his having baptized a child in the Queen's Chapel, she acting as God-Mother, and the Duke of York as God-Father, in the presence of the King, who read in the book used by the Priest the ceremonial of the Baptism. The Duke of York, not being Catholic, another Catholic gentleman answered the interrogatories which are prescribed.

" The King has placed the Great Chapel of St. James at the disposal of the Portuguese Ambassador. Their Majesties, with the Duke and the remainder of the Court, were preparing to go to the country to the house of the Duke of Norfolk, brother of Father Howard.

"I wrote on yesterday a strong letter to the Archbishop of Dublin, exhorting him to keep up friendly relations with the Archbishop of Armagh, and I wrote to the latter in the same strain in regard to the Archbishop of Dublin. I sent to the Archbishop of Dublin the Brief for Dr. Luke Wadding, &c."

The letters of the Primate commemorate many interesting facts connected with this period. Thus he writes on the 20th May, 1671 :—

" The Earl of Inchiquin, a Catholic and influential nobleman, has a relative, named Thady O'Brien, who is a good and learned man. All the bishops of Ireland have prayed that this man might be promoted to the see of Cork, a favour for which the Earl is most desirous.

" This morning, a serious accident occurred here (Dublin). The house within the Castle, in which the armour was deposited, took fire, and about 24,000 scudi worth of arms was consumed. Our Viceroy did not merit this misfortune. Even his own palace ran great risk. I wrote to you already praying you to allow a missionary stipend to three Jesuits who now teach, and will continue to teach in my diocese; if this be not granted, I shall have no means to

---

* Afterwards Cardinal Norfolk.

support them, and the glorious work that I have undertaken will fall to the ground, to the great detriment of religion.

" The adherents of Walsh are now prostrate, nor is there any danger of their raising their heads during the present Government, as the Lord Chancellor is but little favourable to them.

" Dublin, 20th May, 1671."

The letter of Dr. Plunket, without date, but transmitted to Rome, in October, 1672, refers to a striking occurrence of the preceding year :—

" You place reliance [he writes] on the moderation of our future Viceroy, Essex. Up to the present we have enjoyed great peace, and I sailed along with the favourable wind with sails unfurled ; but for the future, till I find what winds will blow, I will steer very cautiously. As to the expense of letters. . . . how many have I written to your Excellency and to the Sacred Congregation, and how many letters have I received ? You have my letters, *but in a certain emergency, when an outburst of persecution was feared in Armagh, I had to burn all my foreign letters, even the Brief of my Consecration. This happened last June twelve months on the Vigil of St. John's, when it was circulated by the Presbyterians that the Catholics had conspired to murder on that night all the Protestants.* The Viceroy was then in London."

Writing on the 2nd August, 1671, after referring to the disturbances that were occasioned in Galway by the recriminations of French and his opponents, he adds :—

" They are anxious that I should go to extinguish this fire, by which the whole province is consumed, and which occasions great scandal. I, however, have no money to undertake such a journey, for it is in the most distant part of the kingdom. I solemnly assure you, that when my debts are paid, 100 scudi do not remain to me in this world : by my visitations of the province, the building of schools, and the maintaining of the Jesuit fathers, my own support, and the expense of letters, home and foreign, *totaliter exhaustus sum.* It is now two years since I left Rome, and I think I maintained this correspondence better than any of my brethren—*plus omnibus laboravi*—and never did I give repose to my mind or hands—let all be to the greater glory of God.

" The good Archbishop of Tuam has suffered, and yet suffers more than can be conceived ; and it grieves the poor man more that he is not able to attend to the government of his province on account of so many summonses before the Courts, than all his other sufferings.

" We are here awaiting from day to day the arrival of our Viceroy, Berkeley, which is wished for by all : those whom he left at the head of the Government acted with great moderation. The poor Catholic gentry laboured hard with their load of taxes this year ; every one had to pay to the King an entire year's income : this reduced them to the straitest circumstances, and also impoverished our clergy, which has no other revenue than the voluntary offerings of the faithful : we are here as in the primitive Church. It is said that a similar tax will not be levied for the future. God grant it may be so ; and with a profound reverence I remain, &c."

Again, on the 9th of August, he writes to the Internunzio :—

"The Earl of Orrery, President of the province of Cashel, has published a most annoying edict against the clergy, in the cities of Cork and Limerick, prohibiting their saying Mass in these cities, and hence they have to go out to the country to celebrate Mass.

" In many of the dioceses of my province there is only one member of the chapter, viz., a Dean or Archdeacon : when the see becomes vacant, this member, *intra octo dies, eligit Vicarium Generalem ; est ne electio valida ?*

" As the Roman climate is not agreeing with Dr. Brennan, and he is, consequently, obliged to return to Ireland, the bishops of this kingdom send as their agent to the Roman Court Dr. Peter Creagh ; he studied in Rome, and knows the Italian language ; he is a gentlemanly man, and I am sure that he will be esteemed by your Excellency, and that he will well discharge the office entrusted to him "

On the 17th of the same month he again writes :—

" A most painful event happened in the town of Ross, in the diocese of Ferns. A certain Nicholas Nugent, of the Society of Jesus, challenged the Protestant minister to a dispute. Amongst other things the Protestant minister asked him did he admit that the King was the head of the Church in this kingdom. Father Nicholas replied that the King was master in temporal or civil things, but that the Pope was head in spiritual matters. During the dispute Father Nicholas also called the Bible used by the Protestants a false Bible, full of errors, and hence not to be styled the word of God. The polite minister cited the good father in the month of July at the assizes of Ross. He was there tried for having used the above language, as also for having said Mass publicly, and was condemned to pay 130 scudi, as well as to one year's imprisonment and the confiscation of all his goods. I must confess that the Father might have kept out of these questions and avoided these odious disputes, from which little good ever results, as experience has convinced us. When a person is found guilty of *præmunire*, the King only can pardon him.

" I wrote to your Excellency how the Earl of Orrery published an edict in Limerick and Cork, prohibiting Mass in these cities. A nice exchange we would have made, did we get him for our Viceroy, as it was desired by some,

" Thanks to God, this province *alta fruitur pace:* God grant that it may continue. Now that the great heat is over, I shall make a visitation of the diocese of Raphoe, which is the most remote one of my province, and distant 120 miles. Nevertheless you can direct your letters as before, for I shall have an agent in Dublin to receive them, and there is little danger of their being intercepted. I suppose you will have received before this the Briefs for those of my province." (17th Aug. 1671.)

On the 2nd October Dr. Plunket informs the Internunzio that he had had a long interview with the Viceroy, who remarked, amongst other things

" That many letters of Airoldi * and Baldeschi † had been intercepted, but that they gave great satisfaction to the Government : and raising his voice, he said, if you follow their wise counsels and do not interfere in political or civil matters, you shall have no annoyance from the King. He also said that he had seen the printed instructions which are given to missionaries, and he praised them, especially the last, which exhorts all not to write about any temporal or political matters. He also said that some of my letters to Airoldi and Baldeschi had been intercepted, and that he always found great praises lavished on himself in them, for which he thanked me. I replied that this was only an act of justice on my part: he then said that he caused all these letters to be diligently sealed and replaced in the post, and that he had given orders to have no further letters of mine intercepted or brought to him. I gave him infinite thanks for this, and after many ceremonies, I took my leave, in order to set out for the extreme north, that is, for the diocese of Derry. Oh! how opportune was the arrival of the Brief for Dr. Conwell ; for, after the death of Terence Kelly, he and the Archdeacon of Derry disputed about jurisdiction : however, the Brief will decide all. You will receive but few letters from me during this month, as I shall be in the extreme north ; but you can send your letters, with the direction, Mr. Oliver Plunket, Dublin : I will always direct mine for the future, a Mons. de Pruisson, Brussels. I pray you to send all my letters to Monsignor Baldeschi, and to keep copies of them, that thus you may not forget the matters of which they treat, and may be able to refresh the memory of Monsignor Baldeschi about them : though, indeed, he has such a disposition to do good to this country, that one might suppose he thought of it alone: God will remunerate him and your Excellency in this world and in the next.

" Dr. Brennan wrote to me more than once, that Monsignor Baldeschi would receive in Propaganda two youths of noble birth from my diocese ; one is of the family of O'Neal, the noblest of this

---

* The Internunzio in Brussels.   † The Secretary of Propaganda.

kingdom; the other is nephew of the Earl of Fingall and of Sir Nicholas Plunket, a most zealous Catholic, as all allow: and as our agent, Dr. Creagh, is about to start for Rome, and in two days will embark for Bourdeaux; and as he knows the French and Italian well, and is of most gentlemanly deportment, they will travel in his company; and I hope that they will become learned and prudent and good labourers and prelates, in this kingdom, at their own good time.

" OLIVER OF ARMAGH.

" 2nd October, 1671."

We learn from Rev. Dr. Lynch's MS. History of the Irish Bishops, that in the month of October, 1871, the Right Rev. Thadeus Keogh, Bishop of Clonfert, received the episcopal consecration at the hands of the Primate, Most Rev. Dr. Plunket, the Assistants being Right Rev. Dr. Plunket, Bishop of Meath, and Right Rev. Dr. Brennan, Bishop of Waterford.

1672.

Early in February, 1672, the Papal Bull, granting a Jubilee to the faithful, in order to conciliate the aid of Heaven in favour of the kingdom of Poland, was received by the archbishops of Ireland. And though the official documents merely commemorate its having been received and published by them, yet we may rest assured that the heroic constancy which that nation had displayed, and the severe persecutions which it had endured, awakened a lively interest, and enkindled an ardent devotion in the faithful people of Ireland.

On the 2nd of April, 1672, Dr. Plunket thus wrote to the Internunzio :—

" I have received your most agreeable note of the 22nd of March, and I am delighted that my letters were pleasing to you.

" In the Diocesan Synod, after Easter, I will make a decree, prohibiting the questing of religious at the parochial Mass; for now, after the late decrees of the King, there is greater toleration, and they can solicit alms *ostiatim*.

" During the past two years I expended in letters £58 sterling, and less than £25 per annum cannot suffice for them. I sent a receipt of Father Superior of the Jesuit Residence for the money which he received from me, and a few days ago I gave him 20 scudi more, as he alleged he had no money for their sustenance. Moreover, as one of the fathers, called Father Browne, was engaged in preaching, I employed another priest to instruct the ecclesiastics; he is a secular priest, and a very worthy man, and is named Edward Dromgole : I gave him his diet and 50 scudi during the past winter, and there were fifty-six priests in his class,"

" The diocese of Ardagh is very far from me, and the journey would be difficult in winter; and hence I did not go in person to arrange matters there, but next May I will visit it.

" The affair of Harold costs me more than 50 scudi, but although I should have to pawn the mitre and the ring, I was resolved not to leave him till I saw him embarked.

" All the orders of the King, in favour of the Catholics, have been punctually executed by the Viceroy in every part of the kingdom, without any actual opposition : the enemies of our religion murmur, however, and say most extravagant things about the King and the Viceroy : the Catholics can now be sheriffs, and some have already been installed ; they also can be incorporated in the cities as they were before the last war of 1641.

" The pension that was allowed me by the King has vanished. The Earl of Ranelagh prevented it, as well as other expenses, under pretext of the poverty of the treasury ; hence, if I do not receive some assistance from their Eminences, I shall be reduced to great misery."

Before the close of the year the Internunzio Airoldi was promoted from Brussels to Florence. Dr. Plunket, whilst he rejoiced at his promotion, laments the loss of his services to the Irish Church, which had been productive of so much good :—

" I have received your letter [he says] of the 6th December, and it occasions consolation at the same time and affliction—joy and sadness ; and it gives occasion of congratulating your Excellency, and of condoling with this nation, which you found disturbed and agitated in spiritual matters, whilst you leave it in tranquillity and peace ; and now that Coppinger has submitted, and that the Archbishop of Dublin and I are reconciled, I do not see what there is to disturb the kingdom. Even the Dominicans and Franciscans are now at peace, of which matters I shall give a detailed account to Cardinals Altieri, Rospigliosi, and my other masters in the Eternal City.

" So then your Excellency goes to Florence, where Galileo and the Crusca are all the fashion ; thence to Venice; afterwards to Madrid, and then to the Purple, which brings with it many other consequences. As hitherto I have been one of your most annoying correspondents from this kingdom, with my long and tedious letters, so I do not know if you will entirely get rid of me in Florence, and I will continue my correspondence, together with my affectionate devotedness to your Excellency.

" OLIVER OF ARMAGH.

" (22) 12th December, 1672."

Writing on the 16th of the same month, he acquaints the Sacred Congregation with the result of the Provincial Chapter of the Franciscan fathers :—

" The Chapter of the Friars is over ; it was a serious business to elect a Provincial and guardians that will last three years ; one would imagine that it was the King of Poland was to be elected. At length a certain Father Kelly was made Provincial. In reality, however, this Chapter appointed four Provincials for the four provinces of Ireland : the Arch-Provincial will reside in Tuam : he has three Deputies, with the title of Commissaries, in the other provinces—Father John Brady, a great defender of the *mare magnum*, in my province : Father James Darcy, in Dublin ; and another, whose name I forget, in the province of Cashel."

1673.

On the 8th of October, 1673, the Archbishop of Armagh thus wrote to the Internunzio in Brussels :—

" Before my arrival in these northern kingdoms, there were but few Irish prelates that kept up correspondence with your predecessors ; and I do not hesitate to say that I wrote more letters during the last four years than the Irish bishops during the preceding thirty years. I moreover stimulated the other prelates to write and to correspond with the Holy See, and I expended about 400 scudi (£100) in this correspondence.

" I found that the Catholic children were frequenting Protestant schools, and hence I brought the Jesuits hither, who, for three years and three months, have held schools, to the great advantage of religion In addition to the 500 scudi which I gave them in the first two years, God alone knows all that I expended, in frequent journeys to Dublin, to reply to the memorials which the Protestant ministers and teachers presented to the Viceroy against the Jesuit schools.

The few pence that I put together are now all gone, and my diocese gives me only 240 scudi a-year. The Protestant primate has all the revenue, which amounts to £20,000 per annum, so that we are precisely in the same condition as the bishops of the primitive Church.

" The whole kingdom, as far as regards ecclesiastical matters, enjoys at present the greatest peace. God grant that the next Parliament may give us no annoyance. Should anything of that nature happen, you shall be informed of it. And, in conclusion, I make a profound reverence."

Q

1674.

The long-threatened persecution 'against the Catholics was in this year let loose in all its fury. The clergy were everywhere obliged to fly to the woods and mountains to seek a refuge : still, as good shepherds, they did not neglect to visit and console their flocks, and often did they sacrifice their lives in this ministry of charity. The details of this persecution, as regards our primate, will be found in another chapter. Early in the year letters were addressed to him by the Sacred Congregation, extolling his zeal and courage in braving the threatening storm, and on the 8th of May letters were again addressed to him renewing these commendations, and exhorting him to constancy and firmness of soul. Other afflictions were added to the sword, and the Internunzio writes on the 11th of August, 1674 : " I received intelligence from various quarters that a great famine prevails in Ireland, and that the greater part of its prelates are reduced to a most miserable condition, as they endure not only persecution, but also the privation of those emoluments which they usually received from their dioceses."*

Dr. Plunket, writing on the 18th October, 1674, sets forth in detail many particular events of this afflicting year :—

" I am now in greater want than ever, and only sixty scudi now remain to me in this world, nor is there any hope of receiving aid from my diocese. the people are so poor. I think none of my colleagues are so badly off, with the exception of the Archbishop of Cashel (Dr. Burgatt) and the Bishop of Waterford (Dr. Brennan). The Archbishop of Cashel, compelled by necessity, sent around to all the gentlemen of the diocese to quest for alms, and he got only eighty scudi (£20), and the Bishop of Waterford receives from his diocese only eighty scudi per annum. The Archbishop of Tuam, too, is reduced to great poverty; but he, after being imprisoned in Galway, by order of the Viceroy, was exiled to Spain a few days ago : he is an exemplary prelate and a true ecclesiastic. The Vicar-General of Raphoe, a learned and exemplary man, Bernard Magorke, is also

* " Da piu parti vengo informato della gran carestia ch' è in Ibernia e dello stato miserabile nel quale si trovano la maggior parte di quei Vescovi, aggiungendosi alla persecuzione la mancanza degli emolumenti che per il loro mantenimento erano soliti di cavare dalle loro diocesi."

reduced to great misery, and has suffered great annoyance from the assize judges: his diocese does not yield sixty scudi per annum; he can scarcely keep clothes on his back. The Vicar-General of Meath, Oliver Dease, after his liberation from prison, having given security that he would leave the kingdom, died a few days ago : he was Vicar-General for thirty-seven years, and a man of great prudence and virtue.

" The Parliament having been prorogued till the month of April we have some hopes that during the winter the assize judges and other ministers will not be so rigorous in executing the decrees.

" Egan, the apostate Franciscan, is come to Dublin from London, in order to preach against the Catholic doctrines ; and the apostate Jesuit Fall has gone to Cashel on a like errand."

1675.

On the departure of the Internunzio, Falconieri, from Brussels, in the commencement of this year, Signor Agretti remained there as acting agent, with the title of Pro-Internunzio. Writing to the Sacred Congregation on 20th of April, 1675, he says :—

" Father Howard has written to state that the King of England made his excuses with him in regard of the late edict against the Catholics, saying that his intention in publishing this edict was to favour the Catholics ; as, had he not published it, the Parliament would assuredly have enacted a similar decree, which would be an irrevocable law ; whilst, on the contrary, when published by the King, it was in his power to connive at the Catholics, and recall the edict when an occasion presented itself."

Whatever may have been the King's intentions, the storm of persecution continued to rage against the Irish Catholics, and in consequence of the imminent risks to which the bishops were exposed, the visiting of the sacred *Limina* was dispensed with in their regard for twenty-five years, and faculty was granted them of making this visit through their resident Procurator in the Roman court.*

A paper presented to the Sacred Congregation in the following year by Father Mollon, of the order of St. Francis, records one of those arts by which the clergy, whilst they

---

* Note of Congregation, 14th January, 1675.

continued their usual functions, succeeded in eluding the vigilance of their persecutors:—

"In Ireland [he says] we are often obliged to celebrate our chapters *in montibus et sylvis*, when, forsooth, there is danger in other parts. The last time, however, it was held in a city and on a fair day, for whilst the world was engaged in trafficking, the religious, with a holy cunning, feigned a similar occupation, but far different was their business, viz., the holding of the chapter; this happened in the month of August, 1675."[*]

1676.

In a note of the archives of Propaganda for the Congregation of 10th February, 1676, we find the following reference to a letter of the Archbishop of Armagh, of which we have been unable to discover any further trace:—

"The Archbishop of Armagh writes for the renewal of faculties for himself and the Bishop of Meath, as these faculties have almost expired. He writes, moreover, that De Burgo, formerly Vicar-Apostolic, has been imprisoned in the province of Tuam, and condemned to perpetual imprisonment and the confiscation of all his property; as this Prelate has no means of subsistence, Dr. Plunket supposes that he shall receive assistance from the Sacred Congregation."[†]

In the preceding year the general Jubilee had been celebrated with great solemnity in Rome; but so violent were the persecutions, so many the afflictions to which the Irish Catholics were subjected, that few of them could visit the sacred shrines of the Eternal City, and perform the works prescribed for gaining its Indulgences. The Archdeacon of Dublin, Isidore Bertach, had come to Rome, in the year of which we are now speaking (1676), to perform the visit *ad limina*, in the name of his venerable bishop;

---

[*] In Ibernia molte volte si fanno li Capitoli in montibus et sylvis, quando vi è pericolo in habitato. Questa ultima volta si celebro in habitato, ed in tempo di fiera, dove essendo il secolo occupato nei suoi traffichi, li Religiosi con santa astuzia fingevano fare il medesimo ma *aliud egerunt*, cioè il Capitolo; e questo successe l'Agosto passato cioè del 1675.

[†] "L'Arcivescovo d'Armagh scrive per la rinnovazione delle sue facoltà e di quelle del Vescovo Midense che stanno per spirare. Scrive inoltre che il De Burgo già Vicario Apostolico è stato carcerato nella Provincia Tuamense e condannato ad perpetuos carceres cum confiscatione omnium bonorum onde non avendo da vivere, stima che la S. Congue. lo sovverrà con qualche sussidio."

and the four archbishops of Ireland availed themselves of this opportunity to solicit through him that a special Jubilee should be granted to Ireland, so that all the indulgences of that holy time might be gained by the faithful without their being obliged to leave the shores of their persecuted island.

It was in this year, too, that Dr. John Brennan, Bishop of Waterford, the bosom friend of our Archbishop, was transferred to the see of Cashel. A little before this translation, Dr. Plunket went on a visit to some relatives in those dioceses, and he availed of the opportunity thus presented to him to examine into the state of ecclesiastical discipline in these parts. " The Archbishop of Armagh, our Primate," thus writes Dr. Brennan, on 16th September, 1676, " is at present in this quarter of the world. He inspected the diocese of Cashel and my diocese to his great satisfaction, seeing that ecclesiastical matters were in as great order as the condition of the times will allow." The Primate himself, writing on the 1st of October, 1676, gives a detailed account of this visit. His letter is as follows :—

" Before receiving yours of the 18th of last month, being already aware, through another channel, of the death of our most glorious common father and pastor, I wrote to the suffragan dioceses, inviting both clergy and people, in a pressing manner, to implore the divine mercy for the eternal welfare of the deceased parent of Christendom ; and for the immediate election of a holy successor of St. Peter; but now, at the request of your Excellency, and in obedience to their Eminences, I shall write again to the different dioceses, nor will I be wanting on my own part to offer my feeble prayers in a matter of such importance.

" During the past four weeks I was on a visit with some relatives and friends in Cashel and Waterford, where, through the goodness of God, and the kindness of the Bishop of Waterford, I saw all the clergy ; they are very orderly, and devoted to the service of God ; and the Catholics, although poor, are rich in spiritual consolations. Had I not myself witnessed the poverty of the Catholics, both ecclesiastics and laity, in the districts in Cashel, I could, with difficulty, have believed it. In the city of Cashel there is not a single Catholic that could give lodging for one night ; there is but one parish priest in the whole city ; in the surrounding districts the soldiers and officers of Cromwell hold nearly all the lands, having expelled the Catholic tenants ; so that in these districts, and in the whole diocese, there are only about twenty priests, who subsist with difficulty, so that the episcopal revenue is no more than eighty scudi per annum ; the late Archbishop had at his death only twenty scudi, whilst his debts exceeded 100 scudi. Hence, I see how justly the Bishop of Waterford refuses to be promoted to this archdiocese ; for, how could a bishop support himself, and also a servant, with eighty scudi a year? To say the truth, there is no one better qualified, either by learning or prudence, or the esteem of the people, for the Pallium of Cashel than Dr. Brennan : and perhaps he would accept it without difficulty, were he allowed to retain the administration of his present diocese, which, indeed, is not half a quarter of an hour's drive ; what do I say? it is not even the distance of a Miserere from the archdiocese of Cashel. The diocese which he now governs has no more than thirty priests, so that both dioceses together have about fifty priests, and thus his revenue will reach about 200 scudi per annum. Now the Bishop of Cork has about eighty priests in his diocese ; the Bishop of Killaloe, seventy ; the Bishop of Meath, seventy ; and the Bishop of Elphin, fifty, with more extensive districts than the Bishop of Waterford would thus have with his fifty priests. The Archbishop of Cashel had at other times the diocese of Waterford in administration, or *in commendam*; and considering the vicinity of the two dioceses, it would be more advantageous for Waterford to be subject to his administration than to be governed by a Vicar-Capitular. The Bishop of Waterford could administer confirmation, perform the visitations, &c., in both dioceses without any difficulty ; and I know that the Catholics of Cashel and Waterford most anxiously desire this. Considering, therefore, the poverty of both dioceses, and their contiguity, I beseech you to obtain from their Eminences that the Bishop of Waterford, when advanced to the sacred Pallium, may retain the administration of his present diocese. Certainly if the bishops of Killaloe and Cork, and others, can govern seventy or eighty priests, and if (to take an example from a diocese nearer to your Excellency)* if, I say, the Bishop of Holland can govern greater districts, and almost more Catholics than are to be found in all Ireland, Dr. Brennan must be able to govern fifty priests ; nor is it becoming that one who taught in Propaganda philosophy for nine years, and theology for five, and who, as his Eminence Cardinal Colonna well knows, worked and toiled in other matters in the service of the Sacred Congregation, should now be left to subsist on eighty scudi a year. I again beseech you, therefore, to procure that Dr. Brennan, when transferred to the Pallium of Cashel, may be allowed by their Eminences to retain the administration of his present diocese, and making you a reverence, I shall ever remain,

" Your Excellency's most devoted servant,

"OLIVER OF ARMAGH, &c.

" Dublin, October, 1676.

"P.S.—The Bishops of Cork and Clogher have arrived in Nantes, and we expect their arrival here in a few days. I pray you to send this letter to Monsignor Cerri."

* The letter is addressed to the Internuncio in Brussels.

Amongst the Irish prelates most exposed to persecution during this eventful period, must be numbered Dr. John de Burgo, Vicar-Apostolic of Killala. In his youth he had served for some years as officer in the Austrian army of North Italy; but, renouncing the world, he dedicated himself to the service of the altar, and was appointed abbot of Clare, in the West of Ireland. From 1647 till the bishop's death, in 1650, he acted as Vicar-General of Killaloe, and we find him three years later arrested by Cromwell, and sent in company with eighteen other priests into banishment. For some years he dedicated himself to the sacred ministry in France and Italy till 1671, when he received a brief from Rome, appointing him Vicar-Apostolic of the ancient see of Killala. In this brief there was a clause, usual, indeed, in the appointments of Vicars-Apostolic in those times, that, *ipso facto*, his appointment was annulled if, within four months, he did not visit his diocese. The appointment was made in the special Congregation of 30th June, 1671; but as De Burgo was then travelling through Italy, it was only on the 22nd of November that the brief reached him in Milan. At the solicitation of Cardinal Litta, a second brief, dated 30th of May, 1672, was granted, without the restrictive clause; and before the close of that year Dr. De Burgo reached the shores of Ireland. Difficulties, however, had been for some time gathering around the path of the newly-appointed pastor. During the vacancy of the see, the Archbishop of Tuam, as Metropolitan, appointed Rev. John Dowley, a venerable ecclesiastic, Vicar-General of that diocese; and the informality of De Burgo's first brief having become generally known, the Archbishop of Tuam, his Metropolitan, refused to acknowledge his appointment, or instal him as Vicar-Apostolic till the second brief was submitted to him. This, however, Dr. De Burgo absolutely refused. He had imbibed the opinion that Vicars-Apostolic were subject *only* to the Holy See, and hence refused to acknowledge any authority in the Archbishop, in his regard, as we learn from a letter of the Internuncio of the 25th November, 1673.

Matters were in this state when De Burgo visited the Archbishop of Armagh, and presented to him the brief of the Holy See. Dr. Plunket recognised at once the genuineness of his appointment, and not being aware of his refusal to acknowledge the authority of the Metropolitan, hesitated not to address the following letter to the Archbishop of Tuam, in which he expresses his surprise how any doubt could be entertained as to the fact of De Burgo's lawful appointment, and corroborates this sentiment by the authority of his friend, the Bishop of Waterford.

We present the original letter of Dr. Plunket, written in English, in its characteristic orthography :—

" DR. PLUNKET TO THE ARCHBISHOP OF TUAM.

"23rd September, 1674.

" MY LORD,—I have perused the Breve Apostolicum that Dr. John Burk got for the Vicarship Apostolick of Killally, dated the 22nd of June, 1672, and I know it to be an Authentick Breve, and, whereas, it is not as the first breve with limitation of four months, I think there can be nothing said against it, or giveing the said Dr. Burk any hindering in his possession. I know alsoe Cardinale Antony Barberini's letter, and the late letter of Cardinal Litta, who doth admire he should be hindered in his possession, and so doe I alsoe, he having gott this second breve. And the Bishope of Waterford, Dr. Brenan, was with me all the last winter, who tould me that this diocess was given to Jo. Burk without that he ever did demand it ; but this was forced, as I may say, on him. And what Doctor Creagh writs to Father Gregory Joice, that there was sentence given by the S. Congregation against the said Dr., if any such sentence was given, it must have beene by misinformation, and on the account of the first breve, which had a limitation of four months ; and my lord, who can ever believe that any should be cast or condemned not being heard: non est mos apud Romanos quemquam inauditum condemnare, qui statuit aliquid inauditâ alterâ æquum licet statuerit haud æquus fuit. Father Burk was not cited or summoned ; how then could sentence be given against him in Rome, or dato non concesso, that it had beene, how can he be hindered or trobled in possession untill he had seen the very sentence under the Secretary's hand ; but as I tould, if any such sentence was given, it was given, it was in condemnation of the first breve and not of the second breve (which is auth)enticall* as

* The words in this, and the following parentheses, are illegible in the original, but the context allows of no doubt as to how they should be supplied.

your Lordship's breve or unqua, and therefore neither in justice (hones)ty, or conscience, can Dr. Burk be trobled ; nai, from the day he (came to) possession, he hath jus to recover all the proxis, and it cannot (be) kept from in conscience, and whoever tooke it he is bound to (make rest)itution, which is the undoubted opinion of

" Your Lordship's most affectionate friend and servant,

"OLIVER PLUNKET.

(On the back) " These
" For Mr. James Lynch,
" at Galway."*

What may have been the reply of the Archbishop of Tuam, we have no means of determining. Certain it is that he convinced the Primate of the justness of his motives in refusing to admit Dr. De Burgo. Nor was he content with this ; he referred the matter to the judgment of Rome, and the Sacred Congregation soon sanctioned the course he had pursued, and appointed the Rev. John Dowley Vicar-Apostolic of Killala.

We cannot conclude without stating, in a few words, the subsequent history of Dr. De Burgo. Before the close of 1674 he was arrested by order of the Crown, accused of " bringing Protestants to the Catholic faith, contrary to the statutes of the kingdom, exercising foreign jurisdiction, preaching perverse doctrines, and remaining in the kingdom despite the act of parliament of 28th March, 1674, &c."

* This letter of Dr. Plunket received the following approbations, which we give in the original :—

" Opinionem antedictam approbo, ut conformem æquitati et justitiæ : Ita attestamur.

" PAT. MIDLE, Epus.
" Idem attestor PAT. CLOGHREN, Epus.
" Idem etiam attestor PAT. Duffius Abbas Benchoren.
S. Th. Mag.

" Idem infrascripti Præsules et ordinarii Provinciæ Connaciæ seu Tuamensis attestamur et censemus dictum Doctorem De Burgo injuste in sua possessione esse molestatum et Diœcesis prædictæ esse legitimum Vicarium Apostolicum.

" D. FR. DOMINICUS ELFINENSIS, Epus.
" FR. THADÆUS CLONFERT, Epus.
" MICHAEL LYNCH, Vic. Ap. Duacensis.
" MAURITIUS DORKANUS, Vic. Gen. Acaden.
" Idem attestor FR. JOANNES REGINALD, Notarius Apost."

For two years he was detained in prison, with irons on his hands and feet;* at the assizes he publicly declared that the Pope, as Vicar of Christ, was Head of the Catholic Church; he rejected with scorn a private offer that was made to him of being promoted to a Protestant Bishoprick, should he conform to the Established Church. Conducted from Ballinrobe to Dublin, he there displayed the same firmness, and was at length sentenced to the confiscation of his goods and perpetual imprisonment. The Earl of Clanrickard, who was his relative, soon after obtained his release, which was accorded, on condition that he should pay the sum of £80 sterling within one month, and retire to the Continent.

During his imprisonment De Burgo had made a vow to visit the Holy Places should he re-attain his liberty. In 1679 he fulfilled this vow; but on his return from Jerusalem was captured by pirates in the Mediterranean, stript of all he possessed, and sold as a slave. He, however, found means to escape to Constantinople, where he took refuge with the Austrian ambassador. He thence proceeded to Venice and Rome, and receiving frequent aid from the Sacred Congregation, seems to have passed in peace the closing years of his eventful life.

1677.

The Internunzio, Tanari, on the 4th December, 1677, writes that he had received intelligence from the Archbishop of Armagh of numerous bodies of banditti having organized themselves throughout the kingdom; whilst, on the other hand, troops of soldiery roamed through the country to exterminate them, "so that great prejudice resulted thence to those who profess our holy religion." †   All that was vile,

---

* " Con ferri alle mani e piedi."—(His own narrative in 1683, Archiv. de Prop.)

† " Riferisce Mgr. Armacano essersi ammassati in quel Regno gran numeri di Banditi, e spingendosi molte soldatesche per esterminarli, risultarne gran pregiudizio a quelli che professano la nostra religione."

and worthless, and immoral, joined these bandit corps, and from them the government of the nation chose its perjured witnesses to lead to the scaffold the Primate of our Church, and to cast opprobrium on the profession of the Catholic faith.

1678.

In this year was decided in favour of the Archbishop of Armagh the controversy which had been long carried on against him by Dr. Fitzsymons, the deposed Vicar-General of Kilmore. The Sacred Congregation not only sanctioned the decision of Dr. Plunket, but commanded that the calumnies which were circulated against him by some over-zealous partisans of the opposite party should no longer be received by any officials of the Holy See, or brought under the deliberations of the Propaganda.

Dr. Fitzsymons, in the commencement of his ecclesiastical career, had given proofs of great abilities and prudence, and conciliated the esteem of the Primate, Dr. Plunket, as well as of his glorious predecessor, Dr. Edmund O'Reilly. For fifteen years he had taught theology in Brussels, and he bore the reputation of being "learned, unostentatious, and prudent." * On the 25th of June, 1666, the Primate, Edmund O'Reilly, appointed him Vicar-General of Kilmore ; and as the bishop, Dr. Eugene M'Swiney was wholly incapacitated by his past sufferings, as well as his present infirmities and age, from attending to the spiritual wants of that diocese, its administration was committed to the newly-appointed vicar. His government of the diocese was not, however, acceptable to all ; and we find that, after many dissensions, the Provincial Council of Armagh, which was held in Owengelley on the 25th of May, 1669, passed sentence of deposition against Fitzsymons, and subjected him to ecclesiastical censures. The Holy See deputed the Bishop of Meath, Dr. Patrick Plunket, to investigate this

* "Fu riconosciuto sempre per savio, modesto e discreto."—(Letter of Tanari, Archiv. della Sac. Congne.)

matter. Before his arrival in the diocese of Kilmore,
Dr. Eugene M'Swiney had closed his earthly career.
However, Dr. Plunket convened the clergy of the diocese,
and on the 25th of October, 1669, whilst he declared
Dr. Fitzsymons lawful vicar-general of the diocese,
published, at the same time, a general absolution of all
those who, in the preceding dissensions, might have
incurred any ecclesiastical censures. This sentence of
Dr. Patrick Plunket received the sanction of our Primate,
a few days after his arrival in the kingdom, on the
7th March, 1670.

For about five years Fitzsymons stood high in the esteem
of Dr. Oliver Plunket, and laboured as a zealous missionary
in the province of Armagh. He had occasion more than
once to inflict the penalties of the Church on some refractory ecclesiastics, and his judgment was invariably confirmed
by the Primate. About Christmas, 1674, having written to
Dr. Plunket that some of those whom he had corrected
still continued contumacious, he received the following
reply:—

" Contemptores superiorum nullo modo sunt tollerandi ; suspende
et priva illos. Nil est in te quod mihi aut ulli honesto displiceat
Si appellaverint ad me eos non protegam sed potius severius puniam.
Qui nolunt solvere Proxim aut ea quæ Concilium Provinciale
decrevit suspendantur. Tu ne cede malis sed contra audentior ito.

" 9 January, 1675 (styl. nov.)

"OLIVER ARMACANUS."

In an address presented in favour of Fitzsymons to Rome,
in April, 1675, it is said, that in the preceding January
Dr. Plunket had written to him in these terms :—" Certus
sis me vivente non alium in ista diocesi quam te futurum
ordinarium : imo, si hodie mihi morituro liceret de Prima-
tiali dignitate ultimum condere testamentum, tibi sane relin-
querum, quia te plus diligo æstimoque quam ullum in
Ultonia ecclesiasticum." It is added, that in a subsequent
letter he had also written :—" Nihil est in te quod mihi vel
ulli honesto displicere queat, imo nullus est in Ultonia

ecclesiasticus quem plus amo vel æstimo ut alias fuse scripsi."

Nevertheless, about this time, Dr. Fitzsymons seems to have passed all bounds in deposing some worthy priests of Kilmore, who appealed from his sentence to the decision of the Archbishop of Armagh.   Dr. Plunket invited by letters the Vicar Administrator to answer the charges made against him.   The only fragment of this letter which has been pre-served to us is the sentence : " Cum tu nihil contumelia dignum agas, mendacia sperne." This investigation resulted in the deposition of Fitzsymons, on the 12th of May following.

The change in the career of this man is most surprising ; but Dr. Plunket, in one of his letters, sufficiently explains it for us, and his sentiment is corroborated by the testimony of the Bishop of Waterford.   Early in the year 1675, Fitzsymons was seized with violent attacks of dysentry, which continued almost without interruption for more than two months.   This long-protracted illness affected his mental faculties, and brought on a sort of childish imbecility, which afflicted him during the remainder of his life.   He thus became the tool of evil-designing men, and his actions seemed inspired alone by enmity to the Holy See, to Dr. Plunket, and to the most deserving priests of his own diocese.

We have no fewer than three letters of Dr. Plunket, wholly devoted to this controversy.   In the first, which bears the date of 2nd December, 1676, he thus writes to the Internunzio :—

" I have received a letter of your Excellency, of the 6th ult., about the affair of Thomas Fitzsymons, who was deposed by me about fourteen months ago.   During the seven years and a half that I have laboured in this Church, I merited but little praise ; but, if ever I merited any, it should surely have been for removing Fitzsymons from his office of Vicar-General of Kilmore.   About two years ago he had an attack of sickness, and since that he has never been sane of mind.   He deposed three parish priests, without even citing them to appear ; and when they appealed to me, though I decided in their favour, yet he refused to obey.   The Vicar whom

I appointed to succeed him, and who still continues, is Bernard Geaghron, who is 60 years of age, a man of holy life, and who was at other times Vicar-General. During the past spring, however, as he was rather infirm, I appointed, as his assistant, Father Bernard Brady, who is 38 years of age, and has been a rural vicar for 12 years. He is a man of sound judgment; and as the diocese of Kilmore is 58 miles in length, the good old Geaghron was not able to discharge all the duty."

The principal accusation made against Dr. Plunket, by some of the abettors of Fitzsymons, was, that he had called in the aid of the civil magistrate to punish some of the clergy of Kilmore. To this Dr. Plunket replies in his second letter, dated 20th December, 1676 :—

"Of this accusation I know absolutely nothing. I never caused any priest to be arrested, nor did I seek the aid of any lay tribunal ; neither was I during the past three years in the diocese of Kilmore. Why not name the priest that was arrested, who was the judge or layman to whom I had recourse, or who issued the writ of arrest ? I am astounded that anyone in his senses should write such falsehoods. On the contrary, it was Dr. Thomas Fitzsymons that had recourse to Boris against me, though in vain. He had also recourse to the sheriff of the County Cavan, whose name is Mr. John Maxwell; and he had recourse to Sir Charles Hamilton. I have the letters of these gentlemen; but, as they saw his imbecility, they refused to give him any support. Not long ago he had recourse to Sir Hans Hamilton, member of the Supreme Council of this kingdom, to have a writ of arrest against Rev. Bernard Brady, as this clergyman informs me.

"I may now assure your Excellency, that I never did anything with more deliberation, or better weighed in point of discipline and canon law, than the deposition of Fitzsymons. When I delivered sentence *ne ciderer inniti prudentiæ meæ*, I called Dr. Cusack, who studied in Rome, and Dr. Dromgole, who studied in Salamanca, who are the two most learned persons of this province, that they might aid me with their counsel. They were both present when I delivered sentence ; and Cusack, though a friend of Fitzsymons, told him publicly that he had not a shadow of reason or of right on his side.

"Nevertheless he is not content with disturbing the diocese of Kilmore ; but, as I learned from trustworthy persons, during the past two months he has been trying, by word and by writing, to excite some of the clergy of the diocese of Clogher against the Apostolic See, and against their bishop, Dr. Tyrrell, a truly learned, exemplary, and amiable prelate."

The third letter of Dr. Plunket details further particulars relative to the sad career pursued by Fitzsymons, after his

deposition, and dwells particularly on the disturbance which
he was creating in Clogher :—

"Fitzsymons [he 'says] has succeeded in exciting some of the
clergy of Clogher against Dr. Tyrrell, a learned and exemplary
bishop ; and for this purpose he wrote a paper, asserting that the
Holy See could not appoint a bishop for that see without their
postulation and election. I wrote, in reply, that his Holiness *dudum
sibi reservavit provisiones Hiberniæ*, and that for 200 years, and more,
such provision had always been made for the Church of Clogher
without the postulation or election of the clergy."

As we have already remarked, the Archbishop of Cashel
received instructions from the Holy See to examine this
whole controversy, and make report on it to the Sacred
Congregation. This he transmitted to Rome on 6th April,
1677. In it he states many things as to the origin of the
controversy, which we have already given in Dr. Plunket's
words, and which it is now unnecessary to repeat. We
shall translate, however, that portion which regards some
accusations made by the partisans of Fitzsymons, who, as
Dr. Brennan remarks, were, for the most part, a few
unworthy members of the Franciscan Order :—

"As to the accusation against the Archbishop of Armagh, that he
is too familiar with the Protestant ministers, to the great scandal of
the faithful, I must say, that during the whole time of my stay in
this country, I never found traces of any such scandal. Moreover,
if they mean by Protestant ministers, ministers of the Protestant
Church, it is indeed true that he is familiar with one of them who is
attached to the court of the pseudo-primate ; and this friendship is
of great advantage to his flock, for when any lawsuits regarding
Catholics, especially in matrimonial cases, are brought to the
Protestant Episcopal Court, this minister remits them all to
Dr. Plunket. I have not received information of his being familiar
with any other minister of the Protestant Church. If by Protestant
ministers, they understand the magistrates and other ministers of
the court, it is true that he is familiar with many of them, and he
derives great benefit from them ; as when any evil persons, whether
lay or ecclesiastical, bring accusations against him before these
ministers, they from their own personal knowledge reject them : and
it is probable, that were it not for his acquaintance with these
persons, he would long since have been banished from the kingdom,
like the Archbishops of Dublin and Tuam, so great is the malignity
of these informers.

"That the primate is not well disposed towards the natives of that province, is certainly a calumny. For, in the whole province but one individual received promotion from his own family, and even that one belonged to the province of Armagh. The Bishops of Down and Clogher, who died about two years ago, were both natives of the province; the present Bishop of Clogher, too, though indeed Dr. Plunket had nothing to do in his appointment, is a native of one of the suffragan dioceses. Moreover, I know for certain that the archbishop bears the greatest love for those of his province, and that he seeks to promote their interests both within and without this realm. Indeed, in my opinion, the present Archbishop of Armagh has attended more to the spiritual administration of that province than any of his predecessors for many years, and I say this without wishing to lower in any way the merit of the preceding primates."

The result of the controversy was, as we have already remarked, wholly confirmatory of Dr. Plunket's decisions. Dr. Tyrrell, the Bishop of Clogher, received from the Holy See the administration of Kilmore, and Fitzsymons retired to Belgium, where he died, in 1680. The principles, however, which he had laboured to disseminate survived him in the Irish Church, and continued for a long time to produce their evil fruits of discord and schism.

1679.

This year witnessed the renewal of the persecution in all its fury. The see of Meath had to lament the demise of Dr. Patrick Plunket, who, in his last moments, was comforted by the presence of the primate; and the whole Irish Church was filled with mourning, her chief prelates being cast into prison, and the remaining clergy being obliged to seek a shelter on the mountain tops, or in the caverns and forests. The occurrences, however, of this and the two succeeding years will hereafter claim a more special attention.

We may refer to this time the correspondence of Dr. Plunket with the learned Mabillon, the most distinguished ornament of the Benedictine Order, relative to a prophecy of St. Malachy, Archbishop of Armagh. This great saint was said to have foretold that after seven centuries of desolation and suffering the Church of Ireland would be clothed with beauty and arrayed in the fruitfulness of sanctity as of old. Dr. Plunket consulted the Benedictine historian as to the authenticity of the prophetic announcement made by his sainted predecessor, in the see of Armagh, and received in reply his weighty attestation removing all doubt of the authenticity of St. Malachy's prophecy. The letter of Mabillon and the text of the prophetic announcement which accompanies it, are the more interesting to us in that the seven centuries from St. Malachy's death (115) have run their course in our own days, and we see the prophecy most fully verified in the renewed splendour of the Irish Church and the marvellous fruits of her missionary zeal in distant lands.

" To MONSEIGNEUR OLIVER PLUNKET, ARCHBISHOP OF ARMAGH.

" MONSEIGNEUR,—In repy to your solicitous inquiries, I have the distinguished honour to state that I have indeed found, in a very ancient archive of the abbey of Einseildelin, the document containing the prophecy relative to Ireland of St. Malachy, your predecessor in the see of Armagh, and herewith I send you a faithful copy of the same.

" The parchment on which it is written is in a very tolerable state of preservation, and, though not of the best quality, is such as was generally used on such occasions.

" The caligraphy is good, and is of the same character as that used at Clairvaux in the time of St. Bernard.

" The style indicates culture and Scripture knowledge. It savours, too, of St. Bernard's school, and bespeaks the author of some note. Indeed, we find that one Reginald was prior of Clairvaux at the period of St. Malachy's death there, and that a certain monk, Theodore, from Clairvaux, became bishop of Autun, towards the middle of the twelfth century. Although no name is subscribed to the document, doubtless these are the two whose names are mentioned therein, and both, or either, may have written it. They may have gone to the " Grange " to meet St. Malachy, as no doubt his feeble health would have compelled him to proceed by easy stages, and in any case the fame of so distinguished a visitor's approach would have reached Clairvaux before him.

" The document was evidently written for St. Bernard, when compiling the Life of Blessed Malachy, and only relates a thing that occurred on one night. Yet this was so remarkable and important, that one might well wonder if a fact so well attested as what it records were not preserved. It did not exactly enter into

St. Bernard's scope, so he barely indicates that St. Malachy was endowed with the twofold gift of miracles and prophecy, and left the document to tell posterity its own tale.

" Events in England subsequent to the time of St. Bernard, as the quarrel about investitures, the martyrdom of Thomas-à-Becket, and the Anglo-Norman invasion of Ireland, would call attention to the document, and keep alive the interest attaching to it. It is certain that there was always at Clairvaux a lively recollection of many of St. Malachy's prophecies, and of this one in particular. And although England had not till thirty years later invaded Ireland, yet our traditions always pointed to England, and not to the northern pirates, as the enemy who were to oppress Ireland for seven hundred years, and that same as the period of their domination in your country.

" As regards ' Pontefract,' I have not been able to discover any place of that name within a day's journey of Clairvaux. There was, however, a ' grange ' belonging to the monastery, at a place now called ' Ligny,' a few miles distant from Clairvaux, and, though the names differ, the place is most probably the same.

" Much of the archives of Clairvaux were transferred to Einseildelin in the last century (16th).

" With every sentiment of veneration and respect, I have the honour to subscribe myself

" Your Lordship's most obedient humble servant,

" J. MABILLON."

THE PROPHECY OF ST. MALACHY, ARCHBISHOP OF ARMAGH.

" When Malachy, the beloved of God, was proceeding the second time from Ireland to Rome, and had arrived at Pontefract, which is a short day's journey from the monastery (Clairvaux), being fatigued with travelling, and already seized with the distemper, which carried him away, he came to a ' grange ' of ours. There he delayed for awhile, and, being requested by some of the brethren who happened to be in the place, stayed for the night. The man, wholly devoted to God and his country, spent a great part of the night in the prayer of God; and at length, seized with a certain divine ardour, his spirit seemed carried away from its earthly tenement. Suddenly a light from heaven shone round about him, while on bended knees, with hands joined, he gazed up into heaven. Two monks, Theodore and Reginald, who were waiting not far distant, ' marvelled to see such things; they were astonished and suddenly cast down, trembling came upon them.' Approaching nearer, and, in their reverential fear, being most attentive, they heard the voice at one time of the holy bishop, and at another as it were of some one speaking with him.

" Woe is me! alas for my ruined country! alas for the Holy Church of God! How long, O Lord! dost Thou forget us! How long, my country! art thou consumed with sorrow!" he exclaimed.

A little after, as if some one spoke to him, although he himself uttered the words, 'Be of good heart, my son,' said he, 'the Church of God in Ireland shall never fail. With terrible discipline long shall she be purified, but, afterwards, far and wide shall her magnificence shine forth in cloudless glory. And, O Ireland! do thou lift up thy head. Thy day also shall come—a day of ages! A week of centuries equalling the seven deadly sins of thy enemy, shall be numbered unto thee. Then shall thy exceeding great merits have obtained mercy for thy terrible foe, yet so as through scourges great and enduring. Thy enemies who are in thee shall be driven out and humbled, and their name taken away. But inasmuch as thou art depressed, in so much shalt thou be exalted. Thy light shall burst forth as the sun, and thy glory shall not pass away. There shall be peace and abundance within thy boundaries, and beauty and strength in thy defences.'

"After this he was silent for awhile, then, with a loud and joyous voice, he exclaimed: Now, 'O Lord! dost thou dismiss thy servant in peace! Long enough have I lived! It is enough! The Church of God in Ireland shall never fail! and though long shall it be desired, my country shall one day stand forth in its might, and be fresh in its beauty like the rose.'

"On the following day the two monks, Reginald and Theodore, conducted the sick prelate, with his deacon, Virgilius, to Clairvaux. The rest, Father Abbot, is known to your Reverence.

"The foregoing agrees with the original.

"J. MABILLON."

CHAPTER XVIII.

DISPUTE REGARDING THE PRIMACY.

As we find dissensions even amongst the Apostles themselves, it surely cannot surprise us that their successors in the sacred ministry should not always be found of one accord when discussing the expediency of measures destined to promote the glory of God and to propagate the Gospel of Jesus Christ. The Archbishops of Armagh and Dublin, at the time of which we speak, were both illustrious ornaments of the Church of God; they had drunk in the waters of truth at the same fountain source; they were alike animated with zeal for preserving to Ireland the rich inheritance of faith; and they were moreover, destined to be one day rivals in their crown of martyrdom. From the preceding chapters it must be manifest that they had long been mutual friends, and it is moreover probable that they were bound together by ties of consanguinity. Nevertheless, when engaged in their episcopal ministry, we find them combating each other's opinions with an ardour which occasionally seemed to verge on mutual schism, and for a while engaged the attention of the whole island, and was a source of many anxious cares to all true lovers of the Irish Church. We shall easily recognise, however, in their dissensions the characteristics of those who are animated with the true spirit of God, who, indeed, when the truth has been proposed to them, hesitate not to acknowledge their errors, and when the storm has passed, embrace anew, in the spirit of mutual forgiveness, charity, and love. In fine, we must remark that whatsoever fault or stain was contracted on either side, was surely washed away in their heroic martyrdom—the one decorating Tyburn with his life-blood, shed for the faith, and the other, though within the prison walls, yet rendering like glory to God by his protracted sufferings and death, which were endured in the same glorious cause.

The question as to whether the primacy in the Irish Church should be referred to the see of Dublin or to Armagh had long been discussed in Ireland; and as no decision had as yet emanated from Rome regarding this controversy, it could scarcely be expected that prelates of such learning and ability as now filled these respective sees, would allow the matter to remain undiscussed. Now-a-days it would be a question of little importance, as modern ecclesiastical jurisprudence allows no special jurisdiction to the primatial see; but at the time of which we speak, many special privileges, not merely as to name, but as to authority and jurisdiction, were involved in the primacy. A like controversy had long been carried on between the Protestant possessors of these sees, which, though it regarded a mere matter of title, could not be settled till the crown, obedient to the learning of Usher, gave its decision in favour of Armagh. Even to posterity the whole controversy is not without its fruits, and three valuable works yet remain which were written in support of these respective claims, and have preserved to us many interesting facts connected with the history of our Church. The first was published by Dr. Plunket in 1672, and is a small octavo of fifty-six pages, written in English, and bearing the title " Jus Primatiale ; or the Ancient Pre-eminence of the See of Armagh above all other Archbishops in the Kingdom of Ireland, asserted by O. A. T. H. P.," which initials represent the words *Oliverus Armacanus totius Hiberniæ Primas.* The second work was written by Dr. Talbot, and was published at Lisle in 1674 ; it is in 12mo, and consists of eighty-five pages, being written in Latin, and entitled " Primatus Dublinensis," &c.* The third was the most learned and elaborate of the three, and was written in 1728, by Dr. Hugh M'Mahon, a successor of Dr. Plunket in the see of Armagh ; his work forms a thick volume in quarto, and is entitled " Jus Primatiale Armacanum, &c." †

The synod held in Dublin in 1670, of which we have already treated, presented the first occasion for the renewal of the controversy. Dr. Plunket was anxious to have the matter at once decided by the assembled prelates, but Dr. Talbot deemed it deserving of more deliberation, and referred its decision to the Holy See. The synod, however, had been convened by Dr. Plunket, and the primacy of Armagh was as if a household word in every diocese of Ireland. Then, too, in the Bull of his appointment to the

---

* " The primacy of Dublin, or the chief reasons on which the Church of Dublin relies on the possession and prosecution of her right to the Primacy of Ireland." In the preface, he tells us that he engaged in the controversy from a sense of duty, believing such to be the rights of his see.

† " The primatial right of Armagh over all the other Archbishops, Bishops, and the entire clergy of Ireland, asserted by Hugh M'Mahon, Archbishop of Armagh, Primate of all Ireland." The initials H. A. M. T. H. P. (Hugo Armacanus M'Mahon totius Hib. Prim.) have been inaccurately translated by some Hugh of Armagh, *Master in Theology and Primate of Ireland.*

see of St. Patrick, he was styled Archbishop of Armagh and
Primate of Ireland; the faculties granted to him by Rome
were addressed to Oliver, Archbishop of Armagh, and
Primate of the Kingdom of Ireland; and in the same document the see of Armagh is styled, " the primatial church of
all Ireland," *Ecclesia totius Hiberniæ primatialis*. Things
being so, the presidency of the synod was without debate
referred to Dr. Plunket, though, as is usual on such occasions,
it was declared that the rights of neither party should be
prejudiced by the order of precedence observed in that synod.
Indeed, so little had this dispute of the noisy character
attributed to it by some writers, that Dr. Peter Creagh
(afterwards Archbishop of Dublin), who was in Dublin at
the time, thus wrote on the 24th of January, 1671 : "There
was some difference of opinion between the Archbishops of
Armagh and Dublin, as to the order of signature, *nevertheless,
the controversy was carried on so peaceably, that the noise
of it was scarcely heard beyond the princints of the place of
assembly*."

The controversy, however, though hushed for a while, was
not terminated in this synod; it was soon rekindled anew,
and for many years continued to engage the attention of the
whole Catholic body. Dr. Plunket, often residing in Dublin,
hesitated not to exercise there his primatial authority, and
amongst the public acts of which Dr. Talbot most complained, was his having publicly absolved from censures the
unfortunate French, who had prosecuted and given evidence
against the Archbishop of Tuam, but whom, on his repentance, Dr. Plunket, pursuing the dictates of his meek and
merciful disposition, received once more into the bosom of
the Church, in the city of Dublin.

Early in 1672 appeared the treatise of Dr. Plunket,
asserting the primatial privileges of the see of Armagh.
But even before this, the opinions of the respective prelates
had found amongst the laity many ardent partizans, and
often had all the true friends of religion to lament the
scandal which was given, and the angry feelings which were

awakened by the offensive tracts which were published by these intrusive partizans, each seeking to cast ridicule and reproach on the persons and pretensions of their opponents. The leading friends of Dr. Plunket were Sir Nicholas Plunket, of whom we have already had occasion to speak, and who, a few years later, was compelled to fly to the Continent, to shun the persecution which was directed against him by the enemies of the Church, and Mr. John Patrick, another Catholic advocate, to whom, towards the close of 1669, a letter was addressed by Propaganda, congratulating him on his efforts in favour of the Catholics, and in reply to which, by letter of the 5th January, 1670, he declares his readiness to ever sustain the Catholic cause, and adds :—" Whatever I may have done in favour of the most illustrious Archbishops of Armagh and Tuam, or of the other prelates of our communion, must be referred not so much to any attention or solicitude of mine, as to the merits of these prelates."* About this time the Valesian faction sought to intrude upon the Franciscan order in Ireland a Provincial chosen from amongst their adherents, and assailed by every means in their power Father Peter Geanor, the lawfully chosen Provincial of the Order. Writing from Dublin, on the 2nd February, 1670, Father Geanor states, that he was accused before the Government by Peter Walsh, for exercising jurisdiction received from Rome ; but, he adds, that he hoped to escape sentence through the ability and the intercession of some individuals, " amongst whom John Patrick is chiefly distinguished, a man truly Catholic, and well deserving of religion in these arduous times, and a warm defender of our cause ; also the most illustrious Nicholas Plunket, a man highly esteemed for his piety and eloquence, as well as for his legal skill, protects and defends our cause ; he drew up and arranged in order our reply to the objections of Walsh."†

* " Quidquid in favorem Illustrorum. Archi-Præsulum Ardmachani et Tuamen. aut aliorum nostræ Communionis Prælatorum præstiti non tam mere curæ et sollicitudini quam ipsorum Præsulum meritis referendum."

† " Eminet D. Joannes Patricius, vir sane Catholicus et de fide Catholica in hac rerum conjunctura benemeritus nostræque causæ

On the side of the Archbishop of Dublin, the most distinguished for his ability, and the most eminent for his services in the Catholic cause, was Colonel Richard Talbot, brother of the Archbishop. He had long figured in the Court of London, and by his talents and address won for himself great influence in the Royal Council. Regarding his merits, it is sufficient to remark, that in the next reign he became Viceroy of Ireland, where he alike distinguished himself by his skill in government, and by his valour in the field. At the period of which we speak he was for many years agent of the Irish Catholics in London. From a note in the archives of Propaganda, we learn that about the feast of Candlemas in 1671,* a meeting of the Catholic gentry was held at Oxmantown ; Dr. Plunket being in Dublin, was invited by the Archbishop to be present at its deliberations ; the chief matter proposed was, that a collection should be made for the purpose of defraying the expenses of Colonel Richard Talbot as agent in London of the Irish Catholic subjects of his Majesty. On this occasion Dr. Talbot contributed £10. A Mr. Francis Barnewall contributed £5. Nothing is said of the other contributors. It is added, that Dr. Plunket promised to contribute £10, which, however, was not to be paid unless the clergy of his province would consent to subscribe to that amount. The clergy of Ulster afterwards refused to collect this sum, and this served to embitter still more the feelings of Dr. Talbot's partizans.

But besides these distinguished personages, of whom we have been speaking, there were others amongst the partizans of both prelates who were secret agents of the Government, and who, by their violence and false reports, sought to keep alive dissensions in the Catholic body. Dr. Burgatt, of Cashel, had written a few years before in his *Relatio*, presented to Propaganda in 1668, that such agents of the

acerrimus propugnator : Illimus. etiam D. Nicolaus Plunket magnæ æstimationis vir tum ob pietatem et facundiam tum etiam ob legum peritiam, nostram causam tuetur et suscepit nostrumque responsum ad Valesii objectiones digessit et in bonam formam redegit."
* Intorno alla Candelora del' anno 1670 (styl. vet.) &c.

Government anxiously approved and stimulated whatever tended to promote "divisions and scandals amongst the clergy, and irreverence for the Holy See." Dr. Plunket, in his letter of the 26th of September, 1671, speaking of the Remonstrants, makes the same remark:—" The noblemen," he says, "who favoured and protected them, cared but little for Walsh and his adherents, but they made use of them as instruments to divide and disunite the clergy and Catholics, *divide et impera.*" Dr. Talbot, too, in his *Friar Diciplined,* which was printed in 1674, but written, perhaps, somewhat earlier, observes that Peter Walsh, in his controversy about the Remonstrance, was all along a mere tool and dupe of the Government, which " for reasons best known to themselves, would let him preach and press a formulary which they foresaw would divide the Catholics among themselves, and discredit their religion," as well as afford a pretext for subsequent arbitrary measures. The correspondence of the then Lord Lieutenant more than justifies this remark of Dr. Talbot, and in a letter of Lord Orrery, cited by Curry (*Historical Review,* book 9th, chap. 14th), that agent of the Court thus wrote to his Excellency:—" I humbly offer to your Grace, whether this may not be a fit season to make that schism which you have been sowing among the Popish clergy, publicly break out, so as to set them at open difference, as we may reap some practical advantage thereby;" and when, some years later, the enemies of the Duke of Ormond strangely enough accused him of having shown favour to the Catholics in Ireland, he replied:—" My aim was to work a division among the Romish clergy, and I believe I had accomplished it, to the great security of the Government and the Protestants, and against the opposition of the Pope and his creatures and nuncios, if I had not been removed;" and he laments that his successors pursued a different policy, " not considering the advantages of the divisions designed."— (Carte ii. Appendix 101.)

However, this policy of sowing dissensions amongst the

clergy did not cease with the Duke of Ormond; it was continued by his successors; and we even see the Earl of Clarendon, whose good qualities have found so many eulogists amongst our historians, pursue the same course. On the 15th of May, 1685, he thus wrote to the Earl of Rochester :—

"This is the day appointed by the titular bishops for a general convention of their clergy in this city,* and there are great numbers of them come to town, and of other gentlemen and persons of quality. I am told one of their businesses is to consider of putting on their habits and wearing of them about the streets; but, no doubt, there are matters of greater moment to be debated. I believe I shall have an account of all they do, but what service I shall be able to do thereby God only knows. One would think these people should not venture to execute anything without first communicating their resolutions to the king, if they will not make me acquainted with them, though they pretend wonderful respect to me, and that they will do nothing without first communicating to me. . . . This general convention, for so it is publicly called and talked of by all sorts of people in the town, is to continue for a week, so that I shall quickly see whether they will give any more account of their proceedings than they did of their meeting. Methinks I should have an answer from my Lord Sunderland to what I wrote to him on the 27th past, whereby I should know how to guide myself in those matters; or if this great meeting be by the king's allowance, methinks his lordship might have given me some directions, though they had been to take no notice of it, for then I should have been at ease, and known I had done no fault in not minding what they did. Suppose the Protestant clergy should appoint a general convention from all parts of the kingdom, to be held in this city or anywhere else, without taking notice to me of it, I am sure I would not suffer them to meet, and would legally punish them for the attempt; and I believe his Majesty would well approve of my so doing; and certainly no Government will permit any part of their subjects to assemble together without the supreme authority.† I would be very glad to know your opinion in these matters, and whether I should send this information, of which I have here given you the substance, to my Lord President or any others, of the proceedings at this convention, for I have

---

* A Synod of the Bishops of Leinster was then being held in the city of Dublin, by the Archbishop, Dr. Patrick Russell.

† Lord Clarendon's good sense seems to fail him in this passage. What has the supreme civil authority to do with spiritual matters? Protestant ministers and their deliberations are mere tools of state policy, and justly would the Viceroy insist on knowing the matter of their deliberations; but the Catholic clergy belong to a higher order. Moreover, as, through

reason to believe I shall have several; but if I do send them I must conceal the names of my informers. The titular Archbishop of Dublin has been with me. He seems to be a good man, but is no politician; he is a secular (priest). I am told by a good hand of their own party that he and the titular primate do not agree. About two days since he asked the primate by what authority this convention was called, to which the other answered that was not a question to be asked; it should be known when they were met. *The more they differ the better; and it is a pity the contests between them may not be encouraged;* but that I must not meddle with."*

Some recent publications have revealed to the world how the same course was pursued in civil matters; and how, as late as the sad era of 1798 the noisiest agitator in the ranks of the Irish confederates was all the time in the pay of the Castle, sowing divisions in that body, and revealing their secrets to the Government. In fact, the whole history of Ireland, for more than two centuries, well justifies the remark of Mr. Plowden:—"It long has been an insidious art of Ireland's enemies to select some ambitious agitator and intriguer from amongst the Catholics, in order to sow and feed dissension in their body."†

The publication of the work on the Primacy by Dr. Plunket gave great offence to the Archbishop of Dublin. Writing some time after to the Secretary of Propaganda, this good prelate gave full expression to his feelings, and with all freedom and earnestness impugns the course pursued by the Archbishop of Armagh. He thus writes:—

" MOST ILLUSTRIOUS AND MOST REV. LORD.

" I cannot say whether my letters may be pleasing to you; however I deem it my duty to inform you how matters here proceed with us. The most illustrious Archbishop of Armagh has just now published in Dublin a book in English, in which he endeavours to prove that the primacy and precedence is due to him; but this is

God's blessing, the Catholic clergy have no connection with the Government, as well might the Viceroy insist on being made acquainted with the private family concerns of each subject of the British Empire as to have the deliberations of the Catholic clergy (which, in the eyes of the law, are their own private matters) made known to him.

* Singer's *Correspondence of the Earl of Clarendon*, vol. i., page 387, *seq.*
† *Historical Letter, &c.*, page 72.

done with arguments so inconclusive, that he might justly be deemed an assailant rather than a defendant of that cause. I was surprised at his imprudence and inconstancy: for it had been agreed on between us that the controversy should be left to the decision of the Apostolic See; in the meantime both should be silent; but to the scandal of the orthodox and the joy of the Protestants, we would seem to dispute *de lana caprina* (about goat's wool), especially after we had learned what grief our dissensions caused to the Roman Court. I, indeed, following the counsel of your Excellency, have avoided every occasion of dispute, and whenever it was impossible to avoid such occasions and meetings. I pretended not to advert to the assumption which the Archbishop of Armagh rashly took upon himself: an instance of which was the absolving, in Dublin, Martin French, the Augustian apostate, from excommunication and other censures, I being uninformed of it, though then residing in Dublin.

" I have consulted the prelates of the kingdom as to the course I should now pursue, being assailed by a public document. I fear, however, that our clergy and people will be ill-contented with my silence, to which I am most inclined, and I hope that your reply will appease the angry and excited sentiments of our subjects; especially should the Holy See deign to renew the ancient decree of Innocent the Sixth.* . . . From that time, during more than three hundred years, there was no contention about precedency or primacy ; both were primates, both were altogether equal. But in these past days Oliver Plunket, more wise, forsooth, than all his predecessors, discovered I know not what force in the word *totius*, by which the custom of so many centuries and peace is wholly upset: but the ingenious prelate did not remark, what is most evident from the very words of the Papal Decree, that the word *totius* indicates merely a distinction from the Dublin primacy, not a higher dignity of the Archbishop of Armagh.

" And lest your Excellency should imagine that the Archbishop of Armagh has any support or patronage from the Court in this cause, I must inform you that the Chief Secretary and Councillor of the Viceroy, being lately returned from England, came to me at once, and after a while presented to me, in the presence of my Vicar-General, an order of his Excellency, to the effect, that Oliver Plunket should, on his knees, ask my pardon for his temerity and for the injuries done to me. Rendering formal thanks to the Viceroy, I sought to excuse, as far as possible, the imprudence of the prelate, and to benignly interpret his intention: his partizan, John Patrick, too, having fallen into the greatest disgrace in Dublin, is compelled to keep away from the Court and Castle.

" Nor is the cause of the primacy of Armagh less wanting in proof than patronage." (He then advances several arguments to

---

* He then cites the words of Ware concerning this decree.

establish the claim of the sec of Dublin, and concludes his letter as follows) :—

" The happy decree of our king was promulgated on the 13th of this month, and by it the Irish Catholics are enabled to retain their ancient privileges and old magistracies in the cities and towns of this kingdom, without being obliged to swear or make declaration of the king's primacy in spiritual matters. It is a most important edict, and a sign of better times.

" Dublin, 26th March, 1672.

" PETER OF DUBLIN."

Some writers have given currency to a story which, if it had any foundation, should be referred to this time :—

" The arrogant pretensions of Dr. Talbot [they write] obliged the Archbishop of Armagh to interpose his authority as primate, and to inhibit him to go to England, where he pretended his presence was necessary, with the object of preventing the success of Peter Walsh's solicitations to have the remonstrance put in force. Plunket, otherwise a mild man, made him upon this occasion a sharp answer, ' that he had good grounds to believe there was no such matter ; that he had the reputation of meddling too much in affairs of state, which was contrary to the canons and order of the Pope :' and for that reason he inhibited him from going. Talbot was, therefore, obliged to send to the Nuncio at Brussels for a licence of absence, under pretence of being required by his Majesty to attend him in England."

It will suffice to remark on this story : 1. That, as appears from various letters, Dr. Plunket was well aware of the efforts and solicitations made to the Court by Peter Walsh to have his Remonstrance enforced. 2. That even in the supposition of the very plenitude of primacy, the Archbishop of Armagh could exercise no such control over the Archbishop of Dublin. 3. That Dr. Talbot, though laying open to the Holy See the various instances of the assumed authority of Dr. Plunket, never even hints at this, which, of all others, would have been the most condemnatory of Dr. Plunket's conduct. 4. Dr. Talbot, in the beginning of 1672, wrote to the Internunzio requesting permission to leave his diocese for awhile, for it was reserved to the representative of the Holy See in Brussels to accord this permission. 5. In a letter of the 5th of March, 1672, and many subsequent letters, the Internunzio announces to the

Sacred Congregation that Dr. Talbot had been chosen by the Court and invited to London for the purpose of being sent to Innspruck as representative of the king : and the Internunzio adds that he readily accorded this permission, "*as the Archbishop of Armagh and the other Prelates of Ireland* were of opinion that great advantage would accrue to religion from this mission of Dr. Talbot."

Indeed, all through this controversy, the personal esteem of Dr. Plunket for the Archbishop of Dublin continued unabated. We have seen how, in his letter of 28th September, 1671, he commemorates his having consulted with Dr. Talbo' on the subject of a letter which he himself had receiveo from Rome. Again, in the same year (24th April, 1671), he thus concisely describes to the Secretary of Propaganda the common danger which both had shared, and his joy that both had escaped unharmed :—

"The Parliament of England sought to give annoyance to the Archbishop of Dublin and to me, but, through the mercy of God, *laqueus contritus est, et nos liberati sumus.*"

Nearly the whole of Dr. Plunket's letter of 22nd March, 1671, is taken up with an account of this threatened danger, and we learn from it that he himself interposed his good offices with the Viceroy to have the Archbishop of Dublin exempted from danger :—

"The rumour is current here [he thus writes], that the Archbishops of Armagh and Dublin will be summoned to London : I do not know for what motive. It is said, however, that it is owing to the indiscreetness of Dr. Talbot in two points. The first was his assembling many of the Catholic nobility to get them to contribute for the support of his brother, who was appointed agent of the Irish Catholics, to lay before the Court in London the grievances of our country from the malgovernment of the Duke of Ormond. Having gone to Dublin to consign to him the archiepiscopal pallium, he one day brought me, wholly unawares, to this assembly ; this assembly gave great displeasure to the Government. The second matter was a work lately written by him, in a very sharp style, against Peter Walsh ; though, in reality, there is more against Ormond in it than against Walsh. The Viceroy, otherwise but little inclined to favour Dr. Talbot or his family, for these and other reasons had resolved to banish him from the kingdom. I opposed this resolution of the

Viceroy with all my power, humbly supplicating him to desist from it. At the same time I assured him, that whatever difference there might be between the Archbishop of Dublin and myself in regard of the question of jurisdiction, yet we were friends ; so that his Excellency was appeased, and declared himself edified by my interference in favour of Dr. Talbot."

But, perhaps, nothing more clearly proves that these prelates, whilst warmly asserting the privileges of their respective sees, allowed not the bonds of Christian charity to be severed, or the peace of God to be interrupted in their breasts, than the letter of the Archbishop of Armagh, written on the 20th of January, 1672. In it he says :—

" I confess I was in some manner displeased with Dr. Talbot in consequence of some defamatory libels and pasquinades, and false letters, in the circulating of which I was informed he had had a part, as he showed them to a certain Colonel Dempsey, who is a fit trumpeter of such things; but Dr. Talbot was with me yesterday evening for three hours, and solemnly assured me that he had no part whatsoever in them, or in their circulation, and that when they were brought to him, he spoke about them, indeed, to the said Colonel, but rather to discredit those pasquinades than to publish them, which was by no means his intention. Dr. Talbot again came to visit me this morning, and with such kindness and affection, that I have now become his servant. I do not hear any report now of his journey to England : I suppose he has changed his intention.

" Thanks be to God, we at present enjoy peace in this kingdom. Dr. O'Molony, of Killaloe, wrote to me about the dread he has of the Duke of Ormond and his satellites. But I pray you to write to him to come to his diocese as soon as possible, and without delay, for I spoke about the matter to the Viceroy, and he replied, that having no royal order against him, he would not, on account of the enmity of an individual, exclude from the kingdom the subjects of his Majesty. Whilst we have the present Viceroy, Dr. O'Moloney need not hesitate to come : and let him not wait looking for the formation of colleges by the French king ; this is a difficult matter, which would require a length of time, and the success of which is very dubious. When he is once in possession of his diocese, it will be difficult to molest him without some great crime, for no subject can be sent into exile without something serious : as is known by experience, and as our laws imply, *turpius ejicitur quam non admittitur hospes.* Though I have often written, yet I received no reply, and know not whether my letters reached their destination. I make you a profound reverence, and will be, unto death,

" Your most affectionate and obliged servant,
" OLIVER OF ARMAGH.

" 20th January, 1672."

Dr. Plunket closes another letter (12th December, 1672), with like sentiments :—

" The reconciliation [he writes] between me and the Archbishop of Dublin will be uninterrupted, because we will no longer give credence to the sowers of discord. . . . We have agreed to send all our respective arguments to Rome, and we will await its decision."

Dr. Talbot often writes in a similar strain ; thus, in his letter of the 4th February, 1671, we read :—

" As regards the Archbishop of Armagh, I am his friend, for I attribute whatever he has done to imprudence, rather than to bad intention. I am and ever shall remain his friend, for this conduces to the glory of God, and is desired by our friends, and in particular by your Excellency, to whom I am bound by special obligations."

When, moreover, some enemies of our holy religion would asperse the character of Dr. Plunket, and extol him as though he were inclined to Protestantism, the Archbishop of Dublin fearlessly denounced the calumny, and asserted our holy Prelate's innocence and orthodoxy :—

" Aliud Dominationi tuæ significatum volo nimirum nomen D. Oliverii Plunket expunctum fuisse a libello Parliamenti (vulgo nominant bill), meo relicto, et ita factum fuit intercedente aliquo haneque potissimum rationem reddente (sed falso), quod dictus Plunket multum propenderit in Protestantismum. Ego autem statim ac hujus injuriæ notitiam habuerim, conabar tueri eum et labem diluere." (14th Aug., 1671.)

Even in the preface of his work, in reply to Dr. Plunket, whilst he warmly combats the arguments of Dr. Plunket, yet he abstains from passing any censorious remarks on the writer, and even speaks of him as a *prelate* eminent for *his learning and prudence*. (Presented to S. Cong. by Peter Creagh, 2nd Aug., 1672.)

When Dr. Plunket, in the commencement of 1672, published his work on the primacy of the see of Armagh, he seems not to have as yet received the decree of the Sacred Congregation, which was enacted the same year, and whilst imposing silence as regarded the public discussion on that question, at the same time instructed the Internunzio to exhort the archbishops to transmit to the Sacred Congregation their respective arguments for the primacy of their sees. It is in this letter of 22nd September, 1672, that Dr. Plunket first refers to this decree of the Sacred Congregation ; in it he thus writes to the Internunzio :—

" As to the primacy, I will observe the promise which I made to your Excellency, and I will send my proofs : I already sent them to you in a compendiated form, and you transmitted them to Rome, and Monsignor Baldeschi seemed satisfied with them. Should you speak to the friars of Louvain on the subject, or with any of the Irish, you will learn whether or not I have reason on my side. The primacy of Armagh is as certain as the archiepiscopate of Armagh. Be good enough to give a glance at the life of St. Malachy, written by St. Bernard ; at Colgan, in his 6th appendix to the life of St. Patrick ; at Barbosa, Azorius, and others, and you will see how unjust are the pretensions of the Archbishop of Dublin.

" I am informed from Rome that Monsignor Baldeschi will go to Paris : I hope that your Excellency will go to Propaganda, which surely would be the case were I counsellor to his Holiness.

" 22nd September, 1672."

Writing eight days later, he again refers to the same subject :—

" In your letter of the 4th of last month you were good enough to inform me that it was the desire of the Sacred Congregation that silence should be observed in regard of the matter of the primacy ; and it commands us to send our reasons and arguments to Rome, that the question may be decided. I will be ever obedient, not only to the commands, but to the hints of the Sacred Congregation, and to every hint of the ministers of the Holy Father. I suppose, however, that this order or desire only commands silence as to writing pro or contra in this matter, and the avoiding of disputes about precedence, all which I will most strictly obey The Sacred Congregation and your Excellency cannot mean that I should omit to exercise my jurisdiction in matter of appeals which are made from the courts of the other metropolitans, which has always been practised, and without any controversy that I know of during past times ; to interdict this to me would be to suspend the rights of the see of Armagh, even before the sentence or decision is made. It would be precisely as if a person should go to law with your Excellency about a vineyard which you possess, and which was already in the possession of your father, and that the judge should command your Excellency not to derive any fruit from the vineyard : not to gather or receive any revenue from it till after the decision or definitive sentence, which would be to deprive him of possession, and, indeed, to his great detriment, if the law-suit continued any length of time, and would seem to be contrary to the course of the civil and canon law. And, hence, I suppose I can exercise jurisdiction in such appeals without being disobedient to the Sacred Congregation, or to your Excellency. You will be good enough to read a work written by Dr. John Lynch, page 71, the title of which is *Alithinologia;* this writer belongs to the province of Tuam; as also a book composed by David Root the, Bishop of Ossory, article the 6th, page 228; this bishop is suffragan of the Archbishop of Dublin, and died here in the time of Cromwell : he was a learned and prudent man. The title of his work is *Analecta de rebus Catholicorum.* Also Colgan, in his 6th Appendix to the *Life of St. Patrick.* These writers, and, in fact, all the other writers are unanimous in granting appeals to the see of Armagh ; nor did I ever read that there was any controversy on that head, though there might have been disputes on other points. So that without acting in contradiction with the desires and commands of the Sacred Congregation, or of your Excellency, I can continue to receive appeals whenever they are presented. I pray you to read the aforesaid books in the cited places for a quarter of an hour. The Canon Joyce will lend you the books, and if he has'nt them he will procure them from the Irish Convent in Louvain.

" I already wrote to Coppinger to meet me about eighteen miles from Dublin ; I shall see what answer he will give. Should he come, I hope we shall do something. I wrote to your Excellency to send either to me or to Mr. Daniel Arthur, a merchant in London, the money which their Eminences were so good as to send me. Father Perez, Jesuit, an excellent man, will find the means for transmitting it to the said Mr. Daniel ; and I pray the Divine Majesty to remunerate your Excellency, in this life and in the next, for the labours and anxiety which you continually give proof of for the spiritual advantage of this poor nation. The Catholics, in consequence of a new edict of the King, can hold situations and offices without taking the oath of supremacy. This information was imparted to Sir Nicholas Plunket by the Viceroy on Wednesday last.

" Dundalk, 30th September, 1672."

But whilst the Sacred Congregation was thus engaged in seeking the necessary information to guide it in its decision, and whilst the archbishops were themselves affectionately united in the bonds of spiritual charity, the question of the primatial rights of Armagh or Dublin was warmly discussed through the length and breadth of the kingdom, and occasioned such dissensions amongst the Catholics as were a source of affliction to all true lovers of religion, and of joy and delight to all the promoters of heresy and error. The most detailed narrative of this controversy is presented in the letters of Dr. Brennan, at this time Bishop of Waterford. Thus his letter to the Cardinal Protector of

Ireland, dated 30th March, 1672, is almost wholly occupied with this subject; it is as follows :—

"MAY IT PLEASE YOUR EMINENCE,—As your Eminence was good enough to permit me to address you occasionally with an obsequious letter, I have deemed it my duty to humbly convey to your Eminence some intelligence regarding the spiritual condition of the Catholic religion in this country.

"During the past two years extraordinary differences have subsisted between the Archbishops of Armagh and Dublin, occasioned by pretensions to precedence, to jurisdiction, to the title of primate, and other foolish notions. At length these differences have degenerated into a clamorous and scandalous discord, to the prejudice of our profession, and the lowering of the dignity which these prelates bear. The first caused lately to be printed in Dublin a little book, entitled *Jus Primatiale*, in which he endeavours to prove that the primacy belongs to the Archbishop of Armagh, and that it is his prerogative to receive ecclesiastical appeals, make visitations throughout the whole kingdom, and other such things.

"The Archbishop of Dublin, displeased at this, is preparing for press an answer, and he addressed a circular letter to the other bishops of this kingdom, asking their counsel on this matter. I wrote to him, dissuading him as forcibly as I could, and I besought the other prelates to do the same; and I suggested that it would be better for all the prelates of the kingdom to assemble together, in order to extinguish this fire; and perhaps this will be done, unless these disturbed times may render the Government jealous of such a meeting. Whilst I was in Dublin I endeavoured, by all quiet means, to reconcile them, and also from this place by means of letters; but I only succeeded in having good promises, and in an apparent reconciliation. I will not cease, however, even for the future, to use all possible endeavours, although there is but little hope, as they are of a hot disposition, and the dispute has become public in England, as well as in Ireland; so that the Catholics are, for the most part, divided, some in favour of the one, and some in favour of the other. I have also been informed, by an important personage, that in Dublin the Protestant ministers speak with delight, even from the pulpits, about this controversy. Confiding in the great zeal and exceeding prudence of your Excellency, I am bold enough to beseech you, even in the name of the other prelates of this kingdom, to devise some expedient for extinguishing the flame, and to impose silence on both parties by the authority of the Holy Father; otherwise it will continue to spread through the whole kingdom, to the great scandal of the Catholics. About other matters of less importance I shall give an account to Monsignor Baldeschi, not to trespass too much on your Eminence.

"Your Eminence's most devoted and obedient servant,

"JOHN, BISHOP OF WATERFORD.

"Waterford, 30th March, 1672."

Writing, a few days later, to the Internunzio, he adds many additional particulars concerning this controversy :—

" MOST ILLUSTRIOUS AND MOST REV. LORD,—I have just received, by way of London, the letter of your Excellency, under date of the 9th of January, in which you impose on me to use every diligence in appeasing the differences between the two archbishops ; but your Excellency may believe me that this would be an extremely arduous undertaking, as these dissensions are daily increasing, and are now arrived to such a pitch, that I do not know in what manner to quiet them. Since my arrival here I have not omitted to exhort them both to peace ; and for the most part I received good promises, though occasionally I came in for a slight mortification. They are, both one and the other, touchy, and of a hot disposition, and they are the first prelates of the kingdom ; and, in my opinion, they would be displeased to receive an admonition from an inferior bishop. I would be desirous to live in peace, without offending either of them, especially as I could hope for but little fruit from my interference. The Archbishop of Armagh lately printed in Dublin a small work, entitled *Jus Primatiale*, of the Church of Armagh ; and he seeks to establish that he has a right not only to precedence, but also to jurisdiction over the Archbishop of Dublin, and the other archbishops, and that he can make visitations and correct abuses throughout the whole kingdom. He lays great stress on the words of his brief, and of the faculties from the Holy Office, in which he is styled primate. The Archbishop of Dublin, annoyed at this, has prepared for the press an answer ; and he wrote to the other bishops, asking their opinion as to its publication. I wrote to him, conjuring him to give nothing to the press (and I besought the other bishops to do the same), for it would only serve to foment dissensions, and to scandalize the world ; the more so, as in Dublin (as I learned from a well-informed person) the Protestant ministers now boast, even from the pulpits, of these dissensions. The Archbishop of Dublin especially complains of the partiality of the Sacred Congregation to use his words) in causing to be omitted in his brief the title of primate, which title was placed in the brief of the Archbishop of Armagh, and gave him ground for boasting. I said to him, in justification of what had occurred, that that title was found in the brief of the late Archbishop of Armagh, whilst it was wanting in the brief for the Archbishop of Dublin. He replied that this was done by Massari, a friend of the late Archbishop of Armagh, and at that time Secretary of the Sacred Congregation ; and that, although it was wanting in the Bull of his predecessor, nevertheless his see enjoyed this privilege by an Indult of the Roman Pontiffs, and was in possession of it for five hundred years, and thus might claim an immemorial prescription. In the end I said to him, that it would not be proper for me to dispute about the rights of one or the other, but that I would exhort them to peace and to patience, considering the circumstances of the country and of the times, and that he should transmit his reasons to the Sacred Congregation, which would surely render justice to him. I think it would be necessary to take quiet measures with the Archbishop of Dublin, for he is, at least, touchy. The Viceroy has now renounced the friendship of the Archbishop of Armagh, and of John Patrick, and he has been reconciled with the Archbishop of Dublin and his brother, who will seek to procure for him a continuation in his office of Viceroy; and for this and other business Colonel Talbot has already taken his departure for London. It is said that the Archbishop of Dublin will also go thither shortly; but if he goes it will be on other business, and perhaps he will go as far as Innspruck. It seems that they both enjoy the favour of the Court in London, and also of the Viceroy; and they are, for the most part, very popular amongst the Catholics of this kingdom, on account of the interest displayed by the Colonel in London in favour of the Catholics.

"The royal edicts have been published, granting the right of franchise to the Catholics in all the cities of Ireland, which has not been allowed since the time of Cromwell; and some of the Catholics are already in public offices. All this is due to the clemency of our Viceroy, whom God may long preserve. Its being carried into execution is also due to the great goodness of the same Viceroy, for it here met with great opposition from the members of the Privy Council and the heretics.

"To-day, being Holy Thursday, I consecrated here the holy oils in an oratory, which since my arrival I gave in charge to the secular priests, who formerly had no chapel whatsoever; and the ceremony was performed with the greatest solemnity and concourse that has been had or witnessed in this city for the last twenty-two years, on which account the Catholics are all greatly consoled. May God grant us perseverance, and preserve your Excellency for many years to console the Catholics of this kingdom.

                                "JOHN, BISHOP OF WATERFORD.
    "Waterford, the 4th of April, 1672."

In another letter, addressed the same year, under date of the 14th of November, to the Secretary of Propaganda, Monsignor Baldeschi, he declares that:—

"The greatest annoyance which they had in Ireland was the continuance of the dissension between the Archbishops of Armagh and Dublin, which now seems irremediable, as the Archbishop of Dublin lately received some sort of a commission from the King, authorizing him, as he says, to superintend all the clergy; and with it he has commenced to annoy the Archbishop of Armagh, prohibiting him to ordain so many priests, and requesting him to recall a decree which he made about the names of some families of his province, to ask pardon of the King and clergy, and other such things. I confess I do not understand this sort of authority: and

I fain believe that it was procured principally for the purpose of molesting the Archbishop of Armagh, as he has hitherto neglected no means of doing so; and I think that in many things he is wrong. As to this commission, it is necessary that your Excellency should give us some instructions as to how we are to manage, for we do not know how to act. The Archbishop of Dublin is supported by the Franciscans in opposition to the Archbishop of Armagh. The reason of this is, that the Archbishop of Dublin favours them in their pretentions, and the Archbishop of Armagh decided against them in favour of the Dominicans; hence they deem the Archbishop of Armagh their adversary, and they say and write against him whatsoever the other may desire . . . The Bishop of Killaloe has arrived in Dublin; he was anxious to try and reconcile our prelates, but he found them more excited than ever, on account of the late commission."

But at this moment, when the controversy was warmest, and the animosity of both parties seemed to have reached its summit, calm and peace were at hand. The letters of Dr. O'Malony, to which the Bishop of Waterford refers, were destined to attain the long-wished-for end, and effect a reconciliation between the conflicting prelates. Dr. Burgatt, Archbishop of Cashel, writing to the Secretary of Propaganda, on the 5th of February, 1673, commemorates this happy result of the intermediation of the Bishop of Killaloe : " My suffragan, the most illustrious Bishop of Killaloe, has not as yet come to his diocese : about three months ago he arrived in Dublin, and he still continues there, not without sufficient reason, as I am convinced, though I am not aware of what his precise motives may be. He has long since been intermediary in the reconciliation of the Archbishops of Armagh and Dublin, and in this he achieved an important work. I have conceived the [greatest hopes in his regard, and that he will be a solace in my declining years."

All joyous and consoled, the Bishop of Waterford hastened to acquaint the Holy See with this happy event, and on the 1st of December, 1672, thus wrote to the Secretary of Propaganda :—

" To-day I have received letters from the Archbishop of Armagh and the Bishop of Killaloe, in date the 19th of last month, and both convey to me the intelligence that on that day a reconciliation had taken place between the Bishops of Armagh and Dublin, which they announce in these precise words, *hodie reddita est pax Ecclesiis Armachanæ et Dublinensi.* This is chiefly owing to the efforts of Dr. O'Malony, who, since his arrival in Dublin, laboured incessantly to effect it. In the same week, a few days before this event, a reconciliation was effected in Dublin between Colonel Talbot and Colonel John Patrick, and this, too, through the efforts of the Bishop of Killaloe and of the Archbishop of Armagh ; and this agreement was a preliminary to the reconciliation of the prelates, because the two colonels were the promoters of either party ; and, as the Archbishop of Armagh writes to me, Colonel Talbot earnestly exerted himself in inducing his brother, the Archbishop of Dublin, to consent to this agreement. This news has rejoiced all the Catholics, who were heretofore disconsolate and scandalized, and I hope great advantage will accrue to the cause of our faith, should God grant a continuance of it. The reconciliation of the two colonels also occasioned great delight, for they are the most active personages of this nation, and when they are united in promoting public measures for the Catholics, a happy result is hoped for. It is true that many have co-operated, both by word of mouth and by letter, to bring about this arrangement; but its accomplishment was reserved for the Bishop of Killaloe, who has thus made a good beginning of his mission, and we are all much indebted to him.

" Coppinger went to Dublin, as I lately informed you, and there presented his submission to the Archbishops of Armagh and Dublin, and he sent submissive letters to Rome and to Brussels, and I think he went thence to the chapter of his Order, to be reconciled with the other members.

" Eight days ago I sent through the same channel by Ostend, two relations of the diocese, and should they be lost, as the former one of the 18th of June last, I shall send a third copy as soon as I receive intelligence of your not having received them.

" I was anxious to convey the above intelligence to you, of which you will have a more diffuse description from the parties themselves, but. perhaps, not so soon as this letter ; and now I make a most humble reverence to your Excellency.

" JOHN, BISHOP OF WATERFORD.

" Waterford, 1st Dec., 1672.
" To Monsignor Baldeschi."

This reconciliation of the two archbishops seems not to have been of a mere momentary duration, and the first letter of Dr. Plunket, in which we have been able to discover reference to it, bears the date 14th of March, 1673. In it the Archbishop thus writes : —

" Our most benign King has been at length compelled to sanction the Acts of Parliament, and hence no Catholic can any longer be employed by the King, the Queen, or the Duke of York, or hold

any office, civil or military, either in the army or navy. This Act of
the English Parliament does not extend to Ireland, because Ireland,
has its own Parliament, and I think our Parliament will not
assemble this year. *The Archbishop of Dublin and myself are like two
real brothers we agree so well;* so also are Colonel Patrick and Colonel
Talbot, the two most important Catholics of this kingdom for their
skill in managing public or private matters, and for their high
position in court; these two gentlemen, by their dissensions,
divided all the Catholics in the kingdom into two factions, to the
great prejudice of our affairs; but now, through the mercy of God,
they are friends, and closely united in friendship, and on Sunday
last they went together to London to oppose every attempt of
those who are but little friendly to us. Dr. O'Malony, of Killaloe,
brought them into harmony, and has remained here till now to
preserve their union, and in doing so, he has rendered a great
service to this kingdom; and he is a person so estimable that I am
sure he will render yet greater services to us, and this especially for
reasons which I cannot now commit to paper, as I have not my
cipher with me, but about this matter *plura alias.*"

It seemed difficult, however, for this harmony to be
lasting till the question of their primatial rights should be
set at rest by the authoritative decision of Rome. Cases
every day presented themselves, in which appeals were
made to one or other of their tribunals, and it was impossible
that some collision would not arise from them. As early
as the 30th of January, 1673, Dr. Brennan, in a letter to
Monsignor Baldeschi, spoke rather hesitatingly about the
continuance of their friendship :* "The Archbishops of
Armagh and Dublin," says he, "get along smoothly since
the reconciliation; but I doubt if it will continue long. At
all events, the Archbishop of Armagh promises me deter-
minedly perseverance on his part; and, indeed, this is
applauded by all the Catholics."

In the beginning of 1674 Dr. Talbot, in a matrimonial
ease which was brought before his tribunal, decided for the
validity of the marriage. The parties deeming themselves aggrieved, appealed to the Archbishop of Armagh.
Dr. Plunket, without hesitation, entertained this appeal;

* " L'armacano ed il Dublinense passano quietamente dopo l'ultimo
aggiustamento, ma dubito che non sia per durare molto. Ad ogni modo
l'Armacano mi promette fermamente la perseveranza della sua parte;
vivamente ciò è applaudito da tutti i Cattolici." (30th Gen. 1673.)

and, following the example of many of his predecessors, erected his tribunal in the very city of Dublin. The existence of a diriment impediment, prior to the contracting of the marriage, having been clearly established, he, by his primatial authority, reversed the sentence of the Archbishop of Dublin, and declared the marriage to have been null and void from the very beginning. But Dr. Plunket soon discovered his error; and learning that Dr. Talbot had, prior to the marriage, obtained a dispensation for the contracting parties, although in his public decision, through dread of *præmunire*, he had not referred to such a dispensation, the primate hastened, without delay, to retract the decision which he had made, acknowledging his fault, and asking pardon of the Archbishop of Dublin. A letter written by Dr. Talbot soon after this occurrence, well reveals to us the true Christian spirit which animated the Archbishop of Armagh on this occasion, and proves, at the same time, the mutual esteem of these worthy prelates :—

"MAY IT PLEASE YOUR EMINENCE,—It was only on the 2nd of February that I received the letters of your Eminence bearing date the 2nd of August last, and I read them with due reverence, but not without sorrow of mind, as I perceived from them that reports had reached your Eminence and the Sacred Congregation of my having passed all bounds in assailing the Archbishop of Armagh by disputes, nowise necessary, about the question of the primacy. No one here is ignorant of his having been the first to provoke this controversy; and his printed book is a standing proof of it: so that I cannot conceive by what arts or means credence was procured for such an imposture in Rome."

He then details the particulars of the matrimonial case, and the erroneous decision of Dr. Plunket, and then continues :—

"On being made acquainted with how matters really stood, the most illustrious Archbishop of Armagh addressed letters to me, in which he avowed his error and his sorrow; and the truly humble prelate, presenting a glorious example of a religious spirit, in the fulness of repentance prayed for pardon of the fault which he had imprudently committed. The Bishop of Killaloe becoming surety for his continuance in these sentiments, we gave our hands and mutually embraced. However, nothing will better perpetuate this concord than a decision of the controversy about the primacy which, indeed, can involve no difficulty, as we have both sincerely submitted our cause to your judgment. Hence, too, in accordance with the commands of your Eminence, I with all possible dispatch, now transmit to you the arguments and proofs which establish the primacy of my see. They would have been long since transmitted, were it not that the letters of your Eminence were delayed for six entire months on the road. Praying that God may preserve your Eminence for many years.

"I remain, &c.,

"PETER OF DUBLIN.

"12th Feb., 1673 (styl. vet.)

"To his Eminence Cardinal Altieri, &c."

In the meantime Rome was not idle in urging these prelates to maintain the concord which had so happily been established; and we find the following decree enacted in 1673* :—

"The Internunzio will urge upon the Archbishops of Armagh and Dublin the necessity of transmitting to the Sacred Congregation the proofs of their asserted title to the primacy; and he will exhort them, at the same time, to mutually love each other, and to persevere in the peace which is now established."

Succeeding events, however, soon gave occasion to new differences.

Before the close of the month of March, 1674, Dr. Talbot was compelled, by the bigotry of Parliament, to seek an asylum on the Continent; yet even whilst far away from the Irish shores intriguing individuals were not wanting to fan the flame of discord, and by misrepresentation and calumny to seek to re-awaken the suspicions of Dr. Talbot against the Archbishop of Armagh. Soon after the departure of the Archbishop of Dublin, his enemies procured from the Government a commission of inquiry into the past conduct of that prelate; and amongst those summoned by the Viceroy to give evidence before this commission was Dr. Oliver Plunket. His evidence on this occasion was misre-

* "De cœtero D. Internuntius instet ut Archiepiscopi Armacan. et Dublinen mittant ad Sacram Congregationem scripturas pro eorum prætenso jure Primatûs Hiberniæ et hortetur eosdem ut invicem se diligant et pacem initam servent."—(Ex Archiv. S. C.)

presented to the exiled archbishop, and became a subject of complaint to the authorities in Rome. However, from the letter of the primate to Dr. Creagh (the Agent of the Irish Church in that city), dated the 15th of September, 1674, we learn that his depositions had been misrepresented, and that Dr. Plunket had merely stated in his evidence such facts as were already well known to the Government :—

"It is said [he writes] that I deposed against Dr. Talbot that he received authority from the King to superintend our clergy; the same had already been deposed some days before by the Bishop of Meath and many others. Dr. Talbot asserted it in the presence of Drs. Burgatt, Lynch, Phelan, the Bishop of Meath, and myself; Dr. Talbot himself wrote about it to the Bishop of Waterford ; and the Bishop of Waterford and I at that time gave an account of it to Monsignor Airoldi and to their Eminences; and it was a matter known to the whole kingdom, and that Dr. Talbot could be displeased with me on that head is all nonsense. Then, as to my accusing him of exacting money for agents, &c, you see how matters are distorted. The whole kingdom collected money for Catholic agents—that is, one *grosso*, for every *rubio* (of land),* and this was publicly exacted. What crime, then, could it be to mention what was publicly done, and with the knowledge even of the Viceroy? and, indeed, the collectors forced all the Catholics to pay it, even by *distraining*.† Dr. Talbot wished also that the ecclesiastics should pay it, but I was opposed to their doing so in Ulster; for in all of Ulster there is only my Lord of Iveagh who has the slightest hope of recovering his property, and should the Protestants hear that the ecclesiastics were contributing for the purpose of having them deprived of the property which they hold, we would be exposed to persecution ; and I asked the Viceroy Berkeley regarding this subject in 1671, when it was first proposed, whether I or my clergy should contribute. He being a very intimate friend of mine, replied, ' by no means, and that we shall leave such matters to the laity ;' and I wrote at the same time to Monsignor Baldeschi about this matter, and about the meetings which Dr. Talbot was holding for the same purpose, and Monsignor Baldeschi condemned and blamed what was done by Dr. Talbot, and approved of the course which I pursued."

The subsequent repeated outbursts of persecution and the

* The *grosso* is equal to *two pence*, and the *rubio* very nearly equivalent to *two acres :* so that the tax voluntarily imposed on the whole nation was *a penny per acre*.

† Dr. Plunket uses this very word even in the original Italian letter. Indeed it would be difficult to find any Italian word that fully expresses the same idea.

continued infirmities of Dr. Talbot hushed, for awhile, all
further controversy, and, at the same time, seemed to have
influenced the Sacred Congregation in deferring the decision
of the subject. We learn, however, from Dr. MacMahon,
in his *Prosecutio contra Anonymum*, cap. 22, that as late as
1678 Dr. Plunket was engaged in preparing for the press a
reply to the work of Dr. Talbot, which had been published
in Lisle, in 1674; but the storm which was then let loose
on the Irish Church, and the arrest of both archbishops,
terminated, at least during their episcopate, the primatial
controversy.   In the prison of Dublin Dr. Plunket and
Dr. Talbot were side by side (being confined in adjoining
rooms), both captives for the faith.   Before the glorious end
of his earthly career in 1680, the Archbishop of Dublin
wished to give a final proof to the world that he was moved
only by a sense of duty in carrying on this controversy, and
that notwithstanding their apparent conflict, the fire of
charity ever glowed in his courageous soul ; and hence, he
addressed from his prison-chamber, in which he was soon to
die, an humble apology to Dr. Plunket, asking his pardon
and forgiveness for any fault into which, in the warmth of
dispute, he might have fallen.*   In this holy rivalry of
Catholic charity and mutual love, Dr. Plunket was not to be
overcome; and we learn from a letter of the Bishop of
Kildare,† that when it was reported to him that the
Archbishop of Dublin was about to enter on his agony,
Dr. Plunket could no longer be restrained, but bursting

---

* This fact is recorded by Dr. M'Mahon in his *Jus. Primat. Armac*,
page 217.

† This passage of Dr. Forstall's letter is so interesting that we here
give it entire :—" Corcagiensis est captus : quæritur ubique Laonensis.
Clogherensis sub gausape et centonibus cujusdam mendicæ et moribundæ
vetulæ sese absconderat et ibidem deprehensus et agnitus vel a sævo
satellite compassionem et veniam meruit. Miserrimus Dubliuensis cerebro
totoque corpore ægrotans plurimum, vix ultima die veneris sanctissimam
non efflavit animam. Primate strenue perrumpente inter reluctantes
satellit s ut cum solaretur et absolveret. Primus ipse in eodem jacet
Tul iano incertus fati futurique. Nemo arctus custoditur ob male
feri.tus nebulones et informatores (proh pudor) ecclesiasticos qui ex
vindictæ libidine falsis crimiuationibus eum consper-erunt."—(5th June,
1680.)

through his guards, rushed to give a last embrace and absolution to the dying confessor of the Catholic faith.

Before closing this chapter it may be expected that we should give some review of the work of Dr. Plunket on the primatial rights of his see—the only work from his pen which has come down to us We shall, therefore, present an outline of the principal arguments which he employed, but we shall present them in his own words, translating the letter which he addressed to the Internuncio, on the 12th of March, 1671, and in which he himself presents a compendium of the chief arguments on this subject:—

" I have received your most welcome letter of the 15th February, and I may assure you that it is nothing new that controversies should arise between prelates in regard of precedence and jurisdiction. I myself saw in Rome how, in the very presence of the Pontiff, Father Marini disputed with Monsignor Celsi, and the chamberlains with the auditors of the Rota about precedence. I remarked that there have been similar controversies in Germany and France, though they are in the midst of heretics; even amongst the Apostles *orta est contentio quis eorum videretur esse major*, nor do I think that there are many who have greater reason than I have for disputing on this head, since my see enjoys an uninterrupted precedence as well as superior jurisdiction for thirteen hundred years, that is, to the time of Henry the Eighth, an heretical king; and that your Excellency may understand this, I will write to you in compendium what I already wrote more diffusely to Rome.

" It is uncontroverted, that from the time of Celestine the I., who sent St. Patrick to Ireland, till the age of St. Bernard, there was no Archbishop in Ireland, excepting the Archbishop of Armagh, and as St. Bernard writes in the life of St. Malachy, *unus ipse omnibus præfuit*, and this was for about 700 years About the year 1000 St. Celsus erected the see of Cashel into an archbishoprick; and thus the see of Dublin is of later date than that of Cashel. In the year 1152, Cardinal Paparo was sent into Ireland as legate of the Holy See, and he erected Dublin and Tuam into archiepiscopal sees, and granted the pallium to the four archbishops. Who will venture to assert that the jurisdiction enjoyed by my predecessors was lessened by these episcopal sees being raised to a higher dignity; their authority was, indeed, increased, but the pre-eminence and jurisdiction of Armagh was not lessened. In the year 1263, Urban the IV., thus wrote to Patrick,* Archbishop of Armagh :—*Primatium totius Hiberniæ quam prædecessores tui usque ad hæc tempora inconcusse habuisse noscuntur ad exemplar Cælestini Papæ Prædecessoris nostri tibi tuisque successoribus auctoritate Apostolica confirmamus*

* Dr. Patrick O'Scaulain, transferred from Raphoe to Armagh in 1261.

statuentes, ut Hiberniæ Archiepiscopi et Episcopi et alii Prælati tibi et successoribus tuis tamquam Primati obedientiam et reverentiam omni tempore debeant exhibere. Again, John XXII. confirmed to Nicholas of Armagh the old privilege of his see to receive, namely, appeals from all parts of the kingdom; the words of the Pope are as follows:—*Quod cum in partibus Hiberniæ ad sedem Apostolicam in quacumque causa appellari contingit seu appellatur de præsenti, hujusmodi appellantes ad eamdem sedem directe, necnon ad Archiepiscopalem curiam (Armacanam) tutorie appellant.* Thus, then, when those of Dublin appeal to Armagh *tutorie appellant:* the Archbishop of Armagh is therefore their superior for *appellatio est recessio ab inferiors judice per invocationem majoris judicis.* At this time the Primate held his consistory in Dublin, and received appeals from the Archbishop of Dublin, and I read in the registers that at the time of Edward the III., in 1349, he carried the cross before him for three days in the city of Dublin, and excommunicated there the prior of Kilmainham. For 150 years the Archbishops of Dublin were subject to the Primate, without any controversy, down to the time of John Leek and Alexander Bicknor, who wished to set aside the jurisdiction of the Archbishop of Armagh, on account of the Viceroy residing in Dublin, precisely as the patriarchs of Constantinople sought to set aside the jurisdiction of the Pope, because the Emperor resided in that city, but *incasum nisi sunt,* and the Archbishops of Armagh continued to exercise their jurisdiction till the time of Henry the VIII., and Edward the VI., that is, till the year 1547. In the fifth year of this Edward, George Browne, Archbishop of Dublin, obtained a royal edict to be called Primate of all Ireland, and George Dowdall, Archbishop of Armagh, a Catholic, was exiled from his see; after the death of Edward, however, Queen Mary, being informed by the legate, Cardinal Pole, and by others, of the jurisdiction and pre-eminence enjoyed by my predecessors for 1100 years, cancelled the decree of Edward, and restored all to Dowdall, and obliged Browne to due submission. Thus, your Excellency may see that the grounds of the Archbishop of Dublin for the primacy of his see is a decree of a Protestant king.

"After George Dowdall, Loftus, a Protestant, was chosen by Queen Elizabeth as his successor, and, nevertheless, he and his successors, *juxta morem antiquum acceptam a Catholicis,* took precedence of the Archbishop of Dublin, even in Dublin itself, and to the present day they hold their consistory there, and decide all controversies according to our canon law.

"But let us come to later times; about the year 1645, when Monsignor Rinuccini came to Ireland, sent by Pope Innocent the Tenth, he assembled all the bishops of Ireland in Kilkenny, in the province of Dublin, and nevertheless, Hugh O'Reilly, Archbishop of Armagh, took precedence of Dr. Fleming, Archbishop of Dublin, and subscribed the Acts before him; soon after they assembled again in Cashel, and the same Archbishop of Armagh again took precedence of all. In fine, in the Bull of the Archbishop of Armagh, we read, *promovetur ad Ecclesiam Hiberniæ primatialem,* and in the privileges granted to him by the Sacred Congregation, he is styled Primate of Ireland. These, perhaps, are mere titles, are *roces nihil significantes, absit :* and hence, the Holy See never gave such titles to the Archbishops of Dublin. Then, too, a primate must have archbishops subject to him ; now, I ask, what archbishops can be said to be subject to the see of Dublin ? Surely, no one recognises it, whilst all recognise the see of Armagh. Even the Archbishop of Cashel claims precedence of the see of Dublin, and not without reason, as his see dates to higher antiquity.

"Your Excellency must now say could I, without incurring the reproach of posterity, cede this right of the see of Armagh, which was preserved and sanctioned during so many centuries ? And is it not evident, that I have jurisdiction over the whole kingdom, and that the province of Dublin is as much subject to me as the province of Armagh? Now, this jurisdiction holds in the following cases :—

" 1. *Quando ad me appellatur.*

" 2. *Quando Ecclesia Metropolitana pastore vacat et a Primate petitur ut de rebus ad Metropolitanum pertinentibus et constituendis siatuat.*

" 3. *Cum. consuetudine ant privilegio, causa ad ipsum defertur.*

" 4. *Cum de gravi et ardua re dubitatur quæ in concilio Provinciali definiri commode nequit, tunc Metropolitanus Primatem consulit.*

" 5. *Cum Metropolitanus negligens est in causis judicandis; tunc enim Primatis est judicare.*

" 6. *Quando juxta leges et consuetudinem Primas visitare debeat totum Regnum.*

" These are the reasons which induced me to defend my right, and which clearly prove, that, as Primate, I have as much jurisdiction in Dublin as I have throughout the province of Armagh ; in everything, however, and under ever respect. I submit myself to the judgment of the Apostolic See, which, in the meantime, I earnestly pray to decide this controversy, that thus every scruple may be removed for the future, and to command the Archbishop of Dublin to render due submission to the Primate, as he alone refuses to acknowledge the Primate's jurisdiction and authority.

" Armagh, the 12th of March, 1671.

"To the Internuncio, Brussels.   " OLIVER OF ARMAGH."

APPENDIX TO CHAPTER XVIII.

The preceding chapter was written when some additional letters came to hand, with which the Primate, the Bishop of Killaloe,* and the Internuncio in Brussels communicated

---

* As the Bishop of Killaloe wrote in Latin, we here present the original letter of that prelate. It is as follows :—

Illme. Dno.

" Non me jam pœnitet unius mensis moræ quam in hac urbe duxi, cum hoc ipso die, non ego sed gratia Dei mecum irreconciliabile bellum Armachani et Dublinensis composuerim, restituta utrique pace et concordia, et toti nostro clero et patriæ charitatis et unanimitatis

to Rome the consoling intelligence of the Archbishops of Dublin and Armagh being happily reconciled, and of peace being thus restored to the Irish Church. The Internuncio, Monsignor Airoldi, thus writes :—

"I may justly demand a recompense from your Excellency for the good news which I now bring of the reconciliation of the Archbishop of Armagh with his Grace of Dublin, through the mediation of Dr. O'Molony, Bishop of Killaloe. This intelligence was the more

exemplo : mecum ambo cum nobilissimo ac strenuissimo Dubliniensis fratre Collonello Talbot prandium hodie alacres et concordes fecerunt : soli Deo honor et gloria ! Ultima hebdomada inter eundem Colonellum et alium virum nobilem a longo jam tempore discordes cum maximo patriæ ac religionis detrimento, pacem similiter et concordiam feci, Dei adjuvante gratia. Jam nullam inter nostrates alicujus notæ aut nominis viros discordiam novi : faxit Deus pacis, et amator charitatis ut ita diu vivamus et sic prospere cuncta succedent.

"Proximo jam die in meam diœcesim sum profecturis, laboraturus si quid possum in vinea mihi commissa. Rogo non gravetur hanc epistolam remittere ad nostrum in curia Romana procuratorem meque semper credas futurum, &c.

"J. O'MOLONY, Bishop of Killaloe.

"Dublinii, 19 Nov., 1672."

It may not be uninteresting to here subjoin the briefs of Clement XI. of 20th December, 1719, by which he put an end to the controversy regarding the primacy, which had been excited again in his time. One brief is directed to Dr. M'Mahon. Archbishop of Armagh, the other to Dr. Byrne, Archbishop of Dublin.

"Ven. fratri. Archiep. Armacan.

"CLEMENS PAPA XI.

"VENERABILIS FRATER, SALUTEM, &c.—Gravi cum animi nostri molestia intelleximus acre dissidium quod inter Fraternitatem Tuam et Ven. Fratrem Archiep. Dublinensem, nuper exortum fuit occasione appellationis ad tuum tribunal interpositæ nomine dilecti filii presbyteri Valentini Rivers a quodam decreto ejusdem Archiepi. per quod administratio Parochialis Ecclesiæ Sae Catherinæ civitatis Dublinensis præfato Rivers adempta, et alteri presbytero Kavanagh cognominato commissa fuit, qua occasione antiquam etiam de Primatu controversiam intempestive redintegrari inter vos ac restaurari cepisse inaudivimus. Cum autem pro pastorali quam gerimus omnium Ecclesiarum sollicitudine, muneris nostri esse arbitremur gravissimis quæ ab ejusmodi contentionibus oriri posssunt malis, opportune ac cito occurrere, causam administrationis (antedictæ Ecclesiæ cum omnibus, illi adnexis ac ab ea dependentibus ab utriusque Vestrum, et quibuscumque aliis tribunalibus, ubi eam forsitan disceptari contigerit, Apostolica Auctoritate ad nos avocandam esse ducimus et avocavimus illamque Congregationi Ven. Fratrum nostr. S. R. E. Cardinalium negotiis Propagandæ Fidei præpositorum cognoscendam finoque debito terminandam commisimus. Quapropter Fraternitati Tuæ tenore præsentium injungimus et mandamus ut authenticum exemplum omnium actorum ejusdem causæ quæ in tua curia hactenus

welcome to me, as it was least expected; indeed, I esteem it rather
the work of God than of man. I have written to both prelates,
earnestly beseeching them to preserve inviolate this happy concord.
I congratulate your Excellency on this event, and I am rejoiced
that, besides the submission of Coppinger, it has been granted to
me to witness the happy termination of this matter before the close
of my ministry.

"Brussels, 24th December, 1672."

gesta fuerunt ad memoratam Congregationem quamprimum transmittas,
et insuper antedictis presbyteris Rivers et Kavanagh denunciari facias
atque præcipias ut jura sibi competentia coram eadem Congregatione
incunctanter deducere non prætermittant. Interim vero donec causa
finita fuerit decernimus et declaramus præfatum Rivers administrationi
controversæ Parochialis Ecclæ. nullo pacto se immiscere debere,
eamdemque Ecclesiam administrari volumus et mandamus a memorato
Kavanagh tamquam ad id a Nobis specialiter delegato, sine tamen
præjudicio jurium ambarum partium. Cæterum quoad Primatum attinet,
cupimus ut jura quæ Ecclesiæ Tuæ suffragari putaveris prædictæ Cognis
judicio discutienda proponas, cujus erit libratis æqua lance utriusque
partis rationum momentis ex justitiæ præscripto litem decidere. Quod
superest Te vehementer in Dno hortamur ac admonemus ut excitatus
isthic de utraque controversia sermones e medio tolli ac penitus aboleri
omni adhibitio studio satagas, cumque in scopum nedum ab antedictis
presbyteris verum etiam a reliquis omnibus Tibi subjectis ecclesiasticis viris silentium custodiri impense cures. Id autem eo mixius a Te
postulamus, quo firmius credimus) non alia magis ratione publicum scandalum
aboleri ac averti posse gravissima pericula et detrimenta quæ ab ejusmodi
inter præcipuos Hiberniæ sacros antistites contentionibus et orthodoxæ
fidei ejusque cultoribus imminere maxime formidamus. Et Apostolicam
Benedictionem Fraternitati Tuæ peramanter impertimur.

"Datum Romæ, &c. die 20 Dec. 1719."

"Venerabili Fratri Archiep. Dublinensi.

"VEN. FRATER SALUTEM, &c.—Vehementer ut par erat commoti sumus
ex iis quæ de gravi contentione inter Fraternitatem Tuam et Ven.
Fratrem Archiep. Armacanum excitata, occasione provocationis ad hunc
habitæ a dilecto filio presbytero Valentino Rivers cui ademptam Paroch.
Ecclæ. S. Cath. istius Civitatis Dublinensis administrationem alteri
Presbytero tradidisti, nuperrime ad nos allata fuerunt. Pro pastoralis
itaque officii nostri debito, non solum scandalo quod quidem ingens ob
hujusmodi dissidium et consequenter instauratam inter vos veterem de
Primatu quæstionem istis in partibus exortum esse intelleximus, salubriter
et opportune consulere, verum etiam gravissima pericula et detrimenta
quæ inde in orthodoxam religionem ejusque cultores derivari possent,
quantum in nobis situm est avertere et etiam arcere cupientes consilium
suscepimus causam administrationis. (Here follow the same words as in the
preceding letter, which are in a parenthesis; then the letter terminates)—
non alia magis ratione publicam bonorum omnium offensionem extingui
posse, neque etiam averti mala quæ sane ingentia a funesto hoc inter
præcipuos sacros Hiberniæ Antistites dissidio, nisi celeriter componatur,
in rem Catholicam redundatura ore summa cum animi nostri molestia
prævidemus. Et Ap. Ben. Fraternitati T. peramanter impertimur.
Dat. Romæ, &c., die 21 Dec. 1719."

T

The Archbishop of Armagh wished to be himself, too, the bearer of these happy tidings, and on the same day addressed the following letter to the Internuncio:—

"I may have written many vexatious letters to your Excellency, but I am sure the present one will not be so annoying, as it brings the news how, through the labours of the Bishop of Killaloe, a perfect concord and reconciliation has been established between the Archbishop of Dublin and myself. Dr. Talbot, with his brothers and nephews, and I, dined together, and in the evening Dr Talbot and his brothers came to visit all my friends, a thing which did not take place before during the past twelve months. We shall send all papers connected with our controversy to Rome, and whilst we await its decision, we shall live in peace and tranquillity. The Bishop of Killaloe brought about a reconciliation also between two other Catholic gentlemen of high character and position; but about this and other matters I will write a more full account by another post. In the meantime I will ever be, &c.,

"OLIVER PLUNKET.

"19th November, 1672."

CHAPTER XIX.

PERSECUTION OF 1674.

TOWARDS the close of 1673, the English monarch, yielding to the well-known bigotry of the Parliament, published an order suspending the few favours which had been granted to the Catholics during the administration of Berkeley, and commanding all the bishops and regular clergy to depart from the kingdom.* Thus were too soon sadly verified the anticipations of Dr. Plunket, which we have already met with in many of his letters. Indeed, the Catholics had as yet scarce begun to taste the sweets of toleration when this new storm of persecution was let loose against them. The use of arms was interdicted to them: "they were disfranchised in all corporations, and deprived of corporate honours and emoluments; the powers vested in the Lord Lieutenant and

---

* "Portano gl'ultimi avvisi di Londra che il Re per incontrare le soddisfazioni del Parlamento, avesse inviato ordine in Ibernia per l'espulsione dei Vescovi Cattolici e di tutti i Religiosi e sacerdoti toltine i parochi; con la proibizi ne delle armi a tutti i Cattolici fuori che ai nobili della sola spada."—Lett del Internunz. Falconieri. 9 Nov. 1673.

Council to regulate corporations were twisted into a legislative authority of new-modelling them, and of imposing oaths and qualifications contrary to law, and subversive of the rights of the subject." *

What were the sufferings of Dr. Plunket and of the Bishop of Waterford, who was the companion of his flight, will be best learned from the letters of the Primate. Soon after the publication of the King's edict in Ireland, he thus writes to the Internuncio on 27th January, 1674:—

"I have received yours of the 12th of December, as also the letter sent to the companions of my sufferings, which, indeed, are very great in this first month of the new year; so that this year begins with a cloud which is truly thickening, and presages a dreadful storm, as you will see from the following narrative.

"In the edict published against the bishops and regulars, there was a clause, that whatsoever bishop or regular would have his name enrolled on the magistrate's list in the maritime forts, with the intention of taking his departure from the kingdom, should suffer no molestation; nay, more, that he should be protected till a vessel would be found ready to sail for foreign countries. Some bishops, as Dr. Plunket, of Meath, and Dr. O'Molony, of Killaloe, entered their names in Dublin; many of the regulars, with the Archbishop of Tuam, gave their names in Galway, and some others in various other parts of the kingdom, hoping that the storm would pass, and that peace and calm would be soon restored. Quite the contrary, however, happened. The Viceroy, on the 10th, or thereabouts, of this month, published a further proclamation that the registered clergy should be treated with the greatest rigour. Another, but secret, order was also given to all the magistrates and sheriffs that the detectives should seek out, both in the cities and throughout the country, the other bishops and regulars; I and my companion no sooner received intelligence of this than, on the 18th of this month (styl. vet.) which was Sunday, after Vespers, being the festival of the Chair of St. Peter, we deemed it necessary to take to our heels; the snow fell heavily, mixed with hailstones, which were very hard and large: a cutting north wind blew in our faces, and the snow and hail beat so dreadfully in our eyes, that to the present we have scarcely been able to see with them. Often we were in danger in the valleys of being lost and suffocated in the snow, till at length we arrived at the house of a reduced gentleman who had nothing to lose; but, for our misfortune, he had a stranger in his house, by whom we did not wish to be recognized: hence we were placed in a large garret, without chimney and without fire, where we have been during the past eight days: may it redound to the glory of God, the

* *History of the Irish Cath.*, by Mathew O'Conor, page 105.

salvation of our souls, and of the flocks entrusted to our charge·
So dreadful was the hail and cold, that the running of the eyes both
of my companion and myself has not ceased as yet, and I feel that
I shall lose more than one tooth, so frightful is the pain they give
me ; my companion, moreover, was attacked with rheumatism in one
arm, so that he can scarcely move it. In a word, we may say with
truth, that *fuga nostra fuit in hieme et in sabbato*; that is on Sunday,
and the feast of the Chair of St. Peter; blessed be God who granted
us the favour of suffering, not only for the Chair of St. Peter, but on
the very day dedicated to the feast of that chair, which, resting
on a rock, will, as I hope, in the end break the violence of these
tempestuous waves.

"Though I have not as yet heard of the arrest of any, except a
certain Father Eugene Cogli (Quigley), of the Order of St. Dominick,
Prior of Tuam, and a Father Francis Brennan, in Mullingar, nevertheless, I fear that for the future room will be wanting in the prisons,
so many will be arrested; for, as I am informed, the sheriffs and
magistrates of the king received orders to hunt out the bishops and
regulars, searching for them even in private houses. May God assist
us. I make you my reverence,

"THOMAS COX.*

"The 27th January (styl. vet.) 1674."

Dr. Brennan added the following lines to this letter :—

"On the 14th of December I gave an account to your Excellency
of my flight, and of the occasion of it. Up to the present God has
protected me in the company of my old Roman companion; we have
been together, sharing the same fate for the last two months, and
he has described above its annoyances. The spies, however,
occasion still greater anxiety, for we are at every moment exposed
to them, especially now that the Lord Lieutenant has avowed his
determination to carry the proclamation into effect, and for this
purpose has already published a new edict. We trust, in the mercy
of God, that He will give us grace to endure all this, and conform
ourselves to His holy will. I will not fatigue your Excellency by
detailing the sad news with which our island is full at the present
time. May God console us, and grant many years to your
Excellency, &c.

"JOHN OF WATERFORD.

"27th January, 1674."

Even after these lines of Dr. Brennan, the Primate added
another postscript, in which he writes :—

"At the moment of closing this, I received two letters from
London, one of the 10th of January, the other of the 12th, and they
bring but little consolation or hope. The Parliament made an

* This was the assumed name of the Archbishop of Armagh.

order that no Catholic could lodge within ten miles of London, and they sent away all the Catholics that have a permanent residence there. The Parliament commenced a suit against the Duke of Buckingham, the Duke of Lauderdale (a Scotchman), and the Earl of Arlington, Secretary of State, and it is feared that the result will not be too favourable to them. It is also said that the Duke of Ormond will be brought upon the stage, and subjected to trial. They obliged the Duke of York and four of the Catholic nobility to take the oath of allegiance ; they are also making an investigation whether there are Catholics in the army. The Parliament is altogether inclined to peace with Holland, and to war against France ; they raise great difficulties about giving money to the king, either to carry on war, or to pay his debts. If such rigour is shewn against the Catholics in the chief and model city, London, there can be but little prospect of relief for us in this country. No matter; the mercy of God is greater than all human efforts and machinations.

" You are reverenced by

" THOMAS COX."

About a fortnight later Dr. Plunket again wrote to the Internuncio, giving further accounts of the laws enacted by Parliament, and although his letter presents no additional particulars as to his own immediate sufferings, still it reveals to us his ardent desire to suffer for the faith, and the true heroism of Christian charity which glowed in his breast :—

" We are here in still greater fear and trembling, for *our neighbour's house is on fire.* In Scotland, the Parliament enacted that for the future it should be considered high treason to hear Mass. It would seem that the days of Nero and Domitian and Diocletian have returned ; the penalty of this crime of high treason is to be embowelled and quartered. So thus we shall have the blood of martyrs in abundance to fertilize the Church. It is true, that in Scotland proper, there are but few Catholic families ; but in the Hebrides there are about 4,000 Catholic families, and I gave a long account of these islands to Mgr. Airoldi. If Scotland is in tears, England has little motive for rejoicing. The Parliament did nothing from the 7th of January to the 27th but discuss matters of religion, and the result of all their deliberations was to assail the Catholics ; they framed a new oath, to be taken by all the Catholics resident in London, and amongst its other beautiful clauses, there is one which deserves to be remarked, that forsooth *the Pope is a heretic.* Whosoever refuses to take this oath is, *ipso facto,* condemned; and amongst the other penalties, he shall lose three-fourths of his goods. They also enacted, that the sons and daughters of the Duke of York should have a Protestant tutor, and should be removed from his palace, on account of his wife being Catholic, lest they, too, should be Catholics. They passed another bill declaring it unlawful for the king, or any of the royal family, to marry a Catholic without the license and consent of the Parliament. I remember the inscription which was over the entrance of Castle Gandolfo, *qui petenti majora negat, minora permittit*. The king can choose any servants he pleases, but he cannot choose a wife ; at this rate in a little while he will not be able to send away a coachman without taking off his hat to Parliament ; it is thus this *bestia multorum capitum* puts its foot upon his neck (you remember the expression of your father). It was also commanded, under the strictest penalties, that all the sons of Catholics throughout the whole kingdom should be educated in the Protestant tenets. It was even proposed that all the priests of the whole kingdom should be imprisoned for life. The treaty of peace proposed by Holland, and favoured by the Spanish ambassador, diverted their attention, and at present engrosses their thoughts ; in my opinion, however, this peace will not be made, for the Dutch are resolved to fish in the British Ocean, and on the coasts of Greenland, whilst the English are equally determined not to yield these fisheries to them.

" I had almost forgotten to mention another clause of the oath of abjuration, forsooth, that when the priest pronounces the words of Christ, there is present naught but the mere substance of bread and wine. Were they to speak only of their own ministers, and say that after their ceremonies and the pronouncing of the words of Christ, there was nothing but the substance of bread and wine which might well be offered to Ceres or Bacchus, it would be true enough ; for when their ministers recite these words, they not only pronounce our formula of consecration, but deliver a sermon, and this at a distance from the bread and wine, and, as they themselves avow pronounce the form as a *gratiarum actio*, not as a *consecratio aut benedictio ;* moreover, when the minister has not received a valid ordination, it matters little how he pronounces the words, for it is certain they will have no efficacy.

" In fine, listen to another edict, or proclamation, which was published on the 24th of last month, and commanded that the 4th of February should be observed as a solemn fast : behold, a general fast now intimated. And for what purpose ? To invoke and implore the Divine assistance against the dreadful machinations and plottings of the Papists. You may easily imagine in what affliction and confusion we are. But *non est abbreviata manus Domini qui dissipat consilia et comitia principum hujus sæculi et reprobat cogitationes corum.* These times are like to the primitive Church ; and I hope that the Church will once more be rendered glorious, and be enriched with the sufferings and martyrdoms of its northern children, who are humble and devoted servants, and imitators of Christ and the Apostles, and that the adverse storm will aid us more even than the favouring breeze

" These edicts, and proclamations, and decrees, do not as yet regard Ireland, for it is not expressly mentioned in them ; but I think there is, as usual, no danger of their forgetting us. Should they come to us. God be praised, we shall welcome them, *aut patiemur aut moriemur*: at least, we will not be mercenaries; with the halter round our throat, they shall have to drag us to the vessel, for otherwise we shall not abandon the sheep or the lambs. I beseech you to procure for us the prayers of the servants of God, that thus *Deus nos protegat a conventu malignantium*, and may grant to us the gift of holy perseverance, and you are reverenced by your most obliged and devoted servant,

"THOMAS COX.

" 12th February, 1674."

Dr. Brennan adds to this letter a few lines, but instead of subscribing either his name, or even his initials, he only writes in the end : "My writing is sufficiently known."

This postscript is as follows :—

" From the place of our refuge I, in union with my companion, cordially revere your Excellency, though I have nothing to add to what my companion has written. Even in this desert he has a most exact correspondence from all parts, and this is the greatest temporal consolation that we enjoy. Such correspondence, however, costs him a great deal.

" From the desert, the 13th Feb. 1674."

The only provision which had been made by the Primate for this flight and concealment, as he mentions in one of his letters, was a collection of books, and with these and his loved companion, this time of persecution, despite its dangers and sufferings, must have been to him one of peace and heavenly calm. He was often obliged to change his abode. If the place of refuge, just described in the preceding letters, was so ill provided with any convenience, that it seemed a prison rather than an abode, the hut to which, at other times, he was compelled to retreat, seemed to have likened him still more to the martyrs of the primitive Church. "The hut in which Dr. Brennan and myself have taken refuge (he writes towards the close of 1673), is made of straw ; when we lie down to rest, through the opening of the roof, we can see the stars ; and when it rains we are refreshed, even at the head of the bed, by each successive shower." At this period, too, a little oaten bread was their only support ; " yet," the Primate adds, " *we choose rather to die of hunger and cold than to abandon our flocks, since it would be shameful for those spiritual soldiers to become mercenaries, who were trained in Rome."* (15 Dec. 1673.)

The other accounts of the persecution of this year corroborate the narrative of Dr. Plunket. Thus, the Bishop of Clogher, Dr. Patrick Duffy, in his letter of 22nd May, 1674, addressed to Cardinal Altieri, whilst aware that the Primate had recently sent a narrative of their sufferings, " de his fusius Illmus. Ardmachanus vobis scripsit et qualiter ipsi nobiles aut amici nequeunt nec audent nobis succurrere ratione publici edicti noviter hic editi contra ecclesiasticos et eorem fautores," adds, that the whole kingdom was most afflicted, and that the persecution raged with such fury that he did not dare to appear in public, but had fled to the mountains and morasses—" montibus et paludibus," to seek a place of refuge. All means of support had been cut off from him, so that unless some aid were sent from Rome, death from starvation should be his lot; " Nevertheless," he continues, " I am resolved not to abandon my flock, and never to depart hence unless when dragged away a prisoner, or decked with the martyr's palm :" " hinc nisi ex carcere vel cum martyrii palma, statui non discedere."

The superior of the Capuchins, Father Patrick Barnewall, writes in a like strain from London to Cardinal Spinola :—

" I have once more returned from Ireland to England, as the persecution is far more intolerable there than it is here. In Ireland no one, under penalty of losing all that he possesses, can receive a religious into his house ; all the convents, as well as all preaching, are rigorously interdicted: the secular priests alone are tolerated, in order not to excite public tumults In London twenty-five scudi are given to whoever discovers a priest ; so your Excellency may imagine in what manner we are able to live here. Nevertheless the bounty of God displays the wonders of His mercy to the confusion of the persecutors, for every day witnesses new conversions to truth."

This persecution seems to have continued during the whole of the year 1674 : even in the first months of the following year the Parliament threatened its renewal with still more rigorous edicts, and on the 5th of March, 1675,

Dr. Plunket thus wrote to Monsignor Ravizza, Secretary of the Sacred Congregation :—

" You will have already heard how a few days ago new rigorous edicts were published in England against the Catholics, so that we are here *cum timore et tremore*.   Should they affect us here we must fly once more to the woods and caverns (*fugiemus ad sylvas, et montes, et ad speluncas*), in which we have now for fifteen months passed a severe novitiate."

However, this threatened storm of 1675 seems not to have reached the Irish shores, and Heaven granted a few years peace, of which the primate untiringly availed himself to visit anew the various districts of his province to correct abuses, and sanction salutary laws of discipline for the safe guidance of the faithful people entrusted to his care.

————

CHAPTER XX.

DR. PLUNKET DECIDES THE CONTROVERSY BETWEEN THE DOMINICANS AND FRANCISCANS.

DR. PLUNKET, at the very outset of his episcopate, found. the regular clergy of his province divided into two conflicting parties regarding the respective rights of the Franciscans and Dominicans to solicit the alms of the faithful in the dioceses of Armagh, Down, Dromore, and Clogher.   Many flourishing convents of the Dominican order had existed in the province of Armagh, and in particular in the dioceses which we have mentioned, till the ruthless invasion of the Covenanters laid waste everything that was national or sacred in our island.   On the restoration of King Charles II. to the British crown, and on some liberty being accorded for the erection of religious houses, the Franciscan friars were the first to re-establish convents in the province of Armagh, and they especially claimed to themselves that privilege in the dioceses referred to.   From the Dominican house of Sligo, somewhat later, a holy community went

forth to gather the scattered stones of the sanctuary, and
re-inhabit their ancient convents of Gaula, in the diocese of
Clogher, of Carlingford, in Armagh, and Villa-Nova, in
Down To their surprise they discovered that these convents
were in the hands of other religious, and that even their
claim was controverted to solicit the alms of the faithful in
these dioceses. The controversy soon grew warm, and an
appeal was made to the Holy See. To our primate was
entrusted without delay supreme authority to examine the
respective claims of both parties, and pronounce definitive
sentence regarding this controversy. It was with reluctance
that Dr. Plunket accepted this commission from Rome, so
conscious was he of the torrent of calumny and reproach
to which he would be consequently exposed.

" If I decide in favour of the Dominicans [he thus writes, on the
16th of April, 1671], behold the whole body of Franciscans will
write and publish a thousand things and a thousand calumnies
against me, and that this primate is an enemy of the Franciscans, &c.,
and *vice versa*, if I decide in favour of the Franciscans. Notwithstanding all this, should your Excellency and the Internuncio write
to me, and state that I have power to decide their controversies, and
command me to decide the matter, I shall intrepidly obey ; and I
am sure that my decision will have effect.

" As regards formulas of allegiance or remonstrances, since that
which we presented in June last, and which was accepted by the
Viceroy, nothing further has been intimated to us ; and I know the
present Viceroy will give us no annoyance of that sort, for he is
aware that Walsh is a knave, and that he excites these disturbances
for his own private ends. The Viceroy is a moderate and prudent
man ; but should the Government be changed, God knows what may
ensue."

On the commands of the Holy See being communicated
to him, he no longer hesitated to apply himself to this
arduous work ; and on the 7th of June, 1671, he thus
expresses his determination, whatsoever the consequences
might be, to deliver his decision in accordance with the
rules of equity and justice :—

" The differences between the Franciscans and Dominicans will be
judged in every part of the province, conformable to the commands
of your Excellency ; and in doing so I will rather appeal to your

authority than to my own. To say the truth, this decision is an arduous and stormy matter ; after all my toils I shall gather no fruit but the thorns of calumny and falsehood. I shall only summon one procurator at a time from each of the three controverted convents, and I will receive their allegations and proofs, and afterwards give sentence in conformity with these proofs and documents,. *pereat mundus et fiat justitia, si fractus illabatur orbis, imparidum ferient ruinæ.*"

Before pronouncing sentence, Dr. Plunket held a visitation in each of the four mentioned dioceses, and by letter of 29th July, 1671, whilst he details the many expenses in which he had been involved in consequence of the many commissions from Rome, he communicates to the Internunzio the result of his deliberations :—

" I received yours of the 22nd of June, with the letter annexed, and this package cost me three scudi and a-half. My poor purse is not able to meet this and like expense of letters. I will not be wanting in toiling and offering my services, and giving an account of everything that occurs ; but unless some assistance comes to me from that quarter the pen must fall from my hands. I expended during the past year 125 scudi in letters alone, and since the month of May ten scudi. If the Sacred Congregation will defray the expense of the letters, I will not fail to work and to write. Moreover, if the Sacred Congregation be desirous that I should continue the schools which I commenced, it will be necessary to give the stipend of missionary priests to three Jesuits who teach them, for I am unable, nor can I for the future support them ; and thus the work which I commenced and carried on for one year will fall to the ground, to the great spiritual detriment of the kingdom.

" I visited my diocese, and I was also in the dioceses of Down, Dromore, and Clogher, to examine the controversies of the Dominicans and Franciscans about their convents and their respective boundaries. In Down it is certain that the Dominicans had a convent called *de Villa-Nova*. But the existence of their convent in Clogher is only attested by an old parchment book, written many years ago, which contains the annals of that diocese ; and some old persons attest that before the war of Cromwell there were Dominicans in that diocese, who went around to quest, in consequence of these convents : the Franciscans, however, always opposed them. Now as to my diocese, the Dominicans have the convent of Carlingford, but the Franciscans pretend that it should not belong to them. I examined the matter, and having heard the witnesses, I find that the Dominicans had formerly a convent there, and that its old walls are yet standing. But the Franciscans have this argument against them, that for many years, and almost within the memory of man, the Dominicans were not permanently in these convents, and that therefore these convents must be considered as *abandoned*; and that, moreover, the Dominicans have lost the right to quest in these parts, on account of the prescription which now exists in favour of the Franciscans. To this the Dominicans reply, that *tempore perse-cutionis dormiunt præscriptiones* (during persecutions, prescription is of no avail), and that these convents were abandoned for many years only on account of the persecution. It cost me a great deal of expense, and a great deal of fatigue, to examine the matter in the three dioceses.

"OLIVER OF ARMAGH.

" To the Internuncio Tanari, Brussels."

The Primate seems to have deferred his final decision for six weeks after the date of this letter to the Internuncio. Writing to the same Monsignor Tanari on the 28th of September following, he informs him, that, having maturely examined the whole matter, and having associated with himself three prudent counsellors, he had at length promulgated his decision in favour of the Dominican Fathers :—

" With extreme fatigue I examined, in three dioceses, during the month of July last, the controversy between the Dominicans and the Franciscans, not without risk even of my health ; and before giving sentence, I called three consultors, forsooth, the Bishop of Meath, Dr. Oliver Dease, a man of great skill and experience, and Dr. Thomas Fitzsymons, that thus I might not presume on my own prudence ; and then I gave my decision in favour of the Dominicans, and I will send a copy of it to your Excellency."

The definitory decree of Dr. Plunket was not published till the 11th of October following, when it was printed and promulgated at Drogheda : it has already been published in the often-quoted repertory of the records of our Irish Church, the *Hibernia Dominicana* of Dr. De Burgo, page 129, and runs as follows :— *

" We, Oliver, by the grace of God, Archbishop of Armagh and Primate of all Ireland, to all Bishops, Prelates, Parish Priests, and

---

* The printed copy of this decree is dated "Dundalk, the 11th of October, 1671 :" the MS. copy sent to the Internuncio, and by him transmitted to Rome on 24th October, 1671, is directed "e loco nostri refugii," without date, and signed "Oliverius Armacanus, totius Hiberniæ Primas." The decree, printed by De Burgo, corresponds with some other ancient printed copies, which are preserved in the Roman archives. The only difference is where De Burgo substituted an *etc.* for brevity sake instead of the name of the dioceses.

Curates of the dioceses of Armagh, Clogher, Down, and Dromore, blessing and eternal welfare in the Lord.

"As many disputes and controversies have arisen between the Dominican Fathers and the Franciscans in the dioceses of Armagh, &c., in regard of certain convents and their limits, for deciding which we, in addition to our ordinary authority, also received delegate power from the Holy See, we, in order to proceed with legality and method, visited, not without great labour and expense, each of the dioceses in which the aforesaid controversies and disputes were carried on, and we received the allegations and proofs of both sides.

"Moreover, not to rest on our own prudence, having called to our deliberations the Most Illustrious and Most Rev. Patrick,* Bishop of Meath, his Vicar-General, the Very Dr. Oliver Dease; and the Very Rev. Dr. Thomas Fitzsymons, Vicar-General of Kilmore, we maturely pondered and discussed the aforesaid allegations and proofs. As, therefore, it is manifest, from the produced documents and proofs, that the Dominicans possessed the convent of Gaula, in the diocese of Clogher; the convent of Villa-Nova, in Down; and the convent of Carlingford, in Armagh, we, with the council and suffrages of the aforesaid consultors, by this present ordain and decree that the Dominicans in the said dioceses may ask for alms, and quest as the other religious do. But as to the diocese of Dromore, in which neither the Dominicans nor the Franciscans have a convent, the Dominicans are not to be prevented from questing there so often as they present to the ordinary of the diocese the permission of their superiors. We, therefore, impose on all and each of you, and strictly command you, under penalty of suspension, which will be *ipso facto* incurred, to obey this our decree and order, laying aside every excuse and tergiversation.

"In sign of which, &c.,

"OLIVER OF ARMAGH,
"Tot. Hib. Primas.

" Dundalk, 11th October, 1671."

Notwithstanding this decision of the Primate, the controversy continued to be warmly agitated on both sides. The laity, for the greater part, united with the Franciscans, and an imposing petition, bearing an endless list of names of the laity, was forwarded to Rome, expressing their desire that the Franciscans alone should be allowed to quest in these dioceses, and claiming, at the same time, the three

---

* Not Patrick *Cusack*, as De Burgo erroneously remarks, but Patrick Plunket, who was transferred from the see of Ardagh to Meath in 1669, and governed it till his death in 1679. See letter of Dr. Plunket, 30th November, 1679.

disputed convents for that Order. It was only the renewal
of the persecution, in 1673, that hushed for awhile this
controversy ; and Dr. Plunket, writing on the 15th
December, 1673, declares that this advantage, at least,
had been obtained by the persecution :—

> "All the convents and novitiates have been destroyed, and the
> novices are scattered. This last decree has put an end to the dissen-
> sions of the Dominicans and Franciscans about the questing and
> the three convents."

With the return of peace there reappeared on the stage
assertors of each party's respective rights, and it was only
in 1678 that the question was finally set at rest, when, as is
recorded in the Acts of Propaganda, a formal letter was
sent by the Holy See, confirming the former decision of the
Archbishop of Armagh.

This continuance of the controversy produced one happy
fruit, for we owe to it a more full and detailed account, from
the pen of the Primate himself, of the course which he
pursued in deciding it.

The following is his letter of 8th September, 1672,
addressed to Monsignor Baldeschi, Secretary of the Sacred
Congregation of Propaganda :—

> "I examined the controversy between the Dominicans and
> Franciscans of the province of Armagh by the authority delegated
> from Rome, as well as by my ordinary authority ; and, finding the
> reasons produced by the Dominicans to be the stronger, I gave
> judgment in their favour. The Franciscans, however, have appealed
> to the Holy See from my decision, and sent a special agent to Rome
> to prosecute their appeal ; and hence I deem it necessary to send to
> your Excellency an account of the whole matter, with as much
> brevity as possible.
>
> "The Dominican Fathers of this province have three convents.
> about which there exists no controversy ; that is, the convent of
> Drogheda, of Derry, and of Bannina, or Culrahan ; about these
> there is no dispute * All the controversy is about three other con-
> vents, videlicet, of Villa-Nova, in the diocese of Down ; of Gaula,
> in Clogher ; and of Carlingford, in my diocese.
>
> "I went to the County Down, called the contending parties, and
> found the clearest evidence that the convent of Villa-Nova belonged

* This justifies the opinion of De Burgo, *Hib. Dom.*, page 130, and
refutes Dr. Crolly, page 43.

to the Dominicans. St. Antoninus makes mention of it in the third part of his history; and Sir James Ware, in his book, *de Antiquitatibus Hiba^e*, speaking of the convent of Down, page 212, thus says: ' *Conventus ordinis Praedicatorum introductus est anno* 1244, *et Capitula ejusdem ordinis ibi habita sunt annis* 1298 *et* 1312 *: sedet in territorio de Ardes prope littus maris ;* ' and witnesses were produced who swore that they had seen Dominicans of this convent questing in the diocese of Down before the time of Cromwell.

" In the diocese of Armagh I summoned before me the parties who were contending about the convent of Carlingford. The Dominicans produced again the authority of Ware, who, at page 203, writes thus : ' *Carlingfordiae conventus ordinis Praedicatorum : Comites Ultoniae patroni fuerunt.*' They, moreover, produced an instrument of the tenth year of Henry VIII., by which a citizen of Carlingford, named Mariman, made over a house and garden to the Dominicans of the convent of Carlingford. Again, in the *Dublin Register*, which s called ' *Defective Titles*,' mention is made of this convent of the Dominicans of Carlingford; and they also adduced the evidence of old persons who had seen some Dominican friars residing near this convent before the war of Cromwell.

" I went to the diocese of Clogher, and near Enniskillen, in the convent of the Franciscan Friars, called the contending parties. The Dominicans adduced the authority of the ancient annals of that town, written in the Irish language, which give the name of the convent of Gaula, the year in which it was founded, the Pope in whose pontificate it was founded for the Dominicans. They also brought forward the testimony of an old priest, who swore that he heard from his father that the convent of Gaula belonged to the Dominicans. They also produced other witnesses, who gave like evidence."

" Now, on the other hand, the Franciscans could bring forward nothing but negative arguments ; that is, the signatures of those who attested that they had never seen or heard of the Dominicans being in these convents : that the people were not able to support both Dominicans and Franciscans ; that the secular clergy were opposed to the Dominicans. They went about seeking the signatures of the gentry and others against the Dominicans, and, what is more strange, they even went to Protestant gentlemen, asking them to speak to me against the Dominicans, and, *de facto*, many of these spoke to me, and almost threatened me if I did not remove the Dominicans from these dioceses.

" The Franciscans, moreover, added, that the Dominicans, in case these convents once belonged to them, must nevertheless have lost their right to them, having abandoned and deserted them for many years, so that prescription now holds against them. The Dominicans, however, replied, that in the time of war, pestilence, and persecution, no prescription can hold good against those who abandon their convents."

" These were, in substance, the principal arguments on both sides,

which, with the whole of the proceedings, I submitted to the Bishop
of Meath, to Dr. Thomas Fitzsymons, Vicar-General of Kilmore;
and to Dr. Oliver Dease, Vicar-General of Meath. They were of
opinion that I should decide in favour of the Dominicans, and I
did so.

"Here it must be remarked that the Dominicans, after the persecution of Cromwell, and on the restoration of the King, that is,
seven or eight years before I came to this country, came to reside in
these dioceses, near these convents ; so that it was not I that introduced them there, but I found them already in possession. Now,
considering the arguments adduced by the Dominicans, and considering that I found them already in possession of their residences
in these dioceses—considering, too, the great good that they do,
having able preachers and learned men ; in fine, considering that
both orders have sufficient for their support in these dioceses, for
they thus supported themselves during the past ten years, notwithstanding their disputes ; and were they to live in peace, they would
be far better supported, for many persons, being scandalized at their
dissensions, will give no alms to either of them ; in consideration of
which things I deemed myself obliged in conscience to deliver
judgment in favour of the Dominicans.

"The sentence being published, the Franciscans appealed to the
Holy See, and it seemed as though hell itself were let loose against
me. Amongst the accusations it was stated that I gave judgment
non auditis partibus; and yet the Very Rev. F. Paul O'Neill, who
goes as their procurator to Rome, was present in the diocese of
Down when I heard both parties, as were also Dr. Ronan Magin,
Vicar-Apostolic of Dromore, and twenty other priests and friars.
In the diocese of Clogher the examination was held in the convent
of the Franciscans themselves ; and whilst I was holding this
session I got a severe attack of illness. As to my own diocese, it
is a most notorious matter that I heard them ; and the concourse
was so great, even though at some miles distance from the city, that
it requires downright barefacedness to say that I did not examine
the matter. However, they threaten me, and that, too very often,
that they will treat me as they treated my predecessor, Richard of
Armagh,* who was summoned to Avignon, and died there of grief.
The guardian of Dundalk told me this to my face.

"It is unnecessary for me to say any more, as your Excellency
has both prudence and solicitude to arrange the matter properly. I
pray you to show this letter, as also all my other letters, to
Dr. Peter Creagh, our agent in Rome, that thus he may be
informed as to the affairs of the province, and I shall ever remain,

"Your most obliged and affectionate servant,

"OLIVER OF ARMAGH.

"Dundalk, 8th Sept., 1672."

Richard Fitz-Ralph, who was appointed Archbishop of Armagh in
1347, and died in Avignon in 1360. (See Ware.)

The accusation of his not having heard both sides of the controversy seems to have been the one on which his adversaries most relied ; and hence Dr. Plunket more than once refers to it in his letters. In his letter of the 4th February, 1672, he thus replies to that accusation : —

"I already sent to your Excellency the attestation of Ardel Matthews, or MacMahon, Vicar-Forane of the diocese of Clogher, to the effect that I heard both sides in that diocese, and that I laboured even so as to bring on a serious illness. I now send a like attestation of Dr. Ronan Magin, Vicar-Apostolic of Dromore, in regard of the convent of Villa-Nova, in the diocese of Down ; and in Dromore, so great was the concourse of friars, priests, and others, that we all ran great risk of being imprisoned by a nobleman very hostile to our religion. But the son-in-law of the High Chancellor was my friend, and, possessing great influence in the County of Down, prevented his evil designs. Now, Monsignore, how can they have the audacity to circulate such falsehoods, that, forsooth, I did not hold an investigation, and that I did not hear both parties ; whilst, when engaged in hearing them, two accidents happened, which were so notorious, that there was not a corner of the whole province but was filled with them, all talking about my illness, and the risk of imprisonment."

The attestation of the Vicar-Apostolic of Dromore is the only one we have been able to discover. In it he declares that about the 24th of June, 1671, the Primate for three days held his session in Dromore, and heard the reasons of the conflicting parties about the convent of Villa-Nova ; and that he, with all his party, incurred great risk on account of the bigotry of George Randon, who would fain believe that they were plotting a rebellion, and under this pretence sought their incarceration.

A letter of Dr. Fitzsymons, Vicar-General of Kilmore, written on 7th September, 1670, also refers to this controversy. In it he eulogizes the untiring zeal of the Primate in celebrating synods and sanctioning ecclesiastical discipline, and declares that the claim of the Dominicans had in its favour "*antiqua documenta, vestigia locorum, et annales patriæ pervetustos, quos ipsemet vidi in antiqua membrana exscriptos et apud antiquarium dicti comitatus Fermaniae custoditus.*"

U

CHAPTER XXI

JANSENISM IN IRELAND.

In one of the meetings which were held towards the close of the year 1659, which will surely form a glorious epoch in the history of the Irish Church, an eloquent speaker well observed that Ultramontanism (for such is, nowadays, the trite designation of Catholic doctrine) was as if implanted by nature itself in the very soil of Ireland. Hence Protestantism never cast any roots there; and hence, too, Jansenism, with its affiliate, Gallicanism, could never take any hold on the affections of Irishmen.

About the year 1665, indeed, a few Irish students in Paris and Louvain had had their minds contaminated with the doctrines of Jansenius, and on their return to Ireland sought to disseminate them in some districts. Gerald Ferrall, afterwards Vicar-Apostolic of Ardagh, when agent of the Archbishop of Armagh in Rome, addressed to Clement IX. an earnest appeal to have chief pastors appointed to the vacant sees :—" The continued series of bishops," he says, " was the chief means by which faith was so well preserved ; and by their authority and piety, and counsel and vigilance, not only was the Irish nation itself preserved Catholic, but also many foreign heretics, with their children and families, were converted to the faith ;" and subsequently he adds, as an urgent motive for appointing bishops, especially at that period,* " that *there were some who now sought to introduce and disseminate Jansenism*" throughout Ireland.

Peter Walsh, to whose name a sad notoriety is attached

* " Non alia potior videtur fuisse ratio, quam Episcoporum continua successio in illo Regno, quorum auctoritate, pietate, consilio ac vigilantia non solum ipsa natio Hibernica permansit Catholica verum etiam advenae multi hæretici cum prole et familiis ad fidem conversi sunt . . . Etenim imprimis necessitas ita postulat ob Jansenismum a nonnullis eo introductum et disseminatum."

in the annals of the Irish Church, seems to have been amongst those who cherished the doctrines and principles of Jansenius. When a member of the Franciscan Order in Louvain, he became acquainted with and an admirer of that broacher of novel doctrines. To him Walsh dedicated his public thesis on philosophy ; and when that heretical work, *Augustinus*, was printed, after the death of Jansenius, he boasts of having been the first to read its proof-sheets as they came from the press.* All the later efforts of this unfortunate man to induce the Irish clergy to adopt his Remonstrance was but an attempt to realize in practice the teaching of Jansenius, for which, in early life, he had professed so great an esteem.

Whilst Dr. Talbot, Archbishop of Dublin, won for himself the title of *malleus Remonstrantium* by his unceasing opposition to Peter Walsh and his followers, Dr. Plunket was not less actively engaged, in union with Dr. Brennan, of Waterford, in checking the silent current of Jansenism, and in exposing the secret evil which threatened to infect the " sainted isle." Some of the decrees of the Synods of Clones and Ardpatrick were directed against the consequences of these erroneous doctrines ; and the necessity of thus enacting special decrees against them sufficiently attests the activity with which the agents of error sought to disseminate such doctrines. On the 27th of March, 1677, Dr. Plunket writes from Dublin to Cardinal Altieri, Cardinal Protector of Ireland, detailing the pernicious errors by which the purity of faith was assailed, and asking for some remedy from Rome to check the growing evil :—

" Though the Parliament lately held in London fills us with alarm by its edicts, threatening to despoil the Catholics of their lands and possessions, yet the Catholics of these kingdoms are far more terrified at the spiritual calamities which seem impending from the remains of Jansenism, and the novelties which continue yet to spread in France and Belgium ; for it is from various parts of these countries that spiritual labourers come to cultivate this vineyard. You are already aware of how dangerous the doctrines are which, in their printed tracts, are circulated everywhere, concerning the infalli-

* *Hist. of Remonst.*, page 75.

bility of the Roman Pontiff, the authority of St. Augustine, as if it were superior to the definitions of Rome ; the invalidity of absolution without the perfect love of God, the necessity of reforming in many things the worship of God, of the Blessed Virgin, and the saints; reproving frequent intercourse to the Sacrament of Penance, deferring absolution solely on account of relapse, or any grievous sin (which gradually deters the faithful from approaching this sacrament); reproving the custom of seeking absolution of mere venial sins ; declaring that invincible ignorance of the natural law can never excuse from sin ; and that works of virtue, unless they proceed from the pure love of God, are never free from sin, and not only do not tend to our salvation, but are absolutely vicious.

"These, and many other things repugnant to the constant teaching and practice of the Church, are a source of much anxiety to us; but, besides the sad results as regards our faithful people, an occasion also may be given to the heretics of these kingdoms to reprove us, as if we sought to introduce some new reformation of the Catholic Church.

"Hence, in order that the purity of faith may be preserved intact and inviolate in this kingdom, which is placed under the patronage of your Eminence, I pray and beseech you, with all reverence and submission, to lay the aforesaid things before his Holiness and the Sacred Congregation, that thus some remedy, embracing all, may be devised, lest this kingdom should become infected with the delirium of the Jansenists. In the meantime, both I and the clergy entrusted to me will not cease, on our part, to maintain the true purity of doctrine, and to impugn all perverse teaching. I know that this will be in accordance with the desires of his Holiness and of your Eminence, for whose welfare I shall ever pray, &c.

"OLIVER OF ARMAGH,
"Primate of All Ireland.
"Dublin, 27th March, 1677.
"To his Eminence Cardinal Altieri, Protector of Ireland."

Dr. Brennan, of Waterford, united his voice with that of the Primate, and on the 30th of March of the same year addressed the following letter to the Cardinal Protector. This letter is specially interesting, being dated from "his place of refuge in Ireland," and being probably the last which Dr. Brennan wrote before his elevation to the archiepiscopal see of Cashel ; for we find another letter, written on the same day, acknowledging the receipt of the briefs from Rome transferring him to that see :—

"Amongst the many things that give us annoyance in this kingdom, one is, the novelty of opinions in matters of faith, in consequence of the greater part of the ecclesiastical labourers of this vineyard studying in France and Flanders, and some of them returning thence with a tincture of Jansenism. In the neighbouring kingdoms many books are circulated which contain most dangerous doctrines, namely, of the fallibility of the Pope; of the authority of St. Augustine being of more avail, especially in the question *de Auxiliis*, than the Pontifical definitions; of the invalidity of sacramental absolution without contrition; of restricting the veneration usually shown to the Blessed Virgin and to the saints; against the frequenting of sacramental confession, especially with only venial sins; that invincible ignorance of the natural law never excuses from sin; that works of virtue performed without the pure love of God are of no avail to our eternal salvation; nay, more, are an impediment to it. These and similar errors have also penetrated this kingdom, but, through the mercy of God, they have but few partizans; even these few, however, have given a stimulus to my humble energies to prevent their taking root here; and as this matter principally regards the Holy See, I, following the example of other zealous prelates, have deemed it my duty to lay it in reverence and submission before the Sacred Congregation through your Eminence, who worthily holds the offices of Protector of this kingdom, and of Prefect of the Sacred Congregation, that thus, in the supreme guardianship of the Holy Father, some remedy may be decreed for the greater consolation of the people of this kingdom.

" And I reverently kiss the purple of your Eminence.

"JOHN, BISHOP OF WATERFORD.
" From my place of refuge in Ireland,
30th March, 1677."

Without delay the vigilance of the Holy See was awakened to counteract the efforts of the emissaries of error, who thus sought to corrupt the doctrines of faith in the Irish Church. We find in the acts of the Sacred Congregation frequent reference made to instructions given to the Internuncio in Brussels to this effect; but the most interesting monument connected with the subsequent history of Jansenism at this period is a letter of Dr. Brennan when transferred to the archiepiscopal see of Cashel. This letter is dated the 15th of October, 1678, and is addressed to the Internuncio, in reply to a communication from Rome, in which some precise information had been requested regarding the Jansenistical works which were being circulated in Ireland. Dr. Brennan not only gives a minute account of these books, but, moreover, affords sufficient data to attest the complete failure of Jansenism in seeking to obtain any footing in Ireland :—

"I have received, with all reverence, the commands of the Sacred Congregation, under date of the 8th of March last, to give a precise account of the books containing the teaching of Jansenius, which have come into these quarters, as also of their authors and partizans. In compliance with these most esteemed commands, I beg to inform your Excellency, that we find here the New Testament, printed in France, in the French language, and having various errors contrary to the Vulgate, and to the Catholic religion. Another work is also met with, entitled *On Frequent Communion*, printed in French, and translated into English, having errors contrary to true devotion, and the practices of Holy Church.

"There is also the Mass, printed in French, and newly translated into English.

"The New Testament in French has not as yet come into my hands; I had, however, the Mass in French, and I made a seizure on it. I saw the book on frequent Communion, and though I could not get possession of it, yet I prohibited its being read. It is true, however, that these books are but very few in these parts, and I am not wanting in being ever on my guard lest they should be introduced or published here.

"As to the followers of the errors of Jansenius, thanks to God, they are but few in this country. There was one regular who was deeply tinged with these errors, but I acted severely with him, and imposed silence on him, so that he retracted, and has become observant; it is for this reason, as also on account of his being a foreigner, that I refrain from mentioning his name, especially as he is neither notorious nor contumacious. There was another religious, and also two secular priests, of the same hue, but they are all now dead. For the future, in consequence of the great vigilance and circumspection which are used, we hope that God may be served here *in veritate et sinceritate doctrinæ*.

"And with this I remain in sincere devotedness,

"JOHN, ARCHBISHOP OF CASHEL.

"15th October, 1678.
"To Mgr. Tanari, Brussels."

Thus was Jansenism soon repelled from our Irish shores. Our bishops sought at the central source of truth the remedy for the threatened evil, as in the early ages of the Irish Church they looked for aid to that see whence the light of faith had come to them, and, as children who have recourse to their mother,* they derived thence counsel, and strength, and consolation.

* Tamquam rati ad matrem. St. Cummian.

We have already seen the erroneous doctrines which were broached by Dr. Fitzsymons, the Vicar-Geneal of Kilmore, in regard of the authority of the Holy See in the appointment of bishops, and how zealously and successfully they were combated and refuted by the Archbishop of Armagh. About the same time the Sacred Congregation wrote to Dr. Plunket, asking for information concerning Dr. Cornelius Daly, whose name had been proposed as Vicar-Apostolic of the united dioceses of Ardfert and Aghadoe. The Primate, deceived by false rumours, wrote in reply that he was infected with the errors of Jansenism, and hence could nowise be promoted to that dignity; but somewhat later discovering his error, he wrote on the 21st of September, 1678, declaring that Dr. Daly was wholly adverse to Jansenism, and having exacted from him a formal condemnation of its teaching, he transmitted it to Rome, and in an accompanying letter declared him fully qualified for any dignity which the Holy See might think well to confer on him. The formula to which Dr. Plunket required the signature of Dr. Daly, and which, thus signed by him, and attested with the primate's own name and seal, was transmitted to Rome, is as follows:—

" I, Cornelius Daly, a priest of Ardfert in Ireland, Prothonotary Apostolic, and also Doctor of the Parisian Faculty, declare myself obedient to the Apostolic constitution of the Sovereign Pontiff Innocent the Tenth, given on the thirteenth of May, 1653, and to the constitution of our holy Father Alexander VII., given on the 16th of October, 1656, and I sincerely reject and condemn the five propositions taken from the Book of Cornelius Jansenius, entitled *Augustinus*, in the sense intended by the author himself, and as the Apostolic See condemned them in the aforesaid constitutions, and I so swear. Sic Deus me adjuvet et hæc sancta Dei evangelia.
" CORNELIUS DALY.

" This has been done in our presence; so we testify this day, the 21st of September, 1678.
" OLIVER OF ARMAGH,
" Primate of all Ireland."

Paris was at this period the great centre of Jansenism, and hence the chief danger of having our Church infected with its errors seemed to impend from that quarter. In fact, Dr. O'Malony, when urging upon the authorities in Rome the necessity of establishing an Irish college in Paris, put forward as a leading motive the danger which otherwise the Irish students would there incur of having their minds poisoned with the tenets of Jansenism. Moreover, he stated from his own experience that some members of our Irish clergy then resident in that city were ardent promoters of these erroneous doctrines. This accusation of the Bishop of Killaloe gave occasion to a large number of Irish ecclesiastics then resident in Paris to enter a formal protest against the doctrines of Jansenism, and present it with their signatures, to Dr. Creagh, Bishop of Cork and Cloyne, and Dr. Tyrrell, of Clogher, who were then hastening to take possession of their sees, and request them to forward it to Rome. It is now preserved in the archives of the Sac. Cong. de P. Fide. It is addressed to the cardinals of the Sacred Congregation of Propaganda, and is as follows :—

" The undersigned, who are Irishmen by birth, and by profession Catholics, through the grace of God, as to orders, priests ; in sacred theology, respectively masters, licentiates, bachelors, masters of arts, and scholars, most humbly lay before your Eminences that they have learned, not with great affliction of soul, that they have been traduced, and, as well in Rome as elsewhere, have been accused of Jansenism ; whilst, as they solemnly protest, they abhor nothing more than each and every doctrine repugnant to the true faith which the Holy Apostolic Roman See professes, and especially the Jansenistic doctrine combined in the five propositions condemned by the same Holy Roman Church. Wherefore, that your Eminences may be convinced of how unjustly they have been accused of the aforesaid Jansenism, they now, by this present letter, protest that they never held or taught such doctrine, and that in time to come, whilst reason remains intact, they never will hold or teach it. Hence, with all due submission, they pray your Eminences to give no credence to any iniquitous report or calumny against them, in regard of this doctrine, or any teaching deviating from the true and Catholic faith, but rather to protect and encourage, with your usual goodness, as well these suppliants as their other countrymen, who, for the faith of Christ, and in an especial manner, on account of their reverence for the Holy See, have been expelled from their country and despoiled of their temporal possessions, and under many difficulties and poverty, now labour and strenuously seek to acquire knowledge and virtue, as well in this holy Parisian faculty as in other Catholic universities; that thus confiding in so great a patronage, they may with more peace and calmness apply to their studies, and these being terminated, may return to their country, and there may attain their own happiness by their virtuous lives, and promote that of their Christian flocks by their learning and example."

The names then follow, and the attestations of Drs. Creagh and Tyrrell, Paris, 26th August, 1676, as to the genuineness of the document and signatures. Amongst those who subscribed this important attestation of fealty to the decisions of the Holy See, we find Cornelius O'Daly, of whom we have spoken above; also, Ambrose Madden, William Daton, and others, who were afterwards distinguished ornaments of the Irish Church.

Such was the vigour of the opposition thus directed against Jansenism, that during the next thirty years, whilst the churches of France and Belgium were rendered desolate by the ravages of its erroneous novelties, its very name was almost unknown in Ireland. The subsequent history of that heresy in Ireland is easily told.

About the year 1709 some travellers visiting the Irish shores brought with them the contagion of its teaching, and by circulating Jansenistical tracts and books sought to imbue the minds of some with its false maxims.* Others, too, in succeeding years, seem to have repeated these attempts, though, happily, without producing any effect on the sentiments of the faithful people. The vigilance, however, of the Holy See was awakened; and in 1719, through Mgr. Santini, the Internuncio at Brussels, an admonitory address was transmitted to the prelates of Ireland exhorting them to earnestly repel these dangers, and, at the same time, expressing a desire that they should, by some public declaration, avow their acceptance of the constitution *Unigenitus*. The bishops of Ireland joyfully responded to this call of the Universal Father, and by their letters testified their abhorrence of the pestiferous errors of Jansenius, their acceptance of the above-mentioned consti-

* See Polidorus' *De Vita et Rebus Gestis Clementis XI. Pont. Max.*, page 215.

tution, and their inviolable attachment to the See of St. Peter. The letter of the Archbishop of Cashel has been fortunately preserved to us by Dr. De Burgo in the appendix to his *Hibernia Dominicana*, page 819. The commencement of it is as follows :—

"MOST HOLY FATHER,—The most reverent and illustrious the Internuncio at Brussels has signified to me, humble as I am, that your Holiness, out of your great zeal for religion, expresses a wish to receive from the bishops of Ireland some testimonial of their obedience to and observance of the constitution usually termed 'Unigenitus.' To this most reasonable desire I am perfectly convinced that all and each of these prelates will accede, agreeably to the obed'ence which is due to the Holy See and to your Holiness, who so gloriously presides therein ; and that amongst them not one shall be found who will not subscribe to the aforesaid most wise constitution without any tergiversation, cavil, or mental reservation whatever. For, although we are poor in the world, yet are we rich in faith ; if we be deprived of our episcopal revenues, we have not, however, forfeited that obedience which we are bound to yield to those who are placed over us; if we suffer under the sword of persecution, we shall never create a schism in the body of Christ, or, to the utmost of our power, allow it to be done. We may be despised and oppressed, but we will be ever solicitous to preserve with *you*, our Head, *the unity of spirit in the bond of peace* ; in short, although we traverse the plains of our native land in distress and affliction, nevertheless there abide within us, even to this day, that fervent love and veneration towards the Mother and Mistress of all Churches, and that desire to preserve all these divine rites, which, more than thirteen hundred years ago, had been established amongst our ancestors by that glorious Apostle, St. Patrick, whom your predecessor, St. Celestine I., had commissioned to preach amongst them. With justice do we glory in the fact, that among our predecessors in the hierarchy not one can be found who, in a matter of faith, has dared to manifest resistance to any constitution, decree, or apostolical diploma. Moreover, were it necessary, we have even additional motives in which to glory. inasmuch as neither by us, or by our clergy, or by our people, have any of these profane and novel terms, *religious silence*, or the *question of right and of fact*, been adopted, in contempt of the lawfully-constituted authority ; nor have those infamous books, which caused so much disturbance and scandal in Catholic countries, been known, unless, perhaps, by name, to the greater part of our nation. That love and reverence for the Roman Pontiffs, which is the first sound that strikes our ears, which in infancy has been planted in our hearts, and, in a manner, forms a component part of our nature, have long since banished these and like novelties from our land.

" Instructed by apostolical documents and by the uninterrupted

tradition of ages, we are confident, most Holy Father, that to you
is committed the important charge of protecting the flocks from the
ravages of the wolf, of leading them into salutary pastures, and of
securing them from whatever may be noxious—a duty which, by the
aforesaid constitution, you have admirably executed. That, therefore, no doubt may remain of the purity and integrity of our faith,
we hereby give our assent, in heart and in mind, to that document and
constitution which, about ten years ago, your Holiness had thought
proper to declare to the Gallican clergy. This our mode of proceeding is in perfect accordance with the faith of our fathers and
with the uninterrupted tradition of ages; it is the rule of the Irish
hierarchy, as well as of the other churches of the Christian world;
while, on the other hand, those convict themselves of having deviated
from it who refuse to subscribe to that most salutary constitution."

Such were the sentiments of affection and reverence with
which the prelates of Ireland ever clung to the See of Peter.
Amongst those who then shared in these noble sentiments
was Dr. Luke Fagan, Bishop of Meath ; and we mention
his name in particular, on account of a fabulous narrative
which a late writer has published concerning him.* This
modern historian of the Jansenist heretics informs us that
in 1715 the agent of that faction being unable to prevail on
any continental bishop to ordain their priests, at length—

" In the person of Luke Fagan, Bishop of Meath, found a prelate
willing to come to the assistance of Utrecht. . . . Von Heussen
gave letters dimissory, as Vicar-General of the metropolitan chapter
of Utrecht, the see being vacant, to twelve candidates, and they
were in four several ordinations raised to the priesthood by Bishop
Fagan. Among the number was Peter John Meindaarts, afterwards
Archbishop of Utrecht. He (Fagan), however, required a solemn
promise from each of the candidates that they would never reveal
the circumstances of their ordination during his life. A curious
event occurred some years afterwards. The secret was not so well
kept as to prevent an indistinct rumour from reaching the Court of
Rome that some Irish bishop had ordained priests from Utrecht.
Fagan, by this time Archbishop of Dublin, received orders to discover which prelate had done so. He convoked the Irish bishops,
put the question to each of them individually, and returned for
answer, that, after examination, he was persuaded that none of the
bishops of whom he had inquired had held any such ordination."—
(Page 236.)

* *The History of the so-called Jansenist Church of Holland, &c.*, by
the Rev. M. A. Neale, 1858.

For this narrative Mr. Neale gives no authority; on the other hand, the acts of Propaganda are silent as to any such commission given to Dr. Fagan, and are also silent in regard to this pretended convocation of our bishops. Dr. Fagan was not transferred to Dublin for fourteen years after the imaginary ordination: undoubtedly he would have never been promoted to a higher dignity if there were any suspicions of his orthodoxy, or rather if he had not given proofs of his zeal and of the integrity of his faith. Besides, during the whole period, that is, from the assumed date of this ordination till after the death of Dr Fagan, the Archbishop of Armagh was the confidential correspondent of the Holy See in Ireland. Should any suspicions have been entertained as to the Jansenistical tendencies of any of our prelates, surely the commission to investigate the matter would be entrusted, not to one who, having studied in France, might himself, perhaps, be supposed to be infected with these errors, but to the Archbishop of Armagh, the long-tried friend of the Holy See, and who had sucked in at Rome's fountain source the pure doctrines of faith. Moreover, as we have seen, it was in 1719, that is four years after the pretended ordinations, and nine years before the elevation of Dr. Fagan to the archiepiscopal see, that the suspicions of the Holy See were awakened in regard to some members of the Irish hierarchy, and whatever may be our judgment as to the fact of this ordination, the letter at least of Dr. Fagan in reply to the encyclical of the Holy Father in 1719 leaves no doubt as to his orthodox sentiments, and his abhorrence of the novel tenets of Jansenius.

CHAPTER XXII.

On the 28th of April, 1670, Prince Cardinal Altieri ascended the Papal Throne, as Clement X. To the acclamations of the Catholic nations on the Continent were united those of Ireland, and many addresses were sent from our shores congratulating him on his elevation to this high dignity. Dr. Plunket, though then engaged in the deliberations of the Synod of Dublin, hastened to lay at the feet of his Holiness the expression of the heartfelt joy with which the hearts of his faithful children of Armagh were filled, and addressed the following letter to him :—

"Most Holy Father,—The universal jubilee of the Christian world, on the elevation of your Holiness to the Chair of St. Peter, has reached also this kingdom of Ireland, ever attached and devoted to your Holiness and to the Holy See, despite the persecutions and afflictions which it has endured since the introduction of heresy into the kingdom of England : wherefore I, as the last of the servants and children of your Holiness, join in this universal jubilee, and prostrate at the feet of your Holiness, in the name of this province of Armagh, entrusted to my pastoral charge by the favour of the Apostolic See, I pray heaven to grant to your Holiness every necessary aid, together with many years of life, that thus you may be able to correspond to the great hopes which the whole world has conceived from your reign, for the glory of God and the public advantage of the Church. We experience in this kingdom, Holy Father, the benign influence of the king of England in favour of the Catholics, so that all enjoy great liberty, and even ecclesiastics may be publicly known, and are allowed to exercise their functions without hindrance. Our Viceroy is a man of great moderation and equity : he looks upon the Catholics with benevolence, and treats privately with some of the clergy, exhorting them to act with discretion ; and for this purpose he secretly called me to his presence on many occasions, and he promised me his assistance in correcting any members of the clergy of scandalous living. I discover in him some traces of religion, and I find that many even of the leading members of his court are secretly Catholics. The nobility, who are natives of this country, are all Catholics, with the exception of three or four ; and comparing the number of Catholics with that of the

heretics throughout the kingdom,* we find that there are twenty
Catholics for one Protestant, if we except Dublin, which is the
metropolis, and in which the Viceroy resides, where the heretics
have a majority. We all continually pray the Most High to grant
to your Holiness His grace and many years of life; and I, prostrate
at the feet of your Holiness, ask your sacred blessing for the whole
Catholic people of this kingdom.

> "Of your Holiness,
> "The most devoted and obedient child,
> "OLIVER OF ARMAGH,
> "Primate of Ireland.

"Dublin, the 20th of June, 1670."

This letter was enclosed in another, addressed to the
Cardinal Protector of Ireland, in which he repeats the same
sentiments :—

"MAY IT PLEASE YOUR EMINENCE,—Although this kingdom of
Ireland be truly poor in worldly riches, yet, nevertheless, it is rich
in virtue, and especially in the true faith; and hence it is just, that
the jubilee of the Catholic people of this nation should be made
known in Rome on the most deserved exaltation of our holy Father
to the See of St. Peter, to which this kingdom has ever been closely
bound and most devoted, despite the afflictions and persecutions
which are known to the whole world, and which we have endured
for more than one hundred years, since the commencement of the
schism in England. I, as the last of the children of his Holiness,
and as a most devoted servant of your Eminence, beg to lay before
you the jubilee of the Catholic people of the province of Armagh,
entrusted to my pastoral care by the favour of the Apostolic See,
and I pray heaven to grant long life and happy rule to his Holiness
and to your Eminence, for the glory of God and the advantage of
the whole Christian world.

"The Viceroy of this kingdom shows himself favourable to the
Catholics, not only in consequence of his natural mildness of
disposition, but still more on account of his being acquainted with
the benign intentions of his Majesty for his Catholic subjects, so
that ecclesiastics may now freely appear in public without suffering
any annoyance, even when recognized as such. The Viceroy himself
privately treats some members of the clergy with great courtesy,
exhorting them to live peaceably without tumult, and without
meddling in state matters, attending solely to their ecclesiastical
functions, on which condition he promises them every protection;
and, indeed, we have reason to believe that this will be afforded
should that condition be fulfilled. I perceive that some of his

---

* Dr. Plunket, on other occasions, states that in some northern counties
the Presbyterians were more numerous than the Catholics and Protestants
put together.

court are secretly Catholics, and even some of the principal members of the government who suggest to him kind measures for the Catholics. May God grant to us a long enjoyment of this calm, and bestow many years on your Eminence, for the public good of the Christian Church.

" P.S.—I have presumed, by the enclosed letter, to express my joy on the exaltation of his Holiness, and to implore his blessing for this nation.

" Your Eminence's

" Most humble and devoted servant,

" OLIVER OF ARMAGH,

" Primate of Ireland."

The Holy Father, notwithstanding the many cares which pressed on him in his guardianship of the universal Church, did not delay to acknowledge the congratulations of his Irish children, and he thus wrote to the Archbishop of Armagh :—

" TO OUR VENERABLE BROTHER OLIVER, PRIMATE OF IRELAND

" VENERABLE BROTHER, HEALTH, &c.

" The most devoted letters of your Fraternity occasioned to us a special delight, and as we learned by them that the Catholics enjoyed peace in these regions, we were truly filled with sincere joy in the Lord, for we place all the glory of the Pontifical dignity entrusted to us by the Holy Ghost in the increase of the divine worship, and in the propagation of the orthodox faith. Whilst you labour in attaining this noble end, as you truly do in your exalted sentiments of religion, your congratulations on attaining this supreme dignity in the Church must be acceptable, whilst you will every day bind us more closely in affection towards you. Go on, therefore, venerable brother, and in those regions pursue with alacrity the carrying out, by word and example, of the commission entrusted to you, and seek to aid with every assistance those orthodox children, to whom, in our paternal solicitude, by night and by day, we are ever present. Thus, indeed, will you well correspond with your exalted office, and have God the rewarder of your renowned labours. In the meantime we embrace, in the bosom of our Pontifical love, the devout expressions of your filial affection ; we promise to you all our patronage, and from the very depths of our heart we bestow on you, and on all the Catholics of that kingdom, our Apostolic blessing.

" Given at St. Mary Major's, in Rome, the 11th October, 1670, the first year of our Pontificate.

" CLEMENS, PAPA X."

After a brief Pontificate of six years Clement the Tenth was succeeded by Innocent the Eleventh, who, even before his elevation to the papacy, was famed for his sanctity and charity to the poor. " Whilst I was in Rome (writes the Primate on the 11th of August, 1677), I knew by experience the holy life of the supreme Pontiff, and the great opinion which was entertained by all of his wisdom, prudence, and sanctity." The Primate seems to have transmitted to Rome, through the Internunzio, a congratulatory letter on the accession of this Pope to the throne of St. Peter, and to it he seems to allude in the beginning of the letter already cited of the 11th of August, 1677,* but we have been unable to discover any further traces of it.

During the first months of the pontificate of Clement the Tenth, Cardinal Barberini filled the office of Protector of Ireland ; but in 1671 he was hurried away by death to be its protector in the heavenly court. His successor in that important post was Cardinal Altieri, a man distinguished for his virtues and learning. At the same time Dr. Brennan, the agent of the Irish clergy, was appointed bishop of the united sees of Waterford and Lismore, and Dr. Peter Creagh was chosen by the Irish bishops to succeed him as their agent in Rome. Dr. Plunket availed himself of the departure of this worthy ecclesiastic for the Eternal City to express his joy on the nomination of his Eminence to that high office : —

" We are obliged to pray unceasingly to God for the long life of his Holiness, in consequence of the favour which he has done us in giving us your Eminence for protector, for in doing so he has rendered to this nation an exceeding great benefit, and a favour the more agreeable as it was most anxiously desired by us ; for we have learned from our countrymen in Rome, and from Monsignor Baldeschi, and we ourselves now daily experience, the special affection which your Eminence bears to this most afflicted kingdom, so that we cannot but hope for most happy results from the protection of a cardinal who, for his prudence in the management of affairs, and for his piety and zeal in propagating our holy faith, receives boundless applause, and is esteemed and revered by the

* See page 17.

whole world. It is certain that the joy here is universal, and that
even the Viceroy, though of a different religion, showed particular
satisfaction at your appointment, and he passed a high eulogium on
his Holiness and your Eminence, praising your moderation, and
prudence, and mildness. I, therefore, and the whole nation, should
rather congratulate ourselves than your Eminence on this event, as
the whole advantage and honour will be ours, leaving to your
Eminence only the fatigue and annoyance, for which you can only
look to the Divine Majesty for remuneration, as this oppressed
nation cannot make any return for the benefits received from your
Eminence, or for those which, through your Eminence, they shall
receive from others, except by continually praying to God for the
long life, health, and prosperity of your Eminence; and the more
incapable we feel ourselves of meriting the slightest of your favours,
the greater merit will the ardent zeal of your charity receive from
God, and so much the more glorious will be the results of your
innate generosity in relieving by your patronage the miseries of
this most afflicted nation, which, on account of its Catholic faith
and the affection and unfailing reverence for the Apostolic See,
has ever been in continual sufferings and trials, from the time
that Queen Elizabeth, with her statutes and penal laws, scourged
the poor Catholics, as your Eminence knows far better than
I do.

"Of all that occurs in this kingdom as regards our spiritual
concerns, I give an accurate and detailed account to Monsignor
Baldeschi, that is to say, through him to the Holy Father and to
your Eminence, and should I be wanting in any particular, it will be
supplied by the bearer of this letter, Rev. Peter Creagh, doctor in
theology, agent of the clergy of this kingdom, a gentleman of
learning and education, and who by birth belongs to the highest
families of his city; he studied in Rome and received the laurea
with great applause; he knows the Italian, Latin, French, English,
and Irish languages, and for years laboured with great spiritual
fruit in this vineyard. I therefore, pray your eminence to protect
and favour him; and all the archbishops and bishops of this nation
most warmly recommend him to your patronage. In conclusion,
making you a profound reverence, I will be whilst I live,

" Your Eminence's
" Most humble and obedient devoted servant,
" OLIVER OF ARMAGH,
" Primate of all Ireland.
" Dublin, 10th Oct., 1671."

The Primate was not the only one of our prelates, who,
on this occasion congratulated his Eminence on this accession
of dignity, or rather their own Irish Church on having so
worthy a protector in the Roman Court. The Archbishop
of Tuam, about the same time, wrote a letter expressing

similar expressions of joy and congratulation, which is well worthy of being preserved.*

One of the subjects most frequently spoken of in the early letters of Dr. Plunket is the sad consequences of the ambitious scheme of Peter Walsh and his adherents in seeking to force upon our clergy and people the well-known Remonstrance. Owing to the zealous labours of the Archbishop of Dublin and the Primate, their efforts were everywhere baffled, and Walsh himself was soon compelled to abandon the Irish shores. Repeatedly Dr. Plunket wrote to the Holy See, detailing the progress of the struggle between the defenders of truth and of error, and laying open to the authorities in Rome the iniquitous designs of Walsh or Valesius; and at length, on the 26th of September, 1671, he was able to inform the Internuncio that the errors of the remonstrants had been wholly rooted out from the Irish Church, and that in the whole kingdom more than five or six could not now be found who would

* We are happy to be able to present it in its beautiful original text to the reader:—

Eme. Dne.

"Inter oblectamenta, quæ Philippus bonus Burgun liæ princeps equitibus ordinis aurei velleris tunc primum instituti exhibuit, virgo spectabatur auro gemmisque fulgens, cui leo additus custos hanc præferebat inscriptionem, Nemo Dominam meam tangat. Hibernia nostra quæ a suscepta semel annis ab hinc mille et amplius religione et S. Sedis Romanæ cultu quantumvis gravibus tentationibus agitata numquam defecit, nacta est jam leonem custodem in persona Eminentiæ vestræ, quo protegente securo quiscere possit. Succedis igitur Eme. Princeps magno Cardinali Barberino invidæ mortis eclypsi nobis erepto et officium quod Deus O. Max. angelicis spiritibus committere solet (ut nempe protectores sint et præsides provinciarum) id imponere humeris tuis voluit, qui Christi in terris vices gerit SSmus D. N. Clemens X. Gratulor non tibi cui onus potius quam honos hoc officio additur sed patriæ nostræ et vineæ huic Hibernicæ quæ tanto protectore gloriari lætarique merito potest, cui certe nihil accedere potest splendidius, nihil felicius aut magnificentius quam patronum habere te quem publica decora et privata etiam virtus inter paucos commendat: quamvis non potest quoque non ingens tuæ incrementum gloriæ afferre, quod talis cura commissa sit præsertim a tanto Pontifice quæ in eos dumtaxit merita sua conferre solet quos suo pariter virtus suffragio comprobat, nec onus tam grave humeris tuis impossuisset, nisi Atlante ipso, quem cœlum ipsum gestare fingunt poetæ, major esses atque illustrior. Sed plura non audeo ne in modestiam vestram impingam. Inter tot autem toto pæne occidente tibi sibique gratulantium applausus, sistit se Hibernia nostra olim

avow themselves partizans of that insidious address. We have already had occasion to refer to this letter, and it contains many valuable particulars connected with this question :—

"Since the return of our most clement King to the government of these kingdoms no question and no art of the demon has so impeded the progress of the service of God in these countries as the perverse efforts and designs of Walsh and his adherents. Oh, how many dissensions, how many scandals, had their origin thence ; and all this commotion was *honorum et turpis lucri causa.* They used all their endeavours to prevent the appointment of bishops for this kingdom, that thus there would be no superior, no pastor, but themselves ; they strained every nerve to attain this *hilares sine regibus umbrae.* But God provided otherwise, and they remain confounded. Since the Viceroy Berkeley and Colonel Patrick were gained over against them, they not only lost a great deal, but rather their whole ground ; and as the Viceroy, Lord Berkeley, a man of prudence and moderation, now returns (as I hope) to the government, the few that remain will cease to follow their evil ways, and will return to the right path; and I am of opinion that there are not in the whole kingdom more than six who publicly and outwardly profess to follow the views, or rather the abortive plans, of Valesius.

"Anthony Gearnon was a great Valesian, but now he professes

sanctorum insula, nunc haereseos tenebris miserabiliter obvoluta, cujus patrocinium eo libentius ut spero, et studiosius assumet Ema. Vra. quod ob solum Deum plane suscipiatur : cum enim ex aliis provinciis tutelae tuae commissis magnam nominis famam et commoda alia sperare fortasse possis, nisi virtus majorem Dei gloriam in omnibus solum spectasset; ab hac certe nostra aliud nihil est quod expectare possis praeter labores et incommoda quae quando pro Deo suscipiuntur omnem mundanam felicitatem longe superant. Sistit quoque se Sedes Tuamensis, quae uti, authore maximo praedecessore tuo, sponsum et praesulem accepit, ita sub auspiciis tuis majorum sperat incrementa gratiarum, cujus quia mihi, immerenti licet, cura mandata est, supplicibus votis rogo ut illam speciali oculo respicias tuoque favore protegere non desistas, et me quoque qui vel ideo mihi propitiam fore curiam Romanam spero quod solus ex confratribus meis hoc tempore contumelias et carceres passus sim, ereptus insuper speciali numinis providentia tamquam alter Daniel e lacu leonum, ex faucibus ipsius mortis quam mihi instigatore praecipue perfidioso et foedifrago monacho fidei nostrae hostes intentarunt. Praesentes necessitates provinciae meae ne longior sim hic omitto : Agens noster in ea urbe eas oblata occasione proponet, cui, ut favere velis etiam atque etiam rogo et simul Eminentiae vestrae annos plurimos ad Hiberniae nostrae et totius Ecclesiae bonum, faustaque et felicia omnia ex animo apprecor et voveo.

"Clunbariae die 4th Nov. 1671,
  "Eme. Dne.   ·· Eminentiae Vrae.
                        "Servus humillimus,
                          "JACOB. Archiep., Tuamen."

obedience. I give, however, very little credence to him, as also to many others who made their retractation. It is certain that they are filled with the desire of Valesius, just as the Jews expect the Messiah, and as the Portoghese are looking out for King Sebastian. The people in authority who favoured them and protected them cared but little about Walsh and his adherents, but they made use of them as instruments to divide and disunite the clergy and the Catholic body ; *divide et impera*. But Berkeley dislikes that manner of governing, and seeks the love of all, and desires that we should be of one accord.

"To say the truth, our just and good God, who permits evil in order to draw good from evil, has drawn great good from the iniquitous deeds of Peter Walsh. This man, about eight years ago, anxious to make a display of zeal, and thus more easily gain partizans, and attract the people, obtained from Ormond a toleration for chapels and convents in Dublin and many other cities ; but he wished that all the convents, and even all the provinces, should be governed by his own adherents. Ormond being removed from the Government, through the mercy of God no other Viceroy molested or molests either the chapels or the convents. In the most wealthy and noble city of my diocese, and of the whole province, there are three chapels, very beautiful and ornamented. The first belongs to the Capuchins, the second to the Reformed Franciscans, the third to the Jesuits. There is also one belonging to the Augustinians, but it is rather poor ; so that we may well repeat what is said of the sin of Adam, *O felix culpa ;* or, again, *necessarium Adae peccatum.* The city to which I allude is called Drogheda, at five hours' distance from Dublin : it is, next to Dublin, the best city in Ireland.

" OLIVER PLUNKET.

" Dublin, 26th September, 1671."

The Act of *præmunire* was one often appealed to by the adherents of the Remonstrance ; and whensoever the defenders of the authority and privileges of the Holy See referred to its decisions, or fulminated ecclesiastical censures in its name, they were sure to find their opponents summoning the cause before the civil tribunals, and seeking to punish their orthodoxy with the severe penalties of that statute. The Irish prelates, when communicating with Rome, had often referred to the penalties of *præmunire ;* and the Internuncio requested the Archbishop of Armagh to give him some explanation of the origin and precise meaning of that Act. On the 30th of September, 1671,

Dr. Plunket at length complied with his request, and wrote as follows:—

"I promised in a former letter to give to your Excellency an exact account of the *præmunire*, this word being the object of the greatest terror which those of my profession have in these kingdoms. Some say that this *præmunire*, as to its etymology, signifies a sort of bulwark which the crown of England has raised in all its kingdoms against foreign jurisdiction, and especially against that of the Pope, which opinion is based on the statute enacted in the 25th year of Edward III., Statute 6, chapter 1st. But some are of opinion that it had its origin in the word *præmonere*, which, being corrupted by the civil jurists, is commonly called *præmunire*, for they often take the effect for the cause; and, as it is said, he who is *premonished* is half-prepared, or *fortified*. I read in an old breviary, or book of old briefs, a citation which thus begins:—*Præmunire facias N. N. ut cum suo procuratore sint coram nobis ad respondendum objectis;* and I think that, instead of *præmunire*, it should be *præmonere*.

"But whatever may be the etymology of the word, it is certain that it is now commonly called *præmunire*, and that it was enforced against the jurisdiction of the Roman Pontiff at the time of Edward III., who was unwilling that the Pope should confer benefices in England, or bestow the favours or provisions which are called *expectative*. He was also unwilling that lawsuits, in matters of benefices, should be brought outside the kingdom; and he, moreover, wished that all such suits should be tried in the secular tribunals; and hence he enacted these rigorous statutes, in the 25th year of his reign (stat. 5. chap. 22), and 28th year (stat. 2, chaps. 1, 2, 3, & 4). But he was well chastised by God for it, as our history records. Richard II. imitated him, by enacting similar statutes in the 12th year of his reign (cap. 15, and anno 13, stat. 2, cap. 2); and he confirmed all the statutes made by Edward III.; and the penalty of whosoever violated or transgressed these statutes was exile, and the confiscation of all fixed and movable property. Henry IV. made similar statutes in the 2nd year of his reign (cap. 2 and 3) ; and although these statutes were made in England, yet they afterwards came into force in Ireland, in the time of Henry VII., an Irish Parliament, during the viceroyalty of Poining, having adopted all these statutes.

"A statute, however, enacted in an Irish Parliament, in the 2nd year of Elizabeth, is the severest of all, as by it is punished with the aforesaid penalties whoever *speaks*, *acts*, or *writes* in favour of the pontifical jurisdiction, even in spiritual matters, or whosoever exercises any act of jurisdiction derived from the Roman Pontiff. Moreover, whosoever says that the king is not head of the Church, and whosoever says that the Pope is head of the Church, incurs the same penalties; and so also whosoever refuses to swear that the king is head of the Church is incapacitated from holding any post or office in the state. This Act of Elizabeth was passed in the

Irish Parliament on a holiday of precept with the Catholics, and
the Protestants availed themselves of the occasion of their absence ;
otherwise it could never have passed, as the Catholics were more
numerous than the Protestants. It is true that in the times of
King James and King Charles I. these laws were not carried out
with such rigour, nor are they even now, under our most clement
king. But it is also true that when a knave accuses any ecclesiastic
before the court, it is with great difficulty that he can escape some
penalty, as lately happened in the case of Father Nugent, and also
of the poor Archbishop of Tuam, who suffered a great deal. It is,
moreover, to be remarked, that whosoever assists or receives into
his house one that has thus incurred the statute of præmunire is
punished with the same penalties.

"Your Excellency sees in what continual danger we are under
the penal laws. I must confess that when I first came to this kingdom, I neither knew nor understood what was meant by the word
præmunire. Since then, however, I wished to read all that appertains
to that matter, and I thought it proper to give some account of it
to your Excellency. I pray you, as I also requested on other occasions, to send all my letters to Monsignor Baldeschi, and to keep a
copy of them, and to let me know if they have safely reached you,
as you have hitherto done with such kindness ; and I shall be unto
death,

"Your most obliged and devoted servant,
"OLIVER PLUNKET."

The correspondence of Dr. Plunket with Rome seems to
have been constant, even in the times of persecution.
Many of his letters are in cipher, but the Internuncio
always transmitted their key to the Sacred Congregation.
His assumed name on these occasions was for some time
Thomas Cox, and afterwards *Edward Hamon* or *Hamond ;*
in fact, all our prelates, when corresponding with Rome,
were compelled to assume other names. Thus Dr. Tyrrell,
of Clogher, signed himself *Scurlog*, which name he afterwards changed for *Stapleton ;* Dr. Cusack assumed the
name of *Fleming*, and Dr. Forstall, Bishop of Kildare, the
more German title, M. F. Von Creslaw. Even the Internuncio was seldom addressed by his proper name, and we
find him at first styled Monsieur *Pruisson*, which in 1679,
for greater security was often changed into *Picquet*. The
year 1675 presents fewest letters of Dr. Plunket. He had
often complained of the heavy expense which his correspondence with Rome entailed on him, and of his inability to

continue it, unless aided by the Sacre Congregation. More than 100 scudi were annually expended by him in letters,* which was nearly half the entire revenue of his diocese. Through the Internuncio about 150 scudi were at intervals transmitted to him to aid in these expenses; but the Sacred Congregation could not devote a larger sum for that purpose, as its care had to embrace not Ireland alone, but the missionary countries of the whole world. The Internuncio was well aware of the motives which impelled the Primate to observe this silence, and on the 21st of December, 1675, wrote to the Secretary of Propaganda:—" For many weeks I have received no letter from the Archbishop of Armagh, as he, in the present afflictions, finding himself in want of means, abstains from writing, in order not to incur the heavy expenses of the post." † However, in 1676, Dr. Plunket resumed his correspondence with his usual vigour, and continued it even when detained in his Dublin prison. His last letter from Ireland is dated the 3rd November, 1680, and was written on board the vessel which was about to conduct him prisoner to stand his trial before a London jury. It is directed to the Internuncio:—

" Six hours before embarking for England I received your letter of the 18th inst., and from shipboard I write these lines to give

* The following extract from Dr. Plunket's letter transmitted to Rome in October, 1672, will sufficiently explain this expense:—" How many letters come inclosed in those addressed to me, how many decrees and commissions and briefs to be communicated to others throughout the province! Before I commenced a direct correspondence with your Excellency, I sent the letters to Ghent, to Mr. Clark; I sent some by Paris, and I think I paid Clark about ten doubloons. Every letter from my diocese to Dublin costs 7½ bajocchi (3¾ pence); from Dublin to London, 10 bajocchi; from London to Ghent or Brussels, 13 bajocchi; from Brussels to Mantua, if I mistake not, 20 bajocchi; from Mantua to Rome, 24 bajocchi Now, my diocese yields only 240 scudi per annum; and when I have supported myself, a chaplain, a servant, and a stable-boy, but little can remain.' Elsewhere he says that each letter he received from Brussels cost him 25 bajocchi, and each letter from Cashel or Tuam, 10 bajocchi.

† " Sono piu settimane che mi mancano le lettere dell' Armacano ed egli nelle correnti angustie ritrovandosi in qualche penuria di denaro si ritiene dallo scrivermi per non soggiacere alle gravi spese della Posta."

you intelligence, that I communicated, in a few words, to those of Cashel, Tuam, and Armagh, as also to the Bishop of Kildare, who is nearest to me, the privilege accorded by the Sacred Congregation. I pray you, however, to reflect that it would be even more necessary to grant the faculty of dispensing for the rich than for the poor, because the rich, by recurring to their Eminences for dispensation. incur greater risk of confiscation of all their property, in accordance with the statute *præmunire*, 2nd of Elizabeth. I do not know who will now correspond with your Excellency. I re-opened communication with their Eminences during the time of Monsig. Baldeschi and Monsig. Airoldi. Before that time scarcely was one letter received from this kingdom in a year. The Bishop of Kildare is nearest to Dublin. and would be best suited. But, believe me, that my poor purse learned what an expensive matter these letters are.

"Tell Mr. Joyce that I received two of his letters, and, no matter what may be the consequence, to send me the money to London as soon as possible. directed *for Mr. John Comin, merchant, in London*, who is my friend, and a Catholic. The expenses here are intolerable, and correspondence is difficult and dangerous. If possible, you will receive letters from London. In the meantime I recommend myself to your prayers, and I have been, and am, and ever will be,

"Your Excellency's most devoted servant,
"EDWARD HAMON."
(Oliver Plunket.)

For some months, so close was the imprisonment in London, that Dr. Plunket could find no means of transmitting letters to his friends. After some time, however, the guard was so struck by his saintly composure, that, moved to compassion, he undertook to be the bearer of an occasional letter; and as soon as sentence was passed against him, greater liberty was allowed him of communicating with whomsoever he pleased. We shall have occasion hereafter to speak at greater length of the correspondence of Dr. Plunket from his London prison. It will be sufficient here to remark, that his letters breathe a true spirit of Christian heroism, and express not only a dauntless courage, but also a heavenly joy on the happy privilege which awaited him of laying down his life for the faith.

There is but one other letter of Dr. Plunket, to which we shall now refer. It is a commendatory letter given to a Capuchin Father, and bears the conjoint signatures of Dr. Plunket, of Armagh, and Dr. Brennan, of Cashel.

We have seen how, during the first outburst of the persecution in 1673-4, these two prelates, united in friendship from their earliest years, had sought for safety in the same place of refuge ; and how again, on its renewal in 1678, they hastened once more to a common retreat. It was precisely at the period when they were compelled to retire a second time before the fury of the storm that they directed in common this letter to Monsignor Cerri, then Secretary of the Sacred Congregation of Propaganda. With the exception of the signature of Dr. Brennan, it is all in the handwriting of Dr. Plunket :—

"Father Barnabas Barnewall, who for many years has been Vice-Commissioner of the Capuchin Fathers in this kingdom, has always been extolled for his prudence and learning, and labours in the vineyard of the Lord ; and he merits special praise for having converted to the faith the wife of my Lord of Slane, and for having conducted the children of that lord into France, by which he delivered them from manifest danger of losing their faith ; and he preserved the spiritual as well as the temporal inheritance of that noble family, which never professed any save the orthodox faith ; and for this and many other labours in affording spiritual assistance, the aforesaid Father Barnabas merits every favour from God and from the Sacred Congregation ; and we supplicate your Excellency to interpose your influence with the Father-General of the Capuchins, that this Father Barnabas may be made Commissary of the Capuchins of this kingdom, which will be of great utility to the cause of religion ; and we make our humble reverence.

"Your Excellency's most humble and obedient servant,

"OLIVER OF ARMAGH, &c.
"JOHN OF CASHEL, &c.

"Dublin, 14th February, 1673."

CHAPTER XXIII.

In the year 1678 the enemies of Catholicity in England, anxious to make a last assault on the Church of their fathers, entered into a conspiracy as dark and as hideous as any known in history. The chief agent in this plot was Titus Oates, whose name has been attached to it by posterity. He had been a clergyman of the Established Church, but preferred to his benefice an infamous and vagrant life. Under ever-varying disguises he insinuated himself into some religious houses on the Continent, and made himself sufficiently acquainted with Catholic usages and distinguished Catholic names to be able to give a semblance of circumstantial accuracy to any anti-Catholic tale which he might devise. Returning to England, he found the Protestant populace in a ferment lest a Papist should succeed to the royal throne, and he soon learned that the leaders of the opposition were eager to second and repay each effort to fan the flame. Such was, then, the disposition of mens' minds, that the monstrous romance which he constructed was hailed with applause, and found credence, not only with the vulgar, but even with the most sober members of the king's council. The Pope, he said, had handed over the government of England to the Jesuits, and these had already, by commissions under the great seal of the society, appointed to all the chief offices in church and state. Once before the Papists had burned London : that scene was to be now renewed, whilst in the confusion they would assassinate the king, and, at a given signal, each Catholic should massacre his Protestant neighbours.

This tale was not merely greeted with applause. Oates became the idol of the people, and through the influence of his patrons, was raised on a sudden from obscurity and poverty to a position of dignity and wealth. Hence he soon found associates and rivals. To give perjured evidence, and lead Catholics to the scaffold, had proved a good speculation, and many wished to share in its profits and honours. We shall allow a Protestant historian to trace the character of the principal of these informers. " A wretch named Carstairs, who had earned a living in Scotland, by going disguised to conventicles, and then informing against the preachers, led the way: Bedloe, a noted swindler, followed ; and soon, from all the brothels, gambling-houses, and spunging-houses of London, false witnesses poured forth, to swear away the lives of Roman Catholics. One came with the story of an army of thirty thousand men, who were to muster in the disguise of pilgrims, at Corunna, and to sail thence to Wales. Another had been promised canonization and five hundred pounds to murder the king. . . . Oates, that he might not be eclipsed by his imitators, soon added a large supplement to his original narrative. . . . The vulgar believed, and the highest magistrates pretended to believe even such fictions as these. The chief judges of the kingdom were corrupt, cruel, and timid. . . . The juries partook of the feelings then common throughout the nation and were encouraged by the bench to indulge those feelings without restraint. The multitude applauded Oates and his con-federates, hooted and pelted the witnesses who appeared on behalf of the accused, and shouted with joy when the verdict of guilty was pronounced." * And hence, as the same writer had already remarked, the courts of justice '' which ought to be sure places of refuge for the innocent of every party, were disgraced by wilder passions and fouler corruptions " than could be found at any other period in the annals of England.

Such an excitement against the Catholics naturally found a response in the Protestant ascendency in Ireland. Ormond was, at this time, Viceroy ; his private letters, indeed, prove that he gave no credence to the accusations against the

* Macaulay, *Hist. of England*, vol. i., chap. 2.

Catholics, but, nevertheless, with his usual duplicity, he enacted such measures and laws as supposed and confirmed the belief of the reality of their treasonable designs. The Council of Ireland met in the presence of the Viceroy, on the 14th of October, 1678. Their first enactment was, that all officers and soldiers should repair without delay to their respective garrisons. A proclamation ensued, commanding " all titular Popish bishops and dignitaries, and all others exercising ecclesiastical jurisdiction by authority from the See of Rome, all Jesuits and other regular priests," to depart from the kingdom before the 20th of November following; whilst a reward was offered of £10 for the capture of a bishop, and £5 for that of a regular, after that period. Orders were, at the same time, given, that all " Popish societies, convents, seminaries, and schools," should be forthwith dissolved and utterly suppressed.

To prevent all excuses for not obeying the foregoing proclamation, another order was issued on the 16th of November, requiring all owners and masters of ships bound for foreign parts to receive " the Popish clergy " on board, and to transport them accordingly.

It was deemed necessary, too, to disarm the Catholics; and a special proclamation enacted, that " no persons of the Popish religion should carry, buy, use, or keep in their houses any arms without license ; and that all justices of the peace should search for such arms as were not brought in within twenty days, and bind over the offenders to be prosecuted at the next assizes."

It was feared, however, that some officers were remiss in executing these laws, and hence positive orders were further issued on the 2nd of December, by the Lord Lieutenant and council, addressed to the sheriffs of the several counties, and to be by them communicated to the justices of the peace, " taking notice of their neglect in not apprehending such of the Popish regular clergy as did not transport themselves, and requiring them to return, not only their names, but the names also of such as received, relieved, and harboured them." They were, moreover, required to return the "names: of all persons licenced to carry arms, and to prosecute those who had not delivered in their arms," according to preceding; proclamations.

These orders were principally directed against the prelates: and regulars, but in reality the officers commissioned with their execution prosecuted alike the secular clergy ; it was, enough for them to raise the cry that anyone was a Jesuit in disguise, to obtain their reward. A proclamation, however, published on the 26th of March, 1679, had the secular clergy for its special object. It commanded that " when, there was any Popish pretended parish priest of any place where any robbery or murder was committed by the tories,. he should be seized upon, committed to the common gaol, and thence transported beyond the seas, unless within fourteen days after such robbery or murder the persons guilty thereof were either killed or taken, or such discovery, made thereof in that time, as the offenders might therefore be apprehended and brought to justice."

A further proclamation ordered the suppression of " Mass-houses and meetings for Popish services in the cities and suburbs of Dublin, Cork, Limerick, Waterford, Kinsale, Wexford, Athlone, Ross, Galway, Drogheda, Youghall,. Clonmel, and Kilkenny," these being the most considerable towns in the kingdom, " in which too many precautions could not be taken."

No soldier had for many years been admitted to the army till he had taken the oaths of allegiance and supremacy. It was now rumoured that some, after entering the service,. had embraced the Catholic religion, and hence a special proclamation offered rewards " for the discovery of any officer or soldier who had heard Mass or been so perverted, to the Popish religion." On the same day with this pro-clamation (20th November, 1678), another was issued,. prohibiting all Catholics " from entering the Castle of Dublin, or any other fort or citadel," and ordering that " no persons of the Romish religion " should be suffered to reside in the towns of Drogheda, Wexford, Cork, Limerick, .

Waterford, Youghall, and Galway, or in any other cor-
poration, excepting such as "for the greatest part of the
twelve months past had inhabited them." *

The result of such stringent measures, though, perhaps, it
did not satisfy the cravings of those who had anxiously looked
forward to the rooting out of Catholicity from the "Island
of Saints," yet was such as even to surpass the expectations
of moderate Protestants; and Carte remarks that, though
all the clergy were not expelled from the kingdom, "which
never was, and never will be, the consequence of a proclamation yet more had been shipped off than could have
been imagined, and the rest lurked in corners, and durst
not come near the great towns." (*Ibid.* 483.)

The illustrious Archbishop of Dublin, Dr. Talbot, returned
to England from his exile on the Continent in 1676, and a
few months before the present outburst of feeling against
the Catholics, through the intercession of the Duke of York,
obtained permission to revisit and console his spiritual
flock. Though subject to violent disease, and apparently
at the close of his eventful career, yet was he chosen by the
malignant policy of Ormond to be the first Irish victim of
the persecution. Dr. Plunket announces his arrest, writing
on the 27th of October, 1678 :—

"The matter being proposed and discussed in the Provincial
Council that I should make a visitation of the province, I commenced with Meath, which is the first suffragan diocese, and then
proceeded to the diocese of Clonmacnoise, where I had scarcely
finished when the news arrived by post, that Dr. Talbot of Dublin
was arrested and imprisoned in the Castle or Tower of this city. I
received this news on the 21st of the past month; immediately
afterwards came a proclamation or edict, banishing all the archbishops, bishops, vicars-general, and all the regulars, commanding
them to leave the kingdom before the 20th of November, and
threatening penalties and fines against any secular who would give
them to eat or drink, or otherwise assist them. I was quite astonished
at the arrest of the Archbishop of Dublin, the more so, as since his
return to Ireland he did not perform any ecclesiastical function.

* Carte's *Ormonde*, vol. ii., 478-82, *Gesta Hibernor.* in Ware ad an.
1668-9; the Protestant Bishop Mant's *History of the Church of Ireland*,
vol. i., page 568, *seq.*

" The convents of the poor regular clergy have been all scattered and destroyed ; so that all the disputes and the reforms which were in contemplation for them are all terminated by this edict. The parish priests and secular priests are not included in it. It is not known what particular accusation has been made against the Archbishop of Dublin ; he is in the secret prison, and no one is allowed to hold communication with him. Some have been imprisoned in London on suspicion of conspiracy against the king, and for maintaining private correspondence with foreign princes, and for the murder of a nobleman who was found dead in London. As to the conspiracy against the king, it is a merely imaginary one. I have not been included by name in the present edict, nor in that passed four years ago, and, therefore, I will remain in the kingdom, though retired in some country place, and it is probable that Dr. Brennan and I shall be together. I heard this morning that Dr. Talbot will be sent to London, to have his trial continued there; howsoever matters may stand, *quidquid erit, superanda omnis fortuna ferendo est.* You will have the kindness for the future to address your letters thus : *for Mr. Edward Hamon, Dublin ;* and I will no longer address your Excellency as hitherto by the name *Monsieur Pruisson,* but by *Monsieur Picquet a Brussells.*

" The Bishop of Meath is very weak after a long attack, with terrible pains, from the gout, and a weakness of the stomach. I hear that in my absence, whilst I was to the west, some letters from you arrived in the north : I will immediately send one to fetch them to me. Should the parliament meet in London the severity of the edicts will continue ; but it will continue also should the parliament meet here.

" To Monsig. de Pruisson
    (The Internuncio Tanari at Brussels),

" Dublin, 27th Oct., 1678.

" P.S.—You will be good enough to send me a copy of the Brief for Dr. Cusack, signed by your Excellency, but without any seal."

The Archbishop of Dublin being confined in the Castle, the other prelates fled to their retreats in the woods and morasses, whilst the flocks were scattered and filled with dismay. The Internuncio thus writes to the Secretary of Propaganda on the 17th Dec., 1678 :—

" The Archbishop of Dublin continues still in prison ; as far as I have been able to learn, none of the other prelates have been as yet apprehended, or compelled to leave the kingdom ; but it is certain that they are all retired to places far away from the public, and the most difficult of access, so that they are no longer able to continue their correspondence with me."

In the following year the Primate, writing on the 15th of May, makes known the fury of the storm to which the Catholics were exposed, and the extreme poverty to which the prelates, and especially he himself, had consequently been reduced :—

"Here matters go on from bad to worse. A proclamation offers £10 to whosoever arrests a bishop or Jesuit, and £5 to whosoever arrests a vicar-general or a friar. The police, spies, and soldiers are in pursuit day and night. Colonel Patrick, an excellent Catholic, and a great protector of the Catholics, although a relative of the Duke of Ormond, was exiled by order of Parliament, which is desirous of prosecuting even the Duke of York, on account of his being a Catholic. The secular priests had some connivance till the present, though in many parts, and especially in the vicinity of Armagh, they have much to suffer. Such is the rigour of the Presbyterians, of whom there is a large number in these parts: they are now the prevailing faction in the three kingdoms, and are the enemies of all monarchy and hierarchy. One might walk twenty-five or thirty miles in districts, and not meet with six Catholic or Protestant families ; for all are Presbyterians and strict Calvinists.

"From my diocese, during the past twelve months, I received only 22 crowns (£5 16s.), and for the future my revenue will be still less. I expended a great deal in building schools, and in maintaining masters to instruct the youth and clergy of my province ; during the past nine years I gave hospitality to all ; indeed, I was the only prelate in Ireland that had a house of his own ; it cost me 100 crowns every year to maintain correspondence with my masters, and the Internuncios, Airoldi and Falconieri, as also Monsignor Tanari, received more letters from me these ten years back than from all the prelates of Ireland ; and should your Excellency give a look to the archives, you will find more letters and *relations* from me during these ten years, than from all the other prelates together; *non dedi requiem temporibus meis ant palpebris meis dormitationem*. I never would have been able to encounter such expense had I not been aided by the charity of Colonel Patrick, who has been a greater benefactor to me than all the diocese of Armagh, or all my friends and relatives in the whole kingdom ; but he now is exiled. Moreover, the severest penalties have been published in proclamations against the lay Catholics who shall receive a bishop or regular in their houses, and thus the rich are afraid of losing their possessions, whilst the poor have nothing to give. Then, too, your Excellency will hold in mind that I served the Sacred Congregation of Propaganda for many years in the chairs of theology and controversies, and also the Sacred Congregation of the Index, not without much labour. I would be ashamed, so to speak, did not necessity compel me, I have done and written and laboured more these ten years than all the other prelates of the kingdom together, and I now find myself without assistance in this diocese, without a benefactor, without a house, and all my money amounts to 53 crowns, *ita est coram Deo et non mention.* His Eminence Cardinal Colonna, when he was secretary, notified to me that the Sacred Congregation, considering my labours and expenses, would give me assistance. Through Monsignor Airoldi I received 100 crowns; Monsignor Falconieri sent me 50 more. This is all that I received for myself during the ten years of my mission here, and, did not necessity compel me, I never would ask aid from my masters; but the charity and liberality of the Sacred Congregation at the present time will be a stimulus and incentive to others to serve it for the future, as I have done these twenty-two years past. I request your Excellency to read this letter for the Holy Father, and for my masters of the Sacred Congregation, and I will ever pray to the Divine Majesty for their welfare, and for the prosperity of your Excellency; and I continually pray for the repose of Signor Francis, your father; and as he loved me whilst he lived, so I am sure it will not be irksome to you to aid me in the present conjuncture.

" 15th May, 1679.

" To Monsignor Cerri.

" P.S.—A matron named Lady Neale, and several Catholic gentlemen, have been accused of a design to burn Dublin; only one ruffian named Murphy, was the accuser; he also accuses three or four of the nobility; *hæc est potestas tenebrarum ac falsorum testium.*"

In another letter, on the same day, to the Internuncio, Dr. Plunket confirms these statements, and declares his resolution never to forsake the flock entrusted to him, and his readiness to suffer exile or death in the discharge of his spiritual duties:—

" I received your letter of the 28th of last month, and all the prelates here thank you for the favour in regard to the matrimonial cases, and, indeed, it might be extended to the rich as well as to the poor in the present times, as petitions regarding such matters are now full of danger, as well for the petitioner as for him who writes; it is also dangerous to solicit indulgences; and already a gentleman who obtained indulgences from the Sacred Congregation has had a deal to suffer. Matters here go from bad to worse; the prelates and regulars were already condemned to exile, and now they do not even excuse the parish priests, several of whom have been cast into prison; and even when a moderate Protestant wishes to show them some courtesy, he is styled by the others a Papist, which to them is a term of great reproach. Colonel Patrick, an excellent Catholic, although a relative of the Duke of Ormond, was banished from Court; and those in London are anxious to accuse the Duke of York himself. A reward has already been offered to spies and gendarmes and soldiers; whosoever imprisons a prelate will have

40 crowns, and for a regular, 20 crowns. I am morally certain that
I shall be taken, so many are in search of me ; yet in spite of danger
I will remain with my flock, nor will I abandon them till they drag
me to the ship. But in case that I should be taken, I must request
you to let me know whither I shall go; for I am sure they will
allow me this choice, as they have allowed it to others. I pray you
again to let me know your advice and counsel on this head, whether
to go to Flanders or to France, or to some other place. I pray you
also to send the enclosed letter to the Sacred Congregation, and to
obtain for me the favour which it solicits. Should you second it by
your letter, I shall surely obtain what I ask for."

The arrest of the Primate was the crowning deed of the
diabolical conspiracy of the enemies of the Catholic faith,
but still it did not appease their fury. The storm continued
unabated, and the rage of the Protestants against the
Catholics seemed every day to become more and more
inflamed. The Archbishop of Cashel thus writes on the
30th of June, 1680 :—

"From the month of April till the present our affairs have become
considerably more perplexed. The demon excited this tempest
principally by means of a friar, the chaplain and companion of
bandits, who, deserving the scaffold, found a means of obtaining
pardon by accusing the Archbishop of Armagh, and many others, of
a general rebellion throughout the kingdom, and persons are not
wanting in other parts of the country to follow the example of this
friar. This diabolical invention added greatly to the afflictions of
the Catholics, and to the fury of the Protestants against us. These,
for the most part, persuaded themselves that the iniquitous imposture
of the friar was a reality, and that all the bishops of this kingdom
have co-operated in setting on foot this rebellion; wherefore, the
mitres are now more than ever hated by the Protestants, who are
convinced that the number of bishops is intended to give offence to
the Government ; and hence, too, the ministers of justice are now
more active than ever in searching after them. It has even been
resolved on by the Government to pass a most stringent act in the
next Parliament (which, it is thought, will be held in September),
prohibiting, under penalty of the scaffold, that any bishop should
ever again enter this kingdom. God forbid that their Eminences
should make any new bishops for the present, as it would only
excite more and more their bile against us, and be of great damage
*in hac terra non suaviter viventium sed in terra tribulationis et augustiæ
ubi manducamus panem arctum. Sed cœlum sursum est et terra deorsum.**

* " In this land, not of pleasure, but of tribulation and of persecution,
where we eat the bread of affliction. But heaven is above, and earth
below."

We hope, without ceasing, in the mercy of the Divine Majesty, that He will free us from these afflictions, and that in His own time He will manifest our innocence of this pretended conspiracy, a thing which we ever anathematized, never desiring anything save the glory of God and the service of our prince. Be good enough to excuse the necessary shortness of this letter, and the absence of titles ; and as usual, I make to you my reverence.*

" 30th of June, 1680."

Again, on the 12th of September following, the same writer not only gives the general details of the persecution, but also adds many particulars regarding the Archbishop of Armagh and some of the other prelates :—

" Never [he says] was there a time more dangerous for writing letters than the present : for when they are intercepted, as very frequently happens, every word is interpreted in an evil sense, and the belief of the conspiracy is so deeply rooted in the minds of all, that an angel from heaven would not suffice to disabuse them of their error ; and, as for us, we pronounce anathema against all conspirators and disturbers of the public peace : for we have no other thought or desire except for the spiritual profit of souls, with the due subordination to the political government. Those, too, to whom our letters are consigned, as well the letters we receive as the letters we send, now hesitate to receive them, fearing imprisonment and the other penalties : hence it is that so few letters are sent ; nor is it expedient to write more frequently, especially for those who keep themselves concealed, and have not as yet come into the hands of the magistrates : for were one of their letters found, every effort would be made to discover themselves, and give them a taste of the prison.

"The Archbishop of Armagh was brought before the courts, accused of conspiracy, especially by a friar, an unworthy student of St. Isidore's : but when the accusations were read, they did not proceed with the trial, as one of the informers, the friar's associate, was wanting, and thus judgment was deferred for six months, and the Archbishop was re-conducted to the prisons of Dublin, where he was confined before. He sustains great sufferings with zeal and resolution, comforting himself with his innocence and with the grace of the Lord. His journey (to Dundalk) occasioned him great expense, as well for himself as for those who were brought thither to attest his innocence.

"The Bishop of Cork being already in prison expected sentence

* This letter is addressed in English. " To my worthy friend Mr. Tanarius, at Brussels :" it begins with *Monsr.*, and no title is given throughout the letter. It is signed merely with the initials *G. C.*, that is, " Giovanni Cassellense," *John of Cashel*. He probably feared that it might fall into the hands of the Government."

during the assizes of the last month : no mention, however, was made of him at that time, and he continues still in prison.

"The Bishop of Limerick has permission from the Government to remain in any part of his diocese, on account of his great age and infirmities.

"The Bishop of Killaloe is not in his own district, but elsewhere : he is in strict concealment, and justly so, for our enemies bear him great ill-will, and speak violently against him.

"Notwithstanding the great afflictions which we suffer, great good is done for the salvation of souls. The Government is moderate, nor do we see that rigour which is felt in England. It is now reported that one of the chief informers of the pretended conspiracy has died, and that before dying, he retracted all that he had said about the conspiracy; and this, perhaps, will mitigate the fury of our adversaries. I request you to communicate the substance of what I write, or to transmit this letter to Monsignor Cybo, who, I hope, will excuse my writing so seldom, which is occasioned by the motives already mentioned, and to one and the other I make an humble reverence.*

"12th September, 1680."

The enemies of the Catholics in England were nowise content with the slow proceedings of the Irish Government. On the 3rd of March, 1680, the Earl of Anglesey wrote to the Lord Lieutenant, that "It is his Majesty's absolute and unalterable pleasure (advised by all the council) to have every individual of the Popish clergy seized and imprisoned till they petition to be sent over seas, and promise never to return or practise against the State ; for there is no other way to cure their madness, and there are those in England who will apprehend them all." To which his Excellency characteristically replied, that "If any in England will undertake it, they shall have the promised reward, and his thanks besides; and to tell him of the insolent deportment and signal perfidy of the popish clergy of Ireland is to preach to him that there is pain in the gout; and he protests that he would be sooner rid of them than of that disease."

Such was their hatred against the Catholic clergy, and

---

* This letter is signed in full *Gior. Arciv. Cassellense*, John, Archbishop of Cashel. He was at the same time Administrator of Waterford and Lismore, but seldom adds this title, except when writing on matters connected with that diocese.

such the premeditated plan, which was worthy of a Diocletian or a Nero, to banish the Catholic pastors from Ireland, or lead them to the scaffold. Several places, particularly in the County Louth, are traditionally marked out as having afforded shelter to the Primate in those days of persecution. In the parish of Faughart, near Dundalk, there is a cave where immemorial tradition attests that Dr. Plunket lay for three days concealed. Again, in sight of the Giant's Causeway, there is a house belonging to a Protestant family, and it is said that for some time he found a safe refuge there. We shall conclude this chapter with the words of the impartial Fox :—

" The proceedings of the Popish plot must always be considered as an indelible disgrace upon the English nation, in which king, parliament, judges, juries, witnesses, prosecutors, have all their respective, though certainly not equal shares. Witnesses of such a character as not to deserve credit in the most trifling cause upon the most immaterial facts, gave evidence so incredible, or, to speak more plainly, so impossible to be true, that it ought not to have been believed if it had come from the mouth of Cato ; and upon such evidence, from such witnesses, were innocent men condemned to death and executed. Prosecutors, whether attorneys or solicitors-general, or managers of impeachment, acted with the fury which in such circumstances might be expected. Juries partook naturally of the national ferment ; and judges, whose duty it was to guard them against such impressions, were scandalously active in confirming them in their prejudices and inflaming their passions."*

CHAPTER XXIV.

ARREST AND IMPRISONMENT OF DR. PLUNKET.

DR. PLUNKET, when rooting out the abuses which had crept into some districts of his diocese, and correcting the vices of some unhappy members of the clergy, had well foreseen that he had to treat with men who deemed his reforms too great a check on their vicious lives—who would refuse to

---

* *Historical Works*, page 33, *seq.*

listen to his words of correction, and pursue him with their
hatred even unto death. But he embraced these consequences of his sacred ministry with joy, and, as a good pastor,
offered his life for the salvation of his flock, and the healing
of the wounds of his suffering Church. He never ceased for an
instant to pursue the reforms which the necessities of his
Church required, and, as he had hoped, the earthly reward
of all these labours was martyrdom : but his death was
the triumph of the holy cause for which he combated;
and, as the Archbishop of Cashel remarked, by his death he
effected more towards the rooting out of these abuses than
he could possibly have achieved by a century of anxious
toil. A letter of the Internuncio, written whilst Dr. Plunket
was as yet in prison, expressly attributes all his sufferings to
the enmity of those who had experienced his zeal in the cause
of Church discipline and morality: it is addressed to Cardinal
Cybo, Prefect of the Sacred Congrgeation de Propaganda :—

"I enclose to your Eminence a letter lately received from the
Bishop of Kildare in Ireland, by which he informed me of his
having been arrested on the 25th of February, without, however,
any accusation being as yet brought against him, save his having
exercised Papal jurisdiction in the kingdom. He, therefore, expects
that after a long imprisonment he will be conducted to one of the
ports, and transported hither after the confiscation of all his goods.
Wherefore he prays that on his arrival in Flanders some succour or
place of refuge should be provided for him : he also hopes to be
recommended to the clemency of the Emperor, at whose solicitation
in Rome he was promoted to the episcopacy ; and he seems also
desirous to remain in the Irish College at Antwerp, where, without
doubt, he will be received if some slight assistance be provided for
him. I have deemed it my duty to notify so much to your
Eminence that you may be good enough, should you think fit, to
lay the matter before the Sacred Congregation, with the news, at
the same time, of the imprisonment, in Dublin, of Dr. Creagh,
Bishop of Cork, who was for many years agent of the Irish clergy
in the Roman Court. From the Archbishop of Armagh I received
no letter since his arrival in London, when he informed me that his
trial had been deferred in consequence of God permitting that his
accusers should struggle amongst themselves, imputing to one
another most enormous crimes. All those who have come to
England to accuse him are Catholics, and even ecclesiastics, regular
and secular. *This is to be attributed to the hatred conceived against this
prelate : hence during the past years the various accusations presented*

against him to the Sacred Congregation. I fondly hope to be able, in
a short time, to give more pleasing news concerning these bishops,
and I make a profound reverence."
" Brussels, 19th April, 1681."

As early as 1678, John MacMoyer, whom Dr. Plunket
had suspended for various crimes, and who, as we shall see
in the next chapter, was noted for his violence, drunkenness,
and immoralities, accused him of conspiracy against the
crown. But so notorious was the character of this
unfortunate man, that the grand jury refused to receive his
testimony, and ordered himself to be arrested, and it was
only with difficulty that he escaped capital punishment.
This check did not suffice to make the enemies of the
Primate desist from their wicked design. MacMoyer could
find no other names for him than Elymas, Simon Magus,
and Oliver Cromwell,* and often avowed his determination
to bring him to the scaffold.

The accusations to which the Nuncio refers as made in
Rome against Dr. Plunket, proceeded from some associates
of this apostate, and were supposed by the Archbishop
to have had for their chief author Fr. Anthony Daly, who
was the friend and companion of MacMoyer.†

A letter penned in Dublin prison by the Archbishop, in
reply to the accusations, presented to Propaganda against
him, discloses to us not only many of these accusations, but
also many facts which sufficiently make known the spirit
which guided these unfortunate men in seeking the destruction of the Primate. It is the first letter written from prison
by Dr. Plunket, and is dated the 17th of January, 1680:—

" May the Lord be praised, who in a twofold way has given me
occasion of spiritual joy. And, first of all, by these prisons of the
tower or royal castle, where I was detained in strict confinement
from the 6th December last till yesterday, when they gave me
permission to converse with some friends and my servant, and this,
because having examined my papers, they found nothing regarding
political or temporal matters, in which I never took any part.

* See Trial, Evidence of MacMoyer and Dr. Plunket.
† From the last letter which was written by Dr. Plunket (22nd
June, 1681), we learn that MacMoyer was Daly's vicar.

Secondly, I am consoled by hearing of the calumnies of an apostate friar, Anthony Daly, *dimidium animæ* of Fr. Felix O'Neil. This Fr. Anthony sought to take away my life here, instigating the tories to kill me; they came at midnight about six years ago, to the house of my vicar-general, where I then was; they broke open the doors, and took away all the money from myself, and my vicar-general, and my secretary, Michael Plunket, who is now in Rome, and they held a sword to my throat. The chief of this band was afterwards taken, and before death declared in prison to the parish priest of Armagh, and to his curate, that Fr. Anthony told him to kill me, and that afterwards he would give him absolution. The curate, Patrick O'Donnelly, is now in Paris, and before embarking *juratus* attested this in presence of the Bishop of Clogher. I have in my possession a letter written by the same Anthony, in which he says *si ipse Deus aliquid detrimenti inferret ordini Sancti Francisci, certarem contra Deum.* He afterwards preached publicly against the Dominicans, and again in the parish of Armagh preached erroneous and scandalous doctrines; and, therefore, in the presence of the Bishop of Clogher, I suspended him from preaching and hearing the confessions of the laity. This was done in his presence, and in the presence of the Bishop of Clogher; he, nevertheless, continued to preach and sacrilegiously to hear confessions, and afterwards went through the province spreading calumnies against me, and against my vicar-general, Bernard Magorth, Dean of Armagh, a man distinguished by his integrity of life and learning, who had endeavoured to restrain the insolence of this madman; then, before going to Italy, he circulated in Paris all that your Excellency writes to me, and even more, viz., that I had become a Protestant, and had taken the oath of royal supremacy. Cardinal Howard is well informed of all the deeds of this apostate friar against me. Under the *seventh* and *eighth* heads, he states that I was the cause of the second last persecution, and that in that persecution, as well as in the present, I found favour, because I betrayed the Catholics. From this alone you may learn the malignant intentions of this man. In that persecution Dr. Brennan, of Cashel, and I were together on the mountains enduring the cold and the frost. In the present persecution I alone of the prelates as yet suffer here, and that solely for communion, and profession, and dependence on my superiors, which I had always held and will hold. This calumniator says that I alone am in favour, whilst others are persecuted, and yet I am in prison and they are free. I declare to your Excellency *coram Deo et non mentior*, that there is not a single one of the eight points which is not mere calumny and falsehood; and though this should be proved, yet what would it avail against a mad friar who defames the first, though unworthy, prelate of an entire kingdom, who lived for twenty-five years in Rome, holding high positions in the schools, and has spent these ten years past in labours, and sufferings, and persecution, and poverty. In the month of August of 1678, two months before this persecution commenced, I held a

Provincial Council, at which the Bishops of Clogher and Meath and the other suffragans or their procurators assisted ; and they gave a most complete attestation as to my labours during the past. Now, to whom is credence to be given, to a friar whom I judicially chastised, or to the attestation of all the suffragans? This was sent to your Excellency, and was, I think, by you transmitted to Rome. But I bear these calumnies, as I hope, with spiritual gain, imitating my Saviour, who suffered in body and in reputation from His adversaries, calling him a magician, a bibber, a glutton, a demon, &c. And now, as far as this sheet will hold, I will answer to the heads which seem of most importance, leaving the others for a future letter.*

" Under the *second head*, towards the end, he says, *bonus presbyter Edmundus Gavanus suspensus est suasu primatis alias non suspendendus ut ipse judex testatus est coram multis.* I never heard even of the imprisonment of this Edmund till after his execution ; he was found in arms amongst the tories, and had been for three months in their company, and on his arrest was at once condemned. I never saw the judge before, or for two years after the trial, and I never spoke to him, nor did I write to him *mediate vel immediate, per se vel per accidens, directe vel indirecte;* nor was I within a less distance than sixty miles from the criminal sessions. But, as this friar, even at the time, circulated this calumny against me, I have under the hand of Ronan Magin, who was the ordinary of the place, and who was present at the sessions, that this was a calumny and falsehood circulated by this unfortunate man and others of his accomplices, and this was three or four years ago.

" In the *second point*, he declares, *me subornasse duos falsos testes qui imposuerunt crimen læsæ majestatis DD. Jacobo Callaghan et Dionysio Raverti;* I neither know such witnesses, who they are, or what their name and surname, or in what they are engaged ; this is the truth, 'coram Deo et non mentior ;' nor was I ever either *per me or per alium* engaged in any criminal session.

" In the second point, he again says, that *Parochi Kilmoren. diœcesis me jubente vocati sunt [ad tribunalia Protestantium.* But he neither names these parish priests, nor to whom I gave the command that they should be summoned to the Protestant courts. I never summoned either by sign or words ; nor was any person, whether lay or ecclesiastical, *me annuente,* ever summoned to any tribunal : and had I any disposition for such things, I would have summoned and prosecuted this very Anthony Daly, who was an abettor of the bandits, and excited them to assassinate me, and, in fact, they did plunder my vicar-general and my secretary, urged on by this friar Anthony.

" In the fifth point, he adds, *me nullam conferre parochiam vel*

---

* He probably thought it useless to trouble himself any more about these accusations ; at least, we have met with no other letter in which he alludes to them.

ordines sine pecunia, et ordinarii a me intrusi idem facere prætendant de jure. So that my suffragans do the same. Testificor coram Deo, to use the words of St. Paul, that I never took nor asked for one half-penny from any person, whether lay or ecclesiastical, or for anything whatsoever, excepting what, *de jure vel de consuetudine*, was due to me and to my predecessors, and that I never received by all emoluments, fixed or casual, £55 per annum.

" To the other points, which are in like manner manifest false-hoods and calumnies, I will answer in another letter, not to render this one too bulky : and with a profound reverence, &c.

" 17 January, 1680.

" P.S.—It is worth remarking what he says, that neither I nor my vicars are able *proponere verbum salutis populo.* I, therefore, must have spent my time very badly in Rome, where I taught theology and controversies for so many years. He says this in the seventh point, towards the end.

" In the first and sixth points he declares *me excludere nativos.* I never gave either vicariate or dignity to any but natives of my pro-vince, nor a parish to any but natives of my diocese, unless when necessitated to call in a priest from a neighbouring diocese ; and Luke Plunket, whom he accuses of simony, is a native of my pro-vince, and is one that has suffered imprisonment and exile for the faith ; but because *coercuit ipsius insolentiam*, therefore does he seek to blacken his character.

" You will be good enough to write to me by return of post, and to tell me the name of my accuser. If I do not greatly mistake, it is this friar Anthony. But whose deputy is he ? As whose agent does he act ? Some letters of your Excellency were found amongst my papers: but they nowise damaged me ; nay, more, your Excel-lency received the praise of prudence and caution in writing. I pray you also to send this letter to Monsignor Cybo."

In the month of November, 1679, Dr. Plunket left his place of concealment, in the secluded parts of his own diocese, and came to Dublin, to assist, in his last moments, his relative, the aged Bishop of Meath ; and we have already seen with what words of affection and Christian charity he announced the demise of this prelate in his letter of 30th November, 1679. Ten days later Dr. Plunket was arrested in his place of concealment in the City of Dublin, by a body of militia, headed by Hetherington ;* and by order of the Viceroy he was committed a close prisoner to Dublin Castle. This was on the 6th of December, 1679.

* Thorpe's Collection of Pamphlets, 1641 to 1690 ; Murphy's Narrative, &c.

For six weeks no communication with him was allowed ; *
but after that term, nothing treasonable having been discovered in his papers, he was treated with more kindness,.
and permitted to receive visits from his friends.

The only crime of which the Primate was as yet supposed
to be accused was that of remaining in the kingdom, despite
of the royal interdict, and of exercising the functions of his
sacred ministry. This is more than evident from many
sources. All the letters of the Archbishop, written for
many months after his arrest, never allude to any other
accusation. In the letter just cited he expressly states that
this was the only ground for his arrest. A relative, too, of
the Primate, named William Plunket, having completed his
course of studies in the Propaganda College in Rome, and
returning to his native land, in the beginning of 1680, to
his surprise learned, on landing in Ireland, that the
Archbishop had been already for some months in prison..
He hastened without delay to convey this intelligence to
Rome, declaring the affliction which overwhelmed him, and
the consolation, at the same time, which all his friends
received, since the Primate was accused of no other crime
than that which was a true glory for a good pastor of the
spiritual flock. His letter is directed to the Cardinals of
the Sacred Congregation de Propaganda, and is dated
20th of March, 1680 :—

"After a long journey I at length arrived at Nantes, a maritime
city of France, in which. though there were many English and
Irish vessels, yet none wished to receive me, fearing lest (should they
bring ecclesiastics to Ireland during the persecution) their ships and
merchandise would be confiscated. At length, after three months'
stay in Nantes, Providence inspired a Catholic master to give me a
place in his ship. The weather was so stormy, and the winds so.
uncertain or contrary, that with difficulty could we reach Ireland
towards the beginning of February, although, if the winds were
favourable, it should be only four days' sail. Having arrived in
Ireland, to my great dismay and grief, I received the news that the
Primate was a prisoner in the Royal Castle of Dublin. I hastened

* (Till 16th January following.) See Lett. mox cit.

thither, and *having heard and learned for certain that he had been
imprisoned only for being a Cutholic bishop, and for not having abandoned the flock of our Lord in obedience to the edict published by
Parliament, I was somewhat consoled, it being his and our glory
that he should suffer in such a cause.* He was arrested on the
the 6th of December last, and no one was permitted to speak
to him till the middle of January, when his friends were allowed
to visit him, and he himself received permission to walk in
an open balcony. No sooner was he arrested than, so to say,
percurso pastore dispersæ sunt oves: the other bishops and prelates
fled to their retreats, and are so concealed that few even of their
most intimate friends know where they are. Notwithstanding
all this, I have this moment received intelligence of the arrest of
Dr. Creagh, Bishop of Cork; and the dread of all this is so much
the more increased, as it is thought a parliament will soon be held,
when the most rigorous enactments will be made against the
Catholics; and, after the manner of the English Parliament, no
Catholic will be allowed to sit in it. As to the state of ecclesiastics
here, all the convents are destroyed, and the friars scattered . . .
The parish priests have as yet some connivance in administering the
sacraments; but in the cities and large towns they are not allowed
to have oratories or chapels, and hence they are compelled to travel
about, and offer the Holy Sacrifice and exercise their sacred
functions, now here, now there, in private houses. Would to God
and to the Blessed Virgin that this same toleration may continue
. . . The times are so disastrous, that it is with difficulty we can
live, the Catholics being so poor, and in continual fear of more
rigorous edicts against us, and inhabilitated to hold any office,
military or civil.

" Dublin, 20 March, 1680."

The Bishop of Kildare writes to the same effect :—" We
are here so terrified that I have not dared to write to you
this length of time. The Primate has been in prison since
the 5th of December, and is kept in close confinement in
the Royal Castle in Dublin; he is in the room adjoining
that of the Archbishop of Dublin; his cause has not been
as yet examined, but it can be no other than that which is
common to all of his dignity and profession, that is, of
having disobeyed the proclamation commanding departure
from the kingdom. One of the three things must soon take
place in his regard, either that he be liberated on security
being given, or that he be compelled to leave the kingdom,
giving security that he will not return, or, in fine, that *le*

dexaran penas a donde esta (he be compelled to suffer where he is)." *

The Primate on his trial declared, " I was a prisoner six months, only for my religion, and there was not one word of treason spoken of against me for so many years ;" and the Attorney-General himself avowed that he was arrested " for being an over-zealous papist." †

Nevertheless, another accusation had been from the commencement presented against him, and if it were kept secret, and disguised for awhile, it was only that the plans of his accusers might be more matured, and the conspiracy so arranged, in all its parts, as assuredly to lead him to the scaffold.

The fact mentioned by the Bishop of Kildare in the above extract is worthy of attention. Side by side with the Archbishop of Armagh in the prison of the Castle of Dublin was the glorious confessor of Christ, Peter Talbot, Archbishop of that see. They had both been pillars of the Irish Church ; they had long struggled together, and sometimes too with conflicting views, in promoting its welfare and defending its rights ; and God now decreed that they should be united in receiving their earthly reward, and be sharers in the same glorious captivity ; and though Dr. Plunket alone was destined to receive the palm upon the scaffold,. yet, perhaps, no less glorious was the crown of lengthened martyrdom which his fellow-confessor received. Dr. Talbot, overcome by the sufferings of prison, died in the beginning of December, 1680.‡

* 17th January, 1679, styl. vet. (1680.)
† The Internuncio Tanari, when conveying the intelligence of his arrest to the Sacred Congregation, had no apprehension of his being subjected to capital punishment, but seemed convinced that he would be only sent into banishment. The Internuncio was, consequently, not aware of any accusation save that to which we have referred :—" E di già incarcerato Mgr. Arcivescovo d'Armach e quando non si tenti cosa veruna in pregiudizio della sua vita, come ho motivo di persuadermi, sarà facile che lo astringhino almeno all esiglio, nel qual caso non dubito che non sia per recoverarsi in Fiandra e per cercarvi un asilo sotto il patrocinio e colla assistenza della S. Congne." (3 February, 1680).
‡ Letter of Nuncio, 21st December, 1680.

MacMoyer, on his first evidence as to the treasonable designs of Dr. Plunket, was treated by Ormond with the contempt which such malignant perjurers deserved.* And when, later still, his evidence and that of the other witnesses was presented to the grand jury, these, though all Protestants, refused to find bills of indictment against the Primate. This fact we learn from the Protestant Bishop Burnet, who, in the *History of his own Times*, page 502, *seq.*, thus writes :—

" Plunket, the popish primate of Armagh, was at this time brought to his trial. Some lewd Irish priests, and others of that nation, hearing that England was at that time disposed to hearken to good swearers, thought themselves well qualified for that employment ; so they came over to swear that there was a great plot in Ireland to bring over a French army, and to massacre all the English. The witnesses were brutal and profligate men ; yet the Earl of Shaftesbury cherished them much : they were examined by the Parliament at Westminster, and what they said was believed. Upon that encouragement it was reckoned that we should have witnesses come over in whole companies. Lord Essex told me that this Plunket was a wise and sober man, who was always in a different interest from the two Talbots, the one of these being the titular Archbishop of Dublin, and the other raised afterwards to be Duke of Tyrconnell. These were meddling and factious men, whereas Plunket was for their living quietly and in due submission to the government, without engaging into intrigues of State. Some of these priests had been censured by him for their lewdness : and they drew others to swear as they had directed them. They had appeared the winter before upon a bill offered to the grand jury ; but as the foreman of the jury, who was a zealous Protestant, told me, they contradicted one another so evidently, that they would not find the bill. But now they laid their story better together, and swore against Plunket that he had got a great bank of money to be prepared, and that he had an army listed, and was in a correspondence with France to bring over a fleet from thence. He had nothing to say in his own defence, but to deny all. So he was condemned, and suffered, very decently expressing himself in many particulars as became a bishop. He died denying everything that had been sworn against him."

It was not till the month of June, 1680, that the witnesses had fully arranged their plans. Armed with commendatory letters from the English court, they now returned to Ireland assured of success. Amongst the many precautions taken

* See Thorpe's Collection, 1641-90, Murphy's Pamphlet, page 29.

by the apostate MacMoyer, one was to have a government order sent from London to the Viceroy, that no Catholic should be a member of the jury:—" Orders had been transmitted to Ireland," says the Primate on his trial, " that I should be tried in Ireland, and that no Roman Catholic should be on the jury, and so it was in both the grand and other jury; yet, there, when I came to my trial, after I was arraigned, not one appeared." Dr. Plunket did not object to this arrangement, though in itself most unjust, so conscious was he of his own innocence, and of the known character of his accusers; and after the words which we have just cited, he again avowed upon his trial:—" If I had been in Ireland, I would have put myself on my trial to-morrow, without any witnesses, before any Protestant jury that knew my accusers and myself."

The Viceroy, however, decreed that the trial should be held in Dundalk, the scene of the reputed treasonable crimes; and, as we shall just now see, this alone sufficed to derange all the plans of the witnesses, for they were conscious that their character was well known in that quarter, and that evidence could be, without difficulty, procured there of their malignity and evil designs and perjuries. Dr. Plunket, writing to the Internuncio on the 25th of July, 1680, the day after his return from Dundalk, gives the following detailed account of the proceedings of this trial :—

" Your letter of the 17th of July consoled me in my tribulations and miseries. The friar MacMoyer, as well in the criminal sessions of Dundalk as after these sessions, presented a memorial that the trial should not be held in Dundalk, where he was too well known, and that it should be deferred till September or March next, but the Viceroy refused.

" I was brought with a guard to Dundalk on the 21st of July: Dundalk is 36 miles from Dublin. I was there consigned to the King's Lieutenant in that district, who treated me with great courtesy, and on the 23rd and 24th July I was presented for trial. A long process was read, but on the 24th MacMoyer did not appear to confirm his depositions and hear my defence: I had 32 witnesses, priests, friars, and seculars, prepared to falsify all that the friar had sworn, forsooth that *I had seventy thousand Catholics prepared to murder all the Protestants, and to establish here the Romish religion and Popish superstition:* that I had *sent various agents to different kingdoms to obtain aid: that I had visited and explored all the fortresses and maritime ports of the kingdom:* and that I had held a provincial council in 1678 *to introduce the French.* He also accused, in his depositions, Monsignor Tyrrell, Rev. Luke Plunket, the ordinary of Derry, and Dr. Edward Dromgole, an eminent preacher. Murphy (the second witness) no sooner heard that the sessions and trial would be heard in Dundalk than he fled out of the kingdom : and hence MacMoyer alleged that he himself could not appear, as he awaited the return of Murphy : and so these sessions terminated, and according to the laws of this country, I must present myself at three criminal sessions before I can be absolved, and as there will be no sessions in Dundalk till the end of March, my counsel and friends recommend me to present a memorial to have the cause adjudged in Dublin at the next criminal sessions of All Saints, and that the jury of Dundalk should be brought to Dublin, which, perhaps, I may obtain. The manner of proceeding here in criminal cases seems very strange to me. The person accused knows nothing of the accusations till the day of trial ; he is allowed no counsel to plead his cause ; the oath is not given to his witnesses ; and one witness suffices for the Crown. They receive, however, the evidence of the witnesses of the accused, although they do not administer the oath to them. The sessions being over, I was re-conducted, by order of the Viceroy, to the Royal Castle of Dublin, to my dear and costly apartment : considering, however, the shortness of the time spent in Dundalk, it was still more expensive, as I had to bring 32 witnesses from different parts, and maintain them for four days in Dundalk, and amongst the guards and servants of the Lieutenant I distributed about 40 crowns. Although the two chief judges are appointed by the crown, the jury is chosen by the Lieutenant of the district of Dundalk. As there are more Catholics than Protestants in the county Louth, MacMoyer, forseeing that some Catholics would surely be on the jury, and knowing that the Lieutenant, who, from his office, is called *sheriff,* was a friend of mine, presented a memorial that no Catholic should be on the jury, and he obtained his petition. I made no opposition, knowing well that all the Protestants of my district looked on MacMoyer as a confederate of the *tories ;* and hence, at the criminal sessions of Armagh, in 1678, he was prosecuted and fined ; and I knew, moreover, that they all deemed fabulous the story sworn by MacMoyer against me, and, moreover, his dissolute life was notorious, and he was always half drunk when he appeared before the tribunals. Murphy fled, because he well knew that the jury of Dundalk would have hanged him. He had been imprisoned in Dundalk and escaped : he was found in the company of the tories, and he concealed the articles which they stole. It is said that he has gone to England to obtain pardon from the king, that he may afterwards appear against me ; not to accuse me *in crimine læsæ majestatis* (of treason), but of exercising papal jurisdiction in this kingdom : another witness, Callaghan, accuses me in like manner, and it is an accusation which I deem most glorious. It is more than two years since MacMoyer commenced his accusations against me, as is clear from the depositions.

"I more than once wrote to your Excellency to request my masters to send me some aid. I am at this moment 500 crowns in debt ; I have to pay here £1 per week for my own and my servant's apartments, and having no means to pay for my food, one of my servants brings it to me in a basket from the house of two Catholic noblemen. This is the truth *coram Deo et non mentior ;* and although you well know I have not now received one halfpenny from my masters, yet Catholics here, as well as Protestants, can with difficulty be induced to believe it. Here there is no such thing as revenue ; as you know, we depend on the benevolence of the Catholics, who are reduced to such poverty, especially in my districts, that it is difficult for the parish priests to find the means of subsistence. So many, between bandits and soldiery, are continually in pursuit of them, that in my district the greater part left their holdings ; in fact, all the military are maintained at the expense of the poor Catholics, and many not being able to pay are imprisoned.

"I request you again to make known my present state to the masters,* and I am sure your letters will have a happy result ; and others seeing their charity towards one that served them these twenty-two years past, will have an additional motive not to abandon their flocks despite every persecution. It is certain, that were it not for my exhortations, many of my brother prelates would have fled on the publication of the edict. But if they see me in prison and reduced to extremities as to food and other necessaries, what will they say ? I submit in everything to the charity and kindness of your Excellency."

In reply to this letter the Internuncio informed Dr. Plunket that he had consigned 150 crowns to his friend, the Canon Joyce in Brussels, and Dr. Plunket, under the impression that these were for the private purse of Monsignor Tanari, again wrote on the 31st of August :—

"I have received yours of the 23rd inst., and it was never my intention to inconvenience the purse of your Excellency, but I was

---

* See in the Appendix, a petition addressed by Dr. Plunket to the Sacred Congregation, stating the many expenses to which he was subjected, and the poverty of his friends, who in consequence of their being excessively oppressed and persecuted (ob minium oppressionem et persecutionem) could yield him no assistance. He then commemorates some special reasons why the Sacred Congregation should not be unmindful of him, and especially his having "for ten years attended to his spiritual charge, despite every persecution."

Z

desirous that you should write without delay to Monsignor Cybo
and the masters to make known my condition and sufferings, and
how I served them in Rome, teaching for many years theology and
controversies in the Propaganda, and labouring at the Congregation
of the Index, and how also I toiled these ten years past corresponding
with the masters and exercising my ecclesiastical functions. God
knows all I spent in this correspondence, and in supporting schools
and teachers for the education of youth and ecclesiastics. I pray
you again to write to the masters: they, perhaps, will be backward
in assisting me, thinking that all my brother prelates would make
like claims; but there is great difference between me and them, and
whilst there are so many special reasons in my favour, I am on the
other hand certain that none of the others will inconvenience them.
No one spent so much as I did in serving them, and had I not
incurred these expenses I would not be now in need. My brother
prelates lived at others' expense, but I lived in my own house and
expended for others more even than I had. I am now 500 crowns
in debt, and until the sessions of All Saints I don't know what will
be my lot. MacMoyer is anxious that the trial should be deferred:
Murphy fled from the kingdom, and they await (*si superis placet*) his
return. You will be good enough to order the 150 crowns to be
consigned to Canon Joyce, and his receipt will suffice. I will ever
pray for the health and welfare of your Excellency.

"31st August, 1680."

But the scene was now to be soon shifted from the shores
of Ireland* to the banks of the Thames. MacMoyer and
his associates felt that it would be impossible for them to
attain their wicked purpose in a country where their crimes
were so public and the Primate so revered: they therefore
petitioned the King that the trial should be transferred to
London. The suggestion was pleasing to the court, and
about the middle of October Dr. Plunket received a summons

---

* We learn from Father O'Heyn that Dr. Plunket, whilst in the
Dublin prison, kept up a correspondence with Dr. de Burgo, Bishop of
Elphin, warning him of the plots that were laid against him, and how
he should best avoid them;—"Vix enarrari potest quantas qualesque
tribulationes perpessus fuerit in horrenda persecutione suscitata contra
omnes promiscue Catholicos in Anglia et Hibernia anno 1680. Consti-
tutæ sunt bis centumlibræ sterlingæ pro quocumque eum (Epum
Elphinen.) prender te, quam ob rem noctu itinerari solebat durante ista
persecutione. . . Eram ejus individuus socius toto anno usquedum
captus fuerit Illmus. et Revmus. Armachanus Archi-Præsul D. Oliverius
Plunket *qui crebro monebat Epum Elphinensem e carcere Dubliniensi de
frequentibus consiliis consilii supremi ac privati ad capiendum illum quibus
monitionibus multum adjutus est Elphinensis Præsul ad eorum insidias et
sanguinolentas manus evitandas.*" (See *Hibernia Dominic.*, pag. 497.)

to appear before Parliament and the King to answer to the charges imputed to him. There are two letters of the Archbishop written on this occasion, one on the 21st of October, announcing this summons to London ; and another, written on board the vessel on the 24th, the day of his departure from Ireland. In the former he thus writes :—

"I have been cited to appear before the King and Parliament in London, and I leave to-day to embark ; may all be for the greater glory of God and the salvation of my soul. Another friar has made his appearance as informer : his name is George Coddan ; he was imprisoned for some crime, and to obtain his liberty became informer against me, and against Dr. Hugo, one of the chapter of Armagh, alleging that he was Nuncio of the Pope. A third friar, also, a certain Paul Gormley, who was prisoner in Derry, being arrested for robbery, now gives evidence in order to save himself : he studied in Prague. I request you to speak to Mr. Joyce that he may transmit the money to Mr. John Comin without delay. The expenses are and will be intolerable, and already I have sold a part of the few things I had, and pledged the remainder, even to the chalice and cross. From London, if possible, you will receive further intelligence. I have been deprived of pen, ink, and paper. I write *sub galli cantu et clam ac furtive*. Let Mr. Joyce not mind the exchange : for *necessitas non habet legem*. One consolation there is, that the captain of the guard which accompanies me is not my enemy. Dr. Tyrrell, Mr. Luke Plunket, and Dr. Dromgole, have been declared guilty of treason by the grand jury. A strange thing that, on the mere depositions of witnesses, sentence should be given against persons who are absent and unheard.

"I request you to communicate this intelligence to Monsig. Cybo, or to send him this letter. There are many of the Irish nobility and gentry here accused of this utopian conspiracy : as my Lord Poer, now Earl of Tuam ; my Lord Brittas, &c. I recommend myself to the sacrifices and prayers of all.

"21st October, 1680."

We have already had occasion to refer to the second letter, dated 24th Oct., 1680 (styl. vet.). Six hours before leaving the Irish shore he privately received a letter from the Nuncio, and he writes from shipboard to acknowledge its receipt, and to announce that he had already been able to communicate the privileges which it contained to the other archbishops and bishops, and he adds :—

"Tell Mr. Joyce that I received two of his letters, and that no matter what may be the consequence, to send me the money to

London, as soon as possible, addressed *for Mr. John Comin, merchant, in London,* who is my friend, and a Catholic: the expenses here are intolerable, and correspondence is difficult and dangerous. If possible you will receive letters from London. In the meanwhile I recommend myself to your prayers, and I have been, and am, and ever will be, your devoted servant," &c.

The Internuncio, when transmitting these letters to Rome, announces to the Sacred Congregation the extreme danger to which the life of the Archbishop was now exposed, and how all his own efforts, even though seconded by the meditation of the Spanish ambassador, had proved fruitless in mitigating the rigour of the Court in his regard.

" The Archbishop of Armagh has been conducted from the prisons of Dublin to those of England, and on the day of his embarking he sent me the enclosed letter, with a desire that I should transmit it to Monsig. Cybo. The fury of the enemies of our faith, and the sad conjuncture of the opening of Parliament, which is furious against the Catholics, occasion great fears for his life, although his innocence of the pretended conspiracy is most manifest; nor are witnesses wanting to establish it should the matter be fairly investigated. I have implored in his aid the intercession of the Catholic ambassador, so much the more, as I have heard that in the persecution during the reign of Charles the First, the then Archbishop of Armagh being condemned to death for exercising pontifical jurisdiction in Ireland, was sent into exile on the promise given by the Spanish ambassador that he would never again return to the British dominions. I can do nothing more than this for Dr. Plunket. I have transmitted to him by a secure person the 150 crowns to which he refers in his letter, and which have been repaid to me by the Sacred Congregation.
" 23rd November, 1680."

In the following month the Nuncio again writes, declaring Dr. Plunket's imprisonment to be so close that it was impossible to open communication with him. His letter is dated the 21st December, 1680, and gives some additional important particulars connected with the persecution :—

" Dr. Talbot, the Archbishop of Dublin, has died of his infirmities, and Dr. Plunket, Archbishop of Armagh, has more than once been examined in London, but it is impossible to discover any particulars, as he is guarded with exceeding rigour. A great number of the usual witnesses have been produced against the Viscount Strafford, nor will his innocence have any weightier support than the dread of the other lords (to whom it belongs to pass sentence), lest the depositions of such wicked and iniquitous witnesses should afterwards be directed against themselves."

The Archbishop of Cashel deemed it his duty on the death of the Primate to collect, as far as was in his power, the particulars connected with his imprisonment and trial, and transmit them to the Holy See. We shall more than once have to refer to his narrative hereafter. The following extract will suffice, as regards the matter of the present chapter :—

"MacMoyer having acted the part of Judas in London, returns by royal command to Ireland, where the conspiracy was then almost wholly discredited, and the Catholics were held in more esteem, till he, with other children of Belial, renewed the accusations, soliciting the Viceroy and the Council that the Primate might be prosecuted for rebellion. The Viceroy consented to this; and thus the Archbishop was conducted to the diocese of Armagh, the place of the pretended crimes, and by the officers of justice was brought to trial on the 20th of June, 1680. The depositions being read, the friar, with his accomplices, was called to prove the accusations; but they, though in the city at the time, were unwilling to appear. The third day, however, the friar made his appearance, declaring his intention to proceed against the accused, but that he was unable to do so in consequence of the absence of the other witnesses. His true reason was, that the Archbishop of Armagh had then present about thirty persons to prove the hatred and declared enmity of the friar against him on account of his having corrected his infamous life; and that it was so likewise with the other accusers, whose testimony could not therefore be admitted as evidence against him. A second reason was, that the goodness and sincerity of the accused was well known in these parts, even to the Protestants, as well as the wickedness of his accusers, so that it was morally impossible that their depositions would be accredited, or the Archbishop condemned. Hence, the trial was adjourned, and the accused was reconducted to Dublin, and confined in the Royal Castle as before.

"In the meantime the friar, with his companions of iniquity, made his way to London, seeing that there was no hope for the success of his evil designs in Ireland. In London he had recourse to the chief promoters of such accusations of conspiracy, giving them to understand that although the accusations against the Archbishop of Armagh were certain, nevertheless it was his opinion that they would not pass in Ireland, and that therefore it was necessary to have the case called to London, and the trial continued there. The suggestion was approved of by these promoters, and they procured a royal order to carry it into effect, and thus the Primate, escorted by a body of the Royal Guards, was brought to England, and arriving in London in the beginning of November, 1680, was lodged in the common prison, where he was kept for six months, without communication even with his servant, who, at the request of the friar was likewise imprisoned at the same place.

"After six months, the judges, on the 3rd of May, caused the Archbishop to be led to the court to stand his trial. But he protested that he could not proceed with his defence without his witnesses, and the necessary documents, which were in Ireland, and thus thirty-five days were granted to him. He consequently sent his servant to Ireland, with the permission of the judges, to procure authentic copies of the depositions and evidence which had been given against him in Ireland, and to collect and bring together from different parts of the kingdom such persons as were able and willing to give testimony in his favour, and to conduct them to London. And having but little money (not as much as would suffice to pay his prison expenses in Dublin and London), he sent with this servant a circular letter to all his friends, beseeching them in their charity to contribute what was necessary for these witnesses, and for the authentic papers already referred to. Being arrived in Dublin, this messenger made a collection amongst the Catholics of Dublin and elsewhere; but although there were thirty persons to give evidence, only five could be found who would consent to undertake so long and so difficult a journey by sea and by land, especially as the collection was small, and it was difficult to assemble so many persons from different parts of the kingdom.

"A petition being presented to the royal council in Dublin, to obtain the authentic copies which were required, the judges opposed this concession, saying, that it was unusual to have such copies transmitted to London; wherefore, the messenger, with his five witnesses was compelled to leave without them. Contrary winds detained them many days in port, without being able to sail, so that the thirty-five days, which were allowed him, passed without their being able to arrive in London; a special messenger, however was sent on to testify that they were on their journey, and the Primate petitioned to have the trial deferred for ten days, in which time he was confident (as it really happened) his witnesses would arrive. But so just a petition was rejected, and the trial was opened on the day originally fixed by the judges, the 8th of June, 1680."

We have seen that after six months' close confinement, in which the prison-guard was his only companion, Dr. Plunket received permission to communicate with his servant, and to write some letters to his friend. In the extract just cited from Dr. Brennan's narrative, mention is made of a circular addressed to his friends in Ireland: the loss of this circular is partly compensated by a letter written to Canon Joyce in Brussels on the 16th of May, 1681, from which it, probably, differed but little in substance, and which translated into Latin by this good canon, was transmitted to Rome, and is now preserved in the Vatican archives. It is as follows :—

" I was brought from Ireland to this city (London) towards the close of October last, and subjected to the sufferings of a rigorous imprisonment, all intercourse with my friends being interdicted, so that no human being, save the guard of my prison, had access to me; but as now permission has been granted to write to my relatives and acquaintances, I could not but write to your reverence, to make known and lay open to you how matters now stand with me. About a fortnight ago I was accused and brought to trial for seeking to introduce the Holy Catholic and Apostolic faith, and to overturn and destroy the Protestant religion. But the accusation being read, the trial was deferred till next sessions. that I might bring my witnesses from Ireland, who, undoubtedly will be an intolerable burden to me. and will exhaust my poor purse, unless I be aided by my friends, to whom I wholly confide myself. I caused eight witnesses to be called to refute all that the friar MacMoyer and his colleagues had stated against me. I shall have a severe trial, for neither the jury nor the judges are acquainted with my circumstances and those of my accusers. I, therefore, earnestly pray your reverence to collect and transmit to me, as soon as possible. whatever my friends can give me, that I may be able to support my witnesses. Each of them will require. at least, £20, considering their stay here and return to Ireland. Show my letters to my friends, and let Michael Plunket know the present state of my affairs. Show them especially to Mr. Picquet or Pruisson, and also to Dr. Cusack, and let Michael Plunket have a copy of this letter ; I will await your answer, to be addressed to Mr. Hugh Reilly.

" OLIVER PLUNKET.

"London, 16th May. 1681."

This letter was itself transmitted through the same Hugh Reilly, and he accompanied it with the following note to Canon Joyce :—

" As I am unknown to your reverence, I will merely state in a few words how the case stands with the writer of the enclosed letter. You must, therefore, know, that he is reduced to the last extremities, so that unless he receives assistance from his friends, it surely is all over with him. A final conspiracy has been entered into and arranged, to effect the total destruction of the Irish, so that whosoever compassionates our priests, bishops, archbishops, and the whole

kingdom, so unjustly and so cruelly persecuted, will surely correspond to this most just and most necessary petition. Please direct
your letter thus:—to Mr. Reilly, stopping at Mr. Booth's, at the
sign of the two sugar-loaves, in Bradfordbury, Covent-garden,
London.

" HUGH REILLY."

The Internuncio Tanari wrote to Cardinal Cybo on the
31st of May, 1681, conveying the substance of this letter of
the Primate, but he erroneously concludes from the passage
relative to the accusations against him, that he had not been
accused of treason; for, as we shall see at the trial of Dr.
Plunket, those two accusations were joined together, and
the treason imputed to him was no other than that he sought
to overthrow the Government, *in order to establish the
Catholic religion, and root out Protestantism.* The Internuncio thus writes :—

" Brussels, 31 May, 1681.
" A letter has, at length, been received from the Archbishop of
Armagh, directed to an Irish Canon of Brussels, with an order to
communicate it to me, whom he styles in his correspondence, Piquet
or Pruisson. The prelate is supposed to be accused only of introducing the Catholic faith into Ireland, and extirpating heresy, wherefore I hope there is no ground for the suspicion that a conspiracy
was imputed to him to expel the English from the kingdom, and
introduce foreign power. The issue of his case has been deferred
till the next meeting of the judges, which will not be for some
weeks, during which interval he has to bring over from Ireland his
witnesses, who may establish his innocence against the calumnies of
his accusers : eight witnesses have been called, but, as twenty pounds
of English money, or eighty scudi (crowns), will be required for the
support of each witness, he implores from every side some charitable
assistance. I fear but little can be got here, on account of the
poverty of the country, notwithstanding that his case is truly
deserving of compassion, and that it is of the utmost importance
that his defence should not suffer through want of sufficient means,
as on it, not only the life of the Archbishop depends, but also the
belief in the pretended conspiracy of the Irish Catholics, and consequently their persecution. In the mean time, the mediation which
has been procured will be most opportune in assisting him, as is
known to your Eminence, to whom I make a profound reverence."

CHAPTER XXV.

THE character of the witnesses, whose perjured evidence led Dr. Oliver Plunket to the scaffold, most clearly establishes the nature of the conspiracy which had been entered into against him, and proves that his death was owing to the hatred of those who looked on him as the pillar of the Irish Church, and the dauntless champion of her discipline and teaching.

John MacMoyer, of whom we have often spoken in the preceding chapter, was the originator of that wicked conspiracy, and his chief associates were another apostate friar, named Duffy, and Edmund Murphy, a suspended secular priest. MacMoyer and Duffy had studied together in St. Isidore's, and were expelled from that convent on account of their irregularities by its venerable guardian, Father Tyrrell, who, at the period at which we are now arrived, was bishop of the ancient see of Clogher, and who, as he zealously co-operated with the Primate in reforming the abuses of some corrupt members of the clergy, so, too, was made the object of their enmity and hatred, and we shall see that in their depositions, side by side with their charges against the Primate were similar accusations against the Bishop of Clogher.

It was about 1673 that the reforms introduced by Dr. Plunket first awakened the fury and enmity of those who sought to maintain irregularity and corruption in the Irish clergy, and whose vicious lives but little corresponded with the sanctity of their profession. Amongst these opponents of the Archbishop none were more violent than the two just mentioned, who afterwards were destined to crown their impiety and guilt by leading him to the scaffold. In the noble library of St. Isidore's, which a few years before had been founded by the great ornament of the Franciscan order,

Father Luke Wadding, a bust of the newly-appointed Primate was erected in 1669. On this bust the two unworthy young men, of whom we have been speaking, resolved to let loose all their rage, and privately entering the library, presented to their indignant fellow-countrymen in Rome the outrageous spectacle of beheading in effigy the most exalted prelate of their Church. Thus did they even then manifest their readiness, were it in their power, to compass the death of him who, animated with Christian zeal, sought to correct abuses, and as a good pastor, to heal the spiritual wounds of the flock entrusted to his charge. Though, in consequence, expelled from the order in Rome, they succeeded by false pretensions in obtaining an entrance to some convent in Germany or France, and returned to Ireland about 1674.

In the narrative of the Archbishop of Cashel we find some further particulars in regard to MacMoyer :—

" In the month of May, 1679, a certain Hetherington escaped from prison, where he was detained for various crimes, and going to London, presented himself before the Earl of Shaftesbury, the principal promoter and the fabricator of the pretended conspiracy imputed to the Catholics. This lord received the fugitive with open arms, and heard from him the welcome information that in Ireland certain friars and priests who were in prison could state positive facts regarding the plot which was on foot in that country to advance the conspiracy. Shaftesbury procured a royal order that John MacMoyer, a Franciscan, Edmund Murphy, a secular priest, and some others, should be sent from Ireland to London, which accordingly took place, and they were examined before the King in council as to what they knew concerning a conspiracy in Ireland. The secular priests declared on oath that they knew nothing of such conspiracy, save what they had heard from the lips of the friar John Moyer; and Moyer being interrogated, answered *tactis evangeliis* (on oath) that in Ireland there was on foot a universal conspiracy, of which the head and promoter was the Archbishop of Armagh, with whom all the Catholics were united in this design ; and subsequently he presented in writing several articles of high treason against the Archbishop of Armagh.

" It is to be remarked that this Moyer was a student of the college of St. Isidore, and it is thought that he was one of those that beheaded the bust of the Primate which decorated the library of that college, and now, by means of his sacrilegious accusations, he has succeeded in giving a like stroke to the prototype. Since his arrival in Ireland he lived in the province of Armagh, where he gave such scandal that his provincial was compelled to declare him *an apostate*, and at his solicitation the Archbishop of Armagh caused this sentence to be published in the parishes of his district, commanding, moreover, that no Catholic should receive from him the sacraments of the church. The friar, enraged at this, had recourse to the then Viceroy, accusing the Archbishop of holding frequent synods for the purpose of setting on foot a rebellion against the Government. But the Viceroy, knowing the loyalty of the Archbishop, heeded not the accusations of the friar, who, however, took care to treasure up his revenge till the favourable opportunity of this pretended conspiracy, when all false witnesses are held in esteem and reputed honourable men."

When, in 1678, MacMoyer presented to the grand jury in Dundalk heads of impeachment against Dr. Plunket for high treason, not only did they refuse to receive his testimony, but he himself was arrested and cast into prison, as an associate of the bandits, and guilty of other crimes : and he seems to have remained there till his design of effecting, by his perjuries, the death of the Primate, was made known to the Earl of Shaftesbury. Even before the order for his release arrived from London, he being assured of the patronage of the court, by a letter of Hetherington, made his escape from prison, and laid his accusations before the Viceroy, Ormond, and the grand jury of Dublin ; but once more his evidence was rejected as worthless, and it was only when summoned to England to appear before the royal council that he found, in the sworn enemies of the Catholic faith, willing and anxious ears to receive his perjured tale.* The facts connected with his subsequent career, till the Primate's trial, have been detailed in the preceding chapter ; returning to Ireland, armed with a royal mandate, and taking the precaution that all Catholics should be excluded from the jury, he yet feared to pursue his accusations before the grand jury of Dundalk ; and at his solicitation London was destined, by the Crown, to be the scene of the trial of Dr. Plunket.

---

* It would appear from Carte, that the Protestant Bishop of Meath, "who had been scoutmaster-general to Oliver Cromwell," and sharer in his many bloody deeds against the Catholics, was the principal patron in Ireland of these perjured witnesses. His words will be cited hereafter.

In his letter of the 2nd July, 1681, Dr. Plunket remarks, regarding MacMoyer and Duffy, that they were sharers in a plot with some other members of their order to accomplish his destruction :—

" MacMoyer and one Friar Duffy were the principal accusers . . . Felix O'Neill was a declared enemy of Dr. Tyrrell and Luke (Plunket) Anthony Daly had some words with Dromgole. I am informed, by persons of credit, that Felix and Daly did contrive all this tragedy before their departure from Ireland. MacMoyer was Daly's vicar, and Duffy is a fosterer, or of that family who fostered Felix ; if so, God forgive them, and I do forgive all who had a hand, directly or indirectly, in my death."

But if MacMoyer and Duffy had long been companions in their career of crime, and of enmity to the Primate, Duffy too was a fellow bandit of Edmund Murphy, and thus it was not difficult to make him a third accomplice in their sacrilegious design.*

Edmund Murphy had been parish priest in the diocese of Armagh, and chanter of the cathedral. As early as 1674 he was suspended from the exercise of all ecclesiastical functions, and hurried away by passion, he soon became one of the most virulent opponents of the Archbishop, and a leading concoctor of the conspiracy against him. Nevertheless, on more than one occasion the dictates of conscience seemed for a while to triumph ; on his first being summoned to London he openly avowed that all he knew of the treasonable practices of the Primate he had learned from MacMoyer ; and again, at the last trial of Dr. Plunket, he used every endeavour to cancel his former evidence—to have the trial deferred, in order that the Archbishop's witnesses might arrive, and to destroy the testimony of his fellow-informers.

In 1680 he wrote a pamphlet (which was published in the following year), entitled " The Present State and Condition

---

* All three were wicked men, and associates in crime, and Dr. Plunket declared, in his last discourse, that " for seven years " he had laboured, but in vain, to effect their conversion.

of Ireland ;" * and in it he details, at length, many of the exploits which won for him the favour of the Court and of the Protestants of England. His career, even as thus pourtrayed by himself, but too well justifies the severity of the Primate in his regard ; and at the same time reveals to us most fully the character of those who found in Dr. Plunket a check to their vicious life, and consequently plotted his destruction.

During the sentence of suspension which he had fulminated against him, Murphy continued to exercise the ecclesiastical functions, and sacrilegiously to administer the sacraments. At the same time he plundered the country, as leader of a band of *tories*, whilst, on the other hand, he corresponded with the Government to betray his fellow-bandits, and obtain the price which had been set upon their heads.

Amongst the many bands of *tories* which then devastated the country, the most powerful was that headed by Redmond O'Hanlon, whose name is yet remembered in many districts of the North of Ireland. Mutual enmity and distrust soon sprung up between the rival leaders, and O'Hanlon caused a proclamation to be made throughout his district, that who-soever would go to Murphy should forfeit, the first time, one cow ; the second time, two ; and the third time, his life. Murphy, on his part, planned the murder of O'Hanlon, and assumed as his chief associates in that design two fellow-tories, Cormack and O'Neill. O'Neill rejoiced to have an opportunity of hastening to O'Hanlon's quarters to betray the plot of Murphy and Cormack ; on his return a drunken brawl ensued, in which Cormac was murdered. Murphy, in his pamphlet, imputes this murder to O'Neill, but the circumstances, even as described by himself, are such as seem to justify the suspicion which was entertained by many at the time that he himself was the author of the

---

* The full title is "The Present State and Condition of Ireland, but more especially of the Province of Ulster, humbly represented to the kingdom of England, by Edmund Murphy, Secular Priest and Titular Chanter of Armagh, and one of the first discoverers of the Irish Plot ;" it is published in Thorpe's Collection, from 1611 to 1690.

crime. Soon afterwards two officers, named Baker and Smith, denounced Murphy as a robber, and the ringleader of a party which kept the country in continual agitation, and eventually he was arrested by the troops under their command, and committed to prison in Dundalk gaol. Carte (vol. ii., p. 514), supplies some further particulars connected with this period of his career :—

" Parties of *tories*, which the Duke of Ormond was careful to suppress, because they were a sort of nurseries for rebellion, served likewise for supplying witnesses for the Popish plot. One Murphy, living in their quarters, and corresponding with them, was prosecuted for that correspondence by Baker and Smith, of Dundalk. The proofs for convicting him were ready, and the assizes were near, when he made his escape out of prison, and put himself under the protection of the Government as prosecutor for the King, of the charge against Oliver Plunket, Titular Primate of Armagh. John Moyer being guilty of the like correspondence, took the same part as Murphy had done, and went to England, whence they returned with encouragement to proceed to the conviction of Plunket, and powers to take up such persons as they saw fit for further witnesses. They had been examined in England as evidences of the plot, but had neglected to take out their pardons, and being prosecuted on their first return, for their correspondence with *tories*, the Bishop of Meath pressed the Earl of Shaftesbury, by frequent letters, to procure their pardons, and get the Titular Primate's trial, which was to be at the next assizes, which were then near, at Dundalk, to be removed from that town, where he would be certainly acquitted, to either Dublin or London. The latter place was deemed most convenient, and the old man was accordingly sent for thither, tried, and convicted by this, and the like evidence, of a charge that was in its own nature incredible, viz , the inviting twenty thousand French to invade the kingdom, and land at Carlingford, and the listing of seventy thousand men to join them."

The officers to whom Murphy was accustomed to betray his companions were Captains Coult and Butler, and he had for his assistants in this deed of infamy his own brothers, and a relative named Hugh Murphy. The occupation of this last individual was to steal the horses of the *tories*, which afterwards were brought by the brothers to Sir Hans Hamilton, and he arrested all who inquired or sought after such horses. Moreover, says the writer of the pamphlet to which we have referred, the same Hugh Murphy being an active partizan of the *tories*, did daily send their state to the deponent (Ed. Murphy), who communicated it in writing to Captain Butler, by a certain damsel, to avoid suspicion. It soon, however, became rumoured through the country that Edmund Murphy was a traitor, and " all or most people were possessed that the informant received a large sum of money from the said Captain Coult, to bring in the heads of several of the chief *tories* and rebels, all which was spread abroad by means of *lying fame*." Elsewhere he commemorates how on one occasion his life would have been sacrificed to their fury, were it not for that Cormack in whose blood he is supposed to have afterwards steeped his guilty hands :—

" All the said *tories* verily believed the report, except the said Cormack, who well knew the informant's design ; but the rest made solemn vows to kill the informant in the first place they met him. The informant getting intelligence hereof, betook himself to a habitation near Dundalk, where he continued a certain season, but one day going there to visit his parish, *accompanied by one Friar Duffy*, as they passed the hill of Carricksticken, they were espied by the aforesaid *tories*, among whom was the said Cormack, and coming violently all together upon the informant, he was thereat surprised ; but Cormack immediately interposed between the informant and them, making oath that whoever should lay hands on the said informant, should in like manner perish ; and Cormack demanding what might be his crime, they told him he was a rogue, and had contracted with Captain Coult, for a sum of money, to bring in their heads; but the informant protested the contrary, and that he never mentioned their names to the said captain, whereupon they were satisfied, and the deponent demitted to resort to his parish."†

Hetherington had met, as companions in Dundalk gaol, MacMoyer and Murphy ; he soon learned their sentiments in regard to the Primate, and having made his escape and arrested Dr. Plunket, he wrote to Murphy, informing him of the royal letters which he had obtained for his release. Murphy could await no longer,‡ but making his escape from gaol, presented himself before the Duke of Ormond and

* This, probably, refers to his design of murdering O Hanlon.
† See Murphy's pamphlet, pp. 14-15.
‡ *Ibid.*, page 29.

accused the Primate and the two officers by whom he was arrested, as being concerned in the Popish plot, and the friends and abettors of the tories. Ormond, however, was already well acquainted with his character, and upbraided him as being actuated solely by motives of revenge in consequence of the excommunication to which he was subjected by the Primate.

"The informant [he thus writes] immediately after this conference with the Duke of Ormond repaired to Mr. Hetherington, and related to him all the passages that had passed between them, particularly of the excommunication that was denounced against the informant, that malice was the original cause thereof; to which the said Hetherington replied, that it was almost impossible, as well as improbable, to have any justice done against the said Plunket by reason of his strong faction, nor in any other matters relating thereunto."

But Murphy was more sanguine in his hopes than Hetherington, and (as his narrator continues), "not taking much notice of this reply, informed the said Hetherington, if he would accompany the informant to the north, he would produce evidence to prove the whole that before he had revealed, and more also." * Murphy soon received a government authorization to gather in these witnesses, and setting out accompanied by Hetherington, "under the denomination of a friar which had lately come from Rome," visited various districts of the north, but he could find none to swear against the Primate, and he complains that his witnesses against the officers "were chained and scourged to sign an instrument for their own transportation."

From facts which he subsequently records we may conclude that the result of his excursion was still more unfavourable to his design. "Lying fame" having spread abroad his purport in visiting the north, a certain Hugh M'Kenna pursued him to Dublin to make known his iniquitous career. But Murphy anticipated his accuser, and caused M'Kenna to be arrested on a charge of making away with government papers necessary for the prosecution

* Page 29.

of the Popish plot. However, on the matter being investigated the truth became known. M'Kenna was released, and Murphy found himself once more cast into prison. The witnesses whom he had succeeded in gathering together were prosecuted for perjury by the officers whom he had accused, and they soon were sentenced to transportation. At the same time his relative Hugh Murphy, met with a dreadful retribution at the hands of Lieutenant Baker, which we may commemorate in the words of the pamphlet:—

"The head of the fore-mentioned spy that the informant employed to look after the tories was brought to the Duke of Ormond, as a piece of good service done by Lieutenant Baker, notwithstanding his being authorized by Sir Hans Hamilton and Captain Butler to betray the tories, under the pretence of corresponding with them, which he was allowed in. The manner of killing of the said spy was, when he was at his house sick in bed, Lieutenant Baker came and knocked out his brains with the but-end of a pistol or musket, and afterwards cut off his head; and then the said Baker taxed the country for money for his head."

Murphy's personal narrative comes down no further, but from other sources we know too well his subsequent history. Having received from the court a full pardon for all his crimes, he was commissioned by Government to co-operate with MacMoyer and Duffy in ensuring the conviction of the Primate. When first examined in private, his evidence was more full and conclusive than that of the other witnesses, as the Attorney-General avowed upon the trial; but he soon repented of his perjuries, and in the words of the Attorney-General:—

"The trial coming on, he ran off and lay hid; I took a great deal of pains to find him out, and sent messengers about; at last I heard he was gone to the Spanish Ambassador's; I sent, and they spied him in the chapel, but the Spanish Ambassador's servants fell upon the messengers and beat them; the Ambassador was sent to about it, and his Excellency promised that he should be brought."

When produced, however, on the day of his trial, all his efforts were directed contrary to the desire of his patrons;

and he was accordingly arrested for contempt of court, and committed to Newgate.

Such were the three chief witnesses who plotted the death of Dr. Plunket; all three unworthy men, whose vicious career the zealous Archbishop had long, but in vain, endeavoured to check, and who, when excommunicated for their crimes, became "renegades from our religion, and declared apostates!" *   Even Murphy, the best of the three, when interrogated on the trial by the judge if he were a priest, made but a slight effort to conceal his apostacy, and answered, "I am indifferent whether I be a Protestant or a priest."

The reader will, probably, have some anxiety to learn the fate of the two former unhappy men after consummating their deed of wickedness. The Internuncio, Tanari, writes to the Secretary of Propaganda on the 10th of October, 1681, that in compliance with his injunctions he had intimated to the superiors of the Franciscan Order the commands of the Sacred Congregation in regard of MacMoyer and Duffy, forsooth that "they should declare them apostates, excommunicated, and entirely cut off from the bosom of religion and of Holy Church."† On the 1st of May, 1682, the Archbishop of Cashel, writing to Rome, informs the Sacred Congregation, that MacMoyer, returning once more to Ireland, accused many others in the province of Armagh, but that his evidence was rejected, and he himself cast into prison, and accused of many crimes, was to receive sentence in the month of August following. The same Archbishop, writing again on the 30th June, 1683, further declares that "Friar MacMoyer and another Moyer, a relative of his, both accusers of the happy Primate, continue still in prison, where they suffer great privations, and are almost dead from hunger, finding none who will give them food, so abhorred are they by all."

* Words of Dr. Plunket on his trial.
† "Per dichiararli apostati scommunicati ed intieramente separati dal grembo della religione e della Santa Chiesa."—Archiv. de Prop. fid.

Similar was the fate which awaited Duffy: he, too, on his return to Ireland, was cast into prison, and, making his escape, joined with a band of *tories*, detested and abhorred by all.* Forty years, full of eventful scenes, rolled on, and at length, old and emaciated, an outcast from the Church, and a prey to remorse, he cast himself at the feet of Dr. MacMahon, a successor of the martyred Primate, and exclaimed in an agony of soul, " Is there then no mercy for me!—am I never to be reconciled to God!" The praye breathed by the holy prelate upon the scaffold, like that of St. Stephen for his executioners, had obtained from God that mercy which he now implored. Dr. MacMahon heard him in silence, then pointing to an open shrine, he said in a solemn voice, " Look here, thou unfortunate man." The head of his innocent victim was before him ; he saw, knew it, and swooned away. Soon after he was once more reconciled to the Church, and closed his career a sincere penitent.†

Before closing this chapter, we may refer to a letter of Dr. James Cusack, Bishop of Meath, who, under the assumed name of James Fleming, details on the 3rd of August, 1681,‡ the motives by which these unfortunate

* See letter of Archbishop of Cashel, 1st May, 1682.
† See Stuart's *Historical Memoirs of the city of Armagh.*
‡ We insert a copy of the original Latin of this important letter, which is as follows :—

" 3 Augusti, 1681.

" DNE. MI,

" Quis, quo, aut cui scribitur per tempus non licet litteris imprimere, nec magis convenit consueto et debito verborum honore uti. Discet ex latore, Oliveri Armachani (piæ memoriæ) consanguineo, hæc esse suspiria gementis et flentis in Hiberna ærumnarum valle obitum vigilantissimi et piissimi illius Præsulis. Certe a centum et sexaginta annis haud unquam Ecclesiæ Hibernicæ gravius inflictum est vulnus. Vix tutum est tam errantes vel admonere ut in viam redeant, et si de iis coercendis alloquatur quis in mortem Armachani tanquam in speculum jubetur minaciter inspicere. Non est in his diebus Rex in Israel, sed unusquisque quod sibi videtur hoc facit. Moliti sunt sacrilegum illud parricidium Franciscani duo MacMoyer et Duffy apostatæ scelestissimi, adjunctis sibi Mac Lanc parocho quodam et quatuor sæcularibus, quorum duo sunt ex familia O'Nellorum, tertius ludi magister quidam Florentius MacMoyer, Franciscani consanguineus, quartus ex familia Hanlonorum, et hi omnes

apostates were urged on to perpetrate their horrid sacrilege
His affectionate esteem for the martyred Primate is dis-
cernible in every sentence ; he declares that he writes this
letter overwhelmed with affliction, "on account of the
death of that most vigilant and most pious prelate :" he
stigmatizes the foul crime of Duffy and MacMoyer as a
*sacrilegious parricide—a crime which contained in itself all
wickedness ;* and he adds, that by this wicked deed, these
two apostates "had inflicted a *worse wound upon the Irish
Church than any it had received for a hundred and sixty
years.*"

iniquitate insignissimi. Tria potissimum præter spem auri et argenti
parricidas istos ad tam nefandum scelus perpetrandum induxerunt.
Primum, quod Ultonia quæ una est ex quatuor Provinciis Hiberniæ
secundum temporalem regni divisionem et pars sola spiritualis Provinciæ
Ardmachanæ (continens tamen plures Diœceses) a Midia et reliqua parte
Provinciæ imo a toto Regno habitantium moribus et antipathia quadam
multum dissentiat : nutrit enim Ultonia rudem et agrestem plebem quæ-
que illibenter mandatis corum qui in Midia aut alibi extra Ultoniam nati
sunt obsequitur, unde fit ut Patritius Clogherensis quia id Midia natus
sicut et Ardmachanus ab iisdem homicidis jam ad necem quæratur.
Secundum est quod Ardmacanus studuerit quantum potuit gentem illam
infelicem et ingratam reformare, et quod digna eorum factis animadver-
sione affecti fuerint sæpe improbi et præsertim MacMoyer et Duffy.
"Tertium quod Ardmacanus in summum cleri bonum, cum aliquibus
Regiis ministris magnam familiaritatem contraxerit quam male interpre-
tati sunt rudiores illi qui Anglos acerbiori odio insectantur ; et quia optime
sciebant quanti hic habebatur ab omnibus Ardmachanus, et quod si hic
in judicium vocatus fuisset nulla ipsis fides adhiberetur, obtinuerunt,
Presbiterianorum opera, ut creditur, in Anglia, ut eo vocaretur ubi tam
ipse quam accusatores erant ignoti et ipsi impossibile vitæ suæ innocentiam
comprobare. Nec aliud jam speratur quam quod alii plures eandem
alcam subituri sint eoque trahendi nisi propter scelus illud in quo omnia
scelera continentur, æternæ aliqua infamiæ nota, translatione sedis
Primatialis (exemplo Innocentii X. ob homicidium Epi. de Castro), aut
alio modo illi genti inuratur. Et forte conveniret ad tempus prohibere
ne Franciscanus ullus huc se conferret nam quamvis duo soli positive,
plures tamen consentur negative in perniciem ejus conjurasse. Hoc
ausim affirmare duos illos plus nocuisse Ecclesiæ Hibernicæ quam profuit
centum bis annis elapsis aut proderit insequentibus tot annis totus ordo
Divi Francisci. Profecto ingratissimus erit populo et clero, ne aliud
dicam adventus ullius Franciscani præsulis, et de facto ita refrigescit
charitas fidelium ratione immanissimi illius sceleris ut non solum parce
et tenuiter fratribus illius ordinis eleemosynas c'argiri sed corundem
conspectum quamplures incipiant abhorrere.
"Sed quæ supra nos nihil nos : expirarunt jampridem magno fidelium
incommodo privilegia Diœcesis Dubliniensis, Ardachadensis, Ardma-

CHAPTER XXVI.

JOHN MACMOYER, Duffy, and Edmund Murphy were the chief originators of the conspiracy which led the Archbishop of Armagh to the scaffold. But they soon associated to themselves a host of other witnesses to confirm their statements, and render plausible the monstrous tale they had devised. Indeed, nothing more clearly proves the sad degradation of Ireland, and the depths of misery and debasement to which long oppression and misrule had reduced its inhabitants, than the number of false witnesses who, at the bidding of an English minister, or attracted by the hopes of reward, started at this period from the Irish shores, and rushed to England to swear away the lives of innocent men,

chanæ, et Midensis, nec audent pro eorum innovatione rescribere arbitratores Juris, sic enim jam nuncupantur qui Ordinariam exercent jurisdictionem, cum Episcopi et Vicarii Generales per mandata publica proscribantur, unde primâ datâ opportunitate transmittenda forent, nec nominandi sunt qui jurisdictionem exercent aut quibus communicabuntur privilegia ne litteræ interceptæ superiores detegant. Et præterea quum incarcerationi, exilio, et etiam morti (si perjuris placeat) expositi sint, putarem privilegia sedibus aut dignitatibus communicanda tum ob prædictam rationem ne personæ detegantur si litteras intercipi contingat, tum ut ad successores transirent si ante eorum expirationem contingeret superiorem aliquem incarcerari, exilio aut morte affici. Nec expedit multas fieri reservationes; hoc enim, si ullo unquam tempore ampliandi sunt favores. Et omnino necessarium est ut facultatibus addatur potestas dispensandi in irregularitatibus provenientibus ex violatione censurarum quæ ab omnibus hic judicatur reservata Ssmo. Dno., cum, hoc tempore ab aliquibus contemptæ sint censuræ et contractæ sæpius irregularitates, in quibus necesse habeant sordescere peccantes propter locorum distantiam et difficilem accessum ad S. P.

"Nulli Hiberno convenit has litteras ostendi, ne auctor earum suspicetur, cum de facto in magno vitæ discrimine versetur, et longe plus sibi a falsis fratribus (quorum aliqui in partibus transmarinis degunt) quam ab adversariis in fide timeat. Dignetur nobiscum orare—ne despiciat omnipotens Deus populum suum in afflictione clamantem et valeat,

"Vræ. Dominationis servus,
"JAC. FLEMING."

choosing as the special victims of their perjury the men most distinguished by their love of country and the practice of religion.

The enemies of the Catholics had, as we have seen, strained every nerve to gain credit for the wicked nonsense of "the Titus Oates' plot;" one thing, however, was sufficient to check the most credulous in assenting to it. Ireland was a Catholic nation, and yet no trace of such a plot had been found in Ireland. "It was a terrible slur," writes Carte,* "upon the credit of the popish plot in England, that after it had made such a horrible noise and frighted people out of their senses in a nation where there was scarce one papist to one hundred Protestants, there should not for above a year together appear so much as one witness from Ireland, to give information of any conspiracy of the like nature in that kingdom, where there were fifteen papists to one Protestant, as that charged upon the papists of England, whose weakness would naturally make them apply for assistance from their more powerful brethren in Ireland."

Welcome, therefore, was the announcement made by Hetherington to the Earl of Shaftesbury, that at length witnesses were at his disposal only too anxious to have a field to labour in his cause, and who, moreover, were desirous of laying the wished-for conspiracy and treasonable plot at the doors of the highest dignitaries of the Church of Ireland. From the extract given in the preceding chapter from the narrative of the Archbishop of Cashel, it appears that Hetherington was at once received into favour by Shaftesbury, caresses were soon heaped on him by that arch-enemy of the Catholics, and the special province was assigned to him to beat up for other witnesses who might confirm the statements of his first friends MacMoyer and Murphy. We find, in fact, an order from the English Council on the 28th November, 1679, "requiring the Lord Lieutenant and Council (of Ireland), to issue a proclamation forthwith for encouraging all persons that could make any further dis-

* Vol. ii., p. 495.

covery of the horrid popish plot, to come in and declare the same by a certain day to be fixed; otherwise not to expect his Majesty's pardon." With these hopes of pardon and reward held out to them, every one who was guilty of infamous crimes, and feared the just chastisement which awaited him, hastened to present himself as *informer*, and thus the scum of society in Ireland found an opportunity of re-acquiring their position in the eyes of the British law by adding perjury to their former crimes. The untiring persecutor of the Catholics, the Protestant Bishop of Meath, was the main supporter of these proceedings : " Nobody," says Carte,* " was more active in procuring these witnesses than the Bishop of Meath, who had been scoutmaster-general to Oliver Cromwell's army, and now exerted himself to the utmost to serve that great and worthy patriot, his very good friend (as he styles him), the Earl of Shaftesbury. The private intercepted letters of his correspondence with the earl, which was carried on by means of Colonel Mansell and William Hetherington, that nobleman's chief agent, manager, and instructor of the Irish witnesses, show something more zealous than honourable in his proceedings in that affair."

With what anxious endeavours the enemies of the Catholics laboured to obtain the conviction of those who were accused, may be seen by the following letter of Lord Massarene† to Sir George Rawdon :—

" I desired that Neal O'Quin, the old friar, might come, because Mr. Bleeks assured me he knows all the whole plot and designs, and was an opposite to Plunket, and of the same faction with Wyer, and so far as I see, Roland MacDonnell, Brien O'Neill, and others, have had differences with Florence Wyer.‡ who has them and others, they say, at malice, whom he accuses, and those who are well known to Sir Hans Hamilton, or Sir George Atcheson, to whom you may please to mention them. My opinion is, that if Neal O'Quin cannot come to us for his age, that Sir Hans Hamilton should examine him, for he

* Vol. ii., p. 493.
† Rawdon Papers, 268.
‡ Florence MacMoyer. He, as we shall see just now, was a layman, and Massarene fears that the other laymen would not agree with him in their evidence.

certainly knows a great deal, and you see none of the other friars
that we have sent to take can be gotten, and those that come at us
either cannot or will not confess the least; and for my part, I really
believe, the popish plot goes still on with the Romish clergy, who
you see are still amongst us, yet you see will neither be taken nor
appear.

" Your servant, M."

The Duke of Ormond from the first seems to have given
no credence to the testimony of these witnesses. Thus, he
refused to listen to Murphy's evidence, and reproved him as
being instigated by hatred and revenge. In one of his
letters also, whilst he gives the history of an individual
witness, he traces the preparatory course of them all.*
" A notorious *tory* in Munster, being ready to be sent by my
Lord Orrery to prison, and at last, actually, perhaps too
hastily, sent thither by his lordship, offers at great dis-
coveries, and names many persons as guilty of the plot. But
orders will go this night for his setting at liberty, and for
protecting him in his way hither. The fellow's name is
Honaghan, as I think, in times past, an attorney in the
presidency court, but since that was suppressed, turned
robber. He has put his tale as well together as any of his
country." In another letter he enters at length into the
character of those who were now feted by the English
Protestants, and whose stories he himself had made the
pretext for new penal laws against the Catholics of Ireland.†
" All the business here belongs to the term and the judges ;
and at Council there is little more to do, than to hear witnesses, some come out of England, and some producing
themselves here, and all of them (I doubt) forswearing
themselves. Those that went out of Ireland with bad
English and worse clothes, are returned well-bred gentlemen, well caroneted, periwigged, and clothed. Brogues and
leather straps are converted to fashionable shoes and glitter-
ing buckles ; which, next to the zeal which tories, thieves,
and friars, have for the Protestant religion, is a main

---

* Carte, ii. 105. The letter is dated 25th **January, 1680-1.**
† *Ibid.*

inducement to bring in a shoal of informers. The worst is, they are so miserably poor, that we are fain to give them some allowance ; and they find it more honourable and safe to be the king's evidence, than a cow-stealer, though that be their natural profession. But seriously, it is vexatious and uneasy to be in awe of such sort of rogues. Now that they are discarded by the zealous suborners of the city, they would fain invent and swear what might recommend them to another party ;* but, as they have not the honesty to swear truth, so they have not the wit to invent, probably. It is for want of something else to say that I fall upon this character of an Irish witness."

A leading witness in the beginning of 1680, was a certain David Fitzgerald, a native of the county Limerick, and a Protestant. In the following year, however, he was seized with remorse, and, as the author of a pamphlet in Thorpe's collection (1640-1690), informs us :—"The said David did order me to write in my information, that one William Hetherington, and the rest of his Majesty's evidence, were all mere rogues and thieves, and gaol-breakers." He had already informed us who ' the rest of his Majesty's evidence ' were, and amongst them we find the names of "Edmund Murphy, John Moyer, Hugh Duffy, George Coddan, Paul Gormley, Murtagh Downing," and others,† most of whom acted as witnesses against Dr. Plunket.

Besides the three witnesses of whom we have spoken in the preceding chapter, there appeared on the trial against Dr. Plunket, Florence MacMoyer, Henry O'Neal, Neale O'Neal, Hanlon, Owen Murphy, and John MacLane. Of these, the five first were laymen, and the last a suspended

---

* Ormond had commenced to fear that the corrupt witnesses whom he sent to England to swear away the lives of the Catholics, might afterwards be employed by his own enemies at court to involve himself in the pretended conspiracy. We shall see just now in the dying speech of O'Neill, how some of the witnesses had formed, in fact, a plan to effect the ruin of Ormond.

† This pamphlet was written by Maurice Fitzgerald, who probably was a relative of this David Fitzgerald, concerning whom he speaks.

secular priest. But there were also others (as we learn from the letters of Dr. Plunket), who, though they were not afterwards produced on the trial, yet privately gave their evidence against the Primate. Thus, in his letter of the 21st of October, 1680, he speaks of George Coddan and Paul Gormley, both apostates whose character is given above, by their former associate, David Fitzgerald.* Dr. Brennan also mentions another whose name was M'Geoghegan.

David Fitzgerald, to whom we have just referred, was a prisoner for having uttered treasonable words, and was about to be brought to trial. Having declared himself a witness for the Government, he was, without difficulty, acquitted of the charge imputed to him; and this being his only object in pretending to an acquaintance with the supposed conspiracy, he now sought to escape from giving further evidence. When sent over to Shaftesbury, he stole away from London, resolving to make good his journey to Ireland. He, however, was re-taken at Bristol, and compelled to accuse many respectable inhabitants of his own county (Limerick) as being connected with the treasonable plot. These assuredly would have been convicted and hanged, were it not that, on the day of trial, he avowed that all he had sworn against them was a pure fiction, concocted by himself and Hetherington. Moreover, he endeavoured, as we have seen, to make known the character of his fellow-witnesses, and so convinced were the friends of Dr. Plunket of the sincerity of his conversion, that they sought to have him produced on the trial, to give evidence in favour of the Primate; his name was called in court by the crier, but he had not courage to appear.

An active witness against the Primate, as well on the trial as in procuring other witnesses from Ireland, was

---

* Perhaps, the *Paul Gorman*, who was afterwards *subpoened* to appear on the trial by some friends of Dr. Plunket, was identical with this Paul Gormley. If so, his evidence was not directed against the Primate, who, he said, "did more good in Ireland than hurt."

John MacLane.* He had belonged to the diocese of Clogher ; but, on account of his many irregularities and vicious life, was suspended and excommunicated by Dr. Tyrrell, and hence he now sought revenge by confirming against him and against the Primate the monstrous accusations of MacMoyer regarding the pretended conspiracy. By his solicitations, too, Henry O'Neal was induced to join the gang of witnesses. Perhaps no document connected with this plot throws more light on the character of these informers, and on the manner of *making* up the evidence, than the dying retractation of this unfortunate man. We shall just now insert this retractation in full, from an original printed copy, which is preserved in the Archives of Propaganda.

But it will be useful to premit to it the following extract from a letter of the Archbishop of Cashel, addressed to the Secretary of Propaganda, and dated 1st of May, 1682 :—

"There can be no question of my desire of more frequently corresponding with you; but the sad condition of the times, and continual vexations, did not permit me to regulate myself according to my own desire ; and, though I could not write without danger, I, nevertheless, contrived to send some account from time to time. I sent a narrative about the glorious Primate, and also information of the death, in prison, of the happy confessor of Christ, the Archbishop of Dublin ; of the imprisonment of the Bishop of Kildare (who has been exiled from the kingdom), and cf the Bishop of Cork, who continues as yet in prison. The Bishop of Killaloe has gone to France, where, it is said, he acts as assistant to the Bishop

* Some dispute has arisen as to the true manner of reading this name. In the letters of Dr. Plunket it is invariably written MacClane. It is also thus written in the printed paper of O'Neill, which we are about to cite in the text. The Bishop of Clogher, however, to whose diocese he belonged, and who must, consequently, be considered best acquainted with his real name, and also the Archbishop of Cashel, always wrote it MacLane. The former manner of writing it is in accordance with the common pronunciation of the name. MacClave (as it is written in the printed speech of Dr. Plunket) is a misprint for MacLane; indeed, anyone acquainted with Dr. Plunket's writing will easily understand how the printer could confound the letters *r* and *u*. Sometimes it is difficult, even for the most expert, to distinguish in his writing one from the other. The *MacLegh*, as the name is written in the State Trials, is one of the usual corruptions of Irish names, and evidently owes its origin to the true name M'Lane.

of Rouen. The Bishop of Limerick lives in his district, and is tolerated on account of his advanced old age. God, in His mercy, has begun to console us; for, during the past month of March, the royal judges, being on circuit to examine and bring to a close the criminal and civil cases, and finding, especially in the province of Cashel, many ecclesiastics and lay Catholic gentlemen accused or imprisoned for two or three years on account of the pretended conspiracy, they caused them to be examined and tried, and all were declared to be innocent, and set at liberty; and some of their false accusers were punished. The same happened in other parts of the kingdom, especially in the province of Armagh, where some accused by friar Moyer and his relative were acquitted, and the two accusers once more cast into prison as guilty of other crimes, and they are to receive sentence in the month of August next. Friar Duffy escaped from prison, and it is said that he is now with the bandits, perhaps, as their chieftain. A priest, MacLane, has been sentenced for some robberies, and he is still in prison. Henry O'Neal has been hanged, and on the scaffold declared that all he had said against the Archbishop of Armagh and others was false; and that he was instigated to accuse them by MacLane, friar MacMoyer, and others, who promised him great rewards for his deed. He passed great eulogiums on the Primate, declaring him innocent, and a great prelate; and he avowed that he deemed his own death permitted by Providence in consequence of the sacrilege he committed in accusing the Primate and other innocent victims. The declaration of this good robber has been printed, and is to be found everywhere throughout the kingdom. I wish to mention these accusers in particular, as they were the witnesses who appeared in London against the Primate, and were the cause of his death; and God wished, in a short time, to chastise them all, that thus He might make known his innocence, and their iniquity. These facts remarkably console the Catholics, and cause confusion to many of our adversaries: and we now begin to breathe and hope more than during these four years past. And the Catholics remark, that, since the death of the Primate, matters have changed for the better, and that happy soul receives every day greater veneration from the faithful."

We shall now insert the dying retractation of O'Neal, to which the Archbishop refers, and which is as follows, in the only printed copy to which we have had access * :—

The last speech of Henry O'Neale, one of the late Irish informers who was executed for a certain robbery at Mullingar, the 18th of March, 1681.

"I, Henry O'Neale, do hereby declare, upon the word of a dying man, as I hope for salvation from the God of truth, my Maker and

---

* Archiv. Propag. Fid. *Carte Riscritte*—Irl., vol. iv. It is to be remarked that the italics are copied from the original.

Redeemer, that I never knew of any plot or treasonable contrivances by Irish or English against his Majesty's person or government; and that whatever I did swear, in this kingdom or in England, to discover a popish plot, was first suggested to me in Dublin, above three years since, by one *Hobbert Tyrrell*, before I was examined by *Sir John Davis;* and afterwards I was brought by *Owen Murphy* into England, who made me great promises that we should get great lands and livings by swearing what people would have us swear, saying that whoever gave evidence to prove the popish plot, he should be largely considered by the Parliament for ever; whereupon I, by the instigation of the enemies of my soul, and being in a very needy condition, to relieve myself, and to free my son out of the gaol of Mullingar, promised to discover a plot; but now, in the sight of God, I never did know anything of it, nor would never say, nor could say anything to it, but what I was taught by Mr. *William Hetherington*, *Hobbert Tyrrell*, *Owen Murphy*, *John MacClane*, *MacMoyer*, *fryar Duffey*, *Florence Weyer*, *Hugh Hanlon*, and others, both here and in *England*, all which was falsehood in me, as I now confess before God and the world. The said *John MacClane* often desired me to swear the plot against primate *Plunket*, and, to induce me to do so, he said he would take the sin of it on himself; this was in *Boossin's-Inn* in *London;* and Mr. *Moyer* and the rest of the informers did use to encourage me, saying it was the best act that ever we did, and that we were the happiest men in the nation, by our interest in the Parliament; but I never gave any evidence against the primate, and I hope in God I am innocent of the blood of that good man, although it was my misfortune to be in the company of those that accused him; and truly, upon the words of a dying man, I think in my heart he was altogether innocent of those crimes whereof he was accused, and for which he died. Nay, I say with my last breath, that I am as morally sure of his being really innocent, as I am of my death now. I also protest before God, that what information I gave in against Bishop *Tyrrell*, and what I said of the Vicar *Brady* and others of the *Irish* clergy, was all false; and that I never knew any such thing, but what the aforesaid *John MacClane* instructed me, what evidence I should give in that point, saying he would take the sin of it on himself; and so he sent me to Dublin to discover such things as he suggested to me, and bid me tell, upon my examination, that himself knew those things, and advised me to swear and discover them, which if I should, I should be very considerably rewarded; to which I now, by my last breath, declare and protest, without equivocation, that I never knew even the least tittle or particular of any thing or things relating to an *Irish* plot, but what (as I before mentioned) I have been prompted and instigated to by the aforesaid *John MacClane;* neither do I, or ever did know, of any meeting or meetings of the Popish clergy, but such chapters and meetings as they publicly have, and alwaies had in their own proper affairs. In a word, as I hope to save my soul, I do not believe there was one word but perjury and falsehood in all that was said by as many of the *Irish* informers and discoverers as I conversed with, and employed me in the aforesaid plot: and now I acknowledge, before God, that I have deserved this untimely and shameful end, or worse, by being engaged or any ways concerned in so horrid a design as that false discovery imported. I have, I say, by my sins in general, and particularly by being so active an instrument as I have been in that hellish contrivance, justly incurred God's vengeance. But as to the robbery for which I am sentenced, I call God to witness I am altogether innocent of it, and that I never saw, to my knowledge, either of the two persons who falsely swore it against me, until they came to give evidence against me in the courthouse of *Mullingar*; and that my sons are innocent of that and all other robberies, as far as I know; but I forgive them from the bottom of my heart, and I beseech God to forgive those two witnesses, and all such as procured or suborned them. I forgive all my enemies, and all such as contributed to my death, my judges and juries, as I hope God will forgive me my sins, through the merits of Christ's bitter passion, ⋅ from whom I hope for mercy by the benefit of His death, communicated to me by the participation of His sacraments in the *Roman Catholick* Church, in the bosom of which I die.

" And upon my death, I declare once again, before God and his angels, I say nothing in this my last speech but the truth ; and as to the evidence as Captain *Morley* desired me to give against Sir *John Davis*, I am sorry for it ; and I now declare I had no ground to accuse him, or any other of the nobility or gentry of this nation, either of contriving or concealing any plot. Mr. *Morley* told me he would make me great friends in the House of Lords, and in London ; and some that he recommended me to did maintain me there, and were my friends ; and he told me that what notice was sent down to the North of what I discovered to Sir *John Davis*, must have been sent by Sir *John* himself, but I replied, it might have been sent by *Hobbert Tyrrell*. I often heard our other informers threatening to accuse the *Duke of Ormond*, the Lord Chancellor, Sir *William Davis*, Sir *John Davis*, and others. I have heard *Hetherington*, *George Murphy*, both the *MacNamarons*, Mr. *Ivy*, and fryar *Bernard Dennis* say, that the Duke of *Ormond* was building a new fortification near *Dublin* to command the city, and that he would bring in the French ; and that the said Duke of *Ormond* was as guilty as primate *Plunket*, but I never had anything to say against them, or any of them, and I am sure the rest had as little to say of the truth as I had ; neither do I believe, if there had been any such a thing as a plot contrived or concealed by any considerable persons, that ever it should be made known to any such men as our *Irish* discoverers were. I know nothing of what *Hawkins* is accused of, and, as far as I know, my sons are as ignorant as myself ; all this I would discover to my Lord Lieutenant when I was removed from *Trim* to *Dublin* by a *habeas corpus*, had not one *John Cooper*, attorney, living in *Corn-Market*, next door to the Black *Dog*, obstructed me.

All which I do before the Almighty and the world declare and protest to be true, which, if not truth, I desire I may be excluded from eternal bliss. As witness my hand this 18th day of March, 1681, styl vet. (*i.e.* 1682).

" HENRY O'NEALE.

" Dublin, printed 1682."

The printed text bears the attestation of being a faithful copy of the original, by Alex. Lockhart, ar. Vic. Com. Westmeath.

It is probably to the retractation of this unfortunate man that Dr. Brennan refers, in the following extract from a letter, dated 10th April, 1682 :—

" In the province of Cashel some priests who were accused of high treason during the past month of March, have been liberated and declared innocent by the royal judges. In the province of Armagh three of the informers against the archbishop were condemned for various robberies, and one of them on the scaffold, like Judas, cried out that he had betrayed innocent blood, and often repeated that the Archbishop of Armagh died innocent; and this is a source of great confusion to the wicked, and of consolation to the faithful, seeing that God has thus so soon punished some of the first assassins of our first prelate. But of this, and of other things touching the same matter, I will give a more detailed account in another letter."

Dr. Tyrrell, too, Bishop of Clogher, in a letter, written on the 1st of May, 1682, gives some further particulars in regard of the witness, Maclane, as also of the unfortunate O'Neal, whose retractations we have just read. It is as follows :—

" By a letter of last month, I informed your Excellency of how matters stood in this country; notwithstanding most diligent investigations, I have not been able to obtain any intelligence regarding Patrick O'Daly; no one in this country seems to speak of him, so, I dare say, he has gone to the continent. Some of the accusers of Dr. Plunket, who were also my accusers (their villanies becoming manifest) are falling into disgrace with the government. The priest MacLane, and friar MacMoyer, with his cousin, the parricides of the primate, and my most capital enemies, are already in prison, and a layman, O'Neal, their partizan in the ministry of iniquity has been hanged, having first avowed the falsehood of all that he had sworn against me in regard of the pretended conspiracy, and that Dr. Plunket was innocent of the matters of which he was accused and condemned. This declaration, together with its attestation by the public official, was printed ; and it, as well as the imprisonment of the above wretched perjurers, occasions a little calm and greater tranquillity. But as there are some others of the same stamp as yet in favour, I do not dare to appear in public, but by letters I do all in my power to attend to those entrusted to my care."

Another witness against the Primate was Florence M'Moyer.* He was the head of the family which enjoyed the hereditary right to keep and guard the *Book of Armagh*. Providence, however, so arranged, that in punishment of his guilt he should lose this long-treasured inheritance, and be compelled, through poverty, to part with, for a mere trifle, that precious relic of the early Irish Church. In Sir W. Beetham's *Antiquarian Researches*, vol. ii., p. 254, we find the fac-simile of its last entry:— " Liber Florentini Maire, June 29th, 1662 ; and the following interesting account of the *Book of Armagh*, and of its last *keeper*, is taken from the catalogue of the learned Humphrey Llyhd :—

" This MS., beyond all doubt, is very ancient, whether it be or be not partly in the handwriting of St. Patrick himself (as is stated at the bottom of page 24), but appears very likely to me to be of a later age, and perhaps it is the text of the Gospels, which St. Bernard, in the Life of St. Malachy, reckons amongst the monuments of the see of Armagh, and relates to have been the text of St. Patrick himself. By Ussher and Ware it is called the *Book of Armagh*, and by the Irish the *Book of the Canons of St. Patrick*. This book was formerly held in great estimation by the ancient Irish, so much so, that the family commonly called MacMaor, in English MacMayre, had their names from the custody of this book, for Maor, in Irish, is keeper, and *Maor-na-Ceanon* is keeper of the canons. All that family were commonly so called, and they formerly held from the see of Armagh eight townlands in the county of Armagh, called the lands of Ballymaire, by the tenure of the safe keeping of the book, in whose hands it remained during many ages until Florence MacMayre went to England in the year 1680, that he should give evidence against Oliver Plunket, D.D., the Roman Catholic Primate of Ireland, who, undeservedly, as is believed, was executed. But

* This man is called, in the dying discourse of O'Neal, *Weyer*, and in the State trials *Wyer*. His name in the contemporary records is generally written Moyer, and was pronounced in Irish, as if it were written in English *Wyer*.

Mayre being deficient of money at his death, this manuscript was left as a pledge for five pounds; fortunately it afterwards came to the hands of Arthur Brownlow, Esq."

The *Book of Armagh*, the invaluable relic of the early Irish Church, to which this extract refers, is now safely preserved in the Library of Trinity College, Dublin.

Florence MacMoyre was interred in the graveyard of Ballymyre, which is situated about ten miles south-east from Armagh. To the present day the people hold the unhappy man in the greatest horror. His grave is distinctly marked out, and everyone that passes by flings a stone upon it. A broken headstone of slate formerly stood at the head of the grave, with the words

BODY OF FLORENCE
WYRE, WHO DYED
FEBRUARY 12, 1713.

The upper part of the headstone was broken off. To prevent further injury, a Protestant gentleman of the neighbourhood removed the remaining portion to his house, where it is still preserved.

The character of M'Geoghegan, who was another apostate and informer against the Primate, is clearly traced for us in the letters of the Viceroy, the Duke of Ormond.* In November, 1680, he landed in the county Waterford, and being armed with an order from council, and accompanied by a guard of six horsemen, set to work at once in earnest to fulfil the desires of his employers. But his old occupations (which we have so often described, as forming the preparatory course of these informers) had still so many attractions for him that he sought to combine them with his new mission; and, as Ormond writes, "during his circuit he committed many outrages;" and at length "his violences, excesses, debaucheries, and, in effect, his plain robberies, became so notorious, and occasioned such disturbance throughout the whole country, that he had to be arrested and

* See Carte, vol. ii., p. 514, etc.

2 B

committed to gaol." In a letter of the 29th December, 1680, Ormond thus reviews the history of this witness :—

"We have already sent you a part of MacGeoghan's life and achievements, till he left Ireland and was re-converted by the Bishop of Durham under the name of Dalton. His exploits, since he came over with the authority of the council to take plotters, are many and remarkable, and shall be sent to my Lord Sunderland as soon as the story is completed to his committal to Newgate, where he now is. I send you authentic copies of examinations, which will satisfy anybody that it was not fit to let him to plunder, beat, and imprison whom he pleased, English and Irish, Papists and Protestants, as his fancy, supported by strong ale and wine, should direct him. There is also Owen Murphy, authorized to search for and carry over witnesses, I suppose, to give evidence against Oliver Plunket . . . He has been as far as the county Tipperary, and brought thence about a dozen people not likely to say anything material as to Plunket: so that I believe he takes them upon Eustace Comyn's mad narrative."

Writing a week later, he continues the history of the informers :—

"Mr. Geoghan's history is brought so far that we have thought it time to transmit it to my Lord Sunderland ; and we hope his villainies will appear to be such as will justify his sending to Newgate. Murphy, sent hither to gather witnesses, by virtue of an order of the House of Lords, is ready to embark with those he has picked up. In Hetherington's letter, produced by Murphy, he was advised to good husbandry, and particularly to take none with him but material witnesses, and yet he has taken some from Carrick that profess here that they are able to say nothing of the plot or plotters."

Again, writing on the 9th of January, 1681, he says :—

"This westerly wind has carried over Murphy with a number of witnesses; and Geoghan, since his imprisonment, has accused my Lord Carlingford, Colonel Garrett Moore, and one Nugent, of treason, that the title of king's evidence may not only defend him from punishment here, but help him into England, where he hopes for more favour than here, where he is best known."

The lawless career of this unfortunate man did not terminate with the martyrdom of Dr. Plunket. Returning to Ireland, he visited again the theatre of his former infamous exploits, and resumed his predatory excursions. But the bubble of the Popish plot had now burst, and the

Government no longer needed his perjuries. He was arrested, convicted of being an associate of *the tories*, and condemned to be hanged. Happy was he, however, that his imprisonment gave him time to repent of his wicked career: we shall allow the Archbishop of Cashel to conclude the narrative. On the 30th of June, 1683, he thus writes to the Sacred Congregation :—

" Here we now enjoy more peace than heretofore : but it is feared that this will not continue long, on account of the many religious coming from abroad, who, together with their brethren here, erect too many public chapels and celebrate too publicly even in the cities, where the garrisons, governors, and royal troops are quartered; for which reason many fear that new edicts will be published against us. I send enclosed a copy of a retractation made on the scaffold by three robbers who were leading informers against the Catholics. Friar James Geoghegan, an apostate Franciscan, a cruel persecutor and informer against the Catholics on the occasion of the pretended conspiracy, being confined to prison two years ago, where he still continues, having been convicted as a robber and a thief, at length wrote and subscribed, with his own hand, a retractation of all that he had deposed and sworn against the Catholics in regard of the conspiracy; and the paper thus signed by him was committed to the parish priest of the place, who now holds it, and exhorted the penitent to renew this retractation in the presence of some minister or royal agent."

In another letter, of the 1st September, 1684, he again writes :—

" I have been informed that James Geoghegan, a Franciscan apostate, was lately hanged. He was the most violent informer against the Catholics in these parts ; he afterwards turned robber, and during the past four years was detained in prison. I cannot be certain of his execution, as he was kept in the Dublin province. This event has given great consolation to the Catholics, and confusion to their adversaries; and, therefore, I have deemed it proper to communicate the intelligence to your Excellency, as I doubt not it will be gratifying to you."

In the paper of O'Neal, which we inserted above, a certain MacNamara is named as instigator and prompter of those who were to act as witnesses. In a few years he too met with a fate well deserved by his wickedness, whilst at the same time the prayers of those he persecuted obtained for him the grace of repentance. We shall describe the close of his career in the words of the Archbishop of Cashel * :—

"On the 24th of August, just passed, John MacNamara, a layman, was hanged at Waterford; he was a famous informer against the Catholics at the time of the pretended conspiracy. Before that conspiracy, he was always a Catholic, but he became a Protestant to acquire greater credit and authority in London, on his going to that city, where he presented to the king and parliament a narrative of the conspiracy, printed and subscribed by him, and in it amongst other ecclesiastics and laymen, he also accused me. But finding that matters had assumed a different aspect in England, and that the art of the informer had become discredited, he returned to Ireland, where he became a public robber (he was, indeed, always supposed to be a thief), and at length, together with other bandits, he was arrested and sentenced to death; whilst he was in prison he became a penitent, and died a Catholic. He declared at the public sessions, and in presence of the royal judges, that all his informations against the Catholics, whether in England or in Ireland, were false, and that he was instigated to give such informations by certain perverse heretics, enemies of the king and of the Catholics, who had bribed him with money, and he named the individuals. He confirmed all this whilst he was upon the scaffold, where he read a paper containing such a retractation, and he afterwards gave that paper to the royal officer who assisted at his execution.".

From the *Apologie pour les Catholiques*, written by Dr. A. Arnaud, and published at Liège in 1682, we learn that a certain *Denis*, who was brought to England to confirm parson Oates' story, accused Dr. Plunket of plotting the overthrow of the English rule in Ireland. In his evidence he described himself as bearer of a letter in 1677 from Oates to the Archbishop of Tuam in Madrid : the Archbishop having read the letter in his presence, immediately remarked, "Oates wishes to be ordained; he will be useful to us; for Dr. Plunket, the Primate of Ireland, has resolved to introduce, on the first opportunity, French troops into Ireland, to support the English and Irish Catholics ; and please God, I will go there myself to assist in accomplishing so holy a work." It is sufficient to have this tale connected with the *Oates' plot*, to reveal its true origin, and the object which its perjured concoctors most iniquitously proposed to themselves.

* See letter already referred to, 1st September, 1684.

On the 8th of June, 1681, Dr. Plunket was placed upon his trial before an English jury in Westminster, charged with overt deeds of high treason committed in Ireland. Such a course was contrary to the standing laws of the realm, and without a parallel in the history of England. Moreover, there was something peculiarly outrageous in sending his case for trial to a London jury; it was nothing less than to hand over the good prelate to sworn enemies, who were thirsting for his blood; it was to procure credence for his perjured accusers, removing them from the country where their perjuries and crimes were known, and where Protestant juries had already refused to receive their sworn testimony; it was also, in the then existing circumstances, to deprive the accused of the possibility of defence, and to oblige him to answer the highest charge against the crown before a court where there could be no witnesses in his favour, no evidence of his innocence.

In the "narrative" of the Archbishop of Cashel, to which already we have so often had occasion to refer, we find briefly recapitulated the various accusations made against the Primate, and at the same time many incidents of his trial :—

"The judges being arrived in court, the accused was placed at the bar, and the indictment read. In the first place he was accused of writing letters to Monsig. Baldeschi, Secretary of the Pope, to the Bishop of Aix, to Prince Colonna, and Cardinal de Bouillon, soliciting them to procure and send aid into Ireland, in order to establish there the Catholic religion and to destroy the Protestants; and in the depositions made against him in Ireland, the apostate friar affirmed that the accused wrote letters to the Pope to the same effect, and that, whilst he himself (the friar) was in Rome, he saw in the hands of Dr. Creagh a letter of the primate to Monsig. Baldeschi, in which he assured him that there were 60,000 men to advance the cause, and that naught was wanting to them but arms.

"Secondly: that he had sent an Irish captain to the King of France, inviting him to send an army into Ireland, and take possession of this kingdom.

"Thirdly: that he had enrolled 70,000 soldiers to unite with the French on their arrival here.

"Fourthly: that he exacted money from the clergy to introduce the French and pay the army.

"Fifthly: that he had visited all Ireland, and examined and explored all the seaport towns and fortresses of the kingdom, in order to introduce the French by a secure port.

"Sixthly: that he had held many synods and meetings, in which a collection was ordered to supply funds for the French.

"These and other heads of accusation were affirmed with sacrilegious oath by John Moyer and Duffy, both, it is said, apostate students of St. Isidore's, who, in addition to these articles of high treason, declared that the primate had appointed some soldiers to enter England clandestinely and assassinate the king.

"The indictment and the aforesaid heads of accusation being read, and the accusers having been examined, the counsel for the crown employed all their deceitful eloquence against the accused. The judges then intimated to the accused to reply to the charges made against him. He stated, that he had already been accused, and had pleaded his cause before the royal court in Ireland, which was the place of his birth and residence, and the scene of the pretended crimes; and that it seemed hard, and without a parallel in past ages, that such a case should be tried in England; and that at least he should be enabled to make his defence by deferring the trial for ten days, in which time his witnesses would arrive; but his petition would not be listened to, and he was compelled to defend himself as best he could.

"He therefore declared, first, that the whole indictment was a mere romance, fabricated by his enemies, who had been chastised by him for their wicked life: second, that he had never written a letter to Monsig. Baldeschi on matters of state, nor any letter whatsoever to the Bishop of Aix, Prince Colonna, or Cardinal Bouillon; and that the English translation of the latter produced against him by Moyer was a mere invention: third, that he had never explored the kingdom, or examined the fortresses or seaports mentioned; fourth, that he had never sent an agent or letter to any part of the world to procure assistance of soldiers and money; fifth, that he had never held synods or assemblies excepting for affairs of the clergy without treating of affairs of state: sixth, that he had never even dreamt of enrolling soldiers or setting on foot an army of 70,000 soldiers, or even of two soldiers; and that it was clear that all the power of the king could not call into existence such an army in Ireland, and that all the revenue of the kingdom would not suffice to maintain it; that all the priests of the kingdom could not maintain 500 soldiers (he might have said 100), and that his statements would be surely accredited by the judges and other lawyers in Ireland acquainted with the condition of the country and persons.

" But all this did not suffice to make the judges understand the truth of his discourse and his innocence. They gave credence rather to the sacrilegious swearing of two enemies of the accused, who procured four of their friends, vile and infamous men, never seen or known by the accused, to ratify all that they had affirmed.

" It was not without interested views that these men apostatized from the faith and renounced all honesty, for having declared themselves informers of the pretended conspiracy, they obtained a royal pardon for their past crimes (for they were wicked men), and sums of money to maintain themselves as gentlemen. In fine, on the evidence of these wicked men he was declared guilty of treason on the 8th of June, 1681, and on the 14th of the same month was sentenced to be hanged and quartered—which is the punishment of treason.

" The primate, on hearing the sentence, and seeing his innocence, condemned to so infamous a death, displayed a dignified composure, and did not lose even one quarter of an hour of his usual repose, as he himself writes, being comforted by his innocence and the justice of the Supreme Judge.

" From the court he was reconducted to prison, where, during fifteen days, he proved himself wholly master of himself, and superior to all the adversities of the world, employing his time in prayer and mortification, and in exhortations to the faithful to persevere in the true faith, and to bear with patience the present tribulation : and he himself gave to everyone the example of a worthy prelate, so that even the guards of the prison remained confused and edified.

" He writes with sentiments of the greatest piety regarding the solicitude and charity displayed by the Catholics of London in his regard, especially from the time that his case was brought to trial, when they were allowed to visit him. They collected amongst themselves a sum of money to pay the counsel and others employed to procure a prorogation of the trial, and to have the execution of the sentence deferred. But this being in vain, they, with a more than ordinary charity and zeal, collected 200 crowns for his funeral expenses, and another sum for the expenses of the witnesses in their return to Ireland, and other expenses that might occur."

According to the truly barbarous policy of the law in the seventeenth century (and, indeed, the same law was enforced till a very late period), no person accused of treason was allowed the assistance of counsel, unless in the case that some purely legal question should arise during the trial. Hence, Dr. Plunket now stood alone at the bar to plead his cause, before judges who seemed to vie with each other in their partiality for the perjured witnesses, and in their animosity against the accused ; whilst, at the same time, the jury had naught to guide them in their decision but the long concocted evidence of these perjurers.

The judges on the trial were the Lord Chief Justice, Sir Francis Pemberton, and Judges Dolbein and Jones, more than one of whom had already imbued his hands in the blood of glorious champions of the faith. As an instance of the ferocity which they displayed against Dr. Plunket, we may remark, that on the panel being called, and the accused being desired to challenge whomsoever he thought fit, Dr. Plunket said :— " My lord, I desire to know whether they have been of the juries of Loughorn, or the five Jesuits, or any that were condemned ? " to which he received for answer, from the Chief Justice : " What if they have ? That is no exception." Again, when, at the close of the first witness's evidence, Dr. Plunket interrogated why, if all he had said were true, he had never, during the past seven years given any notice to Government of this plot ? the Chief Justice, seeing the witness somewhat perplexed, suggested to him an answer, saying : " Of what religion were you then ? " and the witness replying, " A Roman Catholic," Justice Dolbein at once added, " Therefore it will be no wonder that you did not discover the plot."

On the 3rd of May, 1681, in Easter Term, Dr. Plunket had already been arraigned at the King's Bench bar for high treason, but thirty-five days were then allowed him to procure witnesses for his defence. This interval, indeed, might now-a-days suffice, when steam has lent its aid to our modes of conveyance; but it was far from being sufficient at the time of which we treat, when the servants whom the Archbishop dispatched to Ireland took fourteen days from Holyhead to Dublin. Another difficulty which the accused had to encounter was the want of the necessary means to defray the expenses of such witnesses, but this was rendered comparatively easy through the charitable contributions of his Catholic friends : there were, however, some other difficulties which were, indeed, insurmountable. For instance, the officers of the Irish courts refused to give the records of the conviction of MacMoyer and his associates, alleging that the transmission of such documents to an English court would be a violation of the privileges of the Irish nation ; and yet, on the trial, when Dr. Plunket declared the guilty character of his accusers, the judges told him that his assertions were all in vain, unless he produced the records of their conviction. Again, the witnesses who might attest his innocence, and disprove the assertions of his enemies, could not easily be induced to set out for England, where it was more than probable that they themselves would be imprisoned, and brought to the scaffold by the same hired perjurers of the court. Nevertheless, such were the exertions of his friends, that, on the appointed day of trial, a sufficient number of witnesses had arrived in Coventry. On being placed at the bar, Dr. Plunket petitioned that a few days more should be granted to enable these witnesses to arrive, and in feeling terms showed the injustice he was subjected to, and the impossibility in which he was placed of making a proper defence, as those who knew his case had not arrived in London, and copies of the records necessary to establish the infamy of his accusers had been refused by the Irish courts.

But he appealed for justice in vain. The court was inexorable ; and the trial was ordered to proceed without delay. From the speeches made at its opening by Sergeant Maynard and the Attorney-General, Sir Robert Sawyer, it is sufficiently clear that the object of the Government in this trial was to fan the flame of Protestant fanaticism, and evoke against the Catholics the bigotry and passions of the mob.

The former said :—

" You have heard his charge ; it is as high as can be against the king, and against the nation, and against all that is good. The design and endeavours of this gentleman was the death of the king, and the destruction of the Protestant religion in Ireland, and the raising of war. . . . Dr. Plunket was made, as we shall prove to you, as they there called him, Primate of Ireland ; and he got that dignity from the Pope upon this very design."

And the Attorney-General, amongst other things, likewise said :—

"The character this gentleman bears as primate, under a foreign and usurped jurisdiction, will be a great inducement to you to give credit to that evidence we shall produce before you. We shall prove that this very preferment was conferred upon him upon a contract that he would raise 60,000 men in Ireland for the Pope's service, to settle Popery there, and to subvert the Government."

Even the Lord Chief Justice, when passing sentence, betrayed the same sentiments and hatred of the Catholic religion.

"Truly yours [he thus addressed Dr. Plunket] is treason of the highest nature ; it is treason, in truth, against God, and your king, and the country where you lived. You have done as much as you could to dishonour God in this case ; for the bottom of your treason was your setting up your false religion, than which there is not anything more displeasing to God or more pernicious to mankind in the world. A religion that is ten times worse than all the heathenish superstitions ; the most dishonourable and derogatory to God and His glory of all religions or pretended religions whatsoever, for it undertakes to dispense with God's laws and to pardon the breach of them. So that, certainly, a greater crime there cannot be committed against God than for a man to endeavour the propagation of that religion."

Thus did his lordship, from his seat of injustice, rail against the religion of his fathers, the heavenly religion which civilized the Christian world ; and thus did he stigmatize as treason against the king, precisely as the agents of Nero and Domitian were wont to do of old, the preaching and propagation of the Catholic faith.

The swearing in of the witnesses was in full accordance with these sentiments of the court, and must surely have fully satisfied the most sanguine expectations of their patrons, the Protestant Bishop of Meath, Dr. Jones, and the Earl of Shaftesbury. The first witness called was Florence MacMoyer. He swore as follows :—

"I knew there was a plot both before Plunket's time and in his time, for it was working in the years 1665 and 1666 ; but it was brought to full maturity in 1667. For then Colonel Miles O'Reilly and Colonel Bourne (Burns) were sent to Ireland from the King of

France, with a commission to muster as many men as they could, promising to send an army of 40,000 men, with a commission, upon St. Lewis's day, in August following, to land in Carlingford, to destroy all the true subjects, to destroy the religion as it was established there, and to set up the French king's authority and the Roman Catholic religion. And one Edmund Aryle, that was a justice of the peace and a clerk of the crown, sent for all the rebels abroad in the north to come up into the County of Longford; and they marched into the head town of the county, and fired the town. The inhabitants fled into the castle. Then they came up to the gaol thinking to break it open, and by setting the prisoners free to join them with them; but there Aryle was shot, received a deadly wound, and dropt off his horse, and they fled. So, then, when they were without the town, one Charles MacCanal alighted and took away all the papers out of his pocket, which, if they had been found, would have discovered all. This occasioned Colonel Brown to be suspected, and being so suspected, he was taken prisoner, and turned to Newgate in Dublin. Then Colonel Reilly fled away again to France, and the plot lay under a cloud during the life of Primate Reilly, the prisoner's predecessor. This Primate Reilly died beyond the sea. Then many of the Popish religion would have had the primacy conferred upon one Duffy, but the prisoner at the bar put in for it; which might have been opposed if the prisoner had not engaged and promised that he would so manage affairs, that before the present government were aware, he would surprise the kingdom, provided the Pope and King of France would send a competent army to join with theirs for the effecting of it. So the first year of his coming over I was in the Friary of Armagh : I was an acquaintance of the Friars, and they invited me; and one Quinn told the prisoner that they thought Duffy would have been primate. Said he, it is better as it is; for Duffy hath not the wit to do those things that I have undertaken to do ; meaning that he did undertake to supplant the Protestant religion to bring in Popery, and put the kingdom under subjection to the King of France. In his assembly kept by him, he charged his inferiors to collect such several sums of money as he thought fit, according to the several parishes and dignitaries, to assist and supply the French forces when they came over. I have seen the money collected, and I have seen his warrant, *sub pœna suspensionis*, to bring it in to redeem their religion from the power of the English Government. And he procured the MacDonnels a piece of money out of the exchequer, pretending to do good service to his majesty ; but he sent them to France, meaning they should improve themselves, and bring themselves into favour with the King of France, and come over with the French king to surprise Ireland. This one of the rebels told me. So I have seen the prisoner's letter, directed to the grand tory Fleming, desiring that they should go to France, and he would see them, in spite of all their enemies in Ireland, safe ashore, and Fleming should return again a colonel, to his own glory and the good of his country. I have seen the prisoner going about from port to port—to Derry, to Carrickfergus, Corily' Down, and Carlingford, and all about. I heard it among the Church, that he went on purpose to view the seaports, to know the strength of all the garrisons, to see which was the most convenient way to bring in the French army."

The Chief Justice asked, " What place did he pitch on as most convenient?" to which the witness replied, "Carlingford."

On the conclusion of his evidence, Dr. Plunket being interrogated, whether he wished to ask any questions, said :—

" He says, my lord, that ten years ago I had such a design in hand, and he knew the money was collected for these very ends, and that I had a design to bring in the French at Carlingford, and went about to all the ports in Ireland, and pitched upon that as the most convenient ; and yet it is so inconvenient for the bringing in a foreign force, that any one that knows anything of the maps of the world will easily conclude it otherwise. But I say, my lord, why did he not tell some justice of the peace that I was upon such a design, but let me live in Ireland for ten years after, and never speak of it till now ? When he saw me all the time, and to the time of my taking prisoner, and never said one word : for I was a prisoner six months, only for my religion, not one word of treason spoken of against me for so many years ; why did he not acquaint some justice of the peace of it before ?"

Then the scene ensued to which we have already referred ; the Chief Justice and Justice Dolbein suggested to the prisoner the answer which they knew would be most satisfactory to his hearers, that forsooth, he himself was at that time a papist, and MacMoyer continued :—

" I was a papist myself ; the first that did discover it ; Friar Moyer and I did consult about it ; I had him charged to do so, and I had set him to work ; but he was ill-paid for having discovered it, you got him to be trepanned, that he hath gone in danger of his life for it."

Henry O'Neal's evidence was short, and principally directed against the saintly Bishop of Clogher, Dr. Tyrrell ; amongst other things, however, he swore that he had never seen the Primate in his life, which confirms Dr. Plunket's own assertion, that, as to the four laymen who appeared against him, *he had never before seen them.*

Neal O'Neale almost repeated the words of the preceding witness : and Owen Murphy, who was next produced, in fact gave no evidence at all.

Hugh Duffy, however, more than supplied all that was wanting in these witnesses' evidence. On being sworn, he said :—

"I have seen this Dr. Oliver Plunket raising several sums of money to carry on this plot ; sometimes 10s. per annum, sometimes 20s. of all the priests in Ireland, of every priest according to his pension and parish. It was given to his agent in Rome for carrying on this business. I was chaplain to Dr. Duffy, who was infinitely beloved by this man. He was father confessor to the Queen of Spain. There was nothing that happened between them but I was by all the time."

Being asked what was their conversation about, he replied :—

"About the plot : how they could confirm the plot : and this man, Plunket, said he could prevail with the King of France, and the other with the King of Spain. This was in 1673, '74, '75, at his own house* . . . He kept three or four Jesuits there, and a matter of a hundred priests. The discourse was always about the plot, how they could continue the matter between them ; and so they did conclude afterwards to raise so much money upon several priests, all the priests in Ireland, sometimes 20s., sometimes 40s. He talked several times that he did not question but he should prevail with the King of France not to invade Spain : and I have seen his letter to Cardinal Bouillon to expostulate with him about the King of France, why he should wage war with the King of Spain, who was a Catholic, but rather should come and redeem Ireland out of its heretical jurisdiction."

Being asked as to the raising of money, he replied :—

"I have seen several precepts : I was curate to one Father Murphy, and while that man was with Dr. Oliver Plunket and the other Jesuits, I did officiate in his place, and he sent his letters to me to raise 40s. and 20s. a time, several times. It was to send to Dr. Creagh, who was at Rome."

---

* That name is omitted. It was the seminary opened by Dr. Plunket in 1671, and in which there were three Jesuits, with about 150 students, many of whom were sons of the Protestant gentry.

Then in regard to the meetings, he adds that he was present at one

" At Clones, in the County of Monaghan, on the occasion of the confirmation from the bishop, about 1671. It was there agreed that the gentlemen of Armagh, Monaghan, and Cavan should join together, and then they went into a private council to get a list of all the officers that were in the last rebellion, and those that lost their estates. I was in the same consult myself, and was as willing to proceed in the matter as any one in the world. They were withdrawn aside into a garden—some stood up, and some sat down ; and Oliver Plunket stood in the middle of them all as a prelate, and everyone kneeled down before him and kissed his hand. Then they did consult, and gave special order to some of them to get a list of all the officers in the late rebellion, and that lost their estates, and that they should be more forward than others to proceed in that wicked design to destroy all the Protestants together."

Being asked if he heard the prisoner speak on these matters, he replied :—" Yes, and he made a special mention there concerning our own faith and religion." He afterwards swore that he had received a precept from Dr. Plunket to know what men in his district were able to bear arms : that he had accompanied Dr. Plunket to Carlingford, and that there

" He went round about the place where some of the custom ships come in ; there was a great castle there near the sea, and he went to view the place. but could not get a boat. And there was great talk of Carlingford to be one of the best havens in Ireland; there was no great garrison at the place, and any ship might come to the gates of the town and surprise it, it being a little town ; and he concluded thence that he could get the French army to land safely there."

He afterwards added :—

" I have been at Sir Nicholas Plunket's, where there fell some variance about something this man had done to Dr. Duffy. Says Bishop Duffy, I might have had you drawn and quartered if I were as ill a man as you ; and I might have been Primate of Ireland if I would have undertaken those things that you undertook. Upon that, says Sir Nicholas Plunket, What is that ? Why, it was replied. it was to raise 60,000 men in Ireland at any time, whenever the French or the Spanish King should wage war with England. And this man did confess, before my face, to Dr. Duffy, that it was not only to exalt himself, but all the Romish clergy, and all the gentry that had lost their estates."

The concluding question, however, put to this wretched man by Dr. Plunket sufficiently explains all this virulence of his evidence against him :—" Mr. Duffy, one word with you : is not this out of malice to me for correcting some of the clergy ?"

Edmund Murphy was next sworn ; and the Attorney-General on finding that he hesitated in his evidence, declared that in his private examination " he had given the fullest evidence to all instances and particulars of high treason, much fuller than Duffy." But all exhortations to him to proceed in his evidence were in vain. At first he begged the Chief Justice to " respite the trial till next term ;" he then declared that he forgot the evidence he had given on former occasions ; and, when interrogated in detail, belied the various particulars which he had before sworn to, till, at length, the Lord Chief Justice exclaimed, " It is evident the Catholics have been tampering with him ;" and at the desire of the counsel for the crown, in order to strike terror into the other witnesses, who, might, perhaps, in like manner, be desirous of listening to the dictates of conscience, he commanded him to be at once committed to Newgate.

John Maclane then gave his evidence. He said :—

" I was a parish priest in Ireland, in the county of Monaghan, and Dr. Oliver Plunket raised several sums of money in Ireland, and especially in the diocese where I am. I raised some of it, and paid him 40s. at one time, and 30s. at another time ; in 1674 I paid him 40s. ; in 1675 I paid him 50s., and it was about July, and it was for the better advancement of the French coming in. The money was to be kept for arms and ammunition for the Roman Catholics in Ireland. I received an order, *sub pœna suspensionis*, and there was a public order throughout Ireland, or we would not pay it ; nay, several would not pay it, and they were to be suspended.'' Dr. Plunket here asked him :—" Can you show any of the orders under my hand ?" to which he replied :—" Yes, I can show them, but only they are afar off. I did not expect to have them asked for."*

---

* As Maclane did not belong to the diocese of the Primate, it was manifest that he could not have received any such mandate from Dr. Plunket ; to account, however, for this, the witness added this novel theory :—" You being lord primate, you could suspend bishops and inferior clergy together."

He then swore that when he was at Vicar Brady's house,

" Bishop Tyrrell came there with forty horsemen well mounted
and armed; he came into the house about ten in the morning, and
stayed till about eleven at night: I was very much among them,
and as willing to be of the plot as themselves. Then Bishop Tyrrell
said he had orders from Dr. Oliver Plunket and others, to partake
of the plot to bring in the French, and subvert the Government in
Ireland, and to destroy the Protestant religion and Protestants."

He added :—

" In France I landed at Brest, and going through Brittany. I met
with Bishop Tyrrell and Dr. Creagh, who was my lord Oliver
Plunket's agent, and Duke John, of Great Brittany, came unto
them, for he heard of these two bishops being lately come out of
Rome, sent for them, and I being a priest of Tyrrell's diocese, I
went along with them, and they were well accepted, and he showed
Dr. Oliver Plunket's conditions with the king of France, which was
this: to get Dublin and Londonderry, and all the sea ports
into their own hands, to levy war, and destroy the Protestant
religion ; and that they should have him to protect them during his
lifetime."

The Chief Justice interrogated him :—

" What do you know of his being primate?"

He replied :—

" He was made primate by the election of the king of France, and
upon his election he made those conditions with the king of France,
to raise men to join with the French, to destroy the Protestant
religion."

The last leading witness was the ex-friar Moyer. He
declared :—

" I knew the prisoner, my lord, to be made primate of Ireland,
engaging that he should propagate the Romish faith in Ireland, and
to restore it to the Catholic government ; and I know the time by
relation that I came to Rome, within two months after his being
made primate of Ireland, upon the same conditions that have been
related to you; and I was brought into the convent of St. Francis
in Rome, by one Father ——, and this father was very intimate with
Cardinal Spinola ; and when he used to go abroad, he used to carry
me along with him as a companion, and then I found several of the
Romish Cardinals say, that the kingdom of Ireland should come
under the Catholic government by the way and means of the **Lord**
Primate Plunket."

He then produced a copy of a letter of Dr. Plunket which he

"Translated five years ago, and here are the contents following; if you please, they may be read; I will do my best to read them in English, the original were in Latin, and some phrases in Italian. And when I was surprised with Mr. Murphy last year, and taken suddenly, all my papers were taken away before I could return back again, by the soldiers and the tories. I only kept a copy of this letter I had in English, as near as I could, and if I did not diminish anything by the translation, upon the oath I have taken, I have not put anything in it but what the contents of the letter were."

The letter is then said to have been read, but is not given; we can, however, gather its contents from the subsequent examination; that it was addressed to the Secretary of Propaganda; that it destined a sum for the agent in Rome, and Moyer, by the addition of a *zero*, changed that sum from £50 to £500. Dr. Plunket here declared that the sum destined for the agent in Rome was £50; and added :—

"There is never a nation where the Roman Catholic religion is professed, but hath an agent for their spiritual affairs at Rome, and this was for the spiritual affairs of the clergy of Ireland. I deny nothing; *that* is a truth; every nation hath an agent, and that agent must be maintained; and the reason is this, because we have many colleges beyond sea, and so there is no country of Roman Catholics but hath an agent at Rome."

Moyer then swore to the various other heads; the planning of the invasion of Ireland by the French, the collecting of money for that purpose, the exploring the country, &c., and that these matters had been committed to him as a secret by the Primate himself. Being asked in what year this took place, he replied :—

"In 1676, and I being willing that this wicked action should be hindered, *sent to the next justice to discharge myself of it, which justice was as favourable to the business as my lord himself was.*"

Before the conclusion of this witness's evidence, Dr. Plunket produced two letters of the friar. The first was addressed to "My Reverend Father Anthony, Guardian of

2 c

Armagh," and was dated 1st July, 1678. It thus commenced :—

" VERY REV. FATHER GUARDIAN,—Your paternal letter and citation homeward I did instantly peruse. As for my lord Oliver Plunket, I wrote a letter to him the day before I saw your reverence last, that he might cause my fame, which is as dear to me as my life, to be recalled, or I should cause his name to be fixed at every public place, which, by the Almighty, I will do, nature and all reason compelling me to do it."

No more of this letter is given in the state trials, but we learn the remainder of it from the subsequent words of Dr. Plunket :—

" My lord, I say this : he says he came to my house when he came over, and I imparted this secret to him ; yet you see I had denounced him through my whole diocese, and he there calls me by all those names of Elymas, Simon Magus, and Barjesus ; and it is impossible, if I had communicated to him such a secret, that I would deal so with him."

The second letter was dated the 23rd of April, 1678, and was addressed, in like manner, to the father Guardian :—

" I was somewhat comforted by your letter. But now I hope your reverence hath considered what wrong I have sustained by my curious adversaries' calumnies, only for standing, as I have a soul to save, for your rights and privileges, as also for endeavouring to save my native country's ruin and destruction."

As to the remainder, it is said that the witness " read on :" but the letter is not given, and we can only gather from the subsequent discourse, that he stated in it that Dr. Plunket " had fallen into disgrace in Rome." The object of Dr. Plunket in producing these letters was to show the malignity and animosity which this apostate friar bore against him, on account of his having checked his reckless career.

On the Chief Justice asking Dr. Plunket what he had to say in his defence, he replied :—

" My lord, I tell you I have no way to defend myself ; as I have been denied time to bring over my records and my witnesses, ten or twelve in number. Were they here, or were I in Ireland, where both my accusers and I should be known, I would defy all the malice of the world; but when I was to be tried in Ireland, they would not appear, knowing that their statements were false and malicious. These men used to call me Oliver Cromwell out of spite."

The Chief Justice then having recapitulated the heads of the accusations, Dr. Plunket replied to the various charges made against him, pointing out their absurdity and improbability, and proving in a way calculated to convince every impartial hearer, that his accusers were perjurers, and merely animated by a fell spirit of avarice and revenge. He concluded by protesting again that in his present circumstances, without witnesses and records, it was impossible for him to make a proper defence.

The recapitulation of the evidence by the Solicitor-General and Sergeant Jeffries followed, replete with envenomed remarks against the Archbishop and the Catholic religion. Scarce had Sergeant Jeffries concluded, when a stranger stepping forward in the court handed a paper to Dr. Plunket. It contained the names of witnesses who might be called in his defence, and the crier at once read aloud the names; "David Fitzgerald, Eustace Commines, and Paul Gorman;" but Gorman alone appeared, and besides the declaration that he "thought Dr. Plunket did more good in Ireland than hurt, and that he never heard of any misdemeanour of him," the only matter of importance which he avowed was that "friar Moyer, when in discourse with him, said, if there was law to be had in Ireland, he would show Mr. Plunket his share in it."

On the Lord Chief Justice delivering his charge to the jury, Dr. Plunket once more declared :—

"I can say nothing to it, but give my own protestation that there is not one word of what is said against me true, but all plain romance; I never had any communication with any French minister, cardinal, nor other."

The jury without delay came to their decision, and the foreman announcing "Guilty," Dr. Plunket exclaimed, "*Deo gratias*," thanks be to God

Whilst all England was excited to the highest pitch of
fanaticism, and ready to believe every absurd story regarding Catholics, it cannot surprise us that the jury should
have come to such a decision ; and surely any twelve men
ignorant¦ of the character of the accusers, and therefore
judging them to be honourable men, and who, at the same
time, had been taught to recognise in the very fact of the
accused being Roman Catholic Primate of Ireland a *prima
facie* evidence of his treasonable designs, could, with difficulty, have come to a contrary conclusion.   But whosoever,
after reading the preceding chapters, reviews the concocted
testimony of these wretched men, will easily detect not only
evidence of their malignant enmity against the Primate, but,
moreover, manifest indications of the falsehood of their tale.
Thus, to say nothing of the monstrous accusations of preparing a fund for the maintenance of an army of 60,000
men at a time when Dr. Plunket wrote those beautiful
letters which we have seen, and which reveal to us the
extreme indigence to which he and his fellow-prelates were
reduced, and the sad destitution of the Catholics of Ireland,
it is MacMoyer himself, an associate and a leader of a tory
band, who inculpates the tories as having carried away his
papers, whilst the other witnesses were obliged to have
recourse to other like *accidents*, in order to account for the
absence of the document to which they referred, and which
should have been produced :—then, again, the appointment
of Dr. Plunket is sworn to have originated with the French
king, in order to advance his designs of conquest :—another
witness declares the extent of his authority to be to suspend
at his pleasure all bishops and priests throughout Ireland,
who would not contribute to the national fund :—by another,
the sending of a band of tories to France is made a proof of
his treason ; though, in reality, it was the Lord Lieutenant
who had thus removed them from the kingdom, after the
Archbishop had induced them to submit, and obtained the
thanks of the Government as well as of the nation for his
paternal endeavours in their regard.   The seminary at

which the children of many of the Protestant gentry were educated, is made a sort of standing council for deliberating on the best means of extirpating all the Protestants and changing the Government. It is said that he destined Carlingford to be the landing-place of the French ; and yet Florence MacMoyer swore that it was thus destined in 1667, two years before Dr. Plunket was consecrated to the see of Armagh ; that port, too, is extolled by the witnesses; and the Solicitor-General in his recapitulation styles it " a very large port, in which ships of the largest burden may come up ;" whilst, as we learn from the Archbishop of Cashel, and other sources, it was then, as it is now, a most miserable and insignificant little port ; in fine, MacMoyer inculpates the justice before whom he first accused the Primate, as being an accomplice in these treasonable designs, because he refused to receive his evidence ; and yet the Duke of Ormond refused, in like manner, to receive it ; and the Protestant juries not only refused to credit his sworn testimony, but instead of the accused, condemned himself to prison on account of his notorious crimes. But these things being all unknown, perhaps, to the twelve citizens of London, who sat in judgment to try Dr. Plunket for the highest crime of which he could stand accused before the law ; without a dissentient voice—almost without delibera-tion, they pronounced him *guilty*.

The verdict being recorded, the court arose. On the 14th of June, 1681, Dr. Plunket was again brought to the bar to receive judgment in accordance with that verdict. On leave being given to speak, Dr. Plunket again pointed out the difficult position in which he had been placed, refuted the charges made against him, and proved the wickedness and malice of his accusers :—

" My lord, may it please your lordship, I have something to say which, if your lordship will consider seriously, may occasion the commiseration and mercy. I have, my lord, for the offences with which I am now charged, been already arraigned in Ireland. At the day fixed for my trial there, my accusers voluntarily absented them-selves, seeing I had records and witnesses to convict them, and to show what men they were, and the prepensed malice that they did bear to me ; and, so, finding that I could clear myself evidently, they absconded; from that day no one appeared against me in Ireland : but, hither they came and procured that I should be brought where I could not have a jury that knew the qualities of my adversaries, or who knew me, or the circumstances of the places, times, or persons. The jury here, as I say, consisting of strangers to these affairs, my lord, they could not know many things that conduce to a fair trial ; it was morally impossible they should know them.

"I have been accused principally and chiefly for surveying the ports, for fixing upon Carlingford for the landing of the French, for the having of 70,000 men ready to join the French, for collecting money for the agents in this matter, for assisting the French, and enlisting this great utopian army. A jury in Ireland, consisting of men that lived in that country, would immediately understand the folly of such charges, and any man in the world that hath but seen Ireland in a map, would easily see there was no probability that Carlingford should be a place fit for the French to land in. Though never in Ireland, yet by the map he would see the invaders must come by the narrow seas all along to Ulster, exposed to rocks and every other danger, for the purpose of landing at Carlingford, which is a poor town and of no strength, with a very bad harbour, and with a very small garrison, which had not been so if it had been a place of any consideration.

" And then I had influence only upon one province, as is well known, though I had the title of Primate of all Ireland, as the Archbishop of Canterbury hath of all England, though the Archbishop of York did not permit him to meddle with his province ; and it is well known by the gentry there, and those that are accustomed to the place, that in all the province of Ulster, take men, women, and children of the Roman Catholics, they would not supply 70,000. This a jury on the spot, my lord, would have known very well : therefore, the laws of England, which are very favourable to the prisoner, have provided that there should be a jury of the place where the offence was committed, as Sir Thomas Gascoigne, as I have heard, had a Yorkshire jury, though he was tried at London.

" After my coming here, I was kept a close prisoner for six months ; no one was permitted to come to me, nor did I know how things stood in the world. I was brought here the 3rd of May to be arraigned, and I did petition your lordships to have some time to prepare for my trial, proposing to have it put off till Michaelmas, but your lordships did not think fit to grant so long, but only till the middle of this month. In the meantime my witnesses, who were ready at the seaside, would not come over without passes ; and I could not get over the records without an order from hence, which records would have shown that some of the accusers were indicted in Ireland, and found guilty of high crimes ; some having been imprisoned for robberies, and others being men of infamous character ;

so I petitioned, the 8th of this month, that I might have time for but twelve days more ; but your lordships, when the motion was made, thought that it was only to put off my trial, and refused my motion. Now my witnesses are come to Coventry yesterday morning, and they will be here in a few days ; but in the meantime I have been left at the mercy of my adversaries, who were some of my own clergy, whom, for their debauched lives, I had corrected, as is well known.

" I will not deny, that as long as there was any toleration and connivance, I did execute the functions of a bishop ; but that, by the 2nd of Elizabeth, is only *præmunire*, and no treason. But, my lord, whilst I have been left without means of defence, my enemies have had full time to prepare their wicked charges against me. I did beg for twelve days' time, whereby you might have seen, as plain as the sun, what those witnesses are that began the story and say those things against me. And, my lord, for the raising of the 70,000 men, and the monies that are collected of the clergy in Ireland, they cannot be true, for they are a poor clergy, that have no revenue nor land—they live as the Presbyterians do here; there is not a priest in all Ireland that hath, from certain or uncertain sources, above three score pounds a-year, and that I should collect from them sums sufficient for the raising of an army, or for the landing of the French at Carlingford, if it had been brought before a jury in Ireland, would have been thought a mere romance.

" If they had accused me of a *præmunire* for the exercise of my episcopal function, perhaps they had said something that might be believed ; but, my lord, as I am a dying man, and hope for salvation by my Lord and Saviour, I am not guilty of one point of treason they have sworn against me, no more than the child that was born but yesterday. I have an attestation under my lord of Essex's hand, concerning my good behaviour in Ireland, and not only from him, but from my lord Berkeley, who was also governor there, which the king's attorney saw ; but here I was brought—here I was tried, without having time to bring witnesses, so that I could not prove my innocence, as otherwise I might. Hence if any case in the world deserve compassion, surely my case does ; and it is such a rare case, that I do not believe you will find an instance that one arraigned in Ireland should be tried here afterwards for the same fact. My lord, there be anything in the world that deserves pity, this does ; for I can say, as I hope for mercy, I was never guilty of any one point they have sworn against me ; and if my petition for time had been granted, I could have shown how all was prepense malice against me, and have produced all circumstances that could make out the innocence of a person, but having been left without any means of defence, I am at your mercy."

The Chief Justice then proceeded to pass sentence : having said in the course of his address : " I appeal to all that heard your trial, if they could so much as doubt but that you were guilty of what you were charged with. For, consider, here were persons of your own religion, the most of them priests—I think almost all of them in orders." Dr. Plunket corrected him, saying:—

" There were two friars and a priest, whom I have endeavoured to correct seven years, and they were renegades from our religion, and dastard apostates."

And shortly afterwards, the Chief Justice, extolling the evidence of Friar Duffy, Dr. Plunket said:—

" I had sufficient evidence to prove he was an apostate, and was chastised by me, and, therefore, had prepensed malice against me."

On the conclusion of the Lord Chief Justice's discourse, Dr. Plunket again addressed him:—

"May it please your lordship to give me leave to speak one word. If I were a man that had no care of my conscience in this matter, and did not think of God Almighty, or conscience, or heaven, or hell, I might have saved my life, for I was offered it by divers people here, so I would but confess my own guilt and accuse others. But, my lord, I had rather die ten thousand deaths than wrongfully accuse anybody. And the time will come when your lordship will see what those witnesses are that have come in against me. *I do assure your lordship, if I were a man that had not good principles, I might easily have saved my life; but I had rather die ten thousand deaths, than wrongfully to take away one farthing of any man's goods, one day of his liberty, or one minute of his life.*"
Lord Chief Justice—"I am sorry to see you persist in the principles of that religion."
Dr. Plunket—"*They are those principles that even God Almighty cannot dispense withal.*"

With the usual solemnity the sentence of a traitor was then pronounced against him ; but against a man breathing those noble sentiments, such a sentence should be of little avail. His conduct during the whole course of trial, his fearless denunciation of the injustice which was committed in thus compelling him to stand his trial deprived of all means of defence—his solemn protestations of innocence and of the prepense malice of his perjured accusers—but, above all, the exalted sentiments of Christian morality, worthy of a spiritual pastor, who in his own life traced out the path which his children might pursue, extorted the admiration even of his enemies, and the *sentence* which followed, for from being a triumph over him, only crowned his cause and rendered his victory complete.

CHAPTER XXVIII.

THE EXECUTION OF DR. PLUNKET.

FRIDAY, the 11th of July,* 1681, was the day fixed for the execution; and at an early hour Dr. Plunket was conducted from prison to the scaffold at Tyburn. The dauntless spirit which he displayed whilst awaiting in prison the carrying out of the fatal sentence, and the heroic sanctity with which he disposed himself to receive the martyr's crown, belong rather to the next chapter; for the present it will suffice to give some extracts from a manuscript narrative, presented the same year to the Sacred Congregation, and which was not improbably composed by Father Teyling, a distinguished member of the Society of Jesus. It is entitled, "a brief narrative of the imprisonment, accusations, and death of Monsignor Plunket, Archbishop of Armagh and Primate of Ireland, executed at Tyburn, in London, the 11th of July, 1681." Many of the facts, however, which it contains have already been commemorated from other sources, wherefore we shall be content with presenting those passages which add new circumstances connected with the imprisonment and death of our holy prelate :—

"The glorious death of this prelate, deserving of eternal memory, as well for his innocence as for the heroic constancy with which he supported his atrocious penalty, has awakened in many a devout curiosity to learn its circumstances, and especially in those who well remember to have known and conversed with him in this city of Rome, where he lived for so many years, at first as student of the Irish College, and afterwards as professor of theology for many years in the College of the Propaganda. Wherefore, not to defraud so

* This date corresponds to the 1st of July, old style.

holy a desire, whilst we await a more complete narrative of those facts. we shall here relate what is known for certain, partly from various letters, and partly from his own discourse, which may now be had in print in many languages.

" Although he was, from the commencement, sought for with great diligence, nevertheless he, for awhile, escaped every danger, till, at length, detected by the cunning of the spies, he was arrested in the month of December, 1679, in the city of Dublin, and immediately cast into prison, where he was detained with the greatest rigour, being obliged, amongst other things, to purchase, at a price truly exorbitant, and wholly incompatible with his means, the most ordinary conveniences of furniture and food. After suffering for more than six months in that prison he was at length, on the 31st of July, 1680, conducted, under a close guard, to Dundalk, thirty-six miles distant from Dublin, there to stand his trial."

The narrative then proceeds with the various facts till the removal of his trial to London, regarding which iniquitous proceeding it remarks :—

" Every one will see, that nothing less than a heroic virtue and magnanimity was required to receive this blow with that peace of soul, and with that perfect charity for his enemies with which the primate bore it . . . . The good prelate, on the 11th of November, was removed from the Castle of Dublin, and conducted, under a close guard, to London, where he arrived in the depth of the past most rigid winter; and although he was of a most delicate complexion, yet the only relief he received after so severe a journey, was to be thrown into a most opprobrious and disastrous prison, called Newgate, where for a while he had to undergo such trials, as even the accused of most vile condition are not subjected to. Thus the entire winter and spring passed on, and in the meantime his accusers, living at large in London, arranged and matured all their plans to encompass his destruction."

The account of his trial and sentence is then given, and the narrative thus continues :—

" At the same time and place sentence of death was also passed against a certain Fitzharris, a man, for many and heinous crimes, deserving of that punishment ; this served to form a contrast with Dr. Plunket, and add new lustre to his innocence. On the sentence of death being passed, Fitzharris, by the terror of his looks, his trembling, and the complete failure of strength, showed that his heart was not less guilty than feeble. On the contrary, the primate, as well when awaiting sentence, as whilst it was being passed, and after it, displayed such a frankness of soul and heart—such a serene and joyous countenance, and was so composed in all his actions and deportment, that all were able to perceive not only his perfect innocence, but, moreover, his singular virtue, which was master and superior to every emotion of passion. And concerning all this, the Catholics, who were present, wrote endless praises, attesting that none could wish for a deportment more noble, more amiable, more worthy of him whom he there represented. Having heard the sentence (turning his thoughts to his soul, and no-wise solicitous as to the sufferings destined for his body), he asked as a favour from the judge to be allowed to treat of spiritual matters with a Catholic priest. 'You will have,' replied the judge, 'a minister of the Church of England,' But he answered : 'I am obliged for your good intentions, but such a favour would be wholly useless to me.'

'' The primate being re-conducted to prison after this public and so glorious trial, there arose between the Catholics and the Protestants an eager strife who would visit him and converse with him— the former attracted by a singular devotion, the latter by an extraordinary curiosity ; and he, during the few days that he survived, received both with such courtesy, with such a sweetness, and calmness, and amiableness of manner, that the Catholics departed truly edified, and the Protestants were not only exceedingly contented with his deportment, but also rendered more affectionate towards the Catholics. Before his execution he was able to confer with a spiritual father (a man * of great merit, who was then, as he is yet, a glorious confessor of the faith in that prison), to whom he manifested, as that which most disturbed him, his having no horror of death, on account of which he feared that he was not well prepared for it, which shows his humility, and with what worthy sentiments he approached his death, as the only scruple which disturbed him was one derived from a special and excessive grace which God granted to him. On his part he was nowise negligent in disposing himself for this great grace ; for, in addition to the sufferings of prison, to the afflicting journeys so patiently borne by him, to the generous and repeated pardon which he so often breathed for his enemies in exchange for their many outrages, he added, moreover, many voluntary penances, and especially a rigorous fast on bread and water, three times each week, during the whole time that he was in prison in London, as the keeper of the prison, a Protestant, attested after Dr. Plunket's death, not without eulogy and admiration.

'' At length, on the 11th of July, the day destined for the carrying out of the fatal sentence, the keeper of the prison, imagining that the apprehension of approaching death, and horror of the atrocious punishment, would have made some impression on that soul hitherto so resolute, went early in the morning to visit him, and if necessary, too, to give him courage and comfort him ; but he was yet more surprised and filled with astonishment on finding that the prelate,

---

* This was Father Corker, as we learn from the letters of the Archbishop of Cashel.

on being awakened, was as little moved by the approach of sufferings as though his body were insensible to pain, whilst, nevertheless, he was of an ardent and delicate temperament. In a little while the announcement was made that everything was in order, wherefore he was taken from prison, and stretched (with his face uppermost) and tied with cords upon a wooden hurdle (as is there customary), and thus drawn by a horse to Tyburn.

"It had been a hundred years, perhaps, since a Catholic bishop was thus executed there, and hence the curiosity to see a victim of such exalted dignity, and already so famed for his noble deportment, gathered together an immense multitude of spectators, who partly awaited him on the road side, partly at the place of execution. Such as he had shown himself when receiving sentence of death did he now prove himself in this last scene when undergoing death itself, being ever serene and tranquil, even to his last breath; so that he universally excited that esteem and sympathy which is invariably evoked by an heroic virtue oppressed by an extreme rigour; so that few could be found even amongst the Protestants to entertain a doubt as to his innocence.

"On the scaffold he delivered a short discourse, in which, after protesting his innocence as to the charges of conspiracy made against him, he prayed for life and health to the king and all the royal family; gave a most complete pardon to all his enemies and adversaries; and, in fine, supplicated the Divine Majesty to be propitious to him, through the merits of Christ, through the intercession of the Blessed Virgin, and of all the holy Angels and Saints of Paradise. Which form of prayer, so simple and yet so pious, was remarked by the spectators, who never remembered to have heard from any other such an express mention of the Blessed Virgin and the Saints.

"This discourse was the substance of the longer one which he wrote with his own hand in prison, and left with his friends, lest any, by a malignant alteration, might seek to falsify his dying sentiments. Having concluded his discourse, the sentence was carried into execution, and his happy soul sped its flight (as we may hope) to enjoy an eternal repose.

"On the same day, and in the same place, Fitzharris was executed; and to the last the contrast of his manner and actions displayed in brighter light the happy lot of the primate; and whilst Dr. Plunket excited compassion on account of the atrocious and unmerited suffering, and became universally loved for his innocence, and extolled to the skies for his constancy, Fitzharris was abhorred for his wicked deeds, despised for his vile cowardice, and uncompassioned in his suffering, as being his due.

"The primate, before death, asked and obtained permission to be buried with the fathers of the Society of Jesus who, during the present persecution, sacrificed their lives at Tyburn. He was therefore interred with them in the church of St. Giles; and we cannot but remark the devotion and great esteem which the English

Catholics displayed for this sacred deposit ; and together with it they interred a copper plate, on which was inscribed the following inscription :—

"' In this tomb resteth the body of the Most Rev. Oliver Plunket, late Archbishop of Armagh and Primate of all Ireland. who, when accused of high treason, through hatred of the faith, by false brethren, and condemned to death, being hanged at Tyburn, and his bowels being taken out and cast into the fire, suffered martyrdom with constancy, in the reign of Charles the Second, King of Great Britain, on the 1st day of July, 1681.' *

" Here we may remark, that by referring to this inscription it is not our intention to ratify the title of martyr till holy Church will authenticate it : as, also, we must add, that the aforesaid date is not contrary to that given above, as the 1st of July, according to the old style, still used in England, is equivalent to the 11th of July, according to our Gregorian computation.

" Some few circumstances yet remain connected with the death of Dr. Plunket, which cannot be passed over in silence, and which we now add :—

1st. It is deserving of attention that all the accusers, judges, and other opponents of Dr. Plunket were not able to attach the mask of conspiracy to his cause, or conceal its being a manifest and direct cause of religion. The plots in England were pretended to be directed against the life of the king, but neither the death of the king nor the advancement of any other cause could be put forward as the scope of the pretended Irish conspiracy, but only the establishment of the faith.

" 2nd. It has been written that two English lords (who were successively viceroys in Ireland) declared to the king that it was impossible to believe or deem probable any of the accusations against the primate, for they had experienced him a man full of zeal for the public peace ; nay, one of the most efficacious in Ireland in appeasing seditious movements.

" 3rd. It is certain that, on the part of one of the first noblemen in England, his life was offered him, should he consent to accuse others : which offer, although resolutely rejected by him, is said to have been renewed to him on the scaffold, God permitting this temptation for the greater merit of one who thus, in such innocence, sacrificed his life.

" 4th. The Superior of a certain religious order, a man of great prudence, who was present at the primate's death, writes, that on the scaffold, by the singular composure of soul and actions, he

* In hoc tumulo requiescit corpus Rmi. D.D. Oliverii Plunket, quondam Archiepiscopi Ardmachani, totius Hiberniæ Primatis, qui in odium fidei a falsis fratribus læsæ majestatis accusatus ob idque morti adjudicatus Tyburniæ laqueo suspensus, extractis internis et in ignem conjectis Martyrium constanter subiit. Regnante Carolo 2⁰ Mag. Brit. etc. die 1⁰ Julii, 1681."

seemed like an angel descended from paradise, who was joyously arrived at the moment of once more returning thither.

"5th. All write, with one accord, that this innocent victim has done and yet performs great good in England, not only by the edification which he gave to the Catholics, but, moreover, by the change of ideas and sentiments which he occasioned in many Protestants, who now commence to regard all these conspiracies as malicious fictions ; and there are great grounds for believing that the fruit which England will derive from his blood will not end here. The archbishop himself wrote from prison in London (and the letter written with his own hand is still in Rome), that he has experienced in the English Catholics the most exalted piety, faith, and Christian charity, which any one could desire: and he gives the names of many families and individuals who, it seems, gave to him, though a stranger and unknown to them, large sums of money to enable his witnesses to come from Ireland, and offered themselves, moreover, as most ready to undergo any other expense, or render him any service. He, therefore, in the letter referred to, professes an unspeakable love for those so bounteous benefactors: and we may hope, that as he has, whilst living, done so much by his example, so now he will be efficacious in obtaining from heaven most abundant blessings for those by whom he deemed himself so benefited on earth."

Such were the glorious sentiments with which the Archbishop encountered the barbarous sentence which had been unjustly decreed against him. None, even amongst his enemies, dared to insinuate his guilt, or pretend that any deeds of conspiracy could be imputed to him : all felt the attractions of his innocence and sanctity, and could scarce find words to express their admiration and esteem. Even amongst subsequent writers, no matter how ardent defenders they may have been of the Protestant cause, none have reproached his memory with the reputed guilt, but all have uniformly recorded his innocence of the charges thus made against him. We have already quoted the words of the Protestant bishop Burnet : we may now add the testimonies of some few others. Thus, for instance, Echard, in his *History of England* (vol. iii., p. 631), after stating that Dr. Plunket had an attestation of his innocence, under the hands of the two viceroys, Essex and Berkeley, adds that he (the writer) was

" Assured, by an unquestionable hand, that the Earl of Essex was so sensible of this good man's hardship, that he generously applied to the king for a pardon, and told his majesty that these witnesses must needs be perjured; for these things sworn against him could not possibly be true. Upon which the king, in a passion, said, ‘ Why did you not attest this at his trial ? it would have done him good then. I dare not pardon any one.’ And so concluded with the same kind of answer he had given another person formerly, ‘ His blood be upon your head, not mine.’ ”

The continuation of *Sir Richard Baker's Chronicle* (p. 70), not only corroborates this fact of the Earl of Essex, but gives us the general Protestant sentiment of the time in regard of the perjured witnesses, and the accusations which they brought against the Primate.

“ In the meantime [he writes] came on the trial of Dr. Oliver Plunket, Popish titular Archbishop of Armagh, who called himself Primate of all Ireland. He was a worthy and good man, who, notwithstanding the high title given him, was in a very mean state of life, as having nothing to subsist on but the contributions of a few poor clergy of his own religion in the province of Ulster, who having little themselves, could not spare much to him. In these low circumstances he lived, though meanly, quietly and contentedly, meddling with nothing but the concerns of his function, and dissuading all about him from entering into any turbulent or factious intrigues. But while the Popish plot was warm, some lewd Irish priests, and others of that nation, hearing that England was disposed to hearken to good swearers, thought themselves well qualified for the employment, so they came over with an account of a plot in Ireland, and were well received by Lord Shaftesbury. They were also examined by the Parliament, and what they said was believed. They were very profligate wretches, and some of the priests among them had been censured by Plunket for their lewdness, so partly out of revenge, and partly to keep themselves in business, they charged a plot upon that innocent, quiet man, so that he was sent for over, and brought to trial. The evidences swore that upon his being made primate of Ireland, he engaged to raise sixty or seventy thousand Irish to be ready to join in with the French, to destroy the Protestant religion, and to get Dublin, Londonderry, and all the seaports into their hands ; and that beside the French army, there was a Spanish army to join with them, and that the Irish clergy were to contribute to this design. Plunket, in his defence, alleged the improbability of all that was sworn against him ; which was apparent enough. He alleged that the Irish clergy were so poor, that he himself, who was the head of the whole province, lived in a little thatched house, with only one servant, having never above sixty pounds a-year income, so that neither he nor they could be thought very likely to carry on a design of this nature. But the fact being positively sworn against him, and the jury unacquainted with the witnesses' characters, and the scene of action, he was brought in guilty and condemned. It is said that the Earl of Essex was so sensible of the injustice done him, that he applied to the king for a pardon, and told him that the matters sworn against Plunket were so absurd in themselves, that it was impossible for them to be true. But the king answered in a passion, 'Why did you not declare this, then, at the trial? it would have done him some good then; but I dare pardon nobody,' and concluded by saying, 'His blood be upon your head, and not upon mine.' " *

With peace and calm Dr. Plunket prepared himself in prison to receive in a worthy manner the glorious privilege of dying for the faith, with which God wished to crown his earthly labours. On the day after the final sentence had been passed against him, he thus wrote to his friend and fellow-prisoner, Father Corker :—

" DEAR SIR,—I am obliged to you for the favour and charity of the 20th, and for all your former benevolence ; and whereas I cannot in this country remunerate you, with God's grace I hope to be grateful in that kingdom which is properly our country. And truly God gave me, though unworthy of it, that grace to have *fortem animum mortis terrore carentem.*† I have many sins to answer for before the Supreme Judge of the high bench, where no false witnesses can have an audience. But as for the bench yesterday, I am not guilty of any crime there objected to me. I would I could be so clear at the bench of the All-powerful. However, there is one comfort, that He cannot be deceived, because He is omniscient, and knows all secrets, even of hearts ; and cannot deceive, because all goodness ; so that I may be sure of a fair trial, and will get time sufficient to call witnesses ; nay, the judge will bring them in a moment, if there will be need of any. You and your comrades' prayers will be powerful advocates at that bench ; here, none are admitted for

" Your affectionate friend,

" OLIVER PLUNKET."

This composure of soul, and tranquil resignation to the will of God is attested not only by the friends of the illustrious Primate, but also by Protestants who, perchance, had occasion to contemplate and admire his fortitude and

---

* *Chronicle by Sir Richard Baker, continued to the death of King Charles I.* London, 1730.

† A fortitude fearless of death.

heavenly deportment in prison. Sir Richard Bulstrode, for instance, attests that

"Captain Richardson, keeper of Newgate, being asked by the Lieutenant of the Tower, how this prisoner had behaved himself, he replied, 'Very well, for when I came to him this morning, he was newly awake, having slept all night without any disturbance; and when I told him he was to prepare for his execution, he received the message with all quietness of mind, and went to the sledge as unconcerned as if he had been going to a wedding.' " *

In addition to the particulars of the closing scene of Tyburn, which we have already presented from the anonymous narrative, we learn many further circumstances connected with Dr. Plunket's execution, from the often-referred-to letter of the Archbishop of Cashel :—

"The first (i.e., the 11th) of July, 1681, being at length arrived, this great bishop (Dr. Plunket) was brought to the place of execution, destined for public malefactors, being placed upon a sledge trailed on the ground, and drawn by horses, and accompanied by a numerous guard of military, as well as by a multitude of spectators and royal officers; and to all he gave occasion of surprise and edification, because he displayed such a serenity of countenance, such a tranquillity of mind and elevation of soul, that he seemed rather a spouse hastening to the nuptial feast, than a culprit led forth to the scaffold.

"Being arrived at the place of execution, he mounted a car which had been placed there on purpose, and delivered a discourse which lasted an hour, clearing himself of the accusations for which he suffered—calling God and the whole heavenly court to witness his innocence as to the pretended conspiracy—and declaring himself an unworthy Catholic prelate, who laboured to preserve and advance the true faith in a just and lawful manner, and by no other means,— and pardoning his accusers, the friars, and their accomplices, the judges, and all who procured or concurred in his death : and he delivered this discourse with such sweetness and energy that it seems he moved to compassion even his executioner, and much more so those who assisted as spectators. Having finished his address, he made a lengthened prayer to God; and passed to a better life, with a fortitude and spirit truly apostolic.

"His discourse is everywhere to be met with in print, and was applauded even by the adversaries of our religion, who could not fail to admire the singular courage, and extol the many heroic acts of the pretended culprit, and to censure the manner of proceeding of the

* *Memoirs and Reflections upon the Reign and Government of King Charles I. and King Charles II.*, &c., by Sir Richard Bulstrode. London 1721.

2 D

court, and the sentence pronounced against him; the better part of
them, and especially those of the province of Armagh, being well
acquainted with, and having ever esteemed the deceased prelate, as a
man of honour, whilst they knew the accusers to be wicked men, and
their accusations incredible.

"An event so unexpected has overwhelmed the Catholics with
affliction, seeing thus put to death the head of the clergy in this
kingdom, through the perjured testimony of villains, who themselves
had often merited the penalty of robbers . . . . And he being the
first in this kingdom, condemned on account of the imaginary conspiracy, it was feared that all the Catholics of the kingdom would be
deemed culpable, and guilty of the same deeds, as if united with their
head, and this increased their tribulation. But, on the other hand,
when they consider the glorious death of this sacred victim, and the
applause and compassion which he merited even from the Protestants,
and the honour he thus rendered to the Church, to his country, and
to his sacred dignity, they are filled with consolation.

"And in truth, his holy life merited for him this glorious death;
for during the twelve years of his residence here, he showed himself
vigilant, zealous, and indefatigable above his predecessors, nor do we
find within the memory of those of the present century, that any
primate or metropolitan visited his diocese and province with such
solicitude and pastoral zeal as he did, reforming depraved morals
amongst the people, and the scandalous life of some of the clergy,
chastising the guilty, rewarding the meritorious, consoling all; benefiting, as far as was in his power, and succouring the needy, wherefore
he was applauded and honoured by the clergy and people, with the
exception of some wicked enemies of virtue and religious observance.
He held many diocesan synods and provincial councils, to the great
spiritual advantage of both clergy and people. He instituted schools
of moral theology for the young priests, and procured, as far as was
possible to have the children of Catholics educated by Catholic
masters, a rare thing in these parts; and in this and other things
belonging to his pastoral charge, he showed himself untiringly
solicitous. All this was attested more than once by the clergy of
the province of Armagh, in synodal letters addressed to the Sacred
Congregation, with unusual acclamations and applause, extolling their
metropolitan, and reverently thanking his Holiness and the Sacred
Congregation, for having chosen as their primate a person so con-
spicuous and so worthy.

"This prelate merited from the English government more favour
than he received, since he was thus oppressed in London by the
impious calumnies of his enemies. He bore great affection for that
nation, and showed himself ever attentive to the interests of the
king, and to the peace of the present government. He gave signal
proofs of this during the many years that he lived in Rome, having
been attentive to assist its noble youths who went thither to contemplate the grandeur of that city, and procuring for them courtesy and
honours even from the chief nobility of that great court, where, too

on every occasion he spoke of the king of England with esteem and praise.

" His affection and manner of discourse did not change since his arrival in Ireland, where he spoke with zeal of the interests of the king and of the present government, exhorting all to a due subordination to the political laws of the kingdom, to peace and fraternal love among all ; ordering in his synods that the clergy should labour to procure the tranquillity of the subjects, and that they should pray for the king and royal family. Of the sincerity of these desires he gave a great proof, which was applauded by all. There was in the province of Armagh a multitude of famous tories, who pestered that province with robberies and murders, of which Protestants were principally the victims. He, at the desire of the Viceroy, went in search of them, not without his own great risk, and having found them, he exhorted them to live as it became good Christians, and to allow the other subjects of his majesty to live in peace ; and having treated with them in a kind and paternal manner, he induced them to lay aside their plunderings and to submit to the Government ; as in fact they did ; and all going to Dublin, he obtained for them pardon from the Viceroy, and they were placed on shipboard and transferred to other countries, to the great delight and advantage of that province ; and all extolling the charity of the prelate who, by this means, saved the lives of these tories, and, at the same time, preserved the lives and property of the inhabitants of those districts.

"What has been said of his manner of acting in this kingdom, and how devoted he was to the service of the king and the welfare of his country, was known to the king and to many in the kingdom ; and, nevertheless, when his cause was transferred to England, and he himself obliged to appear there, it is not known that any one of them took the slightest trouble to speak or write one word in favour of his merits. Of all that he did in Rome for the English nation, many of the nobility who are now in England can bear testimony ; and yet not one of them took a step to manifest his innocence. From all this we may learn to do good for heavenly motives, and to await its recompense from God alone.

" Many Catholics do not hesitate to call him *martyr*, being convinced that he suffered for the Catholic faith ; and although he was accused on three principal charges, as he himself writes—first, of having sought to establish and propagate the Catholic faith ; second, of plotting the death of the king ; third, of seeking to bring in the French—the second and third were only as if means to attain the first, as even the adversaries themselves laid down. In truth, they might be styled two chimeras : so that the only real cause of his suffering was the propagation of the faith ; and he confessed publicly, in regard of the first accusation, that he had discharged the office of a prelate *ex æquo et bono*, without doing or seeking to do any injury to any being in the world.

" And as Boetius finds a place in the martyrology for having defended the Catholic faith against the Arians, although the pretext of his death was an imaginary conspiracy against King Theodoric; and, in like manner, St. Hermenegild, for having professed and sought to advance the true faith, although the pretext of his death was a similar conspiracy against King Leovigildus and his kingdom, with the aid of the Greek emperor; so, too, they argue in the present instance. But it is not our province to decide this ; *est qui judicet.*

"However this may be, it is certain that the memory of this glorious prelate will ever be revered in these kingdoms, as, on the contrary, the name of his impious accusers will ever be held in abomination, for having, with sacrilegious impiety, shed this sacred and innocent blood, and procured, with like impiety, to insult the Holy See and the court, as well of Rome as of other Catholic sovereigns, by their wicked and sacrilegious depositions, declaring them promoters of the feigned conspiracy, which, in truth, was forged in hell. They included, too, in their accusations against the primate, the Catholics of Ireland as aiders in advancing that engine, from which will result the ruin of our people, unless God, in a special manner, protects them ; and on this account it is that, as I am of opinion, from the time of the institution of the order of St. Francis, the name of *friar* was never less revered in these parts, not only amongst Catholics, but also amongst the adversaries of our holy faith."

These words need no comment ; they present, as if in a picture, the scene of Tyburn—sad, indeed, when looked on with the eyes of this world, but truly glorious when contemplated with the eye of faith. The death of the good prelate corresponded with his life ; and his dispositions of soul and heavenly sentiments fully accorded with the glorious consummation of his career as bishop of God's Church. The discourse which he delivered from the scaffold, with as great calmness and energetic zeal as though he were addressing from the pulpit his own immediate flock, moved all the assembled multitude, and even his executioner to compassion; and surely no one now-a-days can read without emotion even the dead letters of the printed discourse, especially the concluding passages, in which he prays forgiveness to all his enemies, and supplicates from the Almighty pardon for his own faults and eternal rest in heaven. Dr. Plunket composed this discourse in prison, and left it to his friends, written with his own hand ; for he feared lest his dying words should be misrepresented, or any false sentiments be imputed to him. It was immediately printed and translated into various languages,* as we learn from Dr. Brennan. We give it in full, from the printed copy in the archives of Propaganda :—

" I have† some few days past abided my trial at the King's Bench, and now very soon I must hold up my hand at the King of King's Bench, and appear before a Judge who cannot be deceived by false witnesses or corrupted allegations ; for He knoweth the secrets of hearts ; neither can He deceive any or give an unjust sentence, or be misled by respect of persons : *He being all goodness, and a most just Judge, will infallibly decree an eternal reward for all good works, and condign punishment for the smallest transgression against His commandments,* which being a most certain and undoubted truth, it would be wicked, and contrary to my eternal welfare, that I should now, by declaring anything contrary to the truth, commit a detestable sin, for which, within a very short time, I must receive sentence of everlasting damnation ; after which there is no reprieve or hope of pardon. I will, therefore, confess the truth, without any equivocation, and make use of the words according to their accustomed signification ; assuring you, moreover, that I am of that certain persuasion, that no power, not only upon earth, but also in heaven, can dispense with me, or give me leave to make a false protestation ; and I protest upon the word of a dying man, that as I hope for salvation at the hands of the Supreme Judge, that I will declare the naked truth with all candour and sincerity ; and that my affairs may be better known to all the world. It is to be observed, that I have been accused in Ireland of treason and præmunire, and that there I was arraigned and brought to my trial ; but the prosecutors (men of flagitious and infamous lives) perceiving that I had records and witnesses who would evidently convict them, and clearly show my innocency and their wickedness, they voluntarily absented themselves, and came to this city to procure that I should be brought hither to my trial, where the crimes were not committed, where the jury did not know me or the qualities of my accusers, and were not informed of several other circumstances conducing to a far trial. Here, after six months' close imprisonment (or thereabouts), I was brought to the bar, the 3rd of May, and arraigned for a crime for which I was before arraigned in Ireland ; a strange resolution, a rare fact, of which you shall hardly find a precedent these five hundred years past ; but (whereas) my witnesses and records were

* The Italian translation was made in 1681. A printed copy of it is extant in the Casanatense Library, Rome.

† This discourse of Dr. Plunket is taken from an original printed copy, which in the end bears the inscription " *London : Printed by N. Tompson, 1681.*" It is headed " *The speech of Mr. Oliver Plunket, Titular Primate of Ireland, who was executed at Tyburn, on Friday the 1st of this instant, July 1681, written by his own hand.*'

in Ireland, the Lord Chief Justice gave me five weeks time to get them brought hither; but by reason of the uncertainty of the seas, of wind, and weather, and the difficulty of getting copies of records, and bringing many witnesses from many counties in Ireland, and many other impediments (of which *affidavit* was made), I could not at the end of five weeks get the records and witnesses brought hither ; I, therefore, begged for twelve days more, that I might be in a readiness for my trial, which the Lord Chief Justice denied, and so I was brought to my trial, and exposed, as it were, with my hands tied, to those merciless perjurers, who did aim at my life by accusing me of these following points :—

" First.—That I have sent letters by one Nial O'Neal (who was my page) to M. Baldeschi, the Pope's Secretary, to the Bishop of Aix, and to the Prince Colonna, that they might solicit foreign powers to invade Ireland ; and also to have sent letters to Cardinal Bouillon to the same effect.

"Secondly.—To have employed Captain Con O'Neal to the French king for succour.

" Thirdly.—To have levied and exacted monies from the clergy of Ireland, to bring in the French, and to maintain 70,000 men.

" Fourthly.—To have had in a readiness 70,000 men, and lists made of them, and to have given directions to one friar Duffy, to make a list of 250 men in the parish of Foghart, in the county of Louth.

" Fifthly.—To have surrounded all the ports and harbours of Ireland, and to have fixed upon Carlingford as a fit harbour for the French's landing.

" Sixthly—To have had several councils and meetings where there was money allotted for introducing the French.

" Finally.—That I held a meeting in the county of Monaghan, some ten or twelve years past, where there were 300 gentlemen of three several counties, to wit, Monaghan, Cavan, and Armagh, whom I did exhort to take arms to recover their estates.

" To the first I answer, that Nial O'Neal was never my page or servant, and that I never sent letter or letters by him to M. Baldeschi, or to the Bishop of Aix, or to the Prince Colonna; and I say, that the English translation of that pretended letter produced by the friar MacMoyer is a mere invention of his, and never penned by them, or its original, in English, Latin, Italian, or any other language. I affirm, moreover, that I never wrote letter or letters to Cardinal Bouillon, or any of the French king's ministers ; neither did anyone who was in that court either speak to me or write to me, directly or indirectly, of any plot or conspiracy against the king or country. Further, I vow that I never sent agent or agents to Rome, or to any other, about any civil or temporal affairs; and it is well known (for it is a precept publicly printed) that clergymen (living where the government is not of Roman Catholic) are commanded by Rome not to write to Rome, concerning any civil or temporal affairs. And I do aver that I never received letter or letters from the Pope, or from any of his ministers, making the least mention of any such matters, so that the friar MacMoyer and Duffy swore as to such letter or letters, agent or agents.

"To the second I say, that I never employed Captain Con O'Neal to the French king, or to any of his ministers ; and that I never wrote to him, or received letters from him ; and that I never saw him but once, nor ever spoke to him, to the best of my remembrance, ten words ; and as for his being in Charlemont or Dungannon, I never saw him in these towns, or knew of his being in these places ; so that as to Con O'Neal, friar MacMoyer's depositions are most false.

" To the third I say, that I never levied any money for a plot or conspiracy for bringing in the Spaniards or French, neither did I ever receive any on that account from priests or friars, as priest MacClave and friar Duffy most untruly asserted. 1 assure you I never received from any clergymen in Ireland but what was due to me, by ancient custom, for my maintenance, and what my predecessors these hundred years were wont to receive ; nay, I received less than many of them. And if all what the Catholic clergy of Ireland get in the year were put in one purse, it would signify little or nothing to introduce the French, or to raise an army of 70,000 men, which I had enlisted and ready, as friar MacMoyer most falsely deposed: neither is it less untrue what friar Duffy attested, viz., that I directed him to make a list of 250 men in the parish of Foghart. in the county of Louth.

"To the fifth I answer, that I never surrounded all the ports or harbours of Ireland, and that I never was at Cork, Kinsale, Bantry, Youghal, Dungarvan, or Knockfergus ; and these thirty-six years past I was not at Limerick, Dungannon, or Wexfort. As for Carlingfort, I never was in it but once, and staid not in it above half an hour ; neither did I consider the port or haven ; neither had I it in my thoughts or imagination to fix upon it, or any other port or haven, for landing of French or Spaniards ; and while I was at Carlingfort (by mere chance passing that way), friar Duffy was not in my company, as he most falsely swore.

" To the sixth I say, that I never was at any meeting or council where there was mention made of allotting or collecting of monies for a plot or conspiracy: and it is well known that the Catholic clergy of Ireland, who have neither lands or revenues, and hardly are able to keep decent clothes on their backs, and life and soul together, can raise no considerable sum, nay, cannot spare as much as would maintain half a regiment.

"To the seventh I answer, that I never was at any meeting of 300 gentlemen in the county of Monaghan, or of any gentlemen of the three counties of Monaghan, Armagh, and Cavan, nor of one county, nor of one barony ; and that I never exhorted gentleman or gentlemen, either there or in any other part of Ireland, to take arms for the recovering of their estates ; and it is well known that there

are not, even in all the province of Ulster, 300 Irish Roman
Catholics who had estates or lost estates by the late rebellion ; and,
as it is well known, all my thoughts and desires were for the quiet
of my country, and especially of that province

"Now to be brief, as I hope for salvation, I never sent letter or
letters, agent or agents, to Pope, king, prince, or prelate, concerning
any plot or conspiracy against my king or country ; I never raised
sum or sums of money, great or small, to maintain soldier or
soldiers all the days of my life ; I never knew or heard (neither did
it come to my thoughts or imagination) that the French were to
land at Carlingfort ; and I believe that there is none who saw
Ireland, even in a map, but will think it a mere romance ; I never
knew of any plotters or conspirators in Ireland, but such as were
notorious or proclaimed (commonly called tories), whom I did
endeavour to suppress. And as I hope for salvation, I always have
been, and am, entirely innocent of the treasons laid to my charge,
and of any other whatsoever.

"And though I be not guilty of the crimes of which I am
accused, yet I believe none came ever to this place in such a condition as I am, for if even I should acknowledge (which in conscience
I cannot do, because I should belie myself) the chief crimes laid to
my charge, no wise man that knows Ireland would believe me. If I
should confess that I was able to raise 70,000 men in the districts
of which I had care, to wit, in Ulster, nay, even in all Ireland,
and to have levied and exacted monies from the Catholic clergy for
their maintenance, and to have proposed Carlingfort for the French
landing, all would but laugh at me, it being well known that all the
revenues of Ireland, both spiritual and temporal, possessed by his
majesty's subjects are scarce able to raise and maintain an army of
70,000 men. If I will deny all these crimes (as I did and do), yet
it may be that some who are not acquainted with the affairs of
Ireland will not believe that my denial is grounded on truth, though
I assert it with my last breath. I dare mention farther and affirm,
that if these points of 70,000 men, &c.. had been sworn before any
Protestant jury in Ireland, and had been even acknowledged by me
at the bar, they would not believe me, no more than if it had been
deposed and confessed by me, that I had flown in the air from
Dublin to Holyhead.

"You see, therefore, what a condition I am in, and you have
heard what protestations I have made of innocency ; and I hope
you will believe the words of a dying man. And that you may be
the more induced to give me credit, I assure you that a great peer
sent me notice, ' *that he would save my life, if I would accuse others ;* '
but I answered, ' *that I never knew of any conspirators in Ireland, but
such* (as I said before) *as were publicly known outlaws ; and that to
save my life I would not falsely accuse anyone, nor prejudice my own
soul. Quid protest homini, &c. To take away any man's life or goods
wrongfully, ill becometh any Christian, especially a man of my calling,
being a clergyman of the Catholic Church, and also an unworthy prelate,*

which I do openly confess. Neither will I deny to have exercised in Ireland the functions of a Catholic prelate, as long as there was connivance or toleration; and by preaching, and teaching, and statutes to have endeavoured to bring the clergy (of which I had a care) to a due comportment, according to their calling; and though thereby I did but my duty, yet some, who would not amend, had a prejudice for me, and especially my accusers, to whom I did endeavour to do good: I mean the clergyman (as for the four laymen who appeared against me, viz, Florence MacMoyer, the two Neales, and Hanlon), I was never acquainted with them; but you see how I am requited, and how, by false oaths, they brought me to this untimely death, which wicked act, being a defect of persons, ought not to reflect on the order of St. Francis or on the Roman Catholic clergy, it being well known that there was a Judas among the twelve apostles, and a wicked man, called Nicholas, amongst the seven deacons; and even as one of the said deacons, to wit, holy Stephen, did pray for those who stoned him, so do I for those who, with perjuries, spill my innocent blood, saying, as St. Stephen did, ' Lord, lay not this sin to them.' I do heartily forgive them, and also the judges who, by denying me sufficient time to bring my records and witnesses from Ireland, did expose my life to evident danger. I do also forgive all those who had a hand in bringing me from Ireland to be tried here, where it was morally impossible for me to have a fair trial. I do, finally, forgive all who did concur, directly or indirectly, to take away my life; and I ask forgiveness of all those whom I ever offended by thought, word, or deed. I beseech the All-powerful that His Divine Majesty grant the king, the queen, and the Duke of York, and all the royal family, health, long life, and all prosperity in this world, and in the next everlasting felicity.

" Now that I have shown sufficiently (as I think) how innocent I am of any plot or conspiracy, I would I were able, with the like truth, to clear myself of high crimes committed against the Divine Majesty's commandments (often transgressed by me), for which I am sorry with all my heart; and if I should or could live a thousand years I have a firm resolution and a strong purpose, by Your grace, O my God! never to offend You; and I beseech Your divine Majesty, by the merits of Christ, and by the intercession of His blessed Mother and all the holy angels and saints, to forgive me my sins, and to grant my soul eternal rest. *Miserere mei Deus*, &c. *Parce animæ*, &c. *In manus tuas*, &c.

" OLIVER PLUNKET."

To this discourse Dr. Plunket added the following postscript before going out to execution, re-confirming the sentiments of the preceding discourse, and renewing the declarations which it contained :—

" To the final satisfaction of all persons that have the charity to believe the words of a dying man, I again declare before God, as I hope for salvation, what is contained in this paper is the plain and naked truth, without any equivocation, mental reservation, or secret evasion whatever, taking the words in their usual sense and meaning, as Protestants do when they discourse with all candour and sincerity. To all which I have here subscribed my hand.

" OLIVER PLUNKET."

Having concluded his discourse on the scaffold, the Archbishop knelt in prayer, and with eyes raised towards heaven, recited the psalm, " Miserere mei Deus," and many other devout prayers ; and having breathed the aspiration, "in manus tuas Domine commendo spiritum meum," " *into thy hands, O Lord, I commend my spirit,*" the cart was drawn away; and whilst at the hands of the executioner he received the disgraceful punishment of a traitor, he yielded his happy soul into the hands of his Creator.

To conclude this chapter, we will add the letter of a Catholic gentleman, who, as we learn from the Archbishop of Cashel, was present at the execution. It was addressed to that dear friend of the martyred prelate, who transmitted it to Rome ; and, at the same time, deeming it a letter of edification, distributed many copies of it throughout the country, " to the great consolation of the Catholics." * It is dated London, 15th of July, 1681, and is as follows :—

" On Friday last, despite all our endeavours, our good man was conducted to the fatal place of execution ; whither he went to receive and encounter death with a soul so noble and a fortitude so generous, that his adversaries—even malice itself – admired his intrepidity, and compassioned his lot. Never did he preach from the pulpit with greater vigour of soul than he displayed when delivering this discourse at the place of execution. In a word, he won more credit and repute, as well for himself as for his country, by one hour of suffering, than he could have acquired, perhaps, by hundreds of years of life ; and I am persuaded that there was never a victim of the Irish nation which will reflect more credit on that kingdom than this revered and truly Christian prelate, who, as a Jonas cast into the sea, will, we may hope, be a means of appeasing the tempest, and terminating our present persecutions. And of this, indeed, we have already had some evidence ; for on the very day after the death of this martyr, the Earl of Shaftesbury, head of the

<hr>

* See Narrative of the Archbishop of Cashel.

anti-Catholic faction, was committed to the Tower of London, accused of high treason, where also are imprisoned, on the same grounds, Lord Howard, and two others of the same party; so that even already the scales have commenced to change their balance, and we have begun to hope for better times."

Dr. Plunket was the last victim to the anti-Catholic fury with which the English nation was then inflamed; and the next day, which witnessed the fall of Shaftesbury, and saw that arch-enemy of the Catholics conducted to the Tower, saw also the very witnesses whom he had fostered employ their perjured tales to hurry on his ruin. Many, indeed, even in after years, were called to share in Dr. Plunket's crown, but never with the formalities of a trial, or with the public and direct sanction of the Government. With him was brought to a close the bright array of heroes of the faith who at Tyburn received their martyr-crowns. The enemies of the Catholic Church had vainly hoped, by shedding their blood, to destroy the faith; but they forgot that the blood of martyrs is a fruitful seed; that the sword of persecution can only prune the vine, and cause it to put forth new branches; and that the Church of God is, indeed, the mystic field, in which each grain cast into the earth buds forth re-multiplied.

CHAPTER XXIX.

HEROIC SENTIMENTS OF DR. PLUNKET DURING HIS IMPRISONMENT, AND AT THE PLACE OF EXECUTION.

LITTLE remains for us in this chapter, save to allow the reader to draw his own conclusions from some letters of Dr. Plunket, and from other documents connected with his imprisonment and subsequent martyrdom; these documents speak for themselves, and bear with them such an evidence as places in the clearest light the heroic sanctity of this glorious confessor of Christ, and the high degree of perfection to which he had attained. Above all, they attest his calmness and resignation to the Divine will in all his sufferings.

In the first letter addressed from prison he burst forth into the exclamation, " The Lord be praised, who, by these prisons, has given me occasion of spiritual joy." When forced to embark and abide his trial before a London jury, his only sentiments are : " May all be for the greater glory of God and the salvation of my soul." The Archbishop of Cashel declares that in prison he " proved himself wholly master of himself and superior to all the adversities of this world ;" * that he spent his time " in prayer and mortifica- tion, and exhorting the faithful to perseverance in the true faith, and to bear with patience their present tribulations ;" that in his own deportment and resignation he presented to all " the example of a worthy prelate," and filled his very guards with confusion and admiration. The writer of the anonymous narrative, too, continually speaks of his *heroic virtue*, his *perfect charity for his enemies*, the eager desire of Catholics to visit him, and their rapture, as well as edifica- tion, in conversing with him. On the scaffold such was the heavenly unction of his discourse, and the angelic sweetness of his manner, that all were moved to compassion, and the fruits of this closing scene of his glorious career were such that many of his friends could declare him to have merited greater reward, and to have achieved more good by this one hour of his suffering than he could possibly have accom- plished by a century of missionary toil. But in addition to these writers, who thus incidentally declare to us these striking features of the holy primate, many others may be cited, who, in like words, or, perhaps, still more explicitly, commemorate the glorious triumph which he thus achieved in his happy death. The learned theologian, Arsdekin,† declares that—

" The multitude which was gathered together from all sides, pro- claimed with one accord his innocence, his Christian constancy, and

* In another letter of 20th April, 1680, Dr. Brennan writes : " l'Armacano sta tuttavia confinato nel primo regio ergastolo, *constans in adversis*."

† *Theol. Trip.*, p. 230 : " Populus certe undequaque circumfusus summo animarum sensu ipsius innocentiam, Christianam constantiam, et

his incredible contempt for death ; and many, too, affirmed that, did he live for one hundred years, yet never could he have gained such glory for himself, for God, for his country, and for the Catholic faith."

The Internuncio, too, from Brussels, writing on the 19th of December, 1681, after stating that the intercession of the Spanish ambassador with the king of England, in favour of Dr. Plunket, had been in vain, and that the only answer given by the king was, "I can allow no one to make an attempt on my life, though he be a Catholic and an archbishop," adds the following interesting circumstance of his execution :—

"In effect, it is notorious that the most obstinate and most barbarous heretics themselves were forced to feel compassion for him, and many Protestants of the highest name and dignity in their sect declared, that if the government continued to put to death Catholics of such fervour and zeal, they would soon succeed in rendering Catholic all England." *

This well confirms the noble testimony of the Archbishop of Cashel, that the Protestants themselves were filled with admiration at the heroism which he displayed. and that the Catholics, too, were consoled, " considering the glorious death of this sacred victim, and the applause which he merited, even from Protestants, and the honour which he thus rendered to the Church, to his country, and to his sacred dignity."

The letters addressed from prison a little while before his death, perhaps still better than any testimony of others, reveal to us the heavenly calm which reigned in all his faculties—his complete resignation to the Divine will—his spiritual joy at being thus chosen by God for the crown o

incredibilem mortis contemptum ita deprædicavit ut plurimi palam affirmaverint etsi ad centum annos vixisset, numquam sibi, Deo, patriæ suæ, ac religioni Romanæ tantum gloriæ consequi potuisse."

* *Archiv. de Propag.* " In effetti o notorio che gli eretici stessi piu ostinati e piu barbari furono necessitati ad averne compassione, e vari Protestanti di maggior grido e posto nella loro sette dissero che se continuava a far morire Cattolici d'ugual fervore e zelo si sarebbe trovato in breve il modo di rendere Cattolica tutta l'Inghilterra."

martyrdom.   We have already seen one of his letters
addressed to Father Corker, in which he thanked God for
having strengthened him " *with a fortitude fearless of death.*"
In another, addressed to the same worthy ecclesiastic, he
expressed his joy at the prospect of being put to death for the
faith, " since Ireland, so fertile. in saints, has but few
martyrs."*   Nothing, too, can be more calm and dignified
than the following letter, which he wrote to his relative,
Michael Plunket, a student of the Irish College in Rome, on
the day after sentence of death was passed on him :—

" DEAR MICHAEL PLUNKET,

" On the eighth of this month I was brought to trial, accused of
introducing the Catholic religion, of preparing 70,000 men for
rebellion, collecting money for them, exploring the fortressess and
forts of Ireland, and of destining Carlingford as the landing-place
for the French. I applied for time to bring my witnesses from
Ireland, but in vain. I argued that the pretended crime having been
committed in Ireland, it should be there discussed, or that at least a
jury should be brought thence, who would be better acquainted with
the circumstances and condition of those concerned ; but everything
was denied to me. Two Franciscan friars were the principal accusers
against me, the one named MacMoyer, and the other Hugh Duffy,
and a certain priest of the Maclanes. Four seculars also appeared
against me, viz., two of the O'Neils, a certain Hanlon, and Florence
MacMoyer. As to these four I never saw them in my life. Mac-
Moyer swore that he saw with Neal O'Neil, who went to the
Congregation of Propaganda, letters sent by me to the most Rev.
Monsig. Baldeschi, to Prince Colonna, to the Bishop of Aix, soliciting foreign aid for the invasion of Ireland. When I alleged that no
one was ever known, when accused before the tribunals in Ireland,
to have been afterwards summoned to answer to the same charges in
England, the judge eluded my argument by adducing the case of a
certain O'Rourke who was brought from Ireland and tried here in
England ; but I replied that he was outlawed, and that his arrest
took place in Scotland.

" Sentence of death has been passed against me, and there is no
hope of respite or pardon, and thus those who beheaded me in effigy,
have now attained their intent of beheading the prototype. Friar
MacMoyer, by means of two of his brethren, induced another friar
and a priest and the laymen to act as they have done. I pardon them
all, and, with St. Stephen, I cry out, ' O Lord, lay not this sin to
their charge.' I think I will be executed about the end of this month.

* See extract given by Rev. George Crolly, in his *Life and Death of
Oliver Plunket*, p. 226.

Show this letter or its contents to all my friends, and pressingly solicit their prayers for me. I never sought to introduce the Catholic religion unless by teaching and . preaching. My conscience never reproached me with being guilty of any conspiracy or rebellion, direct or indirect. Oh, would to God that I were as free from every other stain and sin against the divine precepts as I am from this. Therefore, it is necessary for all my friends to pray for me, as I confide they will.

" I remain, your friend,
" OLIVER PLUNKET."

This letter was enclosed to Canon Joyce in Brussels, with the following note addressed to the good canon :—

" DEAR MR. JOYCE,
  " By the enclosed letter you see how matters get on with me. I implore your prayers, and the favour to send the enclosed to Michael Plunket, and to show it to your friend Picquet and Pruisson,* and I am, your dear friend,

" OLIVER PLUNKET.

" London, 16th June, 1681."

The Internuncio, writing on the 5th of July, 1681, transmits a copy of both these letters to Rome, and in addition asks for their prayers in the Eternal City, that this innocent victim may be strengthened in his last trial, and receive from God the grace of constancy in his sacred purpose.

A few days later Dr. Plunket addressed another letter to this same relative, Michael Plunket. It is one of the few letters in the Roman archives whose original is in English, and it must be especially dear to the reader, as recording the sentiments of our primate a few days before his execution. It is dated 22nd June, styl. vet. (i.e., 2nd July), 1681, and is as follows :—

" † MR. MICHAEL PLUNKET.

" 22nd June, 1681, styl. vet.

Г " Sentence of death passed against me on 15th, without causing me any fear, or depriving me of sleep for a quarter of an hour. I am innocent of all treason as the child born yesterday. As for my

---

* These were the names by which the Internuncio was indicated.
† It is directed to :—
" A Monsr.
" Monsr. Joyce, de
" Ste. Gudule,
Bruxelles."

character, profession, and function, I did own it publicly, and that being also a motive of my death, I die most willingly, and being the first among the Irish, I will teach others, with the grace of God, by example, not to fear death. But how am I, a poor creature, so stout? seeing that my Redeemer began to fear, to be weary and sad, and that drops of His blood ran down to the ground. I have considered that Christ, by his fears and passions, merited for me to be without fear.

"I was refused sufficient time to bring my witnesses and records from Ireland; the witnesses came eight days after I was found guilty, and would not be heard. The jury here was not informed of the qualities of my adversaries, or of several other circumstances conducing to a fair trial. And I was here arraigned for the same facts for which I was before arraigned in Ireland, of which there could be no precedent given. MacMoyer and one Friar Duffy were the principal accusers. One priest Macclane appeared, but said little. Murphy, at the trial, touched with sorrow, would not prosecute; four seculars, never known by me, appeared, to wit, two of the O'Neills, one Hanlon, and one Florence MacMoyer, open perjurers. And Tyrrell * and Dromgole and Luke were found guilty at Dundalk by the grand jury. Dromgole was out at bonds, but Tyrrell was not then taken. One Paul O'Gormley and Coddon, friars, were brought hither to prosecute, but they did not. Forstall, of Kildare, and Creagh † are, for certain, prisoners in Dublin; and I am told that Tyrrell and Dromgole will be brought hither to their trial. MacMoyer spoke of Brennan and Creagh at the trial of being agents. Felix O'Neil was a declared enemy of Tyrrell and Luke. Anthony Daly had some words with Dromgole.

"I am informed by persons of credit that Felix and Daly did contrive all this tragedy before their departure from Ireland. MacMoyer was Daly's vicar, and Duffy is a fosterer, or of that family who fostered Felix; if so, God forgive them; and I do forgive all who had a hand, directly or indirectly in my death, and in my innocent blood.

"I have recommended you to my friends there; and also my nephews and two nieces. Jemmy and Joseph begun their philosophy, and Mickey ended his prosody. Catty and Tomasina and all will be in a sad condition. You know that Ned is simple, and that by Cromwell's people, what little land and mortgages he had left him by his father were lost; and I believe my friends there will help my nephews, if you speak to Monsignore. I stuck to my care and districts until death.

"The English Catholics were here most charitable to me; they spared neither money nor gold to relieve me, and in my trial did for me all that even my brother would do; they are rare Catholics and

* Dr. Tyrrell, Bishop of Clogher; Dr. Dromgole, Vic.-Gen of Armagh; Dr. Luke Plunket, Vic.-Ap. of Derry]
† Bishop of Cork.

most constant sufferers. My accusers swore that I had seventy thousand men in Ireland to promote the Catholic cause, that I had the harbour of Carlingford ready to bring in the French, and that I levied monies upon the clergy in Ireland, for their maintenance—such romances as would not be believed by any jury in Ireland. As for what was opposed of my profession, character, function, &c., I owned publicly, and die for it willingly: my mind remains unmoved by the terrors of death : fortem servo animum mortis terrore carentem.

" I expect daily to be brought to the place of execution, where my bowels are to be cut out and burned before my face. and then my head to be cut off, &c.: which death I embrace willingly ; I desire to be dissolved : cupio dissolvi, &c. What speech I will have at my death will be sent to you. If I had obtained sufficient time to have brought my witnesses from Ireland, I had, I think, defended myself as to those romances of treason ; but it was not granted, and I was brought to my trial destitute of all legal ways of defence. The judges could not bring one precedent of any arraigned in Ireland. and afterwards brought to England to be arraigned for the same fact. If the trial had been in Ireland, no Protestant jury had believed the romances of treason sworn against me, so with that seventy thousand men enrolled in Ireland to promote the Catholic cause, that I levied monies in Ireland, for their maintenance, and, that I had the haven of Carlingford for to receive a French army, which haven is hardly able to receive fishermen ; yet it passed here, and also the seventy thousand men, for sworn truths.

" Salute all my friends there as if I had named them, and I recommand myself to their prayer : none of them ought to be grieved for my death, being as innocent of what is lodged to my charge as a child unborn, as to matter of treason ; as for my religion and character, 'tis glorious for all my friends that I should die for it. I did expect yesterday to be brought to execution, but finding I am not to be brought to it till Friday or Saturday, I thought fit to write to you these few lines.

" See what you can do with Mr. Cybo and others for Jemmy, Joseph, &c., who, by my untimely death, will be in a sad condition, unless they be relieved. I can hardly believe, though 'tis reported, that Tyrrell is taken ; Dromgole, I know, was, and Forstall and Creagh. If they be, I will lead them the way to a worthy death.

" What pictures are there I leave them to the place where you are, and where I got my first education. I would there were cornices about them. You may write to Joyce, and direct your letters thus :—*For Mr. Thomas Golding, in the Inns, Dublin*, and he will send them to * Acarne. If I will not be executed on Friday, this shall not be the last. These eight days past I have some more liberty than before. I could not get leave to have a priest, though

* Or Acame.

there be eight or nine here condemned ; amongst whom there is one
Mr. Corker, to whom I am much obliged. Yet I am in hopes to get
leave for one of them to come to me. 22 Junii, stylo vet.

"P.S.—Besides two great persons whom I will not name, these
were most kind to me and charitable :—The Lady Goreing, the Lord
Browne, the Lord Bellasis, the Marquis of Winchester, the Lady
Francis Meeth. Mrs. Chavers, Mr. Horgraves, Sir Charley Wilgrave,
Mr. Sheldon, Mr. Dormer, and several other unknown benefactors.
Bringing my witnesses from Ireland, expenses of solicitors, lawyers,
orders, petitions, &c., came to hundreds, and debts I have contracted, above a hundred ; my own expenses in prison came near
one hundred those seven months.

"Another P.S.—I am also much obliged to a clergyman, Mr.
Morsall, Mr. Napper, Mr. Anderson, and to all ; and to the lord of
Strafford, who was executed's family, to Mr. Sheldon's family, and
to several others."

This letter, as was usual, was not sent directly to Rome,
but enclosed in another to Canon Joyce, which has been
preserved to us by Father Arsdekin, and which we translate
from his Latin version :—

"Sentence of death has been passed against me, but I fear it not :
nor does it deprive me of one moment of my rest, for I am as free
from all the conspiracy imputed to me, as the infant of yesterday.
As to what regarded my character, profession, and function, I
publicly professed it, and this being the cause of my death, I
willingly lay down my life, and, as I am the first of the Irish bishops
to come hither, so, aided by the divine grace, I will give example to
the others not to dread such a death. But wherefore have I, a miserable creature such courage of soul, whilst I see that even my
Creator on the approach of death began to fear and dread ? But I
reflect, indeed, that Christ, by his fear and dread, merited for me
to be free from all fear. A sufficient time for bringing my witnesses
from Ireland was denied me ; they arrived eight days after I was
condemned to death, but I willingly embrace it as I die for my
profession, character, and function. I expect every day to be led out
for execution, where my bowels are to be taken out and burned
before my face, and then my head cut off. I ardently desire to be
dissolved, and to be with Christ. I pardon from my heart, and I
pray that God may pardon all who in any way were cause of my
death."

Surely nothing can be more generous or more noble than
the sentiments of these letters of the holy prelate ; the
unaffected piety which they breathe, and at the same time
the ardour which they disclose to us of his desire to suffer for
the faith, and that true Christian courage which, whilst it

joyously reposes on the divine aid, is ever diffident in itself, and loves to dwell on its own lowliness and infirmity, recall to mind the letters of the glorious confessors of the early ages, and cannot fail to fill the soul with spiritual consolation and delight.

Eight days after the Primate's execution, the Internuncio Tanari writes from Brussels, conveying the sad intelligence to the authorities in Rome : —

" It has been impossible to prevent or defer the sentence of death which was passed against the Archbishop of Armagh, the king having obstinately resolved that his cause should proceed in the same manner as that of Fitzharris, whose execution was eagerly desired by his Majesty, in order to strike terror, for the future, into his calumniators. Twelve days were denied him, which the Prelate requested, that the witnesses whom he had summoned from Ireland might arrive ; and after their arrival, their testimony would not be received, as he had already been found guilty, for the Court was afraid to displease the people, should they execute a rebel and calumniator, and declare free from the imputed calumnies a Catholic who was truly innocent, that is, should they put Fitzharris to death and merely detain Dr. Plunket in prison. Perhaps, however, this impious policy has promoted the interests of religion more efficaciously than the zeal of Dr. Plunket could have effected, though he had lived for many years. since all who had conversed with him in prison, or saw him when standing before the judge, or when led out to execution, have admired the sanctity of his manners, the constancy of his soul, and his calm resignation. In a lengthened and able discourse, of which I annex a translation (for he sent the original signed by his own hand to the palace of the Spanish Ambassador), he defended his innocence, so that all present were moved and compassionated his lot, the more so as they heard at the same time Fitzharris acknowledge his guilt, and retract his accusations against the Queen and the Duke of York.

" After his death the Catholics were allowed to collect and put together the remains of the Prelate and inter them, as he had desired, near the Jesuit fathers who suffered in 1679."

The Bishop of Clogher, Dr. Tyrrell, wrote about the same time to the Secretary of Propaganda, conveying the same sad intelligence : —

" What I feared has at length come to pass, that is, the Archbishop of Armagh, falsely accused of treason, against the King and State, was, on the 11th of this month of July, executed and beheaded, having left in writing a last declaration of his innocence and *a glorious example to us of an indomitable patience and constancy.* His accusers were bad priests, degenerate friars, most wicked laymen, though, nevertheless, all pretended Catholics."

Another important document, testifying the heroic sentiments with which the glorious prelate prepared for his happy lot, was presented by the learned Jesuit, Father Teyling, to the Sacred Congregation, and is a recapitulation of various letters which he had received from members of his Order, and others in London.   It is as follows:—

" 1. Dr. Plunket, Primate of Ireland, died with the greatest fortitude and piety that could be wished for ; and with such a serenity and joy of countenance, that the innumerable multitude which was assembled, by repeated exclamations attested his innocence, and even his enemies wept at his death.

" 2. The blessed martyr (as another letter says), had a great esteem for Father Whitbread and his companions, Jesuits, who a short time before had been put to death, so that he asked to be interred with them, as was accordingly done.

" 3. Father Edward Peters, a prisoner in the Tower, was present at the execution, and writes, that the Primate Plunket had the look of an angel who had descended from heaven, and was about to return thither ; and that he has rendered immense glory to the Catholic religion by his angelical deportment in death as well as when conducted through London to the place of execution.

" 4. In other letters it is said that on the days which preceded his death, the concourse was continuous from morning till evening, of persons of every class, and all attested their extreme delight and edification at his manners, discourses, and modesty ; and even the children went to visit him. Such, moreover, was his resignation, that he declared to a friend that he knew not which to choose, were it proposed to him to live or to die. And, moreover, he felt so comforted at the prospect of dying, that he wrote to a Benedictine father, confined in the same prison, that he felt a scruple for the little, or rather, no fear of death. He prepared himself for death on the day preceding his execution, all alone, and with the assistance of a priest, admitted to him by the keeper, who, though most cruel with others, yet with the Primate was merciful and compassionate.*

It now only remains to present* to the reader some fragments of the correspondence of Dr. Plunket and Fathe Corker, as preserved in the Memoirs of the English

---

* It is deserving of remark that Protestant historians, such as Burnet, Echart, Stuart, Leland, Carte, Harris, Hume, and others, write always in the same strain as the Catholic historians concerning the virtues and heroic constancy of Dr. Plunket.

Benedictines, the original manuscript of which valuable work may be seen among the treasures of St. Edmond's monastery at Douai. Father James Corker, to whom the Archbishop's letters are addressed, was an English priest of the Order of St. Benedict, called in religion Dom Maurus. He was one of those accused of treason by Titus Oates, but was acquitted by a London jury on July 18th, 1679. He was not, however, released, but was put upon his trial a second time on the charge of being a priest (under the Penal Act of 27th of Elizabeth), and being found guilty was sentenced to death. Through the influence of powerful friends he was reprieved, and detained in Newgate until the accession of James II. During his years of imprisonment he was indefatigable in bringing relief to the other prisoners who were suffering for the faith, and in reconciling Protestants to the Church. Dom Bennet Weldon, in his "Chronological Notes on the English Benedictine Order" (Worcester, 1881, page 219), states that at this time "he reconciled to the Church above a thousand persons." Being set at liberty on the accession of James II., he was received at Court as the resident Ambassador of the Elector of Cologne, the Prince-Bishop Ferdinand of Bavaria. He was made Abbot of Cismer in 1691, and two years later, of Lambspring in the Diocese of Hildesheim. It was whilst he was a fellow prisoner of the Archbishop of Armagh that the following correspondence was carried on. Other fragments of Letters written at the same time are preserved by some of the old Catholic families of England. The last of Father Corker's letters to the Archbishop concluded with the words : " Lastly I begg for Christ Jesus' sake your last Blessing here and holy Prayers in heaven for your most unworthy servant—J. CORKER." And the postscript was added : " I send you now a capp, an handkerchief, and two guineys to give the executioner at Tyburne. I shall also give a guiney to Cooper and another to Mrs. Hall, for their civilities to you. I lately gave the Captaine three guineys on the same account." On this fragment of letter, in the vacant space opposite Father Corker's name, Dr. Plunket

wrote with his own band the words: "I send you all what
I coulde now, and doe alsoe send awai you my blessing.—
OLIVER PLUNKET." To another letter of Father Corker
asking the Archbishop to bequeath his body to him,
Dr. Plunket replied with the remarkable words: "I see
your great charity that you are desirous to be careful of my
unworthy carcase after my death, which being *opus miseri-
cordiae* in high degree, I ought not to deprive you of it, its
reward being most precious, viz., everlasting glory."

Father Corker, till his death in 1715, continued to venerate
Archbishop Plunket as a true Confessor and Martyr for the
faith, and when he was appointed Abbot of Lambspring, he
caused the quartered limbs of the blessed martyr, which had
been brought thither, to be reverently deposited in the crypt
of the church of that Benedictine monastery.

"FATHER MAURUS CORKER TO ARCHBISHOP PLUNKET

"MOST HONOURED SIR,—I cannot admit of the acknowledgment
your goodness was yesterday pleased to make of my poor service,
which I look upon as an honour done to myself, and beg God's
pardon and yours for my unworthy management of it : and though
I have been frustrated of all my earnest endeavours in your behalf,
yet I do not say or think my undertaking wanted any happy
success, seeing it is not properly happiness to detain a martyr from
his sacrifice, and as from heaven God who sent you to us will now
in a triumphant manner take back his own, and you are upon the
point of enjoying the plenitude of bliss in its original fountain.
Pallium Archiepiscopale mutandum est in stolam jucunditatis et
infula in coronam gloriae. You may justly sing with the Royal
Prophet, "Insurrexerunt in me testes iniqui et mentitia est iniquitas
sibi." "Credo videre bona Domini in terra viventium." Again,
"Funes ceciderunt mihi in praeclaris, etenim haereditas mea prae-
clara est mihi." But I am not so arrogantly foolish as to presume
I can instil into you better thoughts than those you have. However, I am bold to present you in the name of Jesus Christ with an
Epistle dictated by Himself to His followers in your condition.
"Qui credit in me, etiamsi mortuus fuerit, vivet, et omnis qui vivit
(*Joan.* ii.) et credit in me, non morietur in aeternum Noli timere quia
redemi (*Isa.* i. 43) te, et vocavi te nomine tuo, meas es tu, mundus
gaudebit, vos vero (*Joan.* 16) contristabimini, sed tristitia vestra
vertetur in gaudium, et gaudium vestrum nemo tollet a vobis;
confidite, ego vici mundum. Beati eritis cum maledixerint vobis
homines, et persecuti vos fuerint et dixerint omne malum adversum
vos mentientes propter me; gaudete in illa die et exultate quia

merces vestra copiosa est in coelis. Ego vivo et vos vivetis, in illo die vos cognoscetis quia ego sum in Patre meo et vos in me et ego in vobis. Venite benedicti Patris mei percipite regnum, &c. Hodie mecum eris in Paradiso." I wish with all my heart I might be the companion, of which happiness I am, to my sorrow, unworthy. My only request is—Memento mei cum veneris in Regnum tuum—Venerable sir, your truly devoted servant in our Lord.

"M. CORKER."

"ARCHBISHOP PLUNKET TO F. MAURUS CORKER.

"DEAR SIR,—I have received your spiritual and smart lines, which stir up my dull heart and weak will to the contemplation of eternal joys. Oh, if I could but feel one act of true and lively contrition I would be well satisfied. I often endeavour, but still I find some earthly thoughts to obstruct and hinder my good inspiration. Infelix homo, &c., corpus quod corrumpitur aggravat animam, et terrena habitatio deprimit sensum coelestia cogitantem. Pallium Archiepiscopale rubiginem et maculas contraxit ideo purgandum; caput infulam labescit et ideo purgandum. O quot tunc onustus maculis et tabibus. I have need to say, 'dele iniquitatem meam,' and that I deserved 'ut testes iniqui contra me insurgerent.' Your prayers I desire and all your brethren; the passage is but short, yet it is dangerous; it is from time to eternity; it can never be repeated or reiterated. Your prayers I say I beg and your brethren's."

"ARCHBISHOP PLUNKET TO F. MAURUS CORKER.

"SIR,—The Captain sent to me Mr. Cooper to tell me that to-morrow sen-night the execution will be. Whereas it is not upon St. John's Day, I am glad it is to be upon his Octave, and upon a Friday. I am also told I shall be allowed a priest. I desire it should be you. If it will be a person unknown to me I intend to discourse but little with him."

"ARCHBISHOP PLUNKET TO F. MAURUS CORKER.

"SIR,—My man, James, telleth me you are not well, which would be an addition to my afflictions, if I may call them afflictions, they being really comforts and objects of joy. Your infirmity being a motive of grief and trouble to my mind, which is obliged to wish you perfect health and all prosperity, whereas I cannot by any external or outward ways show my gratitude. I wrote to Rome of your charity, and also the names of all my benefactors, that they may be laid before my great master, I mean of all known to me by your list sent to me. I wrote also to Ireland the names of all my benefactors. "Ut non solum Fides sed et charitas vestra annuncietur in universo mundo." Quod Romae divulgatur ubique praedicatur. I long for my man's going to you to know of your condition: a mild purge would not be unprofitable to you. I expect to hear from you, and see your own character which may assure me of your welfare, and also to know something of the warrant for the execution, for believe me " Cupio dissolvi," &c., and that, incolatus meus prolongeretur, it is not coveted by me, knowing that a troublesome world I have, and what a quiet and happy state, by my Saviour's grace, I hope to enjoy, and being the first of any of my countrymen of this age who suffered here, I desire to lead the way to others et quod alios in Hibernia hortatus sum verbo aequum est ut eosdem firmem exemplo. To exhort others to die stoutly is easy and not difficult; but to instruct them by example and practice is more efficacious.

" There are two bishops in Dublin in prison—Marcus Forstall, of Kildare, a great divine and an exemplary prelate, and Dr. Pierce Creagh, a learned, pious, and sweet bishop. He is of Cork: if they be brought hither, I believe they will have the same success I had. There is also a clergyman of considerable parts out on bail, who, I hear, is to be brought hither; his name is Edward Dromgole, a doctor of divinity, excellent preacher both in the English and Irish tongues, well versed in the canons, and profoundly seen and learned in cases of conscience; and which is more, of an angelical life. If these be brought thither (I hope they will not), I do recommend them to your prudent conduct and charity. There is another worthy prelate searched for, viz., Patrick Tirrel, Bishop of Clogher; he was Secretary-General to the Order of St. Francis for twelve years, and Definitor-General; a person of great credit; he is also a Lector jubilatus of his Order, and not unknown to your great master. They might have saved their lives by going over seas; but the Irish prelates are resolved to die rather than forsake their flocks. Forstall Kildariensis had departed, but that I hindered him; for if the captains fly, 'tis in vain to exhort the simple soldiers to fight and stand in battle. 'Jesus coepit facere et docere.' The verb ' facere ' was long in Christ's grammar, and the verb ' docere ' was short. St. Augustine saith of Christ, ' Parum erat hortari Martyres nisi firmaret exemplo.' True it is that Christ saith, ' cum persecuti vos fuerint in una civitate fugite in aliam :' but he doth not say, ' cum persecuti vos fuerint in uno regno fugite in aliud longe remotum ;' and hath these words left in his Gospel : ' Bonus Pastor animam suam dat pro ovibus : Mercenarius autem,' &c., &c. 'Tis objected, why do we not obey the king's edicts? This is an axiom in the civil law : ' mandante consule silet decretum pro-consulis :' Christ is the Consul: the king, the pro-consul. The Consul saith, ' spiritus S. posuit vos regere ecclesiam Dei, et pasce oves meas;' the pro-consul saith, ' leave your flocks, go far from them,' et nolite regere or Pascere oves vestras; for he who is far from them cannot feed them. Are we to obey men rather than God? Shall we despise the Consul, and hear the pro-consul's contrary commands? Shall we hear the Lord Lieutenant's proclamation not agreeing with the king's? Absit.

But they will kill us: by our deaths the number of Catholics will
not be diminished, but rather augmented. When they see we
willingly die and contemn life, which is the only idol of our
adversaries, the Catholics will be induced to contemn lands, riches,
honours, and all other things far less esteemed than life. We lost
by this tempest two or three noblemen here in Ireland, one young-
ship, the Earl of Clanricard's son, and a gentleman called Colonel
Fitzpatrick, ever yet a worldling : but of ours if they had been,
they had not left us : but I dare say and know we have gained
many more, and we have obtained a great and weighty matter, to
wit, the constancy of those who 'non curvaverunt genua ante
Baal,' they are as · aurum probatum igne,' they are armour of proof,
which a musket ball cannot penetrate ; nay, they yield not to a
cannon's ball : habent probam, and they are therefore of great
value and highly to be esteemed, and one of those is worth a
thousand breastplates which yield to every pocket pistol's bullet—
they make number in the arsenal, but in battle serve only for a
show, or a muster ; so that we lost but little or nothing, and we
gained very much ' coram Deo et hominibus.' The Jesuits got more
credit, more esteem, honour, and glory in all the Christian world by
the death of their companions or brethren here, than they gained by
all other actions these many years passed : and the same will happen
to our Irish prelates if they suffer constantly and stoutly. England
from St. Alban's days to these times, was glorious for martyrs ;
Ireland for confessors, but scarce any martyrs. We had none like
St. Alban and his comrades, or St Thomas of Canterbury, &c.
We had St. Patrick, St. Malachias, St. Gelasius, &c., great confessors : now 'tis time for us to imitate the glorious courage of the
English nation, famous for confessors, and more famous for
martyrs. In King Henry II.'s time, learned Cambrensis went to
Ireland, he was John the Earl of Morton's (afterwards King John's)
secretary, and he discoursing with the Archbishop of Cashel, told
him he had read all the histories of Ireland, and found very many
holy men, but no martyrs. The Archbishop Donatus, Aculato
dictus, answered that the Irish race were rude but pious, barbarous
but not bloody ; but, quoth he then (alluding to the martyrdom
of St. Thomas of Canterbury), there is a nation now come to
conquer us, who will teach us to make martyrs and suffer martyrdom
too. This happened after the midst of the twelfth century, as far
as I remember, An. 1172, about the beginning of the English
conquest in Ireland ; so that now by the fervour and constancy of
the English clergy and laity, we are encouraged to be stout souls,
mortis terrore carentes, and to wash away all our past actual
sins by the baptism of blood, as we have our original by that of
water ; and the word water ought not to have more virtue than
blood. Water corpus tangit et cor abluit, blood being ever spilt
upon the ground et extra corpus, agit quasi in distans, wipes away
and cleanseth the soul of all dirt and filthiness. Water cannot
clean us unless it be sprinkled and cast upon us ; blood cast out of

us, and separated from us, sweeps away all, even canker'd and hardened dregs of noxious humours. Happy, then, are we who have a second baptism—nay, a third. Water we received, the Sacrament of Penance we got, and now we have ' tertiam post naufragium tabulum,' to wit, the Baptism of Blood. If, then, we have so many means and ways to save ourselves in the raging billows of our navigation per Scillas and Charybdes, and more than any other profession or pretended religion hath (nay, it hath none) if we will be drowned, if we will perish, 'tis our own fault, and it may be said to us ' perditio tua ex te Israel.' You see how and whither the pen, ' sensim sine sensu,' hath transported me : it begun with bemoaning your corporal infirmity, and now it ends with the meditation of sure antidotes of a certain purgative and corroborative, for the acquiring of everlasting health and felicity. Your sickness, tho' troublesome to you, and to me also secondly, instar hominum loquor, hath brought me to the opportunity of proficuous thoughts and meditations well becoming St. John Baptist's day, who washed himself in water and spilt his blood, though nec vitam levi maculavit crimine linguae. The original dirt he contracted, although he was free from all dust even of venial sins, what then shall we do who have cartloads of actual mire and filthiness ? He had not even venials, and suffered prison and death : we have dunghills of mortals, and what ought not we to suffer? But why should I speak of St. John? His Master, who was free from all original, venial, and actual sins, suffered cold, frost, hunger, prison, stripes, thorns, and the most painful death of the cross for others' sins, compared to which death of the cross, that of Tyburn, as I hear the description of it, is but a flea biting. I ought, therefore, cheerfully to desire it, covet it, and joyfully embrace it, it being a sure way, a smooth path, by which I may, in a very short time pass from sorrow to joy, from toil to rest, and from a momentary time or duration to everlasting eternity, and now say with Boetius :

> " Da fontem lustrare boni, da luce perenni
> In te conspicuos animi defigere vi us,
> Dejice terrenae nebulas et pondera molis
> Atque tuo splendore mica, tu namque serenus.
> Tu requies tranquilla piis, te cernere finis,
> Principium, Dux certus semita terminus idem."

I pray you excuse errors as lapsus velociter scribentis, defuit enim tempus rude revidendi scriptum : quascunque aspicies lacrymae fecere lituras, but I hope there will be soon lacrymarum finis : the happy finis which will draw me to that place where I may, in a great measure, recompense or speak an Interesse with the greatest of princes, to remunerate the favours and charities conferred upon,

" Your obliged friend,

" OLIVER PLUNKET."

ARCHBISHOP PLUNKET TO F. MAURUS CORKER ON THE EVE OF EXECUTION.

" Sir—I do most earnestly recommend myself to your prayers, and to the Most Holy Sacrifices of all the noble Confessors who are in this prison, and to such priests as you are acquainted with ; and I hope soon to be able to requite all their and your kindness. Above all, I recommend myself to the prayers of the holy families of M. Sheldon and the Lady Stafford's, and in general to all the good Catholics in this city, whose faith and charity are great. I do recommend to you and to them my faithful servant, James Mackenna, who served me these eleven years with all fidelity. Some of the good Catholics who came to see me told me they would be charitable to him after my death. I desire that you would be pleased to tell all my benefactors that for all eternity I will be mindful of them, and that I will pray for them until they will come where I hope to come soon, and then also will thank them in conspectu Supremi Domini. They deserve all praise in this, and, by God's grace, a crown of glory in the next world. I doubt not, but that their faith, charity, and good works, will be efficacious with our Saviour, and that there will be soon an end of this persecution, and that iniquitas multorum mox revelabitur, fiat voluntas Dei, fiat, fiat. And I beseech my Saviour to give all the good Catholics perseverance in their faith and good works, and grant me the grace to be to-morrow where I may pray for them non in aenigmate, but facie ad faciem, &c., and be sure that I am still, and will be,

" Your obliged friend,
" OLIVER PLUNKET."

FATHER MAURUS CORKER TO A LADY ON ARCHBISHOP PLUNKET'S DEATH.

" MADAME—I cannot as yet so much as pretend to give you, as you desire, a description of the virtues of the glorious Archbishop and Martyr, Dr. OLIVER PLUNKET. I am promised the particulars of his life and actions, both at Rome, where he studied and taught almost twenty years, and in Ireland, where he exercised his Episcopal or rather Apostolical function. till he became a Champion of the faith ; but these particulars are not as yet arrived at my hands.

" After his transportation hither, he was, as you know, close con-fined and secluded from all human conversation, save that of his keepers, until his arraignment, so that here also I am much in the dark, and can only inform you of what I learnt, as it were by chance, from the mouths of the said keepers, viz. :—That he spent his time in almost continual prayer ; that he fasted usually three or four days a week with nothing but bread ; that he appeared to them always modestly cheerful, without any anguish or concern at his danger or strict confinement ; that by his sweet and pious demeanour he contracted an esteem and reverence from those few who came near him. When he was arraigned, it was true I could write to him and he to me, but our letters were read, transcribed and examined by the officers before they were delivered to either of us, for which cause we had little communication than what was necessary in order to his trial. But the trial being ended, and he condemned, his man had leave to wait on him alone in his chamber. By those means we had free intercourse by letter to each other, and now it was I clearly perceived the spirit of God in him, and those lovely fruits of the Holy Ghost—charity, joy, peace, patience, &c., transparent in his soul: and not only I, but many other Catholics who came to receive his benediction and were eye-witnesses (a favour denied to us) can testify. There appeared in his words, actions, and countenance something so divinely elevated, such a composed mixture of cheerfulness, constancy, courage, love, sweetness, and candour, as manifestly denoted the Divine Goodness had made him fit for a victim, and destined him for heaven. None saw or came near him but received new comfort, new fervour, new desires to please, serve. and suffer, for Christ Jesus by his very presence.

"Concerning the matter and state of his prayer, he seemed most devoted to pathetic sentences taken out of Scripture, the Divine Office and Missal, which he made me procure for him three months before he died; upon these sentences he let his soul dilate itself in love, following herein the sweet dictate and impulse of the Holy Ghost, and reading his prayers, writ rather in his heart than in his book, according to that of the Apostle (*Rom.* viii. 26), Spiritus adjuvat infirmitatem nostram ; nam quid oremus sicut oportet nescimus ; sed ipse Spiritus postulat pro nobis gemitibus inenarrabilibus. Qui autem scrutatur corda, scit quid desiderat Spiritus, quia secun lum Deum postulat pro sanctis, et (1 *Joan.* ii. 27), Unctio ejus docet vos de omnibus. For this reason I suppose it was that, when, with just humility, he sent me his last speech to correct, he also writ me word he would not, at the place of execution, make use of any other set form or method of prayer than the Pater Noster, Ave Maria, Credo, Miserere, In Manus tuas Domine, &c., and for the rest he would breathe forth his soul in such prayers and ejaculations as God would then inspire him withal. He continually endeavoured to improve himself and advance in the purity of Divine Love, and by consequence also in contrition for his past sins, of his deficiency in both which this humble soul complained to me as the only thing that troubled him. Indeed the more we love God the more we desire it ; and the more we desire it the more we love ; for desire increaseth our love and love our desire, and if we may measure this happy martyr's love by the Rule of our Saviour (*Jo.* 13), Majorem hac dilectionem nemo habet, ut quis animam suam ponat pro amicis suis, we shall find him perfect in love ; for in him was fulfilled that of the Canticles (viii. 6), fortis est ut mors dilectio ; by love was extinguished in him all fear of death ; timor, said the Apostle of Love, non est in charitate, sed perfecta charitas foras mittit timorem ; quoniam timor poenam habet: a lover feareth not, but rejoiceth at the approach of his beloved. Hence the joy of our holy martyr seemed still to approach together with his danger, and was fully accomplished by assurance of death. The very night before he died, being now as it were at heart's-ease, he went to bed at eleven of the clock, and slept quietly and soundly till four in the morning, at which time his man, (who) lay in the room with him, awaked him; so little concern had he upon his spirit; or rather had the loveliness of the end beautified the horror of the passage to it. Non sunt condignae passiones hujus temporis, says St. Paul, ad futuram gloriam quae revelabitur in nobis, nam expectatio creaturae revelationem filiorum Dei expectat. After he knew that God Almighty had chosen him to the crown and dignity of martyrdom he continually studied how to divest himself of himself and become more and more an entire, perfect and pleasing holocaust, to which end, as he gave up his soul, with all its faculties, to the conduct of God, so for God's sake he resigned the care and disposal of his body to unworthy me, and this in such an absolute manner that he looked upon himself to have no further power or authority over it. For an instance of this the day before he suffered I sent a barber to trim him: the man asked him whether he should leave anything on the upper lip; he answered, he knew not how I would have it, and he would do nothing without my order; so that they were forced to send to me before the barber could finish his work. Another remarkable instance of his strange humility and resignation therein was, that about an hour before he was carried to execution, being desired to drink a little glass of sack to strengthen his spirits, he answered he was not at his own disposal, but mine, and that he must have leave from me before he could either take or refuse it; thereupon, though I was locked up, yet for his satisfaction, his man and the keeper's wife came to my chamber door, and then, returning back, told him I enjoined it; upon which he readily submitted. But I neither can nor dare undertake to describe unto you the signal virtues of the blessed martyr. There appeared in him something beyond expression—something more than human. The most savage and hard-hearted people were mollified and attended at his sight; many Protestants in my hearing wished their souls in the same state with his: even the most timorous were in love with him. When he was carried out of the Priest's yard to execution, he turned him about towards our chamber windows, and, with a pleasant aspect and elevated hand, gave us his benediction. How he comported himself after he was taken from hence, with all the circumstances of his happy passage, you yourself can give a more exact account than I, or indeed than any other, seeing your piety rendered you so eminently assistant at his death and burial. I shall therefore conclude this letter with blessing and praising the Almighty, who in His faithful servant had confounded the wicked, comforted the good, illustrated the Church, glorified Himself, and increased the number of martyrs in Heaven. Sweet Jesus! grant us the grace to follow the example, to the end we may deserve his present patronage, and future company in eternal glory, which is the daily prayer of, Madam, your devoted servant in our Lord,

"MAURUS CORKER.'

As the Benedictine, Father Corker, had been the admiring friend of Dr. Plunket during life, so did he cherish his memory after death. Dodd, in his Church History, mentions that, on the morning of the execution, the primate bequeathed his earthly remains to this good father ; but, perhaps, he did so rather on the preceding day, when, as we have seen, he alone enjoyed the company of Dr. Plunket, and aided him in disposing his happy soul for its passage to a glorious eternity. Permission was, without difficulty, obtained to collect the scattered members of the mangled body of the martyr, and they were, with due solemnity, interred close by the remains of Father Whitbread and his four companions, all Jesuit fathers, who, two years before, had, in like manner, laid down their lives at Tyburn, and whom Dr. Plunket had ever venerated as glorious martyrs of the Catholic faith. The head and arms, from the elbow were placed in separate cases, as we learn from the following authentic attestation, the original of which, on parchment, is preserved in the Dominican Convent in Drogheda :—

" The under written John Ridley, chirurgien, and Elizabeth Sheldon, doe heareby testifye and declare ; That in this chest are included two tinne Boxes where of the one being Round containeth the Head, and the other, being long, containeth the two Hands armes from the Fingers' End to the Elbow, of the Blessed Martyr Oliver Plunkett Arch-Bishop of Armach, who was hanged, drawne and Quartered at Tyburne on the first Day of July, An: Dni 1681 for the holy Catholick Religion, under pretence of a Plott wrongfully imposed upon him and others of the same Religion. The said Head was cutt off from the Body at the tyme and Place of execution : and on the same Day the two hands armes aforesaid were disjointed and seperated from the rest of the said Body by mee John Ridley in the presence of Elizabeth Sheldon, immediately before the quarters of the said Blessed Body were putt into the Coffin, in order to their Interment, which Head, Hands, and

Armes were reserved by us, out of the Coffin and placed in the said two Boxes of Tinne included in this as above specyfyed. In witnesse whereof wee have hereunto sett our hands and seales this 29th Day of May An: Dni 1682.

JOHN RIDLEY.

ELIZABETH SHELDON.

Signed and sealed in the presence of
EDWARD SHELDON, and
RAPHE SHELDON."

Father Corker, on being liberated from prison, was enabled to translate the venerable relics which had been interred, to the monastery of his order, at Lambspring, in Germany. Dodd mentions that the site where the body was interred was "under the North wall," in St. Giles's; and he quotes from Mr. Wood, in his *Athen. Oxonien.*, page 221, the additional circumstance that, "in the said place, Plunket's quarters continued till the crop-eared plot broke out in 1683, and then they were taken up and conveyed beyond the sea to the monastery of the Benedictines, at Lambspring, in Germany." The exact date of this translation of Dr. Plunket's remains cannot accurately be determined. The author now cited refers it to 1683; on the other hand, Chaloner (page 244) says that it took place four years after his death, which would place it, at least, in 1685. The friend, however, of the martyred prelate, to whose narrative we have had so often occasion to refer, the Archbishop of Cashel, is more precise; and in a letter, which we will more fully cite just now, and which was written in April, 1684, he says, that the translation of Dr. Plunket's body to Germany had then *recently* taken place. Thus it was probably in the month of March, 1684; and, perhaps, if the different manner of computation be taken into account, this will reconcile some of the otherwise conflicting opinions; for 1683, in the old style, did not terminate till the 25th of March, 1684. The account given in Harris' *Ware's Writers*, will also be found to substantially agree; it is as follows:—

" The head was separated from his body, which was divided into four quarters, and they were buried in the churchyard of St. Giles in the Fields, where they rested *about two years*, and then were taken up and conveyed beyond seas to a monastery of English Benedictines at Lambspring, in the dominions of the Duke of Brunswick, in Germany, where, with great ceremony, they were re-buried."

In the Dominican Convent at Drogheda, the brass plate s preserved which marked the martyr's tomb at St. Giles's. The inscription is as follows :—

"In hoc tumulo requiescit corpus Reverendissimi Domini Oliveri Plunkett quondam Archispiscopi Armachani, totius Hiberniae Primatis, qui in odium Fidei a falsis testibus crimine laesae Majestatis accusatus ob idque morti adjudicatus, Tyburniae laqueo suspensus, extractis intestinis et in ignem conjectis, Martyrium constanter subiit, regnante Carolo Secundo Magnae Britanniae Rege etc. die primo Julii, Anno 1681."

We learn from Dr. Chaloner, that when, in 1684, the body of Dr. Plunket was disinterred, it was found to be entire.* It was translated, as we have seen, to Germany, through the care of Father Corker ; and a few years later (1693), this same Father erected a handsome monument in the church of his order, at Lambspring, which bore the Latin inscription :—

"Reliquiae sanctae memoriae Oliveri Plunketti, Archiepiscopi Armachani, Hiberniae Primatis, qui in odium Catholicae fidei laqueo suspensus, extractis visceribus et in ignem projectis celebris martyr occubuit Londini primo die Julii stylo veteri, anno salutis 1681. Hunc tumulum erexit Revmus D. Maurus Corker hujus monasterii Abbas, An. Dom. 1693 :" i.e., "The remains of Oliver Plunket (of holy memory), Archbishop of Armagh, Primate of Ireland, who, being hanged through hatred of the Catholic faith, and his bowels being taken out and cast into the fire, a glorious martyr, laid down his life in London, the 11th day of July, 1681. The Most Rev. Maurus Corker, abbot of this monastery, erected this tomb in the year of our Lord 1693."

* Hugh M'Mahon, Archbishop of Armagh (in the second part of his *Jus Primatiale*, section 22, pages 8-9), attests that many miracles were performed by these sacred remains: "Recens est," he says, "memoria eorum quae egit Illmus Oliverius post gloriosum martyrium adeo signis et miraculis coruscans ut caput et membra in varias deportata regiones, integra et incorrupta permaneant fragrantem spirantia odorem." When the writer of this Memoir had the privilege of visiting the shrine in which the Martyr's head is preserved at the Dominican Convent in Drogheda, on the 26th of September, 1893, the fragrance to which Dr. M'Mahon refers was distinctly perceptible.

The devotion of the good Benedictine did not rest here. In 1684 he petitioned the authorities in Rome to be allowed to keep a perpetual lamp ever burning before the martyr's shrine ; and to strengthen his petition, procured recommendatory letters from the Irish bishops, who, despite the persecution, still remained guardians of their flocks. It was on this occasion that the Archbishop of Cashel thus wrote to the Secretary of the Sacred Congregation of Propaganda in 1684 :—

"The body of the happy Primate has been lately translated from London to a more Catholic country, by a Benedictine father, who assisted him during his imprisonment in London. This father, in a spirit of zeal, desires to have the remains of this great prelate honoured with a lamp continually lighting, and to this effect supplicates their Eminences ; he has warmly pressed me to add my prayers, and, to content him, I wrote a letter to Monsignor Cybo, and another to Cardinal Norfolk, both of which letters I transmitted to himself, according to his desire. I also supplicate the goodness of your Excellency to use your influence in causing to be honoured the memory of this glorious prelate, who was so devoted to you; and, should you judge the desired favour unreasonable, or as yet inopportune, yet I pray you to excuse the liberty which I have taken."

From the fact that the letters of the Archbishop of Cashel, addressed to Cardinal Norfolk and Monsignor Cybo, were sent to Father Corker, it would seem probable that he himself even undertook a journey to Rome to attain the desired end. But the Holy See did not, as yet, deem it opportune, such were the then existing circumstances of the English nation, to declare the holy prelate "*a martyr*." In our own day those petitions to the Holy See were repeatedly renewed, and at length on the 9th of December, 1886, the reigning Pontiff, Leo XIII., signed the decree permitting the introduction of the cause of his Beatification. We fondly hope that the day is not now far distant, when the long-afflicted Church of Ireland will be consoled with the solemn declaration of the Vicar of Christ, that he, who, in the hour of trial, was the pillar of the House of God among his people, and who so nobly

2 F

sealed with his blood the doctrines of the faith, may be ranked among the martyrs * of our Holy Church.

Some further particulars regarding the remains of the martyred Primate are registered in the following note of the Bishop of Limerick, Dr. John O'Molony, presented to the Sacred Congregation of Propaganda, on the 12th November, 1696 :—

"The Bishop of Limerick, in Ireland, begs to state to the Sacred Congregation, that there is at present preserved in the Convent of English Nuns, in Paris, a whole arm of Oliver Plunket, with its flesh and skin, &c., all as perfect and fresh as though still living. He was Archbishop of Armagh, and laid down his life for the faith, being executed in London in the year 1681, under Charles II. The said Bishop of Limerick asks what is to be done in this case. Archbishop Plunket was for many years professor of theology in the College of Propaganda, in Rome, and was always esteemed for his most holy life ; he is at the present day deeply venerated throughout the three kingdoms. The remainder of his body was conveyed from London to Lambspring, in Germany, by the Benedictine Monks, with the exception of one rib bone, which is also kept in Paris. The Benedictines hold his remains in the greatest veneration, and they too are anxious to know what course they should pursue. In Rome there are many witnesses who are well informed about the whole case ; as, for instance, Bishop Ellis, the Vicar of his Holiness in England; the Rev. Father Grims, Prior of the Dominicans, at the monastery of SS. John and Paul ; and many others. It would confer a great blessing on these three kingdoms, should the Sacred Congregation make some inquiry into this matter."

In reply to this note, the cardinals of the Sacred Congregation of Propaganda, ordered the question to be referred to the Congregation of Rites, whose special province it is to inquire into all things connected with the canonization of saints.

In Ireland each memorial of the martyred primate was treasured up with the greatest veneration. As he went to the scaffold he handed his beads to the servant who had

* We have already more than once presented extracts from the contemporary prelates, in which Dr. Plunket receives the title of *martyr ;* we may here add a passage of a letter of Dr. Forstall, Bishop of Kildare, 29th November, 1681, in which he writes :—"Unless the Bishop of Clogher be at once nominated successor of the deceased holy martyr,"&c. *Successore del defonto martire.* In another letter we read :—" *Catholici ipsum venerebantur ut martyrem et quidem fortissimum,*" &c.

waited on him during his imprisonment ; the heirs of that faithful servant still preserve the precious gift. The Dunsany branch of the Plunket family, though they no longer enjoy the blessings of that holy faith for which the Primate laid down his life, yet cherish as priceless heirlooms the watch and some other memorials of Dr. Plunket. In the parish of Termonfeckin, where the Primate generally resided, the site of the hut wherein he dwelt, is still traditionally pointed out, and the inhabitants vividly cherish the memory of the orchard wherein he was accustomed to assemble the little children for instruction in the rudiments of faith ; and of the rude loft, formed of branches of trees, on which he used to seek concealment by day and repose by night.

The Roscommon branch of the Plunket family also preserved among its most cherished heirlooms, a chalice and watch of the martyred Primate. A worthy representative of that family held for some years the responsible post of Attorney-General in New South Wales, and died in Australia, in 1869, highly respected throughout the Australian colonies. His widow presented the above most precious heirlooms to the writer of this Memoir, and by him they have been deposited among the treasures of the Diocesan College of St. Patrick at Sydney.

In Ireland, however, so fierce was the rage of the enemies of the Catholic Church, even after the execution of the Primate, that her persecuted people had but little opportunity of manifesting their reverence and devotion for the memory of Dr. Plunket. The letter sent by the Archbishop of Cashel, when transmitting the narrative, which we have already given entire, discloses the sad affliction to which the Irish prelates were then subjected, and the terror and dismay which everywhere prevailed. It is dated the vigil of the Assumption (14th August, 1681), and is addressed to the Secretary of Propaganda :—

" MONSIGNOR,—I send enclosed a dolorous narrative, the subject of which has filled with affliction all the good in these parts. Our friend died gloriously, if we consider true felicity, but otherwise most sadly: for he was really murdered,* *est qui judicet.* He being the first prelate gave good example, encountering death, confiding in the mercy of God and in his own innocence ; and it is probable that other bishops will follow in the same path, for wicked men are not wanting to accuse them though innocent, and rewards and pardons are held out to stimulate such perjurers. Two bishops are already in prison, viz., those of Cork and Kildare ; but, as yet, it is not known what will be done with them. Of all our prelates, the Bishop of Limerick is the only one who is tolerated on account of his old age. Nothing is known about the metropolitan† of this province, and should he be taken, woe to him. Some say he has left the kingdom, some say no ; but wherever he is, he does not allow himself to be known through dread of some apostates, although everyone of sense knows his innocence ; but innocence does not suffice in these countries, *ubi sedes est Satanæ* (where Satan holds his sway). I omitted writing for some time, though much against my inclination, as those who received and despatched my letters were themselves accused of conspiracy by some apostate friars, wherefore they are now unwilling to receive or despatch any letter; nor can any others be found who will undertake to do so, so great is the terror which has seized on all honest men ; and I omit writing not to expose them or myself to danger or apprehension of danger. I send these papers by a long sea route, and I hope they will reach their intended destination without any danger. Should I live, as I hope, I will procure in a short time some expedient to write more frequently ; but we now live in such a conjuncture, that each one fears his own shadow ; we hope, however, always that God will console our innocence.

" I request you to transmit the enclosed narrative whither it should go, and to excuse the absence of titles, occasioned by the sad state of the times. Be good enough not to send an answer till you receive some further news, and I subscribe myself as usual,

" J. C."

‡ It was the desire of many distinguished members of the Irish Church to have the diocese of Armagh subjected to some signal chastisement by the Holy See, that thus it migh

---

*In the Propaganda archives, there is a letter addressed from Paris by "Patritius Coneus," who styles himself a veteran in the service of Rome (un servitore veterano della corte di Roma) to Monsignor Cybo, Segretario di Propaganda, and dated 26th January, 1682, in which he lodges a complaint against *irreligiosos fratres,* of whom he says, " they presented themselves before the tribunals to give false testimony against the poor Primate of Ireland, now a glorious martyr, and who, through the malice of these wicked men, was condemned to death (si presentarono avanti la ginstizia per portare testimonianza falsa contro il povero primate d'Ibernia ora glorioso martire che per l'invidia di quei scelerati ha perso la vita)."

† He thus speaks of himself as a third person

manifest the common detestation of all Catholics for the deed perpetrated by unworthy members of that diocese. The Bishop of Clogher, in a letter written not long after this occurrence, does not hesitate to say:—

"Should their Eminences refuse to stigmatize that people by some punishment, many here are apprehensive lest the bad example should occasion the worst impressions, and this impunity assume the character of licentiousness. I submit, however, to whatsoever arrangement may be made, and I only add that all our prelates are of opinion, that, for the present, no native of that diocese, and no one nominated by them, should be appointed to that see, lest it should seem to be, as I already said, *pretium sanguinis;* and as the Bishop of Kildare would not accept this dignity, were it offered to him, there is no one, in my opinion, so suited for it as Dr. James Cusack, Bishop of Meath," &c.,

There is in the Propaganda archives another anonymous letter addressed to Canon Joyce by some friend of the primate, which was transmitted to Rome by the Internuncio in Brussels to make known to the Sacred Congregation the sentiments of the Irish Catholics. It is as follows:—

"29th Jan., 1682.

"DEAR SIR,—I received last week your letter of the 23rd November, and I have long since answered yours of the 25th August, giving you the fullest details that I was able about the death of our dear and happy friend. The boys, James and Joseph, will commence their journey next spring or summer.

"Is it possible that an inconsiderate action, such as that of the murder of the Bishop of Castro, could set all Italy in confusion, and that now the long-premeditated death of our primate should be allowed to be passed over without any sign of displeasure? On account of the former deed the episcopate was transferred from that see, and shall this latter so flagitious crime deserve no chastisment? I, for my part, can with difficulty understand how some chastisement is not inflicted for so infamous a deed: the whole world expects it, and the Sacred Congregation has been already three times solicited to transfer at least the primacy to some other part of the kingdom as a punishment, and as a perpetual memorial of so great a cruelty practised against their lawful superior. The crime has not been so personal, as the good bishop represented it to be before his death; '*ut non vinceretur a malo sed in bono vinceret malum.*' The Friar MacMoyer wrote to Dr. Cusack, telling him to exhort Bishop Tyrrell, Dr. Dromgole, and many others, to abandon the kingdom, as otherwise they would share the fate of Dr. Plunket. The

Governor* having learned the contents of this letter, sent an express order to have the letter itself transmitted to him, and in consequence of it Moyer was arrested at Kilmainham, whence he was conducted to Armagh to stand his trial, some say for robbery, others say for this letter; one thing is certain, we are much obliged to the courtesy of our governors, though they be heretics."

None, however, was so vehement in denouncing the wicked sacrilege, and soliciting the Sacred Congregation to inflict condign punishment on its perpetrators, as Dr. James Cusack, Bishop of Meath. In a letter of January, 1682, he thus writes to Propaganda :—

"Again I cry out, again and a third time I knock, if not with clamorous shouts, yet certainly with mournful sighs. I am forced to repeat my cries by the repeated injuries of the wicked men who prolong their iniquity. I mean the murderers of our most illustrious Oliver of Armagh, to whom they rendered evil for good, and hatred for love, all whose fault was, that he reprehended the faults of the wicked. They now add iniquity to iniquity, and seek by new warrants to procure the death of the Bishop of Clogher, Dromgole, Hughes, Maguirke, and others; and the last-named, who is Dean of Armagh, was lately betrayed into the hands of his enemies. All the righteous of heart cry out to you to avenge that sacrilegious parricide by a proportionate chastisement. We hold that the spirit of our prelate, too, with the other souls of the slain, cries out in a loud voice from beneath the altar, and demands revenge, and this the more forcibly, as his blood has been the more recently poured out upon the earth. What does the loved one of the Spouse do? the guardian of the Spouse of Christ? the shepherd of Christ's fold? Does he devise some spiritual remedy to check this so horrid and unheard-of pest? New diseases must be met by new remedies, and such a remedy must, indeed, be found, which, at the same time, will heal for the present the recent wound of the Church, and serve as a warning to posterity. If the spiritual rod of the Church should spare those by whose impulse and perjuries the innocent blood has been poured out upon the earth, who can be ignorant of the consequences which will ensue? How many amongst the clergy will the impunity of these, contrary to all justice and law, cause to be promoted, not through any merit of their piety, but through fear of their own subjects. To avenge so great a crime, something must be decreed of advantage to the Church, that thus the health now received may be transfused into posterity, and the future generations may learn not only what was presumed, but also how it was avenged, lest otherwise the poison should spread, and no antidote being applied, many may come to perish. Let them know that there is a prophet

---

* Perhaps the Viceroy is here referred to.

in Israel. All Ireland vehemently desires and demands this. It is desired by the little and by the great, and otherwise it will be a scandal exceeding great in the Church of God, and I fear that the authority of the Holy See will suffer serious injury and undergo great loss. Nor in a matter so weighty and so universal, should we act tepidly or timidly. Innocent the Tenth has set an example to us in regard to the death of the Bishop of Castro, and Innocent the Third, on the occasion of the death of the Bishop of Herbipolis ; and shall the parricide of the Archbishop of Armagh under Innocent the Eleventh perpetrated with far more deliberation, remain unavenged ?

" At least let the diocese of Meath be cut off from the province of Armagh, and be immediately subjected to the Apostolic See. This the people, the nobles, the clergy of Meath anxiously demand. For, should it not be expedient to stigmatize the province of Ulster with some special mark of infamy, yet surely it behoves, through respect for the most illustrious prelate, that his birth-place should be honoured, especially as between those of Ulster and Meath there exists the greatest dissimilarity, nor can we deem it safe in this or the next century to go to their meetings or synods. The prophet hated the congregation of the wicked, nor would he sit with the impious. But does it behove the prophet alone to have this zeal, and is it not required from every priest of the Lord? And since those from Ulster, in the convent of St. Isidore's in Rome, destroyed the Archbishop of Armagh in effigy, as they afterwards did in reality in London, and as the clergy and people of Ulster now receive these parricides, it is manifest that the crime is not so personal that only the immediate actors in it should receive punishment. A short time since I was struck dumb, and my grief was renewed when I saw, on letters being received here, announcing that one from Ulster was to be appointed to the see of Armagh, how the innocent were filled with ignominy, and how the impious rejoiced that they had done evil, and exulted in their wicked deeds. Truly, if things be so, it must be, not from their own works of justice, but according to the greatness of your mercy, or rather, in order that, where crimes super-abounded, there too favour should super-abound : for, from the time of Judas Iscariot there have been found none who in such a manner rose up against their master and betrayed just blood. Allow not, I beseech you, allow not this to occur ; for all who hear of it will wonder, and none will extol it ; it would give strength to the impious and disarm the zeal for justice. And, if their own wickedness did not suffice, they would boast and exult that they had found defenders in those who should rather have been the punishers of their crime. Wherefore we shall hope that the Lord will not delay to save the afflicted from the hand of the oppressor, and to render retribution to the proud, and, though he should delay, yet will he not abandon us for evermore ; but the protection which is deferred will one day be more powerful, and will more perfectly succour us.

" The clergy of Dublin lately presented the Very Rev. Patrick

Russell for their archbishop: he is now. for the second time, Vicar-General of that diocese during the vacancy of the see,—a man distinguished for his piety and zeal, and so beloved by both clergy and people that a nobleman of high position, on hearing a short time ago that a Franciscan from the Convent of St. Isidore's was to be appointed to that see, exclaimed with an oath: Rome is astray, if it ever think of appointing, at the present time, a Franciscan to this diocese.

"The discord which reigns in Armagh has extended itself to the diocese of Clonmacnoise, where two vicars contend about trifles; one of them, who alone is worthy of being appointed, is named Moriarty Kearney.

"If, urged on by zeal, I have here said anything which I should not, or otherwise than I should have said it, I pray you to hold it as unsaid; whatever I have said right, and in a becoming manner, I hope will not be said in vain. Should not even my zeal merit consideration, you are at least debtors to the wise and to the foolish; and I beseech you to bear with my folly.

"P.S.—After writing the above, I received the letters of your Excellency of the 19th December, with the enclosed letter restoring peace to Armagh,· which, before ¦two days, I will deliver into the hands of Dr. Dromgole himself, and we have easily learned from this how great is the watchfulness and solicitude of their Eminences, and of your Excellency for our affairs. As we can return no thanks equal to such merits, we pray that the Almighty may preserve you many years for his glory and the propagation of the Catholic faith, and, after having happily consummated your earthly course, may crown us with you in glory."

Writing again on the 1st of December, 1683, he urges once more the necessity of inflicting some signal and public chastisement on the see of Armagh :—

"I am importunate, if I conjecture rightly : but I deserve to be excused ; for some illustrious persons, who themselves had often written against the murderers of the primate, solicit me, and I am urged on by the redoubled prayers of the clergy and nobility of Meath. The very Protestants demand it ; nor does anything render more probable, in their opinion, the imaginary conspiracy than that so great a sacrilege should remain unpunished. I add that I proposed nothing save what was conformable to reason and to law, and what I judged best suited to promote the lustre and glory of the Holy See. I thought, and I am still convinced, that that horrid guilt would be punished even less than its demerits by the transla-

* Viz., by the appointment of Dr. Dromgole as Vicar-Apostolic of that see

tion of the primatial see, according to the practice of Innocent the Tenth of holy memory; and thus, if the subjects of Armagh seek to imitate those of Sicily, their sad distemper will be healed by ceasing to give them pastors, and withdrawing the object of their fury, so that, though their fury may remain unabated, yet a fixed pastor will be wanting; and thus, not having a person against whom to vent their rage, they may desist from their temerity; or, at least, in the words of the canon, may cease to be a dire contagion to others. And, as I understand that it was whispered to you that such a chastisement would be displeasing to our nobility, a matter which no one here can understand, it is almost a year since I made known to your Excellency that nothing could be more agreeable to them than to have it decreed that those from Ulster should never, or at least for a hundred and fifty years, should not be promoted to that dignity. And, although as yet we have derived no fruit from our writing, but, on the contrary, the rejoicing of the Ulstermen is heard on every side, who boast and exult that they have found for their protectors those who should have been their chastisers, and that in the last Congregation held on Irish matters, one from Ulster, and he too a regular, was reserved *in petto*, as they say, for the see of Armagh; we will hope for better things. And although it must be left to the prudent and mature counsels of their Eminences to decide whether it be right that they should thus lord it over us, yet it is proper that your Excellency should know how dangerous we would here consider it to have any change made, until he who has actually been appointed Vicar-Apostolic be acknowledged by them. . . . For, though many things must be done and borne with to promote peace, yet we must take care lest, when restoring peace to the diocese of Armagh, the whole province may be put in confusion, and thus the last error be worse than the former. For (in this hypothesis) the Bishop of Clogher will most anxiously solicit to be exempted from Armagh, and the Bishop of Meath will most pressingly, though reverently, demand to be subjected to the Apostolic See or to Dublin, for they will not willingly submit to the yoke of Ulster. Should the Sacred Congregation decree that no appointment would be made until they submit to Dr. Dromgole, and that this should be promulgated by the Bishop of Clogher, before ten days all would return to obedience. The same result should ensue were he absolutely declared primate; for whilst he is movable at will, they will hope to succeed in removing him by their solicitations in Rome, although all confess that he is most eminent in virtue and learning, and most beloved by our own late primate Dr. Plunket."

Even when the Sacred Congregation had shown itself deaf to these solicitations, and appointed Dr. Maguire to the primatial see, Dr. Cusack did not cease his solicitations; and as late as July, 1686, we find the following passage in a letter addressed by him to Cardinal Altieri, then Cardinal Protector of Ireland in the Roman court :—

"I have often set forth how anxiously this nation desired that those of Ulster, that is of Armagh, on account of their parricide of the most illustrious Oliver of Armagh, should receive some chastisement commensurate with their deeds, and how dangerous it would be to allow so great a crime to go down to posterity unavenged ; and now again, with all humility and earnestness, I, by the present letter, pray that, through reverence for him, this diocese, which was the birthplace of the deceased prelate, may be added to the province of Dublin."

Notwithstanding these repeated and urgent solicitations, Rome remained unmoved ; and the Holy Father continued, as heretofore, to nominate worthy successors to St. Patrick in the primatial see. When we now look back on this dark period of Ireland's history, whilst we render the just tribute of our admiration to the zeal and solicitude of these worthy prelates to have such a perennial memorial, such a public tribute, rendered to the memory of their loved martyred primate, surely we must be filled with gratitude for the wisdom and paternal solicitude of the Holy See, which refused to involve alike the innocent with the guilty in the merited chastisement, or impute to the whole body the guilt of some unworthy members, who were already cut off by suspension and excommunication from its bosom, and thus deprive the Irish Church of its glorious privilege of pointing out the series of its primates who, in unbroken succession, have handed down unchanged the sacred deposit of faith which St. Patrick bore with him from the centre of religion and catholicity.

We have seen the reverence shown by the good Benedictine, Father Corker, to the remains of Dr. Plunket ; we may add a few words regarding the manner in which a precious portion of these relics was transferred to its present shrine in the Dominican Convent at Drogheda.

In 1715 Dr. Hugh MacMahon was transferred from the see of Clogher to the primatial see. From his infancy he had learned to walk in the footsteps and admire the virtues and the zeal of his martyred predecessor. When studying

in Rome, in the Irish College, he often heard of the glory
which Dr. Plunket had won for religion by his glorious
death; and often, too, did he there contemplate the shrine
containing the head of that happy prelate, which, as
tradition tells us, had been presented many years before by
Father Corker to Cardinal Norfolk—perhaps at the time of
the contemplated visit of the good father to Rome, in 1684,
of which we have already spoken; and which on the demise
of that cardinal, in 1690, was preserved in the convent of the
Dominican Order in that city.

In 1721, at the request of the Very Rev. Stephen MacEgan,
Provincial of the Irish Dominicans, and afterwards Bishop of
Meath, Dr. MacMahon applied to the General of the Order,
who was soon after decked with the purple, and is known as
Cardinal Pipia, to have a convent for the nuns of his Order
opened in his diocese. The circumstances were indeed most
favourable, and the petition was at once granted. There
was at this time in the Dominican convent at Brussels a
near relative of the martyred primate, by name Catherine
Plunket, mature in sanctity and distinguished for her
virtues. She was at once chosen first Superioress for the
new convent, and Drogheda was destined as the scene of
her labours. This convent was dedicated under the invocation of St. Catherine of Sienna, and it remains to the present
day; never has the primitive fervour of its holy inmates
abated; and it now, as under its first foundress, diffuses
throughout our island the sweet odour of its virtues. No
spot could be better chosen for the shrine of Dr. Plunket;
and Dr. MacMahon hesitated not to place there, without
delay, the precious deposit which had already been granted
to him from Rome—the head of his martyred predecessor.
The foundress of this convent was still living when it was
first visited by the celebrated author of the *Hibernia
Dominicana*, who found Dr. Plunket's head entire, and yet
retaining its grey hair. The reliquary in which the precious
relic is preserved has been thus described:—

" At present it is enshrined in a little ebony temple, at each of the
four angles of which is a Corinthian pillar of silver. The sides are

also inlaid with silver plates. There are two doors, one in the front
and one in the rere, and inside of each there is a glass plate, through
which the head can be seen. On the silver plate in the front door
are the Primate's arms, surmounted by a silver mitre. On each
angle of the roof is a silver flame, emblematical of martyrdom. The
head itself is of a brown colour, and quite perfect, with the exception
of the nose, which is slightly injured. It still retains some of the
white hair of which De Burgo speaks."

The following details taken from the domestic Annals of
the Convent in Drogheda, will not be devoid of interest :—

"July 5th, 1757, Decease of the Venerable Mother, Catharine
Plunkett, our foundress. She was a near relation to the martyred
Primate, and allied to the Barons of Dunsany, the Earls of Fingall,
and the other ennobled branches of the illustrious family of Plunkett.
Her Father was Thomas Plunkett, Esq., of Drogheda. The only
guide we have as to the year of her birth, is the Register of her
death preserved in the convent, which makes her sixty-seven years
of age at that period. She must consequently have been born about
the year 1690. At an early age, she embraced the Order of St.
Dominic in our convent of Jesus and Mary, Galway, and shared in
the vicissitudes of that community, who were several times compelled by religious persecution to quit their convent. Some sought
shelter in the houses of their relations or friends, whilst not a few
experienced the utmost rigours of poverty. Father Hugh O'Calanan,
who was then Prior Provincial from 1709 to 1718, having during the
course of his visitation found the Sisters in this lamentable condition,
and without any hope of their being permitted to return to their
convent, obtained for them from the Archbishop of Dublin, Most
Rev. Doctor Edmund Byrne, permission to settle in his diocese.
Accordingly, in March 1717, eight of them arrived in the metropolis
and took up their abode first in Fisher's Lane, from which they soon
afterwards removed to the ancient Benedictine convent—Channel
Row, N. Brunswick Street. Amongst these eight Sisters was our
future foundress; but she never became a member of that community ; for, with leave of superiors, she repaired to the convent of
our English Sisters at Brussels known as " the Spellicans" in which,
from the time of its foundation by Cardinal Howard in 1660 to the
present day, the spirit of fervour and of regular observance has
flourished in its full vigour. This community, now established in
the Isle of Wight, have a tradition of her residence amongst them.
"From Brussels she was recalled in 1721 by our Very Reverend
Prior Provincial, Stephen Mac Egan, subsequently Bishop of Meath,
to found the Monastery of Drogheda. Letters Patent, dated March
28th, 1722, from our Most Rev. Master General Pipia, incorporating
this monastery with the Order, and appointing Sister Catharine
Plunkett its first Prioress, duly arrived. In the following year, the
Father General withdrew our convent from the jurisdiction of the

Provincial, and took it under his own immediate care. The first dwelling of the new community was a miserable mud cabin on the banks of the Boyne. As the Most Rev. Hugh MacMahon, who then filled the Chair of St. Patrick, was their sincere and zealous friend, we must conclude, either that he was too poor to spare from the many demands on his charity, the means of providing them with a better abode, or that the obscurity of their position was a prudential measure to secure them from the danger of religious persecution. It was only by one of our fathers using the precaution of crossing the Boyne in a little boat so as to celebrate Mass and return before day-break, that our Sisters could have the consolation of assisting at the Adorable Sacrifice and receiving the Holy Communion. It hence appears likely that the mud cabin was on the Meath side of the Boyne. Be this as it may, their privations were real, and cheerfully borne. They at once zealously devoted themselves to the instruction of youth. Their lives must have been very edifying and the fervour of the Drogheda Catholics very great, for even in this wretched abode, postulants were found amongst young ladies of position, willing to join them; one aged twenty-two was professed in 1723, and in January, 1725, two, aged respectively sixteen and seventeen. A few days after their profession, our Father General directed the community of Galway to restore to this House the dowry which our Foundress had given at her profession. Our Sisters some time afterwards removed to Dyer Street; but of the precise time at which this event took place no record has been found. We know only that they then undertook on a larger scale the instruction of youth, that their school and their novitiate were recruited from some of the most distinguished families in Meath and Louth, and no slight evidence of the fervour which animated our foundress, and in which she trained her spiritual children is found in the fact that amidst all their struggles, privations, and dangers, the Divine Office was punctually recited in Choir, and the fasts of the Order observed—though wearing the religious habit or observing enclosure was impossible. The better to conceal the real nature of the establishment, they had pious secular ladies boarding in the house. To the family connection of our foundress with the illustrious martyr, Oliver Plunkett, we are indebted for the precious relic of his head bestowed by his successor and our kind friend Doctor Hugh Mac Mahon.

"Our Venerable Mother filled the office of Prioress three times successively; the dispensation necessary for this purpose was granted probably in consideration of the necessities of the community, all the members of which were so very young. At length our venerated foundress, having the consolation of seeing seventeen professed members of her community—after a long illness closed a holy life by an edifying death at the age of sixty-seven years. She was interred in the burial-ground known as the Cord, because attached to the ancient Convent of Franciscan Friars. This was also the last resting-place of our Sisters till the consecration of our own Cemetery in the present century."

It may not be out of place to add here a few instances of the singular favours which during the past few years have been obtained from Heaven through the intercession of the martyred Primate. I will set them down in the words of one of the devoted Dominican nuns by whom they were communicated to me in the month of October, 1893:—

"A boy named Grey, who lived a few miles from Drogheda, near Slane, was suffering for a considerable time from a swelling in the head. During the month of July, 1881, when a great number of pilgrims were flocking to the shrine on the occasion of the second centenary of Dr. Plunket's martyrdom he proceeded to the Convent knelt before the martyr's head, and prayed that health might be restored to him. Whilst returning home he became quite cured. The fact was witnessed by the boy's mother and several other persons."

"Again, a little more than seven years ago, a young man, named Michael MacIvor, who suffered from a malady in the eyes which almost deprived him of sight, was sent by the Parish Priest of St. Mary's, Drogheda, to the Sienna Convent, with a request that the nuns would do something for him through the intercession of the holy martyr. He knelt before the open shrine containing the head of the martyr, and whilst he prayed there for his cure, one of the sisters touched the sacred relic with her hand, with which she made the sign of the cross on his eyes. From that day the boy's eyes began to improve and his sight to recover, as he himself declared to the nuns when he came a second time to pray before the shrine."

The following cure took place about five years ago:— "A man from Mornington, near Drogheda, who had been for a long time crippled by acute rheumatism, and had been dismissed from an hospital in Dublin as incurable, was perfectly cured by the application of a handkerchief that had touched the head of the martyred Primate. The nuns learned this fact from his wife, who added 'he is now well and strong, able to dig in the fields.' The good woman was filled with gratitude to God and the holy martyr for this signal favour."

" A pious gentleman, Knight of St. John, came several years ago to pray before our holy relic for the conversion of his wife to the faith, she being a Protestant. After some time this gentleman returned, as he said, to make a visit of thanksgiving at the martyr's shrine, his wife having become a Catholic. This gentleman was very fervent in his devotion to Venerable Oliver up to his death (about a year ago). In the year 1884, he expended a considerable sum of money in procuring pictures of the martyr which he sent us for circulation."

" The Rev. Daniel Conway, P.P., Port Glasgow, in Scotland, became acquainted with our community at the time of the celebration of the bi-centenary of Dr. Plunket's martyrdom in 1881. The following year we heard of his hopeless illness from congestion of the brain, and knowing his great devotion to the holy martyr, Mother Prioress thought of sending him the silk cap from the martyr's head, hoping that by wearing this relic he would get relief. Nor was this hope vain. His brother, also a very zealous priest, and the nurse who attended him, attest that they perceived a marked improvement in their patient from the moment the cap was placed on his head—his memory returned and his recovery was rapid. One of the Doctors said :—' I am not a Catholic: I do not believe in miracles performed since the days of Christ or His apostles, but if there is a miracle it is your brother's recovery : not believing in miracles, I say it is marvellous.' The nurse asserted the fact in the following words to the priest on his recovery : ' You mended, and your memory came all right after the cap was put on you. I am sure of that.' This worthy priest when writing afterwards on the subject of his wonderful recovery adds : ' I did not understand all that happened; but I remember wearing the cap, and wearing it for a cure. Those who attended me say that I showed every sign of unmistakable confidence in its power. I esteemed it and valued it even in my most unconscious moments, by words and by signs, as a most precious relic. I hold it still in great veneration day and night, and when I return it, you may easily imagine how sincere and deep will be my thanks for the privilege you conferred on me by sending it to me on so pressing a message of charity." The good priest lived for some years to do much good in the cause of religion, during which time he was more zealous than ever in labouring to have our holy martyr raised to the highest dignity in being inscribed on the Church's list of canonized saints. Finally, by a singular coincidence, this devoted client of Dr. Plunket died happily on the anniversary of the martyrdom of our glorious Archbishop, July 11th, 1884."

On the 11th July, 1881, the centenary celebration of Dr. Plunket's martyrdom was kept with special celebration at the Dominican Convent in Drogheda. The zealous pastor of the district, Archdeacon of the Diocese, Monsignor Murphy, availed of the occasion to erect a new parochial Church as a centenary Memorial, and on the 11th of July the foundations were solemnly blessed. Nothing was left undone to make the ceremony every way worthy of the festival. Cardinal MacCabe, Archbishop of Dublin, was present, as were also the illustrious Primate, Most Rev. Dr. M'Gettigan, the Archbishop of Cashel, and several other members of the Irish hierarchy. One prelate from the Antipodes, Right Rev. Dr. Moran, Bishop of Dunedin, also graced the ceremony by his presence. The building has since been successfully carried on, and as we write these lines in October, 1893, the sacred edifice is well nigh completed, and bids fair in its grand proportions and beau. tiful spire and stately architecture to be a worthy memorial of the Centenary feast. Great was the enthusiasm awakened far and wide among the faithful by the solemn celebration, and within the month of July, 1881, more than 3,000 pious pilgrims visited the holy martyr's shrine at the Dominican Convent.

The monastery of Lambspring was not destined to retain

for ever the whole, at least, of the precious treasure of
Dr. Plunket's remains which Father Corker's loving care had
consigned to it. In the year 1803 the Benedictine monks
were expelled from that territory by the Prussian Government, and the monastery confiscated. The Church indeed
became parochial, but the relics of the martyr continued to
be jealously guarded. In 1883, however, at the urgent request
of the English Benedictine Fathers, the Bishop of the diocese
gave permission for the venerable remains of the martyr to
be translated to the monastery at Downside. The 31st
of January that year was a joyous feast for that great
Benedictine community. Through the kindness of Sir Stuart
Knill, who at present (1893) so honourably discharges the
high duties of Lord Mayor of London, the precious relics
were on that day conveyed to Downside. The prior community, and college students were assembled at the west
porch of the monastery to receive the sacred treasure, and
proceeded in procession to the church where the relics were
deposited in a temporary resting-place. A letter from the
Benedictine Father, under whose care the translation of the
relics took place, will furnish some further interesting details :

" The tomb of Archbishop Plunket in the crypt beneath the choir
of the Abbey Church of Lambspring was on the south side in a
recess formed in the thickness of the wall by the arched opening of
a window which had been rendered useless by some more recent
buildings—the sacristy, in fact, of the church. In this opening on the
old window ledge had been placed a box formed of one piece of red
sandstone, twenty-six inches long, fifteen inches broad at the top
(rather less below), and fourteen inches deep. This box was covered
by a slab of the same stone, which was not fastened to the box, but
lay on the top. The whole of the window recess had been walled
in ; a huge stone with the inscription (given by Challoner) occupying
the greater part of the opening. The removal of a few of the
adjacent stones allowed of an entry being made to the recess ;
and with the assistance of a mason who entered with me I was
privileged to lift out the stone box containing the relics. The Very
Rev. J. A. Gasquet, Prior of Downside ; the Rev. Ferdinand
Stammel, Parochus of Lambspring, and myself, carried the box to
the sacristy, and removed the heavy stone lid. The remains were in
a very perfect condition ; the flesh, though quite black, adhered to
the bones ; and the marks of the quartering were unmistakable on
both flesh and bones. The right hip bone and femur, extracted by

2 G

the parish priest who had been directed by the Bishop of Hildesheim
to retain some relics of the venerable martyr, were not put back
into the stone box; the flesh which was removed from those bones
was replaced, and the stone lid likewise, seals set; and the whole,
relics, stone box, and all securely placed in a strong wooden box
made expressly for the purpose. This took place on January 10th,
1883. The same day the box of relics was forwarded to Hamburg
to be, in due course, shipped to London. Owing to various delays,
especially the severe storms which raged during the month of
January, the relics did not reach London till near the end of the month:
by the intervention of Stuart Knill, Esq., the Custom House
authorities allowed the box to pass unopened, and with seals
unbroken; and in that state it was received with due honour and
solemnity at Downside, on the last day of January. I regret to
say that when the box was opened by the Hon. and Very Rev. W.
Clifford, Bishop of Clifton, on the 12th March, 1883, the flesh had
decayed and crumbled to a powder or dust, and the bones were in a
state of decay. A medical examination of the remains was made,
and such steps taken to prevent future decay of the bones as
science could suggest.

"Written *acta* of all that had been done in the translation were
drawn up; one copy remaining at Downside, another being kept
by the Bishop.

"The relics, carefully preserved in a case specially constructed, and
hermetically sealed, were placed in a handsome stone tomb erected
in the church at Downside, in the south aisle, near the chapel of
St. Laurence; in the same tomb was placed the sandstone box or
coffin in which Abbot Corker had placed the relics."

In various parts of England other relics of the venerable
martyr have long been preserved with pious care. For
instance, in the chapel of the Cardinal Archbishop of
Westminster, there is a small packet containing particles of
linen which at the time of Dr. Plunket's execution were
dipped in his blood. In the Franciscan Convent at Taunton,
there is a reliquary and relic with the inscription: "The
arm-bone of Oliver Plunket, Archbishop of Armagh, and
Primate of All Ireland, martyred at Tyburn, July 1st, 1681."
The same convent preserves two pieces of linen cloth stained
with the martyr's blood. Stoneyhurst College possesses
similar treasures.

One other relic merits particular mention. It originally
belonged to Most Rev Dr. Brennan, Archbishop of Cashel,
and was handed down to his successors in that see till the
year 1791, when on the death of Archbishop Butler, it passed

into the hands of a worthy relative of that prelate living in Ballyragget, in the diocese of Ossory. Miss Margaret Lalor, the last who possessed it, guarded this precious relic with religious watchfulness for forty years, till, for greater security, she consigned it to the curate of that town, the Rev. Nicholas Murphy, to whose great kindness the writer of these pages is indebted for receiving it in charge in the month of August, 1869. It has been deposited by me in the safe keeping of the holy community of Dominican Nuns, at St. Mary's, Cabra, in the suburbs of Dublin, where I trust it may one day, with the solemn sanction of the Holy See, receive that honour and veneration which are due to the martyrs of the Church of Christ.

There is one peculiar feature of the reverence shown to the martyred Primate, which merits special commemoration. During the past years many temperance societies have been formed under the invocation and patronage of the Venerable Oliver Plunket ; the friends of temperance fondly persuading themselves that he who throughout his apostolic career, had laboured so earnestly and so unceasingly to root out from his flock the degrading vice of drunkenness—that accursed plant which has produced and still produces so many evil fruits of bitterness to the Irish people—would not now fail to plead before the throne of God, even more efficaciously than during life, the holy cause in which they were engaged. I may add that instances are known in which families that prayed to God to banish drunkenness from amongst them, and placed their prayers under the protection of the martyred Primate, have had the wished-for blessing granted to them in a most wonderful manner : and some instances are not wanting in which men who had reached the last stage of the dreadful vice of drunkenness, and were already on the very brink of the abyss, have had both their temporal and eternal happiness secured to them through the same most efficacious patronage.

We have brought the " Memoir " of Dr. Plunket to a close ; and whosoever examines the documents which it presents must assuredly confess that the period of his episcopate forms a bright epoch in the history of the Irish

Church. In the centuries which immediately succeeded the conversion of Ireland, heaven seemed to pour out upon her people all the treasures of grace, and, at the same time, all the blessings of peace; for later ages was reserved the ordeal of the faith. But her triumphs in the arena were not less glorious than her crowns in time of peace; and, as the virtues of her children merited the glorious name of "Island of Saints," so the noble heroism displayed by her champions of faith, in the days of persecution, have won the no less peerless title of "Martyr-Island of the Church." From the records we have published, it is evident that Dr. Plunket must be ranked 'amongst the foremost of her heroic children. Neither is his fame confined to his native land. Many are the panegyrists whom his apostolic labours, no less than his 'virtues and his martyrdom, have found throughout the Continent. As regards Ireland, it is not only in the records of her history and the annals of her Church that his name is inscribed; it is yet, after a lapse of near two centuries, a household word in every family, and lives in the tradition of a faithful people.* Well has been verified the prediction of his venerable friend, the Archbishop of Cashel, that, indeed, "*the memory of this glorious prelate will ever be revered in these kingdoms, as, on the contrary, the names of his impious accusers shall ever be held in abomination for having, with sacrilegious impiety, shed his sacred and innocent blood.*"

---

* One of the most learned and judicious of our national writers, Matthew O'Conor, Esq., in his *History of the Irish Catholics*, part i., page 106, *seq.* (Dublin, 1813), after detailing some particulars of the foul conspiracy against the Catholics, thus apostrophises the martyred Primate:—"Illustrious shade! thy memory is embalmed in the tears and honoured by the admiration of six successive generations! The power of thy persecutors was short-lived, and nothing remains of them but the memory of their crimes; your virtues still exhibit a glorious example of patience, meekness, humility, charity, and fortitude. Thou hast received thy reward: *Anima sanctissima aveto salveto.* May the contemplation of thy happiness encourage to the imitation of thy virtues! May the example of thy resignation sustain those who may be exposed to similar persecution!"

ADDITIONAL NOTE.

PUBLIC\TION OF THE DECREE OF THE COUNCIL OF TRENT ON CLANDESTINE MARRIAGES IN IRELAND.

AT the end of Chapter XII. we have made some remarks regarding the publication of the decree of the Council of Trent on clandestinity in Ireland. From Dr. Plunket we learn that it had been published in some parts of Ireland, in the time of Elizabeth, and that it had been proposed in the famous Council of Kilkenny to extend it to all Ireland. If this question were discussed in that Council, no serious result appears to have been obtained ; for if anything had been done, it would not have escaped the notice of Dr. French, who was present.

From other authorities we learn that the decree in question was not published in several parts of Ireland for many years after the time in which Dr. Plunket wrote. In an old MS. copy of the Synods of Dublin I find the following memorandum :—" Certain advices left on record, for new coming missioners by old father Barnaby Barnwall--1st. *That the Council of Trent is received only in the north, in the county of Louth, in Meath, and Elphin in Connaught ; but the decree of clandestine marriages is not published in Meath.*" Father Barnwall was superior of the Irish Capuchins, and is mentioned with great eulogy by Dr. Plunket. It is here to be added, that the Council of Trent was published in Meath, and also in Galway, on the 2nd of Dec., 1827.

In the statutes of Cashel and Emly, published by Dr. Bray, we read, at page 216, "*the decree of the Council of Trent, condemning and annulling clandestine marriages, was duly published and received in the diocese of Cashel and Emly in September,* 1775." In a letter of Dr. M'Kenna, Bishop of Cloyne and Ross, dated October, 1775, it is stated that the decree on clandestinity was published in all the dioceses of the province of Cashel, on the first Sunday of the preceding September, and the following Sundays, for thirty days. " *Prælati hujus provinciæ in mense Julii proxime lapsi convenerunt prope Coreagiam, ibiq. receperunt decretum Conc. Trid. relative ad matrimonia clandestina, promulgaruntque prima Dominica Septembris aliisque diebus Dom. et festivis per trigénta dies.*"

In the provincial statutes of Dublin, enacted in Kilkenny, 1614, whilst the other decrees of the Council of Trent are received, the following exception is made—" *Ob temporum injuriam decretum concilii Tridentini matrimonia clandestina irritans nondum promulgare audemus.*" In another synod, held 24th July, 1685, by Dr. Russell, a similar exception is made— " *Admittimus et recipimus S. Concilium Trid. quod omnia præter decretum irritans matrimonia clandestina.*" Things remained in this state in the province of Dublin until the 2nd December, 1827.

In that year the tridentine decree was published in each parish, as according to Benedict XIV. De Syn. Diœc. l. x. ; no enactment of a diocesan or provincial synod would suffice to introduce the impediment of clandestinity.

We here give a letter of Dr. Troy, written in 1780, before his translation to Dublin, which throws great light on this and other questions. The letter principally treats of the validity of mixed marriages, and the view taken by Dr. Troy appears to have been adopted by Pius VI., who, in the year 1785, declared mixed marriages valid in Ireland, even when contracted clandestinely. It is to be hoped, that letters so replete with erudition and so full of useful instruction as those of Dr. Troy, may yet be collected, and published for the guidance of future generations.

"Kilkenny, 23rd July, 1780.

"MOST HONOURED AND REVEREND DEAR SIR,—My constant and various avocations in the country, since I had the honour of your last favour covering a copy of C. Antonelli's letter to you, of the 20th May, deprived me of sufficient leisure to deliver my sentiments on both, with that degree of satisfaction, my respect for your command, and the importance of their contents required. At present a short respite from business and fatigue, on this day of rest, enables me to observe, that the caution of his Eminence is an indication of his prudence. His dread of evil consequences from a declaration and decision against the validity of the mixed marriages in question, is certainly well grounded; but I do apprehend the smallest inconveniency from establishing their validity.

"No real innovation would thereby be introduced amongst us, because, such mixed marriages have been, and are *de facto* regarded as indissoluble in the very districts where the discipline of the council has been even lately enforced. If I am not mistaken, the laws of this kingdom do not annul these marriages, unless they are solemnized by a Catholic priest. If I should unite two Protestants, the marriage is likewise null and void; and in either case he is guilty of felony without benefit of clergy, as p. stat. 19, Geo. II., chap. 13, sect. 1, anno. 1746, and stat. 23 ejusdem cap. 10, sect. 3, anno. 1750. A degraded minister of the Established Church, or any layman pretending to be a clergyman thereof, is guilty of the same crime; but the marriage performed by either, or a licensed minister is not declared invalid, and the last incurs no penalty. Stat. 12, Geo. 1., cap. 3, sect. 1. I have made these extracts from Bullinbrooke's abridgment, *Titulo Marriages*.

"I said that no innovation would be introduced amongst us, were the declaration and instruction of the Holy See respecting Holland to be extended to this kingdom; because they would only ratify what is already universally practised, notwithstanding the speculative doubts of some prelates about the spirit and meaning of the Tridentine law.

"As to myself, although I have frequently and seriously considered the subject in every point of view. I have not discovered any solid reason for altering my opinion. I still regard the marriages of Protestants with each other, or with Catholics in any part of the kingdom as valid. The account given by Benedict XIV., in his work *De Synodo Diœcesana*, of the deliberation of the canonist and divines, and likewise of the decision of the S. Congregation of the council in 1741, on the subject, appears to me very satisfactory. The arguments in the 8th, 9th, 10th, 11th, and 12th numbers of the sixth book and chapter are remarkably conclusive, and undoubtedly determined him to publish the celebrated decree and constitution—*Matrimonia*.

"I agree with Cardinal Antonelli that the marriages of Roman Catholics

Protestants are unlawful, wicked, and dangerous, and, of course, have been always, and are still reprobated by the Church ; but I do not imagine that a declaration from the Holy See of there being, what they are now held to be, *valid*, would increase them.

"A repeal of the civil laws annulling them, and mentioned above, would multiply them much more effectually. I do not wish it for that very reason.

"His Eminence, in stating the different situation of Ireland and Holland with regard to these marriages says:—'Nam pro Hollandia vehementer ambigetabur an memorautm concilii Tridentinidecretum esset promulgatum in singulis parochiis.' Now, I appeal to you if it does not clearly appear from Benedict XIV. *Ibid.* Num. viii. and ix., that the divines consulted by him, not only abstracted from that question of fact, but likewise established the validity of the marriages, even admitting that the decree of the council had been duly received and promulgated in Flanders — I mean the United States.

"As to the greater or lesser number of Catholics in Ireland and Holland, and other discriminating circumstances between both countries, mentioned by the Cardinal, they are quite extrinsic to the main question, which is plainly this:—Does the decree of the Council of Trent, annulling clandestine marriages, affect Protestants, or other heretical societies, in all and every place where said decree has been received and duly published ?

"This question, as I conceive, ought to be answered categorically and distinctly, without any attention to expediency, which never can alter the nature of things.

"It is the business of those prelates in whose districts the discipline of the council has not yet been adopted, to judge of the conveniency of enforcing it, after receiving a satisfactory answer to the above query; and such bishops as have, after the example of their predecessors, or from their own determination, required an observance thereof, are to abide by the consequences as well as they can.

"Although no positive and explicit answer has been given to the above question, his Eminence seems to deliver his own opinion with regard to it when he says—'Nam cum hæretici non minus quam Catholici, Ecclesiæ legibus subjecti sint, si Tridentinum decretum pro clandestini matrimonii nullitate vim habet pro unis, eandem vim habere debet pro alteris,' &c.

"In my humble apprehension this mode of reasoning savours of what logicians call a *Petitio Principii*. All Catholics must acknowledge that Christians of every denomination are in general subject to the Church on account of their baptism ; but the prelates of Ireland, and many others, doubt whether Protestants, or other heretics are subject to a particular disciplinary law or decree of the Council of Trent, and give very plausible, if not convincing, reasons in support of the opinion which affirms that they are not. In this state of uncertainty the Holy See is consulted, and the prefect of the Sacred Congregation (inadvertently, I am sure) answers by supposing what is questioned:—'Nam cum hæretici, &c., ut supra.'

"From my above remarks you may easily guess my answers to the queries of his Eminence:—Ad primum respondeo—In provincia Dublinensi nondum publicatum fuit memoratum concilii Tridentini decretum: In majori vero parte parochiarum cæterarum Hiberniæ, diversis temporibus receptum et promulgatum fuit. In nonnullis praochiis extant dictæ promulgationis authentica documenta; in omnibus vero dicti decreti observantia repetenda est non a regni legibus quibus matrimonia ipsorum Protestantium inter se vel cum Catholicis, coram sacerdote Catholico celebrata, irrita et nulla declarantur; sed a sacri concilii statuto, ad effectum illud omnimode exequendi. Ad secundum—Perturbationes maximè, aliaque ingentia incommoda certissimè orirentur in hoc regno, si dicta matrimonia irrita et invalida declararentur. Si valida declarentur, nullum incommodum timendum, cum jam pro ratis et firmis habeantur, etiam in iis locis in quibus publicatum fuit Tridentinum decretum. Ad tertium—Cum impediri nequeat promiscua Catholicorum cum haereticis communicatio, nimis frequentia sunt inter ipsos matrimonia istius modi clandestina. Ad quartum—Si nulla declarentur, certum est quam plurima matrimonia jamdiu contracta in iis locis in quibus concili decretum publicatum fuit, cum ingenti familiarum incommodo et dissidio, necnon publico scandalo irritanda etperfringenda fore. Ad quintum—Nihil molestiæ aut detrimenti timendum est ex parte sæcularis potestatis. In impedimento dirimente matrimonium ex consanguinitate vel affinitate, aliisque disciplinæ capitibus, diversa est praxis Catholicorum et Protestantium, quin ea ratione aliquid damni rei Catholicæ obveniat. Ad ultimum—Cum pro ratis et validis jam communiter habeantur matrimonia de quibus agitur, uti supra in responsione ad secundum quæsitum; non possunt multiplicari ea declaratione facienda quod valida sint: si vero leges civiles talia matrimonia irritantes modo supra expresso ad primum quæsitum, aliquando revocari contingat, tunc quidem adeo multiplicari possunt, ut periculo hæresis amplectendæ exponantur contrahentes et proles.'

"You are at liberty to use the above communication of my thoughts as you may think proper. I have worded it in the most unreserved and candid manner in obedience to your command; but would not wish to convey the most distant idea of disrespect towards C. Antonelli, or secretary Borgia. I am long and well acquainted with both, and can assure you they are remarkable for profound and extensive knowledge, consummate prudence, and disinterested zeal. I desire to know your opinion of my reflections, and pray you to communicate it for my instruction.

"It would be madness in us to adopt, and enforce the discipline of the council, until a satisfactory reply shall come from the city; and should it be · pro invaliditate,' I think it (the decree) ought never to be published in this province. In this, and every other matter, I shall always pay due deference to your better judgment.

"Maggiora, auditor-general to the nuncio at Brussels, in a letter of the 29th of May, says the S. Cong. has determined to appoint one of the Armagh suffragans coadjutor to Dr. Blake, and desires me, in the name of the Congregation and his Excellency, to recommend the one I think in my conscience the most worthy and fit. Without much hesitation I answered on the 15th instant. and recommended Dr. Plunket of Meath. This transaction, in my opinion, ought to be kept private; otherwise the disaffection of some, and ambition of others might frustrate this measure, and protract the scandals in Armagh. Pray, what news from Spain and Lisbon? If the colleges there are not speedily re-established the consequences may be fatal to religion in this country. The French modes are already become too fashionable amongst all ranks of our people, Mr. O'Connor enclosed a copy of the decrees you received from the city about the new offices and indulgences. I see the office of the passion has not been granted. Has our friend Charles Kelly given you any communicable news? The above decrees, and the one about the obligation of p. priests to apply their masses on Sundays, &c., for their respective flocks, ought to be published in next year's Directory. I hope the new supplement is in forwardness. It is full time to let you breathe after reading this long scroll. I shall finish it with sincere assurances of being with unfeigned sentiments of respect, esteem, and attachment,

" Most Rev. and Hon. dear sir,

" Your most affectionate and very humble servant,

" ✠ JOHN THOMAS TROY.

" The Most Rev. Dr. Carpenter."

Printed by BROWNE & NOLAN, LTD., *Dublin.*